Bestselling Australian author Robert G. Barrett was raised in Sydney's Bondi where he worked mainly as a butcher before picking up a pen. He appeared in a number of films and TV commercials but preferred to concentrate on a career as a writer, moving to Terrigal on the Central Coast of New South Wales. He wrote over twenty books, including *High Noon in Nimbin, Still Riding on the Storm, Les Norton and the Case of the Talking Pie Crust, Leaving Bondi, The Ultimate Aphrodisiac, Mystery Bay Blues,* and *Rosa-Marie's Baby.* Almost all of Bob's books feature his much loved character, Les Norton – a red-headed, knockabout, old-school Queenslander who works as a Kings Cross bouncer but is forever getting involved in intrigue. *The Australian* called Bob Barrett 'Australia's king of popular fiction'. Over a million copies of his books have been sold and his legions of fans are known as the Norton Army.

To find out more about Bob and his books
visit this website:
www.robertgbarrett.com.au

Also by Robert G. Barrett
and published by HarperCollins:

So What Do You Reckon?

Mud Crab Boogie

Goodoo Goodoo

The Wind and the Monkey

Leaving Bondi

The Ultimate Aphrodisiac

Mystery Bay Blues

Rosa-Marie's Baby

Crime Scene Cessnock

Tesla Legacy

Les Norton and the Case of the Talking Pie Crust

High Noon in Nimbin

Still Riding on the Storm

Maximum Security

Leaving Bondi
Mystery Bay Blues
Rosa-Marie's Baby

ROBERT G. BARRETT

FULL STRENGTH

HarperCollins*Publishers*

HarperCollins*Publishers*

Leaving Bondi first published in 2000
Mystery Bay Blues first published in 2002
Rosa-Marie's Baby first published in 2003
This collection first published in Australia in 2013
by HarperCollins*Publishers* Pty Limited
ABN 36 009 913 517
harpercollins.com.au

HarperCollins*Publishers*
Level 13, 201 Elizabeth Street, Sydney, NSW 2000, Australia
31 View Road, Glenfield, Auckland 0627, New Zealand
A 53, Sector 57, Noida, UP, India
77–85 Fulham Palace Road, London W6 8JB, United Kingdom
2 Bloor Street East, 20th floor, Toronto, Ontario M4W 1A8, Canada
10 East 53rd Street, New York NY 10022, USA

ISBN 978 0 7322 9775 6

Cover design by Matt Stanton, HarperCollins Design Studio
Cover images by shutterstock.com
Typeset in 10.5/14pt Sabon by Kirby Jones

CONTENTS

Leaving Bondi

DEDICATION

This book is dedicated to Major General Peter Cosgrove and all the Australian Forces who served in East Timor. I got a lot of letters from the troops. I know they did a great job up there and they're still doing a great job. And we should all be proud of them.

Despite George Brennan's running gag about Les Norton getting arrested for breaking into a fifty-dollar bill, then being acquitted because it was his first offence, Les wasn't all that mean with his money. A bit tight? Maybe. Careful? Definitely. Distrustful? After watching some of the people around him whilst living in Bondi and working at Kings Cross: one hundred per cent. But mean? No. Definitely not. If it was Norton's turn to shout or he had to spend his money on something necessary, he would. And some of the money he'd come across in his jaunts here and there, Les had certainly spread around. Which, somehow, often came back to him.

However, Les wasn't into the share market or real estate. He owned his own home and was more than happy with that. Even backing some of Price's horses at short odds had lost its allure, whether they were good things or not. As far as Les was concerned, there were only three places to keep any spare cash you had lying around: In the bank. Buried somewhere, where you could get to it easily if you wanted to. Or strapped tightly to your body where pickpockets or such couldn't get to it easily if they wanted to.

So for an extremely cautious person like Norton to invest fifty thousand dollars in a movie, a movie that was virtually just another Australian meat-pie western, would take close to an act of God. Or whoever talked Les into it would have to be the greatest salesperson on the planet. But Les had his reasons for investing such a vast amount of his hard-earned into a dodgy Z-grade flick. It all came about through Les hanging around Ray Tracy's Japanese restaurant next to Bondi Beach Public School.

The way things were going in Bondi, the Gull's Toriyoshi Yakitori wasn't a bad place to hang for a feed and a cool one. The old Icebergs was still a pile of bulldozed rubble money-hungry developers and Waverley Council were constantly arguing over. The Diggers had been sold to make home units, so most of the punters had moved down to The Rathouse in the North Corner, which was good value, except you had to put up with poker machines and cigarette smoke and Les wasn't a member. Les was a member of Hakoah, but mainly for the choice food. The Bondi was all right in the daytime, but you wouldn't go there at night unless you liked drinking elbow to elbow with backpackers full of drink and western suburbs home-boys full of attitude. Redwoods had been turned into an internet cafe and most of the other bars around Bondi were either too smoky or too trendy and charged an arm and a leg for a drink. The old Rex wasn't that bad and the VB on tap was good, only there were too many blokes there either Les or Billy had cuffed on different occasions and Les spent half the night looking over his shoulder. Norton could get all the dramas he needed working at the Kelly Club. And as Les only drank two or three nights a week because of his job, he liked to be able to relax when he did. So a bit of a sneak away from the crowds and the smoke was needed. And in this respect, the Gull's Toriyoshi suited him admirably.

Ray was a good friend of Warren's and Les got on well with him as did just about everybody else. The Gull always reminded Les of Peter Fonda in *Easy Rider*. The same thoughtful, winsome face, the same loose brown hair and steel-framed glasses and the same plausible nature, tinged with polite curiosity. Since Les had poisoned the big Russian swimmer there, Ray had done the Toriyoshi up. The cooking was now done out the back, there was more seating and, being a local waxhead, Ray had filled the walls with old Bondi surfing memorabilia. You could sit out the front if you wanted, where there was a well-stocked bottle shop two doors away, the Japanese staff were friendly and Ray's food was always tasty and well presented and, compared to some of the other feedbags around Bondi, extremely reasonable. Being an actor and a scriptwriter, Ray also had a good-looking French girlfriend who was always good for a perv, a blonde actress called Monique. And if she wasn't around, there always seemed to be plenty of other girls hanging about. Because of his involvement in the film game, Ray's Toriyoshi attracted much of the Bondi and Sydney entertainment industry from TV, film, radio and theatre; some of whom were all right and some of whom were absolute pains in the arse. Les preferred to sit out the front with Ray's old waxhead mates when they were around.

They were good blokes in their thirties who rode mini-mals, liked a drink and a laugh and always had an anecdote about Bondi to relate. Most of them had nicknames like Weasel, Snoopy, Hey Joe, Short-Round, Butch van Bad Skull, Munoz, The Arm, Tounger, or whatever, and all had this strange way of talking now and again in allegorical metaphors tinged with biting sarcasm. Les was sitting out the front one night having a cold one with Weasel and Hey Joe, and evidently Weasel had been seen out on the weekend with a really ugly girl.

'Nnnyyhh,' said Hey Joe, 'I'm glad the chick you were out with the other night didn't have a head on her like a kicked-in shitcan anyway, the Wease.'

'Nnnyyhh,' replied Weasel. 'I'm glad you wouldn't crawl over broken glass with your Morts out to stick it up her behind my back anyway, the Joe.'

Nnnyyhh, thought Les. I'm glad you haven't got me fucked if I know what you're talking about anyway, the boys.

Naturally, being a writer and hanging out with the film industry in beautiful downtown Bondi, the Gull had come up with a film script. It was called *Leaving Bondi*. Thinking Les might be interested and looking for investors, he showed Les the script and the synopsis one night when it was quiet. The story was about an Australian Vietnam veteran who elopes back to Australia with a Japanese girl and was set in Bondi before they got rid of the old sewerage works — the murk — and started pumping all the shit out to sea beneath the ocean floor. Her father is a boss in the Yakuza and comes looking for his daughter. The Vietnam vet shoots the father and his gangsters, then ends up in a massive shoot-out with the police and the State Protection Unit before getting away with his girl through the sewers of Bondi, finally escaping through the main sewerage outlet under the golf links around Ben Buckler Point. There was waffle and moving dialogue and in the end you're left hanging, not knowing whether they got away or drowned in several million litres of shit.

The film was going to be shot around Bondi, Bondi Beach Public School, the Toriyoshi and Ray's father's house in Clyde Street, Bondi. Ray reckoned by cutting costs and using unknown actors he could shoot the film for less than a million dollars. The Gull had called his film company Murke Productions. Les flicked through the script and thought the the film company was aptly named and it was good the movie was about sewers and such, because it was the most shithouse thing he'd ever read. And figured anybody that would invest money in a clunker like *Leaving Bondi* would have shit for brains. Oddly enough, Ray had raised nearly all the money and was just $50,000 short of production. Les handed the Gull back his script, said he'd take a rain check and got another beer.

One night Les was sitting out the front of the Toriyoshi with Warren, Ray Tracy and Ray's French girlfriend Monique. Ron from 99FM was there with a Sydney disc jockey who raved on too much for Norton's liking, and a local film director Les wasn't too keen on either. Along with some lesbian film producer. Evidently they were the main investors in the Gull's movie. Even Warren had sunk some money into it.

The director was Max King, a humourless, narrow-eyed person about forty with a hunched, bony build and a narrow, bony head topped with short greying hair. He rarely smiled and always reminded Les of a snake the way his head sunk between his shoulders and his slitty eyes seemed to dart everywhere as if he was looking for a mouse or a small bird to eat.

He'd made a number of films. His biggest claim to fame being an art film shot in Bali, which won a gong at some obscure film festival in Europe before fading without trace. He'd also been high up in the South Australian Film Corporation where he'd produced several meat-pie dramas and telemovies. King had lived in Bondi for over ten years, but before he moved to Sydney, Eddie said King had been in the army reserve in Melbourne where he'd also done community service for petty larceny. Because of his Balinese film connection, King always liked to wear batik shirts; tonight's fashion statement was black, brown and yellow.

The disc jockey was Nathan David. An average-sized, self-opinionated bigot in his thirties with tinted hair and a squashy little nose rumoured to have undergone plastic surgery. David originally arrived in Sydney from Adelaide via Melbourne. He was single, loved developers, hated environmentalists and was currently right up there in the ratings giving Sydney's talkback kings a run for their money. So far David hadn't been caught up in the cash-for-comment-keeping-the-greed-alive-scandal rocking Sydney radio. And often enjoyed referring to his opposition and anyone else who didn't share his views as vile, rotten swine. Norton, however, after what he'd heard and read in the papers, wouldn't have pissed on any of them, particularly David. And often said so. But if he ever bumped into David at the Toriyoshi, Les kept his opinions to himself. If only for Ray's sake.

The woman was Simone Mitchum. She had dark hair and dark looks, which blended in with her all-black outfit, broken up by a purple scarf and purple earrings. Simone lived in Dover Heights and also came from Adelaide, where she'd worked on a couple of King's movies with the South Australian Film Corporation. She wasn't introduced to Norton as a lesbian. But just her mannerisms, and the way she glared at Les for having the hide to perv on the same woman at the table she was, told him so. Despite her abrasive manner, she seemed to be fairly intelligent, and Les was curious why she, or anybody else, would invest in a Z-grade wobbegong like *Leaving Bondi*. Warren, a mullhead working in an advertising agency, Les could understand. But the others? Maybe they knew something he didn't?

The night Les was drinking there, David had just been berating everybody about his rise in the latest radio survey; mainly because he'd escaped the cash-for-comment inquiry. Now he was berating Les about putting some money into Ray's movie. David was dissecting Les from behind a pair of dark sunglasses he was wearing so no one could recognise him while he was wearing a bright red T-shirt with his radio station's logo across the front so no one could miss him.

'Well, come along, Les,' chirped David, in his familiar radio-announcer's voice. 'Ante up, my boy. This could be a great investment for you.'

'Sure. Come on board, man,' said Ron. 'It's a cool thing.'

'Yeah, why don't you? You miserable big prick,' said Warren. 'You've got plenty snookered away.' He gave the Gull a wink. 'You've been leaching a fortune off me in rent for years. I wouldn't be surprised if you had all my rent money buried somewhere in the backyard in a shoe box,' he added, as a titter of mirth ran round the table.

Les looked at Warren impassively for a moment. 'Yeah, that'd be right, Warren. Trying to kick you out but you won't go'd be more like it. You greasy little bludger.'

The Gull, plausible as ever, seemed slightly taken aback by Les and Warren's rapport. 'Well, hey. Like, you know, Les,' he gestured politely. 'Nathan's got a point there, man. This movie could be big.'

Max King didn't bother looking up from the table. 'I like the script,' he said assertively. His words hanging in the air, as if they were impaled on an invisible wall, to emphasise his approval of the script was all that was needed.

The Gull nodded to Les. 'Hey, he's right. It's a great script, man.'

'A great script?' said Les. 'Turn it up, Ray. A heroin addict could forge a better script than that. I read it. Remember?'

The Gull looked at Les for a moment. 'Not all of it.'

'Ohh why waste your time,' said Warren. 'Les'd rather put his hand in a meat grinder than put it in his pocket.'

Another titter of laughter rang out round the table as everybody got a chuckle out of Warren's remark except Norton.

Simone gave Monique another very heavy once up and down. 'Why don't we talk about something else,' she said.

'Yes. Why don't we,' agreed Max King, his slitty eyes flicking sideways at Les, as if a non-film person like Norton shouldn't even have been sitting with them in the first place.

Les fixed his eyes on the Gull for a moment. 'All right, Ray,' he said evenly. 'I'll back your movie. How much did you say you needed the other night? Fifty grand? Okay. You got it.'

For a moment it looked as if a nerve gas bomb had just gone off as every face at the table froze and all eyes riveted on Norton.

'What was that, Les?' blinked the Gull.

'I said, I'll put fifty grand into your movie.'

'Are you fair dinkum?' said Warren.

'I'm always fair dinkum, Warren.' Les finished his beer and rose from the table. 'Now if you people will excuse me, I have to go. There's a travel documentary about Kakadu on the ABC I wish to tape.' He nodded to the Gull. 'I'll have your fifty down here at the end of the week, Ray. Goodnight all.' Les turned and walked home, stopping briefly at Bates milk bar in Hall Street for a packet of CC's.

When Les got home, he knocked the top off a cold Eumundi Lager, took a swallow, then slipped a tape in the video recorder. Once that was going, he went out into the backyard, sipped some more beer and stared down at where he had all his loot buried next to the garden shed. The Krugerrands had fallen in by accident so he wouldn't miss any, and the arse appeared to be falling out of the gold market so he'd be better off getting rid of them. Fifty grand was a lot of money to waste on a meat-pie western. But it was nice to see the looks on all their faces when he dropped his bombshell earlier, and it would be even nicer to see the looks on their faces when Les Norton, major investor, started hanging round the film set, a big cigar in one hand and a set of worry beads in the other. Also, this would consolidate his position at the Toriyoshi; the Gull would think the sun shone out of Norton's arse now. And although Les couldn't conceal a certain dislike for some of the poseurs and hangers-on in the movie business parading around Bondi — Ray Tracy excluded — they definitely attracted all the choice crumpet. A lot of whom were friends of Monique's and liked to sip white wine and eat the fat-free food at the Toriyoshi. For virtually a handful of coins Les could be the next Sam Goldwyn. He could put a casting couch in the spare bedroom. And even though the government had put the squeeze on the old 10BA rort in the film game, there was still an attractive tax break for investing in a meat-pie western, so he wouldn't lose that much in the wash-up. On the other hand, there was always the chance *Leaving Bondi* could get up. People might actually pay to go and see the lemon. Stranger things had happened. Norton finished his bottle of beer and got the pinch bar out of the shed.

The next day Les saw Price, told him what he was up to and to keep it between the two of them. Price was only too delighted to oblige, as well as cop a nice pile of shiny, bargain-basement Krugerrands to add to his collection. In five minutes Les had his money, and all nicely washed through a bookie so it looked like Les had won it at the races. Five minutes later Les rang his accountant. Norton's last accountant had moved to the Gold Coast so Les had a new one. Geraldine Hardacre. A tall, coppery brunette who did triathlons with her husband Ivor, an insurance investigator. Gerry was one of Billy Dunne's in-laws on his wife's side, so she knew where Les and the rest of them at the Kelly Club were coming from. She also knew a lot of people herself and wasn't adverse to cutting corners and going straight to the heart of the matter if need be. Geraldine quickly got a prospectus on the movie and by the end of the week the Gull had his money and Les had a fifty-thousand-dollar investment in a film by Murke Productions Pty Ltd titled *Leaving Bondi*.

This had all happened before Les went to Port Stephens with Eddie. Since then, they'd both got back safe and sound, Price had slipped Les another ten thousand for the effort, and life went on. Now it was another Sunday night at the Kelly Club in late autumn. The club was empty and Les was sitting in Price's office, wearing a char-grey shirt tucked into a pair of black trousers, about to enjoy an after-work drink. Sitting on his left, Eddie and Billy were wearing leather bomber jackets and dark trousers and deep in discussion about how much chlorine goes in a swimming pool. Price was at his desk, wearing a light green suit with a jade tie, and going over some betting slips with George Brennan. Overweight George was wrapped into a dark blue suit with a blue tie; the suit slightly crumpled as usual. Norton being temporarily left to his own devices was settled back, sipping on a cold Fourex and surmising that all up, things weren't too bad. They could have been better. But all up, they weren't too bad.

Digger and her cousin had certainly made headlines with 'their' discovery of the submarine, and with the money rolling in, they were able to leave for America so Brendon could have his eye operation. Digger even sold her story to a woman's magazine. ANNE ZACCARIAH, MY SECRET AGONY. SHARKS ATE MY FATHER WHILE MY COUSIN WENT BLIND. Because she didn't like travelling to Sydney, Les had been driving to Newcastle when he got the chance. Which sadly wasn't working out. The porking was still sensational. But Digger wasn't the happiest drunk in the world and her cooking would kill a brown dog. Besides that, Les got the distinct feeling Digger was having it away. Not out of any disrespect or lack of affection for Les, but Les had definitely turned her into a mad raving case and having that bottled up inside her all those years, she was making up for lost time. Why buy a book — even if it was a good one — when you can join a library. Digger never let on, but Les could tell. And it wasn't just the phone calls from old friends when he was at her house; phone calls always taken in the other room. Of course what Digger did when Les wasn't around was pretty much her business. Not his. But Les wasn't all that keen on sharing Digger's sweet little whatever with strangers. And now you could bet Digger was cutting a swathe through the medical fraternity in Fort Worth, Texas, while Brendon was recovering in hospital. So Les knew it was only a matter of time before it would be the end of the affair. Oh well, thought Les. You win some, you lose some. I guess I was just born to go through life another broken-hearted clown, laughing on the outside, crying on the inside. That's show biz. And talking about show biz, tomorrow was the first day of filming for *Leaving Bondi*. He took another sip of beer and felt a tap on his left shoulder. It was Billy Dunne.

'You're very quiet there, old mate,' he said.

'Eh? No, I was just thinking about something, Billy,' replied Les. 'You and Eddie were talking anyway.'

Eddie stretched his arms above his head and yawned. 'I know what I'm thinking,' he said. 'I'm thinking of going straight to bed when I get home. I worked on the house all day today, pouring concrete. And I'm rooted.'

'Hey, talking about work,' said George Brennan, locking the safe. 'That lazy, loafing nephew of mine Kevin's got a part in a movie tomorrow. They're shooting it at Bondi Beach Public School while the school holidays are on. He's a cop.'

'Kevin?' said Price. 'How could he do a day's work? They'd have to take an X-ray first to see if he had one in him.'

'He'd make a good cop,' said Billy.

'Yeah,' chuckled Les. 'It runs in the family.'

'Hey, how come you haven't got a part in the movie, Tom Cruise?' said George. 'It's being shot in your backyard. And you're an actor and a model. Did your agent forget to ring you?'

Les brushed his fingernails lightly against his shirt then glanced at them indifferently. 'It's funny you should say that, George. Because I just happen to have a share investment in that very same movie.'

'You what?' said George.

'I bought some shares in the movie,' replied Les. 'It's called *Leaving Bondi*.'

'Shit! You kept that quiet,' said Billy.

'Well,' drawled Les. 'I didn't want to start running around big-noting, Billy. Just because I've become a major player in the Australian film game.'

'Major player in the film game.' Billy shook his head. 'Fuck off, will you, Les.'

'How much did you stick into it?' asked Eddie.

'Enough.'

George turned to Price. 'Can you believe this cunt? Sticking his money into a movie.'

Price gestured with one hand. 'I don't know, George. Taking a punt on an Aussie movie's not a bad idea.' He turned to Les. 'This could turn out to be a very wise investment, old son.'

Les nodded. 'That's right. It could turn out to be another *Crocodile Dundee*.'

'*Crocodile Dundee*,' scoffed George. 'I know one thing. You won't be crying crocodile tears if you do your money. They'll hear you howling the other side of Cape Barren lighthouse.'

'Hey, I'll be down Bondi tomorrow,' said Eddie. 'I got to see a bloke about something. You reckon it'd be worth me hanging round the movie set for a perv?'

'I don't know,' shrugged Les. 'But I'm going to have a look. I might see you down there.'

'Okay. We'll have a coffee,' said Eddie.

Price changed the subject to something that had happened at the club earlier in the night. Then they talked about something else. It was the end of the week and everyone was feeling tired and looking forward to a few days off. They drank and talked for another thirty minutes or so then left. Driving home in the back of Price's new Mercedes, Les was thinking. Yes. Things ain't that bad. I've just earned a few Oxford Scholars tonight. My job definitely isn't the Burma Railway. And I'm getting a lift home in an air-conditioned Merc. Yes. Things could be a lot worse. Eddie dropped him off at his door, Les said he'd see them all later and went inside.

Once more, Les had the house to himself. This time Warren was down the south coast at Ulladulla, in a weekender with a blonde actress he'd met at the Toriyoshi. A blonde Les fancied. But unfortunately Warren tap danced too fast for him. Les got out of his work clothes and into his tracksuit pants and a T-shirt, made an Ovaltine then walked out into the backyard and looked up at the stars shining down on a crisp autumn night. He sipped his Ovaltine and shook his head, finding it hard to believe how time went so fast. It only seemed like a few days ago they were trying to get the money together to make *Leaving Bondi*. Now they were actually filming it. Les yawned and had a slight chuckle to himself. He'd got a postcard from Neville Nizegy early in the week. From San Diego of all places. It didn't say who it was from. But Les knew. I wonder what Nizegy would think if he knew some of his money was going into an Aussie movie? He'd probably be rapt. Naturally, Nizegy didn't leave a forwarding address, so Les couldn't tell him. Les finished his Ovaltine. Yawned again then went to bed. In ten minutes the big Queenslander was snoring soundly.

By the time Les rose from his sleep-in, got cleaned up then climbed into his blue tracksuit and trainers to walk down and get the paper, it was ten o'clock. After throwing his dirty clothes in the washing machine, before taking his own sweet time over poached eggs and coffee, it was after eleven. Outside it wasn't too bad a day; mild, with a few clouds around and a light nor'wester rustling through the few trees in Cox Avenue. An excellent day for filming smiled Les, as he flicked through the sports pages. Filming, I say filming my movie that is, boy.

By the time Les cleaned up in the kitchen and hung his washing out on the Hills Hoist like any other good Bondi housewife, it was getting on for twelve. Les had a glass of filtered water for the road, locked the house up and headed for the film set.

Walking fairly briskly, Les went straight down O'Brien Street then took a left into Gould, slowing down as he crossed Curlewis to wave to a couple of girls he knew going past on ten-speeds. He crossed Beach Road, finally stopping in Gould Street at a metal gate set into the rusty cyclone-wire fence running along the back of Bondi Beach Public School. Behind the metal gate, a set of concrete steps angled down to the old schoolyard, the tar criss-crossed with white markings to form a basketball court. A row of scrubby trees ran below the cyclone-wire fence towards Warners Avenue and on the right a couple of tall pines and other trees stood in front of a grey paling fence that separated the schoolyard from the flats in Beach Road. On the left side of the schoolyard was a children's play station flanked by two basketball hoops and across the playground, opposite Les, was a two-storey block of classrooms, then the rest of the school sprawled across to Campbell Parade. Joining the other interested bystanders in Gould Street, Norton leant against the metal gate and peered into the playground where the circus was well and truly in town.

All over the schoolyard were actors and extras dressed in State Protection Group or army uniforms. Walking amongst them, in a grey dust coat with a holstered magnum on his hip, was the armourer, keeping an eye on the M–16s, Heckler and Koch sub-machine guns and Glock pistols the actors and extras were having a great time playing with. Two make-up girls were bustling about, wiping the actors' faces or whatever while two wardrobe girls were busy double-checking their uniforms and another girl was walking around taking polaroids. Through the sprawl, other film crew were wandering around the playground, sucking on styrofoam cups of coffee as they squawked into two-way radios. Some of the extras, including George's nephew, were leaning up against the school block. Others were seated around a hot-water urn next to one of the basketball hoops. While all this rattle was going on, another scene of organised confusion was being enacted next to the children's play station.

A camera was set up on a cherry picker and beneath it electricians, carpenters, grips and various other film crew were bustling about laying down tracks or securing things with grey gaffer tape. At the epicentre of all this and looking every inch the uber-director was Max King, wearing a red batik shirt and Ray Ban sunglasses. King was staring morosely at the ground, his hand under his chin, in earnest conversation with the cameraman and the first assistant director, who was in earnest conversation with the soundman and the second assistant director, who was in earnest conversation with the assistant to the assistant assistant's whatever. Hovering in the background was the man with the clapper-board. He was in earnest conversation with a girl carrying a stop-watch and a clipboard who was checking the continuity. More film crew were coming and going and the dress was everything from ferocious black to Mambo Surfie and King's batik shirt. All topped with weird haircuts in every colour of the rainbow and facial piercing. It was as if the inmates had taken over the asylum and the inmates were waiting for Max King to rise majestically above the mob, give the nod to the first assistant director who would give the nod to the second assistant director who would then utter the magic words:

'All right. Quiet everybody. First positions please.'

Les leant against the gate to watch all the sizzling action and beautiful girls in the movie business. There was neither. Every girl on the set would have got kicked off a ghost train and the whole scene was about as exciting as watching an endless American gridiron huddle. Les watched everyone on the set play hurry up and wait for a while longer, then decided to walk down to Campbell Parade via Warners Avenue and have a look in the front gate just in case something might be happening there.

Through a line of trees behind the school fence in Warners Avenue, Les could see all the film company trucks lined up along the drive at the main entrance; wardrobe, make-up, generators, etc. The crew and cast had their cars parked nearby and in front of the drive was a grassy area about seventy metres square. Benches and tables were set up on the grass and behind the benches and tables was a dark blue catering van, its back nestled up near some scrubby trees running behind the school fence in Campbell Parade. Les strolled casually round the corner just as a 380 pulled up at a bus stop in front of the fence. As he slowed down for the people getting off the bus, Les noticed his left shoelace had come undone. He walked to the other side of the bus stop then turned round and rested his foot on the seat. Through the trees on his left, a flash of colour caught Norton's eye.

It was a thin, pale man with a shock of pink and yellow hair, wearing a black T-shirt, greasy black jeans and an apron round his waist. The man had come from a set of steps at the back of the catering van and Les surmised he was the cook. He was carrying a small tupperware container in one hand and a fork in the other, and had his back to Les as he picked something up from the grass near the steps. It was a couple of small, dried-up white dog turds. Les watched from behind the trees as the cook carefully put the two turds in the plastic container then clipped the lid on and disappeared back inside the catering van. Les closed his eyes and shook his head for a moment wondering what was going on. Les was still wondering what was going on when he felt a light punch under his floating rib. It was Eddie, wearing a black Balance tracksuit and matching trainers.

'Righto, Shifty. What are you up to?'

'Eddie,' replied Les. 'How are you, mate?'

'Good. What's happening on the film set?'

'Not a great deal,' said Les. 'Hey Eddie, you're not going to believe what I just saw.'

Les finished tying his shoelace and told Eddie what he'd seen, pointing to the catering van on the other side of the trees. Eddie seemed to think for a moment, a smile tugging at the corners of his eyes.

'You reckon the cook was picking up dog shit? And putting it in a tupperware container?'

'Yeah,' nodded Les. 'You could almost smell it. I wonder what he was up to?'

'Buggered if I know,' said Eddie, thoughtfully. 'But I know how we might be able to find out. Follow me over to my car, I'll show you something. It's just round the corner.'

Les followed Eddie across to his maroon Calais which was angle parked on the opposite side of Warners Avenue. Eddie opened the boot and took two aluminium binocular cases out of an overnight bag. He opened the cases and handed Les a pair of black binoculars. They were wider and heavier than normal, with green tinted lenses and there was a switch built into the lens on the right with a tiny light in front of it. Stamped across the top was CANON IMAGE STABILIZER 15×45IS.

'What are these?' asked Les.

'Image-stabilizing binoculars,' replied Eddie. 'I just bought them. You focus on what you want to look at. Then press that button and it cuts out any movement.'

'Yeah?'

'That catering van's facing this way. Come on over the road and we'll have a look from behind those trees. We might be able to see what he's up to.'

Les had another look at the binoculars. 'Righto.'

They crossed Warners Avenue, found a clear view of the catering truck through the trees, then rested their arms on the metal fence and raised the binoculars to their eyes. Les gave a double blink. The catering van was a hundred metres away, but the binoculars were so powerful, you would have thought you were inside it. There were gas bottles behind another door on the right and a white laminex counter at the front with a blue awning over it. Pink Hair was chopping up broccoli behind the counter. Les pressed the image-stabilizer switch and could scarcely believe his eyes. Everything stood perfectly still; there was absolutely no shaking at all. It was like watching TV, only better.

Les could easily make out the cook's facial features now. Under the pink hair, he had a lean, grainy face with a pointy nose and a long pointy chin, where a silver stud glinted through a blond goatee beard. There was a dark-haired girl in another black T-shirt and jeans, wiping over the tables on the grass, leaving the cook alone in the kitchen. The cook finished what he was doing, had a quick look around then reached under the counter and took out the tupperware container. He removed the two white dog turds then very deftly sliced them into six neat portions and placed them on a plate. Through the binoculars, Les could see everything clear as crystal. Next, the cook got a bottle of chocolate sauce from beneath the counter and poured some over the portions of dog shit. While the sauce was sinking in, the cook reached into a cabinet above the counter, got a packet of shredded coconut and sprinkled it liberally over the pieces of sliced dog shit. Satisfied, he put the plate to one side as Les put the binoculars down and turned to Eddie.

'Did you just see that?'

Eddie had his binoculars down too. 'Did I ever. What a cunt.'

They raised the binoculars again and Les pushed the stabilizer switch. A fat, orange blowfly drifted languidly into the catering truck and landed on the counter. The cook kept his eyes on it then picked up a plastic flyswat and carefully flattened the blowfly where it landed. The blowfly had scarcely stopped kicking when the cook descended on it with a small pair of scissors and quickly trimmed off its wings and legs. He flicked them off the counter then got another small tupperware container, opened it and dropped the blowfly inside with several other trimmed-up blowflies. The cook looked at them for a moment before tipping the lot into a pot of bean casserole simmering on the stove behind him. He gave the casserole a stir then put the two tupperware containers into a dishwasher as his assistant came in through the door on the right.

Les brought the binoculars down again, shook his head and looked at Eddie in disgust. 'Ohh yuk!' he said. 'That's enough to turn you off your fuckin day.'

'It is making it a bit willing,' agreed Eddie.

'Making it a bit willing?' said Les. 'It's enough to make you sick.'

'And on your movie too.'

'Yeah. My grouse bloody movie. What's his caper?'

'I don't know. But are you going to cop it?' asked Eddie.

'No fuckin way Jose.'

'Then there definitely has to be a square up.'

'Oh! A square up for sure, mate.'

'You got any ideas?' enquired Eddie.

'Yeah,' nodded Les. 'How about I go over there and pour that casserole down his pink and blond throat. Then force-feed him those dog-shit lamingtons for dessert.'

Eddie wiggled his eyebrows. 'I got a better idea.'

'You have?'

'Yeah. The old exploding-cake-full-of-shit trick.'

'The exploding-cake-full-of-shit trick, Ninety-Nine? What's that all about?'

'Come on. Let's put these back in the car, and I'll tell you.' They walked back across the road to Eddie's Calais. Eddie returned the binoculars to his overnight bag and closed the boot. 'I'll put a thundercracker in a cake full of shit. Then rig it so when Pink Hair opens the box it goes off and he gets a face full of shit. Along with his chuck wagon.'

'Sounds good to me,' said Les. 'How's it work?'

'I'll explain it to you in the morning. All I want you to do is find out his name, so we can write it on the cake box. Then you deliver it to him. You reckon you can do that?'

'I don't see why not, Edward.'

'I got a couple of blokes coming to see me tomorrow morning. I'll bring it over your place about ten-thirty. Is that okay?'

'Good as gold.' Norton turned towards the catering van. 'In fact I can't wait.'

'Okay.' Eddie looked at Les for a moment. 'You still feel like a cup of coffee?'

Les shook his head. 'Not particularly.'

'No. Me either. You want a lift home?'

'No. I might walk. I want to pick a couple of things up at the shop.'

'Okay. Well, I'll see you in the morning.'

'Righto. See you then, Eddie.'

Eddie drove off towards North Bondi. Les had another look at the catering van then walked back to Gould Street. So much for my first day on the wonderful film set. Bloody hell! What's the world coming to?

When he got back to Chez Norton, Les put the groceries away then changed into his old training gear, wrapped a sweatband round his head and went for a lap of Rose Bay Golf Links and back, finishing in the backyard with what felt like a half-a-million sit-ups. Les was in a funny mood while he was exercising. One half of him was dirty on what he'd just seen on the film set. The other half was laughing at the square up coming the next day. After a shower, Les threw a steak under the griller, nuked some vegetables then settled back for a quiet afternoon at home. He wrote a letter to his parents, washed the car, and by the time he'd tidied up and farted around the house the day was over. Les could have watched the news. But instead he thought he might call into the Toriyoshi, say hello to the Gull and congratulate him on the first day of filming. Les changed into a pair of jeans and a grey Toriyoshi T-shirt Ray had given him, put his gaberdine bomber jacket on and strolled down to Campbell Parade. The Gull was on the phone, wearing a red Hawaiian shirt and jeans, when Les arrived at the restaurant. Les gave him a wave through the window, then bought two bottles of Stella Artois, placed them on a table out the front and gave Ray a nod to let him know there was a cool one waiting for him when he was ready. The Gull was out in a couple of minutes.

'That was Monique,' he said, joining Les at the table. 'She can't find her key.'

'She's a blonde,' winked Les. 'Give her a break.'

Ray couldn't help himself. He was absolutely beaming when he picked up his beer. 'Well, what do you reckon, Les?' he said. '*Leaving Bondi*. It's a happening thing, baby.'

'It sure is, Ray. I came down today and had a look. Congratulations, mate.' Les clinked his bottle against Ray's.

Ray clinked his back. 'Thanks, Les. And thanks again for investing your money in it.'

Les made a magnanimous gesture. 'Hey. What else could I do?'

Ray shook his head. 'I swear to God, Les. A lot of my blood, sweat and tears went into that movie, man. And me nearly going over the gap a couple of times.'

'Down and out in Gullsville.'

Ray nodded. 'Yep. Fat city. No soles in my shoes. And no strings on my banjo. But not now, Les. The Gull's back in town.'

'Drinkin' TNT. And smokin' dynamite. Good luck to you.' Les clinked the Gull's bottle again. 'Hey how come you're not doing the catering on the movie, Ray? That would have been a nice little earn for you.'

Ray shook his head. 'I couldn't be bothered making that many pork balls, Les. I'm flat out here.'

'Fair enough. So who's doing the catering?'

'Kreative Katering,' replied Ray. 'Spelt with a K.'

Les snapped his fingers. 'I think I know the bloke who runs that. I used to work with him at Pyrmont. Skinny nosed bloke with a skinny chin. Wears a beard. Do you know him?'

'Sort of,' replied Ray.

'What's his name?'

'I'm not sure. But I can find out for you. I got a call sheet under the counter, I'll get it.'

'That's all right, Ray. You don't have to.'

'Won't take me two minutes,' said Ray, rising from the table. 'Besides, you're a major investor.'

'Thanks, mate,' smiled Les. The Gull walked inside the restaurant, Les had another swallow of beer and looked up at the night sky. Does it always have to be this easy, Boss? Honestly. Where's the challenge? Where is the challenge?

Ray came back out with what looked like a small filmscript printed on blue paper. He placed it on the table and flicked through the first few pages. 'Here it is. Kreative Katering. Albert Knox, Proprietor.'

'That's him,' said Les. 'Knoxie. I must call in and say hello.'

Suddenly some people began to arrive, so Les finished the rest of his beer. 'I'd better make a move, Ray. You're starting to get busy.'

'Hey. Stick around, Les. Have another beer.'

'No. I only called down to say hello. And to offer my congratulations.' Les offered his hand. 'Good on you, Ray. You've killed 'em.'

Ray shook Norton's hand. 'Thanks, Les. And thanks for coming down. It's always great to see you, man.'

'You too, Ray. I might see you tomorrow.'

'See you then, Les.'

Norton got up and left, leaving Ray to look after his customers.

Back home, Les got another beer from the fridge and settled back in front of the TV. Albert Knox. That shouldn't be too hard to write on top of a cake box. Les slipped on a video Warren had brought home from the advertising agency. *Analyze This* with Robert de Niro and Billy Crystal. Les was still laughing when he went to bed. What's a sandwich that ain't fattening? A haf a sandwich. Beautiful. Just beautiful. In ten minutes Norton was snoring like a baby. Tomorrow was definitely going to be another day.

Les was out of bed by seven; feeling good and looking forward to the day. Outside it was pleasant enough again; mild, a bit of an offshore breeze and sunny. Les got cleaned up, had some coffee and a mango smoothie then decided to get his exercise out of the way early. He got back into his training gear again and did the Rose Bay Golf Links, sit-ups in the backyard ghastliness, same as the day before. By the time Les got that over, scoffed some poached eggs and read the paper, it was ten-thirty and the doorbell was ringing. It was Eddie, wearing the same tracksuit as the day before, carrying a white cake box in his hands, sealed with Sellotape.

'G'day, Eddie,' Les greeted him. 'Come on in.'

Eddie followed Les down the hallway into the kitchen. 'Did you find out the bloke's name?'

'Yes. Albert Knox.'

'Good old Knoxie, eh. Well done, Les.' Eddie placed the cake box on the kitchen table.

'So that's it.'

'Yep. That's it,' replied Eddie, looking proud of his work. 'One exploding shit cake to go.'

Les gave the cake box a perusal. 'So how does it work?'

Eddie shrugged. 'It's mainly a lot of fuckin around with electrical tape. And I can tell you one thing, Les. I'm not over rapt in the smell of my own shit.'

'Don't worry, Eddie. I've been on the wrong side of your farts at work.'

'But it's just a thundercracker from Chinatown with a shortened fuse. A matchbox, matches and a mousetrap. The hard part's slowing down the spring on the mousetrap.' Eddie looked at his watch. 'I'll show you how you do it one day back at my place. But believe me, Les. These work a treat.'

'I'll take your word for it, mate.'

Eddie cursed. 'Bad luck I won't fuckin be there to see it go off.'

'You won't?'

'No, bugger it. I've got to go over the north side and I don't know when I'll be back. But when you give it to the cook, hang around and take some photos. I want to see them.' Eddie gave Les a wink. 'And don't piss yourself when you see what happens.'

Les smiled back at Eddie. 'I'll try. But I can't promise you anything.'

Eddie stayed while Les printed the cook's name on the cake box in blue texta colour. He told Les the thing was safe and couldn't go off unless you opened the lid. But keep it upright, don't drop it or knock it around too much. Les promised to obey Eddie's instructions to the letter.

Eddie drove off, leaving Les in the kitchen staring at the cake box. What a weird bloke, thought Les, looking at the cook's name written across the top. I wonder why he did that? Either he's dirty on the world, or there's just some people on the set he wants to get at. Maybe Max King. I wouldn't blame him there. I'll find out somehow over the next few days. In the meantime, Albert's Karma at Kreative Katering is going to katch up with him. Les looked at his watch. Now, what would be the best time to deliver it? I reckon ... about one o'clock. That gives me time to go to the bank, pay a few bills then get to the set when they're all having lunch. That way, everybody will see the cook get splattered and I can mingle in with the crowd. I'll use the telephoto lens first for some action photos then get a few close-ups. The cook won't have a clue who it is, either. Les chuckled to himself. And next day, me and Eddie'll send him a postcard. *We called in to see you. But you were shitfaced so we left. Love, Thelma and Louise.* Les changed into a pair of jeans, a green T-shirt and his Bugs Bunny cap, got his credit cards and whatever else he needed and drove up to Bondi Junction.

Everything went surprisingly easy. He had no trouble getting a parking spot and the queues weren't long. He was back home in time for a cup of coffee and a biscuit before going to the film set. That done, Les picked up the cake box, slung his camera over his shoulder and set off for Campbell Parade.

The big Queenslander was whistling cheerfully as he strolled past the Toriyoshi and through the school gates. The two wardrobe girls were standing near the gate in their multi-coloured clothes and dyed hair. They'd just finished a joint and picked up on Norton's vibe.

'Hey. Someone's in a good mood,' said one, with cherry red hair teased up around her head like a big red broccoli.

'On a day like this,' smiled Les, 'you'd have to be in a good mood.'

Her friend with jet black hair full of dark blue streaks and coloured beads, noticed the cake box. 'Is it somebody's birthday?' she asked.

'Yes. Albert the cook's,' replied Les. 'I baked this for him myself.'

'Oh,' said the dark-haired girl. 'He should like that.'

'Oh yeah,' smiled Norton. 'He'll get a bang out of this, I guarantee it.' Les left them and walked towards the chairs and tables on the grass. He was a little disappointed to find there weren't many people around. One or two film crew, a couple of voyeurs, the ubiquitous Japanese tourist armed with a video camera and the cook's dark-haired assistant, back wiping the tables. Still whistling cheerfully, Les gave the Japanese tourist a smile and a cheeky bow of his head as he went past, straight up to the girl wiping the tables.

'Excuse me, is Albert around?' he asked politely.

'Yeah,' replied the girl, pointing to the blue van. 'He's in the kitchen.'

'What time are you serving lunch today?'

'One-thirty. They're behind with the shoot. So they're having a late wrap.'

'Okay. Thank you.'

Les walked over to the van, tapped on the counter and placed the cake box on it.

'Parcel for Albert Knox,' he called out.

'What?' A lean pink head appeared from behind a wall oven.

'Parcel for Albert Knox. You don't have to sign anything. See you, mate.'

Norton quickly turned and walked off, looking for somewhere to hide while he waited for the cook to open the cake box. The cook, however, was in one of those moods where he didn't have time to be stuffed around. He saw the cake box with his name on top and tore it straight open. Les had just got to the edge of the grass when he heard a muffled explosion and a loud curse. Shit, that was bloody quick. Les laughed and turned around to aim his camera. Next instant, there was a deafening blast and the catering van disintegrated in a spiralling ball of orange flames and a billowing cloud of thick black smoke. Instinctively Les threw his arms across his face as the steps at the rear of the catering van sailed over the school fence before smashing into the back of the bus stop and pieces of metal, wood and fibreglass rained down all over the front of the school, showering the parked trucks and cars with burning debris. The cook, minus one arm and half his face burnt away, was blown through the side entrance at the right of the van, along with the fridge and parts of the stove. Looking like a wobbly mess of charred meat in the remains of his smouldering clothes, Knox was dead before he hit the ground.

His ears ringing like a burglar alarm, Les tried to gather his senses as people started running from everywhere. Some carrying fire extinguishers, others had blankets, most were just startled people from the film crew or bystanders wondering what had happened. By rights, Les should have stopped and offered assistance. But something told Norton the best place for him was out of there. Holding his camera, Les pushed through the people coming in the school gate and walked home as fast as he could.

Back at Chez Norton, Les poured himself a bourbon and ice and with his ears still ringing from the explosion, flopped down in the lounge room dumbfounded. He took a slug of bourbon and tried to get his thoughts together. Jesus bloody Christ! What the fuck did Eddie put in that cake box? Les had another sip of bourbon and shook his head. No, he told himself. No way. There were definitely two explosions. I know I heard the first one. It was just a bit of a bang. Then that other fuckin thing went off. Bloody hell! Les sipped some more bourbon, feeling it burn down his chest and into his stomach. Maybe the thundercracker set something else off? Like those Elgas tanks. No. Les shook his head again. I've heard tanks go. It's a different sound. That was gelignite or some kind of explosive. Les reflected into his glass and was forced to realise the only possible explanation: somebody had let a bomb off in the catering van at the same time he'd bowled up with his firecracker. But why? The cook might have been a low bastard doing what he did. But it wasn't worth killing him for. Was it? Christ! What a lousy, fuckin coincidence. I don't believe it. Then a thought hit Les and it didn't warm his body like the bourbon. It chilled him to the bone. What if somebody saw me leave that parcel there? Saw me leave the parcel? About six bloody people saw me. Those two weird-looking sheilas for a start. The cook's assistant. That Jap with the camera. And anybody else that was there. See me? Fuckin hell! They couldn't miss me. Les stared anxiously at the phone. I think I'd better ring Eddie.

Eddie's mobile wasn't answering. Neither was his answering service at home. That figures, thought Les. Lyndy's taken the kids away for the school holidays so Eddie's up to something. Fuck it. Les put the phone down and started to pace. The more he paced, the more worried he got. Shit! I'm a good chance of getting a tug over this, he told himself. A bloody good chance. He paced some more. Yep. You can back it in. I'm going to get my collar felt. I know it. And what am I going to tell them? Oh, it was only a cracker in a cake box, officer. Yeah. Righto. Les paced some more. No. This is not good. Not good at all. I'd better make another phone call.

'Hello?'

'Yeah. Hello Price. It's Les.'

'Les. How are you, mate? What can I do for you?'

'Price, I think I'm in a bit of serious bother with the cops. I might need a big favour off you later on tonight.'

Les didn't have to spell it out. 'I understand, Les. What time?' asked Price.

'I'm not sure. But I'd reckon early tonight.'

'No worries, Les. I'll make the necessary arrangements. Ring me here. I'll be home all night.'

'Thanks, Price. I appreciate it.'

'You do sound worried, Les.'

'I am.'

'Don't be. Just settle back. And ring me when the time comes.'

'Thanks, Price. I'll get back to you.'

Les hung up and finished his drink. He didn't make another one. Instead he switched on the kitchen radio just in time for the dramatic news.

'One person was killed and several others injured in a bomb blast at Bondi early this afternoon. The device, believed to be remote controlled, was set to go off in a catering van on the set of a movie, *Leaving Bondi*, being filmed at Bondi Beach Public School. Fortunately, the school was closed for the holidays so casualties were kept to a minimum. However, a caterer was fatally injured in the blast and several members of the film crew have been hospitalised. Police have not released any names. But they wish to question a tall, solid man, wearing a T-shirt and baseball cap, seen leaving Bondi Beach Public School shortly after the bomb was detonated.'

'Fuckin hell!'

Les switched off the radio. He'd heard all he needed. A tall, solid man in a baseball cap. That's me. And it'll only be a matter of time before they put a name to the face. Yep. I'm off tap. Les stopped pacing. Okay. No need to panic. But you can bet they'll search the place when they get here. And there's things to be done.

Les got the jemmy from the shed and levered up the pile of wood above where his loot was buried. He removed the slab of wood over the hole then got a shovel and filled the hole with earth. After patting the earth down solid, he dumped the pile of wood on top of it and straightened the tarpaulin. It was going to be a bit of a pain in the arse getting to his swag again, but at least now there was less chance of the police finding it. Next item on the agenda was the boarder's pot. Luckily, Warren had just harvested his plants from the backyard, but he had about half a kilo of juicy heads squashed into a shoe box under his bed. Les took the shoe box out to the kitchen, stood on a chair, moved the manhole cover in the ceiling and hid it in the roof. A thorough search would soon find it, but at least it was better than just sitting under the bed. Warren's lousy fuckin pot, thought Les, after he put the manhole cover back. As if I haven't got better things to worry about than that. Like fuck-all chance of me getting bail for starters. Les gathered his money, wallet, credit cards, passport and anything else he could think of and put them in the pocket of his bomber jacket. He didn't bother ringing his family or Billy Dunne. It was no use alarming everybody for the time being. He'd contacted Price. That was enough. Price would handle it from there. Les could have taken it on the toe and got out of town. But that would only make it look worse and they'd find him sooner or later. No. He had to wear it. It was just plain bad luck. Les had another drink, then made some more coffee and waited. The knock on the door came in the early evening.

Les opened the front door to find two detectives standing there in sports coats, and a uniform cop in overalls with a Jack Russell terrier on a lead. Both detectives were about the same stocky build; one had dark hair going bald, the other had brown hair cut close to his scalp. The uniform cop was tall with a brown moustache. The dark-haired cop had the warrant.

'Les Norton. Cox Avenue, Bondi?' said the dark-haired detective.

'That's me,' nodded Les.

'I'm Detective Caccano. This is Detective Tait and Sergeant Plackett. We have a warrant to search your premises for explosives.'

Les stood back from the door. 'Go for your life.' He turned to the cop with the dog. 'You won't find nothing, mate, so try not to wreck the place will you? There's a tool shed out the backyard too. It's unlocked.'

'Righto, mate,' said the uniform cop indifferently. 'Come on, Oscar. Good boy.'

Les watched as Sergeant Plackett and his sniffer dog started searching round his bedroom, then motioned to the two other cops. 'The lounge is through there. You want to sit down?'

'We'll follow you,' said Detective Caccano.

They went into the lounge room and sat down. Les on the lounge, the two cops facing him on the loungechairs.

'You live here on your own?' asked Detective Caccano.

Les shook his head. 'No. I got a flatmate. A bloke called Warren Edwards. He works for MM and B Advertising.'

'Where's he?' asked Detective Tait.

'Down the south coast with a girl. At Ulladulla. I don't know when he'll be back. About Thursday, I think.'

'You work at the Kelly Club, don't you?' said Detective Tait.

'That's right,' answered Les.

'With a bloke called Billy Dunne.'

'Yeah. We work on the door.'

'Price Galese has gone very respectable these days,' said Detective Caccano.

Les looked at the two detectives expressionlessly. 'I was under the impression he always was.'

The two detectives looked expressionlessly back at Les as Sergeant Plackett and his dog gave the house a swift but thorough going-over. The dog sniffed all over the lounge and kitchen, then they went out into the backyard. Les offered the two detectives some coffee. They declined. There was a modicum of chit-chat then Sergeant Plackett came back into the lounge and shook his head.

'Nothing out there,' he said to the two detectives. He turned to Les. 'How do I get up in the roof?'

'There's a manhole cover in the kitchen. Above the sideboard next to the fridge. The stepladder's in the shed.'

'I won't need it.'

Les watched the cop go into the kitchen then heard him push the dog up through the manhole cover. The dog barked a couple of times as Les heard it running about in the roof. Well, there goes Warren's pot. Now they'll get me for supply. As well as murder, arson, and whatever fuckin else they're going to charge me with. Fuck it, cursed Les.

Les heard the manhole cover being replaced, then Sergeant Plackett and his dog came back into the lounge room empty handed.

Sergeant Plackett shook his head. 'Nothing in there, either,' he said. 'The place appears to be clean.'

'I had a feeling it would be,' said Detective Tait.

'What do you want me to do?'

'Go back to the yard. We'll give you a call if we need you again.'

Les had nearly fallen through the back of the lounge. He knew he had to say something. Anything. Or his facial expressions would give him away.

'If you don't mind me asking,' Les said to Sergeant Plackett, 'that's a funny-looking police dog. I thought they were all German Shepherds. Or Rottweilers.'

'Oscar?' replied Sergeant Plackett. 'Oscar's okay. Oscar used to be with Customs. But he accidentally snorted a big pile of pure heroin one night and nearly died from an overdose. He's been useless with drugs ever since. Couldn't tell dope from donuts. But he's the best in the business when it comes to explosives. Aren't you, Oscar?' The dog panted and smiled up at his handler. 'He's a good boy.' Sergeant Plackett turned to the two detectives. 'Okay. I'll see you later.'

'Righto. Thanks for your help, Geoff,' said Detective Tait.

Les heard Sergeant Plackett and his dog leave and studied Caccano and Tait pretty much the same way they were studying him. From his dealings with police in the past, their attitude and body language told him these two knew what they were doing. They hadn't carried on with any great drama so far and they'd obviously done their homework on him. They were probably mystified why Les would want to set a bomb off on a film set. But by the company Les kept, where he worked and his past form, it wouldn't have surprised them. Up to this point, they'd been very low key. Now Les was waiting for the penny to drop. Though Les had to admit, luck had certainly been on his side so far. Detective Caccano spoke first.

'Well, I imagine you know what this is all about, Les?' he said quietly.

Les made a small gesture with his hands. 'Not ... really. Maybe you'd better fill me in.'

'An explosive device was set off on a film set in Bondi early this afternoon,' continued Detective Caccano. 'In which one person was killed and a number of other people were injured.'

Les nodded. 'Yeah. I heard it on the news earlier.'

'You've been identified by at least five people leaving a parcel in the catering canteen at the precise time of the blast,' said Detective Tait.

'You've been positively identified by the film's director,' Detective Caccano flipped open his notebook. 'A Mr Max King.'

'And there's film of you leaving the parcel on the school's outdoor security camera,' said Detective Caccano. 'Which is what Mr King was able to make a positive identification from.'

There was a brief silence, then Detective Tait spoke. 'So what have you got to say to all this, Les?'

Les studied the two detectives for a moment. 'What have I got to say?' he replied. 'I don't quite know what to say at the moment. But I imagine you'd like me to accompany you to the station. Where I could be of further assistance with your inquiries?'

Detective Caccano half smiled. 'We certainly would.'

Les nodded to his bomber jacket on the lounge. 'I'll just get my jacket.'

Les stood up and so did the two detectives. Detective Caccano reached behind his sports coat.

'If you don't mind, Les,' he said easily. 'Your hands.'

'Yeah,' said Detective Tait. 'It's not that we don't trust you, Les. It's just that we don't trust you.'

Les felt the handcuffs snap round his wrists and knew exactly where he stood with Detectives Caccano and Tait. Two minutes later he was in the back seat of a Holden heading for Waverley Police Station.

Christ! This is getting to be a habit, Les fumed to himself, as the units in Old South Head Road went past. How could anything fuck up so bad? The bloody security camera. I didn't even think of that. But why would Les have thought of that or anything else? It wasn't as if he and Eddie had planned to murder anyone. All they had in mind was more or less a harmless prank. Les would have told the neighbourhood what they were up to. It was a hoot. Now this. Les shook his head and put himself in the two detectives' shoes for a moment. Les was their man all right. They were short on motive, but they had a red hot suspect. And Les knew for sure the best evidence was yet to come.

Waverley Police Station in Bronte Road looked exactly the same as the last time Les was in there. And the time before that. Except there was a platoon of journalists, photographers and TV cameras milling round out the front. Les just had time to pull his jacket up over his head as cameras started flashing and TV cameras began whirling. The police drove down the back of the station and with the media still howling like jackals in the background, Les was bundled out of the Holden and through a door into the station. The only view Les got was his feet beneath his bomber jacket, going up the familiar concrete stairs before he was led into the detectives' room.

'Christ! That was a lot of fun,' said Les, straightening his jacket around him after he walked through the door.

'Yes. Our friends in the media,' said Detective Tait. 'They're all right, aren't they.'

Les had a look around him. He was in the same room as he'd been in last time he was at Waverley Police Station. The same dusty window looking out over the surrounding flats, the same grey metal filing cabinets against the walls. A skinny pot plant in the corner opposite the vinyl chairs and desk. Even the wanted posters on the walls hadn't seemed to change. The only difference was the blue grey carpet looked new, there was a computer on the desk with a TV and a VCR beneath and a video camera mounted on a black metal tripod sat near the computer. Detective Tait motioned Les to one of the seats. Les sat down as the two detectives loosened their ties.

'All right. We won't fuck around, Les,' said Detective Caccano, picking up a video and slipping it into the VCR. 'This is a copy from the school security camera. Have a look and see what you think.'

Les sat back as the video began rolling. It was grainy and jerky with a time lapse. But there was no mistaking Les coming into view and placing the cake box on the counter of the catering van. You could even pick up the maniacal grin on Norton's face as he walked back out of range. Next, there was a great flash of flame and smoke as the van erupted and the chairs and tables closest to the van flew into the others. Then the cook's body tumbled down the stairs through the smoke. Detective Caccano wound it back a couple of times more. Freeze-framed it on Norton's grinning face, then switched it off.

'Well, what do you think, Les?' asked Detective Tait. 'I'd say that's you. I'd even hazard a guess and say you're still wearing the same T-shirt.'

'Yes,' agreed Norton slowly. 'There is a certain resemblance.'

Detective Caccano flipped open his notebook. 'We've also got a statement from a Ms Robyn Cornish, one of the make-up girls on the movie. She said to you, quote, "Is it somebody's birthday?" And you replied, quote, "Yes, Albert the cook's. I baked this for him myself. He'll get a bang out of this. I guarantee it." This is also verified by a statement from the other make-up girl,' the detective consulted his notebook, 'a Ms Jacintha Gillings.'

'Albert the cook certainly got a bang out of your cake, Les, didn't he?' said Detective Tait. 'I'd say half of Bondi did.'

Detective Caccano looked evenly at Norton. 'Do you wish to make a statement, Les?'

Les stared at the handcuffs round his wrists. This was the evidence he knew the two detectives had. And he was stuffed, six ways to Saturday. Or as Billy Dunne liked to say, he had two chances: none and slim. And Slim left town last week. But Les did have two chances. He could tell the truth; not that it would do him much good. And he could make a phone call.

Les sucked in some air. 'Okay. You're right. That is me.'

'Thanks, Les,' said Detective Tait. 'At least you're not playing us for complete mugs.'

'And I want to make a statement. You ain't gonna believe it. But I'll make it anyway. And it's the truth.'

'Okay, Les,' said Detective Caccano. 'Now as this is a very serious charge, I'm going to record it on video.' The detective swivelled the video camera on the tripod, spoke briefly into the recorder, then gave Les the go-ahead.

Without implicating Eddie, Les told them everything that happened. He said he made the device in the cake box, and he was alone when he saw the cook tampering with the food. He left the scene because he panicked, and intended contacting the police the following day, but the two detectives called round before he had the chance. Detective Caccano switched off the video recorder, looked at his partner, then turned to Les. Whether they saw the funny side of the situation, Les wasn't sure. It certainly didn't appear that way.

'You say you made the explosive device in the cake box?' said Detective Tait.

'That's right. At home. In the shed out the back,' replied Les.

'And you bought the cracker from a friend in Chinatown?' said Detective Caccano.

'That's right.'

'What was his name?'

'His name? Ahh, I'm not sure. He's just a bloke I know.'

'And the image-stabilizing binoculars?' asked Detective Tait. 'Where are they now?'

'I loaned them to a bloke. To take to the races.'

'I see,' nodded Detective Tait. 'And the cake you used to put the firecracker in? Where did you buy that?'

'I baked it at home. Out of a packet,' replied Les.

'And you went to all this trouble,' said Detective Caccano, 'because you saw the cook putting flies in the stew. And dog shit in the lamingtons.'

'That's exactly right,' said Les. 'Hey, like I told you, I invested some money in that movie, and I didn't like what I saw going on.'

'I suppose the money you invested in the movie,' said Detective Tait, 'you won that at the races, too.'

'As a matter of fact I did.'

Detective Caccano looked at his partner. Then back at Norton. 'Okay, Les. That's one of the greatest loads of bullshit I've ever heard. It's such a load of bullshit it could almost be fair dinkum. But ...' Detective Caccano shook his head. 'So I am now officially charging you, Les. With murder. Five counts of malicious wounding. Malicious damage. Endangering public safety.' He looked directly at Norton. 'That'll do for starters.'

'Okay,' conceded Les, nodding his head slowly. He'd played his ace. Now it was up to his right bower. 'But bullshit or not, I've been straight up with you blokes, haven't I? I haven't carried on like a cunt. And I haven't treated you like mugs.'

'True,' agreed Detective Tait.

'So how about a phone call?'

Detective Tait pushed the phone across the table. 'Be my guest.'

Les picked up the receiver and dialed awkwardly with the handcuffs still round his wrists. 'Hello Price. It's Les. Yeah. I'm in Waverley Police Station. Okay. I'll put Detective Caccano on the line.' Les handed the receiver to Detective Caccano. 'Just have a talk to Price for a sec, will you?'

Detective Caccano picked up the phone. He didn't speak. He just nodded his head a couple of times. 'All right, Mr Galese,' he said, then hung up.

'What was that all about?' asked Detective Tait.

'I'm not sure,' replied his partner. 'But we'll know soon enough.'

A minute later the phone rang. Detective Caccano picked it up and seemed to stiffen. All Les could hear was a muffled, 'Yes sir. Yes sir. No sir.' Then Caccano handed the phone to Detective Tait. There was another muffled, 'Yes sir. Yes sir. No sir,' before Detective Tait hung up.

Both detectives sat and stared quietly at Les. 'You sure know some people, don't you, Les,' said Detective Caccano.

Les shook his head. 'Not really. But Price does.'

Detective Tait gave a mirthless smile. 'Yeah. Good old Price.'

Les gestured as best he could with the handcuffs on. 'Like I said, he's a very respectable man. Always has been.'

Detective Caccano looked at Norton then undid the handcuffs. 'All right, Les. We'll give you half a break. I'm still charging you. But we'll give you conditional bail. Six days. That means you're back here next Monday at nine-thirty to appear before a magistrate for a hearing.'

'Thanks.'

Detective Caccano tapped the table, then pointed at Les. 'You surrender your passport. You report here every day between nine and three. You don't leave the state. And if we so much as see you walk in an exit door, we'll be all over you like flies on shit.'

'I got the picture,' nodded Les, rubbing his wrists.

'And when you front on Monday,' said Detective Tait, 'we'll oppose bail. The prosecutor will oppose bail. So as well as your lawyer, bring a toothbrush.'

'Fair enough.'

The two detectives then processed Les. He was fingerprinted, they took a photo, and they took his passport. And in no uncertain terms, they warned Les to obey to his bail conditions to the letter. Everything was painstakingly typed up in quadruplicate then they went over everything again with him so there was no mistake. Finally Les was given his bail papers and a report card to bring with him when he came to the station.

'Okay, Les,' said Detective Caccano. 'You're free to go.'

'For the time being,' added Detective Tait. 'And I'll be fair dinkum with you, Les. We're filthy on having to watch you walk out of here. We saw what was left of the cook. There could have been another dozen like him.'

'Fair enough, fellahs,' said Les. He stood up and looked at the two detectives. 'Look, I know how you feel. No one likes being compromised. But this is just one big fuck-up. And that's the truth. I just want a chance to see if I can sort the shitfight out.'

'It's a shitfight all right,' agreed Detective Caccano, emptily. 'See you later, Les.'

'Yeah, see you on Monday. And thanks again, anyway.' Les turned and walked out of the detectives' room.

Fuckin hell, thought Les as he came down the steps to the front desk. How heavy was that? Bloody Price. I wonder what strings he pulled to get me out of there? Yeah. Only for six days. But the way it was going, I'm bone lucky to get that. Then another thought struck Les. Now I've got to get through all those miserable pricks out the front. The last thing I want is my head plastered all over the front of the papers and the late night news. Over at the front desk Les recognised a familiar face. It was the old fat sergeant who farted in the front seat of the wagon when Bob McKenna's daughter got pinched for shoplifting. He wasn't a bad bloke, if Les remembered right. The sergeant was standing next to two other uniform cops who were listening to some woman in a black dress having a beef about an AVO.

'Hey boss,' Les said to the sergeant. 'How can I get out the front without those bludgers swarming all over me?'

The old sergeant recognised Les and remembered what Les had done the day they drove him back to the station. He showed a bit of sympathy. 'Here,' he said, 'take this newspaper and read it walking out backwards.'

'Read it walking out backwards?'

'Yeah. They'll think you're walking in. Christ! They're only journalists. They're not rocket scientists.'

Les hesitated for a moment then took the *Wentworth Courier*. 'You're right. Thanks, sarge.'

This might just work, thought Les. They still don't know for sure what I look like. Les opened the paper in front of him, and went out through the door backwards. The media scrum was still pushing and shoving each other all over the footpath like wild dogs round a dead sheep. Les went round them cooler than Michael Jackson moonwalking; straight into the front seat of a passing taxi. The taxi driver had thick black hair, a moustache and a cap pulled down around his ears.

'Where to mite?'

'Bondi. Cox Avenue. You know it?'

'Sure I do,' said the driver, setting the meter. 'No worries mite.'

Les settled back as the driver headed for Old South Head Road.

'Hey, what you think about the bomb in Bondi todiy mite?' said the driver.

'What do I think about it?' Hello. Here we go, thought Les. 'I don't think much about it at all. It's ... no good,' he answered.

'You know who done it. Don't you, mite?'

Les shook his head. 'No. Who done it?'

'The blackfellahs.'

'The what?'

'The bloody abos, mite.'

'The abos?'

'Yeah mite. Didn't you see the bloke on the tivee the other night. Sayin' burn all the place down for the Olympic games. This the start mite.'

Les looked at the driver. 'You could have something there. I never thought of that.'

'Hey. I know I'm right, mister. Make it hard for me to get the quid now. Should send them all back where they come from, bastards.'

'Come from? They come from here,' said Les.

The cab driver shook his head. 'No. They come from New Guinea.'

'Fair dinkum?' said Les. 'I've lived here all my life and I never knew that.'

'It's the truth, mite. Should send them all back. And Pauline Hanson with them.'

Les stared at the cab driver. 'She's not an abo.'

'No. She's a pom. And they's just as bad. Whinge, whinge, whinge. Allatime.'

'You know,' said Les. 'You might just have something there ... mite.'

'Hey. I know what I'm talkin' bout, mite. Don't you worry.'

The taxi pulled up outside Chez Norton. Les paid the driver and went inside. Fair dinkum. Somebody tell me I'm dreaming, thought Les, as he shut the door behind him.

There were three messages on the answering machine. All from Eddie. Les listened to the last one and the phone rang again. It was Eddie.

'Les. I've been trying to ring you. I just heard all this weird shit on the news. What the fuck's goin' on?'

'What's going on, Eddie,' answered Les. 'Some cunt put a bomb on the film set. And it went off just as I delivered that cake box.'

'Fuckin hell! I don't believe it,' said Eddie. 'So what happened to you?'

'What happened to me? I got pinched. The cops think I did it. I just managed to get bail.'

'You're on bail? Ohh this is fuckin unbelievable.'

'You can believe it all right, Eddie,' said Les.

Les told Eddie what happened. The police coming round to his house. Not believing what he told them and Price managing to squeeze bail for him.

'And you didn't mention me, Les. You wore the lot.' Eddie was impressed. 'Jesus, you're staunch, mate.'

'Yeah. Well, it's not much good the two of us getting nicked,' said Les. 'You're better off helping me out in the street.'

'Hey. Don't worry, Les. I'll be doing everything I can.'

'Thanks.'

'Look. It's not much good talking over the phone. How about I call round your place tomorrow morning? Early. About eight o'clock. That okay?'

'Yeah. Good as gold.'

'And don't worry. We'll sort this fuckin thing out somehow.'

'I hope so, Eddie. Because I'm in deep fuckin shit.'

Les hung up then thought he'd better ring Price.

'Les. How are you mate?' said Price. 'Eddie rang me earlier. And I heard the news. What a gigantic balls-up.'

'Unfortunately the cops don't seem to think so, Price. They've charged me with everything but the Wanda Beach murders. I'd still be up there if it wasn't for you. Thanks for that.'

'That's okay, Les. It's the least I could do.'

Les told Price what happened in the police station and how the cops weren't too happy about letting him go.

'So they've got me on a pretty heavy pinch, Price. After seeing the evidence, I don't suppose you can blame them.'

'Look, don't worry, Les,' said Price. 'We'll do our best to get you bail on Monday. If not we'll appeal or some bloody thing. But we'll work it out. My blokes are the best in the business.'

'Thanks.'

'In the meantime, just hang in. And we'll all get our heads together through the week and see what we can come up with.'

'Okay Price. I'll be in touch.'

'Do that, Les. See you, mate.'

'Yeah. See you, Price. Thanks again.'

They'll do their best to get me bail. Great, thought Les. That cop wasn't joking when he said bring a toothbrush on Monday. Les shook his head in frustration. Why me? Why fuckin me? He went to the bathroom, cleaned the fingerprint dye off his hands and tidied himself up, then got a beer from the fridge and sat in the lounge drinking it, but not enjoying it. About half way through his beer, Les decided sitting around doing nothing wasn't going to help. He had six lousy days to come up with something. So he'd better get his finger out and start asking questions. And there was a very plausible person not too far away who might know something. And if he didn't, a bit of friendly persuasion might jog his memory.

Les was just about to walk out the door when the phone rang. It was Warren, sounding very excited.

'Les. It's Warren. Are you there? Pick up.'

Les reached across for the receiver. 'Hello Warren. How's things?'

'How's things?' replied Warren. 'Christ! I saw the news earlier. I've been trying to ring all night. What the fuck's going on? What happened to the movie?'

'What's happened to the movie?' answered Les. 'It got blown up.'

'Did you do it?' said Warren bluntly.

'No. I didn't fuckin do it, Warren. It's a frame-up.'

'Bloody hell!'

'Warren, I'll give it to you straight,' said Les. 'I've been charged with murder.'

'Murder?'

'Yeah, I'm out on bail till Monday. Then I go for a hearing and they'll refuse bail when I front.'

'Bloody hell!'

'So it looks like you're going to have the house to yourself for a while.'

'Fuck. This is unbelievable. I'd better come home now,' said Warren.

'No. Stay where you are,' replied Les. 'There's no need to spoil your holiday.'

'It's spoiled already,' answered Warren.

'Yeahh. But there's nothing you can do up here. Just be back by Monday to take me to court.'

'Are you sure?'

'Yeah. Positive.'

'All right. I'll come home Saturday, Sunday morning at the latest. You've got my mobile number. If you need me or whatever, call me.'

'Yeah. I'll do that, Warren.'

'Shit! This is unbelievable.'

'Yeah. Ain't it. I'll see you on the weekend, Woz.'

'All right. See you then, Les.'

Les hung up and looked at the phone. Good old Woz. I could think of worse blokes to be looking after the place while I'm away. But I don't need him around at the moment. If me and Eddie should have to drag someone back here for a few answers, I think Warren might get a little squeamish at the smell of burning flesh and blood all over the walls. Les finished his beer. Now, where was I? Out the door if I remember right.

The Toriyoshi was closed when Les got there. So was the bottle shop. The front of the school was roped off with yellow police tape and there was a wagon parked in the driveway. The film crew had long packed up and gone; all that remained was the blackened shell of the catering van sitting near the fence. Mmmhh, mused Norton. Looks like the Gull's flown off. I reckon there's a chance he might be having a drink. And I know where Ray likes a cool one when he's not in his chicken shack. C.C.'s.

C.C.'s was a bar in Curlewis Street just near the TAB. It used to be a wine bar, but a young ex-bookmaker had just taken over and acquired a beer and spirits licence. It was family roomy, with a coloured sign out the front featuring a blinking cocktail glass, and inside was green carpet and green walls dotted with posters for Boags Stout, Caffreys Irish Ale and Jim Beam. Several fans spun under a latticework ceiling, and through an archway at the rear, bands performed on a small stage. There were plenty of stools and tables along the wall on the left as you walked in, the bar was on the right and the windows near the front door opened onto the street to let the smoke out. Les liked C.C.'s and used to pop in for a drink now and again. If C.C.'s had got its spirit licence before Les settled in at the Toriyoshi, he would have drunk there more often. The band had stopped playing and about thirty casually dressed punters were sitting or standing around having a drink when Les walked in the front door. The Gull was perched on a stool at the bar, dressed in a blue Hawaiian shirt, staring into a bourbon and Coke like he wished it was a deep, dark pool of water and he could have jumped in with a Mack gearbox wired to his neck.

Les walked over and stood on Ray's right. 'Nnnyyhhh. So what's happening the Gull? I'm glad you're face isn't looking like a six-month-old passionfruit, anyway.'

Ray looked up and gave Norton a heavy double-blink from behind his steel-framed glasses. 'Les? What are you? I mean ...'

'You mean, what am I doing here, Ray?' replied Les. 'I got bail. That's what I'm doing here, Ray.'

'You did? I mean. I heard on the news ... Hey, what do I know about the news? That's good, Les.'

'Yes. It is. But you don't look too good, Ray me old. What's the matter?'

'What's the matter?' The Gull took a sip of bourbon then shook his head and went back to staring into his glass. 'The police don't know if somebody's going to plant another bomb on the set so they've stopped the shoot. Nearly everyone on the set's getting trauma counselling after seeing what was left of the cook. The rest got hit by flying debris. Max has pulled the pin. Simone's pulled the pin. The whole gig's over, man. Finished.'

'Finished?' said Les.

'Yeah. It couldn't sink any further if they buried it at sea. And I'm sunk with it.'

'Back to Gullsville, Ray.'

Ray nodded. 'Yeah. Not a pot to piss in. Or a window to throw it out.'

'Or a feather to fly with,' suggested Les.

'Right on, baby.'

Ray had another mouthful of bourbon. Les caught the eye of a blonde barmaid in a white top and ordered a bourbon and unleaded for himself.

'Well so much for *Leaving Bondi*, Ray,' said Les, raising his glass. 'It didn't even get on the 380.'

Ray shook his head. 'I don't even want to know about it, man. It's turned out a complete bummer.'

'What about my lazy fifty, Ray? I imagine that left Bondi all right. Never to return.'

'It might be covered by insurance, Les.'

'Yeah.' Les had a sip of bourbon. 'Look, Ray, no matter what you're thinking, I didn't set the bomb off.'

'Hey Les, that didn't even enter my head, man,' the Gull assured Norton.

'But the cops think I did. And I'm in deep shit. So I need some information, Ray.'

'Sure Les. How can I help?'

'I need the Tom Thumb on that cook. Albert Knox. What do you know about him?'

'What do I know about him?' Ray blinked helplessly behind his glasses. 'Shit, Les. I don't know that much about him at all.'

After being grilled at Waverley Police Station for hours in a pair of handcuffs, Norton wasn't wearing his happy hat. 'Well you must know some fuckin thing, Ray,' he said. 'Christ! You knew his name when I asked about him before. You're both in the fuckin food game.'

'Okay. Okay. I'm with you, man.' Ray thought for a second. 'All right. He got the catering job on the movie off his own bat. I didn't do anything for him there. He ... he lives ... I mean, he lived in Darlinghurst. He shared a flat there with some guys.'

'Darlinghurst?'

'Yeah. I heard he was into some weird gay scene.'

'Weird gay scene?' said Les.

Ray nodded. 'Yeah. He's bi. I know that. Was. Whatever.'

'So Albert was AC/DC was he?'

'Yeah. Bowled underarm. Look, the bloke you should talk to is Brett Rittosa.'

'Brett Rittosa? Who's he?'

'Brett and Albert used to be partners in a restaurant at Glebe. The word is, Albert ripped Brett off for a lot of money.'

'Did he now? That's interesting. So where do I find this Brett Rittosa rooster?'

'In rooster territory, Les,' smiled Ray. 'He runs a takeaway breakfast kitchen in Bondi Junction. Near the entrance to the railway station at the back of the mall. It's called Brett's Brekky.'

'Brett's Brekky. I might have seen it.'

'Yeah. He does sausage sandwiches. BLTs. Coffee, whatever. For people on their way to work. It's only a small business. He doesn't make a lot of money.'

Les had a swallow of bourbon and looked at the Gull over his glass. 'What time's he open?'

'Six o'clock in the morning. He closes about eleven.'

Les had a think for a moment as the band came back on. 'All right. Thanks, Ray,' he said, finishing his drink. 'That's a start. I'll go and see him first thing in the morning.'

'Okay. And Brett's not a bad bloke either. He's done it tough.'

'Ain't we all.' Les looked directly at the Gull for a moment. 'Hey Ray. All jokes aside, who do you think did it? You got any ideas?'

Ray shook his head despondently. 'Les, I haven't got a clue, man. I still can't believe it's happened, to be honest. The karma on that set was beautiful. Just perfect. Now this.' Ray shook his head again. 'All I can say is, that Knox cat must've been toting some heavy vibes, man.'

'Right,' nodded Les. 'That definitely makes sense, Ray. Oh, have you heard from Max King and the rest of them?'

'No. Max had split from the set when I went round. The others haven't called me yet. I can't even find my business partner.'

'Okay. Well, I'll see you, Ray.'

'Yeah. See you, Les.' Ray stared back into his bourbon as Les stepped round the other drinkers in C.C.'s and out the door.

Back home, Les had a shower then changed into a clean white T-shirt and a pair of shorts. He got a beer from the fridge and took it into the lounge room to sit and have a quiet think. Unexpectedly, he felt dog tired. Instead of his mind racing at a thousand miles an hour, it was almost blank. All Les could think was, one minute you're up there laughing your head off and life's a bowl of cherries, next thing it's the absolute bloody pits. He ran his eyes around the house at all the creature comforts he enjoyed — along with Warren — and how you take things for granted. Now in six short days he could lose the lot. Along with his freedom for probably the rest of his life. And this time he hadn't done anything. Les looked at the bar and all the bottles of choice booze sitting there. An idea would be to get pissed out of his brain and blot everything out. Then climb up in the roof, get Warren's pot and stone himself into the netherworld with the stereo blasting. Instead, Les finished his beer and went to bed. He intended being up nice and early in the morning and hitting the ground running. He slipped a Steely Dan CD into the stereo in his bedroom, lay back and closed his eyes. By the time 'Aja' had cut out, Norton was in a deep, dark sleep.

L es was out of bed around six. Outside it was cold and the previous day's breeze had turned to a biting sou'westerly. He made some tea and sipped it over a toasted sandwich while he listened to the news. The bombing was the lead story and Norton's name was mentioned; Les finished his sandwich and couldn't wait to read about it in the papers. He got into a pair of jeans, black desert boots and a black leather jacket and drove up to Bondi Junction. The traffic was light and he had no trouble finding a parking spot in Oxford Street around from Newland. He locked the car and walked across to the mall.

Brett's Brekky was a white kiosk with a shutter front and matching awning, in the middle of the walkway near the Grafton Street entrance to the railway station. Les stood back amongst the people hurrying for the trains and checked out the owner and his female assistant. He was lean, with a grainy face and brown hair receding in the front, and had that look of tired humour in his eyes people get after working all their life to get nowhere before finally accepting what life has thrown up. He was wearing white jeans and a white T-shirt with a blue bib and brace and a butcher's apron tied in the front. His dark-haired helper was wearing the same. The owner was cooking food on a small stove next to a coffee urn while the girl was buttering toast; there was one customer. A metal step led up to the back door. Les walked over and knocked lightly on the side of the kiosk.

'Are you Brett Rittosa?' he asked.

'Yeah, that's me,' replied the proprietor, glancing up from a frypan full of sausages. 'I suppose you're from the taxation department?'

'No,' answered Les. 'Quite the opposite. In fact I'd like to give you some money.'

'What?' Brett looked up again. 'Yeah, that'd be right.'

'Do these look all right?' Les flashed a roll of hundred-dollar bills.

Brett looked at them and his thin mouth filled with saliva. 'They sure do, mate.'

'How about making me a flat white with two sugars. And I'll see you on one of those seats in the mall.'

'I'll be there in two minutes.'

Les walked up to the mall, found a wire seat, then sat down and made himself comfortable. Brett was along shortly with a carton of coffee and a can of Coke. He handed Les his coffee and sat down next to him. Les offered his hand.

'I'm Les.'

Brett nodded and shook Norton's hand. 'Les Norton. I've seen you around.'

'I live in Bondi. And I work up the Cross.'

'The Kelly Club. Price Galese.'

'That's me.'

Brett took a mouthful of Coke and smiled. 'So Les. I imagine this is about the unfortunate demise of Albert Knox.'

'You're right on the ball, Brett.' Les smiled back, then tucked a hundred-dollar bill into the top of Brett's apron. 'And you can have that for starters.'

'Thanks. That'll come in handy, I can tell you.'

Les removed the top of his carton and took a sip. The coffee was surprisingly good. 'All right, Brett, I'll get straight to the point. You were partners in a restaurant with Albert Knox. Tell me all about him. Anything.'

Brett looked directly at Les. 'He was a cunt. How's that for starters?'

'Fair enough,' said Les.

'He ripped people off. Dope dealers. Women. Old ladies. Me. Anybody.' Brett shook his head. 'Somehow he managed to keep getting away with it. Up until now.'

'What did he do with all the money?'

'Shoved most of it up his nose.'

'Into the sentimental bloke, eh. That figures. Was he dealing?'

Brett nodded over his can of Coca-Cola. 'Yeah. Not in a big way. Mainly to feed his habit.'

'Did he have many friends?'

'Friends? I'll put it this way, Les, I wouldn't like to be selling sausage sandwiches at his funeral.' Brett swallowed some more Coke. 'He used to hang with some strange people, though. Sort of heavy. In a weird kind of way.'

'What? Dope dealers?'

'Probably. But weird.'

'Gays?' said Les. 'I heard Albert sat on both sides of the fence.'

Brett laughed. 'Albert'd be in anything. No. These people were into Wicca.'

'Wicca? What the fuck's that?'

'Witchcraft. Spells, rituals, all that sort of shit.'

'Albert of the occult,' said Les, taking another mouthful of coffee. 'The plot certainly thickens.'

'He had a place in the Blue Mountains. He used to go there and write poetry and stuff. I went up there a couple of times. But he'd never let me stay overnight. Or have a good look round the house. I thought that was a bit odd, seeing I was his business partner.'

'Whereabouts in the Blue Mountains, Brett? Do you know the address?'

Brett shook his head. 'I can't remember. But it was in Medlow Bath and it had a red gate. And a blue letter box. And there was a big red gum out the front, too.'

'When you say had a place in the Blue Mountains, has he still got it?'

'Oh yeah,' replied Brett. 'He'd never let that go. He has people stay there while he's in Sydney. You know, boarders, some of his weird friends, whatever.'

'Uh huh.'

Brett finished his Coca-Cola about the same time Les drained his coffee.

'Well, Les, there's not much more I can tell you,' said Brett. 'And I'd better get back to the kiosk. Michalina only knows about five words of English.'

'Okay,' said Les, getting to his feet. 'You've been a big help though. Here.' Les stuck another two hundred dollars in Brett's apron.

'Shit! Thanks for that, Les.' Brett offered his hand again. 'If there's anything else I can do. You know where to find me.'

'Okay. Thanks, Brett.'

'Call in anyway. I'll shout you a coffee.'

'I might do that, Brett. It's bloody good coffee.' Les turned to walk away. 'Hey Brett. One more thing?'

'Sure.'

'Where was Albert from? Sydney?'

Brett shook his head. 'Adelaide.'

Les watched Brett walk back to the kiosk, then dropped his empty coffee carton in a garbage bin. He bought the morning paper and headed for Bondi.

Back home, Les had a glass of water and flicked through the paper. The first three pages were headlined BOMB OUTRAGE AT SCHOOL. KILLING ON FILM SET. TEN PEOPLE INJURED. Here we go, thought Les. But it could have been worse.

The photo of him being driven into Waverley Police Station gave nothing away. He'd managed to get his jacket up over his head, so they could have had Elvis in the car for all anybody would have known. And apart from Knox's assistant, the injuries weren't too bad and some of the film crew were probably hitting the workers' compensation trail, seeing that the film shoot was finished. Plus they had him down as Les Norton, a waiter from Kings Cross. That old sergeant was right, mused Les, going over it again before flicking to the sports pages. You definitely don't have to be a brain surgeon to get a job on a newspaper. Les was reading about a disappearing prima donna rugby league player when the doorbell rang. It was Eddie.

'Shit, Les. What can I say, mate?' Eddie waved his newspaper around as Les closed the front door and they walked down to the kitchen.

'We've managed to make the headlines again, Eddie,' said Les. 'It could be worse, though. At least I'm Les, the inoffensive waiter. Not Les, the thug gangster doorman.'

'Yeah. It's still a fuckin heavy pinch they've got you on, mate.'

'Yeah,' agreed Les. 'It sure is. And if I said I wasn't worried, I'd be a liar. And a dill.'

Les told Eddie everything that happened. From the bomb going off. Cleaning out the house. To the police coming round and charging him. Then what Ray Tracy had told him and his meeting with Brett Rittosa earlier.

'So it looks like our mate the cook was a shifty no-good prick,' said Les. 'You almost had to queue up to hate him.'

Eddie shook his head. 'I wish we'd never gone near that silly fuckin film set.'

'You and me both, mate,' agreed Les. 'What about you, Eddie? Have you found out anything?'

'No. I didn't get back home till late last night. And I only got up a while ago. But George'll be ringing you soon. Evidently he's on to something.'

At that instant the phone rang in the lounge room.

'This'll be him now,' said Eddie.

It was Billy Dunne. 'Les, how are you, mate? You okay?'

'As good as I can be under the circumstances, thanks Billy,' answered Les.

'Eddie told me what's happened. Fuckin hell! I can't believe this.'

'It's true, Billy. Eddie's here now. Have you got this morning's paper?'

'Yeah. At least you can't see your head. But everybody around the traps is going to know who it is.'

'Yeah,' admitted Les. 'Great, ain't it.'

'I've spoken to Price and we're all on the case. I've got Big Danny to fill in for you at work.'

'Thanks, Billy.'

'And I reckon you should be sweet on Monday.'

Despite his workmate's effort, Les didn't detect a great deal of confidence in Billy's voice. 'Yeah. We'll see what happens, mate.'

'Look, I'll leave you with Eddie. And I'll call round this afternoon. You be home?'

'Probably.'

'Okay. Well, I'll see you then. Take care, mate.'

'Yeah. Thanks Billy.' Les hung up and walked back into the kitchen. 'That was Billy. He's going to call over this afternoon.'

Eddie nodded. 'I rang him earlier.'

Les was going to say something when the phone rang again. 'This might be George.' It was.

'Hello Les. How are you goin', mate?'

'I'm hanging in, George,' replied Les. 'Hangin' in.'

'Good on you, son.' Les and George might have constantly bagged and poked shit at each other at work, but when it came down to business, that was all forgotten. 'Price told me what's going on, Les. I can't believe your bad luck.'

'I suppose you saw the papers this morning, George?' said Les.

'Yeah, the pricks. At least they didn't get a decent photo of you. And I always said you'd make a good waiter.'

'Thanks George,' laughed Les.

'Okay. I'll tell you what's going on. Evidently they love a bit of scandal and rumour, the show biz mob, and while he was hanging around that movie set, Kevin picked up a bit of gossip.'

'Go on, George.'

'That cook who got blown up. His name's Albert Knox. He was a small-time coke dealer.'

'I already knew that.'

'He'd also been in a bit of strife with the law,' said George.

'Dealing dope?'

'No. You remember about a year ago, a bloke got murdered in the Blue Mountains and they found his body on a walking trail? He was a barrister, had a wife and kids. And it turned out he was a mad raving poof on the side.'

'Vaguely, George.'

'Well, they never found the murderer. But Knox had tried to blackmail the barrister. He was going to out him and a couple of his mates. The cops charged Knox with extortion, but between the bloke getting himself murdered and whatever, Knox beat it.'

'Yeah. According to a bloke I've been talking to, Knox was a bit of a shifty,' said Les. 'Something like that'd be right up his alley.'

'There was also this old bird in the Blue Mountains,' continued George. 'Kicked the bucket and left all this money and real estate in a disputed will. Knox was half pie pally with the old girl and forged her name on a letter giving him part of the estate. He got sprung. But somehow or other he beat that, too. So besides being one step in front of the gendarmes, Knox had quite a few people offside.'

'Christ! You'd think those two coppers'd know all this,' said Les.

'They probably do,' replied George. 'But unfortunately they've got your head on the block, Les.'

'Yeah. Terrific.'

'Anyway, Kevin's calling over this afternoon. He might've found out something else. And me and Price have got our ears to the ground.'

'That's good. Well, thanks for your help, George. I'll keep in touch.'

'No worries. Look after yourself, big fellah.'

Les hung up and walked back into the kitchen. 'George's nephew found out a couple of interesting things.' Les told Eddie what George had said over the phone.

'Fuck. It looks like our mate Knox barred nothing when it came to hustling a quid,' said Eddie.

'Yeah,' agreed Les. 'He'd steal the filling off a shit sandwich and leave you with the dry bread.'

Les and Eddie sat silently staring into space for a while before Eddie spoke.

'Well, what do you think, Les?' he asked.

'What do I think?' shrugged Les. 'I'm fucked if I know, Eddie. Anybody could have murdered that prick Knox. Coke dealers he'd ripped off. People he'd tried to blackmail. That old girl's relatives in case he's still disputing the will. His ex-partner in the restaurant. Witches, warlocks, whatever.'

'Not counting punters who didn't like his nouveau cuisine,' said Eddie.

'Yeah. I forgot about them too,' said Les. 'Christ! It's a cast of thousands.'

'So what are we going to do?'

'What are we going to do?' Les looked at Eddie for a moment. 'I know what I'm going to do. I'm going to take a trip to the the Blue Mountains.'

'The Blue Mountains? What the fuck do you want to go there for?'

'I'm going to see if I can find Knox's house. There's definitely a Blue Mountains connection to this, Eddie. And if I can get into his house, I reckon I might find a clue.'

'Clue?' said Eddie. 'Turn it up, Les. Who do you think you are? Cliff Hardy?'

'Well, I may as well be sniffing around up there, Eddie, as walking around Bondi with every cunt pointing at me behind my back and saying, look, there's the bloke that set the bomb off on the film set.'

'Yeah. I suppose you've got a point,' agreed Eddie.

'I know I've got nothing to lose,' said Les. 'I can punch the bundy at Waverley Police Station on the way up. Stay the night. And be back in time to bundy on again Thursday. And you can keep sniffing around down here.'

'Fair enough,' agreed Eddie. 'When are you going to leave?'

Les looked at his watch. 'By the time I root around here and pack my swag, a couple of hours. I'll get there in time for a late lunch.'

'You know where you're gonna stay?'

'Haven't the foggiest,' shrugged Les. 'First decent hotel I come to in Medlow Bath, I suppose.'

Eddie gave Les a look of grudging approval and got to his feet. 'All right. Well, I'll get cracking and see what I can dig up. And I'll see you when you get back. If you need me, give me a call. I'll be straight up.'

'Thanks mate. I will.'

Les saw Eddie to the door, waved him off, then walked back out the kitchen. He made a cup of coffee and as he was sipping it thought of something the Gull had told him earlier. Les looked at his watch again. Yeah. She'd be at work now, for sure. He took his coffee into the lounge room and picked up the phone.

'Geraldine Hardacre, accountant.'

'Hello Gerry. It's Les Norton.'

'Les?' replied his accountant. 'How are you?'

'Oh. Okay Gerry, I suppose.'

'That's not you in this morning's paper is it, Les? Surely?'

'Yeah. That's me all right,' admitted Les.

'Good lord! What's the world coming to?'

'Well I can tell you now, Gerry, it's not what it seems.'

'I didn't think so. I know you're a pretty willing lot at the Kelly Club, but I didn't think you went around blowing up movie sets.'

'We don't. Especially after one of us has shoved fifty grand into the bloody thing.'

'Yes. That could be looking a bit shaky at this stage. I'm sorry to say.'

'Great,' said Les. 'Anyway, that's the least of my worries at the moment, Gerry. I'm wondering if you could do me a favour?'

'I'll certainly do what I can, Les.'

'Could you ring Ivor and find out if anybody's taken any ... any special sort of an insurance policy out on that movie?'

'I can do that for you, Les. He's busy this morning. But if you ring me back late this afternoon he should know something. Say about four-thirty.'

'Thanks, Gerry. I'll ring you then.'

'Bye Les.'

Les hung up, sipped his coffee and looked at the phone, shaking his head. That's something else we didn't think of. An insurance scam. Add that to the list of suspects. Christ! Forget Cliff Hardy. This is more like Agatha fuckin Christie. Les took his coffee back out to the kitchen and glanced at his photo on the front page of the paper again. Then another thought struck him, giving the big red-headed Queenslander even less joy. Somewhere out there, someone who couldn't believe their luck was having a good laugh at his expense. They didn't even need any luck. All they had to do was hang in and by Monday they were home and hosed. Les threw the paper in the garbage, finished his coffee and started packing for a quick trip to the Blue Mountains. I wonder what the weather's going to be like up there, he mused. Les had a look out the front window. The sou'wester had picked up and it was starting to rain. Cold and wet. Better toss in my GAP anorak. An hour later Les had packed everything he thought he'd need from warm socks to a pair of binoculars and a torch. He locked the house, wished himself luck and drove up to Waverley Police Station.

Signing his report card was pretty much a formality. There were no journalists or TV cameras around and Les was more than likely just one of a host of villains forced to report when told. A grizzled desk sergeant processed him and as soon as he got that out of the way, Les headed for Parramatta Road and the M4, stopping briefly at Camperdown to fill up with petrol.

The rain increased and so did the traffic along Parramatta Road till eventually Les found the entrance to the M4 at Strathfield. He still wasn't too sure where he was going. According to his roadmap, get to the other side of Penrith and climb west. A set of tollgates appeared out of the gloom. Les couldn't see how much it was, so he impatiently flung whatever change he had in the basket and quickly wound the window up. The light turned green and he continued on his way to the steady beat of the windscreen wipers and the rain hitting the roof. The traffic was slow and heavy. Trucks and prime movers hissed by leaving plumes of road water in their wake and every vehicle had its headlights on. Another truck went past spraying water everywhere as the FM station quietly playing in Norton's Berlina pumped out another pop record.

Les caught his eye in the rear-vision mirror and shook his head. You know what I am, he told himself. An idiot. A complete bloody idiot. I'm driving somewhere in the pissing rain, to find a house with a red fence and a blue letter box. With a fuckin gum tree out the front. Then if by some remote chance I happen to find it, what do I do? Knock on the door and say hello, do you mind if I take a stroll around, I'm looking for some evidence in a murder. Unbelievable. The traffic ground on and the radio played another pop song. Ahh fuck it, thought Les, as he crossed the Nepean River. I may as well have some ad-free music on my road to nowhere. He slipped a tape into the cassette and Dutch Tilders and The Blues Club started hoofing into 'Bad Books'. By the time this cut into 'Long Way From Brooklyn — Down to the Bone', Les had gone under Knapsack Bridge and was approaching Blaxland.

At Faulconbridge the fog got thicker and if Les wasn't driving slow enough already, the council was doing up the road. All he could make out in the way of scenery was trees, a few churches and old houses with cars for sale parked out the front. At Hazelbrook Les got stuck behind a tour bus, then when he reached Lawson the fog set in like a monstrous grey blanket over everything and he got stuck behind a petrol tanker. Les shook his head in disgust. What did George say up the club one night? If brains were ink, I wouldn't have enough to write a full stop. He's not wrong. You would have got up here faster in a horse and buggy a hundred years ago.

The road and the traffic ground on. 'Paying Cost To The Boss' — B.B. King and The Rolling Stones were picking and honking out the speakers as Les went past the turn off to Katoomba. Shouldn't be too far now, he mused. B.B. King faded into Mollie O'Brien wailing 'Denver to Dallas' when Les made out a sign on the left. Medlow Bath. Hello. I'm here. Thank Christ for that. Les looked for some shops and houses. I am? There was nothing but trees and a railway line on the right. What the fuck? A railway station came into view and suddenly what looked like a palace appeared out of the gloom on the left. It was all maroon and gold with gold arches out front, set under a huge grey dome next to a bigger building resembling a white castle. A hedge and an old mossy sandstone fence ran along the front with a black and gold sign above the hedge saying MEDLOW ASTORIA — WELCOME. Hey I've heard of this joint, thought Les. Price said he used to come up here for dirty weekends before he got married. It's supposed to be el schmicko. Why don't I prop here? I can't get any closer to Medlow Bath than this. Les swung the Berlina into the driveway and pulled up outside the main entrance.

Norton got out of the car, stretched his legs then took the red carpeted steps to the front doors and into the warmth of the foyer. Hey, this is all right, he thought, pausing to take a look around. Everywhere was beautifully restored art-deco, featuring maroon, gold and white. Arches and small columns stood under a domed ceiling hung with sparkling chandeliers, while thick scatter rugs covered a polished oak floor spread with velvet lounges and plump matching cushions. Alongside the lounges were ornate wooden tables and lamps made to resemble ancient Egyptian figurines. There was an open fireplace under a white archway on the left, and in front of another white archway on the opposite side of the room, two polished oak tables formed the front desk. An attractive, dark-haired woman in a crisp char-grey uniform and matching tie smiled up from the desk on the left.

'Yes sir. May I help you?'

'I'd like a room for the night, please,' replied Les. 'A single.'

'Certainly sir.' The woman consulted a register. 'I can let you have a room in the Concordia Wing at three hundred dollars a night. Or, if you wish to take advantage of our mid-week special, you can have two nights for four hundred dollars.'

Les thought for a moment. 'Yeah okay. I'll take the two nights.'

Even though he intended staying only one night, it was now mid afternoon and in the thick fog outside he'd be flat out finding a herd of elephants with bells round their necks let alone a house. So he'd have to leave his searching till the morning, when hopefully the fog would lift. For the sake of an extra hundred he could take his time checking out and relax a little before he went back to Sydney. The woman took Norton's credit card number, did the details and gave him a key to room 123. Les said he'd be right with his bag, went out and parked the car near the sandstone fence then came back inside, turned right at the foyer and went looking for his room.

The Medlow was huge and plush and was probably *the* place years ago. Long carpeted corridors ran to the left and right with signs saying Del Monte Room, Savoy Lounge, Gaming Room, Caledonia Wing, etc. Les walked past the old gaming room on his right, that was now a conference room, and the breakfast room on the left, where a scattering of punters were taking tea and sandwiches in front of huge windows overlooking the Megalong Valley. Further on, a double-glass door opened into an extensive, art-deco lounge room called The Kurrajong Room. Logs crackled in a big open fireplace on the left and more plush furniture, lamps and ornate tables sat on a polished wood floor spread with thick rugs. On the right was a cigar room, another glass door, then a chrome-railed bar next to a pool table tucked into the corner. Delicate chandeliers hung from the ceiling, paintings and mirrors looked down from the walls, and running past a balcony on the left, massive windows with brown drapes offered stunning views of the Megalong Valley.

From a set of speakers hidden somewhere in the ceiling, a reedy version of 'Pennies From Heaven' played softly in the background. Les stopped and looked around with a half-smile on his face. It was like stepping back in time. Any moment he expected either Agatha Christie and Hercule Poirot to stroll in ready to take tea and cucumber sandwiches, or Fred Astaire and Ginger Rogers to come dancing down the staircase in the corner on the left singing 'You And The Song And The Moonlight'. The doorway to the Concordia Wing was near the staircase. Les picked up his bags and headed towards it.

A corridor with scalloped light fittings along the cornice led to a short set of stairs on the right where two chrome statuettes of women holding outstretched beach balls were set in a wall alongside some glass bricks. Les took the stairs to his room. For three hundred dollars a night, or whatever he was paying, Les felt his room could have been a little bigger. It was no larger than the spare room at Chez Norton. But it was cosy enough, with a comfortable double bed, a small TV, a bathroom and a table with two leopard-skin seats. A sash window offered a sweeping view of the Megalong Valley; only the fog and rain cut the view to a path below and the surrounding trees and ferns. Les tossed his bag on the bed and sat down facing the window. Well, here I am, he thought. Now what? The rain pattered down on the roof and the breeze coming from the valley flicked at the rainwater in the trees. I suppose I'd better drive into Katoomba, buy a map and see if I can figure out where they've hidden the rest of Medlow Bath over a cup of coffee or something. Les unpacked his travel bag, freshened up a bit then headed back the way he came.

On his way out through the Kurrajong Room, Les stopped beneath a painting near the main door, titled *Nile in Flood*. It showed the pyramids and the sphinx and Les was thinking how nice it looked, when a girl about twenty-five came bouncing down the stairs in the far corner carrying a clipboard. She was wearing a light blue pleated dress cut above the knee, long white socks and dainty white shoes. A blue crepe de chine top fitted over her dress and a brimless white sequinned hat sat tight on her head like a bathing cap. She had a pretty pixie face, blue eyes and two thin bangs of blonde hair flicked across her cheekbones from beneath her hat. Les gave the girl a double blink as she stepped daintily across the room. Did I say something about Agatha Christie? It's Vera Claythorne taking a brief holiday after the coroner's inquest. As the girl approached the main door, she dropped a fountain pen from her clipboard. Les bent down and picked it up.

'Excuse me, miss,' he called out. 'You dropped something.' The girl either didn't hear Les or she ignored him. 'Okay,' said Les. 'Bleed to death.'

The girl turned around from the door. 'What was that?' she said.

Les held up the fountain pen. 'You dropped this. I said, okay, if you don't want it, I'll have it.'

'Oh, I'm ever so sorry,' apologised the girl. 'I didn't hear you.'

'That's quite all right,' replied Les, handing her the fountain pen.

'Thank you very much,' she said. 'That's very gentlemanly of you.'

Les gave a slight bow. 'My pleasure, madam. Hugo would have done the same for Vera Claythorne.'

The girl stared at Les and her cheeks coloured slightly. 'Oh my goodness,' she said, then opened the door and bounced off down the corridor like the white rabbit in *Alice in Wonderland*.

Have a nice day, Vera, Les chuckled to himself. Now, what was I doing before I was so rudely interrupted?

Les got in the car and headed through the drizzling rain and fog towards Katoomba. After the warmth of the hotel it seemed colder than it already was, making things even more miserable. Before long he reached the lights at the turn-off and took a right across the bridge over the railway line.

The road curved left past some shops on the right and a few more on the left next to a tunnel beneath the railway station, then it went right again into the main drag. From what Les could make out through the fog and rain, Katoomba was trying to be the art-deco capital of Australia. Most of the shops, especially the restaurants, had that 1930s black and chrome look about them. The main street sloped down on the left, past restaurants, banks, clothes shops, a couple of churches and whatever, before levelling off at a pedestrian crossing on an intersection. Les did a U-turn and came up the other side. It was much the same. More shops and art-deco restaurants, a medical centre, butcher, newsagent, the town centre arcade, an antique furniture centre then the grounds of another old hotel at the top, the Kensington. The hotel was at the back but a set of steps off the street led up to two double-glass doors and a bar. A sign on one of the doors said Piano Man — Thursday Night. Back at the top of the hill, Les noticed a hotel across the railway line called the Gordon. He did another U-turn and found a parking spot, outside a cluster of restaurants opposite the Kensington, then got out of the car and had a look around for a moment. With his breath turning into small clouds of steam in the cold mountain air, Les strolled down to the newsagency and got a map and the local paper. That didn't take long and when he returned Les decided to try Cafe Zappa.

Like the others it was either restored — or just left the way it was to save spending any money — art-deco. The floor was bare boards with booths on either side and a counter at the rear where they did the cooking. Les went for a bowl of pumpkin soup and a flat white; the woman said she'd bring it to him. Even though it was cold and miserable outside, Les chose a footpath table left of the front door, opposite a table full of hippy-gothics on the right.

Along with the men at the table there were three women with prams and babies and everyone had this arty, 'Okay, so I might be on the dole or getting a pension and I dress like a rag picker and I'm half broke. But I'm still really cool, you know' look about them while they sipped their coffees and smoked skinny roll-your-owns from a communal packet of Champion Ruby. Like most of the other punters shuffling past in the rain, carrying string bags or backpacks, the dress code at the table opposite was thick beanies, army pants, loose knitted jumpers and leg warmers. Purple Doc Martens, rainbow-coloured stockings and crushed velvet dresses was another look, along with denim dresses, greasy jeans and ugh boots. And of course nose rings, ear rings, ear studs and cheap Indian jewellery. Some bloke with a cane at a table outside the restaurant next door was wearing a floppy velvet hat, a white jacket and a long scarf. He looked like Dr Who minus the Tardis. Norton's pumpkin soup and coffee arrived. He left the locals to it and sipped and supped while he studied his map.

Medlow Bath wasn't all that big. Just a cluster of cul-de-sacs on the other side of the railway line, not far from a water catchment area, with one long road leading out to the airfield. Depending on the fog and rain, Les felt he was in with a chance. He still didn't know what he was looking for and if he did find the house with the red fence, he was just going to hope no one was home and break in. He'd brought a jemmy with him for that purpose. He still didn't have much to go on. But he didn't have much to lose. And the alternative was the remand yard at Long Bay. Les put the map aside and flicked through the paper while he finished his soup and coffee. The soup was a bit bland and could have done with some chilli and garlic. The coffee was okay. By the time he'd finished, the street was emptying and it was getting dark. Les paid his bill and left for the hotel.

Driving back to The Medlow, Les found himself developing a kind of 'who gives a stuff' attitude. He had nothing much to go on. And he was more than likely wasting his time. So why not to have as much fun as he could before the chop, and try not take it too seriously. If something turned up, great. If it didn't, well, at least he'd had a go. Les was also feeling, although he'd been off his food a bit, the pumpkin soup and the mountain air had put the edge back on his appetite. Dinner at the hotel would definitely be in order. After a few gin and tonics in the Kurrajong Room of course. I wonder should one wear one's tuxedo to dinner? he mused. And take one's ivory cigarette holder? One should certainly give it some thought. He found the same parking spot by the sandstone fence and locked the car.

There weren't many people around as Les walked to his room; a few Japanese tourists, one or two couples and the smiling staff going past. Les took his time having a shower and a shave, then changed into a blue shirt with little white roulette wheels on it Price had given him, jeans, black desert boots and his leather jacket over the top. Then dabbed a drop or two of Eau Sauvage on his face. He also took a book with him to read while he had a few drinks. It was a book he'd bought off Billy Dunne for two dollars. Billy's wife had bought it for three dollars in an op-shop. It was called *The Portable Beat Reader* and had a photo of William Burroughs and Jack Kerouac on the cover. The main reason she bought it was because the photo of Jack Kerouac on the cover looked a lot like Billy. Billy, however, couldn't get into the book. Especially the poetry. Les didn't mind the book. There was a bit of Charles Bukowski, and Burroughs' views on drug addiction made interesting reading. Like Billy, however, Les too thought the poetry was VFO. Very fuckin ordinary.

Apart from a young barman in black, there was no one in the Kurrajong Room. Les ordered a gin and tonic, chose a plush lounge facing the side door and took in the art-deco ambience while he sipped his gin and tonic and read his book. He was looking at a poem that consisted of 'Scissor sceptre cutting prow' repeated four times, followed by 'Ahh, swark, swark', and thinking, did some wally actually get paid to write this? when who should come bouncing down the stairs, wearing the same clothes, but the girl he saw earlier. Vera Claythorne. She too was carrying a book. She couldn't have missed Norton sitting there, but she didn't catch his eye and Les didn't make a point of catching hers. She went to the bar, got a drink, then sat down on a lounge a little to Norton's left. She opened her book and started to read. Les continued to read his and sip his gin and tonic. He was reading a list of instructions some hippy had written during the Vietnam War on how to beat the draft. Three suggestions were: develop a bleeding stigmata, contract tertiary syphilis, when the doctor tells you to spread your cheeks, have a firecracker stuffed in your date. At the word firecracker, Les wasn't sure whether to laugh or cry. He looked up at the same time Vera did. This time he caught her eye.

'Hello,' he said pleasantly. 'What are you reading?'

'Agatha Christie,' replied the girl. '*The Mysterious Affair At Styles*.'

'I should have guessed,' replied Les.

'Oh? What makes you say that?'

'Nothing,' said Les. 'Just a guess.'

The girl looked at Les for a moment. 'Do you mind if I join you?' she said. 'There's something I'd like to ask you.'

'Certainly not,' answered Les, shuffling along the lounge. 'Be my guest.'

The girl came over and sat down on Norton's left. She put her drink on the table in front of them, then placed the book she was reading on her lap. In the process, Les managed to sneak a glimpse of lacy white knickers under the short blue dress.

'You said something to me earlier when I dropped my pen,' said the girl. 'Hugo would have done the same for Vera Claythorne. What did you mean by that?'

'Nothing,' smiled Les. 'It was just a joke. I hope I never offended you?'

'No. Not at all,' replied the girl. 'On the contrary.'

'Really?' purred Les. 'Why's that?'

'That's Agatha Christie. They're two characters in *And Then There Were None*.'

'That's right,' said Les.

'Do you read Agatha Christie?' asked the girl.

'Of course,' said Les. 'Not as much as I'd like to. But I read what I can.' Les hated Agatha Christie. If he could have, Les would have organised a book burning and incinerated every Agatha Christie book he could find, along with the author. When he was at high school, a sadistic female English teacher made the class read three Agatha Christie novels. To Les, it was about as interesting as studying for a degree in law. But being young it got brainwashed into his head and to this day he still remembered most of the corny names and places.

'I study Agatha Christie,' said the girl, patting her book. 'I absolutely adore her.'

'I don't blame you,' enthused Les. 'Agatha Christie's one of the great women writers of our time.'

'Thank you,' smiled the girl. 'I also write poetry.'

'Really?' Les nodded to his book. 'I love poetry.'

'And I'm also working on a novel at the moment.'

Les looked surprised. 'Well I'll be,' he said. 'This is just the most amazing coincidence.'

'Why? What makes you say that?'

'I happen to be a publisher.'

'A publisher?' gushed the girl. 'No.'

'Yes.' Les offered his hand. 'Allow me to introduce myself. Forrest McNamara. Roulette Publishing, Sydney.'

'Oh dear me,' flustered the girl, placing her dainty hand in Norton's huge, calloused mitt. 'This is incredible.'

'Yes. Like I said,' smiled Les. 'It's certainly a delightful coincidence. So what's *your* name? If I might ask?'

'Blythe. Blythe Selby.'

Les shook his head. 'That's poetry in itself.' He took another mouthful of gin and tonic and let Blythe get her breath back. You would have thought she'd just met Elvis.

'And what brings you to the Blue Mountains and the Medlow Astoria, Blythe?' asked Les.

'I was invited to read my poetry at the Blue Mountains Songs of the Wind Festival,' answered Blythe.

Les slanted his head slightly to one side. 'How simply marvellous.'

Blythe gave Les the low-down on how her father ran a furniture company in Bathurst. It was a family business. She did the books and Daddy was picking up the tab at the Medlow. She'd just had a reading and had to go back home in the morning, but she was returning to the Blue Mountains on the weekend.

'I got a really good response,' said Blythe. 'And on Sunday they're doing a play at the Varuna Writers' Centre. Agatha Christie's *Black Coffee*. I'm playing Lucia Amery.'

'Congratulations, Blythe,' beamed Les. 'You're an actress as well as a writer.'

'I'd rather write,' said Blythe modestly.

Les finished his drink and offered to buy Blythe one. Blythe accepted and had a Brandy Alexander. Les had another gin. A double. They sat sipping politely away and Norton found himself starting to feel pretty good along with Blythe's dress starting to look even shorter.

'Are you here for the festival too, Mr McNamara?' asked Blythe.

Les held up a hand. 'Please. Forrest will do. No, Blythe, I'm up here to interview a writer. I'm trying to get him to join Roulette.' Les smiled over his drink. 'It's called head hunting.'

'Goodness,' said Blythe. 'Who is he?'

Les shook his head solemnly. 'I'm sorry Blythe. But I can't tell you at the moment.'

'I understand,' said Blythe. 'You're still secretly negotiating.'

'Exactly.'

Blythe took a healthy hit of her brandy. 'So which poets and writers do you publish, Forrest?' she asked politely.

'Publish?' Les tried to look thoughtful for a moment. 'Adolph Glunshnutter, the German author. Marvin Schwartz, the Jewish author.'

'Marvin Schwartz?' said Blythe. 'I think I've heard of him. What did he write?'

'*Abraham's Ashes.*'

'Oh.'

'Amongst our Australian authors we've got Murray Scrartenvitch, Raymond Tracy, Georgina Brennan, Wilhelmina Dunleavy. To name a few.'

'I can't say I've come across them in Bathurst,' said Blythe.

'You haven't?' Les stroked his chin. 'I must make a note to contact our country rep when I get back to the office and see that he gets some out there.'

'It sounds like you run a pretty tight ship at Roulette Publishing,' said Blythe.

'Oh yeah, we're out there, Blythe,' said Les. 'We've got our finger on the publishing pulse. We're watching the watchers.'

Blythe looked at Les for a moment. 'Would you like to hear some of *my* poetry, Forrest?'

Les nearly swallowed all his drink. 'Why I'd ... only be too delighted, Blythe.'

'It's in my room. I'll get it.'

Les watched as Blythe skipped up the stairs like the white rabbit again, giving him another glimpse of her knickers when she reached the first landing. Christ! This is going to be nice, he thought. Stuck with some bimbo trapped in an Agatha Christie time warp while she reads me her poetry. I think I'd better get another couple of drinks. Still, I wouldn't mind shoving my face into Miss Selby's present participle, if she'd grab me on the personal pronoun. Agatha bloody Christie. God!

If only old Miss Crowther could see me now. Les got two fresh drinks and sat back down on the lounge before Blythe returned with a book binder and made herself comfortable next to him. She opened the folder and started up.

'This one's called "The Singularity Of Narcissism",' said Blythe.

'Fired with desire

I peered into the river of

X-rayed souls

trawling for mythical endurance.

My view obscured

by thoughts

too perceptive to be dreamed.'

Les caught his reflection in a mirror near the bar. He'd seen that expression before. In the meatworks when a steer cops it in the back of the head with a stun-gun. He took another slug of gin as Blythe served up her next offering.

'This one's called "Uncompromisation and Patience":

'She wanted solitude

so she clothed herself in delusion

knowing the demons of antiquity

 would soon be knocking on the door of redemption.'

Before long Les was looking for the cyanide pill. Blythe's poems would stink in a deep-freeze. They made absolutely no sense, and any that did weren't worth listening to. Eventually, after what seemed like days, she came up for air.

'Well,' she asked shyly. 'What do you think so far, Forrest?'

Les looked at her impassively. 'Wonderful, Blythe,' he said quietly. 'Just wonderful. Did it take you long to write them?'

'Oh, yes. Years.'

'I thought they might have. They're so full of hidden passion. Or dare I say, more, an assertive passion. You've obviously written these poems from your heart, Blythe.' Only because your arse was probably blocked up at the time.

'Yes. Yes I did.' Blythe touched Les on the thigh. 'You obviously know literature, Forrest. Would you like to hear some more?'

'I certainly would,' said Les. 'But I've got an idea. How about while you're reading your ... works, I compare them to some of the poets in here.' Les held up *The Portable Beat Reader*. 'I'd like to balance your writing against these people. I feel it would make an interesting comparison.'

'All right,' smiled Blythe. 'That sounds like a great idea. This one's called "Irreligious Shadows Killed The Rainmaker".'

While Blythe waffled away, Les immersed himself in his book, looking up every now and again to smile and nod his head in approval. Norton's book was still heavy going, but compared to putting up with Blythe, it was like reading *Peanuts*. After a while, Blythe ran out of steam and her voice developed a slight croak. Les applauded softly.

'That was absolutely marvellous, Blythe,' he said serenely. 'The comparisons between you and some of the writers in here, especially Diane DiPrima, are absolutely fascinating.'

'Diane DiPrima,' gushed Blythe. 'Surely you're not saying my poetry's in the same class as hers?'

'In the same class?' Les reached over and touched Blythe on the leg. 'It's almost as if Diane could learn from you.'

'Oh dear, I . . . I don't know what to say.'

Les riveted his eyes on Blythe. 'Blythe,' he said quietly. 'There's something I have to ask you here.'

'Certainly, Forrest. What is it?'

'Would you be interested in Roulette publishing some of your works?'

'Publish my works?' squealed Blythe. Her knees started to shake and it was all she could do to stop from peeing herself. 'Oh yes. Yes. That's been my dream.'

'Excellent,' said Les. 'Then how about we discuss it further over dinner? Would you care to join me?'

'I'd love to.'

'All right. Let's go have a literary luncheon. Dinner . . . whatever. And we can have another drink too.'

'I'll just go to the Ladies first.'

'I'll wait here for you,' smiled Les.

As Blythe skipped off to the Ladies, Les caught his reflection in the mirror again. The girls at work have got a name for blokes like you, he told himself. SAAB. A swine and a bastard. Les gave himself a look of grudging approval. Fair enough. But I prefer dropkick, myself. It's got more of an Australian ambience to it. Blythe returned from the Ladies and Les stood up.

'Are you ready to eat?' he asked.

'Yes,' replied Blythe, and picked up her poetry.

'Excellent.' Les motioned with one hand, 'After you, Blythe.'

Les opened the door for Blythe and they took the corridor past the gaming room and foyer, through another door leading into a long, gently sloping corridor lined with huge, velvet chesterfields, lamp tables and indoor plants. Landscapes, hunting scenes and framed etchings hung on one wall, the other was arched windows overlooking the Megalong Valley. The corridor ended at a staircase and access ramp leading into another room full of more art-deco furnishing, mainly cream and white; with chess sets, a library and an enclosed bar at one end. A doorway on the left led along a shorter corridor to the dining room.

Les and Blythe stepped into a dining area with room for over a hundred, one half blocked off where it was divided by an arch across the middle. About twenty diners were seated round polished wooden tables with crisp, white tablecloths. Again it was all very plush; thick red carpet on the floor, cream and gold decor round the walls; chandeliers above and tiny white lamps on the tables. There was a velvet lounge setting as you walked in on the right, with a grand piano in the middle and an old fortune-telling machine against one wall. Music from the 1920s played softly in the background and several waitresses in black uniforms and black bowties hovered round the guests. Wearing an immaculate grey suit, a maitre d with a shaved head stood behind the bookings desk on the left. On his lapel was a name tag. Angelo. Les caught his eye as he looked up from the guest list and had a fifty palmed into the maitre d's hand quicker than it took him to shampoo and condition his hair.

'Good evening, Angelo,' said Les brightly, producing his door key. 'I believe you have a table for me. Mr McNamara. Room 123. Forrest McNamara.'

The maitre d had seen this many times before. He ran a highlighter across the guest list then bowed and scraped like his head was going to fall off and roll across the dining room. 'Of course, Mr McNamara,' he said, then made a gracious, sweeping gesture with one well-manicured hand. 'This way, sir.'

'Easy as one, two, three,' smiled Blythe.

'Something like that,' winked Les.

Angelo led them to a table for four facing away from the other diners. He placed a wine list in front of Norton while a waitress removed the unnecessary cutlery. 'What sort of wine would you like, Blythe?' asked Les.

'I think I'll have the same as what you were drinking before,' she answered. 'A gin and tonic.'

'Make that two gin and tonics please, Angelo.'

'Certainly, Mr McNamara. Tanquerray ... ?'

'Bombay Sapphire.'

'Of course. Thank you, Mr McNamara.' The maitre d laid on some more bow and scrape and sent one of the waitresses hurrying out to the bar.

'Have you been here before, Forrest?' asked Blythe.

'Once or twice,' replied Les.

'They certainly look after you.'

'Yes. I guess it just comes with the territory. Publishing.'

'I can't wait to see my poems in print,' fluttered Blythe.

'Me either,' said Les.

Two crisp gin and tonics arrived and Les proposed a toast to Blythe's success. Blythe modestly accepted that. She had another sip of gin and looked at Les.

'Do you mind if I ask you a question, Forrest?' she said.

'Sure,' shrugged Les. 'What is it?'

'How did you get that broken nose?'

'Playing rugby union at university.'

'You went to university? Which one?'

'New South Wales.'

'I never went to uni. I went straight into Dad's business when I left school.'

Les clinked her glass. 'You never know, Blythe. It might have been all for the best.'

Les went for the smoked salmon and asparagus mille feuille for starters and veal Illawarra with plums and Madeira and macadamia nut mashed potatoes for mains. Blythe sensibly just had mountain stream trout with basil and Spanish onion salsa.

They nattered away about different things. Les said he'd get her phone number and address before he left. She'd send him a copy of her poetry, his company would send her a draft agreement. They'd discuss the advance later.

'I'm going to get an advance?' gasped Blythe.

'Only a small one at this stage, Blythe,' said Les. 'Just a few thousand. It's only your first book, remember.'

'Just a few thousand ...'

Blythe was a completely shot bird. Between the drinks and getting a contract she hardly knew which way was up. However, despite taking advantage of Blythe's gullibility and his outright filthy lies, Les was one hundred per cent certain he wasn't going to throw Blythe up in the air. No one ever got rooted in an Agatha Christie novel. The female characters kept their legs clamped together with superglue; tighter than the women in Barbara Cartland. And you could bet Blythe would play the part to the letter. Still, there was no harm in dropping a quiet sexual innuendo should the occasion arise or making a cultivated lewd comment.

The food arrived and neither could complain. It was tasty, well-presented and served with an absolute abundance of bow and scrape. They had two more gin and tonics and finished with coffee. They didn't bother about sweets.

'Did you enjoy your meal, Blythe?' asked Les.

'Yes. It was absolutely lovely. Thank you.'

'What would you like to do now?'

Blythe smiled and gave her shoulders a dainty shrug. 'I don't really care. I have to be up fairly early in the morning, though.'

'Me too,' inclined Les. 'So how about we go back to the Kurrajong Room and have a couple more drinks before we call it a night. There's something I was thinking of doing.'

'Okay.'

Les put the bill on his room, gave the waitress a fifty, the maitre d gave him some more bow and scrape then they walked back to the Kurrajong Room.

There were a few people clustered around the fire and two couples playing pool in the corner. Les and Blythe sat at the same lounge as before and Les went to the bar, returning with two more gin and tonics. Blythe took Les's book, flopped around on the lounge and started reading one of Bob Dylan's songs as a poem. 'A Hard Rain's A-Gonna Fall.' Whether it was all the gin he'd soaked up, Norton wasn't sure, but he had to admit Bob Dylan's songs made great poems. Blythe hit him with two clunking choruses of Philip Lamantia's poetry then closed the book. Les was more than glad because he was starting to develop corns on his ears.

'And to think you compared my work to what's in here, Forrest,' sighed Blythe. 'I can hardly believe it.'

'Yeah. It's hard to believe all right,' agreed Les. He looked at Blythe over his gin and tonic. 'Blythe, did Agatha Christie ever write a book called *Death in the Cigar Room*?'

Blythe thought for a moment. '*Death in the Clouds. Death on the Nile. Death Comes as the End.* There was *The Body in the Library.*'

'Blythe,' suggested Les, 'why don't you get your drink and that and follow me over to the cigar room?'

'All right, Forrest,' smiled Blythe, rising a little unsteadily to her feet.

A row of full length windows curved round the cigar room to the doorway. Inside was a high ceiling and more plush furniture. A tapestried lounge setting filled one corner and a maroon velvet lounge sat against the opposite wall. Paintings of smokers looked down from above the velvet lounge and next to the front windows was a polished teak cabinet. Sitting on top was a cigar menu, an ashtray and several books of matches. Les had noticed a menu at the bar and it made him curious. He picked up the one on the cabinet and showed Blythe. There were several cigars on the menu: Cuban, Dominican or Canary Islands. They ranged from Tobacos Vargas Capitolios at $9.50 to Galeon Robusto at $15.50 or Romeo y Julieta Dedros de Luxe No. 3 at $18.50.

'How would you like to puff on a nice Cuban cigar, Blythe?' said Les. 'Like Mr Justice Wargrave might do, writing a letter to Constance Culmington.'

'Oh yes,' enthused Blythe. 'That sounds exciting.'

'Wait here, my dear.' Les gave a slight bow and walked round to the bar as Blythe sat down on a tapestry lounge chair in the corner.

In a couple of minutes Les was back with two fresh drinks and two Romeo y Julietas, snipped at the end and ready to fire up.

'There you go, Blythe,' he said, handing her a cigar and an ashtray.

'What do I do, Forrest?' she asked. 'I don't smoke.'

'Neither do I,' said Les. 'But just put your lips round the end and suck. And don't inhale.'

Les struck a match and held it to the end of Blythe's cigar; after about half a dozen puffs she was away. Les got his going and sat down opposite her as swirls of sweet blue smoke drifted above them. Although Les was a non-smoker, the cigar didn't taste too bad. Pretty much like what it said on the menu. Dark, sweet, with a hint of cocoa beans and coffee and a core of earthiness. Les began feeling quite contented as he puffed away and sipped his gin and tonic. Blythe looked like she was feeling quite contented also. She was all over the lounge chair, her top loosening noticeably, giving Les a nice glimpse of snow white breast behind the crepe de chine. And her skirt had crept up considerably, giving Les an eagle's eye view of Blythe's sweet little map of Tasmania beneath her lace knickers.

'So what do you think, Blythe?' asked Les. 'Something different.'

Blythe tapped some ash into the ashtray. 'Yes. They're nice. Sort of sweet. And rich.'

Les blew a smoke ring across the room. 'What was it Ernest Hemingway said? A woman is a woman, but a good cigar is a smoke.'

'I'm not sure,' said Blythe. 'But I don't think it was Monica Lewinsky,' she giggled.

'No,' replied Les slowly.

'What do you think, Forrest?'

'I don't know, Blythe,' replied Les. 'I haven't finished my cigar yet.'

Blythe managed to blow a smoke ring and Les blew one into it. He held up his cigar and smiled. 'Romeo y Julieta. That's us, Blythe. Hasta la vista and buenas noches.'

'Oh Forrest, I didn't know you spoke Spanish.'

'I don't,' replied Les. 'I speak in tongues. And if my tongue could talk right now, you know what it would say, Blythe?'

'What would it say, Forrest?' purred Blythe.

Les nodded to Blythe's crumpet poking out under her pleated dress. 'That looks good enough to eat.'

'Ooohh Mr McNamara,' fluttered Blythe. She spread her legs a little more. 'Well, like Candye Kane says, all you can eat, and you can eat it all night long.'

Les almost ground the end off his $18.50 Romeo y Julieta. 'Why don't we go back to your room when we finish these, Miss Selby, and discuss your draft agreement some more? Mine's a little untidy at the moment.'

'That sounds like a good idea,' smiled Blythe. 'Let's do that, Mr McNamara.'

They finished their gin and tonics while 'Putting On The Ritz' played out of the speakers in the ceiling next door. Then they stubbed their cigars and Les followed Blythe across the lounge and up the stairs back to her room.

Blythe's room was almost identical to Norton's. Only she had a fake tiger skin lounge and a bigger window with a better view. The bed lamps were still on when she opened the door.

'I'll just go to the loo,' she said, dropping her keys by the bed. 'Help yourself to the mini-bar if you want to.'

'I might have a beer,' said Les. 'Would you like something?'

'A small Scotch and water. No ice thanks.'

'Okey doke.'

Les knocked the top off a bottle of Hahn Premium then opened a bottle of Mount Franklin and made Blythe a Scotch. He placed her drink on the coffee table in front of the lounge, sat down and had a mouthful of beer. Blythe came out of the bathroom, sat down next to him and picked up her glass. Les clinked his bottle against it.

'Well. Here's to success, Blythe,' he winked. 'May all your poems be little ones.'

'Thank you, Forrest.' Blythe took a sip of Scotch and smiled at Les. 'I just can't believe my luck. I gave a reading at the writer's festival and now I'm getting a publishing contract. All in two days. It's almost too good to be true.'

Les sipped his beer and shrugged. 'I think it was meant to be, Blythe. Fate.'

'Yes, Forrest,' breathed Blythe. 'Fate.' They sipped their drinks and Blythe moved her knee against Norton's. 'Do you believe in fate, Forrest?'

For a second a picture of the catering van exploding just as he left the cake box there flashed across Norton's mind. 'Do I ever, Blythe,' he said slowly.

'Would you say I had a fatal attraction, Forrest?'

Les put his drink down and placed his hand gently inside Blythe's thigh. 'You've got a fatal something, Blythe. I can tell you that.'

Blythe tilted her head up slightly. Les bent forward and kissed her. There was a slight hint of cigar smoke, but her lips were still sweet and soft and her tiny tongue as delicate as the white lace in her knickers. Whether it was the cigar, the mountain air, or just something about Blythe herself, Les wasn't sure. But in seconds he had a rock hard boner ready to blast off. He kissed Blythe a while longer then stood up, took her hand and led her across to the bed.

'Daddy missed out on dessert downstairs, momma,' he smiled. 'And daddy needs something for his sweet tooth.'

'Ooohh Hugo. Do you think Emily Brent would approve?'

'Vera. Poor old Emily never knew what she was missing.'

Blythe kicked off her shoes and lay back on the bed as Les slipped her knickers off and spread her legs. Then without any further ado, he pushed his face into Blythe's beautiful little ted and went for it.

It was absolutely sensational. Les couldn't remember ever coming across one like it. Blonde and soft and trimmed. It was like a little rosebud. Pink and soft. If you put it out in the morning sun the dew would have settled on it. Blythe had also rubbed some sweet smelling oil around herself, making things even more enjoyable. Les chewed and licked and sucked like it was a slice of watermelon at a country picnic. Best of all, Blythe was going almost spare at the end of the bed. She kicked and bucked and wriggled her hips, screamed and moaned and sighed. It was music to Norton's ears. Before he knew it, Mr Wobbly was frothing at the mouth and Les was ready to blow his bolt all over the inside of his jeans.

'Ohhhhh Vicar,' Blythe was in some kind of Agatha Christie dreamland. All she could do was moan.

Les didn't say a word. He just kept eating Blythe's gorgeous pussy, getting hornier by the second. It was that good, he could have eaten it all night then backed up for seconds in the morning. Suddenly Blythe gave a little scream, grabbed Les by the hair, pushed her hips up and emptied out in his face. Les gave it one more lick then came up for air; eyes sparkling, a grin from ear to ear. He fell down alongside Blythe, pulled a hanky from his pocket and wiped his face while he picked a few hairs out of his teeth. Blythe's eyes eventually stopped spinning around, she got most of her breath back and faced Les with her hands against his chest.

'I'm sorry, Forrest,' she panted. 'But I can't have sex with you.'

'Don't worry, Blythe. I was counting on that.' Les unzipped his fly and pulled out Mr Wobbly, gave it a couple of strokes then put his hand on the back of Blythe's head. 'So get your literary laughing gear around this, sister. And tell the vicar why you weren't at church on Sunday.'

Blythe didn't need much persuasion and Les didn't need any prompting. Blythe hardly had her lips around Norton's knob before he started blowing. Blythe gave it about half a dozen decent sucks and Les almost levitated from the bed as he emptied out. Poor Blythe. It looked like she'd walked in front of a flying lemon meringue pie. It was in her mouth, down her throat, in her hair, across her eyebrows, running down her chin. After he stopped howling, Les gave himself one last stroke and some went on the curtains and the top of the TV.

'My goodness, Forrest,' exclaimed Blythe. 'You certainly were excited, weren't you.'

'Excited,' spluttered Les. 'Blythe, I haven't been this excited since Australia won the America's Cup.'

Blythe slipped her knickers back on and went to the bathroom. By the time she came back, Les had his fly done up and was lying on the bed with his hands behind his head.

'What time are you having breakfast in the morning?' asked Blythe. 'I have to get up early myself.'

Les took this as a hint. Blythe had got her contract. She'd given her publisher a decent blow job. Now he could pack up the casting couch and hit the road.

'I might have a bit of a sleep in,' replied Les. 'I'm not sure. So why don't you give me your phone number and all that, in case I miss you.'

'Fantastic.'

Blythe wrote down her phone number and address. Plus where she worked. Les gave her Warren's phone number at the advertising agency and told her to ring him there. Ask for Warren Edwards, his assistant, just in case he was in a meeting or interstate.

'Well goodnight, Forrest,' said Blythe, opening the door. 'It's been marvellous. I'm so excited.'

'Yes,' said Les. 'Me too. I've got a good feeling about this.'

Blythe batted her eyelids for a second. 'I just hope you don't think I'm awful.'

'Awful?' said Les. He placed his hands on Blythe's shoulders. 'Blythe. You're not in the slightest bit awful. You're wonderful. And you're a gifted writer. Believe me.'

Blythe handed Les *The Portable Beat Reader*. 'Goodnight Forrest.'

'Goodnight, Blythe.' The door closed and Norton was left standing on his own.

Boy, can I find them, thought Les, as he slowly trudged back along the corridor. Blythe bloody Selby. Anyway, I'm sure Mr Edwards will look after her when she rings. Shit! I wouldn't have minded slipping her one though. What about Blythe's grouse little lamington? I wonder did they eat lamingtons in any of Agatha Christie's books? Les picked another tiny blonde hair out of his teeth. Not the way I just did, that's for sure.

The bar was closed and the Kurrajong Room was empty when Les came down the stairs. 'Song Of India' was playing from the speakers in the ceiling. Les went straight to his room, stripped off down to his jox and T-shirt then cleaned his teeth and got under the sheets, leaving one bed lamp on. He yawned a couple of times and stared up at the ceiling for a while, his mind a complete blank. It felt good. Suddenly Les found himself dog tired. Between driving up there in the rain, the booze, the rich meal and the blow job, he was knackered. Oh well, Les thought, as he switched off the light. It hasn't been a bad trip so far. See what happens tomorrow. In less than a minute, the big Queenslander was dead to the world.

Norton's bed was that comfortable and the room was so warm, he probably would have slept in till noon, except that whoever had the room before him had set the radio alarm for eight o'clock. Les was abruptly woken to the news, relayed from a Sydney radio station. Nathan David's station. The news finished with the local weather report and Les was still half asleep wondering what day it was when Nathan David's voice came blustering over the airwaves giving a slant on the news. Instead of sticking to music, it was a law and order rave about the leniency of the courts and Norton got a guernsey.

'Now, as I've been saying,' trilled David, 'I do have an interest in this particular film. But I am one hundred per cent up front with my financial dealings. And always have been. Not like some of the vile swine in this town whom we won't mention at this time. But that has nothing to do with it. I saw the security camera video of this Norton character, allegedly placing the bomb on the film set. Allegedly? It's there in black and white. He even smirks at the camera. Then the bomb goes off and a poor, innocent cook is killed. So how does Les Norton get bail? What? Are the police running some kind of open door policy at Waverley Police Station? Heavens above. Now this Norton character is out there walking the streets, probably to plant another bomb somewhere. I think I'd best leave it at that. But you do have to ask yourself, what in God's name is going on with our judicial system?'

Norton couldn't believe his ears. Thanks David, you prick. I always said I wouldn't piss on you. Why don't you just hang me and be done with it? Christ! Les scowled at the radio as he switched it off. It wouldn't surprise me if you had something to do with it, you little cunt. You and your mate King. And that miserable fuckin dyke. Shit! That reminds me, I was supposed to ring Gerry. It's too early now. I'll do it after breakfast. Les sat on the edge of the bed and stared out the window. The fog had lifted but it was still raining steadily and the thick clouds covering the Megalong Valley looked like huge waves as the wind pushed them over the mountains. Les opened the window, shivered, then slammed it shut again. It was still bloody cold. He took off his T-shirt, got cleaned up then put on his blue tracksuit and walked down to get something to eat.

There were about twenty guests in the breakfast room, but no sign of Blythe. I suppose she'd be halfway to Bathurst by now, thought Les. Still rumblin' from the grumblin' and howlin' from the growlin'. I wonder what she'll tell them at the furniture shop? The register was on the left as you entered and the bain-marie started there. Les told the pleasant woman in charge his room number, then found a table with a view and filled up with fruit, scrambled eggs, bacon and whatever, washed down with coffee and orange juice. A number of thoughts went through Norton's mind while he ate and hearing his name plastered all over the airwaves was one of them. Apart from a good breakfast, the day hadn't got off to much of a start. He had one last coffee and signed the tab.

Back in his cosy, warm room, Les could think of better things to do than be driving round in the rain trying to find some house in the middle of nowhere. He tossed the jemmy and a torch in his backpack, then perused his Blue Mountains street directory, deciding to check out the main cluster of streets first. He put his GAP anorak on, locked up and walked out to the car.

Cars and trucks hissed by in the rain as Les drove past a car yard and some old disused buildings belonging to the hotel, then took a right over the railway line. A hairpin bend brought him alongside the train station and an old red building that was once the Medlow Bath Post Office and had since been turned into a book shop and tea room. The road curved round again to the left, stopping at a dead end in the bush and another road went down to the right. Les followed it down amongst more trees and bush, stopping at a longer street intersected with cul-de-sacs. According to his map, there were two small ones on the left and the rest angled off on the right before the long road to the airfield. Les swung the Berlina right.

Medlow Bath was quite hilly, with more houses than Les thought, most of them built back from the road amongst the surrounding trees, making it even more difficult to find what he was looking for. All the cross streets ended in thick bush and the cul-de-sacs ran down towards a lush green valley dense with trees. A lot of the houses looked new and well built in either polished wood or rumbled bricks and nearly every home had a neat front yard full of flowers or ferns. Clusters of trees were turning from emerald green into beautiful shades of red and orange as they lost their autumn leaves. Others had shed huge strips of bark, which hung in the branches or lay across the road. Even in the mist and rain, Medlow Bath had a noticeable country elegance. There was the odd shack here and there with a rusting car body out the front, plus several overgrown blocks of land. A few had For Sale signs and in one driveway Les made out a truck with Blue Mountains Bushfire Brigade painted on the side. He wound the window down a little and the sounds of magpies and currawongs calling to each other drifted in along with the smell of wood fires burning in some of the homes.

Les drove up and down, slowly crisscrossing each street and cul-de-sac as he checked everything out; there were plenty of yards with red gums or blue gums, but no red gates or blue letter boxes. He found one wooden building on a corner with a Japanese Shinto arch under the trees and a coloured lotus on the front gate. The Blue Mountains Insight Meditation Centre. Les shook his head. I don't think that's what I'm looking for. Les drove around some more then took the long road towards the airfield.

After a few kilometres the houses began to run out and Les was starting to run out of patience. He did a U-turn near a council dump and drove back to where he started. Les drummed his fingers on the steering wheel and peered out the windscreen as the wipers click-clacked back and forth. It felt like he'd been driving round in the rain half the morning. Les looked at his watch. He had. This is fucked, he told himself, shaking his head in annoyance. I knew it was going to be a waste of time. There were two more cul-de-sacs to go, then the ones on the other side of the railway line and that was it. Les shook his head again, hung a left towards the end cul-de-sac and turned right.

It was much the same as the others; a short street full of houses and trees, ending in a turning area at the bottom, and no red gate. Les came back and drove down the last cul-de-sac. A sign on the corner said Red Gum Road. It was almost identical to the other cul-de-sac, except it included a big house built from sandstone blocks on the right with palm trees out front, and further down on the left, a white Holden utility and a grey Ford F 100 parked haphazardly across a driveway belonged to several builders working inside a partially constructed brick cottage. Slowly and a little tiredly, Les reached the end of the cul-de-sac, when — bingo! There it was on the right-hand side. A blue mail box sitting on a low sandstone fence next to a red iron gate. A tall blue gum, covered in peeling bark, leaned over the sandstone fence, all standing in front of a small blue timber house with a red trim and a green-galvanised-iron roof. A vacant block of land sat opposite; Les pulled up in front of the vacant block and wound the window down for a better view.

The front of the house had a small verandah on the left with a seat next to the front door, and on the right, a bedroom faced the street with two gables built over the window. Two windows ran down the right-hand side of the house along the driveway and on the left side was one window. The surrounding yard was fairly neat before it stopped at the bush. The sandstone fence half circled round the front of the house with the gate and the letter box on the right. Painted on the blue letter box was a yellow sun, moon and stars. Parked in the driveway was a black Ford station wagon with a wire grille at the back and sitting out the front was an old brown trailer covered in leaves. A faded sticker was peeling off the back near the tail light. Les could just make out what it said: Witches Do It In Spells.

Les wound the window up then did a U-turn and drove back up the street, parking near the corner so he faced down the cul-de-sac. That has to be Knox's house, he told himself. Rittosa had the tree out the front mixed up with the name of the street. The sticker on the trailer is the clincher. Les smiled tightly. That's the good news. The bad news is, someone's home. And the worst fuckin news is, that station wagon's parked too far down the driveway, so you can't tell if it's gone from up here. Which means I have to wait here to see them go. And if I go away and come back I'll have to drive past the house again. Les looked at his watch. Oh well. May as well make myself comfortable.

Les waited almost an hour. One or two cars went past in the rain and Les could feel the drivers looking at him. He snatched another glance at his watch. That car's not going anywhere. I could be sitting here all bloody day. Les drummed his fingers impatiently on the steering wheel. I may as well ring Gerry. There's a phone booth opposite that book shop. Les started the car and drove back to the old post office.

The phone was out of order and there was a note on the book shopdoor. Back In An Hour. Les shook his head. Warren's right, I've got to get myself a mobile bloody phone. Bit late to be thinking of it now, though. He got back in the car and drove to the hotel.

After parking the car, smiling and nodding to the staff as he walked up to his room, then dialling Sydney, Les had timed it perfectly to find Gerry's phone engaged. He waited and rang another three times. Maybe he had the wrong number? Les checked with Telstra. No. He had the right number. The line was busy. Les stared at the floor, shook his head then walked out to the car and drove back to Red Gum Road. This time he took *The Portable Beat Reader* with him.

The builders were still hammering away and the station wagon hadn't moved. Les did another U-turn then parked in the same spot at the end of the street and continued waiting. Another car went by and not long after that, the white utility belonging to one of the builders backed out of the driveway and drove past. Out the corner of his eye, Les saw a young, thin-faced bloke, wearing a gold earring and with his dark hair tucked under a black beanie, watching him from behind the wheel. Les kept reading his book and waited. Before long the utility returned, and Les didn't have to look up to know this time the driver was staring at him. Les began to feel one of his legs going to sleep and put the book down. Bugger it. I'll try and ring Gerry again. He started the car and drove back to the hotel. Another ten minutes on the phone and her number was still engaged. Fuckin hell, cursed Les. This is getting ridiculous. He pulled his hood up against the rain, walked out to his car again and drove back to Red Gum Road.

When Les reached the end of the cul-de-sac he couldn't believe his eyes. The station wagon was gone. Yes, he beamed. There is a Santa

Claus. Right. No time to fuck around. Les pulled up in front of the gum tree, grabbed his backpack and without bothering to lock the car, walked across to the front gate. He was about to open it when a movement to his left filled Norton's stomach with ice and made the hair stand up on the back of his neck. Two Rottweilers with thick black studded collars raced up to the other side of the gate and snarled at him with gleaming fangs and eyes full of menace. They didn't carry on with a lot of barking or jumping up and down. However, Les knew as he watched the ridges of black hair bristling along their spines, they'd do exactly what they were told to do. Tear anyone to pieces that came through the gate. Les might have flattened one with the jemmy, but the other would have got him and he'd be minus a calf muscle and half his thigh.

'Nice doggies,' said Les, slowly backing away from the gate. 'Nice doggies.'

Without moving, the two Rottweilers watched him get inside the car and drive off. By the time Les got to the old post office, his heart had stopped racing and he pulled over to have a think. Bloody hell! What about those two monsters. Another couple of steps and in two seconds I'd have been minute steak. I didn't even think of that. Les banged a fist into his hand. Fuck it! All that waiting around for nothing. Angrily Les rubbed at his chin and glared out the windscreen. No. He was too close now. The two dogs weren't going to stop him. Les swung the Berlina back over the bridge and headed for Katoomba.

The main street was busy with Thursday afternoon shoppers and there were cars everywhere. Les did two frustrating laps up and down looking for a parking spot before leaving the car unlocked in a driveway next to a bank. He had a quick look around then ran straight across the road into the butcher shop. There were four customers and two butchers serving; an older one going bald and a young one with fair hair and pimples. After a few minutes Les got the young one.

'Yehmadewodillyav?' the butcher asked in perfect strine.

'Gizdoogillosachugstag,' replied Les.

'Rydo.'

'Njobidubwillya,' asked Les.

'Nowurriesmade.'

The young butcher got two kilos of chuck steak from the window, chopped it up and put it in a plastic bag. Les paid him, thanked him and ran back to the car just as a black 4WD pulled up to enter the driveway. Before the woman driving had a chance to start blowing her horn, Les got behind the wheel and was on his way. He was back in Medlow Bath just as a long, freight train rumbled slowly through the station. Les drove straight back to the house and parked in the same place as before. He threw his backpack over his shoulder, opened up the plastic bag and walked across to the gate. Immediately the two Rottweilers rushed up to the other side looking meaner and more threatening than ever. Les decided to try a little animal psychiatry. He wasn't sure who owned the two dogs, but they might recognise a name.

'Albert,' he said, slowly and clearly. 'Where's Albert?' The two dogs looked at Les, cocked their ears up and tilted their heads to one side. 'Yeah. Good boys,' said Les. 'Where's Albert? Albert.' The Rottweilers watched Les suspiciously as he opened the bag of chuck steak. Then they got a sniff and drool started pouring from their mouths like a tap had been turned on. Whoever was looking after the two dogs was probably just slinging them a can of Pal each and a few Meaty Bites. It had been a while since they'd seen choice lean beef. The two dogs gave a little whine and their tails started to wag. 'Yeah. Albert,' smiled Les. 'Good boys. Good boys.'

Les tossed a handful of meat over the fence and eased the jemmy out of his back pack. The two dogs wolfed the meat down in seconds and looked up for more. Les threw the rest over the fence and slowly opened the gate. The two Rottweilers tore into the chuck steak ready to kill each other for it and totally ignored Les. Righto boys, smiled Les as he stepped inside and closed the gate behind him. Time for a different kind of animal psychiatry. He brought the jemmy up and belted the first Rottweiler across the forehead. It gave a grunt of pain, then went cross-eyed and fell face first into the chuck steak with its back legs twitching. Before the other Rottweiler even noticed, Les back handed the jemmy down across its neck. It gave a slight yelp and went down next to its mate with its eyes closed and its tongue lolling. The first Rottweiler looked like there might be a kick left in it. Les gave it another quick belt in the head and it went still. Just to be certain, Les gave the second Rottweiler one in the head as well. That was it. Les slipped the jemmy into his backpack then took the two dogs by their collars and quickly dragged them behind the house. There was a short set of steps leading up to the back door; Les took the steps two at a time and shoved the jemmy behind the lock. Two good wrenches and he was inside the house. He took a torch from his back pack and had a look around.

Norton found himself standing in a small verandah, the windows facing the backyard. An old grey chesterfield sat against the opposite wall, scattered with black cushions, and a tatty green rug covered the floor. Several abstract art posters hung on the walls and the running shelf held assorted bric a brac and thick candles. Les couldn't see anything to get excited about. He moved the torch to a corridor leading inside and followed it.

There was a kitchen and bathroom on the right and two bedrooms on the left. The corridor ended at a lounge room then another room facing the street. The first bedroom had two deadlocks on it. Les left it for the time being and pushed the door to the second one open. It was fairly plain. A brass double bed, a wardrobe, a dressing table, dark curtains over the window and a few prints and rock posters on the wall, Les figured this room would belong to whoever shared the house. Les stepped to the end of the corridor and ran his torch over the lounge.

It was very dark; thick velvet drapes covered the windows, stopping most of the light. A dark blue lounge suite, covered in red and gold scatter cushions with gold tassles, sat on a red rug and faced an open fireplace in the corner. Against one wall was a TV, a stereo and a CD stacker. Around the remaining walls were strange-looking gothic posters and paintings plus a framed poster of *Rosemary's Baby*. There were gold stars and pentangles painted on the walls, bric a brac and candles along the running shelf and a candleholder made from a skull sat on a coffee table. Hanging over the fireplace was a double-handed sword and sitting on a small shelf above it was a copper chalice. Hanging on the wall above the chalice was a framed tapestry containing the words:

> *Drink from the cup of the Wine of Life,*
> *which is the Cauldron of Cerridwen,*
> *and the Holy Grail of Immortality.*

Fill it full of cold Fourex and you've got me, thought Les. Despite his flippancy, the lounge room gave Les the creeps. He stepped through and opened the door to the front room.

There was a little more light and the first thing Les noticed was a chef's hat lying across a wooden chair. Yeah, this is Knox's room, thought Les. If I owned the house it'd be mine. The bedroom was almost twice as big as the other one. A four-poster bed sat against the windows facing the street, the wardrobe was bigger and the dressing table had a full-length mirror. There was a stack of cookbooks on a small table, more gothic posters on the walls and more fat candles in holders round the running shelf along with several incense burners. Amongst the posters was another framed tapestry with a cryptic little poem.

I do not like thee, Dr Fell,
the reason why, I cannot tell.
There's only one thing I know well
I do not like thee, Dr Fell.

So much for Dr Fell thought Les. I wonder if he bulk bills? On the wall near the tapestry were some framed photos. Les ran the torch over them. A couple were of Knox standing outside the house. Another was Knox with the two Rottweilers. Next to that was Knox and Brett Rittosa wearing chef's uniforms in a restaurant called The Moondance Diner. The last photo was of four men, taken from the knees up, standing in front of an old boat — a half-cabin, wooden clinker. There were three portholes along the cabin and on the bow was written *Trough Queen*. It was moored at the edge of a park, next to a sign saying Victor Harbor and in the distance was a rocky island with a jetty running out to it. Three of the men were wearing T-shirts with Victor Harbor Sea Scouts on the front, the fourth man had *Trough Queen* printed on his. The man wearing a sea scout's T-shirt on the left was Albert Knox. The others were all wearing floppy white captain's hats and sunglasses and Les couldn't recognise any of them.

The only standout feature was two had big noses and another was smoking what looked like a joint. They weren't quite facing the camera full on, but all four men seemed to be cracking up at some private joke. Les shone his torch over the photo. I'd say they're the crew of that boat. One of them's the skipper. And Knox and the other two are wearing sea scout T-shirts for a joke. I wonder if they've been using the *Trough Queen* for a bit of dope smuggling? From what I know about Albert Knox, it wouldn't surprise me in the least. Find those other blokes in the photo with him and you never know what might turn up. This could be what I'm looking for. Les took the photo from the wall and put it in his back pack. He flashed his torch around the dead man's room again, had a quick look in his wardrobe and left it at that. Les didn't want to be in the house any longer than he had to. Apart from whoever was living there coming back, the house had a weird feel about it. It belonged in a Stephen King movie. Les stepped back into the lounge room then walked down to the room with the locks on the door. He got the jemmy from his back pack and shoved it in the jamb. The noise in the empty wooden house was horrendous, but three good wrenches and the door was open.

Les gave it a push and walked straight in on a well-organised hydroponic operation. Twenty healthy marijuana plants were growing in tanks placed neatly under Gro-Lights hanging from the ceiling. Each plant was over a metre high and they were all starting to head. Les gave the operation a grudging nod of approval. Very nice boys. There should be a few dollars' worth there. Les, however, wasn't in the least bit concerned about the late cook and his cohorts' indoor drug plantation. He stepped out the back door and closed it behind him. The two Rottweilers were still lying where he left them. Les took the steps two at a time again, got in his car and drove back to the hotel.

The first thing Les did was try to ring Gerry again. The number was still engaged. He changed into a clean blue T-shirt then got the photo out of his back pack and studied it. After finding the hydroponic set up in the house, Les was now convinced drugs were behind all this and Knox and other men in the photo were dope dealers. They'd just pulled off a shipment and that's why they were all laughing and clowning around. And Knox was laughing loudest because he'd ripped the others off. They found out and arranged his murder. Find the men in the photo and you could bet you'd find the killer. Or killers. But where the fuck was Victor Harbor? Les had never heard of it. He placed the photo on the bed then walked down to reception and asked for a booklet of post codes. It didn't take long to find Victor Harbor was in South Australia. But whereabouts in South Australia? Les returned the booklet and strolled back to his room. There was one way to find out. They'd have to have a Victor Harbor Motel or something. Les rang Telstra. They found him a Victor Harbor, Ezy Rest Motel. Les wrote the number down then picked up the phone.

'Hello Ezy Rest Motel. How can I help you?' came a woman's voice.

'Yes. Have you any vacancies?' asked Les.

'How many people?'

'Ahh ... two.'

'No problem. When did you want them?'

'On the weekend. Look, we're new to South Australia,' said Les. 'How far are you from say ... Adelaide?'

'Eighty-five kilometres, if you come via Mount Compass.'

'Thanks. I'll see you when we get there.'

Les hung up and looked at the photo again. Eighty-five kilometres from Adelaide. This bloody Adelaide connection kept cropping up all the time. Knox, King, David. Simone Mitchum. The men in the photo. Yeah, but that's South Australia. This is New South Wales. It's a long way away. Even if this Victor Harbor is just a short drive from Adelaide.

'Ohh shit!' Les sat up on the edge of the bed. 'Oh fuckin hell!'

Talk about short drives. What about a short drive to Sydney? And report in to the police? Les had forgotten all about it. He looked at his watch. There was no way in the world he could get there on time now. And what did those two cops say? If he was one minute late they'd arrest him. If he couldn't report in, don't bother ringing up, they'd come looking for him, with the rest of the NSW police force, and shooting him on sight would be a pleasure. What did Tait say? *We're filthy on having to watch you walk out of here.* They meant every word. They'd had pressure put on them in the middle of an arrest and they didn't like it.

'Shit! Fuck! Fuck it!' Les punched the bed, almost dislodging the mattress.

He felt a film of sweat form on his brow. Les wasn't starting to panic, but there was a cold surge in the pit of his stomach. Things had suddenly changed. For the worse. He'd breached his bail conditions and now he was a fugitive. He could be arrested on sight. And after what he was supposed to have done, you could bet the cops would be looking for him everywhere. What about when Nathan David found out? He'd have a bulletin on him every half-hour. Have you seen this man? What are the police doing about it? How did he get bail in the first place? Les fell back on the bed and looked up at the ceiling. What should he do? Ring Eddie? No. With everyone running around for him, Eddie would think he was a complete dill breaking his bail conditions. Ring Price? After all the trouble Price went to, to get him bail, he'd probably tell Eddie to shoot him. Les cursed and banged at the bed. Then he settled down. No. It was time to do his own thing. He'd been listening to people all his life and got dumped on, and if he hadn't listened to Eddie and his silly fuckin ideas, he wouldn't be in all this shit in the first place. Les stared at the photo on the bed and felt he'd found something to go on. Not much. But it was better than hanging around Bondi. Or Sydney. Les absently looked at his watch and picked up the phone again.

'Hello,' came a familiar man's voice. 'Travelabout Clovelly. Gary Blair speaking.'

'Hello Gary. It's Les Norton.'

'Les. How are you? I'd thought you'd be ... well I don't know where I thought you'd be, to be honest.'

'I'm in the Blue Mountains.'

Gary was the team's travel agent. He was a good style of a bloke and a snappy dresser and always with a twinkle in his eye. Like Gerry the accountant, Gary could cut corners and didn't ask too many questions.

'So Les. What can I do for you?' asked Gary.

'Gary, I need a ticket to Adelaide. Leave tomorrow. Come back Sunday night. A cargo plane. A room at the Y. Anything. I don't give a fuck.'

Gary chuckled over the line. 'Les, you're not going to believe this. I've just had a bloke, some company director, pull out of a trip I had organised. I'm out a bit of time and money ringing Adelaide and that. But it's yours if you want it.'

'I'll take it,' said Les. 'Even if it's in the back of a Hercules.'

'It's not in the back of a Hercules,' said Gary. 'It's a package.'

'A what?'

'A package. You fly business class. You got Golden Wing. A driver's waiting for you at the airport. You stay in a Regency Suite at the Adelaide Grande. And there's a car booked for Saturday and Sunday if you want it. A Hyundai Grandeur.'

'Shit!'

'The plane leaves at twelve fifty-five tomorrow. The driver picks you up again at the hotel, five-thirty Sunday. And you fly out at seven. How's that sound?'

'Unreal.'

'You can pick the tickets up on the way to the airport tomorrow. When you get there, say your name's Conrad Ullrich.'

'I'll tart my hair up and say I'm Kylie Minogue, Gary, I don't give a fuck. How much do I owe you?'

'Ohh for you, Les,' Gary pressed the buttons on a calculator. 'Two grand. You'll have to pay for the car down there. And your meals. But you get a free continental breakfast in the Regency Club. All right?'

'I've got my credit card right here, Gary,' said Les.

Norton couldn't believe it. Some luck at last. He might be going down, but at least he was going down in style. He gave Gary his credit card details, got a few more details himself, and that was it. All he had to do now was get back to Bondi, get his gear, pick up the tickets, hope the cops weren't waiting for him and he was on his way to Adelaide. It might turn out to be a wild goose chase, but if he did find out who those other men in the photo were, at least it was something to offer Tait and Caccano before they flung him in the nick. What did he have to lose? Especially now. Norton's eyes flicked back to the phone. He still had to ring Gerry. This time the line was open.

'Hello Gerry. It's Les Norton.'

'Hello Les,' replied Norton's accountant. 'How are you?'

'Good Gerry. Look, I'm sorry I didn't ring you yesterday. I honestly forgot. I'm in the Blue Mountains and I've been trying to ring you all day.'

'That's all right. I've been super busy. And we've had trouble with the phones and the computers all day. But I spoke to Ivor for you.'

'You did? What did he say?'

'There is another insurance policy on that movie. Max King took it out through his company, King Productions. With one other beneficiary: Simone Mitchum.'

'What a lovely quinella,' said Les.

'The way it's structured, if anything happens to production, they each get two thousand five hundred dollars a week for up to six months. Then another hundred thousand. Plus their original investment back.'

'Nice work.'

'Yes,' agreed Gerry. 'The premium was fairly stiff. But it's quite clever how they worked it. If *Leaving Bondi* never gets off the ground, it's in their best interests. And it's doubtful now it ever will. So they're laughing.'

Les nodded and gritted his teeth. 'Laughing. Like a pair of hyenas.'

'Sorry Les. But . . . that's show business.'

'Yeah. Like no business I know. Okay. Thanks for that, Gerry. I appreciate it.'

'Anytime Les. Bye.'

Norton replaced the phone and lay back on the bed. So. Max King and Simone Mitchum, eh. Maybe one of them did it? It certainly added another angle to the dangle. King especially. All those radio do-dads on the film set. King could slip a remote control device in amongst them, make sure he was safe, then detonate the bomb. And no one would know. His arse was covered and with their money from the insurance policy, he and Simone could go on to make more award-winning movies. But how could you prove it? Not easily. Still. It was something to go on if nothing eventuated in Adelaide. Les smiled bitterly. Not for me though. My lawyers — hopefully. I'll be in the nick. Anyway. What now? Les swung his feet over the bed. Get cleaned up and have a feed in the restaurant. Then have a quiet one at home and pack my bags ready to split in the morning. I suppose I'd better ring the maitre d and inform him Mr McNamara will be dining alone tonight.

Les took his time having a shave and a shower then got dressed again. Outside it had stopped raining, but the wind had picked up and it was still bleak and cold. He had a read, but half the time he kept thinking about his predicament and the room started to get that gaol feel about it again. It certainly was a nice mess he'd got himself into. Eventually he switched on the TV. The reception was awful. But a repeat episode of *Seinfeld* got Les going again. The one where George's mother catches him with a full hand going alone and starts running around screaming: 'My son's a pervert. My son's a pervert.' Still laughing, Les threw his leather jacket on and walked down to the restaurant.

Angelo wasn't on. Instead Les got a fair-haired woman in a black suit. She was extremely charming and polite. But when it came to bow and scrape, she wasn't in the event compared to Angelo. Les got a nice table facing the door and looked at the menu. What he had the night before tasted that good he ordered the same; plus a Hahn Premium, coffee and bread rolls; hold the sweets. Like the previous night, the meal was delicious. Les put it on his tab, gave a tip and left. He paused momentarily in the Kurrajong Room, but didn't feel like sitting on his own listening to Super Hits of the Twenties and Thirties. So he went straight to his room.

There was nothing on TV; and if there had been, the reception was that bad it wouldn't have been worth watching anyway. Les opened *The Portable Beat Reader*. He'd finished all the Bukowski and Kerouac. And after half a page of Joyce Johnson, Les felt it'd be more fun beating his meat. He closed the book and stared out the window again into nothing except cold and darkness. It wasn't much of a night. But Les felt anything would be better than sitting around like a battery hen. What did it say out the front of that hotel yesterday? Piano man Thursday night? Why not go and have a couple of quiet beers and check it out. If I keep my head down I should be all right. Les zipped up his leather jacket and walked out to the car.

Not a great deal was happening in Katoomba when Les got there. A few taxis were parked in front of the tunnel to the railway station, one or two people were walking by and that was about it. He parked the car on a bus stop right outside the Kensington and walked up the front steps.

There was one room as you entered, a small bar on the right then a few stairs led up to another room at the back. Chairs and tables dotted the red carpet and bench seats ran round the walls in the first room. The usual booze posters and sepia photos of pioneer days clung to the walls and a set of stairs on one side of the bar ran up to a bistro. Built above the bar was a wooden stage where a bloke on piano was hammering out Elton John's 'Benny And The Jets', aided and abetted by another bloke on a guitar. About forty punters, mostly men, were scattered around both rooms. There were a few attractive girls and three of the ugliest lesbians Norton had ever seen, wearing Levi jackets and gelled mullets. Sitting along the opposite side of the bar under the stage were four young blokes in sweatshirts and baseball caps, sucking schooners and smoking cigarettes. They were hair raiding the musicians and making plenty of noise in general, somewhere between boisterous fun and drunken attitude. Apart from them, everybody else was quietly drinking and the dress code ranged from corduroy trousers to plastic raincoats, tracksuits to black dresses. The only exception was an overweight woman with a face like a pie tin standing at the bar wearing a long grey woollen dress. She had copper-coloured hair, combed into two braids, junky green earrings and wrapped loosely round her neck was a green, tartan scarf. Sitting on the bar was a cheap bottle of sparkling domestic in an ice bucket and she was carrying on like she'd just won lotto. Les edged his way around her and got a middy of VB then found a vacant bench seat and a table. He sat back looking up at the stage and had an enjoyable sip of beer as the two musicians gave it to Neil Young's 'Heart of Gold'.

The first beer went down easy and was just what Les needed. Feeling a slight glow, he walked over and ordered another one, getting a heavy once up and down from the woman with the ice bucket. Les half smiled back at her and returned to his seat. The two musicians got stuck into Stevie Ray Vaughn's 'Pride and Joy'. Then the piano man announced they were taking a break and he was going to relieve his bladder. One of the young blokes at the bar held up a half empty schooner glass and yelled up to him.

'Here. Fill this up while you're at it.'

All his mates thought it was as funny as all get up and fell about laughing like drains. Les thought it wasn't a bad call and finished his second beer. He got up for a third and got another once up and down from the woman with the ice bucket. Again Les half smiled back and returned to his seat. Over the top of his middy Les could feel her watching him. Finally, she picked up her ice bucket and walked over.

'Mind if I join you?' she said in a throaty voice that vibrated through her double chins.

Les looked at her like she had a tarantula crawling over her face. 'Yeah, why not?' he answered.

Tartan scarf plonked her ice bucket on the table in front of Les and crammed her ample backside into a chair. 'I'm Lareina,' she said.

'How are you, Lareina?' replied Les. 'I'm Marvin.'

'Nice to meet you, Marvin.'

'Yeah. Likewise.'

'Are you from round here, Marvin?'

Les shook his head. 'Stock and Bingle.'

'Oh?' said Lareina. 'What do you do out there?'

'I'm a rabbit trapper.'

'Really. I like to eat rabbits.'

'You'd eat anything,' said Les.

'What was that?'

'I said, you can eat them with anything.'

'Yes. Especially curried.' Lareina swallowed the glass of wine she brought with her and poured another one. 'So what are you doing in Katoomba, Marvin?' she asked.

'I'm here for the Songs of the Wind Festival,' answered Les.

Lareina gave a squeal of delight. 'What a coincidence. I'm a playwright.'

'You're a what?'

'I write plays.' Lareina nodded to the bottle of cheap fizz. 'That's why I'm celebrating. They're performing one of my plays this weekend. And I've won a grant to write another one.'

Les looked at her impassively. 'Fair ... dinkum?'

'Yes. It's called *The Sculptured Chrysanthemum*.'

'Go ... on.' Les had a mouthful of beer and stared at Lareina. Shit! How do I find them? I've got to get a T-shirt made with Come and Talk to Me, I Love Idiots printed on the front. And a matching cap.

Lareina started waffling on about her fabulous play and how Les shouldn't miss it. She could get him a ticket. Then the musicians returned and started flogging Cat Stevens's 'Where Will The Children Play'. While this was going on Les didn't notice a bloke wearing a disposal-store army jacket, jeans and black Timberlands walk in. He had dark hair and an earring and was walking to the hotel across the railway line when he saw the mud spattered green Berlina out the front of the Kensington. Inside there was no missing Norton's craggy red head. The bloke got a middy and quietly watched Les from the bar.

By now Les had had enough of Lareina, and the music wasn't doing anything for him either when Lareina pulled out a packet of Winfields from somewhere in her dress. She groped around for her lighter, got a cigarette going then managed to knock Les's beer over when she picked up her glass of wine.

'Oh I'm sorry,' she giggled, blowing a mouthful of smoke in Norton's face as she flicked ash over the table.

'That's quite all right,' said Les. 'You did me a favour.' He rose from the table and walked straight out the door to his car.

Fuckin fat pain in the arse, Les scowled, zipping his leather jacket up against the cold. I was enjoying that beer. Three would have been just nice, too. He licked his lips. I suppose I can have another one back at the Medlow. He was about to get in the car when he noticed the hotel across the railway line. Why don't I have one more in there. It's not that far and some fresh mountain air would be good after putting up with her. They might have some music going, too. Les shoved his hands in the pockets of his jacket and started walking.

A tunnel ran under the railway station, and the taxi drivers parked in front of the nearby shops thought Les was an approaching fare and nearly ate him. Les smiled as he walked past and took the steps on his right. An opening to the station went off to the left and beneath a grey metal girder the tunnel ran straight ahead. It was fairly well lit. There were some framed posters on the walls and at the end of the wall on the right was a long mural of an indigo night sky full of stars, viewed from over a row of pine trees. Les gave it a grudging nod of approval as he walked past, then turned right, coming up at a pedestrian crossing leading to the hotel.

It was a fairly big hotel featuring a small beer garden out the front beneath an art-deco style verandah and windows. A blue awning with Fosters printed on it swung round to the bars on the right. Les crossed over to the footpath and walked in the glass doors at the end. Inside, one long wooden bar curved around to the left to an alcove with a fireplace. On the right was a games room and in front of that a pool room with one unoccupied pool table. Through a corridor was a lounge with a small ticket office next to a door with a sign, BANDS WED AND FRI NIGHTS $3 ADMISSION. The decor was mainly brown and yellow, with old wooden fittings and lights hanging from the ceiling on chrome pipes. The fire in the alcove was going and about fifteen punters were spread along the bar, including three very sour-faced blokes at the games room end wearing dark tracksuits and trainers. Les had a quick look around, then ordered a middy of VB and walked down to the alcove at the other end.

There was no music and absolutely nothing to perv on as Les sipped his beer and gazed at the fire over a table full of drunks. The crowd was older and more into plain drinking than at the other hotel. It might have been warm and the beer wasn't all that bad, but it was just too boring. Gazing absently at the fire Les didn't notice the bloke in the army jacket walk in the same door he did. He went straight up to the sour-faced men in the tracksuits and pointed to Les. Their sour faces suddenly turned even sourer. Well, there's not much doing here, thought Les. I think I might call it a night. I'd have been better off staying home. No. If it hadn't been for that wobbegong putting her fat head in at that other place it would have been all right. The music wasn't that bad, and the beer was good. Les finished his middy, put the glass on the bar and left through the nearest door.

Walking back through the tunnel, Les stopped momentarily to have another look at the mural and noticed the artist had included a few UFOs in the background. I suppose on those clear nights up this way they'd see a few strange lights in the sky now and again, Les chuckled to himself. Woody should move up here. She'd cough in her rompers if she saw that mural. He'd started walking again when an angry voice shouted out from the end of the tunnel, echoing round the walls.

'Hey, you in the fuckin leather jacket.'

Les stopped and turned around. 'Are you talking to me?' he asked politely.

'You're the only fuckin one here, cunt.'

The three men from the bar, plus the one in the army jacket, marched up to Les. The one doing the shouting had dark hair and a flattened nose, pushed into a mean, sallow face. He was the biggest. The man in the army jacket was about medium build and another one on Norton's right was tall with short brown hair and looked like he might be able to handle himself. The fourth bloke was skinny with a bony face full of acne, and although he was doing his best to look tough, Les felt he was there only to make up the numbers. The four men formed a half circle around Les, who was standing a couple of metres out from the wall.

'What seems to be the trouble fellahs?' smiled Les, taking his hands from his pockets.

The biggest bloke glared at him. 'You were out Medlow Bath today. Weren't you?'

Les shook his head. 'I only just got here a couple of hours ago.'

'Fuckin bullshit!' The big bloke nodded to the one in the army jacket. 'Jimmy was working out there and saw you parked in Red Gum Road. You were cruising around all day.'

Les looked at the bloke in the army jacket. 'I think Colin Combat needs to get his eyes tested.'

'I don't need my eyes tested,' said the bloke in the army jacket. 'That's your Berlina outside the Kensington. And that was you out Medlow Bath today.'

'You got me mixed up with someone else,' said Les.

'We ain't got you mixed up with no one,' said the big hood. 'And I got one dog dead, and another in the vet's with a fractured skull.'

'Well,' suggested Les, 'maybe you shouldn't let your dogs roam the streets. Keep them on a lead and they won't get hurt in the traffic.'

The big hood's face reddened with anger. 'They didn't get hurt in no traffic you cunt. Somebody hit them with something. Something hard. Like this.'

The big hood reached under his tracksuit with his right hand and whipped out a length of pipe. He raised it above his head then swung it at Norton's face. Les had been expecting something like this. He moved in closer, caught the hood's wrist with his left hand, gripped him at the elbow with his right, then twisted left, turning the big hood with him. When the hood's back was facing the tunnel wall, Les swept his right leg away and banged the back of his head into the wall. He followed this with a smashing right knee into the hood's groin. The big hood gave a yelp of pain that echoed round the tunnel and dropped the length of pipe. Les let go of him and snatched up the pipe. In almost the same movement, Les backhanded it against the side of Army Jacket's right knee. Army Jacket gasped in a breath then howled and grabbed at his shattered knee. Before he could howl again, Les gave him an uppercut with the pipe, splitting his chin open and dumping him on his back. Les kept going round in a half circle with the length of pipe and collected the brown-haired bloke across one side of the face, then swung it back across the other. The first blow broke Brown Hair's jaw, the second one smashed several teeth. Brown Hair clutched at his face as blood started oozing through his fingers, then turned his back on Les and sank to his knees. Les split the back of his head open with a quick rap of the pipe and he pitched forward, unconscious. The big hood was sitting on his backside holding his groin: stunned and in a lot of pain, but still conscious. He looked up at Les and the last thing he saw was the length of pipe coming towards his face before it crunched into his forehead, splitting it to the bone. Blood poured into his eyes, he let go of his groin and fell back amongst the others, out cold. This left the last bloke looking down at his mates horrified. His poor, skinny, acned face was contorted with fear and a trickle of urine had started running down the inside of his jeans. Les poked the length of pipe at his groin.

'Hello me old,' said Les. 'How are they hanging? Long and loose and full of juice?'

'Ohh look, mate,' begged the skinny hood. 'I had nothing to do with this. Fair dinkum. I was just sitting in the pub. I don't even come from round here. I'm from Muswellbrook. I drive a bread cart. I swear, mate. I hardly know these blokes.'

Les gave the skinny hood a cursory once up and down. 'You know something? I believe you. You're just an innocent bystander.'

'That's right, mate. I'm telling you the truth. Honest I am. You got to believe me.' The trickle in the bloke's jeans turned into a torrent. 'I've never lied in my life.'

'Yeah. You're an honest man,' said Les. 'So I'll tell you what I'm gonna do.' The skinny hood yelped with terror as Les jammed the length of pipe up under his chin and pinned him against the wall. 'Now listen to me, you pimply faced streak of cat shit,' hissed Norton, his eyes about an inch away from the hood's. 'I'm a secret agent with the taxation department. I'm up here looking for an Israeli banker, stole fifty million dollars from the government. So I'm not in the slightest bit interested in you. Or your shitty mates. You listening?'

'Yeah mate. Yeah,' gasped the bloke. 'Every word, mate.'

'So tell your friends when they're back on their feet: keep their mouths shut about what just happened, and I won't tell the drug squad about their little hydro operation in Red Gum Avenue. You got that?'

'Yeah mate. Every word. No one'll say nothing.'

'Good. Because I don't need the paperwork. But if you don't, you know what I'll do?'

The bloke shook his head. 'No, mate. What?'

Les shoved the pipe between the bloke's legs. 'I'll come back and audit you.'

Les could see the poor bloke was seconds away from crapping his pants as well as pissing himself. He wiped the hair and blood off the pipe on the bloke's tracksuit top and left him.

The taxi drivers were watching Les as he came up the stairs. Les tucked the piece of pipe under his arm, but he thought one driver saw it. When Les got to his car, the piano man and his mate were pounding the life out of Fleetwood Mac's 'Don't Stop'. Les opened the door and threw the piece of pipe on the passenger seat. Whether any of the cab drivers took any notice as he drove past, Les wasn't sure. A couple of kilometres down the highway, Les opened the window and flung the piece of pipe into the bush. He wound the window back up and drove to the hotel.

Back in his room, Les packed his jeans away and changed into his blue tracksuit. He got a little bottle of Jim Beam from the mini-bar, poured it into a glass, topped it with water and swallowed some. It went down well, so Les swallowed some more. He sat on the edge of the bed and looked at the silent TV. What just happened should have had a funny side to it; especially when the skinny bloke piddled himself. But Les wasn't laughing. He was worried. And he felt like kicking himself in the arse. I knew I should have stayed home. There's cops looking for me all over the state. But no. I have to go to a fuckin pub and get into a fight. I need rooting. Les took another mouthful of bourbon. When those heroes drag their sorry arses off to hospital, the doctor or the nurses are going to call the police. Then there's those taxi drivers. They couldn't miss me. And I'm sure one of them saw me with that iron bar. Shit! My only chance is if they don't go to hospital before I get out of here tomorrow. Yeah, right. If they don't get their heads stitched up they'll bleed like stuck pigs all night. Les looked at his bags packed and ready to go. I should piss off now. But where am I gonna go? I can't hang around Sydney or my place. I can't win. I'm fucked if I stay here. And I'm fucked if I go home. Les caught his reflection in the mirror next to the bathroom. You're a nice goose, Norton.

He finished the first bourbon and had another. The second one settled him down a little. Yeah, but surely those hillbillies wouldn't say anything after I drummed it into that dill's head about their hydro system? They couldn't be that stupid. No. I think I'm pretty sweet. And by the time the cops sort all the shit out, how are they going to find me? They could if they wanted to. But I reckon they'd have better things on their minds than a bunch of wallys getting a belting. They're probably local hoods anyway. Les took another sip of bourbon. Yeah. I think I'm drama queening here just a bit. That's me, Les Norton aka Bette Davis. He caught his reflection in the mirror again. You dill. Les was about to switch the TV on when there was an urgent knock on the door.

Norton's blood went cold, and this time he did start to panic. Ohh shit! They're here already. Fuck! How did they find me so quick? God! What am I going to do? He looked at the window. It was a ten-metre drop. Don't answer the door? The cops'd smash the fuckin thing in. Les was trapped. There was only one thing he could do. Answer the door and face the music. Bugger it. Two days he'd lasted. Two lousy, bloody days. And just when it looked like there might have been a tiny light at the end of the tunnel. With a heart full of lead, Les opened the door.

'Mr Forrest McNamara?' It was a woman.

Les gave a double blink. 'Yeah. That's me.'

'My name is Odessa Hatfield. I'm a friend of Blythe Selby's.'

'You are? Well . . . come on in, Odessa. Tell me what I can do for you.'

Totally flabbergasted, Norton stepped aside to let the young woman in. She was almost as tall as Les, with straggly auburn hair combed up at the back. Her face was strong, with a firm mouth and wild green eyes and totally devoid of make-up. A thick black cardigan hung loosely over a maroon dress clinging to her whippy body and across one shoulder was a small leather sling bag. Clutched in her hands was a manuscript. It wasn't far from stepping inside to the mini-bar near the end of Norton's bed, but by the time she got there, Les noticed Odessa had a shapely arse with a swing like a new back door.

Odessa turned around, her chin up, a look of defiance on her face. When she spoke her voice was firm yet eloquent. 'If I've barged in on you like this Mr McNamara,' she said, 'I'm sorry. But Blythe told me you're looking for poets.'

'Yeah. We sure are,' replied Les. 'Are you a poet?'

'Yes,' asserted Odessa.

'Unreal,' said Les. 'So . . . what have you got for me, Odessa?'

'This.' Odessa thrust her manuscript at Norton.

Les took the manuscript and looked at the title, *Silicone Thoughts and Plastic Dreams*. 'Are these all your original works, Odessa?'

'Yes.'

'I thought so. All right. Well why don't you relax and make yourself a drink while I read one.'

'Thank you, Mr McNamara.'

Odessa flustered nervously round the mini-bar and made herself a scotch and water while Les fumbled around opening her manuscript, still not quite sure what he was doing. Odessa watched intently as Les sat on the bed and chose a poem at random. It was called 'Muriel's Milk Box'.

Talk to me in lecherous detail,
my heart demands it.
Is there cream,
yoghurt,
Lite-White,
Ricotta.
I swim in a sea of masochistic love,
with chocolate sharks,
and raspberry stingrays.

Les closed the manuscript and looked at Odessa. Odessa stared back challengingly.

'Well. What do you think?' she said. It was a demand as much as a question.

'What do I think?' answered Les. 'I'm not sure how to put this, Odessa. But you're definitely in the same league as Blythe Selby.'

'I am?' Odessa gave Les a double blink.

'Reckon. Of course I've only read one poem. But hey ...' Les made an open handed gesture.

'So you like them?'

'Of course. They're great.'

Odessa fell back against the mini-bar. 'Oh, I'm so thrilled,' she said.

Les smiled serenely at Odessa. 'But I do have to ask you something, Odessa, before we continue.'

'And what's that, Mr McNamara?'

'Are there any poems in here about sex?'

Odessa shook her head almost imperceptibly. 'I'm trying to keep sex out if it. At this stage.'

'Fair enough, Odessa,' nodded Les. 'What about blow jobs?' Les tapped the manuscript with an index finger. 'Is there any chance of finding a polish in here?'

Odessa's green eyes flashed. 'Mr McNamara,' she smiled. 'There's a sheila in there could suck a medicine ball through a didgeridoo.'

Les nodded cognizantly. 'Did Blythe mention my company's contractual arrangements? Half the advance initially. The rest on publication.'

'Blythe told me everything,' said Odessa. 'Everything.'

'Excellent,' beamed Les. 'Now, why don't I join you in a drink and I'll read another poem.'

'Do that, Mr McNamara.'

Les made another bourbon and found his hands were shaking slightly. What just happened was an astonishing, almost unbelievable turnaround. He had a mouthful of bourbon and settled down at one end of the bed. Odessa cradled her scotch and sat at the other. Les chose another poem at random. It was called 'Prismatic Impulsiveness'.

Moonbeams and rainbows,
nailed her to a wall of proclamation.
But despair and scandal
would never be the sword of righteousness,
in the hands of the separatists.
Nor reticence,
the slings and arrows
of the nebulous ungodly.

Les closed the manuscript and looked at Odessa. 'I don't think I need to read any more, Odessa. Just give me your phone number. And I'll tell you how you can contact me.'

'Marvellous,' said Odessa. 'Oh, I'm so glad I was brazen enough to call around.'

'Me too,' said Les.

She wrote down her phone number and address and her phone number at work. Odessa lived in Blackheath and worked for the council. Les gave her the same phone number he gave Blythe and told her to contact him through Mr Edwards.

'So there you go, Odessa,' said Les, placing her phone number in his wallet.

'You're on your way. I can envisage dual readings. You and Blythe.'

'This is amazing,' said Odessa. 'Absolutely amazing.'

'It sure is,' winked Les. 'Now, Odessa,' he said, undoing his tracksuit pants, 'there's some other contractual arrangements need to be taken care of. I've got a silent partner who'd like to get involved in this deal.' Les whipped out Mr Wobbly and gave him a couple of shakes. Mr Wobbly raised his head up to see what was going on and liked what he saw. 'He's in public relations. You know anything about public relations Odessa?'

'I certainly do.' Odessa moved along the bed. 'And you know something Mr McNamara? You're even better looking than Blythe said you were.'

'Call me Forrest, Odessa.'

Odessa was cool. She kissed Les and let him slip his hand under her dress and give her boobs a squeeze. They were round and firm with hard pointy nipples and her kisses were warm and sweet. It wasn't long before Norton had a rock hard boner and Mr Wobbly was frothing at the mouth. Odessa gave it a few strokes then slipped her mouth over the knob. Les felt a shiver run up and down his spine as Mr Wobbly started to get very red and angry. Odessa got right into it, adding some discreet moaning and groaning to show she was getting off a bit herself. It wasn't long before Les was spreadeagled on the bed, his eyes closed, sighing with sweet agony. Odessa hit the vinegar strokes and Les felt like he was levitating above the bed as he let go. Odessa took the lot. Licked her lips and looked around for more. Les collapsed against the pillows; eyes rolled back in his head and his toes twitching.

Odessa went to the bathroom and came back adjusting her dress. Les pulled his tracksuit pants up and tucked Mr Wobbly back into his little bed.

'I might leave now, Forrest,' said Odessa.

'Okay,' replied Les. 'I'll walk you to your car.'

'You don't have to. Stay where you are.'

'All right.'

'You won't lose my manuscript, will you?'

Les shook his head. 'I'll copy it as soon as I get back to the office. You've got other copies just to be on the safe side?'

'Oh yes.'

'Good.'

Odessa gave Norton a kiss. 'Goodnight, Forrest,' she smiled. 'I look forward to seeing you again.'

Les smiled back. 'Me too, Odessa. It's been a delight.'

Odessa stepped out the door, closed it behind her, and was gone.

Les looked at the door for a moment then placed Odessa's manuscript on the table and stared out the window. Suddenly he felt beat. It wasn't just driving around and being stuck in the car half the day. Or the beers, the fight and the romp with Odessa. When he heard that knock on the door, Les thought he was gone. When he opened it and it wasn't the police, the feeling was almost indescribable. Shock, followed by sheer elation. Like diving into a pool full of chilled champagne. Les knew the cops wouldn't be around now. He could relax. He cleaned his teeth, left his tracksuit on then crawled under the doona and switched off the bed lamp. Norton's last thoughts before drifting off were that he couldn't really blame that big bloke and his mates for wanting to sort him out after he'd killed one dog and fractured the other one's skull. But he honestly didn't think he'd hit the dogs that hard. And maybe he shouldn't have smashed the blokes as much as he did. But on the other hand, what would those blokes have done to him if he hadn't got hold of the iron bar? He probably wouldn't be walking. And Odessa wouldn't be getting a contract with Roulette Publishing. Les yawned and jammed his head into the pillows. Anyway, it was all behind him. Tomorrow was another day. And with a bit of luck he'd be in Adelaide and something might turn up. Les yawned again. It wasn't long and he was out like a light.

Les was out of bed, washed and in the breakfast room by eight wearing the same tracksuit; not being out to impress, and knowing he was only going to be sitting in his car all morning, he didn't bother getting changed. He filled a bowl with cereal and fruit and a plate with bacon and eggs, got some toast and coffee and found a table overlooking the Megalong Valley. Outside it was cold and raining again. He didn't bother turning on the radio or reading the paper. David would only be screaming his name to the rafters and some journalist would be doing the same. Les felt what he didn't know wouldn't hurt him. After one last cup of coffee he checked out, and by nine o'clock Les was in his car and heading for Sydney. He'd worked it so he had plenty of time to get home, grab a change of clothes, pick up his tickets and get to the airport, yet not be hanging around long enough for the police to arrest him. If he could make it to the airport Les felt he'd be able to hide in Golden Wing and he'd be all right.

Because of the weather, the drive down was slow and Les didn't like being a fugitive one bit. Five kilometres the other side of Linden a highway patrol car pulled in behind him and he began to sweat. He kept to the left and drove like Grandma Duck, when the cop suddenly switched on his siren making the butterflies in Norton's stomach start line dancing. But the cop went round him and pulled over a driver towing a trailer with no brake lights. Les exhaled audibly. That's it. Time for some music. He found a tape and Jools Holland and his Rhythm and Blues Orchestra started tickling the ivories with 'Travelling Blues'. After that the trip went noticeably smoother. The other side of Penrith, Bob Margolin was cranking out 'Up and In' like there was no tomorrow and B. B. King had just belted out 'Pauly's Birthday Boogie' when Les switched off the stereo and came down O'Brien Street, Bondi. He pulled up on the corner of Cox Avenue and Lamrock and peered through the windscreen. He couldn't see any police cars out the front of his house or the State Protection Unit hiding somewhere. Oh well, thought Les. Here goes nothing. He screeched to a halt outside Chez Norton, grabbed his bags then quickly locked the car and sprinted inside.

There were two messages on the answering machine. Les didn't bother to listen to them. It would only be Price or Eddie telling him what an idiot he was and he could do without that. Instead Les rang for a taxi. While he was waiting, he dumped his dirty clothes out of his bag, filled it with fresh ones and whatever else he thought he'd need in Adelaide then changed into a clean pair of jeans and a black Lee Kernaghan T-shirt. A horn bipping out the front told him the taxi had arrived. Les threw his leather jacket on, picked up his bags and Wednesday's paper from where he'd left it in the kitchen, then made sure the house was locked and ran outside.

'Clovelly Road. Then out to the airport,' said Les, jumping in the back seat of the taxi.

'No worries,' replied the driver.

Les buried his head in the paper, kept quiet and avoided any eye contact with the driver. Gary wasn't in his office when the taxi pulled up out the front of Travelabout Clovelly. One of the girls working there handed Les his tickets and wished him a good trip. The traffic wasn't too bad and he was outside Ansett Departures before he had a chance to re-read the sports pages. At the desk it was automatic drive. Mr Ullrich had his bags tagged Priority and was politely told his plane was leaving from gate sixteen. Les couldn't help the butterflies fluttering a little as he passed through the uniforms at security, but nothing happened. Safely through there, Les stopped at a newsagency and bought a map. Suburban and Regional Adelaide. He took the escalator to Golden Wing, got a smile from the girl at reception when he showed his card, and stepped inside.

There were a few casually dressed people in Golden Wing, but it was mostly suits waffling into mobiles or using the phones provided. Les found a table in the corner, made a cup of tea, got a plate of cheese and crackers and a *Bulletin* and spread his map out. The drive to Victor Harbor looked like a piece of piss. Les saw Mount Compass on the map and from there, Victor Harbor was almost straight down a highway, sitting in a long, wide bay. You can't tell which way the train went by looking at the tracks, thought Les, and you can't tell much about a town by looking at a map. At least I know where it is. Les folded his map up, put it in his backpack and read the *Bulletin* while he kept an eye on the other punters. By the time he had another cup of tea and a few more crackers it was time to board the plane.

Les had the very front seat to himself and plenty of leg room and one of the flight attendants had dark hair and a pretty good pair of legs in her black stockings. She gave Les a nice smile and a glass of orange juice. She came back to make sure Mr Ullrich's bag was stowed in front of him and they were on their way. Les had decided to brush *The Portable Beat Reader* for the time being. He'd read and heard enough nutty poetry to last him a lifetime. Instead he got a book from Warren's room. *Once A Jolly Swagperson* by Lawrence Held. *Politically Correct Tales For Our Times*. Les had just finished 'The Differently Statured Adult Male of Notre Dame' when it was time for lunch. Salad with sesame soya vinaigrette and mixed grill with honey carrots and sautéed wild mushrooms. This went down easily with another glass of orange juice and Les picked up his book again. He'd just finished 'Beauty and the Superficially Non-Humyn Animal' when the pilot announced they were making their descent into

Adelaide. The plane bumped down on the tarmac and a few minutes later Mr Ullrich got another smile as he disembarked.

Adelaide airport was nowhere near as big as Kingsford Smith. It was only a short walk to the arrivals lounge and standing on the right, wearing a grey uniform, cap and sunglasses, was a driver holding a sign: ULLRICH. Les walked up to him a little cautiously.

'I'm Conrad Ullrich.'

The driver was about thirty, dark complexioned and looked fit. 'Thank you, Mr Ullrich,' he replied pensively. 'I'm Vincent. I'll get your luggage.'

Les followed Vincent over to the carousel without saying anything. Vincent seemed to expect this. Norton's bag arrived, Vincent picked it up and Les followed him out to a white Ford LTD and got in the back. The weather was cloudy and cold and it looked like there had been some light rain. Vincent didn't say anything as they left the airport. Les thought it might be best if he did the same and peered out the window.

After the smog, traffic gridlocks and high rise of Sydney, Adelaide was like a big country town. Long flat roads, roomy wooden houses and plenty of parks and trees. A sign ahead said BURBIDGE ROAD A–6 CITY. Further on Les noticed a nice old hotel with a verandah round it called the New Market. Before long they were in the city. Vince turned this way and that, then came out on a wide, straight road divided in the middle. There were office blocks on the right and railway lines on the left. Behind the railway lines was a park with a river running through it. Vincent turned left into a curved driveway and pulled up in front of the Adelaide Grande.

The hotel looked quite swish. Thirty storeys high, plenty of chrome and glass, neat gardens and a split-level restaurant out the front. On the right was a casino. Vincent got Norton's bag from the boot and gave it to a porter with a brass luggage trolley then opened Norton's door.

'I'll see you at five-thirty on Sunday, Mr Ullrich,' he said.

'Okay. See you then, Vincent. Thanks,' replied Les.

'Enjoy your stay in Adelaide, sir.' Vincent got back in the LTD and drove off.

'Just the one bag, sir?' asked a porter in a black vest.

'Yes.'

'This way, sir.'

Les followed the porter into the lobby. Inside was even more swish than out. A ring of marble and gold columns rose out of a shiny parquet floor and circled a set of marble stairs with brass railings, leading down to a ballroom and function centre. The lifts were on the left next to a spacious bar called the Torrens Room. Just round from this were the doors to a sundeck overlooking the river, then an open doorway to a large dining room. To the right from the main entrance was the concierge, then behind a barricade of shiny black marble was the reception desk. Les followed the porter to reception. Checking in was automatic drive again. An extremely pleasant woman in a blue suit soon fixed everything with a minimum of fuss. Les signed in as C. Ullrich, Clovelly Road, Sydney, and was given his key and charge card. He then checked with the concierge about the car. No problems. Avis was straight across the road, the car was available at nine, bring it back to the hotel and it would be valet parked for him. Les followed the porter across to the lifts and even though Les would have made two of him, he let the porter carry his bag and they swooshed up to the twenty-third floor.

As he stepped out of the lift, Les walked to the windows at the end of the lift lobby to check out the view. On the right was the park and the river, ahead in the distance was the ocean and to the left a ring of hills surrounding the city. Walking to his room Les looked down two floors onto the Regency Club, a tastefully furnished, lovely green area with a bubbling fountain, servery and a bar where Gary had said the continental breakfast was on the house. Les couldn't wait for breakfast.

After the Medlow, Norton's room was like a home unit with a fabulous view over the city, the casino, and all the way to the distant hills on the left. There was a queen-size bed, a TV, ample furniture and wardrobe space and a marble bathroom with a shower and spa. The mini-bar was well stocked with assorted booze, chocolates and nibblies. And to think I would have settled for a room at the Y, Les chuckled to himself. He gave the porter two dollars and got a bottle of Heineken from the mini-bar. While he sipped that, Les unpacked then checked out the hotel directory and the room service menu. He had another look at the city as he finished his beer and noticed the clock radio: Adelaide was half an hour behind Sydney. It just gets better. Now I've got thirty minutes up my sleeve. Les lay back on the bed, closed his eyes and wondered what to do. The bed was very comfortable and Les lay on it longer than he intended. Another minute and he would have dozed off. He got up, splashed some water on his face and took in the view over the city again. Why don't I go for a walk? Check out beautiful downtown Adelaide. I won't get much chance tomorrow. Or Sunday. Les threw his leather jacket on and got the lift to the lobby.

He walked past the entrance to the casino and turned left at the old railway station. Les hadn't gone five metres before he tensed up. Three uniform cops were standing just inside the station. Les watched them out the corner of his eye, but they didn't appear to notice him. Shit! This is ridiculous, he told himself, I'll finish up in the rathouse. Les went right at King William then strolled past an office block and a group of girls huddled on the footpath, puffing desperately at their cigarettes. They were all dressed in black or purple with long dark hair and chalk-white skin. Very different to the girls at Bondi.

After unexpectedly seeing the wallopers, Les felt like something soothing. A Jack Daniels or a coffee would be nice. He sprung a health bar that was all bright colours and vinyl stools called the Boost Juice Bistro. Les ordered a shot of wheatgrass and a Brain Boost. Carrot, beetroot and apple with ginseng and ginkgo. The wheatgrass tasted exactly like licking the blades on a lawn mower, but you got a slice of lemon for a chaser. The brain booster was delicious and went down splendidly. It might have been Norton's imagination, but as he strode off, his head did feel clearer and there seemed to be an extra kick in his step as he crossed King William Street to check out Rundle Mall.

Les found himself walking down a long flat mall crammed with shops on either side and entrances to arcades and malls with more shops. There were crowds of shoppers and groups of unfamiliar mall hangers amongst the shoppers. Skinheads wearing black T-shirts with Korn, Fear Factory, Witchery and Crypt on the front and pale-skinned Gothic chicks wearing dark dresses and layers of weird dark make-up who looked like they'd just flown in on broomsticks. Fruit barrows and paper stalls were scattered along the middle and near one fruit barrow were several bronze pigs, one on its haunches eating out of a garbage tin. Les wished he'd brought his camera.

There were plenty of music shops catering mainly for thrash and grungeheads. Les had a look in one. It was all dark and mysterious with dark and mysterious-looking staff. On a bookshelf was a whole section on Wicca, Paganism, Ritual Magic, Goddess Studies. I wonder if I could get *The Beach Boys Greatest Hits* in here and a few Barbara Cartlands. I don't think so. Les crossed an intersection and now it was hotels, restaurants and sidewalk cafes. The mall ended near a gift shop selling cute little portable fountains. Les crossed over and came down the other side. It was much the same, except for the ubiquitous McDonalds and the usual kids, with faces full of pimples, that like to hang out the front. Les walked back to where he started, crossed over from the mall and found himself in Hindley Street.

Traffic drove back and forth and now there was a noticeable sleaze. Head shops, disposal stores, adult book shops, triple-X videos, video games arcades, Wild Night Review, takeaway food shops, tourist trap hotels. Bigger and better Gothic shops. Strip joints. Hello, thought Les, I'm home. I'm back at the Cross. All that's missing is a few hundred assorted hookers and junkies.

Although he knew he shouldn't go near it, something about the local police station fascinated Les and he had to have a discreet look. There was only one young cop in there with his head down and his window was shaded by a venetian blind, so his view was restricted. What fascinated Les was the other window. It was covered in posters for missing persons. MISSING. MISSING. CAN YOU UNRAVEL THE MYSTERY? DO YOU HAVE A CLUE IN MICHAEL'S MURDER. REWARD. DISAPPEARANCE. SUSPECTED MURDER. There were photos of at least forty missing people, most of them young girls. Not counting all the Murder–Reward posters. Christ, thought Les, that's a lot of missing people for a small city. Then he remembered he'd heard a few stories about South Australia. They had some good murders and things in Crow Eater Territory. It wasn't long ago they found eight bodies stuffed in barrels in an old bank vault. They still hadn't found out what happened to the three Beaumont children. I'll bet there's a few Jeffrey Dahmers and Charles Mansons running around out there, mused Les. What about all those Witchcraft shops? And those spooky looking Gothics?

There was one bright light in Hindley Street, a music shop called The Blue Note. It had the best selection of blues and rock 'n' roll music Les had ever seen, plus Latino and Cuban and all that. There were blues bands Les had never heard of. The proprietor was a friendly young bloke wearing a stars and stripes vest with his hair combed across his forehead in two thick bangs. He offered Les assistance. But how was Les going to tell him that if he wasn't going to gaol on Monday he'd have bought half his shop out? Les browsed round for a while, drooling over the CDs and told the bloke he'd be back.

Outside, Les noticed it was getting dark and took a glance at his watch. Across the road was a lane leading down to the Grande. There was a hotel on one corner with an enclosed verandah around the top and an unused picture theatre on the other. Les crossed Hindley Street and walked down, passing a dirty little alley on the left with a skip bin out the front. Further down on the right was the foyer of another glitzy hotel that ran down to a bar on the corner. Les had a quick peek in the window as he went past. It looked all right; black furnishings and shiny chrome fittings. But not many customers. Les waited for the traffic then jogged over to the Grande.

Back in his room Les sucked on another Heineken and stared out the window as the lights came on across the city. Now what will I do? he asked himself. I know, there's a heated pool downstairs and it doesn't close till nine. Why don't I have a mullet and bream. I tossed my Speedos in before I left. Les changed into his black swimmers and got a white bathrobe out of the wardrobe. He took a nice fluffy towel from the bathroom and barefooted it for the lift down to the pool.

The pool was on the third floor, down a corridor and in the open. When Les stepped outside, the wind felt like it was coming straight from Antarctica. Shit! I don't know if this is such a good idea, he shivered. No wonder I've got it to myself. When he dropped his robe the wind flayed him like an icy whip. Oh well, here goes nothing. Les bolted across the sundeck and plunged straight in. It might have been cold out, but the water was beautiful. At least ten degrees warmer. Even though the pool was only fifteen metres long, Les started doing laps like he was Ian Thorpe. Freestyle, breaststroke, backstroke any stroke or style you like. It was great and the water seemed to wash away his cares. It was almost like he was in Adelaide on holidays. Les flopped around, duck dived, lay on his back and spurted water in the air. Soon he noticed people looking down at him from the rooms above. Evening everybody, grinned Les, then pulled his Speedos off, rolled over and mooned the surrounding windows. Would you like another look? Sure you do. Les rolled over again and spread his freckly, white cheeks. There you go. What do you reckon that is? A cut or a burn? Les flopped around a while longer then got out and climbed back into his robe. He tossed his towel over his shoulders and dripped water in the lift all the way to the twenty-third floor.

Back in his room, Les showered and shaved and changed into his back-up tracksuit, a dark blue Brooks. He got a bottle of Hahn premium from the mini-bar and studied the room service menu. Les picked up the phone and ordered hoummos, taramasalata and toasted pita bread plus a Caesar salad with Cajun chicken for starters. Lamb rack with mashed potato and vegetables for mains. And coffee and bread rolls. The person at room service told Mr Ullrich it should be there in thirty minutes. Les flopped back on the bed, swivelled the TV round and watched *Seinfeld*. It wasn't a bad one: Kramer is a theatre guide, Elaine shows a bit of cleavage and George gets dressed up as Henry the Eighth. Les was still laughing over a bottle of Hahn when his meal arrived. He gave the waiter two bucks and got stuck into it over Adelaide's version of the *7.30 Report*.

Les couldn't knock the food. It was delicious. The vegetables were steamed to perfection and the lamb was tender. The Caesar salad was exceptional. Les bored in then put the trolley out on the landing, saving the hoummos for a late-night snack. He started flicking through the TV guide. There wasn't much on the commercial channels and SBS were having another racist witch hunt. A doco about the Vietnam War on the ABC looked interesting. Les got his map out and went over it again while he waited, when the phone rang. It was Gary Blair from Travelabout.

'Gary,' said Les. 'What's up?'

'Nothing,' replied Gary. 'I just thought I'd ring up and see if everything was okay. All part of our after-sales service.'

'Thanks, Gary. No, everything's as a bean, Gary. The driver picked me up okay. The hotel's the grouse. In fact I've just been for a swim in the pool.'

'You've been swimming? What's the weather like down there?'

'Cold and cloudy. But the pool was heated.'

'It's pouring bloody rain up here.'

'Fair dinkum?'

'Hey, I just thought I'd tell you, Les. The reason that bloke never picked up his ticket. The poor bastard got run over.'

'He what?'

'A motorbike collected him near Rose Bay golf links. He died on the way to hospital.'

'Shit!'

'So you won't have to worry about Mr Ullrich wanting his room back.'

'Jesus, Gary. I hope this isn't some kind of omen. Like the *Twilight Zone* and he turns up delivering my room service or something.'

'Hey, you never know, Les. Adelaide's a spooky place.'

'Thanks, Gary.'

'Anyway, I'm glad everything's all sweet. Anything goes wrong, give me a ring.'

'No worries. Thanks, Gary.'

Les hung up the phone. Bloody hell! One minute I'm going through a dead bloke's house. Now I'm staying in a dead bloke's room and using his name. Not a very nice coincidence. Les gazed absently out the window for a moment. Not much I can do about it though, I suppose. Les got the last Heineken from the mini-bar and settled back in front of the TV.

The doco wasn't bad and showed how easily the Vietnam War could have been avoided if the Yanks had used their heads. Instead they blew JFK's off then managed to kill three million Vietnamese along with fifty thousand Americans. After that there was nothing. Les switched off the TV and stared out the window at the city lights. It was too early to go to bed, and that cooped-up feeling started kicking in again. You know what I should do, he told himself, instead of flopping around after all that food. Go for a walk. Even if it's just up to that music shop and have another look through those CDs. Yeah. Why not. Les put his Nauticas on and walked out to the lift.

The bar on the corner had picked up and so had Hindley Street when Les got there. Les stopped outside the empty theatre at the end of the lane and had a look around. Gangs of youths were roaming around in baggy clothes and baseball caps on back the front, swearing and trying to act tough, while packs of hoons cruised up and down the street like sharks in old Kingswoods and Commodores, yelling out at any passing girls. Across the road in front of a Time Zone, gangs of black kids, aged from ten up, swarmed around the footpath managing to swear louder than anybody. Young girls hobbled past in long black boots with high heels, each one wearing a black mini, a black top and five layers of make-up. Mecca appeared to be the hotel and strip joint on the opposite corner. Several lumpy girls in minis and high-heeled boots were bumping and grinding out the front to a blaring disco version of Rod Stewart's 'Do Ya Think I'm Sexy', trying to entice any passing blokes to come in. Behind the enclosed verandah upstairs, you could be a star for the evening and dance on a little stage placed in full view of the street below. Rod Stewart finished and 'Bus Stop' started thumping out from the hotel at a thousand decibels plus. Les walked across to the music store.

Latino music was playing and the owner was busy behind the counter talking to a South American bloke when Les walked in. Although the shop was crowded, Les managed to earwig the conversation. The customer had just bought some tickets to an Afro-Latino Fiesta and he and the owner were discussing Latino bands. Les stepped over to the blues section and started flicking through the CDs. There were bands Les had never heard of. Sax Gordon, Red Rivers and the Rocketones, CJ's Blues Band. Eddie The Chief Clearwater. Blue Katz. It was torture. All that music to be bought and he was going in the nick. Les would have loved to have heard a few tracks. But all the headphones were being used and the owner was playing Latino for the benefit of the people buying tickets for the concert. Les could only take so much. He flicked through the CDs again and left.

There was a Lebanese takeaway two doors up from the music store with a few chairs and tables out the front. Les walked in and got a bottle of OJ from the fridge. As he paid for his drink, Les inadvertently flashed several one-hundred dollar bills. A young black homeboy standing out the front in a Sweat Hog jacket noticed and hurried back to the Time Zone to tell four of his mates. Les stopped next to one of the tables and downed his OJ, not noticing the severe eyeballing he was getting from five young hoods wearing baggies and floppy beanies. Three were blacks, another was white and the fifth could have been anything from a Yemeni to an Eskimo. The oldest was around fifteen. Les dumped his empty bottle in the nearest bin then sidestepped through the passing cars across Hindley Street and proceeded down the lane. He was level with the skip bin at the alley when he heard a young voice behind him.

'Hey mister. You got a cigarette?'

Les stopped and slowly turned around. The tallest of the gang, wearing a red beanie, was doing all the talking. The others were grouped behind him, rocking up and down on their toes.

Les didn't need a degree in atomic physics to know what their intentions were. 'Sorry,' he said slowly. 'But I don't smoke.'

'Then give us all your fuckin money. You cunt,' snarled Red Beanie.

Norton's face turned to stone. 'Get fucked. I'll give you nothing.'

'Yeah? Then I'll fuckin stick you.' Red Beanie pulled out a knife and waved it in front of Les, close enough to put a tiny nick in Norton's jacket. 'I'm tellin' you, I'll fuckin stick you, man. Give us your fuckin money.'

Les looked at his jacket. 'My fuckin good tracksuit,' he howled. 'You little cunt.'

Norton wasn't in the mood to play games. If the kids wanted to be men, then they'd better learn to take it like men. He pivoted slightly on his left foot and with his right instep kicked the knife straight out of Red Beanie's hand, breaking the kid's wrist. The young hood screamed with pain and grabbed his shattered wrist as the knife landed in the skip bin. Les followed up with a full-blooded right into the young hood's face, almost taking his skinny head off. Before the kid hit the ground, Les turned and left hooked his nearest mate, dumping him on his skinny backside with blood pouring down his chin and no front teeth. Realising things weren't quite going as they'd planned it, the other three turned and went for their lives. One wasn't quite quick enough and Les was able to kick him fair up the arse. He yelped with pain and lost his balance for a moment then tottered forward before catching up with his mates.

'We'll fuckin remember you, mate,' one called out.

'Good,' Les called back. 'Make sure you do.'

'Fuckin white cunt.'

'At least I know what I am,' said Les. 'Do you?'

Les looked at the two young hoods moaning on the ground and felt like doing a bit of Balmain folk dancing on their heads. Instead he gave them a kick in the thigh each and walked briskly to the end of the lane. He ignored the people in the bar on the corner, jogged straight across the road and up the driveway into the Grande.

Les stopped near a column in the lobby to gather his thoughts. Can you believe that? he asked himself. I go up to have a lousy look at some CDs and I nearly get rolled. Bloody hell! Does trouble follow me around or what? Shaking his head, Les felt like a drink. But not in his room. Why don't I have one in the Torrens Bar? he thought. Maybe with a bit of luck somebody'll pick a fight with me in there, too. Or pull a gun on me. Or a knife or something. They'd be mad not to. I mean, that's what I'm here for.

A bar built low to the floor with low seating ran around as you walked in on the left with a sunken lounge on the right and plenty of chairs and tables in between. A mirrored ceiling looked down on the punters and at the rear a three-piece jazz combo was backing a girl in a silver-blue lamé dress wailing 'My Baby Don't Care For Me'. The air was thick with smoke, most of it coming from a plentiful selection of cigars available in a cabinet near the entrance. Along with the cocktails and beers going down, every second man in the place was smoking a cigar and every woman was smoking a cigarette. Everyone was dressed up, mainly in black, and the average age was thirty plus. There was a casually dressed group of people at one end of the bar that looked like flight attendants on a stopover. Looking around, Les surmised the Torrens Bar was one of the places to be seen in Adelaide. He walked over to the bar, ordered a bottle of Hahn and a JD and ice and charged it to his room. Some bloke in a dark jacket got up from a table near the cigar cabinet leaving a butt smouldering in an ashtray. Les took the table, dumped the cigar butt into a pot plant and sat facing the bar. He took a belt of JD and washed it down with almost half the bottle of beer.

Well that's it, Les told himself. No more going out while I'm away. I'm a walking fuckin disaster area. Kids with knives, blokes with iron bars. Coppers. Stop the fight! He took another hit of JD with his beer chaser and looked at the nick in his tracksuit. No. Tomorrow night I'll be in my room watching TV or reading a book. In fact I shouldn't even be in this rotten bloody smoke box. Knowing my luck, the cops'll come in here looking for whoever belted those little pricks, and I'll get charged with assault. Along with every bloody thing else I've been charged with. Fuck it. I'm out of here. Les downed the rest of his drinks and caught a lift to his room.

The room temperature was perfect. Les took his tracksuit off, cleaned his teeth and turned the TV on. There was still nothing worth watching, but Les lay on the bed and watched it for a while anyway before turning everything off and getting under the doona. As he squashed his head into the pillows, Les couldn't help but think about Conrad Ullrich being dead. It *was* a little eerie. And Gary saying Adelaide was a spooky place. I wonder why he said that? Buggered if I know. Buggered if I know anything to be honest. Les yawned and stretched out a little more. This bloody bed's comfortable. I know that. Before long Norton was snoring peacefully.

Les was out of bed, cleaned up and staring out the window at eight o'clock the next morning, picking over the remains of last night's hoummos. Outside it was windy with patchy rain and it looked cold. So. What should I wear today in my search for the good ship Lollipop or whatever it is? thought Les. I'll probably be doing a fair bit of running around. I reckon my tracksuit and gym boots. And my Bugs Bunny cap. Les got changed, put what he thought he'd need in his backpack and left it on the bed then got the lift down to the Regency Club to sample the continental breakfast.

A smiling girl in a black uniform checked Norton's room charge card when he walked in. There were plenty of comfortable chairs and glass tables and about a dozen guests seated round the fountain. Les placed his room key on a table near the entrance and walked across to the servery. He didn't go far. Next to the fresh fruit and stewed peaches was a tub of fresh Bircher Muesli thick with blueberries. Les got the biggest bowl he could find and ate enough to fill a pothole in a road. He followed that with toast, smoked salmon and coffee and more toast, and finished with two sparkling glasses of fresh OJ. Nothing wrong with the continental breakfast, thought Les, rubbing his stomach as he took the lift back to his room. I can't wait for tomorrow. He checked his map again, made sure he had everything, and headed for Avis.

There were two girls in red uniforms looking after two customers at the far end of the office when Les walked in, and a man at this end using the phone. The man was wearing a button-down collar shirt with the collar buttons undone and a crumpled red tie. He put the phone down and moved his eyes wearily to Les, looking like he'd sell his soul if he could get out of having to work that morning.

'Yes, sir,' said the bloke, expressionlessly. 'How can I help you?'

'Have you got a car here for Ullrich?' said Les. 'Through Travelabout in Sydney?'

'Just one moment, sir.' The bloke punched the keys on a computer like he was shifting furniture. 'That's right, sir. A Hyundai Grandeur. For Mr C. Ullrich.'

Norton couldn't help himself. He had to try an impersonation of Jelly in *Analyze This*. 'Mr Ullrich's been detained,' said Les. 'Not only that. He ain't going to be here. So I'll be taking it instead. My name's Norton.'

The bloke looked at the computer screen again. 'No problem, Mr Norton. Do you have your driver's licence and credit card?'

'I sure do.'

Les soon filled out the forms and was handed a receipt, the keys, a small map of Adelaide, a pamphlet for the Avis Navigator and told where to collect the car.

'You know how to work the Avis Navigator, sir?' asked the bloke.

Les looked at the pamphlet like it was a Chinese newspaper. 'I wouldn't have a clue.'

'Just read the pamphlet, sir. It's quite simple.'

Les looked at the pamphlet again. 'Simple, eh?'

'Yes, sir. Just read the instructions, sir,' repeated the bloke, tireder than ever. 'It's quite simple.'

'Yeah righto,' replied Les, staring blankly at the pamphlet.

He walked out of the office into a small arcade with a few Saturday shoppers and through a doorway into the car park. The Hyundai was up on the next level in bay 37.

The car had a silver duco with a neat grille and looked a little like a small Mercedes. Les clicked the locks up with the remote, opened the door and got behind the wheel. Inside it was all soft leather seats that adjusted every which way and a wooden dash that looked like it belonged in a MiG 21. Les had a look around and tried to familiarise himself with everything. The handbrake was a footbrake with the release in the dash, you couldn't take the keys out of the ignition unless the gear shift was in park and the electric windows were especially designed so you'd push the wrong buttons all the time. There was a small screen below the dash and sitting near the gear shift was the control module, something like a TV remote. Les had another look at the pamphlet.

Avis Navigator is easy ... Control Module. Cursor direction control. Repeat direction. Confirmation key. Main menu. Plan an alternative route. Volume down. Volume up. 1. Turn on ignition. Les turned on the ignition and the screen lit up. Main Control. Destination input. Stand-by. Settings.

Les pressed a minus button, and a woman's voice said, 'Softer.'

Les pressed a plus button, and the voice said, 'Louder.'

Well, I'll be buggered, thought Les. How about that. Les pressed more buttons and the screen changed to: Destination input. Country. Junction. Guidance. Les pressed buttons and more buttons and got nothing except the woman's voice saying softer and louder. After a while he threw in the towel. Fuck this! You'd have to be Bill Gates to work one of these. Les locked the car, went back to the office and got the bloke to come and have a look at it. The bloke followed Les like he was being led to a firing squad.

'Fair dinkum, mate,' said Les, as they both got in the front seat, 'I can't work this thing out to save my life. It took me all my time to find the handbrake.'

The bloke looked at the pamphlet. 'They can be a little tricky,' he conceded.

'A little tricky?' echoed Les.

'Where are you going, sir?'

'Victor Harbor.'

Even the man from Avis had a little trouble. But eventually he pushed the right buttons and the screen lit up like the keys on a typewriter. He ran Les through it; Les nodded, understanding less than a third of what he was saying. Finally the bloke punched in Victor Harbor. And told Les how to punch in his way back to Adelaide.

'There you go, sir,' he said. 'You'll be all right now.'

Les had another look at the pamphlet. Approximately ten to twenty-five per cent of the traffic network is changing each year. Because of this one hundred per cent accuracy is not possible.

'Hey mate,' asked Les. 'Do these things play up much?'

'No more than anything else, sir,' replied the man.

'Yeah. But do they play up?'

A polite half-smile appeared on the man's face before vanishing. 'No more than anything else, sir,' he repeated.

'Thanks.'

Les watched as the man got out of the car and dragged himself back to the office.

Terrific, thought Les. That means they can play up. Knowing my luck, I'll probably finish up in Perth. Les got his backpack from the back seat and put it next to him with the map on top. Oh well, here goes nothing, he thought, and started the car. The engine was that quiet and smooth you hardly knew it was running, and after fiddling around with the seat, the car seemed to mould itself around you.

Les drove to the boom gate, gave the parking attendant his ticket, then turned right into a lane and came out facing the Grande. There was a break in the traffic and Les turned left looking for West Terrace then Anzac Highway and South Road. He took a quick glance at the map when an arrow and a number appeared on the radar screen and the woman's voice said, 'In two hundred and fifty metres, turn left.'

'Huh? Oh, thanks sweetheart.'

Sure enough, there was West Terrace. Les waited for the lights and took off. He was about to check the map again, when the voice said, 'In five hundred metres, turn right.'

'If you say so, sexy,' smiled Les.

A little further on a sign said Anzac Highway. And another, A.13 Noarlunga. Cape Jervis. Victor Harbor. Yes, smiled Norton. We're on our way.

The traffic was constant, but compared to Sydney it was a drive in the country.

There were plenty of parks and trees and the road was wide and flat like the old houses going by on either side. Les passed a hotel on the left called The Avoca and smiled as he briefly remembered walking along the beach with Jimmy Rosewater. The traffic thinned out a little and he came to a slight rise so Les put his foot down to see what the Hyundai could do. Instantly it kicked silently down into second and took off. Les found himself congratulating the late Conrad Ullrich on his choice of cars. The Grandeur was a real pocket rocket. Les zipped effortlessly past the other cars then eased up. The last thing he needed was to get pulled over and a check done on his licence.

'Right turn — ahead.'

'What?'

Les looked at the radar screen and an arrow saying 2700 metres. Minutes later, Les found himself cruising up a winding hill and noticed in the distance a low range of mountains that ringed Adelaide. He crossed the Onkaparinga River, and the voice said, 'Left turn ahead.'

After that it was plain sailing. A shower would fall now and again, but mostly it was light drizzle. The countryside was green rolling hills with patches of forest here and there, but it still looked a little barren; probably because it was such a miserable bleak day. Les didn't notice many birds. The only signs of life were cows standing around waterholes with ibises picking at the grass near their hooves. He went through Mount Compass. It was more a big hill than a mountain, with a set of lights, then a few shops and a hotel on the left. Les was tempted to put on a tape but he thought it might be best to concentrate on the road rather than start bopping. The road curved up and down. The weather had probably turned away the weekend drivers, so there wasn't a great deal of traffic. A sign on the right said MINIATURE VILLAGE. It's certainly bloody miniature, thought Les, cause I'm buggered if I can see anything. The farms thinned out and houses began to appear. Then a Lutheran church with a sign out the front. YOUR CHILD'S TOMORROW DEPENDS ON YOUR LOVE TODAY. I'll go along with that, thought Les. Unless it's got a skateboard that should be wrapped round its pointy little head. A garage loomed up on the left and Les got a glimpse of ocean. A sign on the left pointed to Goolwa and another on the right said VICTOR HARBOR.

'Right turn ahead.'

'Thanks, baby,' smiled Les. 'I couldn't have got here without you.'

The road curved down a hill with houses on either side, the ocean on the left, and surrounding hills off to the right. Ahead was just a huge bay edged by a strip of sand. There were a few rocky islands and waves breaking over reefs near the shore, a long row of pine trees faced the ocean and in the distance a long jetty ran out to another rocky island, and that was it. It looked nice enough. But Les was expecting wharves, jetties, piers, marinas, boats, fishing fleets. Not just a big, blue bay. The smile vanished from Norton's face. This is Victor *Harbor*, he asked himself? Railway lines appeared on the left, and coming up was the shopping centre. Suddenly a sign on a small blue wooden building on the right in front of a brown wooden fence caught Norton's eye and he pulled over. 1ST V.H. SEA SCOUTS. Hello, thought Les, I'll bet that's where Knox and his mates got their T-shirts. I'm definitely on the right track. The building was locked and the wind blew a sudden patch of rain against the car, so he didn't bother getting out. He doubted if he'd find what he was looking for in there anyway. But he'd keep it in mind. Heartened by what he'd found, Les drove on.

He bypassed the shopping centre and followed the road as close to the coastline as he could with no idea where it would lead. Around him were mostly houses or holiday lettings, a few small blocks of flats and the odd motel. Parks and reserves overlooked the bay and he crossed a couple of creeks. A smile flickered in Norton's eyes for a moment. Next door to a bowling club was The Ezy Rest Motel. The sealed road finished at a blue building called The Whalers Inn Resort and Conference Centre, then a narrow dirt road curved round the water's edge towards a low bluff. There were still no boats or jetties, not so much as a canoe or a paddle-pop stick floating in the water. Just a few clumps of granite rocks smeared with bird shit sticking up through the seaweed with the odd pelican sitting on top. Les followed the dirt road till it ended at a turning circle next to a small wharf and a low granite wall facing the ocean. Parked near a granite cliff was an old white station wagon and sitting on the wall were two surfboard riders. Les pulled up near the wharf, got out of the car and stretched his legs. The rain had eased, but a gusty offshore wind was blowing and it was quite cold. Les shoved his hands in his pockets and had a look around.

The wharf was a fish-measuring station, with a noticeboard at one end showing the different kinds of fish. Across the bay, houses built on the low hills overlooked the ocean and there was another island in the distance, but still not a boat in sight. Les was shaking his head, completely baffled, when he heard the two board riders clapping their hands and calling out to something in the water. He sauntered over for a look. Swimming next to the rocks were half a dozen seals. Les watched fascinated as the seals rolled on their sides, dived under the water then came up again, snorting and blowing as they floated on their backs, wiggling their flippers and looking up at you with big soft eyes. Les had never seen a seal before. He got his camera from his backpack and, despite his disappointment at not finding any boats, took a few photos. The two surfies gave him a smile, then got in their car and drove off. Les was about to take another photo of the seals when a movement on the right caught his eye.

A woman wearing just a pair of check shorts and a black T-shirt rattled up on a battered old push bike. A white helmet sat loosely on her head and a pair of well-worn thongs clung to her feet. She had black hair and a plain face and Les would have put her age at around forty. The cold didn't seem to worry her at all. Les caught her eye as she rested her bike against the granite wall and smiled. She smiled back, then turned to watch the seals. Les walked over to her.

'Excuse me,' he said. 'Would you mind doing me a favour?'

'Ohh yeah,' answered the woman. 'What is it?'

'Would you mind taking a photo of me standing next to the car?'

'Okay.' The woman looked at the camera as Les handed it to her. 'How do you work this?'

'It's easy.'

Les showed her how, then sat against the bonnet of the Hyundai with the ocean in the background. The woman clicked off a photo. Les got her to take another one of him standing on the wharf.

'Thanks very much,' he said, taking his camera back.

'That's okay.'

The woman seemed quite friendly, so Les thought he'd try a few questions. 'You from round here?' he asked.

The woman pointed to the houses facing the bay. 'Over there.'

'You lived here long?'

'All my life,' she replied, sounding rather proud of the fact.

'Hey, how come there's no boats around? It's supposed to be a harbour.'

'The marina's at Goolwa. They keep them there.'

'Oh? Where's that?' asked Les.

The woman pointed across the bay. 'About twenty kilometres that way. It's nicer than Victor Harbor, too. Not so touristy.'

'Right,' nodded Les. Yes, she's a local all right, he smiled to himself.

'There's another marina on Hindmarsh Island, too.'

'How do I get there?'

'You get the ferry at Goolwa.'

'Fair enough,' nodded Les. 'Hey, have you ever heard of a boat called the *Trough Queen*? I'm looking for the owner.'

The woman looked at Les and shook her head. 'No. Can't say I have.'

'Okay. I'll ask around Goolwa.'

'If you don't do any good there, ask the fishermen in the pub.'

'Fishermen?'

'Yeah. They'll all be in the pub Saturday night. They'd know.'

'Which pub?'

'The Harbor Hotel. There's two pubs near the jetty. The Harbor and the Royal. They'll be in the Harbor.'

'Thanks,' said Les. 'You've been a big help.'

'No worries.'

The woman went back to watching the seals and Les got in the car. Well, there you go, thought Norton as he drove back along the dirt road. All you have to do is ask the locals. I'll take a run over to Goolwa. If I don't do any good I'll come back and ask the fishermen in the local boozer. Be funny if I bumped those blokes in the photo. Les stopped at the end of the dirt road and had a quick look at his map. On the way to Goolwa was a place called Port Elliott. I suppose I'd better have a look in there while I'm at it, he thought. It says Port. Yeah. Like this place says Harbor. Les bypassed the shopping centre again, figuring he'd check it out later and get a coffee. Just past the sea scout building on the left, Les noticed a sign. VICTOR HARBOR, WHERE YOU'RE ALWAYS WELCOME. Yeah. That's me all right, Les smiled to himself. Everybody's mate.

The road to Goolwa was straight and flat through wide green fields and barren hills. Sitting amongst the farms and houses on the side of the road was an abandoned drive-in and an old sign, TEN DOLLARS A CAR LOAD. At a row of shops Les turned right into Port Elliott. The street leading to the ocean was narrow and flanked by old heritage buildings preserved in the original red-brick and sandstone. It was all very colonial and beautiful, but not what Les had come to see. He drove to the end and came out at a bluff overlooking a wide, deep bay with a rocky island in the middle. The wind had picked up, pushing a light drizzle before it and the ocean looked grey and uninviting. On a fine day it probably would have looked a picture. But not today. And again there was not a boat to be seen. Les turned around and got back on the main road.

Entering Goolwa, Les drove past more old red-brick and sandstone buildings with verandahs built out over the footpath, and a sign said WELCOME TO GOOLWA. SOUTH AUSTRALIA'S TIDIEST TOWN. At the start of the main street another sign near the local war memorial said HINDMARSH ISLAND FERRY. Les hung a right then followed the signs, almost going round in a circle, before coming out at a railway line opposite a row of pine trees in front of a floating motel. Towering over a strip of water was a bridge under construction and just past that two rows of cars were waiting for the ferry. One lane said PRIORITY. Les pulled into the other and turned off the motor There were other buildings back amongst the trees and a restaurant on the wharf. Norton's timing was good. Just as he pulled up the ferry pulled in. The cars in front started moving and a bloke in overalls guided them onto the ferry.

The ferry took about a dozen vehicles and two minutes to reach Hindmarsh Island. Les followed the other cars off the ferry and started looking for the marina. The road was sealed, but all Les could see was reclaimed swamp covered in flat tundra with patches of scrub and no trees. The only touch of colour was an Aboriginal flag painted on a sheet of corrugated iron at the end of a paddock. Secret women's business, thought Les. Christ! Why waste millions of dollars arguing over the joint? It's a swamp. The roads seemed to circle every which way till eventually Les came across some new homes, bulldozers clearing the swamp and a blue-grey tavern with an olive green roof. Near a ring of townhouses down from the tavern was the marina.

Les drove down to a parking area in front of a long, flat green building with a radio antenna on the roof that overlooked the marina. He parked the car and got out. Several grey wooden jetties pushed out from the grass in front of the parking area and along the jetties, rows of boats moved gently at their moorings. There was no one about; the only sound was the wind and a solitary crow squawking in the scrub. With a light drizzle softly swirling around him, Les pulled his collar up and started combing the jetties, looking for the *Trough Queen*.

The boats were all cruisers and yachts named *Wind Move*, *Lazy Life* or *Lady Celene* with numbers on the bow: MR 6034, IF 1731, TQ 555. Definitely no old wooden clinkers. Les went over the last jetty then got back in the car. Well, it's definitely not there. I'll try the one in Goolwa. He started the car and drove back to the ferry. This time there were more cars and he had to wait a little longer. While he was sitting in the car Les noticed the other marina off to the right on the mainland. After cooling his heels for fifteen minutes they were herded aboard for the two-minute journey then he bumped off the ferry behind a small white truck.

Les circled round once more then came down the main street of Goolwa. Like Port Elliott it was all old red-brick and sandstone buildings with galvanised-iron roofs and verandahs built out over the footpath. There was a hotel amongst a row of shops, a garage that looked like it had been shut since nineteen fifty, craft shops and cafes and a small horse-drawn tram displayed in a shelter. Very interesting, thought Les. He did a U-turn at a motel, stopping for a woman with a pram, then drove back and took a left at an op shop on a corner. There were more heritage buildings and houses, then Les bumped over a railway line and the marina was on the right, running alongside a park and a long patch of bullrushes. There was a small parking area in front of a brown building with BOAT SUPPLIES on the side. Les stopped the car and got out.

The Goolwa marina was much the same as the one on Hindmarsh Island only more spread out and the boats looked a little less expensive. They had names like *Big Bird*, *Onawa* and numbers on the bow. LP 2545, MJ 663. At the end of one pier Les thought for a moment he'd found the *Trough Queen*. But it was only an old grey wooden clinker called *White Coffee* TF 3192. Les went over it just to be sure it wasn't the *Trough Queen* renamed and done up. It wasn't. Feeling a little disgruntled, Les walked back to the car.

Well, that's that, thought Les. My only chance now is to ask those fishermen tonight. He looked at his watch. But I don't fancy hanging round till dark. I may as well drive back to Adelaide and come back tonight. This little car's fun to drive and I'm doing nothing else. I wouldn't mind a quick bite to eat right now, though. What about some fish and chips in Victor Harbor? I still haven't had a look at the place yet. Les started the car and headed for Victor's shopping centre.

When Les got there, he went past the main street and turned left further on, doubling back down a wide road running alongside the bay. He had a quick look around then parked near a row of pine trees next to the tourist centre, where you caught a horse-drawn tram across the jetty to Granite Island. Over the road were two hotels with a park and a fountain in between and a building to the right with ENCOUNTER COAST DISCOVERY CENTRE on the side. Behind the building was a much larger park where a longer row of pine trees faced the ocean. Two small streets and a number of shops ran up from the hotel on the left and the main street started behind the hotel on the right. There weren't many cars and people around. The main activity was a group of bike riders in coloured lycra and safety helmets. Les locked the car and crossed the road.

The hotel the woman had mentioned, the Harbor, was the one on the left and looked quite modern with long, wide windows facing the ocean. The other hotel on the right, the Royal, had a green verandah above the footpath with signs on it saying DANCE CLUB SATURDAY, BAND FRIDAY. Set in in pavers around both pubs were lovely old gaslights and small trees. Les walked past the Royal and up the main street.

There were the usual coffee shops, a newsagent, clothes and sporting stores, fish shops and banks. Les heard music playing — The Eagles, 'Hotel California'. A little further on was a radio station, 99.9 FM, Great Southern Radio, and a DJ in his forties sitting in a window facing the street. Les turned back and found a fish and chip shop opposite the bank with a wooden table and bench seat out the front. This'll do, he thought, and went inside to see what was on offer.

There was a dark-haired woman in a white tunic standing behind the counter and a blackboard menu on the wall. Les ordered three King George whiting fillets and chips and an OJ. This didn't take long to cook. Les paid the woman then went outside and sat down at the wooden table. He spread his fish and chips out to cool and started eating. The whiting fillets were delicious and the chips weren't bad either. A car parked in front of where Les was sitting pulled out, and seconds later a flock of seagulls arrived, squawking and arguing with each other around Norton's feet, waiting for a handout. Les threw them a few pieces of batter and some burnt chips to shut them up. But the more he gave them the more they wanted and the more they fought amongst each other. Les was tossing the seagulls another couple of chips when a bloke driving an old, white Jaguar with Victorian number plates pulled into the vacant parking spot, scattering the seagulls. The bloke got out of the car and locked the doors. He was wearing a blue-check shirt tucked into a pair of blue King Gee trousers and he was bigger than Les, with a beefy, florid face and long black sidelevers. For some reason he gave Les a dirty look before crossing over to use the ATM outside the bank. As soon as he left, the seagulls returned for another handout. A couple landed on top of the bloke's restored Jaguar and shat on it. Les tossed the seagulls some more chips as the bloke came back from the ATM. As soon as he saw the seagulls sitting on his car, his florid face turned purple.

'Ahh get off the car, you mongrels,' he cursed, scattering the two seagulls. 'I just washed the fuckin thing.' The bloke looked at Les finishing his fish and chips and muttered something under his breath.

Les smiled up at the bloke good naturedly. 'They reckon that's a sign of good luck,' said Les, nodding to the two piles of white shit on the roof of the car.

Sidelevers glared at Les. 'You're lucky I don't shove those fuckin fish 'n' chips down your throat, you prick,' he growled.

Norton's eyes narrowed. It hadn't been a good day, even without the weather.

'Yeah?' replied Les. 'Well how about you shove your old bomb Valiant up your fat arse instead, you big goose.'

'What did you fuckin say?' snarled Sidelevers.

'You heard,' said Les. 'What? Are you deaf as well as ugly?'

'Why you smartarse fuckin cunt.'

The big bloke came charging round on the left to grab Les by the front of his tracksuit and pull him out from behind the table. Les edged back a little, then quickly stood up and slammed the top of his head into Sidelever's nose, stopping him dead in his tracks. The big bloke howled with pain as blood started pouring out of his mangled nose, and down his chin. Les pushed Sidelevers back, then bent slightly at the knees and belted him under the ear with a short, devastating left hook. The big bloke's legs went from under him and he fell down in the gutter next to his car, out cold. Les looked at him for a moment, then picked up the wrapping paper from the table and scattered what was left of his fish and chips all over Sidelever's chest. In a squawking, screeching frenzy, the seagulls immediately swarmed onto the big bloke's check shirt and started gobbling up the scraps. One dropped a shit on his forehead. Les scrunched up the wrapping paper, tossed it in the nearest bin along with his empty OJ container and walked back to the car. On the way out of town he saw the sign again: Victor Harbor, where you're always welcome. Yeah. That's me, nodded Les. Making friends wherever I go.

Les stopped at the garage near the Goolwa turn-off and bought a packet of jaffas and some mineral water. He had a fiddle with the navigator while he was sitting there, getting Route Selection, Optimise Distance. And the woman's voice saying softer — louder. Les had a pretty good idea how to get back to Adelaide anyway, so he just left the navigator turned on and kept his map next to him. Well. So much for beautiful downtown Victor Harbor in the daytime, thought Les, popping a jaffa in his mouth. I wonder what it'll be like when I come back tonight? Cold, I'd reckon. He hit the blinker and headed for Adelaide.

The farms and turn-offs to local hamlets went by. Les wasn't thinking about much. There wasn't much to think about. Things hadn't quite turned out the way he expected. But it wasn't over yet. He still had one shot left. And trying not to be over optimistic, Les had a feeling something would turn up in the hotel when he met the local fishermen. He took a tape from his backpack and popped it in the stereo. Next thing Lee Kernaghan was twanging 'Aussie Dog House Blues'. Mount Compass went by and further on a turn-off to some place called Yundi. It didn't seem long and Professor Ratbaggy was singing 'Love Letter' and Les was in downtown Adelaide.

'Right turn. Five hundred metres.'

'Okay, baby,' said Les.

'In two hundred and fifty metres, take the next turn on your right.'

The navigator hadn't been saying all that much and whether it was working properly or Les had somehow fluked it, he didn't know. But the Bar Kings' 'Treat Me Right' faded out just as Les pulled safely into the driveway of the Adelaide Grande. He opened the door to get out and pushed the minus button on the navigator.

As the concierge approached, the voice said, 'Softer. Softer.'

Les gave him a smile. 'Be nice to my girlfriend, won't you.'

The concierge smiled back and gave Les his receipt. 'No problems, Mr Ullrich. We'll look after her.'

Les caught the lift to his room and got out of his damp tracksuit. After spending most of the day sitting in the car, he felt like another swim in the heated pool to stretch out a bit. He put his Speedos on, climbed into the bathrobe and with a towel over his shoulder, caught the lift down to the pool to give the guests another glimpse of his freckly backside. Except when he got there, two other guests were in the pool — a couple of young Japanese honeymooners who went awfully coy when Les dived in alongside them. Les gave them a smile then spent an enjoyable time flopping around and breaststroking up and down the pool. The only chilling thought, apart from the weather, was knowing it all had to end and he wouldn't be doing any swimming in the remand yard at Long Bay. Les finally got out and went back to his room. He rang room service and ordered another Caesar salad, plus a club sandwich and coffee. Then he got under the shower. His food arrived, Les switched on the TV and ate it watching a wildlife documentary. After putting the empty tray outside the door, he changed into a pair of jeans, a clean grey T-shirt and his leather jacket. He checked everything he needed was in his backpack, then went down and collected the Hyundai.

Minutes later Les was taking a night drive through the suburbs of Adelaide. Somewhere along the way the voice said, 'Right turn, five hundred metres.'

'Righto, sweetheart,' replied Les. 'You don't have to nag. I think I know where I'm going by now.'

A bit further on the voice said, 'In two hundred and fifty metres, take the next turn on your right.'

'Hey, I won't tell you again,' said Les. 'Knock up on the nagging. You don't know who you're dealing with, woman.'

Bloody sheilas, smiled Les. You can't tell them anything. He slipped on a tape and Steely Dan started bopping out 'Cousin Dupree'. The Hippos were 'Three Steps From The Blues' when Les drove into Victor Harbor.

Les pulled up facing the park opposite the Harbor Hotel and switched off the motor. He got out of the car and there was a bitter wind blowing straight in off the ocean; as he'd surmised earlier, it was cold all right. There weren't many cars around and the surrounding cafes were almost empty. From the hotel further down Les could hear music coming from upstairs and see the punters drinking in one of the bars below. Across the road at the Harbor Hotel two bars faced the street; a lounge on the left and a smaller one on the right. Oh well, here goes nothing, thought Les. He shouldered his backpack and walked over to check out the lounge first.

A long bar faced the door as you entered and inside it was split into two sections: a raised lounge on the left with a gaming room behind, and a betting room on the right. The barmaids wore white shirts and rugged-up in jackets and scarves was an average crowd of all ages and sexes, seated or standing around enjoying a drink and a smoke. The betting room was full of TV sets showing the prices and a TAB doing brisk business on the trots. Above the bar were photos and paintings of racehorses and a wooden cabinet full of cups and trophies. Set up in the lounge was a duo called Joe and Danny who were currently on a break. Les had a quick look around then walked into the lounge first. Nothing much was happening in there so he walked back to the betting room. After checking out the punters, Les got a feeling he was in the wrong part of the hotel. He stepped across to the bar and caught one of the barmaid's eye.

'Excuse me,' asked Les. 'Where do the fishermen drink?'

'Fishermen?' said the barmaid.

'Yeah.'

She pointed to the left. 'Try next door.'

'Thanks.' Les walked back out into the street and went into the other bar.

It was smaller, just a room with two pool tables, more betting facilities, a juke box against the far wall and blue-curtained windows looking out on the street. There was a solitary barman in a shirt and tie and behind the bar were sporting photos and one of two blokes standing next to a monster crocodile they'd just shot and hung from a rope. About a dozen men were standing or seated on stools round the bar, with one bloke in a floppy captain's hat sitting at a table pencilling a betting card. All Les knew about drinking in South Australia was, certain beers were pretty ordinary and instead of pots and middies, they drank butcher's. He walked over to the bar and ordered a butcher's out of a red tap, then stepped over to one of the windows and took a mouthful. It tasted like dog's piss. Bloody hell, thought Les. No wonder they call them butcher's. A couple of these and you'd be butcher's hook all right. You'd be dead. He took another sip to make sure he wasn't imagining things, shook his head and placed the beer on a small table beneath a glass noticeboard. Something inside the noticeboard caught Norton's eye. J.D. won Friday night's meat raffle. Under that another short notice said: *Victor Harbor Angling Club will close if we don't get members' support.* Les read it again then stared out the window. Angling club? Les was expecting professional fishermen. Not anglers. And the angling club was folding up. No wonder that woman on the bike didn't feel the cold. She wouldn't know what day it was. There wouldn't be two fishermen in the whole bloody joint. Les stared out the window and shook his head. I don't believe it. After a few moments, Les shifted his gaze from the window back to the bloke in the captain's cap. He had a trimmed beard and a weathered face. Fuck it, thought Les, I'm here now, I suppose. He took the photo from his backpack and approached the man in the captain's cap.

'Excuse me, mate,' said Les.

The bloke looked at Les indifferently. 'Yeah, what's up?'

'I'm looking for the crew of a boat. You wouldn't know these blokes, would you?' Les showed the man in the cap the photo.

The bloke looked at the photo for a second, laughed and called out to the bar. 'Hey Merv, Harry. Come over here.' Two rugged-looking men in their late twenties, wearing check shirts and beanies, left the bar and came over. One of them had a brown moustache, the other had two teardrops tattooed next to his left eye. 'Have a look at this. This bloke's looking for the crew of this boat. What do you reckon?'

The two men looked at the photo then all three of them started laughing amongst themselves. Les couldn't see what the big joke was. The bloke with the tattoos stopped laughing, took a drag on his cigarette and turned to Les.

'So you're looking for the crew of that boat, are you, mate?' he said, breathing smoke all over Les.

'That's right,' replied Les.

'You're not a poofter, are you?'

'What?' said Les.

'Are you a poofter, mate?' asked the bloke with the moustache.

'No. I'm not a bloody poofter,' said Les indignantly.

'You sure?' said the bloke in the captain's cap.

'Yeah — I'm sure,' said Les.

Tattoos shook his head. 'I reckon you're a poofter.'

'So do I, mate,' added Moustache.

The bloke in the captain's hat gave Les a very indifferent once up and down. 'I reckon you are, too.'

Les could feel his fuse starting to burn out rapidly. Another half a minute and they'd soon know whether he was a poofter or not. Les took a deep breath, slid the photo into his backpack and closed it.

'Sorry,' said Norton quietly. 'I was just trying to find those blokes in the photo. It appears I've made a mistake. Thank you for your trouble.'

'That's all right — sweetheart,' said Tattoos.

Moustache gave Les a wink. 'Are you sure you wouldn't like a pink lemonade before you go?'

'They got straws,' said the man in the captain's cap. 'And little umbrellas.'

Les smiled thinly. 'No thank you. I'm not thirsty. And I think it's best I leave.'

Les swallowed his anger and headed for the door. Fuckin wallys. I should have known better. He was just about to open the door when who should walk in but the big bloke with the sidelevers he'd flattened earlier. He was wearing a black leather jacket and white sticking plaster all over his nose. Two enormous black eyes blinked painfully from behind the plaster and his jaw was wired up. Close behind him were two blokes almost as big. One was wearing a grey gaberdine trenchcoat, the other had on a bulky white jumper. As soon as Sidelevers recognised who it was, his face darkened and he turned to his two mates.

'Grrhhnngggmmgh. Grmrngh brrghh,' he grunted, pointing angrily at Les.

'Ohh go fuck yourself,' replied Les, and stormed past them out the door. He was across the footpath, heading for his car when he heard a voice behind him.

'Hey. You with the fuckin backpack.'

Les stopped and turned around. It was the bloke in the woollen jumper. Sidelevers and his two mates had followed him straight out of the hotel with Sidelevers bringing up the rear.

'Yeah, fuckin what?' replied Les.

'We want to see you,' said the one wearing the trenchcoat.

Norton's fuse suddenly burnt out. 'You're going to wish you hadn't,' he hissed, and dropped his backpack on the footpath.

Les walked up to the bloke in the woollen jumper, feinted a left to his chin then belted a short right under his floating rib. The bloke's eyes bulged and his mouth gaped open as Les doubled up with another short right over the top. The bloke's legs wobbled as it slammed into his jaw and he fell down on his backside, eyes glazed, wondering what hit him. The bloke in the trenchcoat on Norton's right swung a left at Norton's head. Les stepped outside it and grabbed the bloke by the arm with his left hand then pulled him forward and back-fisted him in the mouth, ripping his lips open. Les gave him another one then straightened his right arm under the bloke's chin and thumped his right knee into the bloke's kidneys. The bloke fell back over Norton's leg and banged the back of his head on the footpath as he landed at Norton's feet. Les left him and walked across to Sidelevers who was looking for a hole he could crawl into and something he could drag over the top with him.

'You big weak prick,' said Les. 'Look what you've done.' Les jerked a thumb at Sidelevers' mates lying bleeding on the footpath. 'I hope you're happy.'

Sidelevers looked like he was ready to crap his pants. 'Nnghhh. Nghhh.'

'Shut up,' ordered Les. 'This is all your fault. And now you're going to have to pay the penalty.'

'Nnnnhh. Nnnhh. Gmmh nnh unh mghh.'

Les was going to belt Sidelèvers in the jaw again and smash it up some more. But he just couldn't be that cruel. Instead, he stepped back and kicked him hard in the balls. Sidelevers grunted with pain and sank to the ground clutching his groin. The worst part was he couldn't scream and everything bottled up inside him. Eventually the strain and the pressure were too much and the capillaries in his eyeballs burst, sending blood seeping onto the white sticking plaster across his nose. Les watched him for a moment then looked up. The three blokes he'd shown the photo to had come out to see what was going on.

Les smiled at them. 'Now. Which one of you hillbillies reckons I'm a poofter?'

The one with the tattoos shook his head vehemently. 'Not me, mate,' he said, and scurried back inside.

'Me either,' added Moustache, turning to join his mate. 'Never said a word.'

'What about you, Captain Ahab?' asked Les. 'What have you got to say?'

'I was just thinking,' said the bloke in the captain's cap, 'that was a really clear photo. What sort of camera did you use?'

Les picked up his backpack and got in the car. A few people had gathered in front of the hotel and he knew the best move now would be to put as much distance between himself and Victor Harbor as possible, before the wallopers arrived.

Rather than take the main street after reversing out, Les turned left, past a video arcade and a second-hand bookshop, and came round a back way near a garage. On the way out of town Les saw the sign again: VICTOR HARBOR, WHERE YOU'RE ALWAYS WELCOME. Yeah terrific. Unless you feed the seagulls or you're a poofter looking for a boat.

The turn-off to Goolwa went by, then the farms and countryside. Les stared into the twin beams of light splitting the darkness ahead of him and shook his head. The trip to Adelaide had turned out to be a complete waste of time and money. And deep inside Les had had a feeling it would. He just didn't think it would end in so much violence and people laughing at him and calling him a poof. On the other hand, it would have been no use staying in Sydney. He had to take a punt. Maybe if he hadn't breached his bail conditions it would have worked out differently. Who knows? Anyway, it was too late now and he was looking at a very dismal future when he got home. Very dismal indeed. He started thinking about some of the things that had happened on the trip and flashed on to the romp he had with Blythe at the Medlow. That was fun all right, mused Les. But you still can't beat a good root. Les laughed mirthlessly. That's something I can forget about, starting Monday. My sex life. Unless I want to chase drag queens around Long Bay. Yes, it had certainly turned out a bummer all right. Les blanked his mind and just stared through the windscreen, totally zoned out. He didn't bother listening to a tape; he didn't even notice any of the hamlets or turn-offs going past. Les just stared ahead, thinking about absolutely nothing.

'Right turn. Five hundred metres.'

Les slowed down and swung the Hyundai right. He didn't notice the name of the road, but glimpsed a sign saying WATCH OUT FOR LOW-LEVEL BRANCHES. Les drove on down a narrow sealed road covered with a thin layer of mist, the headlights picking up dense forest on the right side of the road and a plantation of tall pine trees on the other. Beyond that the car was enveloped in total darkness.

'In two hundred metres, take the next turn on your right.'

Les slowed down again and turned right into the forest. A narrow, dirt road full of potholes and gutters rose up through the trees. Next thing a bumping, banging sound came from under the car. The noise seemed to snap Les out of his trance.

'Hey! What the fuck am I doing?' he exclaimed. 'This isn't the way to Adelaide.'

Les stopped the car and looked around him. Christ. Am I a nice goose or what? I was bloody miles away. I deserve to have that navigator shoved up my arse. What was that noise though? Shit! Knowing my luck, something's probably gone through the fuckin petrol tank. Les quickly turned everything off, found the torch in his backpack, then got out and shone it beneath the car. A branch had jammed itself under a firewall. He wrenched it away, tossed it to one side of the road then switched the torch off and stood next to the car. It was quite eerie standing out in the middle of nowhere, surrounded by a black, leaden silence that seemed to close in on everything. It was also very exhilarating. Suddenly the sky lit up and great shafts of light beamed down through the trees. At first Les thought it was a UFO. It turned out to be the biggest, brightest full moon Les had ever seen, drifting momentarily between a bank of clouds like a huge ball of beautifully polished silver. Les stared at it in awe before it disappeared back behind the clouds again and darkness returned. Shit! What about that? thought Les. That was unreal. Les was about to get back in the car when somewhere in the distance he heard the most awful scream he'd ever heard in his life. It split the darkness like a bolt of imaginary lightning and clamped an icy hand around Norton's heart. It was a woman's scream. Not of pain. A scream of sheer, hysterical terror. There was another scream, followed by a horrific wail.

'No. No. Help me. Somebody. Please HELP me.'

It seemed to be coming from somewhere near the top of the hill. Another scream sent a chill up Norton's spine, then it abruptly stopped. Les found his heart starting to quicken. Shit! I don't like the sound of that. Some poor sheila's in bad trouble. Les stared into the darkness towards where the screams had come from. Fuckin hell! As if I can't get into enough trouble as it is, he cursed, without playing Dudley fuckin Do Right. Why me all the time? Shit! Leaving the car where it was, Les picked up the branch, broke off the skinny end to make a club, and followed the dirt road up the hill.

As he approached the top Les could hear people chanting, ringing bells and beating drums. When he got there, he could see a driveway leading back to an old abandoned farmhouse with cars parked around the front and lights glowing out the back. Les stopped near some trees for a closer look. The farmhouse was red-brick and sandstone, just like the old buildings in Goolwa, but not very big. The front door and windows were boarded up and two chimneys along the side squatted on a rusty galvanised-iron roof. A stone wall with several gaps in it formed a perimeter around the farmhouse and the remains of a high wooden gate stood out the front. At the end of the driveway, a man wearing a Driz-A-Bone and a woollen beanie was leaning against a tree with a gun over his shoulder. He had his back to the road and seemed more interested in what was going on at the back of the farmhouse than anything else. Quieter than a silkworm tiptoeing on a silk hanky, Les snuck up on the man and belted him across the side of his head with the branch, knocking him unconscious. As the man fell silently to the ground, Les grabbed the gun; it was a fully loaded pump-action shotgun. Les cradled it for a moment, then left it against the tree, knowing it was there if he needed it. There was a piece of cord hanging from the man's coat; Les ripped it off, tied the man's thumbs together then stuffed his beanie in his mouth. Gripping the piece of branch, Les kept low and snuck across to a gap in the stone wall to see what the man in the Driz-A-Bone had been looking at.

The stone wall formed a backyard at the rear of the farmhouse. Outdoor heaters were placed round the yard and candles and hurricane lamps flickered on the walls. A wooden table sat against one wall, draped with a sheet of black satin. Placed on the sheet was a solid bronze candelabra, a chalice, several animal figurines and black velvet cushions embroidered with gold stars and pentangles. Standing in the yard were about twenty naked old people in varying degrees of ugliness and obesity. The men wore chains and medallions round their necks and carried small drums. The women had weird masks made from bird feathers over their eyes and held tiny bells. One particularly grotesque old man was wearing a fur hat made from a ram's head complete with horns; in his hands was a long silver knife with a black handle. Next to him was another old man wearing a silver mask shaped like a hawk; he was carrying a ram's horn painted with gold to look like a penis. They were all grouped around a wooden altar covered with a sheet of white satin. Tied to the altar by her hands and feet with a gag over her mouth was a struggling, terrified young woman, her blonde hair tied at the back and adorned with flowers. She was dressed in a long white gown, cut low across her shoulders with wide billowing sleeves and laced round her waist was a maroon bodice. Standing behind her was an old woman holding a hypodermic syringe. She removed the gag from the young woman who immediately started screaming again. The man wearing the ram's head started waving the knife about, reciting some ritual, while the others beat their drums and tinkled their bells.

'Oh mighty Azalzak, lord of earth, water, wind and fire, wand and sword. Prince of Darkness, Ruler of Spirits, come ye unto life as the sacrifice is made.'

'Azalzak. Azalzak. Azalzak,' chorused the others.

'Hear the offering's screams, oh mighty Azalzak. As they waken ye from the night. And beckon ye unto our desire.'

'Azalzak. Azalzak. Azalzak.'

'Oh ye mighty Azalzak, hear her screams. Soon you shall taste her body. Then you will drink her blood from the witches' blade.'

At the word 'blood', the woman on the altar almost screamed her lungs out and started thrashing around that much it looked as if she'd break her bonds. The man wearing the silver bird's mask then lifted the young woman's dress up and began working the ram's horn towards her vagina. The man in the ram's head gave the woman with the syringe a nod and with the help of another woman she was able to prepare a vein in the young woman's arm and stick the syringe in. A steady push with her thumb and the woman went completely comatose.

Watching grimfaced through the gap in the stone wall, Les was almost sick as he realised what he had stumbled across out in the Adelaide Hills.

It was a coven of Devil worshippers, Satanists, AntiChrists, or whatever their ungodly trip was. Not a bunch of flower-smelling, spell-casting, flute-blowing Wiccas. These were full-on, black magic, murdering nutters, complete with a high priest ready to perform a human sacrifice. You could bet this was where half those people in the photos outside the police station had finished up — as offerings to Azalzak or whoever. The chanting, drum-banging and bell-ringing got louder. The man in the ram's head raised the knife above his head.

'Now mighty Azalzak. Now. Taste her blood.'

'Taste the blood. Taste the blood. Azalzak. Azalzak. Taste the blood.'

That was enough for Dudley Do Right. Les stood up and flung the branch at the high priest. It turned end over end and the thick part whacked the high priest in the mouth. He gave a surprised shout and fell back, dropping the knife over the altar. A hush went through the coven and they all stopped chanting and banging their drums and ringing their bells. The man with the bird mask turned to see what had happened to the high priest as Les leapt through the gap in the wall, shouting and yelling at the top of his voice to get the coven off guard.

'Go on. Get back. Get back,' Les clamoured. 'Keep away from her. Leave her alone. Piss off, the fuckin lot of you. You horrible-looking bags of shit.'

Les ran across to the altar and picked up the knife from where the high priest had dropped it. He brandished it at the coven and kept yelling at them.

'Go on. Get back you rotten, evil fuckin things,' he shouted. 'Get back. Or I'll cut your fuckin heads off. I'll kill the lot of you. I'll rip your guts out.'

The coven drew back with shock as Les slashed the cords tying the woman's arms and legs, and took her round the waist. She was a completely dead weight and it was like trying to pick up a wobbling sack of jelly. Still shouting his head off, Les managed to get the girl over his shoulder in a fireman's carry while he waved the knife at the coven.

'Go on. Keep away, you motherless bastards,' he howled. 'Fuck off.'

The coven withdrew from Les. A couple started to taunt him and hiss obscenities. Les didn't see one old woman sneak up behind him with the heavy brass candelabra. She raised it and swung it at his head just as Les bent a little to shrug the girl from round his neck. The candelabra missed his head but thumped down hard on Norton's shoulder, making him drop the knife.

'Ow shit,' yelped Les, the pain almost paralysing his arm.

He spun around just as the old woman brought the candelabra up to hit him again. She was fat and ugly with grey hair and great, droopy breasts and looked eighty-five if she was a day, and was probably somebody's dear old grandmother. Les smashed her with a straight left that split the old woman's mouth open, cracked her top plate and dumped her on her flabby, wrinkled backside. Les reshuffled the young woman on his shoulder as the man in the bird mask picked up the knife.

'Come on. Get the unbeliever,' he called to the others.

The coven advanced on Les. Some started picking up rocks, another had hold of the brass candelabra as they grouped behind the one holding the knife. On his own Les would have left them for dead, but juggling a dead weight on his shoulders slowed him almost to a walk. Under a hail of rocks, Les got through the gap in the wall and made it to the tree where he'd left the shotgun. He dropped the woman on the ground, took the shotgun and aimed it at the parked cars.

'Blam! Blam! Blam!'

Les shot out the three nearest windscreens, sending wiper blades and pieces of glass flying everywhere.

'Look out,' shouted the old man with the knife. 'He's got Martin's gun.'

Blam! Les sent another blast into one of the outdoor heaters, spewing gas and sparks across the backyard.

'My bloody oath I have', shouted Les. 'Now piss off, before I blow the lot of you to hell. Where you fuckin well all belong.'

The coven stopped in their tracks. Les fired another shot into the galvanised-iron roof, then picked up the girl and jogged back to the car. He opened the door and dumped the girl in the front seat, quickly doing up her seat belt. Before he got in alongside her, Les emptied the shotgun into the trees near the farmhouse, then threw the gun into the scrub. As soon as he was behind the wheel, Les shoved the Hyundai into drive and spun it around in a tight circle, sending rocks and clods of mud everywhere. He straightened up, belted back down the dirt road, did a screeching left turn at the end, then further on fishtailed a smoking right onto the main road back to Adelaide. A few kilometres along the road Les slowed down a little, took a deep breath and tried to stop his heart from pounding its way out of his chest and through the seat belt.

Bloody hell! What about that. Those ratbags were just about to cut that poor girl's throat. Thank Christ I came along. Or thank Christ that navigator's on the blink, or whatever. I don't know about those other directions it was giving me. Half the time I was looking at the map. But that was just sheer coincidence. Les looked at the night sky and shook his head. Or an act of God. The girl had slid around inside the seat belt. Les adjusted it and straightened her up so she didn't bang her head on the door. I don't know who you are, sweetheart, but you've got a guardian angel, that's for bloody sure. Les started checking her out.

She looked to be in her early twenties with a pretty face, nice lips and corn-blonde hair, which looked quite beautiful with the flowers in it. She had big breasts and could have been a little overweight, but a bit of exercise and she'd be a stunner. I wonder who she is? thought Les. And I wonder where she comes from? Then another thought struck Les. What am I going to do with her? Shit! I can't take her to the police, or I'll go with her. And I can't just dump her somewhere. She's out like a light and anything could happen to her the way she is. Les caught his reflection in the rear-view mirror. Good old Dudley Do Right. I'm going to have to take her back to the hotel. Let her sleep there and if she doesn't wake up by the morning, call a doctor before I split for Sydney. I wonder what they hit her with? That old tart looked like she might have been a nurse at one time, the way she prepared her arm before she shoved the pick in. Probably valium or something like that. Christ! I wonder what she'll think when she wakes up? I hope she doesn't start screaming blue murder. Les looked at the girl, her head down, moving with the motion of the car behind the seat belt. Poor bastard. After what she's just been through, you wouldn't blame her if she did.

Les cruised on into the night and started to relax. Even though his trip to Adelaide had turned out a complete disaster, it did have one redeeming feature: he'd saved some poor girl from a terrible fate. Les laughed mirthlessly. I wonder if the beak'll take that into account when he throws me in the slammer? Whether or not, Norton's good deed did make him feel better. A bit further along he switched on the radio and got some FM station playing mouldy oldies. Sam the Sham and the Pharaohs were singing 'Little Red Riding Hood'. Les looked at the unconscious girl and started singing a bodgie version of the lyrics.

'*Hey there little Miss May Queen baby, watcha doin' out in that South Australian bush alone.*'

He topped a hill and suddenly beneath the night sky the lights of Adelaide burst across the horizon like a ribbon of beautiful flowers. Les turned to his unknown passenger again and smiled at the uncanny resemblance in her hair. How about I nickname you the May Queen, sweetheart. It suits you in that outfit. The next song on the radio was 'Lucy in the Sky With Diamonds'. Les was singing away as he swung onto the Southern Expressway. He'd reached the traffic lights at the end when he heard a familiar voice.

'Right turn, five hundred metres.'

'Yeah, that'd be right, you dope,' said Les, turning left to follow the traffic into Adelaide. 'I'll finish up in Port Lincoln.'

'In two hundred metres, take the next turn on your right.'

'Sure. Straight into the oncoming traffic you moron. Right. That's it for you, you low-life slut,' said Les. 'You're sacked. You'd think Muhammad Ali was a street in Cairo.' Les jabbed at whatever buttons on the navigator he could find. 'Piss off. I never want to see you again.'

'Softer. Softer.'

'Ohh shut up. You're nothing but a slaggy moll.'

Some more old pop songs played, Les saw a familiar street sign, then another and another. He hung a right and finally pulled up in front of the Adelaide Grande. The concierge came over and opened the passenger door first. He gave a double blink when he saw the girl lolling behind the seat belt wearing a long puffy gown, a maroon bodice, flowers in her hair, no shoes and no knickers. Les picked up his backpack, came round and got the girl out of the car and put her left arm around his neck.

'Can you manage all right, Mr Ullrich?' asked the concierge.

'Yes. My fiancée's just had a few too many magic mushrooms, that's all,' replied Les, and dragged the girl into the foyer.

As luck would have it, there was a ball downstairs in the hotel, so plenty of half-plastered girls wearing long gowns were getting shouldered all round the foyer by plenty of half-plastered men in tuxedos. None, however, were completely out on their feet with their boobs flopping everywhere like the girl with Les, and they were wearing a lot more under their evening gowns as well. The more sober patrons gave Les a double blink as he dragged the May Queen over to the lifts, as did the three young Japanese tourists waiting for a lift and two young girls with their shoes off behind them. A lift pinged and Les bundled the May Queen inside. From there it was an embarrassing silence all the way to the twenty-third floor.

Les dragged the May Queen back to his room, pulled the sheets back and lowered her onto the right side of the bed, lying her on her left side. He got a towel from the bathroom and placed it under her head, then put a small rubbish bin by the side of the bed in case she woke up sick. He checked the girl's pulse again then watched her for a moment and wondered what else he could do. Nothing. But at least she was safe. What Les felt like now was a drink and a debriefing. He splashed some water over his face, then got a lift down to the foyer.

The Torrens Bar was packed with revellers from the ball along with the normal Saturday night punters. A duo in black, comprising a skinny brunette and a skinny dark-haired bloke, were warbling 'My Guy' in front of a half-full dancefloor. Like the night before, the place was full of cigarette smoke and the cigar cabinet was doing a roaring trade. Les blinked at the smoke and had half a mind to give it a miss. He got a JD and ice with a bottle of VB and fluked a stool next to a pillar facing the dancefloor. The duo cut into 'Blame It On The Boogie' and the dancefloor filled up with shuffling couples. Les took a belt of JD and washed it down with beer. Yeah, he thought grimly, don't blame it on the sunshine, don't blame it on the moonlight, don't blame it on the good times, blame it on the devil. Bloody hell! What a fuckin freak-out. Imagine if that old sheila had clobbered me with the candelabra. I'd have finished tied up on the altar with the May Queen as an offering to Zamzak or whoever it was those lunatics were praying to. He swallowed some more booze. Gary sure was right. This is a spooky fuckin joint. I haven't got much to look forward to when I get home, but I'll be glad when I'm back in Sydney. Les sipped his drinks and let his eyes drift around the bar at the punters in basic black with sequined bolero jackets, silver belt buckles or whatever as the duo struck up 'Celebration Time'. Les finished his drinks. Celebrate without me, folks. It's all yours. He left the revellers to it and got the lift back to his room.

The beer settled Les down and on the way back to his room he began to feel weary. Plus he was aching where the old woman had hit him with the candelabra. When he opened the door, the May Queen still hadn't moved. Les checked to see if she was all right, then stripped off and got under the shower.

He had a nice bruise coming up on his left shoulder and another near his kidneys where someone had got him with a rock. Les stayed under the shower for a while letting the hot water soothe his aches and pains, then dried off and got into a clean white T-shirt and jox. He took a bottle of mineral water from the mini-bar, stared out the window while he drank it, yawned a couple of times, then switched off the lights and got into bed with his back to the girl.

It was odd being in bed with someone after sleeping on his own, and Norton's share of the pillows weren't comfortable the way he was. He was forced to roll over. He tried to close his eyes, but he kept staring at the May Queen. The rise and fall of her shapely body looked truly delicious bathed in the soft light coming through the hotel window. Christ, this is going to be nice, thought Les. Trying to sleep with that lying in front of me. The girl still hadn't moved and it didn't even look like she was breathing. Les thought he'd better check her pulse again to make sure she hadn't expired. No. Her skin was warm and there was a steady pulse in her neck. Les slipped his hand under the May Queen's arm. She also had a good heartbeat. She also had a great pair of tits. Les knew he shouldn't do it and there was guilt written all over his face, but he started giving them a little squeeze. They felt sensational. Mr Wobbly started to thinking the same thing too. As Les squeezed the May Queen's boobs, Mr Wobbly forced Les to rub his evil little head against her shapely backside. Within minutes Les had a horn that hard you could have shattered roof tiles on it, and he was in a pitched battle between himself, his conscience and Mr Wobbly.

By rights the girl shouldn't even be there. She should be dead. Another half a minute and she would have been. Les had risked his neck to save her from the devil. So, literally, she owed him her life. Okay, it was wrong. Very wrong. It was statutory rape. But on Monday he was going to gaol anyway. What did he have to lose? And what could they do if they found out? Give him another ten years on the life sentence he was already going to get? Besides, the May Queen was that out of it she wouldn't know anyway. Les squeezed her lovely big boobs. Christ! I'd kill for a root right now. And she definitely owes me one. What the fuck, I'm going to give her one. Better the devil you don't know, my child, thought Les, slipping off his jox, than the devil you almost did. Mr Wobbly wholeheartedly agreed. Les lifted up the May Queen's gown, placed his hands on her hips and slipped Mr Wobbly in from behind.

Right wrong or indifferent, the May Queen's ted felt fabulous; warm and tight and juicy. Plus it was the taste of forbidden fruit. Les also didn't have to worry whether he was going too hard, too fast or too slow. Just do your own thing in your own time. It still wasn't as good as going off with someone. But hey, it was on the house. And who's complaining? The May Queen certainly wasn't. She didn't bat an eyelid. Didn't say a word. Les felt the vinegar strokes coming on so he started going for it. A minute or two later he squeezed his eyes shut, groaned with ecstasy and emptied out.

'Whoah ho! Shit! Bloody hell! Oh yeah, ohhhhh yeah.'

Les finally shuddered to a halt and pulled out a very happy Mr Wobbly. After he got his breath back, Les smiled to himself, put his jox back on and got a towel from the bathroom. He gave the May Queen a wipe, wiped around the bed then dropped the towel on the floor and rolled over. That, Les chuckled to himself, I say that, should solve any problems I've got about sleeping. Les reached behind him and gave the

May Queen a pat on the behind. Goodnight, sweetie, he smiled in the darkness. Les closed his eyes and crashed out.

Les was in a field somewhere. He was naked. Covered in flowers. He started running. All these strange people in weird masks were chasing him. They had shotguns. A flock of seagulls flew over his head. They started shooting the seagulls. Dead seagulls started to fall around him. The field turned into a tunnel. At the end of the tunnel was a pack of snarling dogs. Rottweilers. Albert Knox had them on a lead. He dropped the lead. Les woke up and blinked at the clock radio. It was four in the morning. The girl was still lying just as he'd left her. Les checked to see if she was all right. She was. Next thing, Mr Wobbly wanted to know if the girl was all right too. Still half asleep, Les started giving the May Queen another one. It felt just as good as the first. Maybe better and it took a little longer. Les emptied out and wiped up again. Well, he thought as he closed his eyes, that should keep me going for the next thirty years or so. Les crashed out. He didn't have any more bad dreams.

Les woke up about nine. The girl had rolled over onto her back during the night and now she was gently snoring. Although the flowers in her hair had wilted, she still looked beautiful in the morning light. Les got out of bed and had a shower. He dried off, got back into his tracksuit and a clean T-shirt and stared out the window. There were patches of blue in the sky, but the trees below were moving steadily with the wind and it still looked cold. Les was starving hungry and would have loved to have gone down and eaten another bucket of Bircher Muesli. Only he didn't fancy leaving the May Queen on her own in case she woke up totally freaked out and started running round the hotel screaming her head off. He made a cup of tea and chewed a hotel biscuit. Les was staring out the window and thinking of ringing room service for some food when he heard movement behind him. He turned around and saw the girl was starting to sit up. Les put his tea down, got a bottle of soda water from the mini-bar, opened it and sat on the end of the bed like a family doctor on a house call. The girl rolled her head around as if it weighed a tonne, then blinked her eyes open. They were a soft hazel. She looked up and saw Les at the end of the bed and a puzzled look came over her face. Then she noticed what she was wearing and saw the flower petals on the bed and her face went white. She shrank back, wide-eyed with terror and looked as if she was going to scream. Les placed his hand gently over her mouth.

'It's all right. It's all right,' he said softly. 'You're okay. You're safe. No one's going to hurt you. Don't scream. Don't scream.' He took his hand away and offered the girl the bottle of soda water. 'Here. Drink this. It's only soda water and it'll make you feel better. Come on. Take a sip. It'll do you good,' Les assured her.

The girl's hands were shaking as she took the bottle. She had a few mouthfuls but never took her eyes off Les. Les eased back to the end of the bed as the girl drank some more soda water, then belched lightly into her hand. She took a quick, nervous look around the room and stared at Les again.

'Where am I? Please tell me where I am,' she pleaded. 'I'm all confused. Who are you? What's … ?'

'Take it easy. Everything's all right,' said Les. 'You're in a hotel in Adelaide.' Les opened his wallet and showed the girl his driver's licence. 'That's me. My name's Les Norton.'

The girl looked at the driver's licence. 'You're from Sydney?'

'That's right,' nodded Les. 'This is my hotel room.'

'How … ? How did I get here?'

'I'm going to tell you. But would you like a cup of tea first? Or a coffee?' The girl shook her head. 'All right. Well, I'd better warn you, it's not a very pretty story. What's your name, anyway?'

'Roxy. Roxy Boswell.'

'Okay Roxy. This is what happened.'

Les picked up on driving back from Victor Harbor and taking the wrong turn because of his Avis Navigator. How he heard her screams. Knocking out the guard. What he saw. Everything. Roxy stared at Les wide-eyed as she gulped down the rest of the soda water. Les told her how he got her in the car then wasn't sure what to do. He was a bit shook up himself. So he brought her back to the hotel and put her to bed. If she hadn't woken up before long, he added, he was going to call the hotel doctor.

'And that's about it, Roxy,' said Les. 'Like I told you. It wasn't pretty.'

'Oh my God,' she gasped. 'It's all coming back to me now. Those horrible old men and women. And that man with the … Oh God!' Roxy started to hyperventilate.

Les read her mind, took her by the arm and steered her towards the bathroom. 'Why don't you have a shower and that while you're in there,' he said. 'There's plenty of towels. And there's a hair dryer next to the mirror.'

'Thanks,' mumbled Roxy.

Les closed the door behind her and settled back on the bed. Everything had turned out fine. Apart from being very shaken up, Roxy wasn't too bad. She didn't start screaming and she didn't faint. Considering what she'd been through, she showed a lot of heart. Les switched on the TV and got *Sunday* with Jim Waley. He watched it till Roxy eventually came out of the shower. She'd taken off the bodice and let her hair down and the colour had returned to her face.

'How do you feel now?' asked Les, switching off the TV.

'A lot better thanks,' answered Roxy. She gave Les a coy smile. 'I hope you don't mind, but I borrowed your swimmers.'

'That's okay,' said Les. 'Would you like a coffee or something?'

'I wouldn't mind another bottle of soda water, if that's all right. I'm so dry.'

'Sure,' said Les. He got a bottle of mineral water from the mini-bar and handed it to her. 'Are you hungry?'

Roxy took a healthy swig on the bottle of mineral water and belched quietly into her hand. 'I'm absolutely starving.'

'Good. So am I. And they do a continental breakfast here, make you jump fences.'

'All right.' Roxy finished the bottle of mineral water, closed her eyes for a moment and shook her head. 'God, I'm still ...'

'Don't worry about it,' said Les easily. 'Come on. Let's go and eat, and we'll have a talk over breakfast.'

They caught the lift and Les escorted Roxy into the Regency Club. The May Queen got a few second looks from the other guests before Les settled her down at a nice table by the fountain. He told her to stay there and be his guest then got a tray and loaded it up with Bircher Muesli, fruit, coffee, toast and OJ and they both ripped in. They followed up with smoked salmon on toast and ham and finished nibbling croissants and sipping more coffee.

'Well, how was that?' asked Les.

'It was delicious,' replied Roxy, patting her stomach. 'Thank you very much, Les.'

'I'm glad you enjoyed it.' Les sipped his coffee and smiled at the May Queen. She definitely looked more relaxed after a good meal, but Les sensed she was still nervous. He decided to try a little light conversation. 'So tell us a bit about yourself, Roxy. Are you from round here? Or ... ?'

Roxy flicked some long blonde hair across one eye. 'Tell you a bit about myself. There's not really that much to tell, Les.'

Roxy was twenty-nine. She grew up in Adelaide but she'd lived in Victor Harbor with her mother for the last ten years since her parents were divorced. She had an older brother in Adelaide who owned a computer shop. He was married with two children. She worked in an office in Victor Harbor for her uncle who had a car dealership there. Roxy wasn't seeing anyone in particular at the moment. She had a boyfriend, a musician. But he moved to Melbourne and he was too into drugs for her liking anyway. She liked Victor Harbor. It was quiet and it suited her because she was trying to write a book. She'd done a writing course and had a couple of short stories published in women's magazines. She didn't go out that much. If she did, she'd go to Adelaide and stay at her brother's house in West Beach.

'And that's about it, Les,' said Roxy. 'I'm just a battling little Crow Eater doing her best.'

'You're writing a book,' said Les. 'Unreal. What's it about?'

Roxy shrugged a little self consciously. 'It's about a girl who joins a rock band and gets involved in murder and drugs and ... has to sort it out.'

'Yeah? What are you going to call it?'

'I was thinking, *While My Guitar Gently Screams*.'

'Hey. I like it,' smiled Les. 'I reckon you could be on a winner.'

'I hope so. I'd love to be a writer.'

'Well, I hope you get there, Roxy.'

'Thanks, Les.'

Les got two fresh coffees and another croissant between them. Roxy had opened up, but Les sensed she still had something bottled up inside her. He decided it was time to uncork the bottle.

'So how come you finished up with those ratbags in the old farmhouse?' he asked.

'How come?' Roxy took a deep breath and stared into her coffee for a moment. 'I was out having a walk. I walk for an hour nearly every day. I was near some bush not far from home when this old couple in a campervan pulled up and asked me how to get to Hindmarsh Island. When I told them, they asked me to come closer to the car because they were a bit deaf. I went over and the next thing I knew, someone had come from behind and put a cloth over my mouth with something on it. I went all giddy and they bundled me into the back of the campervan. I didn't have time to yell out or anything.'

'What time was this?' asked Les.

'About six. It had just turned dark and I was on my way home.' Roxy sipped some more coffee. 'They tied me up. Gagged me and blindfolded me. I came to a couple of times, but they put that cloth back over my nose. I remember coming to and I was in these clothes. Then I woke up in that farmhouse tied to an altar or whatever it was out in the open. There was a huge full moon for a few moments. Then I saw all those horrible old people standing around me beating drums. And that man with the knife and that other man with the ... ram's horn. Then they took the gag out and I started screaming.'

'That's about when I arrived,' said Les. 'I heard you half a kilometre away.'

'Thank God you did.'

'Yeah,' conceded Les.

'After that it was a nightmare. That man waving the knife around. The other man with that ... that thing. Then I heard one say something about drink my blood. And the other said ... something else. And I just flipped out. I went crazy. Then that woman stuck a needle in my arm and that was it. Next thing I remember waking up in bed and you offering me soda water. I didn't know where I was.'

'I'm sorry I had to put my hand over your mouth. But I thought you were going to start screaming again,' said Les. 'You've sure got a good set of lungs on you, Roxy. I mean ... noisewise,' added Les. 'But you didn't, you were cool. You're a brave girl.'

Roxy shook her head. 'I don't know about that. I was absolutely terrified.'

'Who wouldn't be?'

Roxy gave Les the same coy look she gave him when she borrowed his Speedos. 'Les,' she said, a touch of colour in her cheeks, 'there's something I have to ask you.'

'Sure,' replied Les. 'What is it?'

'That man in the bird mask holding the ram's horn. Did he ... ?'

Les nodded slowly. 'Yes, I'm afraid he did, Roxy. I just didn't quite get there in time to stop that. I'm sorry.'

'That's okay,' said Roxy quietly.

'But it was only for a few seconds or so. It wasn't long. What makes you ask, anyway?'

'Oh. It's just that I'm a little sore down there. That's all.'

Les sipped some coffee. 'Yeah, well. At least I got there before that other nutter got in the act with the knife. Or ... well, we won't go into that.'

Roxy reached over the table and took Norton's hand and squeezed it. 'You're very reassuring, Les. You know that. And you're very understanding too.'

'Whatever,' shrugged Les. 'But I know how you feel, Roxy. You've been through hell. And now you've got to try and put it behind you.'

Roxy let go of Norton's hand sat back against her chair, taking him in. She seemed a lot brighter now that she'd faced up to what happened and got certain things off her chest.

'Anyway, what about you? Mr Les Norton from Sydney,' she smiled. 'What brings you to Adelaide? I suppose you're on some sort of business trip?'

Les threw back his head and laughed. 'A business trip? Yeah. That'd be right.' He smiled at Roxy for a second or two. 'All right, Roxy. I'll give you the whole deal. Shit! I got nothing to lose.' Les took another sip of coffee. 'Was there anything on the news down here about a film set getting blown up in Bondi?'

'Yes,' answered Roxy. 'I saw something on TV. And there was a photo in the paper.' She gave Les a double blink. 'Wait a minute. Norton. That wasn't you, was it?'

Les nodded. 'It sure was.'

Les gave her pretty much the whole story. Where he lived. Where he worked and what he did. What happened on Tuesday. How he was trying to clear his name. And how he finished up in Victor Harbor looking for a boat called the *Trough Queen* and the crew. He didn't say he killed the bloke's dog. But he did tell her how he broke into the house at Medlow Bath.

'So that's it, Roxy,' shrugged Les. 'It was a waste of time coming down here. But I was desperate. Now I'll get bundled off to the nick on Monday. Probably when I get home tonight. It's not much to look forward to.'

Roxy was both surprised and sympathetic. 'Golly. That's tough,' she said. 'And it wasn't even your fault. That's awful.'

'Try telling that to the two cops who nicked me,' said Les.

Roxy shook her head. 'So what do you intend to do now?'

'What do I intend to do now?' Les looked at his watch. 'Well, I intend driving you back to Victor Harbor, for starters.'

'Oh. Thanks very much.'

'Then you're going to have to go to the police. You've got to report those nutters before they do the same thing to somebody else. And you can bet you're not the only one they've abducted.'

'Yes. They've probably been watching me walking for a while,' agreed Roxy.

'But we'll discuss that on the way to Victor Harbor. Anyway, I have to go back to my room and get a couple of things. We've got plenty of time. But I have to fill the tank and all that.'

'Okay,' said Roxy. 'Let's go. And thanks again for the lovely breakfast.'

'My pleasure, Roxy,' replied Les. 'And I'd like to rephrase something too.'

'Oh? What's that?'

'Well, when I said it was a waste of time me coming down here, it wasn't. It was one of the best things I ever did.'

'Thank you, Les,' replied Roxy. 'In fact I don't even know how to thank you.'

They walked round and caught the lift. On the way up Roxy started giving Les some odd looks. Les couldn't quite pick up on the vibe. But he had a feeling Roxy suspected he'd been doing a bit of heavy tampering through the night. Les smiled at her and said nothing. Back in his room, Les started sorting a few things out. Roxy had to use the bathroom and Les offered her a T-shirt to put on under her dress if she wanted it. Les was staring out the window when he felt Roxy come up behind him and slip her arms around his waist.

'You know what, Les,' she said.

Les turned around. 'No, Roxy. What?'

'How did you sleep with me last night without ... you know?'

Les looked at Roxy as if he had no idea what she was talking about. 'I was tired. I crashed out. Besides, what sort of a cad do you take me for, Roxy?'

'You're a decent sort of man, aren't you, Les,' said Roxy.

'Ohh, I don't know,' said Les. 'Maybe if I'd taken my Viagra things might have been different.'

'Are you tired now?'

'No. I had a terrific night's sleep,' replied Les. 'Why?'

Roxy went a little coy again. 'Well, I was thinking. You going to gaol. And me living down here and all that. We might not get the chance to see each other again.'

'Yeah,' agreed Les. 'It's a bit of a bummer.'

'Well. And don't get me wrong about this, Les, because I don't do it very often. But seeing as I owe you my life, why don't we make love before you drive me home? I owe you one.'

'You don't owe me anything, Roxy,' smiled Les. 'I just did what any half decent, red-blooded Australian man would have done. That's all.'

'All right,' conceded Roxy. 'I don't owe you anything. But shit! I don't know. For some reason I'm as horny as buggery this morning.'

'You sure it wasn't the Bircher Muesli, Roxy? It's full of vitamins, you know.'

Roxy shook her head. 'No, Les. It wasn't the Bircher Muesli.'

'Well, in that case.'

Les put his arms around Roxy's waist, bent his head a little and kissed her. That's what was missing last night. The kissing. And Roxy's lips were soft, warm and horribly inviting. And when she slipped her delicate little tongue in, Les felt like putting his foot straight through the hotel window. He ran his hands up Roxy's ribs and lifted her dress up over her head. Roxy stood at the end of the bed with Norton's Speedos tied round her waist and her huge boobs sticking out.

'Jesus Christ, Roxy,' said Les. 'You've sure got one hell of a good body.'

'Don't say things like that, Mr Norton,' replied Roxy. 'You'll only make me hold it against you.'

Les got out of his tracksuit, slid the Speedos off Roxy and eased her back onto the bed. He spread her legs then pushed his face in and gave Roxy's blonde ted a monster eat. Roxy oohed and ahhed and wriggled on the bed while she jammed Norton's head into her. Les came up for air and Roxy reached under and gave his knob a polish that sent Norton somewhere into the fifth dimension. Just when Les thought he was going to stay permanently cross-eyed she stopped and he got between her legs. Roxy gave a howl of joy as Les slipped Mr Wobbly in and started going for his life. They made love on the bed from all angles. Les got Roxy's ankles behind her head, sat a pillow under her behind. She got on top. They had a doggy. A sixty-niner. It seemed to last forever till Les finally pulled the plug and emptied out, with much moaning and groaning from him, and plenty of wailing and flailing from Roxy. On a scale of one to ten, Les gave it a nine point nine. He reluctantly deducted a percentage of a point because she had been wearing his old Speedos. In a pair of knickers, Roxy would have romped in a ten.

They got cleaned up a little, pulled the sheets back over them and lay on the bed getting their breath back. Les had one arm around Roxy. Roxy had her head on Norton's chest.

'Well, I have to say one thing Mr Norton,' said Roxy, running a finger around Norton's chest.

'Yes. What's that, Ms Boswell,' answered Les.

'You certainly don't need Viagra.'

'Oh? What makes you say that?'

'You're there for the long haul, aren't you? You don't just squeeze the trigger and empty the magazine in one burst.'

'Yes, Roxy,' admitted Les modestly. 'I am a bad mamma jamma, a couple of metres out from the fence and the track's good.'

'Between that and the Bircher Muesli,' replied Roxy.

Yeah. And having a couple earlier in the piece slows things down a bit. 'Bad luck I've got to get you home, Roxy,' kidded Les. 'Or I'd be very tempted to pounce on you again.'

'Sounds good to me,' smiled Roxy. 'But how about when we get back to my place?'

'Whatever you say.' Les gave Roxy a cuddle and a big sloppy kiss on the forehead and they got dressed.

Les gave Roxy his address and phone number. He probably wouldn't be there, but she'd get his friend Warren and he'd tell her what was going on. Roxy gave Les her home details and said she'd be in touch and for Les to at least write to her. Les promised he would. They finished dressing. Roxy put Norton's Lee Kernaghan T-shirt on. Bad luck his shoes didn't fit. But it would be warm once they got in the car. He tossed a couple of bottles of mineral water in his backpack and they caught the lift downstairs. It was a different concierge from the night before, but he knew who Les was.

'Good morning, Mr Ullrich,' he said brightly.

'G'day mate. How's things,' replied Les.

'Good morning, ma'am.'

The concierge opened the car door for Roxy, getting a good look through the gown at her boobs and black Speedos, as he closed the door.

'I got to get some petrol,' said Les, as they turned right at the front of the hotel. 'Do you want anything while I'm there?'

'No. I'm all right thanks, Mr Ullrich,' replied Roxy.

'Roxy. Please,' said Les. 'After what went on upstairs. Call me Conrad.'

Roxy gave Les a clip under the ear. 'Keep that sort of talk up and they'll be calling you an ambulance.'

'Hey Roxy. What do you call a woman with no clitoris?'

'I don't know. What?'

'Call her what you like. But she won't come.'

'Right. That's it.'

Les stopped at the first garage he came to, filled up and they proceeded on their way to Victor Harbor. He didn't put the Avis Navigator on. But he pointed it out to Roxy and told her again that was what saved her life. Roxy went a little quiet so Les thought this was the time to get serious.

'Okay Roxy,' he said. 'I've told you all about me. And this is what I'd like you to do.'

'Sure Les. What?' answered Roxy.

Les suggested she didn't go to the police till around six. Say she was still in shock. This would give him time to be on the plane back to Sydney. But tell the police the truth and give them all his details, then they'd extradite him back to Adelaide to give evidence. In the meantime, tell the cops to check round the local panel beaters and find out who was getting new windscreens put in their cars and if there were any signs of shotgun pellets. Also check the hospitals for an old lady with a busted mouth, an old man with a lacerated face and some tall bloke with dark hair who could have a broken jaw. Les wasn't sure where the farm was. It was pitch black. But it was a turn-off to the right coming back from Victor Harbor. There wouldn't be too many abandoned farmhouses out there. A helicopter would find it in five minutes. And tell the cops to make copies of any tyre prints in the mud and match them up with the cars getting new windscreens. The coven had to be stopped before they killed someone else. They might even come back looking for her. This sent a chill up Roxy's spine. But on the plus side, if they got rounded up and the police found out who they'd murdered in the past, there would probably be a reward. Which she could claim. Roxy agreed this all made sense and she'd do what Les asked.

The trip back to Victor Harbor seemed to take no time at all with Roxy in the car and Les found himself getting quite attached to the May Queen. He was going to be very sorry when it was time to say goodbye. He sensed Roxy was feeling much the same way, too. She started to go quiet just before they reached the turn-off to Goolwa.

'You okay, Roxy?' asked Les. 'You're very quiet there.'

'Yes. I was just thinking of something,' deliberated Roxy. She turned to Les. 'You know how you were saying you came to Victor Harbor looking for a boat, but it turned out there was no Harbor?'

'Do I what,' replied Les.

'Well there used to be a boat in Victor Harbor. But it wasn't in the water.'

'Wasn't in the water?' Les stared at Roxy. 'What do you mean?'

'It used to be in a park. I'll show you.'

Wondering what Roxy was on about, Les followed the road into Victor Harbor. The long wide bay curved round in front of the car and in the distance Les could see the island with the jetty running out to it. They went past the houses and shops then, before they reached the shopping centre, Roxy told Les to turn left. They crossed a railway line and she told him to pull up next to a big green park with a long row of tall pine trees alongside the footpath. Les turned off the engine and had a quick look around. A row of two-storey holiday homes stood across from the park and on the corner was a red-brick and sandstone restaurant with a lattice-work balcony around the top floor. An old cannon sat in the park, facing out to sea, and near where the park met the ocean was a row of young pine trees protected with hessian.

'It used to be over there,' said Roxy, pointing out her window. 'Come on. I'll show you what I mean.'

Les got out of the car and followed Roxy across the park to the rocks at the water's edge. The wind had eased and the sea was calm and grey under a leaden sky. The thin strip of beach was covered with seaweed up to the rocks. Roxy looked at the rocks for a moment then walked back into the park a little and turned to Les.

'It used to be here,' she said, pointing to her feet.

'What used to be here?' said Les. 'I'm not sure I follow you.'

'An old wooden boat,' said Roxy. 'It had something to do with the bad old days of whaling. People were always getting their photos taken next to it.'

'Photos,' said Les.

'Yes. The tourists. And there used to be a wooden sign saying Victor Harbor.'

'A sign?'

'Yes. Next to the old boat. But some vandals set fire to the boat one night. They burnt the sign too. The council never replaced it.'

Les stared at Roxy for a moment. 'Roxy. Just wait here for a second, will you?'

Les jogged back to the car and got his backpack with everything still in it from the night before. He jogged back, pulled out the photo he stole in Medlow Bath and showed it to Roxy.

'Is this the boat?' Les asked her.

'Yes. That's it,' replied Roxy. 'It wasn't called the *Trough Queen*, though. It never had a name.' She looked up at Les. 'Are the men in the photo friends of yours?'

Les shook his head dumbly. 'No, Roxy. They're not friends of mine. The one on the left is the bloke that got blown up on the movie set. Albert Knox.'

'Oh.'

Les stared at the photo then lined it up with the ocean. From the way it was taken and if you didn't know better, you'd think the old boat was sitting in the water. The name *Trough Queen* on the bow also started to take on a different perspective, and you could bet if you examined the photo under a magnifying glass or a loupe, you'd see it was held on with tacks or something.

'How long ago did they set the boat on fire?' he asked.

Roxy shrugged. 'About five years. Something like that.'

'Five years. Thanks, Roxy.' Les stared at the photo, had a look round the park and felt like his arse had just caved in.

'Are you all right, Les?' asked Roxy.

Les looked at her for a moment and an ironic half smile crept over his face. 'Am I all right? Yeah, Roxy, I'm all right. For a complete Dubbo I'm real good.' He put the photo back in his bag and took out his camera. 'Anyway, let me get a photo of you with the ocean in the background.'

'Okay,' smiled Roxy. 'And I'll take one of you.'

They clicked off the photos then Les placed the camera back in his bag. 'Come on, Roxy,' he said, putting his arm around her. 'I'll get you home. It's too cold to be standing round here in your bare feet.'

Roxy lived back towards where they drove in. She told Les to take a left next to a park and a garage, then he followed a hill up past a wedding reception building that looked like an old medieval castle. Roxy's street was on the right a bit further along. The house was a single-storey brick house with a garage underneath and a verandah with a skinny iron railing round the front. There were trees on either side and a well-kept garden out the front. Parked in the driveway were two Ford Lasers, a blue one and a white one. Les surmised these would both be from her uncle's dealership. Les pulled up in the driveway behind the white one.

'So this is your place, Roxy,' he said, switching off the engine.

'Yes. It looks like Mum's home,' she replied. 'Would you like to come inside and meet her? I don't like your chances of getting my Speedos off again, though.'

'No. I think I'd better make a move,' replied Les. 'By the time I get back and all that.'

'Okay,' replied Roxy softly.

There was a silence between them for a few moments as they looked at each other. Les tried to smile, but all it did was make Roxy's eyes well up and a tear rolled down her cheek.

'Hey, Roxy,' soothed Les. 'What's all this, mate?'

'I don't know,' answered Roxy.

'Well, don't start. Because I feel pretty ordinary as it is.'

'Oh Les.' Roxy buried her head in Norton's chest and put her arms around his neck. 'It's not fair.'

Les held Roxy and stroked her hair. 'What's not fair?'

'Everything. You going to gaol. Me down here. And I'll never see you again.'

'Hey. You'll see me again. Even if I have to tunnel my way out. I'll smuggle a spoon in with me. Or a hacksaw blade.' Les was putting on a brave face, but inside he felt as empty as an old mailbag. In a very short space of time the May Queen had managed to bore her way right into the big Queenslander's heart.

'Yeah. You'll see me,' said Roxy. 'How?'

Les got his hanky out and wiped away her tears. 'You never know what might happen, Roxy. Your guardian angel could fly up to Sydney and keep an eye on me for a while.'

'Les, promise me you'll keep in touch,' said Roxy. 'You saved my life. Besides, I like you. A lot.'

'I know. And I like you too, Roxy. A lot. And I will keep in touch.'

'You promise?'

'I give you my word. Hey, I got to come down and give evidence when the police round up those ratbags. I'll probably see you then.'

'Yeah. From across a courtroom.'

Les put a finger under Roxy's chin, lifted her face up and kissed her. The kiss was long and hard and he could taste the salty warmth of Roxy's tears as they trickled down her face onto his lips. After a while Les had to finish.

'Roxy, I have to go,' he told her.

'All right,' sniffed Roxy. She placed her hand softly on Norton's cheek. 'I'll never forget you, Les.'

'And I won't forget you either, Roxy.' Les kissed her again. 'Goodbye, Roxy.'

'Goodbye, Les.' Roxy got out of the car and looked at Les for the last time. 'It's still not fair.' She closed the door and ran up the driveway. Les watched her disappear into the house, then started the car and drove off.

Norton's jaw ached and his mind was full of sadness as he went past the Goolwa turn-off. He got a bottle of mineral water from his backpack and swallowed almost half of it. Yeah, you're not wrong, Roxy, mused Les. It's more than not fair. It's completely fuckin shithouse, if you ask me. Les swallowed some more mineral water and stared at the road ahead. Just when I meet a girl I truly like and I might be able to share some good times with, I get the rug pulled straight out from under me. She wasn't only a good sort, she had something going for her. She's trying to be a writer. Well, I hope she cracks it and makes a bundle. She deserves it, after what she's just been through. Les swallowed some more mineral water. Christ! I'd have loved to have shouted her a trip to Sydney. Then taken her away somewhere, like a top resort and just given us both a spoil. But, I guess it just ain't to be. The only holiday I'll be getting is a long one care of the government. Les drained the bottle and dropped it on the floor of the car. Still, I've had a bloody good run. I guess my karma had to catch up with me sooner or later.

Les put his foot down, put Roxy out of his mind and brooded on something else. Shit! All that fuckin trouble for nothing. There was no dope smuggling. The boat was just an old relic sitting in a park for people to take photos of. And that's all the photo was. Knox and his three mates having some sort of a joke when he lived in Adelaide. And me and my Sherlock Holmes, super-deduction brain went spare. I need rooting. The witchcraft thing in the house? That'd be just part of Knox's weird and wonderful lifestyle. Like putting dog shit in lamingtons. Me stumbling across those other ratbags down here was just a coincidence.

Then despite himself, Les started to laugh. No wonder those three blokes in the pub called me a poof and started poking shit at me. Why wouldn't they? Some big goose comes in with a photo of a boat that used to be in the park down the road. There's four grown men standing in front of it wearing sea scout uniforms or whatever. And the big goose says, I'm looking for the crew of this boat, have you seen them? And I got the shits because they took the piss out of me. They were entitled to boot me fair up the arse. But I'll learn not to make an idiot of myself one of these days. I don't know which day it'll be. But I will learn. Even if it takes Tjalkalieri and the boys to come down from Binjiwunywunya with the first lesson written on a message stick and jam it fair up my silly big arse.

Still, if I hadn't come down here, Roxy would be lying in a shallow grave somewhere with her throat cut. Yeah. Bottom line, I saved a lovely girl's life. My oath I did. And they can never take it away from me. Feeling a little better, Les switched the radio on and listened to some pop music till he pulled up in the driveway of the Adelaide Grande.

'Will you be needing the car again today, Mr Ullrich?' asked the concierge.

'No. I'm finished with it,' replied Les. 'In fact you can tell Avis to come and pick it up if you like.'

'No problem, Mr Ullrich.'

Les picked up his backpack and got the lift to his room. He didn't have much to pack and there was plenty of time, so he ordered a club sandwich and coffee. When it arrived, he ate it watching TV while he waited for the driver. It was strange. Instead of waiting for a driver, Les felt like he was waiting for the hangman. It had that feel about it. Somehow the afternoon seemed to fly and soon it was time to check out.

Les caught the lift down to the lobby, handed in his key and signed for the extras on the bill. He paid cash, put his wallet away and turned around to find Vincent walking towards him carrying a small attaché case in one hand and a manila envelope in the other.

'Good afternoon, Mr Ullrich,' said Vincent. 'Ready to leave, sir?'

'Yes, thank you, Vincent. I am.'

Vincent handed Les the attaché case and the envelope and picked up Norton's overnight bag. 'There's the briefcase you've been expecting, Mr Ullrich. The key is in the envelope.'

'Thank you, Vincent,' replied Les.

They walked out to the LTD. Vincent opened the back door, Les got inside and they proceeded to the airport.

Vincent caught Norton's eye in the rear-vision mirror. 'Did you enjoy your stay in Adelaide, Mr Ullrich?' he asked politely.

'Yes thank you, Vincent,' replied Les. 'It was good.'

'Everything went smoothly?'

'Absolutely. Couldn't have been better.'

'Excellent, Mr Ullrich.'

'The Hyundai Grandeur went well too.'

'They're a very nice car, sir.'

They drove to the airport in silence. Les played it cool and aloof. Softly, he drummed his fingers on the attaché case. I wonder what the fuck this is all about? Probably Ullrich's strategy for a corporate takeover. Some insider trading? I'll make sure Gerry gets it. Could be something to her advantage. Maybe mine too. Yeah. Fat lot of good it'll do me. The houses and shops went by, and in what seemed like no time, Vincent pulled up outside the Ansett terminal. He opened Norton's door then carried his bag into the terminal.

'Goodbye, Mr Ullrich,' said Vincent. 'Have a pleasant trip back to Sydney.'

'Yes. Thank you, Vincent,' replied Les. 'I'm sure I will.'

Vincent drove off. Les walked over to a row of seats across from the check-in counter and sat down. He placed his overnight bag and backpack at his feet and rested the shiny black leather attaché case on his knee. It had gold-plated locks and looked expensive. Stamped in gold near the handle it said CONDOTTI. Les slit the envelope with his finger, took the key out then opened the letter.

Well there you go, thought Les. J's cool. N's a dropkick. Now let's see what we've got here. Les clicked the key in the two locks and opened the attaché case. On top was a layer of white paper. Les peeled it back and underneath were rows and rows of hundred-dollar bills, all tied with rubber bands in neat stacks of ten. Les counted one hundred and fifty. He took out one bundle of notes and tucked it in his jacket pocket, then put the letter in the case, locked it and packed the case in the bottom of his overnight bag. There were a number of people waiting to check in. Mr Ullrich went through as smooth as butter and was told he was leaving from gate ten. Les thanked the girl, skirted round the other punters and took the escalator to Golden Wing. He flashed his card, got a smile and joined the other people inside. Five minutes later Les had a nice table facing the tarmac and was sitting down sipping tea and munching cheese and crackers while he waited for the fruit bats flapping around in his stomach to settle down before they kicked his ribs out.

Holy mother of God, whooped Les. A hundred and fifty fuckin grand. And it's all bloody mine. Ullrich's dead. And the other bloke — K — has hit the toe somewhere. Don't contact him for a couple of years. I'm bloody sure I won't. I haven't got a clue what it's all about. But thank you very much K and C and the Sunshine fuckin Band. Or whoever. Les stared out at the darkened tarmac in amazement. I can't believe my luck. Then a thought hit him and he silently laughed that ironic laugh again. Yeah. Luck. What am I going to do with it? Les turned his eyes to the night sky. You sure giveth, but you sure taketh away, don't you, boss. But thanks anyway. One thing it will get me is a truckload of good lawyers and barristers. I might even be able to get to the judge. Les tapped the thousand in his pocket. So I've got back the fifty I lost on the movie. Plus another hundred for good luck. Not bad for a quick trip to South Aussie. Christ! If only I didn't have that other shit hanging over my head, life'd be gravy. Les was sipping his tea when he felt some one sit down on the lounge next to him.

'Hello Les me old. What's happening?'

Les turned slowly to his left. It was a dark-haired man with a trimmed beard and a dark complexion, losing his hair. He was wearing jeans, a denim shirt, a black leather jacket and black Wallabees. 'Pieman,' said Les. 'What are you doing in Adelaide? Or need I ask?'

'I suppose I could ask you the same thing, Les,' replied Pieman.

'Yes, I suppose you could, Pie.'

Pieman, or Pie, was Spiro Pythagoras. A Bondi boy from a Greek family. Pie rode a surfboard and lived up the north coast with his wife and kids where he had a fishing boat and used to supplement his fishing income with a little bit of pot dealing here and there. He was a good mate of the Gull's and all the team that hung out the front of the Toriyoshi, and despite his occasional dabbling in prohibited substances, Pie was a good bloke with a good sense of humour. However, he was also keen on a dollar, and all you had to remember when dealing with the Pieman was *caveat emptor.*

'That wasn't a bad photo of you in the paper the other day, Les,' said Pie.

'Thanks. I hope you cut it out and hung it up in your boat,' replied Les.

'I did, to tell you the truth.'

'Good. Anyway,' gestured Les, 'feel free to join me, Pie. I'm on the run from the law. All I need is to be seen hanging around with a notorious drug dealer.'

'Fair enough,' chuckled Pie. 'So what are you doing in Adelaide? You're a long way from Bondi.'

'To be honest, Pie, I came down here looking for some blokes I thought might be able to help me with all that Elliott I'm in back home. But I fell on my arse. Now I'm on my way back to stick my head in the noose.'

'Bad luck, mate.'

'Yeah,' Les sipped the last of his tea. 'So what about you, Pie? What's your John Dory? Surely you're not moving dacca down here. It's semi legal. They give the stuff away with green stamps.'

'I know. The bastards,' answered Pie. 'No. I need some cash in a hurry. So I came down to do a little business. Now I'm on my way back to a Sleaze Ball in Zetland with a thousand caps of Ebeneezer.'

'A Sleaze Ball and a head full of eccy,' said Les. 'You'll excuse me if I don't come along and join in the festivities.'

'Oh, I don't know, Les,' said Pie. 'Someone told me you were very partial to a Sleaze Ball. I even heard you were the Trough Queen.'

Les turned slowly to the Pieman. 'You heard I was the — what?'

'The Trough Queen. The Trough Monster. The word's out it's you, Les.'

Les stared at the Pieman. 'Tell me more about this — Trough Queen, Pie. Who is he?'

'No one knows, Les. It could be a she. I reckon it's you. But whoever it is, it's been a legend in the urinals at Sleaze Balls the last few years.'

'Why? What's this Trough Queen do?'

'The only way to find out, Les,' smiled Pie, 'is to go to a Sleaze Ball and hang out in the brasco. And take a torch with you.'

Norton's demeanour was calm, but his mind had kicked into overdrive. 'Say I wished to purchase a ticket to this Sleaze Ball in Zetland, Pieman. How would I obtain one?'

'You wouldn't,' replied Pie. 'It's a Sunday night special, it's been sold out for months. I happen to have one because of my ... business activities.'

'You want to sell it to me?' asked Les. 'You won't need it if you're just dropping off a bundle of disco biscuits.'

'True,' answered Pie. 'But tickets are as rare as rocking-horse shit. Any donut puncher worth his sequins would kill to get one. If I was to sell you mine,' Pieman patted the inside pocket of his leather jacket, 'I'd have to charge you the full black-market price.'

'How much is that?'

'Five hundred dollars.'

'You got me.' Les pulled out the thousand, whipped off five hundred dollars and handed it to the Pieman. 'Come on. Give me the ticket.'

'Jesus! You are keen, Les.'

Pie pocketed the money and handed Les his ticket. It was black in a black envelope. Embossed in silver on the front was a likeness of Oscar Wilde and the words *Take A Walk On The Wilde Side.*

Les turned it over in his hand. 'How do I know this isn't a forgery, Pieman?'

Pieman pointed to the likeness of Oscar Wilde. 'There's a magnetic strip at one end. They'll run it through a scanner to make sure. Believe me, Les, that's one hundred per cent kosher.'

'For five hundred fuckin bucks it'd want to come straight from Tel Aviv.'

Pie rested his hand on Norton's knee. 'And don't worry, Les. Your secret is safe with me.'

'Thanks, Pie,' said Les. 'Now fuck off while you're still in front.'

Pie gave Norton a wink. 'It's been a business doing pleasure with you, Les.' The Pieman got up and vanished amongst the other passengers as quietly as he arrived.

Les put the ticket in his backpack, took out the photo he stole from Knox's house at Medlow Bath and started thinking. He put the photo away, got another cup of tea and was still thinking when it was time to board the aircraft.

Mr Ullrich got another nice smile as he was shown to his seat. Les buckled in and stared straight ahead. He was still staring straight ahead when the plane took off. A few minutes into the flight Les ordered a can of VB. Another two cans of VB later and Les was still staring straight ahead and thinking. He was thinking that much he even knocked back the evening meal. By the end of VB number three, Les was starting to think maybe he hadn't been barking up the wrong tree after all. Just barking at the wrong boat. And the nucleus of a plan had formed in Norton's mind.

It wasn't much of a plan and it was pretty risky. The risky part involved sneaking back to Chez Norton and getting his car. Followed by some very risky skulduggery at this Sleaze Ball. And even if he did pull the plan off, the end result would be no more than a bone to throw the two cops who pinched him. Then he was going to have to spend Sunday night in gaol. But this was his last roll of the dice. He'd pretty much stuffed things up in the Blue Mountains and South Australia. What else could go wrong? And once again, what was the alternative? Thirty long years in the puzzle. Les stared out the window at the stars etched into the inky blackness of the night sky and the clouds below tinged with silver in the moonlight. He was going to give it a go. That money falling in and bumping into the Pieman in Adelaide had to be an omen. Maybe Roxy's guardian angel had flown in?

Before Les knew it, the lights of Sydney were spread out below the plane and they began making their descent. The pilot circled the plane then they bumped down at Kingsford Smith Airport.

'Goodbye, Mr Ullrich,' smiled the young lady flight attendant, as they filed off.

'Thank you,' replied Les, and strode down the corridor.

He took a left straight onto the moving walkway as a uniform cop went by. His adrenalin now on the rise, Les looked straight ahead and kept moving till he got to the baggage carousel. There was the usual wait then his overnight bag came round with the other luggage; Les picked it up, feeling for the edges of the briefcase on the bottom. With his overnight bag in one hand and his backpack in the other, Les walked out to the taxi rank. There were about ten taxis and twenty punters. Les ducked and dived and pushed and shoved a little rudely before jumping in the back seat of the first cab he found empty.

'Bondi Beach, driver. Cox Avenue.'

The taxi took off and the driver smiled in the rear-vision mirror. 'Hello big Les. What's doing, mate?'

Les stared back at the rear-vision mirror. 'Bananas. I didn't know you drove a cab.'

'I don't normally. But I'm doing a bloke a favour. And I need the cashhhhh.'

'Christ! I think the last time I saw you was at the game,' said Les.

Nobody knew Bananas' last name. His first name was Louie. And everybody knew him as Lou Bananas. He was a dumpy faced, dumpy built, balding bloke with Italian parents who came from Coogee and ran bars. He once worked at the Kelly Club for a while. Lou was a likeable bloke with a dry sense of humour and an abbreviated way of talking. His main claim to fame was four daughters he called Bananarama and his love for a punt and a dollar.

'So where have you been hiding, 'Nanas?' said Les.

'I've been managing a pub in Taree,' replied Lou.

'What was that like?'

'They all got two heads and question marks on their foreheads. I stuck it out till I got back to civilizaish. Evench.'

'Fair enough, 'Nanas,' said Les.

'So how have you been, Les?' asked Bananas, as they stopped in the traffic coming out of the airport. 'Nice photo of you in the paper early in the week. If your melon hadn't been covered up, I would have thought it was Brad Pitt.'

'Thanks, Bananas,' said Les. 'You know I didn't do it, don't you?'

'Oh, of course, Les. Bombs aren't your go. You just pulverise people with those big fists of yours.'

'Exactly, Lou. I hate violence.'

They headed for Mascot and Les started thinking again. It had to be an omen. First the money. Then the Pieman. Now Bananas. This could be just what he was looking for. It meant not having to go back to Bondi and get his car.

'So you're chasing a dollar, Lou?' said Les.

'Get four daughters, Les, and see if you don't chase a dollar.'

'How would you like to earn five hundred bucks for about an hour's work, Bananas? Cash.'

The sudden glow in Bananas' eyes shone back at Les from the rear-vision mirror like twin laser beams. 'Did you say cashhhhh?'

'Of course.'

'What do I have to do, big Les? Nothing too ridic?'

'No. Instead of going to Bondi, Take me to a Sleaze Ball in Zetland. Do you know where it is?'

'Yeah,' replied Bananas. 'Lachlan Street. I've been dropping freaks there all night. It's roaring.'

'That'll be the one,' said Les.

'I didn't know Sleaze Balls were your go, Les. How long ... ?'

'Get stuffed, Bananas. All you got to do is wait out the front. I'll be thirty minutes at the most. Here,' Les gave Bananas the other five hundred dollars he had in his jacket.

The sparkle in Bananas' eyes was like a pair of headlights on high beam. 'Sensaish. Thanks, Les.'

'That's all right,' Les picked at his chin for a second. 'On the way, stop at one of those dollar bargain joints. I want to buy something.'

'There's one in Kingsford, should still be open,' said Bananas.

'Okay. And have you got a mobile phone?'

'In the glove box.'

'Good. I might want to use it later,' said Les.

'No worries.'

'After I'm finished at the Sleaze Ball, Bananas, we'll probably be going to Waverley Police Station.'

'The wallopers, Les?'

'Yeah. I won't be coming back out. So I want you to take my overnight bag up to the Kelly Club and give it to Billy Dunne. Make sure he gets it. And tell him where I am. Billy'll know what to do.'

'Righto,' said Bananas. 'Shit! This is all very Mission Imposs, Les. Any chance of an explanaish?'

'Evench, Bananas,' said Les. 'Evench. Now take me shopping.'

Les stared out the window, still not quite sure what he was doing. Whatever it was, he couldn't finish up in much more hot water than he was already in. From now on, thought Les, I'm just burning my bridges as I come to them. Les was still thinking along those lines when Bananas pulled up on a bus stop in Kingsford outside an el-cheapo store between a Chinese restaurant and a newsagent. Lou waited in the taxi while Les ran inside. Five minutes later he was back with a plastic raincoat, a scarf, a cheap pair of women's sunglasses, rubber gloves and a Bic lighter. Plus a toy sword made of grey plastic, about the same size as a carving knife.

He put the raincoat and sunglasses on then tied the scarf over his head and got back in the taxi.

Bananas couldn't believe his eyes. 'What in the fuck are you doing, Les?'

'Nothing,' replied Norton. 'Why?'

'You know who you look like holding that knife. Don't you?

'No, Bananas,' said Les. 'Who?'

'That old sheila in *Psycho*. The one who did all the murders.'

'Norman Bates's mother.'

'Yeah,' nodded Bananas. 'That's her. You're a dead ringer with the raincoat and the scarf over your head.'

Les checked himself out in the rear-vision mirror. 'Well, it is a drag scene I'm going to, Bananas.'

Bananas shook his head. 'You're kiddin,' aren't you? Fair dinkum.'

Bananas cut through Kensington, swung into Dacey Avenue and got a green light near the hotel at Lachlan and South Dowling. He followed Lachlan about half way along then pulled up on the footpath.

'There it is, Les,' said Bananas.

'I know this joint,' said Les. 'It's the old Jaeger Smallgoods Factory. I used to deliver meat here when I worked for Fields.'

'Yeah? Well the only meat you'll get in there now, Les, is straight up the blurter.'

The old factory was a long two-storey brick building with a small metal door at this end and a shuttered loading dock at the other. A wall of glass bricks dotted with air conditioners faced the street and along the footpath out the front was a row of black metal posts embedded into the footpath. At the far end of the street was a park and at this end was a spare parts wholesaler. Opposite was a massive block of land that had been levelled to build a housing commission complex. There were no signs on the old building to say what was going on. The only sign of life was half-a-dozen security staff standing out the front in dark blue trousers and matching windcheaters.

'Okay, Bananas,' said Les. 'Wait here for me. I shouldn't be long.'

'Hey, Les,' replied Bananas. 'Take your time. Enjoy. You might meet the man of your dreams inside.'

'Keep smiling, Bananas,' said Les. 'You're going to look pretty funny kissing your daughters goodnight with your mouth full of stitches.'

Les got out of the car and walked across to the front door. Although he looked like a nutter, the security staff scarcely gave Les a second look. To them he was just another freak. There was a table near the door with an electronic scanner on it. A burly security man swiped Norton's ticket then another opened the metal door. Les stepped into a small corridor where a third security man opened another door. Les stepped through and it closed behind him.

Inside was complete pandemonium. At least two thousand people were either milling around or dancing at the speed of light beneath several rotating mirror balls and a bank of Bose speakers pumping out techno house music loud enough to shake the fillings out of your teeth. Lights flickered everywhere and coloured laser beams arrowed through the smoky atmosphere, making criss-cross patterns on a towering row of scaffolding hung with balloons and streamers.

Les moved away from a set of speakers and got his bearings while he checked out the punters. It was big on micro leather shorts with studs and leather caps and white satin shorts with gold and silver stars on each cheek and G-strings wedged up your backside. There were outrageous drag queens big enough to play front row for the Broncos. Shirley Temples, Xenas, Barbara Cartlands, Tina Turners, Marilyn Monroes, Marj Simpsons complete with towering blue beehives. Groups of Village People were there, along with Boy Georges, boy scouts, girl guides, nurses, nuns, archbishops, rabbis, fairies, pixies. Platoons of elegant Oscar Wildes in velvet and silk mingled with legions of bull-necked lesbians in overalls, spike collars and Brando jackets, ugly enough to scare a herd of warthogs away from a waterhole. Whatever outfit you could think up with the backside cut away and a freshly waxed bum sticking out of it was in there getting down and getting dirty. There was even an Adolph Hitler, an Idi Amin and a Joe Stalin, with their freshly waxed behinds sticking out of their uniforms. And that was only near where Les walked in. Who knew what else you'd find? But there was only one Mrs Norman Bates.

Now if I remember right, thought Les, the shithouse was in that corner down there to the right. In the distance Les could make out a green sign saying EXIT. He started weaving his way through the punters, getting a great giggle when he'd stab the plastic knife around. Les was correct. There was a short corridor to the right and a sign said TOILETS. Les got the rubber gloves from his pocket and slipped them on. The Norman Bates's mother outfit was a hoot, but it also gave Les head to toe protection from the various creepy crawlies he expected to find in a Sleaze Ball toilet. The open door was just a little further down on the left. Very gingerly, Les stepped inside.

Every light bulb had been broken and it was almost pitch black. The only light was a few faint beams snaking in through a row of dusty windows high above a wall at the far end. Les could make out a row of cubicles on the right and a line of stainless steel urinals on the left. All through the middle was a congestion of seething, jostling silhouettes, sucking, fucking, licking and groping or otherwise happily engaged in all manner of sexual acts. All the lewd activity was accompanied by a chorus of squealing and moaning that hung in the dark along with the almost overpowering smell of body oil and perspiration. Good Lord, thought Les, bumping past a pair of leather clad silhouettes with their hands in each other's shorts and their tongues down each other's throats. How off's this? Les squinted into a cubicle where a silhouette with its shorts down was spreadeagled against the cistern, with another silhouette behind, choc-o-bloc up it and putting in the big ones.

It was all too much for Norton, and besides that, it was too dark. Fuck it! He cursed to himself. Looks like I've blown it again, I don't even know what I'm looking for, and even if I did, you wouldn't find it in here. No. They can stick this up their arse. They are anyway. Unexpectedly, Les suddenly found himself busting for a leak. Shit. What a time to want to have a piss. Oh well. Les weaved past several darkened figures doing whatever they were doing and stepped up onto the urinal. In the darkness he bumped into someone at his feet.

'Sorry mate,' said Les, unzipping his fly.

'Piss on me,' said a muted voice from near Norton's feet.

Les looked down but couldn't see anything. 'What?'

'Piss on me,' the tinny voice repeated.

Les pulled out the Bic lighter and flicked it on. Sitting in the urinal, with its feet out in front of it and its arms by its side was a ghastly figure, clad in a full-length black leather bodysuit, complete with rubber booties and gloves. Clamped tightly on its head was a hideous black leather face helmet with yellow stripes on the front and a zipper down the back. The mouth was a small mesh grill and the eyes were a pair of dark blue swimming goggles. It was a macabre sight and reminded Les of the repulsive creature they kept locked in the cellar in the film *Pulp Fiction* — the Gimp.

'Piss on me,' the figure in the urinal pleaded again.

'Sure mate. My pleasure,' replied Les, whipping out his old boy. 'Here. Have one on you.'

After three cans of VB on the plane, Les was only too willing to oblige. He pissed all over the figure in the urinal from head to toe, giving whoever it was a real good hosing in its face while he tried to get as much as he could in its mouth. The Gimp revelled in it. Rolling its head from side to side, rubbing its hands across its face and chest and delicately flicking warm, frothy urine from its fingertips. Les gave the figure a final burst in the eyes then shook the last few drops out in its face and tucked his old boy back inside his pants.

'There you go, mate. How was that?' asked Les. 'Enjoy yourself?'

'Fantastic,' murmured the figure in the urinal. 'Please come back again.'

'I will,' promised Les. 'In the meantime, try this.'

Les stepped back and kicked the Gimp in the solar plexus. The figure gasped a tiny, shrill scream then clutched at its chest, unable to move. Les grabbed the figure under one arm and lifted it up from the urinal then pushed it out of the darkened toilet and started steering it through the crowd. Under the strobe lights and darting lasers, nobody took a great deal of notice. Any freaks who did, thought it was just part of the night. Mrs Norman Bates holding the Gimp and slashing at everybody with a toy sword. Les reached the first door where two security staff were standing with their arms folded.

'What's the problem?' asked one.

'My friend's having an asthma attack,' shouted Les, camping it up. 'For heaven's sake open the door. I've got to get him into the fresh air.'

'Okay.'

One of the security guards opened the door. Les hustled the Gimp along the corridor to the next door and banged on it. The door opened and Les stepped outside still holding the paralysed figure in the black leather bodysuit.

'What's happened?' asked one of the security guards standing out the front.

'My friend's had an asthma attack,' said Les. 'I've got to take him to a hospital.'

'Stay there. We'll call an ambulance.'

'It's all right,' said Les. 'I can see a taxi.' Before the security guard had time to blink, Les hustled the figure across the footpath straight into the back of Bananas' taxi. 'Righto, Bananas. Waverley Police Station.'

Bananas looked at Les, looked at the Gimp and took off. 'God strike me. You've got some funny friends, Les. Who's that?'

'I don't know,' answered Les. 'But we'll find out soon enough. Give me your mobile.'

'Here you are.' Bananas got the phone from the glove box and handed it to Les. 'Phew! You're mate's not on the nose enough, Les. Where did you find him? In a shithouse?'

'As a matter of fact, Bananas, I did.'

Bananas shook his head and drove towards Centennial Park. 'You're kiddin', aren't you, Les. Fair dinkum.'

Les got onto Telstra. Got the phone number for Waverley Police Station and dialled.

'Hello. Waverley Police,' came a policewoman's voice.

'Yeah. My name's Les Norton. Would detectives Tait and Caccano happen to be working tonight?'

'Yes. They are. But they're busy at the moment.'

'Okay. Well tell them Les Norton will be there soon. And I'm turning myself in.'

There was a pause at the end of the line. 'What was your name again sir?'

'Norton. Les Norton. You know? The bomb on the film set.'

'I don't quite follow you, Mr Norton,' came the policewoman's voice. 'What's the problem again?'

'Just tell detectives Tait and Caccano. Les Norton rang. And I'm coming in to give myself up,' said Les.

'Yes, all right, very good, Mr Norton. I'll see that they get the message.'

Bananas looked at Les in the rear-vision mirror. 'What was all that about?'

'I'm giving myself up to the cops, Bananas,' replied Les, handing Lou back the phone. 'And I'm taking the Gimp with me for company.'

'Fair enough.' Bananas kept looking at Norton in the rear-view mirror. 'You're dead set mad, Les. You know that, don't you?'

'You're probably right, Bananas,' agreed Les. 'But being mad's the only thing that stops me from going insane.'

They went past Centennial Park. Les got out of the plastic raincoat and everything else and dropped them on the floor of the taxi. Bananas came up through Charing Cross and pulled up almost out the front of Waverley Police Station. The Gimp looked like it was starting to breath normally again so Les gave it a short right under the ribs to settle it down a bit.

'Okay, Bananas, you know what to do,' said Les, picking up his backpack.

'No worries, Les.'

Les had some more cash in his pocket. 'And here's another couple of hundred to help clean your cab.'

'Shit. Thanks, Les. Do you want me to wait around for a while, then come inside and find out what's going on?'

Les thought for a moment. 'No. Don't bother. Just make sure you get my bag up to the Kelly Club and give it to Billy.'

'No worries, Les.'

Norton shouldered his backpack and bundled the Gimp out of the taxi. 'I'll see you when I see you, Bananas.'

'Good luck, Les.'

Well. Here goes nothing, thought Les. He grabbed the Gimp under one arm and steered it across the footpath straight through the door into Waverley Police Station.

For a Sunday night it was very quiet. There was a young couple talking to a policewoman behind the counter on the right. Another policewoman was on the phone behind her and a burly sergeant was going through a file at a desk behind her. At the end of the counter, near the noticeboard in the corner, Les could see the two detectives in sports coats and jeans. Caccano was on the phone and Tait had a notebook out, listening to what his partner was saying. Les walked past the stairs in front of the door, and bowled straight up to them, his backpack in one hand and the Gimp in the other.

'Okay fellahs. It's all right,' exclaimed Les, dropping his backpack near the counter. 'I'm here to give myself up. I'm unarmed so you won't need your guns.'

Detective Tait turned around and looked at Les without seeming to notice the Gimp. 'Hello, Les,' he said shortly. 'What do you want?'

'What do I want?' said Les. 'I want to hand myself in. That's what I want.'

'Yeah, well, we're busy at the moment, Les. Can you wait till we're finished on the phone?' Detective Tait turned back to his partner.

Les stared at the two detectives, totally admonished. What's up with these two hillbillies? he asked himself. The last time I saw them they wanted to shoot me on sight. Every cop in Australia's been looking for me. Now no one wants to even talk to me. Les looked around the police station. No one, including the young couple at the counter, seemed to notice he was there. But they certainly noticed the Gimp standing behind him. They were all wrinkling their noses and staring at it like it had just landed from another planet.

Eventually Detective Caccano got off the phone. He discussed something with his partner then turned to Norton.

'What's your problem, Les?' he asked.

'What's my problem?' echoed Norton. 'I'm here to give myself up. And to prove my innocence at the same time.'

'Prove your innocence?' said Detective Caccano.

'That's right,' said Les. 'I can prove I didn't do it.'

'We know you didn't do it,' said Detective Tait.

'You what?' said Les.

'We know you didn't do it,' repeated Detective Tait.

Norton's voice rose. 'What do you mean, I didn't do it?'

'Well, if you want to be like that,' said Detective Caccano.

'No. That's not what I mean,' said Les. 'I mean ... Shit! What the fuck's going on?'

'Didn't your mate Eddie tell you?' said Detective Tait.

'Yeah. Where have you been?' asked Detective Caccano.

'I've been away. I mean ... Look, tell me what's going on, will you?'

'Eddie Salita came in and saw us on Thursday morning,' said Detective Tait. 'And he brought in one of those crackers in a cake box, Like you were telling us about.'

'He did?' said Les.

Detective Tait nodded. 'He showed us how it worked. And I have to admit, we were very impressed.'

'And you got another mate. Ray Tracy,' said Detective Caccano. 'Runs a Japanese restaurant next to the school.'

'That's right,' said Les. 'The Gull. It was his movie I put my money into.'

'Well, his partner is out here at the moment. A Mr Kobayashi,' said Detective Caccano. 'He was in the school with his video camera when the bomb went off. Ray brought him up when Eddie was here and they showed us the video. Compared to the school security camera, there's a good two second's difference between the explosions.'

'Two second's difference,' said Les.

'That's right,' nodded Detective Caccano. 'When you watch Mr Kobayashi's video, you can clearly see the cake box blow up in Knox's face. Then you see the second explosion come from the left and blow Knox down the side of the catering van.'

'We've got other forensic evidence to back this. So your story would stand up in court,' said Detective Tait. 'And even though you weren't quite fair dinkum with us at the time because you were covering for Eddie, we can see you were telling the truth. So we've dropped the charges.'

'You've dropped the charges,' muttered Les.

'That's right, Les,' said Detective Caccano. 'You've walked.'

Norton could scarcely believe what he was hearing. All he had to do when he came back from the Blue Mountains on Thursday was pick up the phone. And that would have either been Eddie or the Gull telling him he was in the clear. Instead he'd gone to all that trouble flying to Adelaide and gone through all that anxiety for nothing. On the other hand — he was laughing. Not only was he off scot-free, he had one hundred and forty-nine thousand dollars on its way to the Kelly Club completely GST-free. And a good sort's phone number in his wallet. Norton was totally out of the shit, back stroking in gravy. It was a beautiful world after all.

'I don't know what to say,' said Les. 'I'm flabber and gasted.'

'Thanks, officer, would be nice,' said Detective Tait dryly.

'Yeah,' agreed Detective Caccano. 'We'll settle for a thank you.'

'Thanks,' said Les. 'I'll give you more than thanks.' Les turned and pointed to the Gimp. 'I'll give you the bloody murderer.'

'Yeah. What the fuck is that thing?' asked Detective Caccano.

'Christ! It doesn't half stink,' sniffed Detective Tait.

'What is this thing?' said Les. 'This *thing* gentlemen. Is the Trough Queen. Sometimes known as the Trough Monster.'

A sudden, inexplicable high hit Norton as if the heavens had just opened up and the sun shone only for him. Maybe it was hanging around with the poets in the Blue Mountains playing Agatha Christie? Or just the exhilaration of not having to go to gaol. He wasn't sure, but suddenly Les thought he was Hercule Poirot or some great courtroom barrister and he started to soar.

'This foul fiend,' orated Norton. 'This devious denizen of the night. This malodorous monster. Frequents the urinals at Sleaze Balls. And other dens of iniquity. Where. It gets its perverted, lascivious pleasures. By enducing persons using the toilet. To urinate upon it.'

'It sure bloody smells like it,' agreed Detective Tait, waving a hand in front of his nose. 'Christ!'

'And I. Les Norton, concerned citizen,' continued Les. 'Have just made a citizen's arrest of this diabolical beast. Because it is my belief. This. Is the perpetrator of the foul deed. Wherein an innocent cook. One Albert Knox. Was blown apart by a bomb.'

'Keep talking, Les,' said Detective Tait. 'I like it.'

'And it is also my belief,' said Les, pointing indignantly at the figure in the swimming goggles and black leather. 'That if you take the same sniffer dog you brought to my house. Oscar. And search this insidious fiend's premises. You will find evidence of bomb making.'

Detective Caccano sounded interested. 'Can you prove this, Les?'

'Can I prove this?' replied Norton.

No. He couldn't. Les was completely bluffing. It was just a gamble he'd taken to try and get some of the heat off himself. All he had was a photo of four blokes standing in front of an old boat. But who gives a stuff. He'd beaten a murder charge. He'd got around statutory rape. What could they charge him with now? Abduction and assault? The way Les felt, he'd beat that standing on his head.

'Yes. I can,' said Les. 'The proof is in my bag. But first. I will unmask this wretched miscreant.' Les undid the zipper, then reached behind the Trough Queen and gripped its mask. 'Gentlemen, I give you — the Trough Queen.' An audible gasp echoed around the police station as Les tore the Trough Queen's mask off.

'I don't fuckin believe it,' said Detective Tait.

'Well, if I hadn't been here to see it,' said Detective Caccano, 'I wouldn't have believed it either.'

Les stepped back and like the others stared in astonishment at the Trough Queen. Most of all Les. Possibly in amongst all the bullshit he'd done it? Maybe this was the murderer? The motive was there. Blackmail. The connection was there. Adelaide. The timing was there. Had a nose job been done? Could the Trough Queen make a bomb? Insurance coverage? Who cared? Les was off the hook.

The Trough Queen's lips curled back, trembling with anger. Eyes blazing with hatred, the figure in black glared furiously around the police station, shaking with rage. 'You vile, rotten swine,' it screamed. 'Get me my lawyer. And my agent. This is absolutely outrageous.'

Shaking his head in amazement, Les took his camera out of his backpack then handed the Trough Queen back its mask and swimming goggles. 'And to think I used to go around telling people I wouldn't piss on you. You've certainly made a liar out of me. Haven't you, Nathan.'

THE END

A MESSAGE FROM THE AUTHOR

Firstly, thanks for all your letters. It's great to hear from you and I'm doing my best to reply. But I get bogged down and I am lazy, so please be patient. Especially my readers in various big houses across Australia. I also want to thank all those people who came to the book signings for the *The Wind and the Monkey*. Particularly Newcastle. When I walked into Charlestown Mall it was like Beatlemania. I've never seen so many people. Anyway, the book went to Number One, and I'd like to thank everyone for that.

Now. People keep writing to me and asking me what's going on with the Les Norton movie. Well, things have fallen in a bit of a hole there. I can't elaborate on this for legal reasons. But the movie will get made. I'm just going to have to come at it from a different direction. So what I've done is this. I've paid a bloke an arm and a leg to write a film script for *Davo's Little Something*. The script is finished, it looks sensational and I reckon *Davo's Little Something* will make a red hot movie. We'll find some investors and get it up. Then when we do, I'll use the same team and make Les Norton movies the way they should be made. And it's about time. In the meantime, I hope you enjoy *Leaving Bondi*. I'm not sure what's coming up next. I might even give Les a break next year and do something else. Who knows? No matter what, thanks for your support and I'll see you in the next book.

Robert G. Barrett, 2000

STUMBLE IN THE JUNGLE

Robert G. Barrett goes to Pohnpei and explores the mysteries of
Nan Madol

In my house I have two computers, one in my office and another downstairs in the den. I like to get a bit loose occasionally and knock out what I call 'roughs' on the den computer, which I tidy up in my office when I straighten out. Both computers are brand new and cost me a bundle. A while back the screen went on the one in the office and recently the one downstairs completely shat itself. Nothing would make the prick of a thing work and the bloke was away on holidays when I rang. As anyone knows, computers can be the most frustrating, maddening things ever invented when they play up. I kicked a hole in the door, threw tantrums and was seriously thinking of putting an axe through the one downstairs before I left it till the bloke got back from holidays. I needed it, too, because I wanted to knock out some roughs about something before I left for Nan Madol.

Don't worry if you've never heard of Nan Madol. Hardly anyone has. It's way out in the middle of the Pacific in Micronesia, on an island called Pohnpei. Just past Kapingamarangi, somewhere between Nauru and Guam.

I got hooked on Nan Madol through Erich Von Daniken and recently it featured in a series on the ABC called *Quest for the Lost Civilizations*. Thousands of years ago some race built these enormous structures there out of crystalline basalt logs and nobody knows how or why. Von Daniken claims it was visitors from outer space. Whatever, the place absolutely fascinated me and I always wanted to go there. I'd just finished my seventeenth book and I needed a break. So I booked a ticket, packed my swag and split for Micronesia.

You fly to Brisbane then pick up Air Nauru with a stopover at Nauru on the way. Returning Nauruans take enough luggage on the plane with them to fill the MCG, so they overloaded the aircraft. After kicking a dozen fat Nauruans off the plane, along with their outboard motors and TV sets, we were able to take off an hour late. We flew into Nauru, superphosphate centre of the galaxy, at 3.00 a.m. and when the door opened you'd swear you'd landed in a monster chicken coop. By the time the plane was unloaded, we were bundled into Nauru's one hotel at 4.00 a.m., handed our luggage, pointed towards our rooms and told to get stuffed. After a bit of sleep, I stumbled downstairs and had breakfast thrown at me then went for a walk in the heat with the romantic scent of Dynamic Lifter wafting gently though the palm trees. What can I say about Nauru? It's hot, it stinks and the locals hate tourists and anybody else that can get out of the place. Before long they bundled us back on the plane and we took off for Pohnpei.

We approached Kolonia airport late afternoon, right in the middle of a violent rainstorm. On the old scale, Pohnpei gets 190 inches of rain a year on the coast and 400 inland. When we arrived they were getting about two feet. You couldn't see a metre out the window and the 737 was shaking in the turbulence like a ride at Dream World. The pilot took the plane down then had to abort the landing. 'I'll just have to circle over to the left for a few minutes,' he said, 'till the rain eases.' We circled the airport for forty minutes and made four aborted landings. After the fourth one, my hair looked like Don King's and my ring was hanging out that far you could have cut washers off it. Finally the pilot said, 'I'm sorry. I can't land the plane, it's too dangerous. We're flying on to Guam.' I swear, I've never been so terrified in my life. We got to Guam around 9.00 p.m., got bundled into another hotel and given a feed, then it was up at 3.30 a.m. to catch the 4.30 a.m. back to Pohnpei.

It was still raining when we returned to Pohnpei. However, the pilot was able to land the plane at Kolonia airport, where it was a pleasant 85 degrees F with 90 per cent humidity. A driver met me and I was bussed miles out of town to my hotel. I had picked the hotel off the internet. Beach hut, fabulous views it said. Waterfall just up the road. My US$90-a-night room had no fridge, no air-conditioner, no TV, no phone and two sloppy water beds with mosquito nets. A gap ran round the thatched ceiling and at night the room filled up with bugs. The room was 150 metres from reception, down steps hacked in the jungle and the beach was a mud flat half a kilometre down a llama trail. I wasn't expecting the Mirage Resort, but Papillion had a better digs on Devil's Island. Plus I'd paid eight days in advance. However, the hotel was the main spot in Pohnpei where they arranged reef dives and trips to Nan Madol. I booked a visit to Nan Madol the next day, Saturday, then hired a car and drove back into Kolonia to check it out. On the way back I stopped at a saccau bar.

Saccau is the local version of kava and a saccau bar is several seats and tables on a dirt floor under a thatched roof. After straining the saccau through a Romanian weightlifter's jockstrap, they pour it out of plastic containers and you drink it with beer chasers. It resembles thin grey mud

and tastes like a horrible vegetable health drink. After about six glasses
you feel as if you've had a couple of Serepax and some toothache drops. I
drove back to the hotel, lay down in my room and sweltered for three
hours, then got up feeling like I'd just eaten a mouldy Chiko roll and
been stabbed in the guts with a rusty fishing knife. I drove back into
Kolonia to get some soda water then came home and crawled onto the
water bed. If the heat wasn't bad enough, a family of Pohnpeians living
down on the mud flat had at least fifty dogs and they barked non-stop
from 9.30 p.m. till 4.00 a.m. My first night in paradise and I had to sleep
with earplugs.

After a shithouse night's sleep, I dragged my tortured back off the water
bed in time for breakfast and met Sunni, who worked at the Japanese
Embassy. Sunni was also going to Nan Madol. We got our snorkelling shit
together then climbed down another llama track with Allan, our Pohnpeian
guide, to the boat, where we waited for Sarah. Sarah was from California
and she'd been backpacking around Micronesia. Once we were organised,
Allan got behind the twin outboard motors and flogged the skiff at warp
speed out to some reef where we all went snorkel sucking for a couple of
hours.

Probably because of all the rain the water wasn't all that clear, and
probably because the locals had fished everything out I didn't see all that
many fish. We got back in the boat and Allan hit warp speed again to a
desert island where we had a nice lunch, drank coconut milk and
frolicked in the ocean. All this time genious me didn't bother to wear a T-
shirt like everybody else and soon my back looked like 20 kilos of boiled
silverside. Allan said we had to catch the tide, so we cleaned up our mess
and weighed anchor for Nan Madol.

You don't arrive at Nan Madol. Nan Madol creeps up on *you*. Allan
cut the motors as we came in off the reef and started pushing the skiff
over the shallows. The heat is absolutely crushing and an eerie silence
suddenly seems to settle over everything. Then from out of nowhere these
colossal stone walls appear all around you, stacked up out of huge
crystalline basalt logs. It's the most astonishing sight imaginable. We
floated silently over shallows before Allan pulled up in front of what
looked like a fortress made from these massive stone logs. I got off the
boat and started snapping and filming everything in sight. Next thing we
were joined by a Japanese film crew shooting a documentary. When our
little party settled down, Allan gave us a talk on the people who
supposedly built Nan Madol. Logic says it was the Saudeleurs who
floated the logs out on huge bamboo rafts. Legend says it was two

brothers, Olo-Chipa and Olo-Chopa, who 'flew the logs through the air by magic'. I'll take the legend, because some of the stones are as big as shipping containers and there wouldn't be enough bamboo in Micronesia to make a raft big enough. Evidently some archaeologists tried the bamboo raft trip with just one small stone log and — no pun intended — it sank like a stone.

I could have spent ages there, but we were running late and had to catch the tide again to visit Kepirohi Waterfall. Finally we returned to the hotel. I booked out and booked into the South Park Hotel, land of a thousand moggies, in beautiful downtown Kolonia, and dropped six nights at US$90 a night straight down the gurgler. The South Park wasn't the Hilton but at least my room had a fridge, air-conditioning, and a bed that didn't give you spina bifida. I caught up with Sarah and some local girls in the bar next door and had a cool one with her while the girls chewed beetle nut. Me being a Trekkie and Sarah coming from California, we bonded and got into a cosmological, New Age, UFO rap about Nan Madol. Both of us agreed it was one weird trip and vowed to return on Monday for a closer look. This time we'd drive around Pohnpei then walk in through the jungle and the canals. I had a few more beers, told Sarah I'd see her in the bar again on Sunday night then kicked my way back to my room through fifty hungry, miaowing cats.

That night I slept a little better. However, when I got up my back felt like Captain Bligh had laid a lazy 500 lashes on it with a cat o'nine tails. After breakfast at the hotel I thought I'd take a drive around Pohnpei to take my mind off the pain. Driving in Pohnpei is fun. It's left-hand drive, there's no rules, you don't have to wear a seat belt and there's potholes in the roads big enough to swallow up a Russian nuclear submarine. Pedestrians meander all over the place with the pigs and chickens and you have to steer around them. Cars pull out in front of you and cut you off. But there's no road rage because it's too hot. Everybody drives like Grandma Duck after she's had a few Valium. Your average, ethnic, Sydney westie wouldn't last a day over here. The people live in corrugated-iron shacks with dirt floors and old sacks for curtains. Yet as you drive past they all smile and call out 'Kaselehlie', the local version of 'G'daymateowyergoin'. I loved it.

One thing they do have in Pohnpei is dogs. Thousands of them. All the same size, shape and colour, only in different stages of malnourishment. This had me curious. Pohnpeiens appear to be flat out feeding themselves, let alone families of dogs. Then according to my guide book, dog is on the menu. Between the pot lickers and the moggies, I made a mental note to be wary of any chicken or rabbit dishes. I met up with Sarah in the bar that night and shouted her dinner. I have to rap the food at the South Park Hotel, though. Especially the sashimi. The local tuna is sensational and they pile it up on your plate like Weetbix. I had a couple more beers and told Sarah I'd see her about nine the following morning. And hopefully when we got to Nan Madol the tide would be out and we'd be safe wading through the canals before the tiger sharks came in at high tide.

Sarah rang me the following morning to say she was running late. She didn't have a watch and the wind-up thingy she had to tell the time wasn't working. Did I mention Sarah came from California? It was raining when she called round. Being a gentleman I offered to let Sarah drive. The truth was, between my sunburn and the potholes the day before, my back was buggered. Being a Yank, Sarah was rapt. Yanks love to drive cars. A Seppo would rather drive twenty miles than walk fifty feet. Even in a little clapped-out Japanese hire job. I gave Sarah the keys, we checked our roadmaps then set off in the rain for the mysterious lost city of Nan Madol.

By now Sarah and I had bonded enough to swap star signs. Sarah was a Gemini; the twins. Which figured, because it was like having three people in the car — Larry, Curly and Mo. We'd decided to check out some rock carvings first at Madolenihmw and all we did was keep getting get lost. Sarah was a good driver, but she had absolutely no sense of direction and I couldn't read the map. We finished up in three piggeries, the local tip, a mangrove swamp and every backyard in the area. Between us we couldn't find peace of mind.

We drove as far as we could, then set off on foot just as it started to pour with rain. Before long we were soaked to the skin and *completely* lost. We never found the rock carvings. But as we stumbled through the jungle, I found an old stone building two metres high and 20 metres square totally hidden in the undergrowth. It had probably been there thousands of years and nobody knew. Evidently things like this are all over Micronesia. Soaking wet and reeking of BO in the humidity, we somehow managed to find the trail back to the car and stunk the seats up as we drove around getting lost again. Finally, we found the back way into Nan Madol, left the car, and set off through the canals.

Walking in was a different buzz again. You slush through mangrove swamps and age-old pathways in almost indescribable heat, then these massive stone walls and buildings loom up in the jungle like something out of a Tarzan movie. It is absolutely mind-blowing. I started filming and snapping away again, then we came to the canal leading out to the reef and one of the bigger buildings. This time we had the place to ourselves and the eerie silence of Nan Madol sends shivers up your spine. It's got a spiritual quality about it you can honestly feel. Sarah and I walked around filming and taking photos and looked for answers. But instead of answers, all we found were questions.

The stone logs in the photo weigh up to 50 tonnes. There's 250 million tonnes of stone logs in the buildings they know of so far, not counting the underwater columns out towards the reef. But this is the best part: they're all built on 92 artificial islands. Before they brought the basalt logs over from Sokehs, about 40 kilometres away on the other side of Pohnpei, they built the islands, the foundations, out of coral. Put bluntly, thousands of years ago some race of ignorant savages with no electricity, no cranes and no bulldozers, no hard hats, work boots or work gloves, no paper to draw the plans on, no wages and no fresh water, in a place that hot and humid you can hardly breathe, was able to construct fantastic buildings to rival the pyramids. Buildings I don't believe we could duplicate today. How?

Evidently, basalt is not only crystalline, it's magnetic. I rubbed a piece of stone against one of the logs and it made an odd ringing sound. According to a book I got hold of, basalt would be an ideal stone to levitate. Levitation by sound has been experimented with by NASA and some physicists claim that gravity is really a frequency, part of Einstein's Unified Field. Crystalline blocks of basalt need only be resonating at the frequency of gravity, 1012 hertz, and they lose their weight. Maybe that was the way the stones 'flew through the air by magic'. In other words, humankind today can put a man on the moon, build atomic bombs, jumbo jets and cars, but thousands of years ago ignorant savages could move gigantic boulders around by sound waves. Is that how they built the pyramids? The Mayan temples? Nan Madol? Buggered if I know. But if somebody's got a better answer I'm willing to listen.

Sarah and I hung around Nan Madol taking photos and shooting videos for as long as possible. Then the tide started coming in. And the tide in Micronesia doesn't come in, it rushes. So rather than risk being tiger shark sashimi, we left. I pocketed a piece of stone for a souvenir. But as we were walking back I took it out and tossed it into one of the canals. I'm not all that superstitious, but I honestly felt Nan Madol was one place that's truly spiritual, and after what happened flying in, it wasn't worth the risk.

We only got lost twice on the way back to Kolonia. That night I shouted Sarah dinner at the South Park before she caught the eleven o'clock plane to Australia. I gave her a book and a couple of Team

Norton T-shirts and told her to ring me when I got back and I'd look after her. I was a little sad to see Sarah go. We shared a lot of laughs together and she was one of those zany, happy people you can't help but like.

I spent the rest of the week hanging around in the heat, buying T-shirts and so forth. I called in on Mr Timothy Cole, the Australian consulate, and left him with a couple of books. Then I flew out on Friday. And I must say it was great to touch down in Sydney. However, there was another mystery waiting for me when I arrived home.

I got back to Terrigal just after midnight and the stereo in my garage gym was glaring out FM radio. During my absence there was a power surge. And whenever this happens it turns on any stereos in the house not switched off at the power point. Lucky neighbours. I settled in, got my photos developed and made cassettes from my video camera. Sunday night I was downstairs in my den getting a little loose, listening to some music and thought, Shit! I'd love to knock up some roughs about my trip. But the computer wasn't working. Just for fun I pushed the button and — bingo! The prick of a thing lit up like a Xmas tree. Windows 98. It had to be the power surge. So away I went. The next day I rang the bloke up to tell him what happened and asked could he explain it. He couldn't. It was a complete mystery to him. Sorry.

So I figure, between that and what I saw at Nan Madol — not counting all the money I lost in Pohnpei, the plane nearly crashing, the heat and getting sick on saccau — I'm entitled to write a mystery story. A science-shock thing set on a fictitious island somewhere in Micronesia. Complete with magic crystals, UFOs and mysterious force fields. Plus the usual gratuitous sex, drugs and violence you find in my books. And just to stir things up a bit, I'll throw in a third world war. Sort of *Independence Day* meets *Wag the Dog*. How's that for a mystery story?

But of course the literary establishment has always considered me a mystery writer. It's a complete mystery to them why anybody buys my books.

Mystery Bay
Blues

DEDICATION

This book is dedicated to Judge Michael Finnane in Sydney.

Yes, thought Norton, as he stepped right from Campbell Parade, Bondi into Hall Street. You might know how to hand it out, but you sure know how to kick a man in the nuts too. Don't you, boss. Les stopped for a moment to look upwards and smile mirthlessly at the sky before continuing steadily towards Cox Avenue and home. It was a pleasant Tuesday afternoon in early spring and Les was in a pair of green cargos, a white T-shirt, cap and an expensive pair of brand new trainers. Despite the day and his new trainers, Les wasn't striding out in the sunshine. He wasn't dragging his feet either. He was just walking along steadily. Very steadily. Thanks again to Eddie Salita. And just when everything was going along absolutely swimmingly.

The harrowing business with the Gull's movie was well and truly behind him now. In all the smell and confusion, the Trough Queen had simply run out of Waverley police station and disappeared never to be seen again. The police searched his unit but so far hadn't found any incriminating evidence. So whether the Trough Queen did the deed could not be proved conclusively. Nevertheless, it did seem more than a little odd, vanishing from a nicely furnished unit and a top rating radio program. Subsequently, police were rather keen to find the Trough Queen so he could help them with their investigations. Not that Les gave a stuff whether the wallopers found him or not. Les was as free as a bird. He'd even had his fifteen minutes of fame. A flicker on TV and a photo in the papers with a few words saying 'Bondi Waiter Cleared On Murder Charges'. Alongside 'Mysterious Disappearance Of Radio Announcer Has Police And Friends Puzzled'.

Now, Les was just another innocent man wronged and his good name almost ruined due to the bunglings of the NSW police. In fact the big Queenslander was so aggrieved and full of self-righteous indignation over what had happened, he was thinking of suing the police for malicious arrest and post-operative, traumatic, something or other. But, balancing that against all the villainy Norton had got away with in the past, he decided to cop it sweet. And speaking of villainy: while all this rattle was going on Les had the money he'd stolen washed quicker than a cup and saucer. He gave it to his accountant who changed it into Euros. She then bought shares over the net in some French IT company, resold the shares and bought into a Belgian IT company. Sold the shares again and cashed them back into Euros, changed the Euros into Hong Kong dollars, then US dollars. Before finally changing them back into Australian dollars. Somehow, amongst all the confusion between the internet, share traders and money changers working out what a Euro was, let alone how much it was worth, when the money got back to Les — all quite legally washed, folded and dried — another two thousand had fallen in, as well as his accountant getting her whack. Les was laughing.

Roxy had done the right thing in Adelaide also. Due to her drugged state and the trauma she'd been through, all she could recollect in her statement to the police was that a tall man named Conrad had saved her, then brought her back to his hotel before driving her home the next day. The police checked the hotel register along with an identikit photo from Roxy, and found no trace of Conrad Ullrich either. However, Roxy was able to identify the ratbags who'd kidnapped her, who were promptly arrested and were now awaiting trial. And Les didn't have to appear in court. Roxy also got her fifteen minutes of fame. She sold her story to a newspaper for thirty thousand dollars; now she was in line for another fifty thousand in reward money. So Roxy was laughing too.

Les flew Roxy to Sydney. She stayed at Chez Norton for a couple of days, then they both flew to Coffs Harbour and booked into the same resort Les had stayed at with Perigrine. Les hired a car and they both had a lovely time swimming, snorkelling and taking in the sights. Porking, drinking expensive cocktails and eating that many lobsters their eyes started poking out on stalks. Then Roxy went back to Victor Harbor and threw in her job to concentrate on her novel. They kept in touch. But between the conspiracy of distance and Roxy immersed in her work they didn't see as much of each other as they would have liked. But Roxy wasn't interested in any men at present and was quite happy seeing Les when she could. Les felt very much the same way about Roxy. One day — he told her, when she was kissing him goodbye at Adelaide airport — you just never know, Roxy. You just never know. Now Roxy was in Perth before heading for Broome to research another part of her book. And Les was in Sydney, back at the Kelly Club and training like a man possessed on his days off. Maybe it was knowing he wasn't going inside that gave Les a new lease on life. Maybe it was Roxy. But Les just had this wonderful feeling of freedom and fitness; along with being unexpectedly cashed up. Then, everything came to a shuddering halt.

After all the drama Eddie had caused him with his exploding cakebox, Les reckoned the little hitman should shout him the other pair of stabilising binoculars. That was okay by Eddie. He even tossed in a spare pair of inversion boots he'd got from the same villain. They were pretty much like the ones Sylvester Stallone used in the Rocky films. A pair of rubber-lined metal tubes, with a hook facing backwards, that you clamped round your shins. Then you swung up onto a bar and hung upside down like a fruit bat doing sit-ups or whatever took your fancy. Les had a chin-up bar in the sunroom which was ideal. He'd only had the inversion boots a week and he loved them — hanging upside down stretching his spine and everything else.

One afternoon Les came home from a run jumping out of his skin and decided to play Batman for a while. He clamped on his inversion boots, swung up on the bar in the sunroom and started swaying back and forth and jigging around. He did a stack of sit-ups then started doing press-ups, pushing and shoving and clapping his hands in between. It was a hoot and Les was loving it. Until Les felt a stab of pain in his lower back. It didn't worry him all that much until he climbed down. Then the stab of pain suddenly turned into searing, gut-wrenching agony and Les could hardly move. The best he could manage was to roll around the floor with what felt like a burning arrow sticking out of his back. It was frightening and Les didn't know what he'd done. But he was almost paralysed, sweating with pain and convinced he'd broken his spine and would never walk again.

Somehow he got to the phone and pulled it onto the floor where the only person he could get was Warren. Going by the urgency in Norton's voice, Warren came straight home from the office. It was definitely no laughing matter. But when Warren found Les all grey-faced and crawling round the floor like a carpet snake with a ruptured hernia, Warren laughed that much he nearly threw his own back out. With Les bent over and barely able to move, Warren got him into his Celica and off to a chiropractor they knew in Rose Bay: Bernie Trelaw. Bernie could hardly see and wore Coke bottle glasses. But he had amazing feeling in his hands and people swore by him. Bernie got Les on the table and after a bit of prodding and pushing told Les he'd slipped a disc. Slipped it almost into another postcode. And if Les thought the pain was bad before, when Bernie started on him Les almost fainted. Bernie cupped one hand under Norton's chin, another round his knees, then Bernie stuck his own knee in Norton's back and bent him backwards like he was a longbow as he worked his disc back in. Les didn't bother about stoically holding everything inside and showing how tough he was. He swore and screamed and cursed Bernie all the way back to Bernie's hometown of Grenfell. After twenty minutes of indescribable misery, Les got off the bench to find his back didn't hurt as much. He still couldn't stand up straight; that would take several more visits, and even then Les was as stiff as a board. But the improvement was remarkable.

Surprisingly, Warren had been a great help, coming home from work to take Les to the chiropractor then the doctor for a further check up and pain killers. Nevertheless, Warren did buy a big cigar, and a pair of horn-rimmed glasses with a false nose and a moustache attached, that he insisted Les wore when he drove the stooped-over Norton around for treatment. Les went along with the Groucho Marx impersonations. But he swore to Warren that as soon as he came good, he was going to buy every Marx Brothers video there was and shove them all up Warren's arse; along with a harp and a rubber horn. Les's back slowly started getting better. But both Bernie and the doctor told him to take it very easy for a while. No running and no strenuous exercise of any kind. A little swimming, breaststroking only. Yoga would be good, and long, steady walks. It was frustrating at first. But Les just took the time off from work and got used to it. Warren often joined Les on his walks and sometimes Warren's latest girlfriend, Clover, would come along too.

Clover was an attractive, well-shaped brunette with long, soft hair and soft, grey eyes that studied you from behind a pair of delicate, steel-rimmed glasses. She worked for a glassware company and lived in Dover Heights, but had moved to Sydney from a small town on the South Coast: Dalmeny. Warren met her at a wine promotion and they'd been an item ever since. Les liked Clover. She was a cheerful, outdoors girl who liked to get out on her boogie board or go snorkelling. She had a cheeky sense of humour, but good country values and always showed Les respect whenever she was in his house. Consequently, Les never had to take a dump in the sink to remind people the dishes needed doing if Clover ever stopped over at Chez Norton.

Through Clover, Les got to meet other people. One in particular was a flamboyant, young man about town, or Bondi at least — Edwin Everton. Tall and fit with a big, white smile and a square jaw, set beneath a well-groomed head of thick, dark hair, Edwin was handsome and popular, and a good surfer and tennis player. He ran a small import business, mainly T-shirts and clothes from Asia and South America, and once had a few XXL T-shirts over which he let Les have for a bottle of good bourbon. He called round the house now and again and, like most people, Les quite liked the stylish Edwin.

However, if Les got on all right with Edwin, he couldn't cop Edwin's girlfriend Serina. Serina was very good looking and super fit, with orange Astro-punk hair and cool, green eyes, that looked at you as if you were an electrical appliance on special that she was deciding whether to buy or not. Serina was into skydiving, scuba diving, rock climbing and all that thrill-seeking kind of rattle. She taught aerobics and had moved to Sydney from Narooma, a small town on the south coast. Les wished she'd piss off back down there. For some reason Serina had it in for Les, and if they all happened to be out together somewhere, like the Gull's Toriyoshi, Serina had this annoying habit of running her hair back, effecting a supercilious smile then quietly putting Les down by asking him vague questions. Which Les always answered equally as vaguely.

'There's plenty of other jobs around Les, and you own your own home. How come you still work on a door?'

'Dunno. I can't figure it out myself at times.'

'You dress reasonably well, Les. And you can run half-a-dozen words together if the wind's blowing the right way. How come you can't find a lady?'

'Dunno. It's got me buggered.'

'You seem to know a lot of people around Bondi. How come you never get invited to any good parties?'

'Dunno. I haven't got a clue.'

If Serina wasn't doing that, she was always inviting Les to jump out of a plane with her, or abseil down one of the pylons on the harbour bridge. Or go scuba diving someplace with a name like Shark Reef. Les would always politely decline the offer; although underneath he would have loved to have told Serina to go fuck herself with a broken umbrella. But for the sake of good manners Les kept his feelings to himself. Les knew Edwin felt the bad vibe. But Edwin would never tell Serina to lay off. He seemed in awe of Serina to the point of fearing her. If Serina said jump, Edwin would say how high? Les figured that despite all Edwin's machismo and style, he was more than a little pussy whipped. Serina *was* a strikingly good-looking woman, with a lot of nerve.

Although both Clover and Serina came from the same area down the south coast, they weren't close friends. But through Clover, Norton learnt something about Serina that nobody seemed aware of. At least it was never mentioned. Serina got done in WA for conspiracy to import cocaine. She'd been trawled up with a firm who all finished with big sentences. Yet somehow Serina was able to walk. She had vanished overseas for a while, now here she was in Bondi with Edwin in tow, bigger and brighter than ever.

Sadly, it was because of Edwin that Les was out walking in the afternoon. Flamboyant Edwin had unexpectedly committed suicide. There had been a church service, now all Edwin's surfing friends had just held a moving ceremony near the middle of Bondi Beach. Over eighty surfers formed a circle on their surfboards about a hundred metres out from the shore, where they scattered Edwin's ashes over the still, blue water. Les had taken his camera with him and got some nice photos; including a couple through the zoom lens of super-fit Serina in a red bikini, holding the urn.

It was a mystery to everybody why Edwin topped himself because he was a young man who appeared to have everything going for him: good looks, money, a beautiful girlfriend. What also had people talking was the bizarre way Edwin had done it. Evidently, he'd paddled out at South Bondi, wrapped a leg-rope with several lead-weights tied to it around his neck, then just slid off his surfboard. Nobody noticed until his unmistakeable surfboard with the big rainbow on the bottom started 'tombstoning' and a couple of surfers dived down and brought him to the surface. The lifeguards got Edwin to the beach in their rubber ducky where the paramedics tried to revive him. But it was too late.

After their escapade in Port Stephens, Les and Eddie thought they might have smelled a rat. Edwin's parents put on a bit of a turn at the service too, saying their son had fallen into bad company which caused his death. Les and Eddie discussed this on a couple of occasions over a beer at the refurbished North Bondi RSL. But they ended up letting it slide. Oddly enough, Les had been down the beach the day Edwin committed surfboard Hari Kari.

It was a fine Saturday morning and Les was walking round to the bogie hole at Ben Buckler to go snorkelling. He was with a diver–photographer he'd met through Warren, named Ray Bissett. Ray was a jovial, balding, Bondi boy who was also an accomplished artist and cartoonist. Les liked snorkelling around North Bondi or the bogie hole with a disposable, underwater camera, taking photos of colourful little fish or whatever was around, and one day in the bogie hole a huge, silver salmon swam right up to him. The ocean was clear and Les caught the sun shining through the water behind the fish and fluked several photos that were good enough to appear in *National Geographic*. Les had one blown up poster size and it now took pride of place on the loungeroom wall at Chez Norton. Ray had brought his camera along and this particular Saturday morning he was going to show Les some of the intricacies of underwater photography as Les was thinking of investing in an expensive camera and housing.

The water didn't look all that clear as they walked around the rocks at North Bondi. But it was calm enough. However, when they got round the front of Ben Buckler, the wind was pushing a heavy north-east swell through the bogie hole and past the point that was getting bigger and rougher all the time. After watching it for a while, Ray suggested they brush the bogie hole and just fartarse around in front of the boat sheds. Les agreed. They headed back, only to walk straight into a scene of complete pandemonium when they got to the Big Rock.

A group of scuba divers were standing around the Big Rock; some looked exhausted, others were yelling and pointing. One was screaming for help while he dragged in another scuba diver who was floating on his back. Someone jumped in the water and helped him get the unconscious diver onto the rocks. Then the first diver, an instructor, started screaming and pointing out to sea saying another diver was missing. Not realising the swell was rising, a dive school had gone out and one diver had almost drowned. Another *had* drowned and was still out there floating around on the bottom. Ray snapped off several photos as they watched, then the rubber duckies from the surf club arrived and next thing the place was swarming with paramedics, police, the police rescue squad, and before long a helicopter appeared overhead. There was nothing Ray or Les could do and it was fast turning into a complete shitfight of voyeurs, rescuers and milling scuba divers. Ray took a few more photos and they decided to leave; Les didn't bother taking his underwater camera out of the wrapper. Ray's car was parked up near the bus terminus. Les said he'd walk home; he'd give Ray a ring and they do it again when conditions were better.

Les set off along the beach thinking he'd have a quick swim on the way. By the time he reached Bondi Surf Club another helicopter was circling the point and two police boats had arrived. Then, as he got to the south end, Les was surprised to find another drama being played out on the wet sand.

A crowd had gathered next to a rubber ducky where two paramedics were frantically trying to revive someone. Les didn't stop to rubberneck. But he did have a look as he went past and got a shock to see the person in the black rashy they were trying to revive was Edwin Everton. Les couldn't help but stare for a moment or two, before he continued down to the end of the beach. He left his gear on the sand, then dived in and just floated in the shorebreak, trying to get his head around what he'd just seen; especially poor Everton, blue-faced and belly up on the beach. It was an eventful day and certainly made the evening news. And it was certainly something to talk about that night at the Kelly Club, where Les made a macabre joke about getting two deaths for the price of one.

But, that was then and this was now. Edwin was gone, Les had a sore back and life went on. Les stopped for an apple at the fruit shop next to the butcher's, then proceeded up Hall Street thinking it would be nice to get out of Bondi for a few days. No particular reason. Just a change of scene. Book into a nice resort again somewhere and lie around the pool all day drinking piss and getting his back massaged. Les finished his apple just across the road from the Hakoah Club and stopped. He might have had a rotten, sore back, but that wasn't going to stop the big, red-headed Queenslander from doing his good deed for the day.

A little old lady in a floppy, blue linen hat was trying to cross the road. A shock of white hair stuck out from under the hat and a blue cardigan was buttoned up almost to her chin over a pair of grey slacks and white bowling shoes. She could have been anywhere from ninety to a hundred and fifty, was stooped, and might have reached Norton's armpit if she was lucky. From behind a huge pair of glasses Les could read the worry on her dear old face.

'You having a bit of trouble with the traffic there, sweetheart?' said Les, ambling up alongside her.

The old dear recoiled a bit at first and clutched her handbag tighter. Then she sensed Les meant no harm. 'Yes. I have trouble seeing sometimes,' she replied. 'And the traffic frightens me.'

'Well have no fear. Big Les is here,' smiled Norton. 'Just get on my arm and we'll have you across the road in no time.'

'Oh thank you so much, young man. That would be wonderful.'

'No worries.'

The LOL took Norton's arm and they proceeded across Hall Street. Les could scarcely believe how frail and light she was. It was like a bag of air hanging on his arm. 'Where are you going?' he asked her.

'Into the club. I meet my friend Vera there every Tuesday afternoon for a nice cup of tea. And maybe a little cream cake.'

'Sounds good,' said Les.

'Vera's Polish,' said the old lady. 'She lost her husband during the war.'

'Oh. That's no good. You been friends long?'

'Over forty years.'

'Yeah? Isn't that great.' Les walked the old lady to the steps of the club and gently removed her arm. 'There you go, sweetheart. Now don't go shoving all your money through the poker machines while you're in there.'

'You needn't worry about that,' assured the old lady. 'Though sometimes on pension day, Vera and I might put a few shillings through.'

'Well, I s'pose a few "shillings" won't hurt,' smiled Les. 'Bye bye. And take care now.'

'I will. And thank you very much again, young man,' said the old lady, then entered the club.

Norton waited for the traffic and walked back across the road; he felt that good he almost burst into a run. Having all that strength and being able to help somebody so weak. Then Norton's face clouded over when he reached the footpath and thought of the low excuses for human beings that prey on old ladies like that; bashing them and taking their handbags. Les shook his head moodily. If ever he came across an old lady being mugged and caught the dirtbag doing it, the police would definitely have him up on another charge and no getting out of it. One hundred percent guilty of choking someone to death; then ripping their head off and dumping it in the nearest garbage tin. Les was wondering how many years a bleeding heart would make sure he got for that when he heard a voice to his left.

'How much did you get out of her bag, Les? Enough for a slab of piss and a couple of pies?'

Norton's eyes narrowed menacingly as he turned around to where the voice came from 'What?' he replied slowly.

Standing a couple of metres away was a lean figure, medium height with lank, dark hair falling over a pair of sunglasses perched on a lean face. The figure was wearing jeans, trainers and a black cotton jacket over a black T-shirt with SUN RECORDS on the front.

'The Zap,' Les nodded carefully. 'What are you doing in Bondi? You low life, little piece of shit.'

'Hey. That's not very nice, Les.'

'No. And neither's brassing me for two hundred dollars. You prick of a thing.'

The Zap was Frank Zammit. A part-time musician who surfed and played keyboards in various rock bands around the Eastern Suburbs. When he wasn't doing that, Frank did what a lot of other blokes from Bondi did for money. His best. Frank was about thirty and when he was younger, grew a thick moustache and a line of fuzz under his bottom lip like Frank Zappa. And with his skinny face and black hair Frank uncannily resembled the zany American musician. Naturally he got nicknamed Zappa, which soon got shortened to The Zap. A friend of Warren's once stayed at Chez Norton for a few days and ran up a fair phone bill along with the food and other incidentals. When the time came for him to leave, and in a bit of hurry, he couldn't weigh in. So he gave Warren his surfboard: a near new, DHD, Joel Parkinson signature model. Warren offered it to Les, Les didn't want it, so he sold it to Frank for two hundred dollars. The Zap absconded to Hawaii a week later. The last Les heard of Frank, The Zap had tried to move some dope on the North

Shore in the wrong territory and got a ferocious pummelling from the Black Shorts. He was lucky they didn't shoot him. Now here he was, back in Bondi and still in hock to Les for two hundred dollars.

Frank made an open-handed gesture. 'Les. That money I owed you. That was just a matter of bad timing. That's all.'

'Owed?' answered Les. '*Owe* is the word, Frank. Not fuckin owed. And talking about timing. How much time do you think it would take for me to break all your ribs down one side? Say both sides.'

'Not long, Les,' sweated Frank. 'That's for sure. But Les, I'm sorry. I really am.'

Norton shook his head and and started to take off his watch. He was only foxing, but it was fun watching Frank sweat. 'No Frank. You're not sorry. But you soon will be.' Les dropped his watch into his pocket. 'And not so much as a fuckin postcard from Hawaii either. Let alone my two hundred. That's what hurt, Frank.'

Frank took his sunglasses off and put them in his pocket also. If he was going to get some more black eyes there was no use getting his good Ray Bans smashed as well. He made a defensive gesture. 'Now hold on a minute, Les. Before you start. Maybe we can strike a deal here.'

'A deal,' echoed Les. 'I'd deal with the merchant of fuckin Venice before I'd deal with you.' Les cocked his chin. 'Nevertheless Frank. What's your deal?'

'These.' Frank whipped a manilla envelope from his jacket and handed it to Les.

Norton recoiled. 'What's this? Drugs?' His eyes narrowed. 'Frank. If you're offering me dope in a main street in Bondi in the middle of the day, fair dinkum, I'll drag you over to the Hakoah Club, run you through the nearest twenty cent poker machine, and feed you to the Jews. You greasy little turd.'

'It's not bloody dope,' said Frank. 'Read what's on the front of the envelope.'

Gingerly, Les took the envelope and read what was near the left hand corner: Great South Coast Blues Festival. He opened it and took out what looked like three movie tickets. 'Tickets?' said Les.

'Yeah,' nodded Frank, enthusiastically. 'It's a long weekend this weekend and there's a big blues, rock 'n' roll festival at Narooma. Thirty bands. Three days and nights of non-stop rock 'n' roll. Those tickets are worth over a hundred each. You like music, Les. This'd be right up ...'

Frank kept talking away, thinking the more he talked the longer it would take before Norton started raining left hooks and short rights to his scrawny head and body. On the other hand, Les was half interested and he'd forgotten it was a long weekend coming up.

'Hang on, The Zap,' interjected Les. 'Before you start getting too carried away. Are these tickets kosher?'

'One hundred and ten percent,' exclaimed Frank. 'On my delicatessen's life.'

'Yeah?' Les had another look at the tickets.

'Think on it, big Les,' said Frank. 'Pulverising me might be good in the interim. But it's not getting you your two spot back. This is a beautiful way out. And believe me, Les. Being a muso, it breaks my heart letting them go.'

Les studied the tickets for a moment or two more then slipped them into the right side pocket of his cargos. 'All right The Zap,' he said, offering his hand. 'I'll take these and we'll call it square.'

With huge beams of relief shining from every pore on Frank's face, he took Norton's hand in both of his like he was shaking hands with the Pope. He was a split second away from genuflecting. 'You're a good man, Les,' he said. 'Like I just witnessed with that poor old lady a moment ago.'

'Thank you Frank,' replied Les. 'And despite our minor differences, I've always considered you a man of principle also.' Les let go of Frank's hands. 'So what are you doing now, The Zap? Would you like a cup of coffee? I'll shout you one over at the Hakoah. Or a cool one. Name your poison.'

'Les. Your offer is more than generous. But I have to see a bloke about … about things you have to see certain blokes about.'

'I understand fully, Frank,' nodded Les. 'Well, if you're going past the Gull's Toriyoshi and I'm there, I'll shout you one.'

'Thanks Les. I look forward to it. I'll see you later.'

Les watched Frank walk off down Hall Street then continued merrily on his way home. Only a few minutes ago he'd been thinking of getting away for a few days; this could be just what the doctor ordered. Plus he owed Warren a favour. He could offer him the spare tickets. Woz might like to go and take Clover with him. She came from somewhere down there. Les arrived home, put his camera away and made a cup of tea. He took it into the lounge with a few biscuits, sat down and opened the envelope again. As well as the tickets, there was a small brochure.

Frank wasn't lying about the bands. There was a heap. Both Australian and international. Little Charlie and the Nightcats, Rusty Zinn, Dave Hole, The Blue Cats, Jeff Lang, amongst others. There were even the two bands he'd seen when he was in Cairns white water rafting. And best of all, Jo Jo Zep and The Falcons. Re-formed especially for festival. With Wilbur Wilde on sax. Shit! Grooving to the old 'Honey Dripper' would be worth the price of admission alone. Les folded the brochure and put it back in the envelope. He was going. Then something dawned on him: where the fuck was Narooma? All Les knew was that it was down the south coast. And where was he going to stay? Being a long weekend in a tourist resort, everything would probably be booked out. It'd be nice driving all that way then having to sleep in his car. That would be real good for his back. Like fuckin hell! Shifty bloody Frank. Maybe this wasn't such a good deal after all. Then the phone rang and the answering service cut in. Les placed his cup on the coffee table. 'Hello. Who the fuck's this?'

'Les. It's Warren. Are you there. Are you there, Les? Les. If you're there, pick up. Les ...'

'Yeah all right. Don't shit yourself.' Les walked over and picked up the phone. 'Yes Warren. What's up?'

'Les? Ohh thank Christ you're there.'

'For you mate, I'm always here. What's your problem?'

'Les. In my room. In the left side drawer next to the computer. See if there's a floppy disc there, will you.'

'A floppy disc. Hang on.'

Norton took the remote into Warren's room, opened the drawer and had a look through the rubber bands, biros, stapling machines, hi-liters and other odds and ends. On a spare mouse pad was a floppy disc. 'Yeah, there's one here,' he said.

'What's it say on it?'

Les had a look. 'On a piece of black it says "Verbatim". Under that "IBM Format". And under that in biro it says "NSW Tourism Promo. 2 August".'

Warren breathed a huge sigh of relief over the phone. 'Ohh thank Christ! I thought I'd lost the fuckin thing.'

'Is it important?' asked Les.

'Reckon,' said Warren. 'There's two months' work in there. It's part of a job we're doing for the NSW Department of Tourism.'

'NSW tourism,' said Les, walking back to the loungeroom and sitting down again. 'There might be a bone there for me, Woz. I've done TV commercials before. And I ain't doing nothing at the moment.'

'Les. You're a fuckin one-eyed Queenslander. Getting you to promote NSW would be like asking a Shi'ite Muslim to sell kosher wine.'

'I dunno,' said Les. 'I can soon be a cockroach if the price is right.'

'Yeah terrific. So what have you been doing today?' asked Warren, changing the subject. 'Shuffling around Bondi, like Marriane Faithfull with an axe-handle stuck up her blurter?'

'No. Not really,' sniffed Les. 'Actually, I've had quite an interesting day.' Les told Warren about the ceremony down the beach then bumping into Frank and getting the tickets for the blues festival. 'And the tickets are right here in front of me, if you're interested, Woz.'

Warren thought for a moment. 'That doesn't sound like a bad idea. Clover might like to take a run down the south coast and see her oldies.'

'Yeah. Where's she come from again?'

'Dalmeny. Just next to Narooma.'

'Right,' nodded Les absently. 'The only blue's finding somewhere to stay down there. You can bet the place'll be booked out on a long weekend.'

'That mightn't be a problem,' said Warren. 'Clover's parents own a house right in the middle of Narooma.'

'They do?' said Les. 'Yeah. But I don't fancy imposing on people.'

'No. They don't live there,' assured Warren. 'They just own it. It's a real old joint. Been in the family for years.'

'Yeah? Maybe they'll rent it out for the weekend. I'll pay the freight.'

'Leave it with me,' said Warren. 'I'll ring Clover and see what's the story.'

'Unreal,' said Les. 'That'd be the grouse if we could get a place to stay.' Les sipped the last of his tea. 'So what's doing? You going out tonight?'

'No. I'll stay home. There's some work I got to catch up on.'

'All right,' said Les. 'I'll knock up something to eat.'

'Okay. See you when I get home.'

'See you then, Woz.'

Les took his mug into the kitchen then had a look in the fridge. There was some chicken and vegetables and things not doing anything. Les started cooking a chicken stew with okra and eggplant and a pot of rice. While that was simmering he put on some music, got his rubber mat out and did some yoga exercises from a book Clover had loaned him. About the only pose he could do properly was a *Cobra*. His back may have been getting better all the time, but it was still sore and if he didn't do as Bernie and his doctor told him, he'd throw the thing out again for sure. Les did what he could then just lay there on his back listening to the stereo. Finally he got up, had a shower and changed into his blue trackies. By the time he sorted out the chicken stew over a couple of cool ones, it was dark and Warren had arrived home. Les heard him go into his bedroom then Warren walked into the kitchen, his Shooter denim shirt hanging out over his designer denim jeans.

'So what's doing, Woz?' said Les. 'Everything okay?'

'Yeah. Good as gold,' said Warren, taking a Carlton long neck from the fridge. 'I'd just forgotten where I put that floppy. That's all.'

'That's all that pot you're smoking,' said Les. 'Your memory's gone. You've got CRAFT syndrome. Can't remember a fuckin thing.'

Warren blinked at Les over his beer. 'Are you talking to me? Hello. Where am I?' He looked at his reflection in the kitchen window. 'Is that me over there? What am I doing here? Whose house is this?'

'Yeah righto,' nodded Les. 'You hungry?'

'Yeah. That smells all right too.' Warren lifted the lid off the pot. 'Chicken?'

'No. It's Alaskan musk rat.' Les sipped some beer. 'So did you ring Clover?'

'Yeah. Everything's sweet. In fact I'll ring her right now and you can talk to her yourself.' Warren went into the lounge then came out a few minutes later and handed the phone to Les.

'Clover,' said Les. 'How are you?'

'Good thanks, Les,' came Clover's cheery voice over the phone. 'Warren told me about the tickets to the blues festival.'

'Yeah. You interested?' asked Les.

'I certainly am,' replied Clover. 'Just because I drop the odd disco biscuit and hit a rave now and again, doesn't mean I don't like good, head-banging, foot-stomping rock 'n' roll, big daddy.'

'You're beautiful, Clover,' smiled Les. 'So what's doing with this house your oldies have got down there?'

'Yes. It's right in the middle of town. About two minutes walk from where they hold the festival.'

'Unreal. Can I rent it over the weekend?' asked Les.

'No. You can't rent it, Les. Sorry.'

'I can't? Ohh shit!'

'No. But you can have it for free. Until the Wednesday after the long weekend.'

Les shook his head. 'Fair dinkum, Clover. You're unreal. When are you going to piss Warren off and get with me?'

'I can't, Les. I'm hopelessly in love with him.'

'Fair enough. So what do I do? Pick the key up from a real estate agent?'

'No. Mum and Dad hardly ever rent it. It's ... it's a kind of family heirloom.'

Les shrugged. 'Okay. So what do I do?'

'You got a piece of paper and a biro?'

Les got a notepad and a biro and Clover gave him instructions. The address was 3 Browning Street. Close by was a Christian Op-Shop. Ask for Edith or Joyce. They'd give him the key. The house was empty at present. Les could move in when he liked. He just had to be out by Wednesday before some people came to steam clean the carpets.

'That sounds fantastic,' said Les, doing a little doodle above the notes and the map he'd drawn, from the instructions Clover had given him over the phone. 'Are you going to stay there too?'

'No,' replied Clover. 'I'll stay with my parents. You and Warren can have it.'

'Okay.'

'But you'll love the house, Les,' said Clover. 'It's got a great view, it's even got a piano. And it's got ... it's got charisma.'

'Sensational,' said Les. 'We can all stand round the piano singing charismasy carols.'

'Les. Give me a break.'

'Sorry Clover.'

'So how's your back?' she asked.

'Getting better. I even managed a bit more yoga this afternoon.'

'Good.'

'All right,' said Les. 'I'll put you back onto Warren. If I don't see you before, I'll see you in Narooma.'

'Okay. Bye Les.'

Les handed the phone to Warren. Warren took it back out to the loungeroom, finished his beer talking to Clover, then walked back into the kitchen.

'So have I got connections? Or have I got connections?' he asked, dropping his empty into the kitchen tidy before getting another beer from the fridge.

'You sure have, old mate,' replied Les. 'The tickets are on the coffee table. Open the envelope and check out the lineup.'

Warren got the envelope, brought it out to the kitchen and studied the brochure. 'Shit!' he said. 'There's everybody here but the Morman Tabernacle Choir.'

'They arrive on Sunday,' said Les. 'Along with the Russian Cossack dancers and Kylie Minogue. All wearing gold hot pants.' Les got another beer also. 'I'll drive down early Thursday morning and beat the traffic. So when you arrive, I'll have the house stocked with plenty of food and piss.'

Warren nodded. 'I'll get away from work as early as I can on Friday. Allowing for the traffic, and picking up Clover, we should be there by about eight or nine o'clock Friday night.'

Les rubbed his hands together with glee. 'That's about when it kicks off.' He winked at Warren. 'I reckon this could be good.'

'So do I,' nodded Warren. 'I can't wait.'

Les served up the chicken which turned out even better than he thought it would. They both stuffed themselves and talked about this and that. Then after they cleaned up, Warren had a shower and locked himself into his computer. Les propped on the lounge in front of the big screen TV he'd shouted himself with the money from Adelaide and watched a video Warren had brought home from work, *Black Hawk Down*. There was heaps of action and bombs going off, which all sounded pretty good coming through the stereo. And Eric Bana wasn't too bad as the laconic, Delta Force, all-American, superhero. But Eric's Kentucky fried, suthin' accent? Les wasn't too sure. By eleven o'clock Norton was on the nod and so was Warren. Les hit the sack looking forward to a long weekend of 'head-banging, foot-stomping' rock 'n' roll.

Les was up before Warren, wearing a blue cotton tracksuit and his new black trainers with the little plastic springs on the bottom. He had some coffee and toast then set out for a walk, leaving a cheap overnight bag with a towel in it at South Bondi. It was another lovely spring day with a light, off-shore breeze, hardly a cloud in the sky, and the morning sun sparkling on the ocean. Les followed the cliffs to Clovelly and back, pleased that his walks were getting brisker all the time. He retrieved his bag then had a swim and a shower at North Bondi, stopping for a while to talk with a couple of blokes he knew from the Cross. When Les returned home with the paper and a road map of NSW, the morning was almost over. He toasted a couple of bacon and tomato sandwiches and washed them down with a mug of tea, then decided he'd clean the car out before he started packing his gear.

Les was jangling the car keys and about to open the driverside door, when he noticed the car was due for registration on Friday. The slip from the RTA had been on his dressing table for a month and he'd forgotten all about it. He'd also forgotten the front tyres were bald and there was a small hole in the muffler. Les shook his head. And I've got the hide to bag

Warren about him losing his memory. Bugger it! Without any further to-do, Les locked the house then drove over to Chicka's garage at Bronte.

Chicka was happy to see Les; but he was flat out. He'd order the tyres and a new muffler. Les would have to leave the car and pick it up in the morning; it should be ready by nine, he said. There wasn't much Les could do except nod his head. He told Chicka he'd see him in the morning and caught a taxi home.

It was warmer now and much too good a day to be inside. Les got his banana chair, walked back down to North Bondi and propped on the sand with a book. He went for another swim then caught up with the same blokes he'd been talking to earlier and they had steak, chips and salad at the Rathouse. They followed this with a good, strong coffee at Speedos then Norton went home.

Les spent what was left of the afternoon preparing for the trip. He packed his camera, his snorkelling gear and the binoculars Eddie had given him — along with, what he imagined would be more than enough clothes, a few other odds and ends and his ghetto blaster. He also cleaned his thermos and made some ham and salad sandwiches, figuring on eating something half decent on the way down, rather than a diabetes-burger, fries and Coke. By the time Les had this organised, he'd finished two beers, the sun had gone down and he was eating last night's leftovers while he studied his road map. Narooma wasn't that far away. Four or five hours at the most. Even counting on a trip to the RTA, he should be there in time to pick up the key. He rang Price and left a message on his answering service to say where he was going and when he'd be back. Not that there was any drama at the Kelly Club. Big Danny was filling in admirably and Les could take all the time off he needed to recuperate. Les was checking what was on TV when the phone rang. It was Warren.

'Woz. What's happening old mate?' said Les.

'Not much,' replied Warren. 'I'm at Clover's. We're going to the pictures and I'll stay at her place tonight.'

'Half your luck.'

'Listen. She said if we get down there late, and you've already gone to the festival, there's a welcome mat outside the front door. Leave the key under it so I can get in.'

'Okay mate. No worries,' assured Les. 'Anything else?'

'No. Let's just hope the weather stays like it was today. Did you do anything?' Les told Warren about his day knowing exactly what his reply would be. 'Hah!' chortled Warren. 'And you've got the fuckin hide to bag me about my memory. You wally.'

'Yes. You've got me again, Warren.' Les hadn't told Warren he'd been sneaking a bit of his pot and having a little joint sometimes when he did his yoga with the stereo on. It wasn't a bad buzz. 'I apologise.'

'So you should. All right dude. We'll see you Friday night,' said Warren.

'Okay Woz. See you then.'

There wasn't a great deal on TV. Les watched some rubbish, then *Foreign Correspondent*. After that he climbed into bed with his book, *The Perfect Storm* by Sebastian Junger. All Les could think when he finally turned off the light was there had to be better ways of earning a living than fishing for swordfish off Grand Banks. Before long Les was snoring peacefully.

Les had a sleep-in the next morning. But he'd finished breakfast, changed into a pair of jeans and a T-shirt and was pulling up in a taxi outside Chicka's garage right on nine to find the mechanic putting the last wheel on his car. Les checked the two new tyres, picked up his rego sticker and green slip, paid Chicka and was soon driving out the door heading for the RTA in Bondi Junction. It was a beautiful, sunny day and Les wasn't enjoying the morning crawl along Bronte Road. He found a parking spot near the Cock 'n' Bull and walked round to the Roads and Transport Authority. The queue was surprisingly short and Les was back home attaching the new rego sticker to his windscreen before he knew it. He put his gear in the boot and placed several tapes and an overnight bag next to him. He took a last look at the house and had a quick glance at his watch, then started towards the Princes Highway. Les listened to the radio as far as Sutherland before he slipped on a tape. Seconds later, Barbara Blue was reggaeing the old Janis Joplin song, 'Piece Of My Heart', and Les was heading for the south coast.

The first tape finished and a surfboard sticking out from the roof of a hotel caught Norton's eye as he drove through Berry. He slipped another tape in and The Bellhops started rocking 'Sick and Tired'. After that it was rolling hills full of dairy cattle, with the odd winery on the right and green fields leading towards the ocean on the left. Les cruised through Nowra and Down To The Bone were cruising into 'Bridge Port Boogie' when a green dinosaur with yellow spots attracted his attention approaching the fishing port of Ulladulla. Les kept going, then pulled up before the bridge at Batemans Bay and ate his sandwiches watching the Clyde River pushing out towards the Tollgate Islands. Next came

Moruya and Bodalla and Les was thinking the countryside around the south coast looked pretty good. Red Rivers was bopping 'The Girl Likes To Rock It' and it was late afternoon, when the road wound gently down through the surrounding hills and there was the sign: NAROOMA. POPULATION 8000.

Les crossed an iron bridge over a beautiful blue lagoon that spread away to a ridge of green hills on the right. On the left it pushed against a rocky treeline and grassy sandbars before it angled round into a deep channel running towards a narrow breakwater. Over the bridge, a flat stretch of shops and garages on the right faced a long camping area and a tourist centre, then a park at the end. The park was fenced off with hessian and inside were three huge coloured tents amongst a maze of caravans, trucks and trailers swarming with workers. Behind the park was an indoor pool. Les switched the car stereo off as the highway curved to the left and climbed past several shops. The road kept rising, but down on the left a narrow street, protected from the highway by a guard rail, ran past a hotel, a Chinese restaurant, a cake shop and several other shops. The last shop, next to a vacant lot on a corner, was the op-shop where Les had to pick up the key. Les had missed the side street below and there was no way in except to go back. So he decided to keep going.

Past the vacant lot was a house almost hidden by trees, a dive shop, then the narrow street ended across from a hardware store, near Narooma's one set of lights. Amongst the shops opposite was the newsagency and post office and a large motel overlooking the town. On the left were more shops and an arcade, then an old wooden hotel on a corner. The road levelled off to the right past a camping store and a bit further on Les came to a shopping plaza, with a supermarket and bottle shop. He turned left at the plaza, and drove down past a small lagoon alongside a golf course leading to Narooma Beach. Les did a U-turn at the surf club and took a street to the right that went up to a beautiful, tree-lined golf course overlooking the ocean. Another street full of neat houses and gardens dipped down and up and brought Les back to the wooden hotel on the corner.

Driving back through the lights, the courthouse and police station were up off the main road on the left, then came a modern RSL, a small picture theatre and a garage. Traffic was light and there weren't many people around, and for all the shops doing business, Les noticed plenty with FOR LEASE signs sitting in the window. So this is Narooma, he mused, gazing down towards the lagoon. It sure looks nice. But shit! I reckon it'd get a bit quiet down here. Especially during winter. Les did a

U-turn at the garage, then swung past the first hotel into the narrow side street and pulled up outside the op-shop.

It was only small and made of plain, blue fibro, with two windows either side of the front door. On an awning above the door, a sign said: NAROOMA CHRISTIAN OPPORTUNITY SHOP. A table sat in front of each window covered with cups, teapots, salt shakers, and other odds and ends. And another sign tucked in the corner of one window said: DON'T WALK IN FRONT OF ME, I MIGHT NOT FOLLOW. DON'T WALK BEHIND ME, I MIGHT NOT LEAD. WALK BESIDE ME AND BE MY FRIEND. My sentiments exactly, mused Les, and walked inside.

Stacked around the little shop were wicker baskets full of well-worn cutlery, pots, pans, china and other items people had donated, next to racks of clothes and piles of books. Les couldn't see anyone, then he heard voices coming from behind a faded curtain drawn across a small room on the right.

'Hello. Is anybody there?' Les called out.

A few seconds later, an elderly woman, wearing a pair of cheap jeans and a blue hand-knitted top came out from behind the curtain. She had thick, grey hair and peered at Les through a pair of glasses with solid red frames.

'Can I help you, young man?' she smiled.

'Yes. I'm looking for Edith and Joyce,' said Les.

Another elderly woman appeared from behind the curtain wearing smaller glasses, and a white tracksuit. Her hair matched her tracksuit and she wore a hearing-aid in her left ear.

'I'm Edith,' said the first woman. 'And this is Joyce.'

'My name's Norton,' said Les. 'I have to pick up a key for a house in Browning Street. I'm a friend of Clover's.'

'Oh yes,' said Edith. 'The Merrigan house. Miss Merrigan rang us.'

'Yeah, that's her,' said Les. 'Clover Merrigan.'

The two old ladies smiled serenely at Les. 'We've been expecting you,' said Joyce.

Les made an open-handed gesture. 'Well here I am,' he said. 'I just got here.'

'How lovely,' said Edith. 'And how do you like Narooma, Mr Norton?'

Les looked at the woman in the red glasses for a moment. 'Hey, what can I say?' he replied. 'That bridge. They don't make bridges like that anymore.'

'No. They certainly do not,' agreed Edith.

'I'll get the key,' said Joyce.

Edith tilted her face and smiled up at Les. 'Do you know anything about the Merrigan house, Mr Norton?' she asked.

Les shook his head. 'I've got the address in the car. That's all.'

'All right then,' replied Edith. 'Well, it's just up there on the corner,' she pointed. 'Number three. A lovely old house. You can't miss it.'

'Ohh yeah,' nodded Les. 'I think I saw it as I was driving in.'

Joyce returned with a solid brass key tied to a piece of blue cord. 'There you are, Mr Norton,' she said.

Les jiggled the key up and down in his hand. 'They sure don't make keys like this anymore, either.'

'No. They certainly do not,' said Joyce.

Edith studied Les for a moment.' Are you a religious man, Mr Norton?' she asked.

'I sure am,' replied Les. 'Only the other day I was doing a bit of carpentry, and I hit my thumb with a hammer. The first thing I did, was tell Jesus Christ all about it.'

'Oh that's so nice,' beamed Edith.

Joyce studied Les too. 'He looks like a good Christian,' she said.

'Yes he does,' agreed Edith.

Les dangled the key. 'Yeah — well, I suppose I'd better get going,' he said. 'I have to unpack, and everything.'

Edith smiled up at Les. 'Do that, Mr Norton,' she said. 'And enjoy your stay in the Merrigan house. And should you need us, we're always here.'

'And the church is just up the top of the hill,' smiled Joyce.

'I'll keep it in mind,' said Les. 'Goodbye ladies.'

'Goodbye Mr Norton.'

Les turned and walked back out to the car. So that was Edith and Joyce, he mused. Friendly enough for a pair of old bible bashers, I suppose. Are you a religious man, Mr Norton? Les drove to the next corner and stopped.

Browning Street was a short, steep road running down to the water. On the other side was a big, white, weatherboard house with a green roof and a wide verandah overlooking the ocean. The foundations were covered by crisscross, wooden slats; a low, post and rail fence ran beneath the trees surrounding the front yard. There was no gate, just a gap in the fence. Les drove in and pulled up on the grass alongside the front door. He switched off the motor, then got out and had a look around.

The sloping yard was wide and green. Runners and flower beds spread colour around the house and dotted amongst the trees were healthy aloe vera plants and thick ferns. Les walked across to a wooden fence that ran past an overgrown vacant lot, to a barbecue down the side of the house. Pecking around a bush near the barbecue were a couple of magpies. They stopped for a moment to watch Les. Norton gave them a whistle then walked back to the where he'd left the car. Three thick wooden steps led up to the front door. Les worked the heavy brass key into the lock, gave it a twist and stepped inside leaving the door open behind him.

A long, wide hallway, with a bathroom on the left and a kitchen on the right, led past two bedrooms on either side to a large loungeroom with a bedroom on the right. There was a library full of old hardbacks in one corner of the loungeroom, a piano in the other and a sandstone fireplace faced a door leading out onto the verandah. The furnishings were a wooden coffee table and a tan Chesterfield that matched the burgundy carpet. Mirrors and paintings hung on the whitewashed walls along with framed, black and white photos of old Narooma. The ceilings were high and small chandeliers hung from them; a teak rail ran around the walls below the ceiling and all the doors and windowframes were edged with teak panelling. The light switches were the original brass fittings. Les opened the door and stepped out onto the verandah.

The view over the houses and the boats moored along the jetty below was absolutely spectacular. It went up to the trees and the golf links on the right, out to the breakwater, across to the hills behind the bridge and along the coast all the way to Dalmeny. There was a table and chairs in one corner of the verandah and round the other side was a second bathroom. A set of stairs led under the house; Les followed them down. Sitting on the dirt floor were several empty boxes and a stack of splintery timber next to a room with no door. Inside was a wooden wheelbarrow, some old tools and rusty tins of paint, a small pile of rusty horseshoes and some other junk covered in dust and cobwebs. Les gave everything a quick once over, then went back upstairs to check out the bedrooms.

They were all big and full of antique mahogany furniture and beds. In the back bedroom were a double and two singles; there were also two singles in the nearest bedroom along the hallway and one double in the room across from the kitchen. Les gave the last mattress a push and walked into the kitchen.

As well as an electric stove near the sink, it still had the original wood burner set into one wall. Sitting on the wooden floor in front was a solid table and four highback chairs. There was ample cupboard space, a two door fridge and a large pantry in one corner. A laundry led out to another room at the side with a red cedar table and eight matching chairs. Les walked back to the loungeroom, eased back on the Chesterfield and put his feet up on the coffee table.

The house was like a time capsule left from around the turn of the twentieth century. The only things out of place were the electric stove and the new fridge in the kitchen. So this is the Merrigan house, Les smiled to himself. Apart from being a little gloomy, it's the absolute grouse. And what about that view? Thank you Clover. Les turned to the piano in the corner and couldn't help himself. He went over and lifted the lid then clunked tunelessly up and down on the keys several times before closing the lid again. Whistling cheerfully, Norton went out to the car and brought his gear in.

Les chose the bedroom across from the kitchen; the double bed was comfortable, there were plenty of blankets in the wardrobe and a reading light sat on the dressing table. A door in the corner opened out onto the verandah and there was a window across from the bed. Les opened the window and the curtains swirled gently in the ocean breeze. He tossed his bags on the bed and unpacked.

The bathroom had been modernised a little; shiny green tiles covered the floor and walls and the shower looked new. Les put his shaving tackle in a cabinet above the sink and left a towel on the rack. In the loungeroom, a wooden mantelpiece rested beneath a mirror above the fireplace; the ghetto blaster sat there perfectly above a power point. Les tuned to a local radio station and got Graham Nash wailing 'Military Madness'. He turned the volume down and walked out onto the verandah. The sun was heading for the mountains behind the lagoon and the water in the channel looked like rippling turquoise as it wound its way in from the sea. Les stared at the view for a while then his eyes moved to his watch. He clapped his hands together and minutes later, he was in the Berlina heading for the shopping plaza.

Les hit the supermarket and stocked up on bread, milk, a barbecued chicken, mineral water, and other groceries. At the bottle shop he bought two bottles of Jack Daniels, plenty of mixed beers and a bottle of Bacardi for Clover. On the way back he stopped outside a real estate office across from the older hotel and went to the newsagency. It was quite big and well-stocked; Les got the Sydney paper and a 'What's On' around Narooma. A coffee table book — *Narooma's Glorious Past*, by Jasmine Cunneen — caught Norton's eye and he bought that too. As he placed them in the car he glanced across the road at the arcade. There was a new age clothes store and a food shop at the entrance. Les felt like some corn chips, so he walked over and bought a packet of Dorritos. While he was there he decided to have a look in the arcade.

On the right was a health food store, the other side was taken up by a second-hand shop. Les strolled in munching his Dorritos. The shop was crammed with furniture, office-chairs, electrical appliances, packets of sunglasses, plates, cups, clothes and countless other odds and ends. On the floor was a big box of dolls and sitting on a dressing table next to the box was a kooky-looking bear about the same size as a pineapple. It had a silly smile on its face, sunglasses, and a white tuxedo. Les smiled and absently poked his finger in the little bear's fat tummy. Instantly the little bear went into action, waving its arms around and shaking its head, while from a tiny speaker came Ricky Martin singing two bars of 'Livin' La Vida Loca'. The bear's actions took Les by surprise, then he started laughing at the bear and himself. The bear finished and Les poked it a second time. It didn't take much to set it off and immediately the bear went into action again; arms waving, head rolling, fingers pointing and Ricky Martin belting out 'Livin' La Vida Loca'.

Les was hooked. He finished his corn chips and called out to the owner, a thin faced man in a white shirt, sitting behind a desk near the door.

'Hey mate! How much for the bear?'

The owner knew a mug when he saw one. 'Ten bucks, mate,' he replied. 'It's from Costa Rica.'

'You got me,' said Les, fishing out a ten dollar bill. He picked up the bear and away it went again, waving its arms around, 'Livin' La Vida Loca'. Les was buggered if he could figure how to turn it off. 'Hey mate,' he pleaded, as the bear kept dancing around in his hands. 'All right if I borrow a chair and break it over this things head? I can't bloody stop it.'

'Hang on a sec,' replied the owner. He fished around under one of the bear's feet and found the switch. The bear stopped immediately. 'There you go.'

'Thanks mate,' smiled Les, feeling a little foolish. He gave the owner the ten dollars and walked back to the car.

Before long, Les had everything put away, eaten some chicken sandwiches and read the paper. The bear was sitting on the piano and Les was standing on the verandah with a cup of tea, watching some people fishing off the jetty. After four hours in the car his back was a little stiff and Les felt he could do with some exercise. There was still an hour of daylight left, and a brisk walk over the bridge to the breakwater and back would be ideal. Les tossed the last of his tea onto the dirt drive separating the Merrigan house from the houses below, got into a pair of shorts, an old T-shirt and cap and his new trainers and set off.

Les came down the hill and passed by the jetty, just in time to see a plump woman pulling in an equally plump bream. The pool was closed, but there was still plenty of movement around the trucks and trailers in the park behind. In the camping area alongside the lagoon, people were sitting outside their mobile homes enjoying an afternoon cool one; several raised their beer holders as Les strode by and he waved back. Past the camping area, the walkway rose alongside the mangroves to a footpath over the bridge. Les peered down into the water at a school of blackfish hanging around an old pier, amazed at how clear it was.

Past the bridge, the footpath curved right, down to a long boardwalk. Les followed it across the shallow end of the lagoon and beneath the tree-studded cliffs above. Apart from one or two others and a few people fishing, Les had the boardwalk to himself, before it ended at a car park and a boat ramp, near a safe beach inside the channel with a shark net across the front. A sandy trail led out to the end of the breakwater, and at Bar Beach a group of surfers were getting some hot lefts running off the granite boulders. Les watched them for a few moments in the fading light then headed for home.

When he reached the jetty Les was feeling good, so he double-timed it up the hill to the house. Yes, he smiled, as he opened the front door, my back is definitely getting better. Another week and it'll be as good as gold. And the first thing I'm going to do is have a paddle and get back on the heavy bag. Maybe have a spar with Billy. After a shower and a shave, Les put on his Levi's shorts, a white T-shirt and his blue And 1s. With a bottle of mineral water in one hand and the tourist magazine in the other, he wandered down to the loungeroom, switched the verandah light on then walked outside and sat down.

It was dark now and cool, but not cold. Les watched the coloured shipping lights blinking on and off at the entrance to the channel; the lights of a boat coming up the lagoon then started flicking absently through the magazine. Amongst the ads for riding schools, joy flights, restaurants and little maps of the Eurobodalla area was a section titled 'This Week In Narooma'. The Blues Festival was the main story. But tonight, they were having the Battle of the Bands and a fireworks display, near the golf course above the ocean. That could be all right, thought Les. And it's close to home. I may as well walk up and put my head in for a while before I hit the sack. Les finished his mineral water and looked at the empty bottle. It was quite refreshing and there was beer in the fridge. But what he really felt like was a nice draught beer — or three. There was a hotel just down the road. Les switched off the light, got some money and headed out the door.

From the house to the hotel via the op-shop was just a quick stroll. The hotel had a red brick front plastered with beer signs and was called McBride's. An entrance next to the bottle shop ran through a gaming room and via a patio on the left was another entrance through two solid glass doors. Well raise my rent, Les smiled to himself, stepping back to check things out. I'm two minutes from the pub. There's another one just up the main drag if this one's no good. Across the road is a bright, shiny 'rissole'. And the Blues Festival is five minutes away along the jetty. What did Jack Nicholson say in that movie? Maybe this is as good as it gets. Les took the side entrance to the hotel.

There was a CD jukebox and a piano on the left as you stepped inside and the bar faced the entrance across several chairs and tables. Around the walls were photos of fishing clubs and football teams and blown-up photos of old Narooma. On one wall was a glass cabinet full of Harley-Davidson memorabilia and above the entrance was a big screen TV. The bar was well-stocked and angled round to the gaming room and the other entrance. Further to the left were more chairs and tables then a bistro surrounded by blackboard menus. Another glass door led from the bistro onto a balcony with a view similar to the one from the house. There were about forty people inside. A few were standing around the bar, some were seated, others were near the bistro eating. Les stepped across to the bar and waited alongside four burly, older men on his left, wearing yellow polo shirts. He wasn't there long before a dark-haired barmaid came over and Les ordered a middy of Carlton Draught.

The four men alongside him were morose, half drunk, and arguing loudly amongst themselves. Les checked out what was written on one bloke's polo shirt: Narooma Big Rock Fishing Club. That'd be right, thought Les. I don't know a fisherman yet that hasn't got the shits about something. Especially when he's on the piss. Les was about to give them a wide berth when the barmaid placed his middy in front of him. Les paid her, then picked it up to take a sip so he wouldn't spill any before he moved. He'd just got the glass to his lips when the fisherman next to him cursed belligerently to the others, waving his arm around to emphasise the point. His arm caught Norton's and knocked most of Les's middy into his face and down the front of his T-shirt.

'Ohh take it easy will you mate,' said Les, flicking beer from his face and half-soaked T-shirt.

The bloke knew he'd done it and half turned his head. 'Get fucked,' he said

'What?' scowled Les.

'You heard. I said get fucked.' The fisherman then ignored Les and continued arguing with his mates.

Les tapped him on the shoulder. 'Hey mate. You just knocked my beer all over me. I think you could at least say you're sorry. Not tell me to get fucked.'

The fisherman turned around and pushed a miserable, fleshy face, stinking of beer and cigarettes in front of Norton's. 'Well, I'm telling you again. Get fucked. And don't poke your fingers in me, you cunt. Or I'll take your beer and shove it up your fuckin arse.'

One of the bloke's mates put his head in. 'What's up, Mick?' he said.

'Ahh this whingeing big prick reckons I spilt his beer.'

'Tell him to get fucked.'

'I just did.'

Norton's face started to turn purple. He couldn't believe it. Isn't this lovely, he fumed. I've got a bad back. I'm in town just to have a good time. And I need a fight like I need an enlarged prostate. But I'm fucked if I'm gonna cop that. With a friendly smile on his face, Les turned and tapped the bloke on the shoulder again. The fisherman turned around and scowled.

'What the fuck do you want now?' he snarled.

'Hey Mick,' said Les. 'You like fishing do you mate?'

'What?'

'I said, you like fishing, mate?' repeated Les. 'Well, hook into this.'

Les thumped his head onto the bloke's nose, smashing it across his face like a soft-boiled egg. The fisherman screwed his eyes up with pain and blood started running down his chin as Les slammed his knee into the bloke's groin then dropped an elbow into his jaw. The burly fisherman fell to the floor out cold, splitting his head open against the bar on the way down. The other three looked at Mick lying on the floor for a second, then came at Les swinging. Les blocked their punches then stepped in and nailed the one on his left with a straight left, breaking the bloke's nose. Les hooked off the straight left into the next bloke's face, splitting his cheekbone open like a ripe plum. Then Les set himself and slammed a murderous, short right into the last bloke's face, pulverising his mouth and knocking out his front teeth. The bloke's legs folded like a card table and he slumped on his backside next to the first fisherman. The two left standing were still wondering what was going on, when Les kicked the one on the left in the knee. The bloke screamed, tottered for a second then dropped to the floor, clutching his leg. This left the last member of the Narooma Big Rock Fishing Club groggily holding onto the bar with one hand trying to stay on his feet. Les palm-heeled him under the jaw and the fisherman went flying across the chairs and tables, knocking drinks everywhere, finishing up sprawled out on his back in front of the jukebox.

The whole thing didn't take a minute. But it was long enough for any women in the place to start screaming blue murder. Les took a quick look at the four blokes lying all over the floor, oozing blood everywhere, and figured it was time for a bit of travelling music. He put his head down and hurried out the same way he came in. When Les got to the bottle shop he started to run. Then he stopped and cursed out loud.

'Ohh shit! My fuckin back.'

Walking briskly, Les got to the house as fast as he could. He couldn't see anybody following him, so he opened the front door and switched on the light. He shut the door behind him then walked down to the loungeroom and moved gingerly around. He hadn't thrown his back out again. But he'd aggravated it. Bugger it, thought Les angrily. Just what I need. Les circled the loungeroom a few times, rubbed at his back then took his beer soaked T-shirt off and tossed it in the shower. He cleaned himself up, put on a dark blue T-shirt then got a bottle of beer from the fridge and went back to the loungeroom. He had a swallow and turned on the stereo. The radio station was playing The Eagles' — 'Peaceful Easy Feeling'. Yeah. That'd be right, thought Les. Rubbing at his back again, he took his beer out onto the verandah.

Les had another swallow and stared balefully at the harbour lights then up at the stars. I've deadset got a pumpkin for a head, he told himself. I could have walked away and copped it sweet. Or at worst, just given that old mug a backhander. But no. I had to flatten him. And everybody else. Now, as well as stuffing up my back, you can bet the cops'll be looking for me. Shit! Les drank some more beer. Maybe I ought to piss off while I'm in front. Les stared into the night and thought about it for a moment. No, fuck it, he told himself. I'm here now. And this house is too good. And after the trouble Clover went to, she'd think I was a nice idiot. He had another, thoughtful sip of beer. No. I'll just keep my head down and stay away from that one pub. Then blend in with the crowd when it gets here on the weekend. If anyone does say anything, I'll just say it wasn't me. Les looked into his bottle. Sounds all right in theory. Norton finished his beer and belched. Anyway, bugger it! I'm going to see the battle of the bands. He turned for the loungeroom, winced and shook his head. Serves me right for being a mug, he told himself as he stepped inside. Les put his cap on, pulled it down over his eyes, then got his camera and headed out the door.

Going right at the bottom of Browning Street it didn't take long to climb the hill to the golf course and Les felt the walk was doing his back good. He was convinced the worst thing he could do would be to lie down and let it stiffen up. When he got to the top and went past the clubhouse, Les was surprised at the crowd. There were thousands. Mostly parents with kids or young people between twelve and eighteen. The event was being held in a reserve alongside the golf course. Les walked through a parking area then followed a dirt drive that separated the reserve from the trees, and blended in with the crowd. Next thing a band started up.

Across from the trees on the other side of the crowd was an outdoor stage. On it, four young girls in hipsters and T-shirts were belting out some kind of grunge rock. The words were totally indecipherable and they possibly knew three chords between them; the drummer sounded like she'd just got her drum kit that afternoon. But they were up there going for it, and what they lacked in talent, they more then made up for with enthusiasm. Les took his camera out and eased his way through the crowd. When he got closer to the stage, Les aimed his camera and took a couple of photos.

The band stopped and took a bow then began to move off stage. From somewhere an announcer said that was Murdering Mary's last song, give them a big hand and next up was Frenergetic; to be followed by the fireworks. Les moved back from the stage and watched as four skinny young blokes all in black got up, gave their guitars a quick tune then attacked some song they'd written, racing each other like crazy to see who could finish first. Les took a photo and gave the race to the bass player with blue hair. Frenergetic galloped their way through another song and that was it. Apparently because of a heavy lineup and the fireworks display, each band was only allowed two songs. From what Les had heard so far, that was plenty. He moved to the back of the crowd and was lucky enough to find a milk crate near the trees. He sat down, rubbed the sore spot in his back and watched some kids running around like wild things, waving luminous, plastic tubes in the air. Les was wishing he'd brought a few beers with him when the announcer said it was time for the fireworks. The technicians were positioned between the reserve and the clubhouse and, as soon as the announcer stopped, a star shell exploded over the trees with a loud, whistling bang and a huge shower of pink and green.

For a small country town, Les was surprised at the fireworks display. It was quite spectacular and seemed to last forever. Great bursts of red star clusters and showers of gold and blue exploded into the night then rained down from the sky. Les had a great view and sat back and was enjoying it immensely. He tried for a couple of photos and smiled to himself as he watched a trail of bursting silver climb into the night. I know what would go well now, he thought. Some of Woz's pot. Wouldn't that put some colour into the fireworks? Finally, the fireworks finished with one last spectacular explosion that brought a great roar of approval and applause from the crowd. The announcer said that was it and now it was back to the battle of the bands. Next up was Cybertronical Biped. I think that might be enough for me, thought Les, as another band got up and blasted away into the night. He left his milk crate and drifted off with some of the crowd who'd also seen enough.

Les walked back to the road going past the clubhouse and paused. To the right was home, bed and safety. But Norton was still stubbornly determined to have a draught beer. There was a street to the left and if Les wasn't mistaken it was the one that took him into town earlier. Les followed it down then up and, sure enough, just ahead was the main drag and the old wooden hotel on the corner.

The hotel had a restaurant at the back and Les noticed several punters through the windows before he turned the corner. There was an entrance round the corner off the main road, windows faced the street, and at the end another door led into a gaming area. The usual beer ads covered the blue, timber front of the hotel and above was an enclosed verandah and a sign in white: LAWSON'S HOTEL. The old pub seemed to have a nice feel about it, so Les pushed open the door and walked in.

Part of the bar angled round to the restaurant, the rest faced the windows and ran down to a makeshift stage at the end. Lights and fans hung from the ceiling and the wood-panelled walls were covered in old photos and framed newspaper clippings. Two attractive girls were working the bar; one wore a white top and had black hair with a flower in it, the other wore a mauve floral top and had brown hair. Behind them, two older men in white shirts and plain trousers were looking at the till. A duo between songs was standing in front of two microphones and a pair of speakers at the far end of the bar. A brown-haired bloke in a red check shirt and holding a guitar was on the left, next to a dark-haired bloke in all black on the right. About a dozen casually dressed people were seated or standing around the bar drinking and laughing. The smoke wasn't too punishing and Les couldn't see anybody looking for a fight, so he took a stool near the corner of the bar, facing down to the duo. He put his camera on the placemat and ordered a middy of Tooheys from the barmaid with the flower in her hair. The beer was cold and delicious and just what Les had been looking for. Then the guitar player hit a few notes, the drum machine kicked in and the singer in black started warbling 'Teddy Bear'. And the duo wasn't real bad.

Les sipped his beer and ran his eyes around the bar. He was still a bit edgy, but no one paid him any mind. Two blokes wearing polo shirts walked in and Les stiffened as they looked at him. But it was no more than a cursory glance before they went to the bar and got into a shout. Les finished his middy about the same time as the duo finished 'Teddy Bear' and started into 'It's Not Unusual'. Les ordered another middy, with a Jack Daniels and ice on the side for a buzz, and found himself tapping his foot to the music. The duo played 'Eagle Rock' and a few punters got up and started dancing; including one of the men who'd been standing at the till and the barmaid in the mauve top. Les got his camera, walked down and took a few photos. He sat down again and ordered another beer and a JD and ice.

Les was about to take a photo of the barmaid with the flower in her hair when he noticed a woman standing next to him. She had a lean, attractive face with no makeup, inquisitive, hazel eyes and long brown hair parted in the middle. A thick, beige shirt hung over a blue T-shirt getting pushed out by a healthy bust, and the T-shirt hung out over a denim dress, with splits in the side tied by leather laces. Handpainted across her T-shirt were little orange and yellow birds. Les put her age at no more than thirty and figured she was some kind of hippy. He quietly sipped his beer and avoided eye contact.

'Did you get any good photos?' she asked.

'Yeah. I think so,' replied Les, a little indifferently.

'Am I in them?'

'Possibly,' Les gave her a sideways glance. 'Were you up dancing?'

'Yes,' nodded the woman.

'Then I could have got one of you.'

'I'd like a copy. If that's all right?'

Les shrugged. 'Well, I haven't finished the roll of film yet.'

'Are you from around here?' asked the woman.

Les shook his head. 'Canberra. I just got here.'

'Oh? Where are you staying?'

Les started getting suspicious. 'At that big motel near the post office.'

'The Islander.'

'That's it,' nodded Les.

'Are you down for the Blues Festival?' Les nodded. 'Maybe you could leave it at the desk for me?'

'Sure,' said Les.

The woman smiled. 'I'm Grace.'

'George,' replied Les, politely but not over friendly.

Grace stood there a moment. 'Okay George. I might see you again before the night's over.'

'Yeah. Okay.'

Les went back to his beer and watched Grace walk off to join some people near the other end of the bar. She had a shapely behind and her hair bobbed silk-like across her shoulders when she walked. What a bummer, thought Les. Grace isn't a bad sort. If I was a little more friendly, I might have been half a chance there. But after what happened tonight, I don't know. A little town like this, she could be a friend of a friend or something and saw the fight. She might even be a cop. Who knows?

The band finished a fair version of 'I Saw Her Standing There' and took a break. Les ordered another beer and a JD and was starting to get a bit of a glow on. He still didn't drop his guard and kept an eye on the door. But the night was turning out to be all right. Even his back felt better. He took a sip of JD and looked up as a lean, wiry bloke, with a lived-in face, and untidy black hair going a little grey at the sides, walked in the door on his own. He was wearing a black T-shirt with Blondie on the front, a pair of grease-stained, black jeans and scruffy, black gym boots. The bloke nodded to Grace and her friends and the two girls behind the bar then walked round and took a stool near Les. The barmaid with the floral top came over and the bloke exchanged a smile and a few words with her, before ordering a can of VB. He took a long, enjoyable pull on his can of beer when it arrived, then belched into his hand and turned absently to Les. The bloke turned away and looked curiously at his beer for a moment then turned back and stared at Les with an odd, half smile on his face. Les picked up the vibe. It was a look of knowing admiration. The exact look a punter would give some stranger he'd just seen flatten four blokes. Fuck it, Les cursed to himself. I've been sprung. Les ignored the bloke in the Blondie T-shirt, but he could feel his eyes on him. Finally the bloke leant over.

'Hey mate,' he said. 'I know your face.'

Les shook his head. 'I doubt it, me old,' he answered quietly.' I'm not from round this way. And I only just got here.'

'Yeah, fair enough,' the bloke nodded slowly, continuing to stare at Les. 'You're from Sydney but, aren't you?'

'Why? What makes you say that?' shrugged Les.

'I'm a chef,' answered the bloke. 'A couple of years ago I was working in a restaurant in Paddington called Forty Four. One of the waitresses didn't turn up so I had to help on the tables. You were there with another bloke and two real good sorts. And you left a five hundred dollar tip.'

Les thought for a moment then remembered the night. He was with a notorious drug dealer known as Mullets. Mullets had run out of money one night at the Kelly Club and Les had loaned him a couple of hundred dollars. Which Mullets managed to turn into fifty thousand. Mullets repaid the loan: plus. Then lined up two glamours and shouted Les to dinner at Fourty Four. One reason Les had left the five hundred dollar tip was because Mullets was trying to act low key so he gave Les the cash to pay for the night out. The second reason was that the waitress was absolutely hopeless. She tried her heart out to please them. However, the harder she tried, the more she stuffed things up. But in a crazy, bumbling way. It was like something out of a movie and she had them in stitches all night. So Les left five hundred extra of Mullets' ill-gotten gains on the table. The girl thought he'd made a mistake and chased them up the street. When Les told her no, that was all right, he was just so impressed with her service, the poor girl burst into tears.

Les looked at the bloke and shook his head. 'Well, that proves it definitely wasn't me, mate. Because I wouldn't leave a five hundred dollar tip, if it was to save my life.'

The bloke smiled and nodded his head. 'All right. But I know I've seen the other bloke's face somewhere.'

You're not wrong there pal, thought Les. Mullets got banged up over a huge shipment and was still on remand in Long Bay. It had been all over the news. Nevertheless, the bloke seemed friendly enough and he hadn't lamped Les from the fight at the hotel. Plus he was spot on with his assumptions.

'So you're a chef are you, mate?' enquired Les.

'That's right,' said the bloke, getting into his beer. 'I work at the other pub down the road. McBride's. I just knocked off.'

'Oh?' said Les. 'I've never been in there. What's it like?'

'All right. I help run the bistro. The food's really good. And I'm not just saying that because I work there.'

Les nodded and had a mouthful of beer. 'Fair enough. I'll have to come down and put my head in.'

'Do that,' said the bloke. 'I'll look after you.' He swallowed some beer and laughed to himself. 'It's a good thing you didn't put your head in tonight though.'

'Oh?' replied Les. 'Why's that?'

'There was an unbelievable fight in the bar.'

'A blue? In a quiet town like this,' Les raised his eyebrows. 'What happened?'

'Four fisherman picked a fight with some bloke and he absolutely creamed them. I came round just after it happened and had to help clean up the blood. It was everywhere.'

'Fair dinkum?' Les looked shocked. 'Who was the bloke? A local?'

The chef shook his head. 'One of the barmaids saw him. Said he was tall and skinny. With brown hair and tattoos.'

'That sounds like a pretty good description,' said Les. 'And did the police come?'

The chef laughed out loud. 'Not for those blokes. It was probably a cop that done it.'

'Yeah?' Norton's eyes lit up. 'What makes you say that?'

'One of the blokes that got belted was Mick Scully. He's a real old thug. Him and his nephew Morgan just about run the place. They even bashed some cops down at Bermagui. Everybody knows it was them. But no one could ever prove it.'

'Fair dinkum?' said Les. 'He sounds like a nasty piece of goods this bloke — what did you say his name was?'

'Scully. Mick Scully.' The chef looked pensive for a moment. 'It would have been a different story though, if Morgan had of been there.'

'Yeah? Why's that?' enquired Les.

The chef made a dismissive gesture. 'When it comes to fighting, Morgan'd beat anyone. He's unbelievable. Him and his uncle have got half the south coast terrorised. Actually, we were all having a bit of a laugh when Mick copped it.'

'Go on,' smiled Les.

The bloke finished his can of VB. 'I wouldn't like to be the bloke though, if Morgan gets hold of him.'

Les shrugged. 'How's he going to find him?' he asked.

The chef shook his head. 'I doubt he will. If the bloke knows what's good for him, he'll have pissed off out of town by now.'

Les looked serious. 'From what you just told me, mate,' he said, 'I can't say I blame him.'

'No,' agreed the bloke.

A warm glow started to spread though Norton, and it wasn't from the Jack Daniels. Suddenly, wonderfully, a whole new vibe had come over the night. There was no heat from the local police. And instead of belting a bunch of drunken fisherman, Les had been right all the time. That bloke in the hotel had mug and bully written all over him. Norton had galloped into town on his white horse, and done a Clint Eastwood. Bad luck about his back. But he preferred that to an assault charge. As for this nephew Morgan, he'd be running around looking for some skinny bloke with tattoos. Norton had done it again.

'So what's your name, anyway, mate?' asked Les.

'Olney.'

'I'm Les, Olney.' Les shook the chef's hand. 'And I've got a confession to make.'

'Yeah? What's that Les?' asked the chef.

'That was me in the restaurant that night, left the five hundred dollars on the table.'

Olney's face lit up. 'I thought it was.'

'It's just that the bloke I was with that night ...'

Olney nodded. 'I know. I saw him on TV.'

'Yeah, well I'm not in the same caper. I help run a small security business in the eastern suburbs.'

'Fair enough Les,' said the chef.

Les patted the chef on the shoulder. 'Anyway Olney, since you caught me out telling porkies, how about letting me buy you a drink. What do you want? Anything.'

Olney looked at his empty can then at Les. 'One of these. With a bourbon chaser?'

'A man after my own heart. And we'll make the bourbon a double.' Les looked seriously at the chef. 'Are you driving?'

Olney shook his head. 'No. I only live up the road.'

'Well, let's make it a triple.'

Les bought the drinks and he and Olney toasted food in general, then Les explained how he was down for the Blues Festival. Olney came from Narooma. But he went to Sydney when work got scarce. He didn't mind working in the city and he managed to save some money. Now he was working at the hotel and hoping to open a place of his own one day. Les noticed Grace checking them out, laughing and having a good time. Les caught her eye, smiled and beckoned her over. She picked her drink up from the bar and came round.

'Grace,' said Les. 'This is my friend Olney.'

'We know each other,' said Olney. 'How's it going Amazing?'

'Amazing?' said Les.

'That's what they call me, George,' said Grace.

Les smiled at her. 'Grace. I have to be honest. When you came over before I was bullshitting you a bit. My name's not George. It's Les.'

'Oh?' said Grace.

'And I don't come from Canberra. I come from Sydney.'

'I had an idea you weren't quite telling the truth,' said Grace.

'Yeah,' confessed Les. 'It's just that I used to take this girl out in Sydney. And you reminded me of one of her friends. We had a bit of a messy breakup. And I thought you'd come over to punish me about it. I'm sorry.'

'That's all right,' said Grace. 'I can be a little forward at times.'

Les looked at the little birds getting pushed out by Grace's ample breasts. But he decided against being smart. 'Also, I'm not staying at the motel. I'm just down the road in Browning Street.'

'Seaview flats?' said Grace.

'No, the big house on the corner.'

Grace raised her eyebrows. 'The Merrigan house?'

'That's the one,' nodded Les.

'Are you staying at the Merrigan house?' said Olney.

'That's right,' said Les. 'The old white joint. It's the grouse.'

'Who are you staying there with?' asked Grace.

'I'm on my own at the moment,' replied Les. 'But my flatmate's joining me tomorrow. His girlfriend's parents own it.'

'And you're on your own there at the moment?' said Grace.

'Till tomorrow. He's going back on Monday. And I'm there till Wednesday.'

'Lucky you,' said Olney.

'Yeah.' Les looked up at Grace. 'Have you ever been inside the house.'

Grace shook her head. 'No. But I'd love to.'

'Okay,' smiled Les. 'Maybe when the hotel closes you can walk me home. Have a cup of coffee or something,' he suggested 'You live far away?'

'Central Tilba.'

'Where's that?'

'About twenty minutes south of here,' replied Grace. 'But I'm staying just over the bridge tonight. Near Bar Beach.'

'Ohh yeah,' said Les. 'I know where Bar Beach is. I walked round there this afternoon.'

'I won't come tonight,' said Grace. 'I'm going home with Julie.' She nodded to the barmaid in the floral top. 'But will you be home tomorrow?'

'Sure,' nodded Les.

'How about I come round in the morning?'

'Okay,' said Les. 'Why don't you make it about nine or so? I'll do my Denise Austin workout early. Then we might have breakfast somewhere.'

'If you're gonna have breakfast,' said Olney, 'go to Carey's.'

'Where's that?' asked Les.

'Just over the road. The red and yellow place.'

'I know it,' said Les. 'I drove past this arvo. That sound all right to you, Grace?'

'Yes,' replied Grace. 'That would be lovely. Thank you.'

'Righto. That's breakfast organised.' Les had a mouthful of beer and picked up his camera. 'Now. How about another a photo? Grace, hop in there next to Olney. Olney, give us your best smile.'

Les took a couple of photos, then got the barmaid with the flower in her hair to take a photo of the three of them. After that the night went swimmingly. Grace was drinking vodka, lime and soda. Les pointed to the money on the bar and said the drinks were on him. The duo got up and slipped into 'Big Girls Don't Cry' and soon had the small crowd dancing and singing. Grace even got a reluctant Les up for a dance. Grace was a bit of a hoofer with a few vodkas under her belt. She shook her boobs and shimmied and showed what the Good Lord gave her. Les with his back, however, shuffled around pretty much as Warren had described him. Like Marianne Faithfull with an axe handle stuck in her date. Olney was a surprise packet. The duo bopped into 'Roll Over Beethoven' and when he got up with the blonde barmaid Olney jived like a hep cat in an old Bill Haley movie. Before long the night was over. The duo finished with 'CC Rider'. Les got another photo taken as they finished their drinks and it was time to go. Les was a shot bird anyway.

'Okay Grace,' he slurred. 'I'll see you tomorrow morning.'

'All right Les. See you then,' she smiled. 'And don't forget your camera.'

'Yeah, right,' Les retrieved it from the bar. 'Olney, I'll see you next time I'm looking at you, mate,' he said.

'See you then, Les,' answered Olney. 'Thanks for the drinks.'

'No worries. G'night.' Les stepped out the door and swung into the street.

After the warmth of the hotel it was quite cool outside and a light breeze coming off the sea hit Les in the face. There were no cars and nobody about. He pulled his cap down, jammed his hands in his pockets and headed down the hill. Les started moving along to keep warm and could feel a painful twinge in his back. Shit, he thought, I wish I hadn't let Grace drag me up on the dancefloor. And why did they have to play 'Let's Twist Again'? Les was still contemplating this as he turned the old brass key in the front door a few minutes later.

The first thing Les did was hit the bathroom, then the kitchen for a tall glass of mineral water. He poured another one and walked into the lounge room. I should watch TV for a while, he smiled. But they didn't have TV at the turn of the century, did they. He decided against putting some music on and took his glass out onto the verandah.

Les drank some more water and felt his head spinning. Bloody hell! Didn't I get myself nice and pissed, he told himself. Thank Christ the pub closed at twelve. But why wouldn't you? What a great result. Everything's sweet. And breakfast with that girl tomorrow. Les stared happily up at the stars and noticed the difference after the air around Sydney. They were everywhere. He'd just started enjoying their brilliance, when one zipped across the night sky. As well as being clear, however, the night was cool; especially in a T-shirt and shorts. Les yawned and looked at his watch. Well, if I'm getting up for a walk and breakfast by nine, I suppose I'd better hit the sack. He finished his mineral water and went inside.

After cleaning his teeth, Les changed into a clean T-shirt and climbed into bed. He turned off the dressing table lamp and scrunched his head into the pillows. The old double bed was roomy, he had plenty of blankets and through the window Les could hear the sea. The big Queenslander was literally as snug as a bug. He was almost asleep and vaguely thinking about Warren and Clover arriving when suddenly it was as if the room had turned into a freezer. A dense, clammy cold settled over the bed and Les felt an icy chill run up his back that made the hairs on his neck stand on end. Holy shit, he thought, pulling the blankets tighter around him. I expected the south coast to be a bit colder than Sydney. But not like fuckin Antarctica. Les rolled himself into a ball and pulled the blankets around him even tighter. But there was no way he could get warm. Ohh bugger this, Les grumbled to himself.

With his teeth chattering like castanets, Les turned on the bed lamp then got up and banged the window closed. Shivering and puffing clouds of steam through the half-lit room, he put on his tracksuit and a pair of socks, then got another blanket out of the wardrobe and spread it over the bed. Trying to rub some warmth into his arms, Les got back under the covers and turned off the light. After a couple of minutes he settled down and started to warm up. Ahh yes, he sighed, contentedly. That's a bit more like it.

With the window closed the room was silent now. Les was almost asleep, when from far away he heard Ricky Martin singing 'Livin' La Vida Loca'. Les half-opened one eye. What the fuck? Ricky Martin kept singing in the distance. It's that fuckin bear, cursed Les silently. I thought I switched the bloody thing off when I put it on the piano. Ricky Martin stopped. Then he started up again. Stupid prick of a thing. I knew there was something wrong with it when I bought it. Les pulled the blankets around him. I'm buggered if I'm getting out of bed though. It's too fuckin cold. But tomorrow, the batteries are coming out. Ricky Martin stopped and Les dozed off.

Les was only asleep for a short while when another noise woke him. This time someone was playing the piano. Not a tune. Just inane clunking like Les had done earlier, only softer. Les half woke up and listened for a moment. The piano stopped. Then it started up again. Les shook his head and shoved it into the pillows. It's all the piss I drank. I'm hearing things. But I couldn't really give a shit if Jerry Lee Lewis was out there playing 'Great Balls of Fire'. There's no way I'm getting up. The piano playing stopped. If it started again Les couldn't tell. He fell straight into a deep, drunken, snoring sleep.

Les woke up the next morning feeling seedy. A knot of pain in his back told him where he was and why he was hungover. He yawned and scratched, then got into a pair of shorts and opened the bedroom window. Outside, it didn't look like too bad a day. He plodded into the bathroom, freshened up, then walked across to the kitchen.

'What the fuck?'

Something had been in there during the night. Lying under the table was a packet of wheatmeal biscuits, the loaf of bread, tea-bags, and a few other things out of the cupboard, along with some cutlery and a broken cup.

Les put his hands on his hips. 'Hello. Looks like the Merrigan house has got rats.'

Les walked across to the pantry. Sitting on a shelf amongst the other odds and ends were two old wooden rat-traps. I thought so, nodded Les, picking one up. Well, I'll be setting you tonight. Something suddenly jogged Norton's memory. That's what was running around on the bloody piano last night. Jerry Lee Rat. Okay Jerry Lee, smiled Les. See how you like tickling the ivories with a broken neck. And when you're lying there all bruised and broken rat, don't, I say don't, expect uncle Les to give you any mouse to mouse resuscitation ...

Les replaced the rat-trap then switched on the jug and dropped two slices of bread in the toaster. While he was waiting Les cleaned up the mess. He noticed the rat hadn't broken open the packet of biscuits. So you don't like Shredded Wheatmeal, Jerry. See if you like sinking your teeth into a nice piece of tasty cheese — tied to the trap with cotton. Les made a mug of tea, buttered the toast and walked out to the loungeroom. The bear was sitting on the piano facing the wall. Les placed his mug on the piano and turned the bear round the way he'd left it.

'Go on. Start singing now, you fat bastard,' he said.

Nothing happened. Les pushed the bear in the stomach then lifted up its leg.

It was switched off. Les switched it on and immediately the bear went into action; head nodding, arms waving, singing Ricky Martin.

Les shook his head. 'You've got a mind of your own, haven't you. You little shit.'

Les switched the bear off and left it on the piano. He changed his mind about removing the batteries and took his tea and toast out onto the verandah.

Despite a light southerly blowing, it looked like being a delightful spring day. A band of clouds stretched across the horizon and the sun was sparkling on the harbour. The tide was rapidly pushing in through the channel and a charter boat with a half-dozen people on board was backing out from the jetty. People were fishing and a couple of kids were paddling around on skis. That's what I'd like to be doing right now, thought Les. Having a paddle on that big, blue lagoon. He gingerly bent down and tried to touch his toes. Yeah. Bad luck about that. Les finished his tea and toast and looked at his watch. Well, I suppose I'd better make a move if I'm going for breakfast. The breeze was flicking at the trees above the hill. Les decided to walk up to the golf links and follow the cliffs. He got into his training gear, pulled an old cap down over his sunglasses and set off, locking the front door behind him.

The clubhouse looked bigger in the daytime, when Les reached the top of the hill and golfers were teeing off on the fairways or whizzing around the greens in golf buggies. Watching out for golf balls, Les strode off across the greens in the cool fresh air. The grass felt soft beneath his feet, and the morning dew seeped into his trainers. Les would have loved to have ripped into a good, hard run. But he strode steadily along telling himself how much good the walk was doing his back. He found a path behind the trees and followed it along the cliffs. Out to sea Les noticed a long, flat, rocky island with a lighthouse on it. That must be Montague he surmised. I may as well take a trip out while I'm down here and do a bit of snorkel sucking. I imagine the water'd be clear and there's supposed to be a big seal colony out there. Les followed the cliffs as far as Narooma Beach and stopped.

The view up and down the coast was spectacular. The morning sun sparkled on the water as tiny clouds drifted across the sky, and solitary seabirds hovered lazily above the ocean, taking advantage of the on-shore breeze ruffling the surface. Below the cliffs, fishermen were scattered along the water's edge or around clusters of tall rocks thrusting out of the sand like huge stone fingers. Les saw a flash of silver as one fisherman pulled in what could have been a nice tailor, watched him carry his wriggling catch up to a bucket then headed home. When he got back to the house, an old, box-shaped, maroon Jackaroo, with a WILDERNESS NOT WOODCHIPS sticker on the rear window, was parked behind his Berlina. Grace was bent over in the yard examining an aloe vera plant, and in a pair of tight jeans and a short-sleeved purple shirt, the view from behind was even better than the one from the golf links. Les waited a moment or two before he called out.

'You looking for something, mate?'

Grace stood up carrying a camera in one hand and turned around. 'Hullo Les,' she smiled. 'How are you this morning?'

Les returned her smile. 'A bit seedy from last night. But I'm getting there.'

'Have you been for a jog?'

Les shook his head. 'A walk. I went around the golf links.'

'Isn't it a lovely view from up there?'

'Yeah, fantastic.' Les took his sunglasses off and wiped some sweat from his eyes. 'You been here long?'

'Not long,' replied Grace. 'I've been looking around the yard. All right if I take a few pieces of aloe vera?'

'Help yourself.' Les took the key from his pocket and motioned to the door. 'Come inside and have a look at the house.' He opened the door and ushered Grace through.

Grace entered the old house, then stopped in the hallway and gazed around. 'Oh yes,' she said. 'This is even better than I imagined.'

'It's something else, isn't it,' agreed Les, shutting the door. 'Anyway, why don't you take a look around while I have a shower. There's coffee and that in the kitchen.'

'Okay.' Grace held up her camera. 'All right if I take a few photos?'

'Go for your life,' answered Les.

Les left Grace with her camera and got under the shower. He rinsed his training gear and the beer-sodden T-shirt, towelled off then put on his shorts and a green polo shirt with a denim collar. He got a bottle of mineral water from the fridge, then took his washing out onto the verandah and hung it on the line. Grace was round the other side. She heard Les and came around.

'This view,' said Grace. 'It is absolutely beautiful.'

'It's tops, isn't it,' said Les, taking a drink of water.

'In fact this whole house is fantastic,' said Grace. 'I just love the old piano in the corner and the library. Did you know some of those books are a hundred years old?'

'Yeah?' said Les. 'I hadn't noticed.'

'I got some great photos.' Grace smiled at Les. 'What about the bear? Where did that come from?'

'I bought it at the second-hand shop in the arcade. Have a look at this.'

Les took Grace into the loungeroom and switched the bear on. Grace started laughing as it went into action and took a photo.

'That thing is so cute,' she said.

'Yes,' agreed Les. 'He's certainly got a style all of his own.'

Les switched the bear off and they went back out on the verandah. Grace leant against the railing watching Les and gave him an angled, once up and down.

'So how did you sleep last night, Les?' she asked.

'Sleep?' replied Norton. 'If you'll excuse the expression Grace, I was that drunk last night, I would have slept under a horse pissing.'

'Okay,' said Grace.

'But Christ, it sure gets cold night down here at night.'

'Cold?' said Grace. 'How do you mean — cold?'

'I mean, bloody cold,' answered Les. 'Like Siberia. I had to get up and put my tracksuit on, and throw another blanket on the bed. I was freezing.'

'Where was it cold?' asked Grace.

'In the bedroom,' said Les. 'I closed the window and it was okay.'

'And you slept all right after that?'

'Like a top,' said Les, thinking it best not to tell Grace about the rat. 'Until I woke up this morning. Me and my hangover.'

'Okay.' Grace smiled and continued to watch as Les drank his mineral water. 'Do you know anything about this house, Les?' she asked.

Les shook his head. 'No. Only that it belong's to Clover's parents.'

'It used to be the old government surveyor's hut.'

'This was a surveyor's hut?' said Les. 'Not a bad hut.'

'What I really meant was,' said Grace, 'the government surveyor, Edward Ruddle. His original slab hut used to stand here. In those days there wasn't much down here but rainforest. Then the Merrigans built the house.'

'They sure picked a good spot,' said Les. He turned from the view to Grace. 'So who were the Merrigans? What happened to them?'

'Lander Merrigan owned a sawmill. He and his wife Hildreth drowned when their sulky got swept away during a flood.'

'They got drowned? Oh. What a bummer.' Les ran his eyes around the verandah. 'I suppose having a house like this, they would have left about twenty little orphaned Merrigans too.'

Grace shook her head. 'No. Only one. A son. Eachan. He lived here on his own — before he went insane, and died in a mental hospital.'

'Christ!' said Les. 'The Merrigans sure had a lot of luck — didn't they?'

Grace looked at Les for a moment. 'Have you ever heard of a place called Mystery Bay, Les?'

Les indicated his 'What's On' still sitting on the table. 'I think I saw it on a map. Is it further down the coast a bit?'

'That's it,' said Grace. 'On the way to where I live. Edward Ruddle disappeared there early in the nineteenth century. Along with three other men.'

'Disappeared?' Les found himself interested. 'What? Nobody knows what happened to them?'

'That's right,' said Grace. 'Their boat was seen drifting off Mutton Bird Point before it got washed into the bay alongside. The authorities left it there till it rotted away. And the place ended up getting named Mystery Bay.'

'They left it there? What sort of boat was it?' asked Les.

'A solid wooden clinker. With a big hole in the bottom where the staves were forced out.'

'Forced out?'

'Yes. That's another part of the mystery. The bottom was stove out. Not in. They found most of the men's things still in the boat. But the men had vanished without trace.'

'Fair dinkum? And how do you know all this, Grace?' asked Les.

'Oh, I sort of dabble in local history,' said Grace. 'It gives me something to do during winter.'

'Right.' Les finished his mineral water and indicated with the empty bottle. 'Well. Between Edward Ruddle and the late Merrigans, you wouldn't actually call this spot Happy Valley — would you?'

'It gets even better, Les. At the time of his disappearance, Edward was about to marry a farmer's daughter from Bodalla, Gwendolyn Monteith. He had a gold ring with tiny opals in it, made specially for the occasion. Which Edward swore to wear on his own finger until their wedding day.'

'And he had it on when he disappeared,' said Les.

'That's right,' replied Grace.

Les stroked his chin. 'So what happened to Gwendolyn. Who did she finish up with?'

'No one,' answered Grace. 'She never married. She moved to Moruya, and died of a broken heart.'

Les looked blankly at Grace for a moment. 'I don't quite know what to say, Grace. Until you turned up this morning, I was having a pretty good time living here. Now I feel like moving into a motel.'

Grace laughed. 'I'm sorry, Les,' she said. 'I didn't mean to be like that. It's just that for such a lovely old house, and such a lovely spot, it's got a very sad past.'

'You can say that again.' Les tapped the empty bottle against the railing. 'The mystery of Mystery Bay, eh. Any theories? You give me the impression you're keeping something up your sleeve.'

Grace shook her head. 'No. No theories. Edward Ruddle didn't have any enemies. None of the men had any money on them at the time. And it wouldn't be worth killing four men for a wedding ring.'

'What about the local abos?' asked Les. 'They'd have to be a walk-up start to get the blame.'

Grace shook her head again. 'No. Edward was good friends with both the Murring and the Pyender tribes. So was Gwendolyn.'

Les shrugged and indicated to the sky. 'Maybe Edward and his mates were beamed up to the mother ship.'

Grace gave a shrug also. 'Maybe they were,' she said. 'Who knows?'

Les looked at Grace looking at him, then looked at his watch. 'Anyway. How about we beam over and have some breakfast. I'm getting a bit peckish.'

'Okay,' said Grace. 'We may as well walk up. It's not far.'

'Suits me.' Les started for the loungeroom door.

'Before we go,' said Grace, 'let me take a photo of you.'

'If you want,' shrugged Les. 'You want me to stand on the verandah with the ocean in the background?'

'No. Lean in the doorway. I'll get the light.'

'Okay.' Les propped in the doorway and Grace took two quick snaps.

'That's good,' said Grace. She followed Les into the loungeroom then stopped and pointed to the ghetto blaster sitting above the fireplace. 'Is that working?' she asked.

'Yeah,' replied Les. 'I got it tuned to some local FM station.'

Grace switched the radio on and fiddled with the dial. Next thing there was a blaze of trumpet-playing as a song ended and a gravelly voice went, 'Zatzoo-zatzoo-zazoo-zah'. Then a smoother voice came on. 'That was Louis Armstrong singing "Ain't Misbehavin'". Now let's hear Helen Forrest and the Artie Shaw band, with "I Have Eyes".' Grace turned up the volume and the house filled with some woman's tinny voice, accompanied by muted trumpets, clarinets and a slow riff from a double bass.

'What's this?' asked Les.

'It's a local station. Season FM. They play nothing but old twenties and thirties music.'

Les listened for a moment and was reminded of the old hotel he stayed in at the Blue Mountains. 'It takes you back in time,' he said.

'Doesn't it,' smiled Grace. They listened for a while longer then Grace turned the ghetto blaster off. 'But what do you think?' she said, waving around the room.

'Yes, I see just what you mean,' replied Les. 'It definitely adds a certain ... ambulance to the house.'

'That's ... the exact word I was looking for. Thanks Les.'

'No worries,' smiled Norton. 'Now let's go and have breakfast. After you, Grace.' Les placed his camera in his overnight bag and ushered Grace out the door.

They turned left where Browning met the divide and followed the side street past a small dive shop, an empty shop, then a bigger dive shop. Grace stayed slightly behind Les, watching him as he walked up the hill. They got to the lights just as they were about to change and Grace jogged across to the other side of the main road. Les followed her as fast as he could and nearly got run over by an elderly woman driving a silver Corolla. The woman bipped her horn at Les and frowned at him like he was an idiot. Grace waited on the footpath till Les caught up.

'You've got something wrong with your back, haven't you,' she said.

Les felt a little embarrassed. 'You noticed,' he answered.

'What happened?'

As they were walking up the hill past the shops and the people, Les told her how he'd slipped a disc. Then he told her his back was just coming good when he got a flat on the way down and strained it changing tyres.

'I had physio and every bloody thing,' said Les. 'Now I've stuffed it up again. Talk about give you the shits.'

Grace smiled at Les. 'I think I can help you,' she said confidently.

'You can?' said Les. 'What? Are you a chiropractor or a physiotherapist?'

Grace shook her head. 'No. I can do a little massage. But there's something else.'

'Not aromatherapy or crystal balancing? I got to admit Grace — you do come across as a bit of a hippy.'

'No,' laughed Grace. 'But you'll have to come out to my place.'

'All right.' Les gave his back a quick rub. 'Shit! I'll try just about anything.'

Grace took Les's arm for a moment. 'Okay. We'll see what we can do.'

The red and yellow restaurant was on the corner opposite the hotel. There were windows all round and a sign above the plastic strips in the door said CAREY'S. Les followed Grace inside. Carey's was roomy with polished wooden floors, and the counter and blackboard menu faced the door with the kitchen behind. Near the counter was a rack full of magazines and a computer linked to the internet. The people in black polo shirts and aprons behind the counter were friendly, and knew Grace. Les ordered scrambled eggs on toast with the works and a flat white. Grace opted for an omelette and a cappuccino. Les paid and instead of a number, you got a small wooden object on a stand. Les got a lemon, Grace got a slice of watermelon. They took their little wooden stands and sat facing each other at a table near the far wall. Les had time to check out a few paintings around the walls and the other diners, when their coffees arrived and they got into a bit of chitchat.

Les told Grace pretty much the truth. His family was in Queensland, he lived at Bondi and worked security for a club in Kings Cross that he had shares in. Single, white, heterosexual male. He owned his own house and car, liked music and was down for the Blues Festival.

'That's about my story,' said Les. 'What's yours, Grace.'

'My story?' replied Grace. 'It's a little different to yours, I suppose.'

The food arrived and over the bacon, eggs and toast Grace opened up. Her family came from Narooma. She'd gone to work for a law firm in Sydney, at Ryde, where the lawyers were cooking the books. Grace saw what was going on so she cooked a bit for herself and got away with it before she left. She stayed in Sydney for a while then returned to Narooma where she bought an old farm on five acres at Central Tilba. She made T-shirts and she also had shares in a company in Sydney. Like Les, she did her best to keep fit and, also like Les, she enjoyed good music. Les ordered another two coffees and was wiping his plate with a piece of toast when Grace told him she had a twelve-year-old daughter, who lived with her grandparents in Wollongong.

Les swallowed his piece of toast and gave Grace a double blink. 'Did you just say you've got a twelve-year-old daughter?'

'That's right,' said Grace. 'Ellie. She's got my eyes. But lighter hair.'

Les stared at Grace a little open-mouthed. 'Well how old are you?'

'How old do you think?'

'Somewhere in your twenties. Thirty at the most.'

'I'm forty-two.'

'Forty-two?' Les gave another double blink. 'Christ! You don't look it.'

'I know,' smiled Grace.

Les couldn't help himself staring at Grace. Apart from a few, tiny laugh lines around her eyes, her face was exceptionally smooth and healthy. Her teeth weren't perfect. But there were no gravity lines at the sides of her mouth and the skin round her neck was unwrinkled as were her hands. Forty-two wasn't all that old. But Les had seen a lot of women in their forties. And after years of drink, smokes, coffee and cream cakes, and lying in the good old Australian sun, they looked every minute of it. Not Grace. However, that was just her face.

'Yes,' conceded Les. 'You've certainly looked after yourself. But I still haven't seen you down the beach.'

'What?' said Grace. 'You haven't seen me down the beach?' She unbuttoned the front of her shirt and threw it open. 'How do you think these would go down the beach?'

Sitting up confidently under her shirt, in an almost invisible wisp of lacy black bra, Grace had breasts like two, big, juicy, honeydew melons.

Beneath the two gorgeous big melons was a neat six pack. As quickly as Grace unbuttoned her shirt, she did it up again.

'Well,' she said, easing back in her chair. 'How did they look?'

'How did they look?' blinked Les. 'I don't know, Grace. I think I just hallucinated. Maybe you better show me again to be sure.'

'I think you've seen all you need to,' smiled Grace. She looked up as their second coffees arrived.

Les regained his composure, sugared his coffee and took a sip. 'So, were you ever married?' he asked, politely.

'Two years,' replied Grace. 'Russell sold plumbing supplies. Then lost his job a year after we were married. He tried selling paintings door to door and got run over one night walking back to his car. Leaving me with no insurance, a daughter to raise, and a mortgage on an old house in Botany full of cockroaches.'

'Not a bad place, Botany,' smiled Les.

'Yes, delightful,' replied Grace. 'I stuck it out long enough to sell the house without having to owe the bank any money. Then when I got what I thought was fair from the lawyers, I couldn't get out of Sydney quick enough.'

Les looked across Grace and through the restaurant window at the ocean, blue and sparkling along the coast. 'To live down here. I couldn't blame you.'

'Yes. It might be dullsville at times, Les. But when you walk out to your car in the morning, it's still there and it hasn't got an inch of grime all over it.'

'I know what you mean.'

Grace checked Les out over her coffee. 'When were you born, Les?' she asked. He told her and Grace smiled. 'That makes me old enough to be your aunty.'

'Well, you'd be an unreal aunty,' said Les. 'In fact Grace, you're an amazing woman all round.'

Grace smiled across the table. 'That's what they call me, Les. Amazing Grace.'

The girl came and took away the plates. Les thanked her for the excellent food and had another sip of coffee.

'That Olney the chef's not a bad bloke,' remarked Les.

'Olney? We went to school together. He's a really nice person.' Grace looked at Les for a moment. 'Did you really leave a five hundred dollar tip?'

'Yes,' replied Norton. 'But it wasn't my money.'

Grace had a sip of coffee. 'You'll have to call in to the hotel where he works and have a meal. Olney's a good chef.'

'I intend to,' said Les.

'Did Olney tell you what happened down there last night?' asked Grace.

'He said there was a fight in the bar, or something.'

'Or something?' said Grace. 'It's the talk of Narooma.'

'Really?' said Les.

'And it couldn't have happened to a nicer bunch of blokes either,' said Grace. 'I laughed my head off when I found out who it was got beat up.'

'Yes. Olney said they weren't much good.'

'Old Mick Scully and his cronies. Pity his nephew Morgan never got beat up as well,' said Grace.

'Olney might have mentioned him too,' said Les. 'Who's he?

Grace's cheeks coloured. 'A local bastard.'

Les picked up the vibe. 'I gather you and this Morgan aren't the best of friends.'

'You could say that,' replied Grace.

'What happened?' asked Les. 'Not that it's any of my business.'

'Nothing happened,' she replied. 'Luckily my parents showed up. But the next day he tried to run my father off the road. He could have killed him.' Grace shook her head. 'He's a nut. But bad as well as mad.'

'He sounds like it,' said Les. 'So do they know who it was give it to the blokes in the hotel?' he asked.

Grace shook her head. 'They think he plays football for Ulladulla.'

Les finished his coffee and thought he might change the subject. 'So what's doing tonight, Grace?'

'Well, I don't know about you, Les,' answered Grace. 'But I'm going to the Blues Festival. Aunty Grace has got a three day pass.'

'Me too,' said Les. 'Who are you going with?'

'No one in particular.'

'Would you like to come with me? Warren and Clover should be here by eight. We can all go together.'

'All right,' said Grace. 'I know the guy who runs it. I'll introduce you to him.'

'Unreal. And if you want to have a few drinks, there's a spare room in the house.'

'No thank you,' said Grace. 'I mean, if I do have a few drinks I'll stay at Belinda's.'

'Fair enough. Well, just call round the house about eight. Unless you want to come earlier and have a bite to eat somewhere.'

'No, that's all right thanks. I have to do a few things at home. In fact what is the time?' Grace looked at Les's watch. 'I'll have to get going.'

'Okey doke,' said Les. 'But before we go — my turn to take a photo.'

'What? In this old thing?' smiled Grace.

'That old thing looks pretty good to me,' said Les.

Les popped two photos of Grace and got her to take one of him, then they headed out the door. On the way back to the house, Les got the paper and checked out the dive shops when they crossed the road. The big brown one looked the busier of the two. But Les liked the smaller white one down from it. There were photos in the front window of diving at Montague Island with the seals and stingrays, and the shop had a regular charter boat that went out there game fishing or diving. They got back to the house and Grace stopped at the door of her car.

'Well, thank you very much for breakfast, Les. It was lovely. And thanks for letting me see inside the house,' she said.

'That's all right,' smiled Les. 'Anytime.'

'And I am serious about your back. I can help you.'

'Hey, you've got me,' assured Les. 'I'm coming round to your place.'

'Make sure you do.' Grace opened the door of her car.

'Before you go. What about your aloe vera?' said Les.

'Oh. I almost forgot.' Grace got a plastic bag from the front seat of her car and walked across to the trees. She broke off three pieces, put them in the bag and placed them in the car. 'Thanks for that,' she said.

'I'll see you tonight,' smiled Les.

Grace blew Les a kiss as she backed down the driveway and Les blew her one back off his fingertips, then she drove away. Les went inside to the bedroom and gave himself a double blink in the mirror. *Did I just see what I think I did? What about those with breakfast? What about Grace? And she wants to fix my back. I wonder if that's all she wants to fix?* Les laughed and tidied up the bed. *Imagine if Grace did throw me up in the air. Forget having a slipped disc, I'd finish up looking like the Hunchback of Notre Dame.* Les kicked off his casuals, got the paper and his book about old Narooma then walked out to the table on the verandah and made himself comfortable.

Les finished the paper and started flicking through *Narooma's Glorious Past*. 'Noorooma' meant clear water in the local aboriginal dialect and it was once a gold mining and timber town. White people had first been through there in 1797 and people started settling in the area around 1840. Les looked at photos of sawmills and old steamers. Serious men with full beards in high-collared shirts and stern women in black crinoline dresses with white hats that looked like tea cosies. As Les turned the pages, something Grace said earlier intrigued him. Edward Ruddle had sworn to wear his betrothed's wedding ring until the day they were married. If that was the case, Edward must have had very dainty hands.

Les turned a few more pages and couldn't believe it. There was an old black and white photo of Edward Ruddle standing alongside Gwendolyn Monteith, seated in a high-back, wicker chair. Edward had untidy dark hair and a full beard, tiny glasses, and wore a frock coat, watch chain and striped trousers. Gwendolyn was wearing a heavy, pleated dress and a straw hat with the brim turned up. The photo wasn't the best. But Edward looked like a reasonable style of a bloke. Gwendolyn, however, was an absolute beast. She had a miserable, fat face, pushed into a bony, hog head, with that many double chins she could have shuffled them and done card tricks. Resting in her ample lap, her hands looked like two small bunches of sugar bananas, topped off with a body that made Jabba the Hutt look like Elle MacPherson. Gwendolyn was nineteen. Edward was thirty-seven.

'Oh my God!' said Les. 'What a walrus gumboot.'

Les stared at the photo in disbelief and closed the book. Well that's the mystery of Mystery Bay solved, he told himself. Edward's pulled out a photo of his girl and everyone's jumped out of the boat. Edward's got the shits and kicked a hole in the bottom, no one could swim and they all drowned. And you can see why Edward was able to wear his beloved's little band of gold. If the bloody thing could fit round Gwendolyn's pig's trotter, it'd double as a serviette ring. Les opened the book again. Still, he conceded, there probably weren't many stray women down here in those days. And at thirty-seven, plucking a nineteen-year-old's not a bad effort. But, fair dinkum, to marry something like that Edward must have been absolutely desperate. Or too lazy to pull himself. Les turned to the next page. A few pages on he came to a photo of the Merrigans.

'Hello,' said Les. 'It's Lander and the team.'

The photo was taken standing on the verandah with the ocean in the background. There was no breakwater then and the channel was more a wide, sheltered bay with a long wooden jetty running out from the park on the right. Lander was all done up in a check, three piece suit and had grey hair, combed neatly over a full, happy face. Hildreth wore glasses and had her hair in a bun; she also looked happy, in a simple, floral dress with a shawl over her shoulders. Their skinny son, Eachan, had a cap plonked on his head and a crumpled coat over a pair of crumpled short trousers, and was staring into the lens like he'd never seen a camera before. Les smiled at the photo and pictured exactly where they were standing on the verandah when it was taken. He had a good look then turned the page. Towards the end of Jasmine Cunneen's book, was 'The Mystery of Mystery Bay'.

Apart from an old pencil sketch of the boat, sitting on the beach with a hole in the bottom, there were only the names of the other missing men and all the police and officials investigating the case. There wasn't a great deal more than Grace had told Les already. Police initially thought it was foul play, then said there'd been an accident at sea. Important evidence was never properly examined and prominent people thought the police had botched the investigation. The Select Committee of the Legislative Assembly investigating the incident concluded it was murder. The police, the police magistrate and the mining warden said it was an accident. A lot of theories were put forward over the years. But the mystery of Mystery Bay remains unsolved to this day.

Les ran his eyes over the page again, then closed the book. Unsolved to this day? I just solved the bloody thing. The surveyor did it. Les put Jasmine Cunneen's book on the table then went inside and got *The Perfect Storm*. He made himself comfortable and rejoined the crew of the *Andrea Gail* having a wonderful time battling twenty metre waves and two hundred kilometre winds off Grand Banks.

Les read on into the afternoon. He was that engrossed in his book, he didn't notice Narooma coming to life. Cars were arriving down the side street or up Browning and stopping in front of the surrounding holiday flats and houses. Car boots and garage doors were opening and closing, bags and suitcases were getting dumped on footpaths, keys were rattling and getting pushed into locks. Shades were being pulled up and down, taps were being run. The sun began to to go down and lights started coming on. Bottles clinked, cans fizzed open and voices drifted over from the surrounding balconies. Les heard music and looked up. Canned Heat. Coming from a flat on the corner. Other balconies followed suit. John Lee Hooker, John Mayall, Dave Hole. From a house below, Les heard Buddy Guy and Junior Wells, chugging out 'This Old Fool'. From another balcony, Johnny Johnson started tinkling 'Drink of Tanqueray'. Hello, thought Les. Looks like the bloody tourists have hit town for the Blues Festival. And I'm caught in the battle of the ghetto blasters. Trapped in a rock 'n' roll no man's land. He put his book aside, stretched his legs and looked around. Well, if I don't want to finish up missing in action, I'd better start fighting back.

Les walked into the loungeroom and switched on his ghetto blaster. It was still tuned to Season FM. A smooth voice said, 'That was "Thanks for the Boogie Ride", with Anita O'Day. Now let's hear the dulcet tones of Kay Starr and "Secretary to the Sultan".'

'Yes. Let's not,' said Les. He switched the radio off, got a tape and took the ghetto blaster out onto the verandah. He put it on the table facing the jetty and found the power point. 'Instead, why don't we hear Katie Webster, from her CD *Two-Fisted Mama*! And "The Katie Lee".' Les hit the play button and Katie Webster's honky tonk piano joined the other music. 'Fire one for effect,' smiled Les, then went inside and got a bottle of beer.

Les had an enjoyable late afternoon, sitting with his feet up on the verandah, drinking beer, listening to music and watching the world go by. Around in the park someone did a sound check which thumped out across the channel. Les changed tapes and kept drinking beer. Before he knew it, it was well and truly dark and he was getting drunk. He looked at his watch. Shit! I'd better take it easy. Grace'll be here before long and I don't want to open the door with my wobble boot on talking in Icelandic. Les finished his beer and got under the shower.

He had a shave and mulled over what he should do about dinner. Going down to the pub or the RSL might still be a bit risky. There was chicken and salad in the fridge and tins of salmon in the cupboard. Les made some sandwiches and read the paper again over a mug of tea. He cleaned up, then changed into a pair of jeans and a white T-shirt with a hang out denim shirt, and dabbed a little Calvin Klein on his face. Satisfied everything was in order, he went to the kitchen and made a delicious: JD and mineral water with a slice of lime. Les was glancing at some maps in his 'What's On', when there was a knock on the door. Les opened it and Grace was standing on the step wearing a pair of red jeans and a short-sleeved maroon shirt, over a mauve T-shirt with tiny yellow parrots on the front. She had her hair in a ponytail and pinned to her shirt was a little wooden lorikeet with mother-of-pearl eyes.

'Hello Grace,' said Les, cheerfully. 'How are you?'

'Good. How's yourself?' she replied.

'Terrific. Come on in.' Les glanced along the driveway. 'Where's your car?'

'I left it at Belinda's and got a lift over.'

Les closed the door and ushered Grace into the kitchen. He gave her another once up and down and noticed the neat cut of her shirt and the tiny green emblem near the pocket.

'That's a nice shirt,' said Les. 'Where did you get that?'

'I buy them at the Hemp shop in Central Tilba,' she replied.

'It looks good over that T-shirt,' remarked Les.

'Thanks.' Grace fingered the emblem. 'Yes, they look good. They feel good, and they last forever.'

'Don't let Warren see it when he gets here. He'll try and smoke it.'

Grace shook her head. 'He could smoke ten tonne of these and it wouldn't do him any good.'

'I know,' said Les. 'I was only joking. But I'll buy a couple of those before I go home. They look all right.' Les rubbed his hands together. 'Can I get you a caarrktail?'

Grace pointed to Norton's glass on the table. 'What are you drinking?'

'Jack Daniels and soda. Or there's beer and Bacardi.'

'How about a Bacardi?'

Grace placed her bag on the table and looked around the kitchen while Les made a Bacardi and orange. He handed it to her and clinked glasses.

'Cheers Grace.'

'Yes. Cheers Les.'

'Would you like to go out on the verandah?' suggested Les.

'All right. After you.'

On the verandah it was quite mild. The sky was full of stars and the moon shone brightly on the channel. The surrounding balconies were down to only a couple of ghetto blasters. But coming from the park was a blur of music and the solid thump of a bass.

'Sounds like the show's started,' said Les.

'Yes. The first band was at seven-thirty. But there's no hurry.' Grace sipped her rum. 'So what did you do this afternoon?'

'Read a book. But you should have heard it out here earlier. It was like the battle of the bands.' Les pointed to his ghetto blaster on the table and told Grace how he was reading when all the people arrived and things started happening. So he put his book down and joined in over a few beers.

'What were you reading?' asked Grace.

'*The Perfect Storm* by Sebastian Junger. Before that, however, I was reading *Narooma's Glorious Past* by Jasmine — someone-or-other?'

'Cunneen,' answered Grace.

'That's her.' Les had a sip of bourbon and looked pensively at Grace. 'You didn't tell me what a ravishing beauty Gwendolyn was, Grace.'

Grace pursed her lips. 'You saw the photo, Les.'

'Saw it? I'll probably have nightmares.'

'Yes,' agreed Grace. 'Young Gwendoline was something else. Wasn't she?'

'Yeah. A sumo wrestler in drag.'

Grace looked out over the railing. 'Just think, Les. Edward and Gwendolyn probably held hands and made love on this very land.'

'How truly romantic,' said Les. 'Lucky Edward.'

Grace turned to Les. 'You have to wonder what he used to stop her from rolling down the hill. Logs, rope, giant tent pegs ...?' Grace put her hands over her mouth and looked around. 'Ooh. I shouldn't have said that.'

'No, you shouldn't,' chuckled Les, having to look away. 'I also found a photo of the Merrigans. They looked fairly normal.'

'Yes,' agreed Grace. 'About your average, eighteen fifties nuclear family. Except young Eachan looks like he's just entered the twilight zone.'

Les raised his glass. 'You haven't got a bad turn of phrase, Grace.' Grace was about to say something when Les noticed headlights pulling up in the driveway. They stayed on for a moment, then they were switched off. 'Hello,' said Les. 'I've got an idea who this might be.'

'Your friends?'

'Something like that.' A minute or so later there was a loud banging on the front door. Les placed his drink on the table. 'I won't be a minute.'

Les walked through the house and opened the front door. Warren was standing one step below wearing a black tracksuit and cap, with a bag in each hand. He looked like he was ready to kill someone.

'Yes,' said Norton. 'Can I help you at all, mate?'

'Ohh get fucked will you,' Warren exploded. 'Why don't you park your car right outside the front fuckin door, and take up the whole fuckin driveway. You dopey-looking cunt.'

'I thought I had.' Les moved aside to let Warren in. 'So how was the drive down? They say the south coast is beautiful this time of the year.'

Warren glared at Les. 'How was the drive down ... How do you think the fuckin drive down was? Fuckin hell! I didn't think I was ever going to fuckin get here. And if I have to listen to another one of Clover's fuckin Bob Dylan CDs I'll smash the fuckin thing over her head.'

Les closed the door. 'Where is Clover?'

'I dropped her off at her place. Fuck! That was another shitfight. Getting from fuckin Dalmeny back to here at night. You should have ...' Warren stopped and looked around. 'Hey. So this is the old house. Fuck me.'

'Haven't you been in here before?' said Les.

'No. Shit! What about all these old photos and paintings?' Warren had a look in the kitchen and bathroom. 'Hey this joint's fuckin unreal.'

'I'm in that bedroom. There's one across the hall and another off the loungeroom.'

Warren had a look at the bedroom in the hall, then followed Les into the loungeroom. 'I'll take that one.' Warren threw his bag on the double bed and came back out. 'Fuck! What about all the grouse old furniture? Check the old fuckin piano.' Then Warren noticed something missing. 'Hey, wait a minute,' he said. 'There's no fuckin TV. Where's the fuckin TV? You've taken it into your room, haven't you? You big cunt.'

Les placed a soothing hand on Warren's shoulder. 'Warren. They didn't have TV during the First World War. Anyway, come out onto the verandah.'

Warren followed Les and stopped dead when he saw Grace standing next to the table. 'Shit! How long have you been there?'

Grace raised her glass. 'This is my first drink.'

'Grace, this is Warren. Warren, this is Grace.'

'Hello Grace,' said Warren. 'How are you?'

'I'm fine thank you, Warren. Les told me about you. Where's Clover?'

'She's . . . she's at her parent's place. She'll be here later.' Warren stared at Grace, then turned to Les.

'Would you like a drink, Woz?' asked Les.

'Yeah. I wouldn't mind.'

'There's Jackies and ice in the kitchen. Help yourself.'

'Okay.' Warren had another look at Grace, then headed for the kitchen.

Grace smiled at Les. 'So that's Warren.'

Les smiled back and picked up his drink. 'That's him. AKA, the boarder.'

It didn't take Warren long to knock up a double, triple Jack Daniels and return to the verandah. 'Well, cheers everyone,' he said.

Les raised his glass. Grace spoke. 'So how was the drive down, Warren?'

Warren winced as the bourbon bit in. 'Oh, it was . . . nice. The south coast's quite lovely this time of the year.'

'Yes it is,' nodded Grace.

'Are you from down here?'

'Central Tilba.'

Warren had another hit on his drink. 'So where do you know gorilla-head from?'

'You mean Les? We met last night. I'm going to help fix his back.'

'He's not still putting on the bad back act is he?' said Warren. 'There's nothing wrong with it, you know.'

'Is this true, Les?' asked Grace. 'You told me you were in agony.'

Les shook his head and held up his empty glass. 'How about we have a refill.'

Grace handed Les her glass. He went out to the kitchen and made two fresh drinks. When he got back to the verandah, Warren and Grace were talking and laughing away. Les handed Grace another Bacardi and orange.

Grace thanked Les and put her drink on the table. 'I might go to the loo,' she said.

Warren waited till Grace was halfway down the hall and turned to Les. 'Fuck! Where did you find her?'

Les gave a casual shrug. 'You know how it is, Woz. They find me.'

'She's not a bad sort,' said Warren, sucking lustily on his JD. 'What about her set?'

'You noticed, Woz.'

'Christ! How could you miss it.'

Les took a sip of JD also. 'So what's doing with Clover? How long before she'll be here?'

'I don't know,' answered Warren. 'About an hour or so.'

Les looked at his watch. 'Well instead of waiting around, we might meet you down there.'

'Please yourself,' said Warren. 'I want to have a shower and unpack my gear anyway.'

'Okay,' said Les. 'I've been to the supermarket. There's coffee and tea and all that in the kitchen, as well as booze.'

'Good on you.'

Warren offered Les some money. Les told him not to worry about it. Then Grace returned. She got her drink from the table and smiled at the boys.

'Warren doesn't know for sure how long Clover's going to be,' said Les. 'So I suggested we meet them down there.'

'She might be a while,' added Warren. 'And I still have to get cleaned up.'

'Suits me,' nodded Grace. 'Little Charlie and the Nightcats are on in about half an hour.'

'Did you say Little Charlie and the Nightcats?' chorused Les and Warren.

'Yes. Haven't you got a program.'

Les shook his head. 'I got a brochure with the tickets. But no program.'

'They never sent you a program?' queried Grace.

'Haven't you told Grace how you got the tickets?' said Warren.

'Didn't you buy them like everybody else?' asked Grace.

'Not really,' said Les. He explained to Grace how he managed to get the tickets. 'So in a way Grace, if I hadn't bumped into The Zap, we probably wouldn't be here.'

'That's not a bad bartering system you have in Bondi,' said Grace.

'It's another world up there. Believe me,' said Les.

Warren gave Les a punch on the arm, 'Where he's known as Lucky Les.'

'I wish.' Norton raised his empty glass. 'Well, what do you reckon Grace? We make a move?'

'That might be a good idea,' agreed Grace. She turned to Warren. 'There's a souvenir stall inside where they sell T-shirts and CDs. How about we meet you and Clover there after Little Charlie?'

'No problem,' said Warren. 'We'll find it and wait for you.'

They proceeded inside. Grace got her bag from the kitchen. Warren made himself another drink. Les got his camera and gave Warren the key, telling him to leave it under the mat. They said goodbye and Warren started to unpack.

Les and Grace walked down the hill and around the jetty and joined the crowd. It was a different scene to the evening before when Les had the place almost to himself. Now there were people everywhere, heading for the festival. Music was coming from inside the park and just past the local pool was an entry for the performers and their trucks with security people in black standing on either side. They rounded the corner and joined a queue at the entrance next to the tourist centre. Les handed over his ticket and was given a plastic tag to put round his wrist that he was assured would stay on for the three days, then Grace had her bag politely searched and they went inside.

There were people everywhere, but the park was long and wide so there was no shortage of room. The souvenir stall selling T-shirts and CDs was on the left next to some other stalls and opposite was a big red and blue tent with a stage and seating. Further on to the right was a much larger red and yellow tent and round to the left was a smaller green one. Between the largest tent and the entry backstage, a striped booze tent was doing a roaring business. Overlooking everything were two huge trailers full of Portaloos.

Les glanced at his watch. 'Why don't we have a quick look around before Little Charlie comes on,' said Les.

'Okay,' said Grace.

With Grace by his side Les checked out the rest of the park. At the far end were food and drink stalls selling everything from chilli-dogs to authentic bush tucker, from fresh fruit juice to Turkish cuisine and Thai noodles. Other stalls sold alien masks and new age clothing, bottles of oil, jewellery, all sorts of things; and doing a brisk business. Grace went to get two orange juices while Les cast an eye over the punters.

There were plenty of young people. But definitely no ravers with bottles of mineral water. Most of the crowd were in their late thirties and on and some people had brought their kids with them. The dress code was very casual. Plenty of leather and denim, baseball caps and Akubras. Vests and cowboy boots and T-shirts saying what the owner drank or where they came from. The men were all shapes and sizes with a sprinkling of Willie Nelson and ZZ Top look-alikes. The women were either fit with big breasts and long hair, and squeezed into faded jeans, or had their hair shorter and their clothes looser and appeared more into taking life easy. In general, the crowd was pretty much Aussie working class. All enjoying the music and the food, definitely enjoying a drink; and everybody with a smile on their face. Grace came back with two fresh squeezed orange juices and handed one to Les.

'Hey this could be all right,' said Les, picking up a good vibe in the air.

'It always is,' replied Grace. 'And the weather's good this time of year too.'

'It's definitely not cold tonight.'

'Why don't we head over to the tent and find a seat? The band will be on in a few minutes.'

'I'll follow you.'

They weaved their way through the crowd across to the big tent and fluked two seats on the side about ten back from the stage. The stage was all set up and they weren't there long before a huge man, with dark hair and a long face and wearing jeans and a Blues Festival T-shirt, came out on stage. He towered over the microphone and adjusted it to suit him.

'Christ! Check the size of this bloke,' said Les.

'That's the guy that runs the festival,' said Grace. 'Norman Dadd. Everybody calls him Daddy.'

'I wouldn't like to call him names,' said Les. 'He's a big boy.'

'I'll introduce you later. I've known Norm and his wife for years.'

Daddy tapped the microphone and started talking. He had a booming voice and didn't like to waste words.

'Righto,' he said. 'I want to welcome youse all to the South Coast Blues Festival. I know youse are gonna have a good time. And it's good to see youse all again. Now I want youse to give a big South Coast welcome to one of the stars of the show. All the way from the west coast of America. Come on. Put your hands together for … Little Charlie and the Nightcats!'

Three men, an Afro-American and two whites, walked out on stage led by Ric Estrin, wearing dark glasses, an oyster grey suit, a white shirt with a hand-painted silk tie and two-tone shoes. He looked immaculate and confidently took hold of the mike.

'Alllriiiggght,' he said, as the band got behind their instruments. 'I just want to say how great it is to be here in Narooma.' Ric took out his harp, nodded one, two, three four to the band, and then they slipped straight into 'Dump That Chump'. Seconds later the whole tent was rocking.

'Hey, how good's this?' said Les, bopping around in his seat.

'Open your orange juice,' said Grace.

Les took the lid off and Grace tilted a hip flask into it. 'What's this?' asked Les.

'Stolly.'

'Well done, Grace.' Les took a sip, gasped and kept on bopping.

Little Charlie and the Nightcats ripped into everything from 'Don't Do It' to 'Gerontology'. And brought the house down. Between bopping and drinking vodka, Les and Grace managed to get some good photos. The band did one encore, 'I'm Just Lucky That Way'. Then walked off to a standing ovation. Les had a glow from the vodka and so did Grace.

'Weren't they good,' said Grace.

'Were they what!' agreed Les. He looked at his watch. 'I suppose we'd better find Warren and Clover.'

'Yes. We don't want him getting all excited again,' said Grace.

They got up with the rest of the crowd leaving the tent and walked over to the souvenir stall where Les immediately started to drool at the stacks of CDs on sale. He made a mental note to come back with his Visa card and fill his overnight bag. Les felt Grace tap him on the shoulder and turned around as Warren and Clover walked up. Warren was wearing designer jeans, a shiny, grey shirt and a black leather jacket. Clover had on a powder blue top an inch above her navel, a denim mini with a white belt six inches below her navel and red, white and blue cowboy boots.

'Hello Clover,' said Les. 'How are you sweetheart?'

'Good Les,' smiled Clover. 'The house all right?'

'All right? It's sensational. Clover, this is Grace.'

'Hello Grace.'

'Hi Clover.'

Clover looked at Grace for a moment. 'I think I know you. Do you work at a craft shop in Central Tilba?'

'Sometimes,' said Grace. 'My friend Alysia owns it. I sell T-shirts there.'

'Grace Holt originals.' Clover pointed to Grace's T-shirt. 'You're wearing one now.'

'That's right.'

'They're beautiful.'

'Thank you,' smiled Grace.

Les gestured. 'Well, there you go. We're all friends.'

'We just caught the last of Little Charlie and the Nightcats,' said Warren. 'Can he play a harp or what?'

'He doesn't dress too bad either,' said Les.

At that moment, Ric Estrin came over to the souvenir tent to sign autographs and CDs. Considering he'd just performed a scorching gig, he still looked immaculate; not a hair out of place, not a crease in his suit. Coming through the crowd behind him was Norm Dadd. It looked like a tree moving across the park.

He got near and Grace called out 'Daddy'.

Norm looked around. 'Amazing,' he boomed. 'How are you? Everything okay? You got your ticket? You got in all right?'

'Yes thanks,' she answered, reaching up to give the big man a kiss on the cheek. 'Daddy, I want you to meet some friends of mine.' She introduced the three of them, then Daddy looked at Les.

'Les Norton. You work at the Kelly Club with George Brennan.'

'That's . . . right,' hesitated Les.

'George and I are old mates. When I lived at Balmain, we knocked around together.'

'Go on.' Les recollected Norm waiting in a car outside the Kelly Club one night to give George a lift home.

Daddy nodded slowly. 'He told me a bit about you.' Les discreetly placed his index finger in front of his mouth. Daddy understood. 'About when you played football,' he said.

'Yeah. I played for Easts,' said Les. 'But I didn't last long.'

'When did you get here?' asked Daddy.

'In Narooma?' said Les. 'I arrived here late Thursday night.'

'Late?' said Daddy.

Les picked up a certain tone in Daddy's voice and a twinkle in his eye. 'Yeah. I saw the end of the battle of the bands up at the golf links. Then I had a drink at Lawson's hotel. That's where I met Grace.'

'You'll have to come down the other pub and have a drink,' said Daddy. 'McBride's.'

'I intend to,' replied Les. 'I met Olney the chef last night.'

'Olney's a good chef,' said Norm. 'So where are you staying down here, Les?'

'Clover's parent's own a big house in Browning Street. Warren and I are staying there.'

'The old Merrigan house?'

'That's the one. You know, Norm,' said Les, 'there's something I've always wanted to know about George.'

'Oh. What's that Les?'

Les winked at Grace. 'Excuse me a second.' He pulled Daddy aside. 'Are you on to me about what happened in the hotel last night, Norm?' Les said quietly in his ear.

Daddy nodded. 'I was in the bottle shop, and I thought I saw you running out of the hotel. I wasn't sure if it was you. But when I saw what had happened inside, I knew who it was.'

'You haven't told anybody?'

Norm shook his head. 'No. There's half-a-dozen descriptions of you getting around. But one of them's right on the money. So be careful. One of the blokes you flattened has got a real nutty nephew. And he runs with a bad team.'

'So I heard.'

'Any trouble, come and see me. I'll see what I can do.'

'Thanks Norm.' Les slapped Daddy on the shoulder and laughed. 'So that was George.'

'Yeah. That was him all right,' said Norm. He was about to say something else, when a solid bloke with fair hair, wearing a Blues Festival T-shirt and an urgent look on his face came over. 'What's up Spike?' asked Norm.

'One of the women's toilets is playing up, Daddy,' said Spike.

'Ohh shit!' cursed Norm.

'That's part of the problem,' said Spike.

'I have to go,' said Daddy. 'I'll see youse all later. See you, Les.'

'Yeah. Nice to meet you, Norm,' he replied.

The others said goodbye then Warren turned to Les. 'What was that all about?' he asked.

'Oh, George got barred from a hotel in Balmain for fighting,' said Les. 'But he'd never admit it.'

'Knowing George,' said Warren, 'he'd never admit to anything.'

Grace had been to the souvenir tent. She handed Warren and Les a program each. 'There you are,' she said. 'Now you know what's going on.'

'Thanks Grace,' said Les.

'So what are we doing now?' asked Clover.

'Blue Katz are on in fifteen minutes,' said Grace. 'In the middle tent.'

'Blue Katz,' said Les. 'They'll do me.'

'I got time to get some cool ones,' said Warren.

Les looked at Warren, who seemed to be a little on the nod. 'Did you have a few more cool ones after we left?' asked Les.

Warren nodded. 'And a hot one.'

'He's half wasted,' said Clover.

'I'll give you a hand with the drinks,' said Les.

Les and Warren left the girls and walked over to the drink tent. Warren bought four tickets and went to the bar. While Les was waiting for Warren to get served, he didn't notice he was getting a very deliberate once up and down from a beefy bloke with lank black hair, wearing a Jim Beam T-shirt and an earring. The bloke was also waiting for a mate at the bar, who was wearing a red T-shirt. When the bloke in the red T-shirt came back with four drinks, the bloke with the earring pointed Les out. They both gave Norton a very heavy perusal before taking the drinks over to the two denim-clad women they were with. Warren got the drinks, Les took two and they walked back to the souvenir tent. Les handed Grace a Bacardi and took a sip of JD.

'We'd better see if we can find a seat,' suggested Grace.

'Yeah,' yawned Warren. 'I'm knackered. And my back's that stiff from the drive down.'

'Ohh shit, Warren,' said Les. 'Not your back.'

They found four seats on the aisle behind each other. Warren and Clover took the front two, Les and Grace sat behind. They weren't there long when a dark-haired bloke in a Blues Festival T-shirt walked out on stage and took hold of the mike. He had a husky voice and was even more succinct than Daddy.

'Ladies and gentlemen. All the way from South Australia, will you please welcome Blue Katz!'

To generous applause from the people seated, or standing around the tent, the three-piece band came on stage. They were all dressed fairly neatly. But the leader in a dark blue suit and hand-painted tie could have almost given Ric Estrin a run for his money. Without any further to do, Blue Katz slipped into 'Beef Bong Boogie'. Soon the tent was rocking, people were clapping, others were up in front of the stage dancing. Les told Grace he'd have to put any dancing on hold for the time being: Grace understood. Warren was too tired for any dancing and Clover was content to sit and get into the music.

Blue Katz cruised through 'Katman', 'Louise Louise' and 'Red Hot'. More tracks from their CDs, and for their encore did 'Rock Big Daddy Rock'. Then they left the stage to thunderous applause and much whistling. Norton's hands were sore from clapping, but he got some good photos over Warren's head. Grace took some in front of the band. The four of them waited for the tent to empty a little.

'Well, that's one of the best nights of boogie I've had in a while,' said Les.

'Yes. They were unreal,' said Clover. 'What did you think Warren?'

'Yeah. Great,' said Warren, stifling a yawn.

'I took some photos of the dancers,' said Grace. 'And I got one of this guy doing a spin just as his wig came off. I can't wait to get it developed.'

Les had his program out. 'It says on the program, Jimbo's Blues Band is on at one o'clock tomorrow. I saw them in Cairns. They're a hoot.'

'If you're coming to see them, I might join you,' said Grace.

'I'll be here for sure,' said Les. 'That bloke in the war bonnet cracks me up.'

Les and the others hadn't noticed a bloke in a red T-shirt and another in a black Jim Beam T-shirt sitting two seats behind, listening to their every word. The two men nodded to each other then got up with their women and left.

'Are you going back to Central Tilba tonight?' Clover asked Grace.

Grace shook her head. 'No. I'm staying with my girlfriend Belinda in Eastaway Avenue.'

'How are you getting home?' asked Clover.

'With her. She works at Lawson's Hotel. But I'm not sure what time she's finishing because of all the people in town.'

'Mum's picking me up at the house in about thirty minutes. We can give you a lift home if you like.'

'That'd be great, Clover. All right if we call in to the hotel for a second while I tell Belinda?'

'Sure.'

'There you go, Ugly,' smiled Warren. 'Saves you having to drive Grace home.'

'Yeah,' said Les, hoping Grace might have come back for a cool one.

Warren could read the look on Norton's face. 'Lucky Les,' he said. 'You've done it again.'

'Well, I suppose we'd better make a move,' said Clover. 'I don't want to keep mother waiting.'

'Yes. Come on Les,' smiled Grace. 'I'll help you up the hill. You poor old thing.'

'Thanks, Amazing,' he replied.

Part of the crowd were hanging back to see a Creole band still playing in the smaller tent. Les and the others joined the people leaving the park. It was only a short walk to the house and they discussed the bands they'd just seen, and cracked a few jokes. Warren yawned a few times while Les had one quick whinge about his back, then they were standing in front of the driveway.

'Do you want to wait inside?' asked Les.

'No thank you,' replied Grace.

'No. Me either,' said Clover.

'I don't know how you can just piss off and leave me like this,' sniffed Warren.

'It's ... relatively easy Warren,' replied Clover. 'I simply say goodnight. And go home to mother.' She put her arms around Warren. 'But I'll be around for breakfast tomorrow darling, pet, dove.'

'Do you want to have breakfast again, Grace?' asked Les.

'Yes. That would be nice. Same place, same time?'

'Yeah. Carey's. Nine o'clock. You going to join us Clover? We had breakfast there this morning. It's pretty good.' Les winked at Grace. 'The view's not bad either.'

'I know Carey's,' replied Clover. 'But why don't we make it about ten. Have a bit of a sleep in.'

'Good idea,' said Warren.

'Okay then,' said Les. 'Ten o'clock it is.'

A metallic blue Holden station wagon with a woman behind the wheel pulled up out the front. The woman gave the horn a quick beep.

'Here's mum now,' said Clover.

Warren walked across to the car with Clover. Grace smiled and put her arms around Norton's neck.

'I had a lovely time tonight,' she said. 'Thanks Les.'

Les put his arms around Grace's waist. 'I didn't do much,' he shrugged.

'You didn't have to. You were just nice company.'

Les smiled. 'You weren't bad yourself.'

Grace returned Les's smile then kissed him full on the mouth. Her lips were warm and firm and Les returned the kiss avidly. He felt a tiny snap of Grace's hot, sweet tongue and was just getting into the swing of things when she stopped. Les opened his eyes and looked into Grace's.

'I'll see you in the morning, handsome,' she said.

'Okay,' said Les. 'See you then.'

'And when the band's finished ... we might take a look at your back.'

'Righto.'

Grace gave Les a quick kiss, untangled herself then walked across to the station wagon and got in the back seat next to Clover.

'See you, Clover,' Les called out.

Clover waved through the window. 'Bye Les.'

They drove off and Warren walked back. 'I left the key under the mat,' he said.

'Well, why don't you get it and open the door,' said Les.

'You're closest,' replied Warren. 'You open it. If you can get your fat arse round your car.'

Les shook his head, got the key and opened the door. He closed it behind them and turned the light on in the kitchen. 'You want a cup of tea or something.'

'No,' Warren called out from the bathroom. 'I'm fucked. I'm going to bed.'

'Yeah. Me too,' said Les. He left the electric jug and had a drink of water.

Warren propped in the doorway and yawned. 'I'll see you in the morning, dude. If you get up early, try not to wake me will you.'

'I'll be like a little mouse. See you in the morning, Woz.'

Warren dragged himself off to his bedroom. Les went to the bathroom, cleaned his teeth then started climbing out of his clothes and into his tracksuit. He looked at the bedroom window and decided to leave it open. If it got cold again he had plenty of blankets this time. He yawned, closed the bedroom door then switched off the light and got under the covers. Les thought about Clover for a while and mulled over what Daddy had told him. Before long, however, he was snoring. What sounded like thunder woke Les during the night and he noticed it was chilly again. But he went straight back to sleep.

Les had a dry mouth and a sore back when he got out of bed the next morning. But no hangover. Outside it looked like being another nice day. He stretched, got into a pair of shorts and went to open the bedroom door. It was jammed.

'What in the fuck!'

Les pulled and wrenched the solid old door, but it wouldn't budge. Something was jammed underneath. A piece of rusty metal. Les picked up a shoe and belted whatever it was back out, then opened the door. The piece of rusty metal was a horseshoe. Les picked it up, looked at it for a moment then placed it on the kitchen table and walked into the bathroom. Their shaving gear was scattered all around the floor, along with the towels, and there was water all over the toilet seat.

'What the ... ?'

Les stared at the mess. Not the rat again, surely? Then a humourless smile appeared on his face. Warren. He'd stumbled into the bathroom during the night, pissed everywhere then thrown a wobbly looking for his headache tablets. Same as he did at home when he was out of it. The goose. Les cleaned up the mess, got himself together then walked into the kitchen. While he was waiting for the kettle to boil, the reason for the horseshoe sitting on the kitchen table dawned on him as well. Warren again. He would have had a good look around the house when he unpacked, gone downstairs half-tanked on bourbon with a torch, and spotted those old horseshoes. Would Warren go to all that trouble? Ohh shit yeah. Anything to annoy the landlord. That's why he kept calling him Lucky Les all night. And locking Lucky Les in his room with a horseshoe would be hilarious. Hah-hah-hah! But just to rain on Warren's parade, the landlord wasn't going to bite. Les picked up the horseshoe, opened the front door and threw the thing right up under the trees. It never happened. Les dusted his hands and shook his head. If you ask me, Woz has been in that advertising agency too long.

Les made a mug of tea and a couple of slices of toast and went out into the hallway. The door to the loungeroom was closed; Les opened it and stepped inside. The bear was on the piano facing the wall and Les could hear snoring coming from Warren's room. Les had half a mind to turn the bear on and push it inside Warren's door. Instead, he took his tea and toast out onto the verandah.

There were more clouds around than the day before and the southerly was up a little. But people were fishing or strolling around the jetty and the activity on the lagoon had increased. Les stared across the channel as he sipped his tea and ate his toast. He did a few light stretches and decided to walk around the golf links again. He rinsed his mug, changed into his training gear and set off.

With the southerly in his face, Les found the walk the same as the day before. Enjoyable, but again he would have loved to burst into a run. However, Les kept going, crisscrossing the greens, and before long he started to get a sweat up. He stopped at the beach and noted there were more fishermen than yesterday and the waves were bigger. Les touched at his toes a few times and attempted some sit-ups and crunches but was forced to give the idea a miss. So he headed home. Warren was still in bed. Les had a shower, got into a green Nautica T-shirt and cargos and walked up to get the paper. The two dive shops were open. Les called into the smaller one on the way back.

The counter was on the left with a doorway at the rear leading to a filling station. The wall behind the counter was arranged with certificates and the wall opposite was shelved with snorkelling gear and spear guns. The front of the shop was stacked with scuba tanks and racks of wetsuits, and on the wall near the front window were blown-up photos, as well as maps and posters. A fair-haired bloke, wearing a white T-shirt with Wagonga Dive Shop on the front was behind the counter, fiddling with a spear gun trigger mechanism. As Les approached, the bloke looked up and smiled.

'Yes mate? What can I do for you?' he asked, cheerfully.

'I'd like to take a trip out to Montague Island,' answered Les. 'Have a look around and do a bit of snorkelling.'

'Okay,' said the bloke. 'We're pretty well booked out till next week. But wait till I check.' At that moment the phone rang. 'I won't be a sec.'

The proprietor started talking on the phone and going through his bookings. Les browsed amongst the posters and photos on the wall. Even behind a face mask there was no mistaking the proprietor looking through the porthole of a rusting wreck and another of him stroking a big potato cod. One photo blown up to poster size stood out from the rest. Printed across the top was: 'How We Don't Run A Dive School'. In smaller print in the bottom right hand corner, it said: 'Photo By Ray Bissett'. The photo was taken at Ben Buckler the day Les was there with Ray and the diver drowned. Norton's face lit up. Well I'll be buggered, he thought.

Les stared at the poster-size photo in astonishment. It was like living the moment again in IMAX. He could see the anguish on the instructor's face as he worked on the diver he'd just rescued. Sense the shock and exhaustion amongst the other divers lying or milling around the rocks.

You could pick out a woman diver standing apart from the others with her head down being sick. Les was amazed at the clarity and detail of the photo. He could read the brands on the wetsuits, spot a lock of light brown hair poking out from under the woman diver's hood. See the vomit on the face of the rescued diver. Almost count the barnacles on the rocks.

'Hey, you're in luck mate,' said the bloke, hanging up the phone. 'There's been a cancellation. And I can get you out there tomorrow morning.'

'Okay.' Les walked back to the counter. 'Hey mate, where did you get that big photo?'

'The photographer's a mate of mine,' replied the proprietor. 'He sent it to me and I had it blown up.'

'I was there the day that happened,' said Les, excitedly. 'I was with him.'

'You were with Ray? Really?'

Les told the proprietor how he'd arranged to get some tips from Ray on underwater photography, but it was too rough. Then they came across all the drama as they were walking back. 'Looking at that photo,' said Les, 'is just like being there again. It's uncanny.'

'It certainly is,' agreed the bloke.

'Where do you know Ray from?' asked Les.

'Ohh shit. We're old mates. I come from Clovelly. Me and Ray used to dive together all the time.'

'I'm only a snorkel sucker,' said Les. 'But I like underwater photography.'

'Well, you won't find a better bloke to teach you than Ray. He's won over ten awards.' The proprietor laughed. 'He's a funny bastard too.'

The proprietor's name was Ian. He could get Les on a boat called *The Kingfisher*, leaving the jetty at nine the next morning. And seeing Les was a friend of Ray's, he'd give him a ten percent discount. Les thanked him and paid with his Visa card.

'It's funny,' said Les. 'The day that happened, I was walking back along the beach and a surfer committed suicide.'

'That's right,' said Ian. 'I saw it on the news. What a day.'

'It was.' Les shook his head. 'I don't know about surfing, Ian. But you can keep scuba diving. I had one go at it. I'll stick to snorkelling.'

'Yeah. I know what you mean,' said Ian. 'You got to be super careful. Any people we take out, we give them the full-on, silkworm treatment.' Ian glanced over at the photo. 'I'd hate to have something like that on my conscience.' As he spoke, a young Japanese couple walked in. The man was wearing Coke bottle glasses, the woman was about four feet tall and looked like she'd never been in anything deeper than a spa bath. 'Hello,' winked Ian. 'Talking about silkworms ... Mushi, mushi.' The two Japanese smiled and bowed towards the counter.

'I'll leave you to it, Ian,' said Les, waving his receipt. 'Thanks for everything,'

'No problem, Les. Have a good time out there.'

Les pocketed his receipt and walked back to the house. The front door was open, Warren was in the kitchen in a T-shirt and shorts holding a glass of orange juice and Glen Miller was swinging in the loungeroom.

'Hello,' said Les. 'You finally dragged yourself out of bed.'

'Hey, what about this fuckin unreal radio station,' said Warren. 'They've just played Cab Calloway, The Andrew Sisters, Rudy Vallee. If I'd known about this, I would have brought my white dinner jacket.'

'Maybe Brian Ferry'll lend you one of his.' Les tossed the paper on the table, got a glass of water and looked at Warren. 'So how are you this morning, Woz?' he asked.

'All right,' answered Warren, glancing at the headlines. 'But Jesus! Doesn't it get cold down here.'

'Cold?'

'Yeah. That room's like a fuckin deep freeze. I had to get up and put every blanket I could find on the bed. I felt like Omar Sharif in *Doctor Zhivago.*'

'It did get a bit chilly at one stage last night,' admitted Les.

'Oh and one other thing, Les,' said Warren. 'I know you like your little jokes and all that. But did you have to get up in the middle of the night and play the fuckin piano? And set that stupid bloody bear off?'

'*I* was playing the piano last night, Woz?'

'By playing, I mean clunking up and down on it like a moron. I'm in there freezing to death, trying to get to sleep. And you're playing Elton John.' Warren turned back to the headlines. 'But if that's what turns you on, so be it.'

'Warren. I've got some news for you, mate.' Les told Warren about finding the mess in the kitchen the day before then got a rat-trap from the pantry to prove his point. 'So there's rats in here. They get in the kitchen and they like to run up and down on the piano. I meant to set this last night. But I forgot.' Les put the rat-trap back in the pantry. 'As for the bear, there's something wrong with it. It goes off on its own.'

'It wasn't you then?' said Warren.

'No Warren. It wasn't me,' said Les, deliberately. 'I don't do childish fuckin things.'

Warren shrugged. 'If you say so. Actually the bear's a ripper. Clover had it going. She loves the bloody thing. Where did you get it?'

Les told Warren where he got it and how much it cost. 'I might give it to Clover for letting us have the house.' Les looked at his watch. 'They should be here soon.'

'Ohh yeah, for sure. Clover thinks punctuality has to do with flat tyres.'

Les read the paper out on the verandah, then gave it to Warren and tidied up his room. Warren read it then they both sat on the verandah, enjoying the view. A couple of ghetto blasters were playing CDs on the surrounding balconies.

But Warren insisted on listening to Season FM. He was tapping his toes to Andy Kirk and his Twelve Clouds of Joy playing 'Boogie Woogie Cocktail', when there was a knock on the door just before eleven.

'Look at that,' said Warren, holding up his watch. 'Right on time.'

Footsteps sounded along the hallway then Grace and Clover stepped out onto the verandah. Grace was wearing faded jeans and one of her originals in white, with a beige pelican on the front. Clover was wearing hipsters, and a blue Hawaiian shirt four sizes too big for her. There were pecks on the cheek and smiles and greetings all round, then Grace and Clover leant against the railing sizing the boys up. Grace spoke first.

'So how did you sleep last night?' she asked.

'Yes. Did you sleep all right?' said Clover.

'Yeah. It got a bit chilly at one stage,' said Les. 'But I was okay.'

'Forget chilly,' said Warren. 'It was bloody freezing. I've never been so cold in my life.'

Clover looked at Warren over her glasses. 'Freezing cold?'

'Where was it cold?' asked Grace.

'In my bedroom,' said Warren. 'Are there any electric blankets, Clover?'

Clover shook her head. 'Was there anything else besides the cold?'

'Only the rat in the piano,' smirked Warren. 'And the bear going off.'

'Rat in the piano?' said Clover.

Yeah,' replied Les. He told them about the noise the night before, then waking up to the mess in the kitchen and finding the rat-traps in the pantry. 'Only I forgot to set the trap last night. Jerry Lee Rat'd be in rock 'n' roll heaven right now.'

'What was that about the bear going off, Warren?' asked Grace.

'Les said there's something wrong with it,' shrugged Warren.

'I think it's the batteries,' said Les. 'They're wired wrong.'

'And it went off on its own,' said Grace.

'Yeah. It even dances round in circles,' said Les. 'I told you, it's got a mind and style all of its own.'

'Anything else, Les?' asked Clover.

Les thought for a moment. But he didn't have the heart to tell Clover her boyfriend got up during the night and pissed all over the bathroom. 'No. Nothing else,' he replied.

Grace and Clover exchanged glances. 'A piano-playing rat and a dancing bear,' said Grace.

Clover shook her head. 'What next?'

'I'll tell you what's next,' said Warren. 'How about breakfast.' He glanced at his watch. 'Oh shit! Look at that. Ten o'clock already.'

'We stopped to pick some flowers,' said Clover.

'You could have picked half of Amsterdam.' Warren got to his feet. 'Come on, let's go. Whose car are we taking?'

'Car?' said Grace. 'It's five minutes up the hill.'

'There's a hill?' said Warren.

Les locked the front door, Grace locked her Jackaroo and they set off. Les told them about booking a trip to Montague Island and about the photo in the dive shop. They crossed the road, wended their way through the Saturday morning crowd and were soon at Carey's.

The restaurant was packed; even the tables outside were taken. But they were lucky enough to arrive just as four people were getting up from the same table Les and Grace had the day before. They ordered, Les picked up the tab, then they got their little wooden objects and sat down. This time Les got a banana. Their coffees arrived and they got into a bit of chitchat about the night before, about clothes, the house. Les told Clover about the photo of Lander Merrigan in Jasmine Cunneen's book.

'That was my great, great uncle,' said Clover. 'We've got the original photo at home. Poor old Lander and his wife were drowned.'

'Yeah, Grace told me,' said Les. 'And their son Eachan finished in the rathouse.'

'My hundred-and-forty-eighth cousin removed, or something,' said Clover.

'So how did your parents end up with the house?' asked Les.

'It's been in the family for years. Now dad owns it.'

'It's the most beautiful house,' said Grace.

'How come your parents don't live there?' asked Warren. 'It's a fantastic spot.'

'They're happy at Dalmeny,' said Clover.

'Do you ever rent it out?' asked Les.

'Now and again. But only to people we know.'

'Like us,' said Warren. 'Your hunk of a boyfriend, Warren Wonderful. And Lucky Les.'

'Lucky Les, eh,' said Les.

Warren reached over and punched him on the shoulder. 'That's you, baby.'

'Yeah.'

The food arrived and they had a lovely, long breakfast talking and cracking corny jokes. Warren ordered more coffees and they continued the conversation. When they finished their second coffees they decided to make a move. On the way home, Les called into the dive shop to show the others the photo. Ian was on the phone again; Les gave him a wave and pointed the photo out to the others. They were impressed. Grace was still talking about it when they were standing on the verandah back at the house.

'That's hard to imagine,' she said. 'You see one drowning. Then you walk along the beach and see another.'

'Yeah. Poor bloody Edwin,' said Les.

'He was such a nice person,' said Clover. 'Everybody liked him.'

'Bad luck about his girlfriend,' grunted Les.

'Yes,' said Clover. 'You and Serina never quite hit it off, did you?'

'I'd like to hit it off with her. With a size twelve Doc Marten. Right up her thrill-seeking Khyber.'

'Now don't be like that, Les,' smiled Clover.

'I still can't get over the view from here,' said Grace, looking out across the channel. 'It's so beautiful.'

Les snapped his fingers. 'Hey, I just thought of something. I won't be a minute.'

Les got his keys and walked out to the car. He'd completely forgotten that the stabilising binoculars Eddie had given him were still in the boot. He got them out and returned to the verandah.

'Have a look at the view through these, Grace,' he said, taking them out of their case and handing them to her.

Grace held them to her eyes. 'Oh yes. Don't these make a difference!' She had a good look around then handed them to Clover.

'Look at that,' said Clover. 'I can see right up to Dalmeny. These are great, Les. Where did you get them?'

'Off a friend,' said Les. 'I forgot they were in the car.'

They all had a look then realised it was time to make a move if they were going to see Jimbo's Blues Band. They left the house and walked down to the Festival. At the entrance they showed their wrist tags and joined the people inside.

'Does anybody want a cool one?' asked Warren.

'Not on top of all that food,' said Clover.

Les agreed. 'Count me out.'

Grace pointed out the big tent where Jimbo was playing. 'Why don't we find a seat?'

There were plenty of people around, but it wasn't as crowded as the night before. They got four seats, six back from the stage, and weren't there long before Jimbo strolled on stage wearing a red hat and a Hawaiian shirt. The band followed and Jimbo walked up to the mike. He rambled away about having a singalong, then produced a piece of cardboard with the lyrics to 'What A Wonderful World This Would Be' on it.

'So you got it,' he said pointing to the words. 'Don't know much about . . . Don't know what a . . . Okay. Here we go.'

The crowd got into into it. Les and the others sang along. When the band finished that song, they slipped straight into 'Bye Bye Baby'. And behind all the fooling around, Jimbo and his band were tighter than a vice done up, and he had one of the best blues voices in the business. They scorched it and several other songs. Les and Grace took photos. The band played some more howling rock, then Jimbo stood on his head and sang two songs. He stood up, put on his Indian war bonnet and wore it till they finished the set. They did 'Statesborough Blues' for an encore and finished to a tumultuous applause.

'That guy,' said Clover. 'He is . . . what can I say?'

'They can boogie,' said Warren. 'I know that.'

Grace pointed to her program. 'They're on again tomorrow.'

'I'll be here,' said Les.

Warren rose to his feet. 'I got to have a snakes.'

'Okay.' Clover pointed towards the middle of the park. 'See that table and bench seats? We'll wait for you there. You want anything?'

'Yeah. Grab me a fruit juice, will you.'

Warren left for the toilet. The others moved across to the wooden table. Clover and Grace went for the drinks while Les minded their bags, then they stood around waiting for Warren. They finished their fruit juices and after a while Les looked at his watch.

'Where's Warren gone for a leak?' he said. 'The state forest?'

'Yes,' agreed Clover. 'He's certainly taking his time.'

'He might have stopped at the souvenir stall,' suggested Grace.

A minute or two later, Warren appeared walking unsteadily through the crowd. He looked pale and the two men who had been checking Les out the night before were standing on either side of him. One was holding Warren's arm and another man with a thick moustache followed behind. Walking in front as if he owned the park, was a tall, heavy-framed man with thick, tattooed arms, wearing black jeans and a yellow Big Rock Fishing Club polo shirt. He had a mop of unruly black hair pushed back from a wide, bony forehead, and on either side of a flat nose, two beady, dark eyes glared menacingly at everything in sight.

'Oh shit,' said Grace. 'It's Morgan bloody Scully.'

The man holding Warren pushed him towards Les and the others. Warren bumped against the table and Clover took hold of his arm.

The tall man gave Les a heavy once up and down. 'So you're Les Norton.' He had a dull, rasping voice and when he opened his mouth, his teeth looked like a row of charred railway sleepers. 'You're a shitty fuckin waiter. You live in Cox Ave Bondi. And this is your little bumboy, Warren Edwards.'

'I don't know what's going on, Les,' said Warren. 'They grabbed me coming out the toilet and went through my wallet. They found out where we live and I told them you were a waiter.'

'That's okay, Woz,' said Les. 'Are you all right?'

Warren winced and held his stomach. 'Yeah. I'm all right.'

Les turned to the tall man. 'Okay. That's me. I'm a waiter. I work in a restaurant at Bondi. Now what's your problem . . . ?'

'Morgan,' rasped the man in the polo shirt. 'And you're the cunt with the problem. That was my uncle, and his mates, you bashed up in the pub last night.'

Les slowly shook his head. 'I'm not sure . . .'

'Ohh don't give me the fuckin shits,' snapped Morgan. 'It was you.'

'All right,' said Les, tightly. 'It was me. So what?'

'So what?' Morgan's eyes blazed. 'So you're pretty good bashing up old blokes when they're drunk. Let's see how you go against someone a bit younger.' Morgan jabbed a thumb in his chest. 'Me.'

'You want to fight me over those four clowns?' said Les. 'You're kidding.'

'No I'm not fuckin kiddin'.' Morgan nodded towards the entrance. 'You and me. Outside.'

Norton's mind started racing. He was seething at what Morgan and his thugs had done to poor Warren and under normal circumstances he would have ripped straight into Morgan on the spot, big and all as he was. But these weren't normal circumstances. Norton's back was buggered. If he went outside he was on a hiding to nothing. And even if could put up half a fight, Morgan had three big mates with him. It was time for Les to do a Brer Rabbit. And Brer Rabbit better be able to tap dance pretty bloody fast. At that moment Norman Dadd loomed up in a bulky T-shirt and jeans with four nervous-looking security people.

'Not in here, Morgan,' he said, loud and clear.

'Ohh don't shit yourself, Daddy,' said Morgan. 'Nothing's gonna happen in here.' He turned and glared at Norton. 'But it will outside.'

Les looked back at Morgan and half smiled. 'Hang on a moment, Morgan,' he said easily. 'You're going about this all the wrong way, baby. You're blowing your cool.'

Morgan glowered at Les. 'I'm what?'

'You're blowing your cool, brother. When you come to a fork in the road, take it. You're walking backwards when you should be putting your best foot forward. There's fire in your eyes, but you got water on the brain. You're surrounded by yes men and stuck in nowheresville. You've got the world on a string and enough rope to hang yourself.'

'What the . . . ?'

'You're that far down, Morgan,' continued Les, 'rock bottom is three flights up. Someone's pulled the rug from over your eyes. You're a cool swinger, but you can't handle the heat. You've got to roll off your high end and adjust your tone control dude. Opportunity's knocking . . .'

Morgan's face coloured and he turned to his team. 'What's this cunt talking about?'

'I don't know,' shrugged the man with the moustache. 'But fuck him anyway.'

'What am I talking about?' said Les. 'What am I saying? What am I trying to tell you? Is that what you're asking me?'

'I'm not asking you anything,' said Morgan. 'I just fuckin want you outside.'

'That's what I'm saying,' said Les. 'Anything and everything. And anything's better than nothing.' Les smiled at Morgan. 'In other words, why don't we do it for money?'

Morgan stared at Les, looked at his mates for a moment then stared back to Les. 'For what?'

'For money,' said Les. 'I'll fight you for five thousand dollars.' Les watched Morgan's eyes knit together and he could hear the boulders slowly rumbling around behind the big man's forehead. Morgan's mates stayed quiet. Standing in front of his security staff, Daddy looked surprised as well as interested. Warren and the others were still mystified.

'Well. What do you say, Morgan?' said Les.

'I'm ...'

'Look at it this way, Morgan,' said Les. 'If we go outside and fight, the cops'll come and break it up. We'll both get pinched and it'll cost you money. I'll leave town still in one piece. And you'll have proved nothing. Right?' Morgan half nodded in agreement. 'There's no way I can beat you,' continued Les. 'But with money riding on the result, at least I'll have a go.' Les gestured to Morgan. 'Well. What do you reckon? You're a big, hard man. Are you game enough to back yourself in a fight?'

'He's got a point there, Morgan,' said Daddy. 'Are you game?'

'Game? Of course I'm fuckin game,' asserted Morgan.

'Have you got five grand?' said Daddy.

'Yeah.'

'Righto,' said Les. 'Then it's on. In here one o'clock Monday afternoon after lunch, when there's no one around. Just the blokes packing up.' Les motioned for Morgan and Daddy to come in closer. 'That all right with you?' he asked Morgan.

'Yeah,' grunted Morgan.

'Will you hold the money, Norm?'

'No worries,' said Norm.

'I'll have my five grand here in half an hour. Can you do that?'

'Yeah,' nodded Morgan.

'And if anybody gets pissed and starts fighting before Monday, he forfeits his money. Right?'

Morgan nodded morosely. 'Right.'

'Good idea,' said Norm.

'Okay,' said Les, stepping back. 'That's the rules. We'll meet here again on Monday.'

Morgan pointed a calloused finger at Les. 'Forget the fuckin rules. You just be here Monday, you big-mouthed prick. Because if you're not, I know where you live. And I'll come looking for you.'

'He's not joking,' said Norm seriously. 'I know these blokes. They'll come after you all right.'

Les held his hands up. 'Fair enough. I'll be here.'

'Make sure you fuckin are.' Morgan gave the nod to his mates and they left.

There was a brittle silence for a moment as Les looked pensively around him, then caught Clover's eye.

'What in God's name was that all about?' she asked.

'How about I explain everything back at the house.' Les turned to Daddy. 'Norm. Okay if I have a word with you on your own?'

'Sure,' replied Daddy. 'Come over to the souvenir tent.'

Les caught Clover's eye again. 'I won't be long.'

Norm dismissed his four, relieved, security people. Les walked with him and the others as far as the souvenir tent, then followed Norm. At the rear of the tent was a caged-off annexe with a wire gate. Norm opened the gate and they stepped into a room full of T-shirts, cartons of CDs, brochures and other merchandise. There was a table and two plastic chairs in the middle. Norm sat down on one chair and Les sat facing him across the table on the other.

'Well Norm,' said Les. 'You saw what happened outside.'

'I sure did,' answered Norm. 'You're not bad on your feet, are you?'

'Norm. I've only got about a grand on me. And my credit cards. Can you spring me the five grand? You know me and who I run with. I'll have it back to you first thing next week.'

'Spring you the five grand?' said Norm. 'Mate, I'm backing you. I'm going to organise the side bets.' Norm grinned and rubbed his big hands together. 'You'll be the underdog. I'll get three to one.' Norm threw back his head and laughed. 'Morgan's bloody good. But he sure ain't you.'

'Norm. Before you get too carried away,' said Les, 'I've got a fucked back.'

'You've what?'

Les told Norm about his back and how he aggravated it in the fight. 'What I was mainly doing out there was buying time. I couldn't knock a sick pygmy off a piss pot at the moment.'

'Oh,' said Norm. 'That could be somewhat of a handicap if you're going to fight Morgan.'

'Yeah,' agreed Les. 'But I'm getting some treatment on my back. I might be all right.' Les looked directly at Norm. 'If not, I'll ring Eddie. He'll be here in four hours.'

Norm put his hands in front of him and looked away. 'I didn't hear that.'

'I know,' said Les. 'That is taking things to extremes. And I'll cop all the heat if the big goose suddenly disappears. But I don't fancy finishing up a cripple either.'

Norm stared at Les. 'So what happened in the pub?'

Les shook his head. 'It was half my fault.' He told Norm how the fight came about. How he lost his temper then simply went into the swing of things. 'In a way I don't blame that bloke for sticking up for his uncle. I did go a bit overboard, I suppose.'

'Hey,' said Norm. 'Don't be too concerned about sorting out old Mick and his mates. They're cunts. And my missus has had to go around Mick's place plenty of times and patch his wife up after Mick's had a few drinks.' There was a rap on the gate. It opened and a woman half the size of Daddy, with long dark hair and glasses walked in, wearing slacks and a Blues Festival T-shirt. 'Hello. Talking about wives,' said Norm. 'Here's the Handbrake now. Les this is Marina. Marina, Les Norton.'

'Hello Les.'

'Hello Marina. Nice to meet you.'

Marina looked at Norm. 'We need some more extra large T-shirts.'

'Okay. I'll bring them out.'

'And some Little Charlie CDs.'

'No worries.' Marina left and Norm turned back to Les. 'All right. I'll put up the five grand. What are you getting done to your back?'

'I don't know. Grace thinks she might be able to help me.'

'Amazing's working on you? Well, you're in good hands.' Norm lumbered to his feet then opened a drawer in the table. 'Before you go. Have this.' He handed Les a length of black cord, with a plastic ticket on a swivel that said: Narooma Blues Festival — GUEST.

'What's this?' asked Les.

'It lets you go backstage and meet the bands. Have a coffee and a bite to eat if you want.'

Les stood up and put the backstage pass in his pocket. 'Thanks Norm. That's unreal.'

'No worries,' said Daddy.

'And thanks, for everything else, Norm. I really appreciate it.'

'That's okay, Les. I'll see you later.'

'Yeah. See you.'

Norm started going through the cartons. Les left him to it and headed for home, instinctively looking around as he walked out the front of the park. But Les felt he was safe for the time being. Nothing would happen before Monday. When he got to the house the door was open and the others were out on the verandah with a pot of tea sitting on the table. The colour had returned to Warren's face, but he wasn't doing any stand-up comedy. They all stared silently at Les. Les gave them a weak smile and a half wave.

'Hi.'

'Yeah hi,' said Warren. He took a sip of tea. 'Shit it's good living with you, Les. Next time, as well as getting kidnapped, I might get knifed. Or shot.'

'Are you all right, mate?' asked Les, genuinely concerned.

'Yeah. One of those clowns punched me in the stomach, that's all.'

'Which one?'

Warren ran a finger across his top lip. 'Groucho Marx.'

'Right.' Les patted Warren on the shoulder. 'And thanks for the bit about the waiter, Woz. You're bloody staunch, mate.' Warren shrugged a non-reply.

Clover gave Norton a very calculated once up and down. 'All right Les,' she said. 'Exactly what is going on?'

Les indicated to the teapot. 'Okay if I have a cup of tea?'

Les poured himself a cup of tea, added milk and sugar and told the others the whole story. 'I suppose I should have told you about the fight. Except I felt like a dill and I honestly thought no one knew it was me. But they must have seen us out together. So they grabbed you, Woz, to get some info on me. Sorry about that mate.'

'So it was you all the time, that beat up Mick Scully and his friends,' said Grace.

'Yes Grace. It was me,' admitted Les.

Grace looked at Les and shook her head. 'You're certainly something else, Les. Aren't you?'

'I have to go to the toilet,' said Warren, getting out of his chair.

Clover put her hand on the pot. 'I'm going to put the kettle on again.'

They left, leaving Grace and an uncomfortable Les on the verandah.

'Yes. You're something else all right,' said Grace, continuing to stare at Les. 'One minute you're George from Canberra. You're staying at the Islander Motel. You had a terrible breakup with your girlfriend — oh, and I look like one of her friends. You hurt your back changing tyres. Then you're asking me about the fight and do they know who it was? Do you ever, sort of, get round to say, going within flying distance of the truth at all, Les?'

Les looked at Grace for a moment. 'Okay,' he said. 'I don't blame you having the shits with me. But I wasn't really lying to you, Grace. I was only trying to cover my arse. That's all.'

'Ohh yeah.'

'Look. What happened in the hotel was just bad luck. And you don't
really think I want to fight this gorilla on Monday do you? Christ! I'll
probably get my head kicked in. As well as lose five thousand bucks.
Which I just talked Daddy into putting up for me. And if I remember
right, Grace, when I did mention the fight, you said "Oh, couldn't have
happened to a nicer bunch of blokes. Pity Morgan wasn't there too."
Right?'

Grace shook her head. 'Yes. But ...'

'No buts. The thing is, Grace, you said you could help me with my
back. And now I need your help. Bad. And that's the truth.'

'The truth?' said Grace. 'Hah!'

Clover returned with the jug of hot water and poured some in the
teapot. Warren followed her out and sat down. Les looked at Grace who
was staring at the ocean.

'So what's the story, Grace? Are you going to help me?'

Grace continued to stare at the ocean, then she looked at Norton.
Finally she turned to Clover. 'Clover, have you got a biro in your bag?'

'Sure. Here you are.' Clover handed Grace a biro and a notebook.

Grace placed the notebook on the table and clicked the biro. 'Here's
how you get to my place.'

A huge grin spread across Norton's face. 'Grace,' he said, 'you won't
ever regret this. I promise.'

'Yeah, yeah.' Grace started writing directions on the piece of paper.
'Your name is Les, isn't it? That is your car out the front?' Grace paused
for a second and looked around her. 'This *is* number three Browning
Street?'

'Now come on, Grace,' said Les. 'Don't be like that.'

Grace drew a little map with her address and phone number on it and
handed it to Les. 'I'll see you about five.'

Les looked at the piece of paper. 'Grace. What can I say?'

Grace picked up her bag. 'How about goodbye as I back down the
driveway.'

Grace farewelled the others and said she'd catch up with them later
that night. Les walked Grace out to her car and opened the door. He felt
like kissing her. Instead, he smiled as she started the engine.

'Five o'clock?'

'Five o'clock,' replied Grace. She looked at Les for a moment, then
blew him a kiss. Les blew one back off his fingertips and watched her
drive off. Then he walked back out to the verandah where a fresh cup of
tea was waiting for him

'Are you fair dinkum going to fight that dopey, big relation of yours on Monday?' said Warren.

'I got to, haven't I, Woz,' said Les, taking a sip of tea. 'Five grand is five grand.'

'What about your back?'

'Don't matter. Grace reckons she can fix it. Besides, I told Daddy you were going to back me up.'

'What?' said Warren. 'I'll be leaving for Sydney straight after breakfast.'

'Not without me you're not,' said Clover. 'I've heard about Morgan Scully. He's all mean and horrible.'

Les shook his head. 'Jesus. You sure know who your friends are, don't you.'

They finished their tea then Warren had to to drive Clover back to Dalmeny. Les didn't know what time he'd be back from Grace's. He'd catch up with them later. Les put everything away then walked back out onto the verandah. It hadn't been the best of days. And the thought of having to either fight Morgan Scully, or bury him somewhere with Eddie, weighed heavily on Norton's mind. What should have been a few days resting and listening to music had turned out to be a giant pain in the arse.

Out in front of the house the water running through the channel looked blue and inviting. And if there was anything to ease a troubled mind, it was an hour or so of snorkelling. While you were floating around looking at the fish or whatever, you switched off. And Les needed to switch off. He climbed into a pair of Speedos and his rubber vest, tossed his disposable camera in with his towel and snorkelling gear and strolled down to the jetty.

People were walking by or fishing near the boats and on the right, a large, white catamaran bobbed peacefully at its mooring. Facing the catamaran was a bench, where two fishermen had finished cleaning a catch of salmon. Beneath the bench a concrete landing sat at the water's edge. Les stood on the landing, rinsed his face mask then pushed out into the channel.

The water was beautiful and clear, running over a white, sandy bottom covered in sea grass. There were fish everywhere: whiting, bream, leather jackets, schools of fat blackfish. It wasn't deep near the jetty and Les drifted along with the current, diving around the boats and under the catamaran. Lying on the sand beneath the catamaran was the skeleton of a huge marlin, picked clean. Spread across the sand, it had a sad beauty about it so Les dived down and took a photo. In barely two metres of water, he came across a school of blackfish feeding on the bottom. Les swam amongst them and they appeared completely oblivious to him, munching away on the seagrass right in front of his face mask. It was amazing. Les floated amongst the blackfish for a while taking photos, then chased a big leather jacket through the piers, watching its tiny fins going a hundred to the dozen, before photographing it framed in front of a mooring rope. Les floated out to the deeper water and got several shots of a big black stingray moving across the bottom, as well as some mullet, before swimming back to the piers. After a while Les looked at his watch. He went on to photograph several big whiting that had joined the blackfish, then got out of the water and walked back to the house.

Les rinsed his gear under the shower and had a shave. He figured Grace would probably be giving him some kind of massage and he'd end up covered in oil, so he wore a pair of dry Speedos, shorts and the T-shirt he had on in the fight. He put a sweatshirt in his overnight bag, then locked the house, leaving the key under the mat for Warren. He fired up the Berlina and took the road out of town.

It didn't take long to leave Narooma behind. Traffic was light and the drive through the countryside in the late afternoon was pleasant. He crossed Coruna Lake and at the top of a rise a sign on the left pointed to Mystery Bay. That's not far at all, thought Les. I'll check it out for sure. Further along a sign on the right said Central Tilba and Tilba Tilba. Les took the road for Central Tilba.

A yellow barn with a sign saying CENTRAL TILBA ENGINEERING appeared amongst the trees on the left, and further on a little wooden church stood on the right. Past the church the countryside opened up into green rolling hills full of granite boulders. Down on the right, opposite a long, wide valley, Les could see the red roofs of Central Tilba snuggled against the surrounding hills. He continued on, then turned right at the war memorial and slowed down as he entered the main street.

It was very pretty. All the old heritage cottages and houses on either side of the road had been colourfully painted and preserved and turned into craft shops and cafes. The post office was on the left and further on the local hotel. Amongst the shops on the right, a big one had a sign in the window: THE HEMP EVOLUTION. That must be where Grace gets her shirts, mused Les. Most of the shops were closed and apart from the hotel, there weren't many people around and few cars. Les drove past a Tibetan Import shop up on the left, more colourful shops, and further on where the road dipped down was the old cheese factory. He checked the map Grace had given him. Two kilometres on the left past the cheese factory.

Les followed a narrow, winding road that climbed through green hills studded with granite boulders, and the odd farm with a few cows nosing amongst the grass. Further on, next to a blue oil drum letterbox, a white gate hung back in a driveway surrounded by trees. A white sign welded on top of the letter box said: GRACELAND.

Les followed the driveway up until it levelled off at a clearing circled by trees. Opposite the trees, Grace's 4WD was parked in front of a yellow picket fence; beyond the fence and in front of the house sat a garden full of flowers. The house was all wood and painted white and green with a yellow roof and looked like one of the old heritage homes in Tilba. Steps led up to a front door set beneath an arch supported by two wooden poles, with windows either side. A narrow verandah ran from the left of the house and around the front. Les took the steps to the front door and stopped. A black female Staffordshire, with a huge head and a bark like a dinosaur, came skidding around the corner of the verandah. Bristling and snarling, it took up a position between Les and the front door.

Les stepped back from the door and held his palms up. 'Good girl,' he said quietly. 'Good girl. You're just doing your job. Good girl.'

The dog continued to snarl at Les when the door opened and Grace came out wearing a blue hemp shirt with her hair combed in two pigtails either side of her head.

'Morticia. What's the matter, baby,' she said, and put her hand inside the dog's collar. The dog settled down a little but continued to growl at Les. 'This is Morticia,' said Grace. 'She's our little baby.'

'She's a little beauty,' said Les. 'And she does her job too.'

'Yes. She looks after us.'

Grace reached over and gave Les a peck on the cheek. Les pecked her back. The dog noticed this and stopped growling. Les knelt down and softly called the dog.

'Morticia. Come here girl. Come on. I'm a friend of Grace's.'

Morticia looked suspiciously at Les, then reluctantly came over. Les patted her on the head, then put his fingers where her spine met her tail. He started scratching and rubbing and Morticia began wiggling her muscly behind and wagging her tail. She rolled her eyes back and looked up at Les.

'How's that, sweetheart?' The little dog continued to wag its tail and smiled up at Les as he kept scratching and rubbing. 'Yes. Your head's not the best, Morticia. But you've got a great little arse.'

Grace was impressed. 'You've got quite a way with women, haven't you Les. I don't think I've ever seen her like that around strangers before. Especially men.'

'It's just a matter of pushing the right buttons.' Les gave Morticia a pat on the head and stood up.

'Anyway. Come inside,' said Grace. 'You found the place all right.'

'Yeah, easy,' said Les. 'And I saw the turnoff to Mystery Bay.'

Inside was a little like the Merrigan house. High ceilings and a long hallway, with the kitchen and bathroom opposite, and two bedrooms either side. The polished timber floor along the hallway led to a large loungeroom and another door opened onto an enclosed verandah. Facing an open fire, a red velvet lounge suite sat on a Persian carpet and against one wall was a TV and stereo. Paintings of birds and old photos of Tilba hung on the walls, tasselled lamps sat in the corners and near the door to the verandah was a large, black, fitness ball.

'This is a really nice old house,' said Les. 'By old I mean like the ones in Tilba. Heritage style.'

'Yes. This was a gold merchant's home,' said Grace. 'It was built in the eighteen hundreds.'

'It's in bloody good nick.'

'Thanks. Can I get you something to drink? There's some beer. Or white wine.'

Les shook his head. 'A mineral water will do thanks.'

Grace went to the kitchen and came back with a bottle of sparkling and handed it to Les. 'So what did you do this afternoon?'

'Went for a snorkel with my disposable camera,' he replied. He told Grace about the fish round the jetty. 'What did you do?'

'Finished a few T-shirts. Cleaned the house.'

Les nodded then looked at Grace over his bottle of water. 'So how are you going to fix my back, Grace?' he asked.

'I'll show you later. But first, come with me.' Grace slipped on a pair of trainers. 'I want to show you something while there's still light.'

Grace put two empty wine bottles and a screwtop jar into an overnight bag, then took Les out through the enclosed verandah to a set of stairs leading down to an open yard. The yard backed onto the surrounding valleys and granite-studded hills and a trail led from the yard through a small patch of trees. Morticia trotted over from the verandah and Les followed Grace up a steep hill as the trail followed a small stream running below on the right. After they'd climbed for a while, Les paused to catch a glimpse of the sun setting on surrounding valleys. He could see a couple of farmhouses below, the roofs of Central Tilba to the right, and the ocean in the distance. Les commented to Grace about the view, then they climbed further up the trail, before Grace stopped at some trees facing a huge mass of granite boulders. There, the stream gushed and bubbled down the hillside from out of the rocks. Morticia had a drink and Grace pointed along the watercourse to a rocky pond edged with small trees, down in the valley below. Alongside the pond was a timber-built pumping station.

'You see that pond down there? That's on the Hillier property. They've got cattle living to twenty-one and still producing calves at eighteen. Twins.'

'Shit!' said Les. 'That's amazing for cattle.'

'Their sheep live to fifteen. Joe Hillier and his wife are both in their eighties and they're as fit as fiddles. She still rides horses.'

Les looked at Grace. 'You're not going to tell me it's the water?'

Grace nodded. 'Exactly. These scientists from the CSIRO heard about the cattle. So they came here and tested the water. It's full of minerals. Especially magnesium bicarbonate.'

'What's that do?'

'Flushes the toxins and carbon dioxide out of your blood.'

'And you've been drinking it?'

'I started just after I bought the property. Believe me Les, Amazing Grace wasn't looking too amazing when she left Sydney. Not after having Ellie and going through all that other drama.'

'So that's your secret,' said Les.

'That. Plus exercise and a fairly healthy lifestyle. But remember I told you I had shares in a company in Sydney. It's a soft drink company. They're bottling the water as Eureka Water. And because it comes through my property they're paying me a percentage on every case.'

'How's it going?' asked Les.

'They've only just started. But they're hoping to get a big spread in the papers and on TV. So it could take off. And if it does . . .'

'Aunty Grace is laughing.'

'Exactly.'

'Well, good on you,' said Les. 'I hope you sell a million.' He bent down, cupped a hand and took a drink. 'It sure tastes all right.'

Grace flashed Les a sly smile. 'That's just Eureka lite, Les. Follow me.'

With Morticia trotting alongside, Grace took Les further up the hill to the end of the trail. After that, they scrambled up the hillside and over rocks to a clearing, where a tiny spring seeped from a crack in a huge wall of granite and gently overflowed into a small rock pool at the base. The water was crystal clear and shone like silver in the rays from the late afternoon sun. The bottom of the pool was covered in what appeared to be fine, white sand.

Grace placed her bag in front of the rock pool. 'This is the other Eureka water,' she said. 'The high octane stuff.'

'It is?' said Les.

'Yep. I didn't tell the soft drink people about this one. It starts way back under all this granite. I don't know what's in it. But it's anti-inflammatory. Every time Ellie or I get a bruise or a sprain, we drink some. And it heals in no time.'

Les cupped his hand again and took a mouthful. 'It's got a kind of bitter-sweet taste. Not bad actually.'

'You have to stir up all the sediment on the bottom,' said Grace. 'That's where all the goodies are.'

'And you reckon this will fix my back, in time for Monday with Morgan.'

'It should. With a bit of massage.'

Les stared into the little rock pool. 'I'll take your word for it.'

Grace took the screw top jar from her overnight bag and scooped it into the pool, till the sediment on the bottom swirled through the water like snow. She filled the jar and the two wine bottles, sealed the tops then put them in her overnight bag and hoisted it over her shoulder.

'Righto,' she said, indicating down the trail to Les. 'Let's get back while we've still got light.'

The sun had gone when they reached the house. Morticia went round to her kennel at the side and Les followed Grace up the back stairs. As they kicked off their shoes and walked through the enclosed verandah, Les noticed a screen printing set-up near several clotheslines hung with neatly printed T-shirts.

'So this is where the Grace Holt originals originate,' he said.

'Yes. It keeps me out of mischief.'

'You've got a big fan in Clover.' Les watched as Grace put her bag in the loungeroom then followed her out to the kitchen.

Grace's kitchen was nicely set up. A double window above the sink looked out into the valley, a wooden table and chairs sat in the middle, and a rack of copper cooking utensils hung above the stove. Amongst the magnets and things pinned to the fridge was a photo of a pretty, fair-haired girl in denim, holding Morticia.

'Is that your daughter?' asked Les.

'Yes. That's Ellie. Smelly Ellie. She'll be home on Tuesday.'

'She's half a good sort,' smiled Les. 'A bit like her mother.'

'She's going to be good-looking when she grows up,' said Grace. 'That's when I'll buy a shotgun. Are you hungry, Les?'

'I'm always hungry, Grace. And even when I'm not hungry, I can still eat something.'

Grace pointed to the table. 'Have a seat. I baked some eggplant parmigiana.'

Grace took a large container from the fridge, scooped a pile of food onto a plastic dish and placed it in the microwave. When it pinged she served up two platefuls with rice and crispy bread and butter. Les had a mouthful and nearly fainted. The eggplant was cooked to perfection in a beautiful tomato and onion sauce, and over the top was a layer of lightly baked cheese with more bite than an alligator. Les had another mouthful and looked at Grace.

'Grace,' he said. 'This is absolutely sensational. I've never tasted anything like it.'

'Amazing's not a bad cook on her day,' said Grace. 'But it makes a difference if the eggplants are fresh. And I get a special cheese in Tilba.'

'It's delicious,' said Les, stuffing some more into his mouth, along with a lump of bread.

They finished with coffee, Grace placed what was left back in the fridge then put the dishes in the sink and turned to Les.

'Have you had enough to eat?'

Les patted his stomach. 'Plenty.'

'Okay. Come inside, and we'll have a look at your back.'

'You want me to get my gear off?' said Les. 'I got Speedos on.'

'Okay,' replied Grace.

Les followed Grace into the lounge and got down to his blue Speedos. Grace rolled the fitness ball over and told Les to sit on it with his hands resting on the back of the lounge and facing away from her. Les had seen these big rubber balls, but had never used one. He did as he was told and as soon as he sat on it he could feel his spine straighten and his stomach muscles contract.

'Hey, these are all right,' said Les, bouncing lightly up and down.

'Didn't your physiotherapist put you on one of these?' asked Grace.

'No. All I got was ultrasound.'

Grace ran her eyes over Les. 'You're in pretty good shape, aren't you.'

'I train a lot with a mate who used to be a top middleweight fighter.' said Les.

'What about you, Les. Can you fight?'

'I can handle myself a bit,' shrugged Les.

'So I believe.' Grace smiled at Les and put her hand on his back. 'Are you a gangster, Les?'

Les smiled up at Grace. 'No. But some of my best friends are.'

'Yeah, right. So where is it sore?'

'Just above my kidneys.'

Grace ran her hand along Norton's spine. 'Yes. I can feel the swelling. Does this hurt?' Grace pushed her knuckle into Norton's vertabrae.

'Ow!' winced Les. 'Does it what.'

'Okay.' Grace walked over to a cabinet and came back with a small bottle. 'You know what this is, Les?'

Norton had a look and shook his head. 'No.'

'Hemp seed oil. It's the best massage oil there is.'

'If you say so, Grace,' said Les.

Grace tipped a little on her hand and rubbed it into Les's back. Gently at first then a little firmer. 'How does that feel?' she asked.

'Unreal,' said Les, rocking gently on the rubber ball.

Grace stopped and rubbed some oil on her right knee then got a footrest. She placed her foot on it, put her hands on Les's shoulders and pushed her knee against his spine. 'Okay Les,' she said. 'Start bouncing up and down on the ball. Not too fast. Just nice and steady.'

Les did as Grace instructed. It hurt a little at first, then the pain eased. After a while, Grace's knee in his back began to feel good.

'Ohh yeah,' said Les, closing his eyes. 'That feels unreal.'

'I told you I could help you,' said Grace. 'Your spine's sitting straight, and the sore point's getting massaged at the same time.'

Les kept slowly rocking up and down. 'Whatever it is, it's certainly working.'

'Good. How about we listen to some music?'

Grace walked over to the stereo, put a CD on, then returned to the rubber ball and pushed her knee back into Norton's spine. Les started bouncing up and down again and some good rock 'n' roll drifted over.

'Hey, this is all right,' said Les. 'Who is it?'

'Jools Holland's Big Band Rhythm and Blues. I ordered it from Sydney.'

Grace pulled Les back against her knee as he gently bounced up and down to the music. It was so relaxing, Les kept drifting off; he lost all track of time. Another track finished, Grace took her knee away and pushed her knuckles into Norton's back. She massaged his spine for a while then gave Norton's neck and shoulders a rub before she finally stopped.

'There you go,' said Grace. 'How do you feel now?'

Les opened his eyes, blinked and arched his back. 'That's unreal,' he said. Les turned around on the ball and looked at Grace. 'The sharp pain's nowhere near as bad as it was. I just feel kind of stiff.'

'That's understandable. You've just had a really deep massage.' Grace went to the kitchen and came back with the jar of water. She shook it up, unscrewed the lid and handed it to Les. 'Here. Drink this.'

Les gulped it down easily, sediment and all. 'Thanks,' he said, and handed Grace the empty jar.

'That will get your system used to it. Too much can make you upset in the tummy, if you've never had it before. But the two bottles — I want you to drink one when you get up tomorrow morning, and the other one before you go to bed Sunday night. You got that — George?'

'No worries,' smiled Les.

Grace put the jar back on the coffee table then stood in front of Les and smiled down at him. 'And by Monday afternoon, you should be fighting fit.'

'Are you going to come down and cheer me on?' asked Les.

Grace shook her head. 'No. I'd like to see Morgan Scully get what's coming to him. But I wouldn't like to see you get hurt.'

Les smiled softly up at Grace and leant back against the lounge. 'Grace. Come here,' he said.

Les took Grace's hand and drew her down onto the rubber ball. She spread her legs, sat on Norton's knees and placed her hands on his shoulders. As she did, her skirt rose and Les glimpsed a pair of very lacy, white knickers. He put his hands on Grace's ribs and they started slowly rocking around on the ball.

'What are you doing, Les?' asked Grace.

'Nothing,' answered Les. 'Just seeing if you can straighten two spines at once. That's all.'

'Ohh yeah.'

Les kept rocking away against Grace in time to the music. Whether it was the sudden infusion of minerals, or Grace's sensational melons moving up and down in front of his nose, Les wasn't sure. But suddenly Mr Wobbly had eaten a can of spinach and turned into Popeye the sailor man. Grace felt it as Les kept rocking steadily away.

Grace looked directly into Norton's shining, brown eyes. 'You're a bit of bastard. Aren't you, Les?'

'That's not very nice, Grace.'

'It's true though.'

'No. Not really. It's just that I keep meeting people who bring the bastard out in me.'

'Do they now?' said Grace.

Les looked directly back into Grace's lovely hazel eyes. 'Do they what.'

Les kissed Grace's lips and Grace kissed him back. It wasn't long before the kissing got very passionate as they rocked up and down on the fitness ball. Les felt the tip of Graces's tongue like a whiplash and slipped his hands under her shirt. He ran them gently over her back, then unbuttoned her shirt. A moment later, Grace's magnificent, unfettered melons were out in the open. Mr Wobbly started tossing his head around and thumping his chest.

Grace stopped kissing Les and looked into his eyes. 'Les,' she said quietly.

'Yes Grace,' replied Norton, knowing it was all too good to be true, and he would have to put his toys away.

'Rub some oil into my boobs.' Grace took her shirt off, dropped it on the floor then reached down and got the bottle of hemp seed oil. 'Can you do that, Les?' she smiled, tipping a little into Norton's hand.

'I'll ... manage somehow,' said Norton.

Les rubbed the oil into his hands then placed one on each of Grace's melons. Grace closed her eyes and rocked slowly up and down on Norton's lap as Les started smoothly massaging. Sideways, up and down. Around in circles. Tenderly squeezing her nipples till they firmed and stuck out like big, pink arrowheads. Les massaged away, scarcely able to believe how firm Grace's boobs were for their size. And they were the absolute real deal as well. Mr Wobbly, meanwhile, could believe. He started howling and screaming and trying to rip his way out of Norton's Speedos. Grace arched her back, rubbed herself against Les and sighed. Les watched her pigtails swaying from side to side and leant forward and kissed her. Grace kissed Les back and soon the kissing went from passionate, to steamy delicious.

Grace chewed Norton's bottom lip then slipped her tongue in his ear. Les winced as he felt Grace's hot breath and kissed the tenderness of her neck. He kissed her eyes then ran his hand up and down her spine and over the firmness of her stomach, before slipping his hand between Grace's legs. Grace crushed her mouth onto Norton's as he stroked the beautiful, wet tenderness of her ted. Finally, Les lifted Grace to her feet, stood in front of her and eased her knickers off. He turned her around and sat her back down on the fitness ball facing him. Grace took hold of the lounge behind her as Les spread her legs apart, then he got to his knees and pushed his face into her ted.

Grace moaned and writhed on the fitness ball, gripped the back of the lounge and kicked her legs as Les slid his tongue inside her and sucked tenderly. He squeezed her behind and rolled his head around in unison with the bouncing ball pushing his face hard against her as Grace moaned and licked her lips with delight. Les went for it, flicking his tongue around like a rattlesnake and before too long Grace gave a long squeal of ecstasy and got her rocks off. Les came up for air, picked a few pubic hairs out of his mouth and got into it again.

Naturally, Les was soon filled with lust and yearning desire. But Mr Wobbly had become possessed. The werewolf had completely taken over and he was foaming at the mouth, howling his angry little head off, wanting to play hidings. Les fought the beast as long as he could before his willpower collapsed and he was forced let Mr Wobbly have his evil way.

Les stood up, helped Grace to her feet then got out of his Speedos. He sat back down on the ball and made himself comfortable, then drew Grace towards him. Grace spread her legs as Les held her backside then she laced her hands behind Norton's neck and straddled him.

Les pushed himself in and the warmth and firmness of Grace made him shudder. Grace groaned and came down, then she brought her knees up and it didn't take long to get a steady rhythm going, up and down on the fitness ball. Every so often Les would lean back, Grace would come down, and he'd go in deeper.

'Ohh. You know what that ... feels like, Les,' said Grace.

'No,' panted Les. 'What Grace?'

'Like ... one of those stalls ... at the show. Where you ... hit the stump with a mallet. And see how ... high you can go.'

'How am I goin'?'

'Ohh. Every now and again ... you hit the top. Ohh yeah, like that. Oh fuck!'

With Grace clinging to him, Les relaxed and bounced away into the evening. The pain in his back was bearable and Grace and the ball were doing all the work; Les felt he could go all night. Grace's pigtails were whirling like the blades on a helicopter, and from the expression on her face it looked like she hoped he would. She hooked her ankles up over Norton's shoulders, Les went in deeper and the ball went faster. Then Les felt the urge engulfing his body; building up inside him like a volcano.

Grace started to howl, Les screwed his face up and sweat trickled down his back. Then it was all systems go. Les had ignition, he had lift off. He jammed his eyes shut and blasted off into the galaxy.

'Ohh shit! Ohh Christ! Aarrgghhhh!'

'Oh my God! Oh my God! Oh! Oh! Owwhhhh!'

Finally the ball stopped bouncing and Grace stopped trying to choke Les. Les stopped trying to rip Grace's backside off and Morticia stopped barking at the front door. Les blinked his eyes open and stared at Grace. Grace stared back at Les.

'I have to go to the bathroom.'

Norton's chest was heaving. 'Okay.'

Grace stood up and left. Les got to his feet and climbed unsteadily into his Speedos then flopped on the lounge. The last track on the Jools Holland CD cut out as Grace sat down alongside him wearing a yellow shower robe with a fluffy white towel over her shoulder. In her hands were two bottles of sparkling mineral water. She handed one to Les.

'Just what I need,' said Les. 'Thanks.'

Les gulped down half the bottle, Grace drank some of hers and started wiping Norton's shoulders.

'Your soaking,' she said.

'Yeah,' he replied. 'I hope I haven't messed up your lounge.'

'That's okay. How's your back feel?'

'All right, I think.' Les winked at Grace. 'The rubber ball worked splendidly.'

Grace smiled back at Les over her bottle of water. 'That wasn't quite what I had in mind.'

'No,' said Les. 'Amazing what they can do though.' Les gave Grace's leg a gentle squeeze. 'Any chance of putting that CD on again Grace? I missed the last tracks.'

'I wonder how that happened?'

Grace put the same CD on again and they sat on the lounge with their bottles of mineral water listening to Jools Holland. Grace had a good stereo and Les was thoroughly enjoying it. He settled down and Grace rested her head against his shoulder. Les massaged Grace's scalp and, as she relaxed, one of her oil-glistening melons slipped out from under her robe. Les spotted it about the same time as Mr Wobbly. Next thing, the werewolf took over again and Mr Wobbly started climbing out of Norton's Speedos, angrier than ever.

'Hello,' said Les. 'I think there's some one here wants to see you, Grace.'

Grace looked down at Norton's throbbing boner. 'You just behave yourself, Mr Norton,' she said. 'Or you're going to hurt your back.'

'Not on the magic ball I won't.'

'Maybe. But aunty Grace is a little sore.'

'Oh. Oh well,' said Les. 'It doesn't matter.'

Grace smiled at Les with a strange glint in her eye. 'Doesn't it?'

Grace slipped Norton's dick out of his Speedos, dipped her head and proceeded to give him a spanking blow job. Les didn't know what hit him as Grace sucked and licked and gently squeezed his balls, while she sighed with delight. Before Les knew it, sweat formed on his brow, his face began to twist out of shape and, feeling like he was going to have a heart attack, Les collapsed back onto the lounge; groaning again, he got his rocks off.

Grace had a drink of water and gave Norton a minute or two. 'So how was that, Les?' she asked.

Norton was laying back on the lounge with tears in his eyes. 'Ohh. Ohhh shit!' he mumbled.

'Well, if that's all you've got to say — bugger you.' Grace started hauling Les off the lounge. 'Come on. If we're going to the Blues Festival tonight. You'd better go home and get ready.'

'Okay,' said Les, stumbling back into his shorts. 'So what's doing? Do you want to come with me this time, and I'll drive you home in the morning?'

'No. I'll have a shower. And meet you at the house in about an hour. I'll stay at Belinda's again.'

'Okay.'

Les put his T-shirt on, Grace put the two bottles of mineral water in his overnight bag, gave him the instructions again, then walked him to the door. Les gave her a quick kiss goodbye, patted Morticia on her massive head and walked to his car. It felt a bit nippy out in the hills now, so he put his sweatshirt on before getting behind the wheel. He tooted the horn and drove off.

Apart from a few people in the hotel, it was all over as Les drove through Tilba. He hung a left at the war memorial towards the turnoff. When he got there, Les caught a glimpse of the ocean in the distance and noticed the sky was full of clouds and the southerly had picked up. It didn't appear as if it was going to rain. But the weather had definitely changed. He slipped a tape on then swung left and headed for Narooma. As Red Rivers started thumping out 'Baby Blue Buick', Les started thinking. What started off as a rotten day had turned out gravy. He'd been sucked and fucked. Fed beautiful food. Given a fantastic massage. And with a bit of luck Grace's special mineral water might fix his back.

There was a break in the clouds and the moon appeared for a few moments. Les looked up at the sky and grinned. You like me boss, don't you. Despite all the shit you lay on me. And the pain and suffering you put me through. Underneath, you like me. Come on. Admit it. As he cruised along something else occurred to Les. He felt he'd made a friend in Grace, and he remembered saying to her that if she helped him, he promised her she'd never regret it. Les smiled and stroked his chin. Besides the gigantic mumble on the grumble he gave her, there could be another, even nicer way to return the favour.

There were people and cars around as Les drove through Narooma. When he pulled up at the house, Warren had parked his car against the front door. The key was under the mat; Les opened the door and stepped inside. Ray Anthony and his Orchestra were hitting 'In The Mood' in the loungeroom and Warren and Clover were in the kitchen hitting the sauce. By the smell, they hadn't long finished a hot one. Warren was wearing black jeans, a blue check shirt and his leather jacket. Clover had on a red cap, a tiger-striped top under a red cardigan that went past her knees, jeans, and cherry red Doc Martens.

They were very cuddly and by the looks on both their faces, Les surmised they'd made good use of the empty house while he was away.

'Righto,' said Les. 'Who owns the bloody yellow Celica out the front? You couldn't park it any closer to the front door could you.'

Clover narrowed her eyes at Norton. 'Don't get too cheeky big fellah,' she said. 'Remember your bad back. I might just jump up and sit you right on your arse.' Clover then had an attack of the giggles and spilt her drink.

Warren raised his JD and soda. 'What she said, dude.'

Les shook his head. 'Jesus Christ. What are you pair into?'

'Just a few cools ones,' said Clover. 'And the odd hot one. You want some.'

'Maybe after I have a shower,' said Les.

'Actually,' said Clover, 'I've got something special for us besides pot. I'm saving it for tomorrow.'

'Clover,' replied Les, sagely. 'If you think I'm going to drop a disco biscuit, and start dancing and talking at a hundred miles an hour and tell Warren I love him, you're playing with yourself.'

Clover shook her head. 'No. Better.'

'Yeah, righto.'

'So how was your day with Grace?' asked Warren. 'Bit of nudge, nudge, wink wink, there Ugly?'

'No,' replied Les. 'We went for a walk in the hills. I had an absolutely fantastic meal. Heard an absolutely fantastic CD. And had a ... terrific massage. It was great day all round.'

'What's her house like?' asked Clover. 'She invited me out tomorrow.'

'Nice. But watch out for the dog.'

Les left Warren and Clover to it and got under the shower. He had a shave, dabbed on a little CK then got into his jeans and a blue, Margaritasville T-shirt he'd bought in Florida; he put a hang out denim shirt over the top. He gave himself a detail and walked back to the kitchen. Warren and Clover were drinking away steadily and going over the Blues Festival program.

'Hey. You seen who's on tonight?' said Warren.

'No. Bjork? Celine Dion? Surprise me, Woz.' Les got a tall glass and made himself a super, monster delicious.

'Dave Hole. Holy Dave. And that other band you saw in Cairns, that you're always on about. Rock Solid Steve and the Scorchers.'

'You're kidding,' said Les. 'Rock Solid and the boys. I might even have a hot one.'

'Are they any good?' asked Clover.

'Only if you like rock and a roll,' smiled Les.

'Well, I like rock and a roll, Les,' mimmicked Clover. 'In fact you and I might get up for a dance big guy.'

'Okay. But only if the masseur says so.'

'So what did Grace do to you?' asked Warren.

Les told them how Grace massaged him with her knee on the fitness ball. He said nothing about the porking and polishing. And he kept quiet about Grace's secret spring. But he told them about the other one and what was in it and how Grace was hoping to make some money through the soft drink company.

'So that was my day kiddies,' said Les, making himself another delicious. 'But Grace should be here soon. She'll tell you anything else you wish to know. I imagine.'

'If she's forty two,' said Warren. 'I'm going to buy a forty-four gallon drum of that Eureka Water. She is absolutely amazing.'

'Evidently that's what they call her,' said Les. 'A ...' There was a soft rap on the door. 'Hello. I'd say this is the person in question now.'

Les put his drink on the table then walked across and opened the door. It was Grace, looking very foxy in a brown, suede Mao jacket, beige jeans and a light green T-shirt, with a goanna on the front. She had her hair down and two mother-of-pearl seahorses dangled from her ears. A brown leather bag that matched her boots hung loosely over one shoulder. Les stood at the door, staring down at her.

'Well. Are you going to let me in?' smiled Grace.

'I'm sorry,' said Les, moving aside. 'But I was just thinking. They have to bring in a law against women like you looking so beautiful.'

'And there should be a law against men like you being such dropkicks.' Grace stepped inside and gave Les a kiss as he closed the door. 'How are you?'

'Terrific,' said Les. 'My back feels that good, I'm thinking of getting up later and showing the locals some new dance steps.'

'I'd advise against it after the massage,' said Grace. 'Give your back time to settle down.'

'Okay. You're the doctor,' said Les.

Grace entered the kitchen to warm greetings from Clover and Warren. Clover gushed a little over Grace's clothes. Warren just stared at her. Les made her a Bacardi and orange. Grace took a sip and noticed Norton's T-shirt.

'Margaritasville,' she said, pointing with her drink. 'You're not a parrot head, are you Les?'

'Warren and I have been known to have a few Jimmy Buffett CDs amongst our collection,' admitted Les.

'So have I,' said Grace. 'My favourite's "Fruit Cakes".'

'Mine too,' said Clover, quickly. 'Hey Grace. You know anybody in Miami can gimme a passsssssport real quick?'

Grace sat down and they all got into a tipsy, light conversation. Grace had been to Florida and saw Jimmy Buffett in Miami. Les had also been to Florida and they'd all been to Hawaii. Clover arranged to give Grace a lift home again and as they were talking Clover rolled a couple of joints. She put them aside and turned to Grace.

'Have you ever tried mushrooms, Grace?' she said.

'You mean Tiger Stripes? Not for a while.'

'Tiger stripes?' said Les.

'They're the local variety,' said Grace. 'Somewhere between Victorian Blue Meanies and Queensland Gold Tops.'

'I bumped into a friend from school,' said Clover. 'She gave me some.'

Clover walked over to the fridge and came back with a brown paper bag. She opened it and inside were half-a-dozen mushrooms with brown and orange stripes on top.

'That's them,' said Grace.

'I'm going to make some coffee tomorrow night,' said Clover. 'Care to join in?'

'Sure. Why not,' shrugged Grace. 'It'll certainly put some colour into the last blast of the festival.' She smiled at Norton. 'You ever tried these, Les?'

Les shook his head. 'No.'

'What about you, Warren?'

Warren shook his head also. 'No.'

'They're fairly mild,' said Grace. 'They only last about six hours.'

'And you get a flashback, a couple of days later,' said Clover.

'A flashback?' said Les.

'Yes,' smiled Grace. 'But only for a little while.'

Clover turned to Warren. 'You still keen, Warren?'

'Yeah, why not.'

'What about you, Les?'

'Yeah I suppose so. Though I hate bowing to peer pressure.'

'Hey unreal,' said Clover. 'Sunday night at the Blues Festival, off our trolleys.'

'I can't wait,' said Les.

Grace looked at the two joints sitting on the table and the bag of dacca. She opened the bag and squeezed one of the heads. 'These look all right,' she said. 'Where's this from?'

Les pointed to Warren. 'The boarder's. He grows it in the backyard.'

'Really?' said Grace. 'I put a few plants on the property next door, now and again.'

'Do you get helicopters and sniffer dogs down here?' asked Warren.

'Yes. The pains in the arse,' said Grace.

'It's a pain in the arse all right,' said Warren. 'Fair dinkum. If they carried on about people importing heroin and cocaine as much as they carried on about people smoking pot, there wouldn't be a drug problem.'

'Yes. But you have to understand,' said Clover. 'The government gets votes out of busting people for having a bit of pot. And it makes the cops look like they're doing something about the drug problem.'

'Yeah. While they're selling heroin and cocaine,' said Warren. 'It gives me the shits. You have a smoke after work, and they jump all over you. Shoot up after robbing an old lady and they give you a safe house.'

Les gave the others a frosty look. 'I don't know how you can say that about the NSW government and the police,' he said seriously. 'I happen to have friends in the police force.'

'Ohh wonderful,' scoffed Warren. 'And your boss wouldn't have ever bribed any of them either. Would he?'

'Price? Never.'

'Never stopped, you mean.'

Les pointed a finger at Warren. 'Warren. I will not have you bad mouthing the integrity of Mr Galese and the Kelly Club. We run a very respectable business up there. Next thing, you'll being accusing us of money laundering and organising murders.'

'Sorry Les. I forgot. Eddie only does the cleaning.'

'And very efficiently too.' Suddenly Norton's eyes narrowed. 'Hang on a minute. What's this?' Les reached over and undid a couple of buttons on Warren's shirt. He patted him down, then pulled Warren's hip flask out of his leather jacket and shook it. 'You rotten little bastard, Warren. You're wearing a wire. It's you that's been ratting us out. Jesus Christ! When Eddie finds out about this. You'll have more holes in you than a gas ring.'

'You really are a gangster. Aren't you, Les,' said Grace.

Warren laughed derisively and snatched his hip flask back from Norton. 'No. But some of his best friends are.'

'Hey, talking about holes,' said Clover. 'We'd better make a move if we're going to see Dave Hole and Rock Solid.'

'Yeah, you're right,' said Les. 'Bloody women. You'd talk all night.' Clover and Grace looked at Les like he was a dud TV commercial they were watching for the two hundredth time. 'Sorry about that ladies,' smiled Les. 'Just making sure I hadn't lost my touch.'

'Hey. What about de ganja, mon,' said Warren. 'Are we goin' to smoke de spleefs?'

'I think so,' answered Clover. She put the mushrooms back in the fridge, fired up a fat joint and it started going the rounds. 'Hey, I just thought of something,' she said. 'What if Morgan Scully and his gang are down there?'

'Yeah. That's a worry,' agreed Warren.

Les shook his head and blew out a great cloud of smoke. 'I can't see any problem if he shows up.'

'I hope you're right,' said Grace. 'But I'd keep away from him. He is a bit mad you know.' She took a toke and handed the joint to Warren.

'I hope you're right, too,' said Warren, disappearing behind a cloud of smoke. 'Because if anything starts, I'm saving the women.'

They finished the joint and Les felt it definitely put a spin on the night. Even the old music coming from the loungeroom sounded better. They decided not to bother about the other joint. Les turned the ghetto blaster off in the loungeroom, then they picked up their bags, cameras, hip flasks and whatever and headed for the door.

'Hey just a minute,' said Les. He went to his room and came back with the GUEST pass Norm had given him round his neck. 'What do you reckon gang?'

'Where did you get that?' said Warren.

'Daddy gave it to me,' replied Les breezily. 'In case I want to go backstage and mingle with the other stars. I might even get up and do a gig man.'

The others looked at each other. 'You don't have to be seen with us, if you don't want to,' said Grace.

'Yeah. And don't worry about doing a gig, Les,' said Warren. 'You are a gig. Now open the door, you big goose.'

Les shook his head. 'The good old tall poppy syndrome. You couldn't wait to cut my legs off. Could you.'

The walk down seemed to take longer this time. But it was a lot more fun. They got to the jetty and the music coming from the festival seemed to be everywhere. Grace had hold of Norton's arm as they threaded their way through the people and Clover had hold of Warren. They arrived at the entrance to find Norm standing there checking some receipts. He saw them and smiled.

'Hello Grace,' he boomed. 'Les. How is everybody?'

'Good thanks, Daddy.'

'Morgan's in there.'

'Really?' said Les. 'I must make sure I say hello before the night's over.'

Norm pulled Les aside. 'I put him in the picture. He won't start anything tonight. But shit, he's mad keen for Monday.'

'Fair enough,' nodded Les.

'Listen. He's put his five grand up. And I can get three to one about you. How's your back?'

'A little better,' said Les. 'Don't say anything though. We might get fives.'

'Sweet.'

Les rejoined the others; the security gave their bags a quick flick, and they went through.

'Oh my God!' said Clover. 'Did you hear that. Morgan Scully's inside.'

'Shit! I don't like it,' said Warren.

'Ohh for Christ's sake,' asserted Les. 'You're just being paranoid. Nothing's going to happen. Trust me.'

'I'm not paranoid, Les,' said Grace, taking hold of Norton's arm. 'But don't go away. There's a lot of people here that are. And they're all out to get me.'

'Why don't we buy some drinks. Then find a seat,' suggested Les. 'Do you think you can make it to the bar and back with me, Woz?'

Warren looked around. 'Christ! I hope so,' he replied.

The queue wasn't too long and Les and Warren came back with a tray of drinks. They walked over to the middle tent and managed to get four seats together about a dozen rows from the front, then settled down amongst the crowd. Warren and Grace pulled out their hip flasks and topped up all their drinks then after a quick 'cheers' they had a mouthful each. The band hadn't come on stage yet and some good music was coming quietly through the speakers. Les was nicely out of it and would have been content to sit there all night and listen to what was playing.

'Hey, how good's this?' said Clover. 'We're right in the middle of the speakers.'

'I don't know what this music is,' said Warren. 'But it's unreal.'

Les sipped his drink and checked out the other punters. They were a happy-looking crowd, a few heads were bopping around here and there and Les surmised he and the others weren't the only ones who had been partaking in illegal drug activities that night. His eyes wandered back towards the stage, then Les gave a double blink. Sitting five rows in front of them was a huge, unmistakable man's head wearing a black cowboy hat over a black T-shirt. The man in the cowboy hat was with two ordinary-looking blondes in denim and leather and another big man in a check shirt and a black baseball cap.

Les turned to the others. 'Hey. Look who's sitting right in front of us.'

The others stared then Clover gasped and put a hand over her mouth.

'Oh my God! It's him.'

'Oh shit! It is too,' said Warren.

The others held their drinks and sank back in their seats. Les sipped his bourbon and stared at Morgan's tree stump neck sitting beneath his hat. That was the only thing Les didn't like about smoking pot. It brought out the Bugs Bunny in him. He sipped some more bourbon and looked around the grass near his feet. Lying under the seat in front of him was a thick, juicy apple core, that someone had left from the previous concert.

'Grace,' said Les. 'Would you hold my drink for a second please?'

'Sure,' replied Grace, taking Norton's bourbon.

Les picked up the apple core and got to his feet. He aimed carefully then flung the apple core at Morgan as hard as he could, splattering it all over the big man's neck and his mate sitting next to him.

'Hey Boofhead! Yeah, you in the hat,' Les yelled out. 'Take the bloody thing off. You're blocking our view.'

Grace's jaw dropped, Warren went grey and Clover buried her face in her hands. The people around them thought it must be some kind of joke. Morgan lumbered to his feet and spun around hyperventilating with rage. He saw Les standing there with a silly look on his face and started to shake.

'Well. You heard me possum eyes,' said Les. 'What, are you deaf as well as stupid ... Get the bloody thing off. Or do you want me to come down there, rip it off your head and shove it up your blurter. You inbred moron.'

Morgan's mate stood up alongside him; it was the bloke with the thick moustache who had punched Warren. Before they got a chance to do anything, a tall bloke in a Blues Festival T-shirt appeared on stage and took hold of the mike.

'Ladies and gentlemen. Will you please give a big welcome on stage. To ... Rock Solid Steve and the Scorcherrrssss.'

The audience erupted into wild applause as Morgan stared daggers at Les. Les gave him a friendly little wave and sat down. Still shaking with rage and his face absolutely purple with anger, Morgan turned and sat down too. So did his mate. The band got behind their instruments and did a quick sound check.

Warren stared at Les, his eyes like dinner plates. 'Are you fucking insane?'

Clover stared into her drink. 'We're dead. I know it.'

'Les,' said Grace, urgently. 'If you're like this after one joint, I would seriously reconsider the mushrooms tomorrow.'

Les had been keeping his eyes on Morgan. He turned to the others. 'I told you nothing would happen.' Les smiled and pointed towards Morgan. 'Look.'

The others followed Norton's finger. Morgan had removed his hat and placed it on his knees.

'My God,' said Clover. 'He's taken his hat off.'

'I don't believe it,' said Grace.

'Well why wouldn't he?' replied Les. 'Shit! I asked him politely enough.'

The band was just like Les remembered them in Cairns. The happy-faced bloke with the goatee beard and the Hawaiian shirt on bass, the lead singer in the horn-rimmed glasses with the rigger's belt full of harmonicas and the guitarist with the Elvis hairstyle hunched over his Fender. Behind them, their long haired drummer was poised ready to start hammering the tubs. The lead singer said something Les didn't quite catch, then the band ripped into 'Love So Much' and the tent erupted.

'Oh yeah,' said Grace.

'Rock and a roll,' squealed Clover, banging her head from side to side and almost losing her glasses.

'I told you they were good,' smiled Les.

People started dancing in front of the stage and by the time the band had scorched through 'Burn Rubber Burn' and 'Queensland Moon', Grace and the others were down the front as well; Clover and Grace were dancing and taking photos at the same time. Les couldn't join in the dancing. But he went down and took photos. He noticed Morgan and his friends giving him filthy looks, so he smiled back at them and took their photo as well.

Les sat down and after a while the others joined him, then they topped their drinks and rocked happily away till the Scorchers finished with 'Skinny Skinny Skinny'. The band waved to the audience then left. When the applause died down, Les and the others went into a huddle about the band and finished what drinks they had left.

'I got some great photos of you dancing,' said Les.

'I got a great photo of you taking photos,' said Grace.

Clover glanced towards the stage as the tent emptied. 'Hey look. Morgan's gone.'

'Thank God for that,' said Warren. He looked at Les. 'Why don't we get some more drinks, and find a seat before Dave Hole comes on.'

Everybody agreed so they got up and walked to the front of the tent. Waiting outside was Morgan, his mate, and the two women, all looking like they'd all just bitten into a plate of bad oysters. Clover saw them first.

'Oh my God!' she said, and hid behind Les with the others.

Les was still very much in Bugs Bunny mode. 'Great band, Morgan,' he said cheerfully. 'If you're into that sort of music. Or are you more a techno-house, dance club, kind of guy?'

Morgan stepped in front of Les and pointed to his hat. 'You see this hat?' he rasped.

'Is that what it is,' replied Les. 'I thought you'd brought your washing with you.'

'It's only an old one. But when I'm finished with you on Monday, I'm going to shove it right up your arse.'

'Fair enough,' said Les. 'But make sure you take it off first won't you.' He turned to the others. 'Come on. Let's go and get a drink.'

Les ignored Morgan and led the others to the booze tent. The queue wasn't long and soon Les and Warren returned with a tray of drinks. They all toasted each other and took a sip.

'I have to give it to you, Les,' said Grace. 'The spinnaker's on the wrong end of your yacht. But you're bloody cool. I was shitting myself back there.'

'So was I,' said Clover. 'I still am.'

'I told you before. Nothing's going to happen tonight.' Les smiled and raised his drink. 'It's all sweet.'

'Don't count your luck,' said Grace. 'We're not home yet.'

Les put his arm around Grace. 'Why shouldn't I count my luck? I've got you with me. Amazing Grace.'

'I like you, Les,' smiled Grace.

'I like you too, Grace.' Les gave Grace one on the cheek and they walked over to the main tent.

This time they had to sit apart. Les and Grace got two seats on the side. Warren and Clover found another two further down from them in the middle. There was no sign of Morgan and his friends. Les swallowed some bourbon, then Daddy lumbered out on stage and took hold of the mike.

'Orrrright. Here he is. Come on, give a big welcome. Dave Hole. Come on!'

The crowd started clapping and cheering as Dave Hole led his band on stage wearing a vest and a baseball cap. He plugged his guitar in, nodded to the band, and they tore straight into 'New Way To Live'. From that it was 'Every Girl I See' followed by 'More Love Less Attitude'. And the crowd loved every note. Dave scissor-kicked and duck-walked across the stage. He worked the slide on his guitar till it screamed and sparks were flying off the frets. Les and Grace took photos, bounced up and down in their seats and listened in awe as Dave racked up more blistering solos, through 'Cold Women With Warm Hearts' and 'Take A Swing'. The band did a swag more songs off all their albums, then came back for an encore with 'Bullfrog Blues', before finally walking off to a standing, cheering ovation.

'Well Grace,' said Les, 'I don't think we can complain. It hasn't been a bad night of rock 'n' roll.'

Grace shook her head. 'Wow! I don't think I could take any more after that.'

The crowd started to leave. Clover and Warren came over. Les and Grace put their cameras in their bags and stood up.

'What did you think?' asked Les.

'Unreal,' said Warren. 'Especially when he finished with "Bullfrog Blues".'

'I like "Crazy Kind Of Woman",' said Clover. She turned to Grace. 'I suppose we'd better start walking up to the house. Mum will be here soon.'

'Any sign of — you know who,' said Warren, running his eyes over the crowd.

'No,' answered Les. 'But I wish there was. I'd like to put the hard word on his girl. She wasn't a bad sort.'

'Yes,' agreed Clover. 'If you fancy Harpo Marx in drag.'

They joined the crowd exiting the tent and kept going. Les had his arm around Grace as they went by the jetty and Warren was arm in arm with Clover. Although the pot had worn off, they were still laughing and joking as they strolled along. Nevertheless, Warren was avoiding any shadowy areas and looked very relieved when they reached the front yard.

'So what's the story tomorrow?' asked Les. 'I'm going to Montague Island at nine o'clock.' He glanced up at the cloudy sky. 'Don't look like being much of a day for it though.'

Grace turned to Clover. 'I told Alysia I'd help her in the shop till one. Why don't you call over after then and we'll have lunch?'

'Okay.'

Warren yawned. 'I'm having a sleep in.'

Clover took hold of Warren. 'Then why don't we all do our own thing tomorrow. And meet back here at six. For a double shot, decaf-mushroom latte.'

'Sounds good to me,' said Warren, leaning against Clover.

Les shook his head. 'Like I said, Clover, I can't wait.'

The station wagon pulled up out the front. Warren waved to Clover's mother without bothering to walk across to the car. Les hadn't met her. But he gave her a wave also, then put his arms around Grace. Grace slipped her arms around Les and he kissed her.

'Thanks for everything today, Grace,' he said. 'I'll see you tomorrow night.'

'I'll see you then.' Grace shook her finger at Les. 'Now don't forget to drink your water in the morning. Every last drop.'

'No I won't. Goodnight Grace.'

'Goodnight Les.'

Les said goodnight to Clover, then she and Grace piled into the station wagon and it drove off.

Warren let go another huge yawn. 'Shit I'm tired,' he said.

The yawn was infectious. 'You're not Robinson Crusoe,' said Les. He got the key from under the mat, opened the door and they stepped inside. Les locked the door and walked into the kitchen.

'You feel like anything, Woz?' he asked, getting a bottle of water from the fridge.

'Yes. About ten hours sleep,' said Warren. 'I'm rooted.' Warren went to the bathroom then came back and propped in the kitchen doorway. 'I couldn't believe it, when you hit that big goose with the apple core,' he laughed. 'You're fuckin insane.'

'I know what I'd like to hit him with,' said Les.

'Yeah,' agreed Warren. He let go another yawn. 'Shit! I hope that bloody rat doesn't wake me again tonight.'

'Hey. Thanks for reminding me, Woz.' Les put the bottle of water back in the fridge, took out a packet of cheese then got a rat-trap from the pantry. 'See how Jerry Lee Rodent likes this.'

Les broke off a piece of cheese and tied it to the trap with a thread of cotton from a tea towel. Warren watched absently as Les baited the trap, when the temperature in the kitchen suddenly plunged to what felt like below zero.

'Shit!' said Warren, as clouds of steam formed in front of his face. 'How fuckin cold is it.'

'There must be a bloody draught in here.' Les put the trap down and rubbed the goose bumps on his arms while his breath also turned to steam. 'It's probably coming from under the house.'

'Coming from fuckin Siberia'd be more like it,' shivered Warren. 'Ohh fuck this. I'm going to bed. It's freezing. See you in the morning, Les.'

'Yeah, see you then.'

Warren moved off into the hallway leaving a cloud of steam behind him in the kitchen. 'Hey, what *is* under the house?' he called out from the hallway.

'What was that?' Les yelled back.

'Doesn't matter. I'll see you in the morning.' The loungeroom door closed followed by the door to Warren's bedroom.

Les knitted his eyebrows for a moment then shook his head. He sprung the trap and left it on the floor under the table then turned out the kitchen light. After going to the bathroom, Les took off his clothes and climbed into his tracksuit. He got under the blankets and switched off the bedlamp. It didn't seem as cold in the bedroom and before long Les had warmed up and was almost asleep. Warren was right, he smiled. The look on Morgan's face when he turned around in the tent was a hoot. But one way or the other, there wouldn't be much laughing on Monday. In the quiet darkness of the old room, Les let his mind drift off to more pleasant things and soon he was sound asleep.

When Les woke up around seven the next morning he felt pretty good. He'd slept well, he had no sign of a hangover and although his back was still stiff from Grace's massage, the pain in his spine had eased. A quick peek out the window said it didn't look like being much of a day however. He went to the bathroom, then changed straight into his training gear and walked into the kitchen. Rubbing his hands together, Les had a look under the table. The trap wasn't there, or anywhere else in the kitchen. Mystified, Les picked at his chin for a moment, then smiled. I've got him. He's wounded and dragged the trap somewhere. All I have to do now is find Jerry's mangled corpse before he stinks the place up. Les pointed. Probably in that side room. But first, a cup of tea and toast. With just a little grated cheese. Les put the kettle on, popped two slices of bread in the toaster, then opened the fridge and reached inside.

'WHACK! ! !'

'Shit a fuckin brick!' Les flew back as the rat-trap slammed down a centimetre from his thumb.

Norton stared at the rat-trap sitting next to the tomatoes and milk with the piece of cheese still attached. Gingerly he took the trap out and placed it on the table. Fuckin hell, he scowled. That could have broken my bloody finger. Norton's eyes narrowed towards the front bedroom. Fuckin Warren. He's getting sillier by the minute. No, Les shook his head. Not even Warren's that stupid. You know what, I reckon the poor, silly bastard's walking in his sleep? I think I'd better have a word with the boarder. Before he does somebody an injury. Particularly me.

Les removed the piece of cheese and placed the trap back in the pantry. He made his tea and toast then walked down the hallway and opened the door to the loungeroom. The bear was on the piano facing away from the wall and snoring was coming from Warren's room. Les stepped out onto the verandah and leant against the railing.

There was still no sign of rain. But the sky was grey and it was cool with a southerly blowing. Not much of a day for a boat trip out to

Montague Island. Les watched the people round the jetty and listened to some music coming from the nearest balcony while he worked out his game plan. He'd walk to the pier again and check out Bar Beach. Les finished his tea and toast, put his cap on and set off.

Whether it was the festival atmosphere or he just had a good vibe about him, Les wasn't sure. But almost everybody he passed on his walk either smiled or said hello. Even some old ladies picking up rubbish by the side of the bridge stopped for a moment and smiled when Les strode past. Les smiled back at everyone as he ambled steadily along and in what seemed like no time at all he was standing on the breakwater. There was a decent wave running and a group of surfers were getting some hot barrels off Bar Beach, while some fairly solid swells were pushing into the Bar. Les couldn't tell how rough it was out to sea. But it looked very bumpy and, beneath a grey sky, the water was dark and uninviting. He did a few light squats and watched the surfers for a while then headed for home.

Les kept the two bottles of mineral water Grace had given him in his room and it wasn't hard to gulp one down after the walk; the bitter-sweet taste was quite good. He had a shower and put on his tracksuit, then walked up and got the paper and some more film. He didn't notice Ian in the dive shop on the way and Warren was still in bed when he got back. Les made a couple of toasted sandwiches and washed them down with some fresh tea while he read the news. After that, he checked his cameras and got his diving gear and everything else together. He couldn't see himself getting in the water on the day. But part of the island might be sheltered. Making sure he had his ticket, Les shouldered his bag and walked down to the jetty.

The Kingfisher was moored between the catamaran and the other boats. It was all white with a red cabin at the front, wide beamed and ten metres long. Aerials and fishing rod holders poked up in the air, a flag dangled off the stern and a radar dish sat on top of the cabin. There were no steps; you climbed straight in from the jetty. Standing at the rail holding a clipboard was a beefy, bearded, red-haired bloke wearing sunglasses, shorts and a white T-shirt with Kingfisher Cruises across the front.

'Are you the skipper?' asked Les.

'That's me, mate. Neville. Everyone calls me Nev.'

'Okay Nev,' Les handed Nev his ticket. 'I'm Les. Ian sent me.'

'Good on you, Les. Climb aboard. We got two more to come and we'll shove off.'

'Righto.'

Les piled on board. There was a seat running along the stern and two other seats below the cabin. A set of steps went up to the cabin on the right and another set in the middle went down to the galley. Above the steps in the middle was a storage space full of orange life jackets. A young couple in warm clothes were standing near the stern and an older bloke and his wife wearing shorts were seated next to the steps beneath the cabin. The young couple were your average Australians. The older bloke had glasses, thin hair and ears like frying pans; his wife was dumpy with a worried look on her face. Les gave them a half-smile and took the seat opposite on the other side of the storage space. He placed his bag between his legs, took out a bottle of water and had a sip while they waited for the others to arrive. Les was looking around, avoiding eye contact, when two young girls wearing blue tracksuits and sunglasses — one girl much heavier than the other — climbed on board. They had jet black hair and very olive skin and Norton guessed by their complexions and mannerisms they were European or Middle Eastern. They sat down on the seat along the stern and Nev put his clipboard down.

'Okay folks,' said Nev. 'This is *The Kingfisher*. I'm Neville. Welcome aboard.' Neville then went into his tourist spiel for the thousandth time.

Montague Island was nine kilometres south east of Narooma, around eighty-two hectares in area and pinched in the middle. After Lord Howe it was the second largest island off the NSW coast. The trip out and back, going around the island, plus snorkelling would take the best part of four hours. Neville went on about other things of interest. But Les was only half listening. Big Ears thought he was being funny and kept interrupting all the time making stupid remarks. Finally Neville pointed to the life jackets and informed them it was deadly imperative everybody wore one when they were crossing The Bar. The Bar was deadly and dangerous. Ships had sunk there. People had drowned. Great sea monsters lurked beneath The Bar. Neville made crossing The Bar sound like going around Cape Horn in the *Cutty Sark*. Oh. And if anyone was interested, the sunglasses he was wearing were special polaroids. A snap at twenty bucks each.

'Okay folks,' said Neville finally. 'Let's put our life jackets on and we'll get going.'

They all took a life jacket from the storage space and while they were strapping them on, Les got into a little polite conversation with the two girls and the young couple. The young couple were from Penrith and down for the Blues Festival so they'd decided to take a trip to Montague

Island while they were in Narooma. The two girls were Iranian and came from Yagoona. They too were down for the festival and the thinner one was, like Les, going to Montague to go snorkelling; particularly to dive amongst the seals. Les ignored Big Ears. He took a photo of everyone putting on their life jackets and when Big Ears saw Norton's camera, he offered to take his photo. To keep him happy, Les handed Big Ears the camera, then watched as he looked at it like it was the control panel on the space shuttle and went on to stuff up two photos. Les took his camera back as the skipper checked them all out.

'Okay,' said Neville, satisfied everybody was secure. 'Let's get going.'

Neville cast off then climbed up to his cabin and started the motor. Les and the others either found a seat or somewhere safe to stand as the skipper carefully manoeuvred *The Kingfisher* away from the jetty. Soon, they were motoring slowly up the channel.

They got to The Bar as four decent swells came through and the boat started dipping up and down and rocking from side to side. Les held on to a pipe above his head and realised what Neville had meant about having a life jacket on when crossing The Bar. As well as being quite narrow, the water wasn't all that deep at the mouth; if any sort of a sea was running it would be extremely dangerous. They hit another couple of swells as they cleared the entrance, then Neville veered right and gunned the motor.

The Kingfisher was noisy and vibrated like a floor sander. Out to sea, the ocean was rougher than Les had anticipated and sheets of spray came splashing over either side of the boat as it pitched up and down in the swells. Nevertheless, Neville yelled down from his cabin that it was safe to take their life jackets off if they wanted to. As soon as they did, Big Ears got up on his seat and poked his head around the corner of the cabin, straight into a huge blast of water that immediately soaked him to the skin. Everybody tried not to laugh and Les took a photo as Big Ears sat down and tried to appear nonchalant while his dumpy wife looked more worried than ever. They bumped and rolled through the troughs and Les remembered Neville saying they'd probably see dolphins on the way out. They might even see whales. The others were looking out to sea and Les was watching the landward side of the boat when he gave a double blink. Swimming slowly along the surface a hundred metres from the boat was a huge shark. There was no mistaking its triangular black fin and the black tip of its tail flicking through the chop. Les poked his head up the stairs.

'Hey Nev!' he yelled out. 'Did you see that?'

Neville turned around from the wheel. 'See what, Les?'

'That bloody big shark out there,' pointed Les.

Neville shook his head. 'Nah. No sharks out here. It was probably a dolphin.'

Les stared at the skipper for a moment. 'Yeah righto,' he said, and returned to his seat.

Les knew a shark when he saw one. He'd seen them up close and personal. He'd seen them eating people. And that was a bloody shark. A big one. Les gazed at the deck and gave his head a slow, thoughtful shake then sat back with his bottle of mineral water as they bumped and rolled their way out to Montague island. Eventually they got there and Nev slowed down on the leeward side. Les stood up with the others to check it out.

There wasn't much to see. A long, low, uneven island of lumpy, grey rock with a small lighthouse on top near some old houses. Sitting in a small cove down from the lighthouse, was a landing with a crane and a lifeboat next to a rail leading up to a white shed with a red roof. There were no trees and little colour. The only vegetation was brittle scrub and patches of green and brown kikuyu grass. The place reminded Les of documentaries he'd seen about bleak, windswept islands off Scotland and Northern England. Maybe if the sun was out it might have looked all right. But on a cloudy day with a southerly blowing — VFO. Les took a few photos and returned to his seat. Nev left the engine idling and came down from the cabin.

'Well, this is it,' he said, warmly. 'Montague Island. Only land mass between Australia and South America.'

With Big Ears butting in again, trying to be funny, Nev went on with his spiel about the island. The tuna industry. When Zane Grey started big game fishing off the island. Penguins, whales, giant squid. How an entire tribe of Aborigines paddled their canoes out over a hundred years ago then got caught in a storm going back and they all perished. Les, however, wasn't the slightest bit interested. He was wishing he was somewhere else, instead of bobbing up and down on a boat out in the middle of nowhere on a lousy day, having to put up with Big Ears. Les stayed in his seat and did his best impersonation of a Trappist monk, till Neville said they'd check out the rest of the island, along with the seal colony, and they got going again.

Les took his binoculars out and scanned the island. It looked even worse. Then Neville informed them the seal colony was coming up and went in closer to the rocks. There were two seals: an old, brown bull and his mate.

The only sign of any other seals were patches of white seal shit splashed all over the rocks, as if a team of gyprockers had just emptied their work buckets. Nev yelled down that the seal colony must be out chasing fish. Les couldn't really have given a toss and went back to searching around with his binoculars hoping he might see a whale or something.

They got to the south side of the island, with Les focusing out to sea, when charging up the coast came a fleet of over thirty yachts under full sail, taking advantage of the southerly. They were all shapes, colours and sizes and made a great sight, ploughing through the white-capped swells about half a kilometre out from the island. Les saw them before the others and yelled up the stairs.

'Hey Nev! What are all the yachts in aid of?'

Nev peered out to sea. 'Ohh yeah. That's a special Bermagui to Ulladulla and back yacht race they organised for the long weekend. I forgot all about it.'

'They look good,' said Les.

'Yes, they do,' agreed Neville.

Les went back to peering through his binoculars, as the others crossed over for a better view.

The yachts were tacking and straining, their sails billowing in the wind, and as they drew closer Les could make out some of the names. *Trumpeter. Witchy Woman. Wind Dancer. Emily. Barbarella. Kerouac.* Hey, that's a good name for a yacht, thought Les. I've read *On the Road* twice. I'll check it out and see if its spinnaker's at the right end.

Les zeroed in on *Kerouac*. It was a wide-beamed, blue and white, ten metre ocean-going job with a sizeable cabin and the name along the side in red. A black rubber ducky was lashed securely across the bow, and an Australian flag flew off the stern. There was a man at the helm and two other men and a woman sitting up on the far rail. The yacht was tilted towards him and Les hit the stabilising button. The crew were all wearing sunglasses and dark sailing outfits with laced up hoods. Les could make out thick moustaches on the men and a strand of bright hair wisping across the woman's sunglasses. He zeroed in on the woman when the yacht tacked and the crew all ran across to the opposite rail and sat with their backs to him as the yacht angled in towards the rest of the fleet. Les watched the yachts move up the coast before they disappeared, as Neville brought *The Kingfisher* back around to the leeward side of the island.

They stopped in the same sheltered place as before. Neville cut the engines then came down and went into a bit of a spiel about the seals.

While he was talking, he picked up a bucket and started tossing pieces of fish over the side of the boat. There was a swirl of shiny black in the water as several seals came in and took the pieces of fish.

'There you go,' said Nev. 'I knew they were here somewhere.'

'Oh look at that.' The thinner of the two girls turned to her friend. 'Quick Massoameh. Get the camera.'

By now Grace's mineral water, along with the other water he'd been drinking, had flushed through Norton's system and he was bursting for a pee. He got up and went downstairs to use the toilet. Like all fishing boats, the galley stank of rotten bait and diesel, and when he opened the door, the toilet was jammed. Les looked around for something to piddle in. But there was nothing, and the smell downstairs, along with the pitching boat, was making him sick. Les went back upstairs to find Big Ears and the thinner of the two girls had stripped down to their costumes to go snorkelling with the seals. The girl noticed Les watching them as Neville handed out the diving gear.

'Come on,' she said. 'Before they swim away.'

Les turned to Neville. 'What about sharks?'

Neville ignored the worried look on Norton's face. 'Nah. No sharks out here,' he replied, breezily.

Les peered over the side of the boat. They were in around fifteen metres of water next to a ledge that dropped into bottomless, cobalt blue. Running beneath the water towards the island he could make out some huge, white rocks edged with grey and black. It was overcast, the water was deep and gloomy and full of fish pieces, and seals were a shark's favourite food. Especially White Pointers. And Les had already seen a possible Great White on the way out. Les turned to watch as the young girl and Big Ears got into their face masks and flippers while Neville kept tossing more bloody pieces of fish to the circling seals. By the time Big Ears and the girl had geared up, the boat had drifted well away from the seals. Nevertheless, Big Ears and the girl pushed off the back and swam blissfully out to them. Les watched in horror. But he was absolutely busting for a pee. He also felt like a big blouse still standing by the side of the boat with his snorkelling gear in his bag.

'In you go mate,' said Neville.

Les stared across at Big Ears and the girl swimming around out in the middle of nowhere circled by half a dozen seals chewing on pieces of fish.

'Oh,' squealed the girl. 'One just swam between my legs.'

'Go on,' her friend said to Les, holding up her camera. 'I'll take a photo of the three of you.'

Les looked at everyone watching him. 'Yeah righto,' he said.

Les got into his rubber vest, slipped into his flippers then shuffled to the landing bay at the back of the boat and rinsed his face mask and snorkel. He put them on, saw Neville give him the thumbs up, then took a deep breath and pushed off the landing bay.

The water was deep and dark and cold, and edged in gloomy blue-black, with huge, shadowy boulders tumbled across the bottom. No seaweed and no movement except for a few clusters of small school fish. Exactly as Les had seen in other documentaries about White Pointers in The Great Australian Bight. All that was missing was the shark cage and a six metre Great White, with its teeth bared, either coming in out of the gloom or up off the bottom. Without letting go of the landing bay, Les strained and pissed as hard and as fast as he could, feeling blessed relief and the water warming up around him. As soon as he finished, Les gave Mr Wobbly a quick shake, then hopped back on the boat and took his face mask off.

'Yeah,' he said, brightly. 'It was good. Didn't see any seals though.'

Ignoring the others, Les pulled his vest off then wrapped a towel around his waist and got his camera. If Big Ears and the girl were going to get taken he may as well get a photo. Nothing happened, however. The seals swam off, Big Ears and the girl snorkelled in and got back on the boat safe and sound. Les put his camera away, got dressed, then went back into Trappist monk mode, as Neville started the engine and they headed for Narooma.

With the wind behind them going home, it wasn't long before they were approaching The Bar and it was time to put their life jackets on again. They crossed The Bar without incident and Les was the first one off the boat when they tied up at the jetty. He thanked Neville for a wonderful day, said goodbye to the others and walked up to the house glad to be back on dry land.

Warren's car wasn't outside, the key was under the mat and there was no sign of Warren when Les let himself inside. He made a cup of coffee then had a shower and rinsed his snorkelling gear. By now Les was getting hungry. He put on a blue T-shirt, cap and cargos, got his overnight bag and Visa cards and headed for the festival.

The venue was fairly crowded with people getting the most from the last day of the concert. Les showed his wristband and walked straight across to the foodstalls at the back of the park. The Turkish stall smelled enticing and the owner in his braided vest had a swarthy friendliness about him. Les got a plate of beans, lamb, rice and vegetables and other things that looked tasty, then found a seat at the table where they'd had the drama the day before, and washed everything down with a freshly made pineapple and orange juice. While he was eating Les checked out the punters and listened to some music drifting across from the tents. It sounded like Jimbo's Blues Band. Les finished his meal then got a takeaway coffee and found a seat in the red tent and sat back to watch Jimbo and his band do their thing. They were just as tight as the day before and had the crowd rocking. Jimbo finished in his Indian headdress, Les applauded loudly with the rest of the crowd, then left the tent and walked over to the souvenir stall.

There were that many CDs Les didn't know where to start. So first off he bought a stack of T-shirts and caps for Billy, himself and anyone else he could think of, including Roxy in South Australia. Then he started on the CDs. He just pointed to the ones with covers he liked and finished up with everything from Ronnie Dawson to Pete Cornelius and the DeVilles to Blue Katz. And a stack of compilation records. *Big City Blues* to *Blues Road Trip* featuring everybody from The Johnny Nocturne Band to James Harman to Pat Boyack and the Prowlers. Most of the musicians and bands Les had never heard of. After leaving both his Visa cards quivering wrecks, Les crammed as much as he could into his overnight bag and carried everything back to the house.

There was still no one home. Les got a beer and packed all his purchases into two cardboard cartons. He was drooling at some of the music but decided to wait till he got back to Chez Norton then get into it with the help of Warren's prohibited substances. Les tidied his room and sorted out a few other things and later, when he was sitting in the kitchen reading the paper, a car pulled up in the driveway. Warren walked in wearing a T-shirt and jeans, designer sunglasses and driving gloves.

'Woz,' said Les. 'What's happening baby?'

'I found a nice, winding road in Bodalla State Forest. So I thought I'd see what the Celica could do.'

'The westie finally come out in you, eh.'

'You bet. I was chucking donuts and burnouts. It was megaramic.'

'That's good, Woz. I like to see you enjoy yourself.'

Warren got a glass of water from the fridge. 'So how was Montague Island?'

'In a word Woz, up to shit.'

They exchanged pleasantries about their day. Les told Warren about the trip out to the island, seeing a shark and shitting himself when he went in the water. The only thing of interest was the yachts. Warren had a sleep in then breakfast on his own at Carey's. He read the paper at the house and listened to the radio then went for a burn along the backroads. He didn't have a bad day. Les showed Warren what he'd bought, then Warren made two mugs of coffee, tuned the ghetto blaster to Season FM and Les followed him out onto the verandah. They sat facing the ocean. Despite the overcast sky, it was still pleasant watching the boats bobbing up and down at their moorings and the people walking around the jetty. Les held up his mug.

'I wonder what your crazy girlfriend's coffee's going to be like tonight?'

'Yes. I wonder,' replied Warren.

'What if we trip out and never come back.'

'Yeah. We might finish up living in Nimbin or somewhere. Just another couple of hippies with our brains fried.'

'I think yours are fried now.' Les was about to mention Warren's sleepwalking, but he thought he'd wait until Clover and Grace arrived so Warren would have to face up to it in front of the others.

'At least you don't have to worry, Ugly,' said Warren. 'You ain't got any brains to fry.'

'If I take too much lip like that from you, I'm sure I ain't.'

'So how's your back now, anyway?' asked Warren. 'Grace going to give you another massage?'

Les looked into his coffee. 'I'll let you in on a little secret, Woz.' Les told Warren about his romp on the rubber ball with Grace and how she topped him off afterwards. 'You know me, Woz. I never say too much. But it was some of the best porking I've ever had. You ought to get one of those rubber balls and give it a run with Clover.'

'And she just handed you the bottle of oil, and said rub it into that giant monster set of hers.'

Les shrugged. 'I could only do what she asked, Woz.'

'Fuck! What are they like? Are they as good as those photos of Tara Moss in *Black + White* magazine?'

'Are you kidding, Woz? They make Tara Moss's tits look like a couple of old football socks.'

Warren drained his coffee and raised the cup to Les. 'You are truly the chosen one, Les. You have been blessed.'

'They don't call me Lucky Les for nothing,' winked Les.

Warren looked at his watch. 'Well it's not getting any earlier. I might have an Eiffel Tower and get my shit together.'

'Okey doke.'

They rinsed their cups and Warren got in the shower. Les lay on his bed and read some more of his book then had a shave when Warren finished. He dabbed a bit of CK on his craggy face then got into his jeans, And ls and a blue and white polo shirt with a light blue collar. When he walked into the kitchen, Warren was wearing black jeans, a brown shirt with black stripes and his black leather jacket. He'd just made them a monstrous delicious each.

'Cheers Woz.' Les took a mouthful and blinked. 'Christ Warren. How much bourbon did you put in this?'

'I'm not sure,' replied Warren. 'But there wasn't much room for the ice, the slice and the soda water.'

Lionel Hampton and his Octet were wailing 'Jack the Fox Boogie' on Season FM in the loungeroom while Les and Warren were hitting the trail to deliciousville in the kitchen, and it wasn't long before they had a glow up. It was Norton's turn to make the drinks when there was a knock on the door. Les walked out and opened it. Clover was standing on the bottom step in a pair of white hipster jeans, a collarless white shirt and a blue T-shirt with yellow parrots on the front that she'd obviously got from Grace.

'Yes young lady? Can I help you?' he asked.

'You're the one that'll need help if you don't get out of the road,' said Clover. 'Where's that man of mine?'

'You must mean Mr Edwards. Do come in.'

Clover walked into the kitchen and threw her arms around Warren as Les closed the door.

'My God,' she said, smelling Warren's breath. 'How long have you two been on the turps?'

'Not long,' said Warren. 'Would you like one?'

'Yes. I wouldn't mind.'

Warren snapped his fingers and nodded to the fridge. 'Another delicious, Riff Raff. Plenty of ice.'

'Yes master,' bowed and scraped Les. 'Coming right up.' Les just about had the drinks made, when there was another knock on the door. 'Ohh shit!' he groaned. 'Who the bloody hell's this?' Les opened the door again and it was Grace. Her brown hair was down and shining like silk and she was wearing tight blue jeans, a Wrangler jacket and a black T-shirt with magpies on the front. A pair of black coral earrings caught the light as they dangled from her ears, and over her shoulder was a smart, black denim bag.

Les looked down at her. 'I suppose you want to come in too.'

Grace shrugged. 'It doesn't worry me that much. I can go over the RSL and have a drink if you like.' She stepped inside and gave Les one on the lips. 'How are you, George?'

'Good,' smiled Les, closing the door. 'Clover's inside. She beat you by about two minutes.'

They walked into the kitchen and the old house seemed to light up with the arrival of Clover and Grace. Les got all the drinks together then they sat back and talked about their day.

'So your trip out to Montague Island wasn't so good, Les,' said Grace.

'On a nice day, it'd probably be all right,' replied Les. But today ...' He shook his head. 'And I was certain Big Ears and that girl were going to get eaten.'

'What did you do when you came back from Grace's?' Warren asked Clover.

'Helped mum round the house then read a book,' Clover replied.

'What are you reading?' asked Les.

'*Fetish*. By Tara Moss,' answered Clover.

Warren caught Norton's eye. 'We were only talking about that earlier.'

'You were?' said Clover.

'Yeah. It didn't get a bad write up in the paper.'

'She's a really good writer,' declared Clover. 'I'm quite enjoying it.'

'Cool,' replied Les. 'If it's all right, I'll borrow it off you when you've finished.'

They talked away and ripped into the delicious while Season FM pumped out the hits and memories from the flapper era. Before long everyone was starting to feel no pain.

'So what's doing with these mushrooms?' asked Warren.

'Yes. I think it's about time I made the coffee,' replied Clover.

Clover put the kettle on then got the Tiger Stripes from the fridge, emptied them out onto a chopping board and started dicing them up while the water boiled. She tipped the mushrooms into a jug, added instant coffee, plus a little evaporated milk and honey, gave it a stir then poured out four mugs and handed them around. It looked like a cross between greasy dishwater that had run out of detergent and lumpy mushroom soup.

'Well. Here we go.' Clover raised her coffee and took a mouthful.

Les took a mouthful of his and nearly gagged. 'Ohh yuk!' he said. 'It definitely isn't Moccona.'

Warren screwed up his face. 'Christ! It tastes like someone eating curried rat just shit in my mouth.' He blinked and swallowed some bourbon.

'You get used to it,' said Grace, sipping away on hers.

'Yeah. I'll bet you do. Ohh bugger this,' said Les, and drained his mug, washing away the taste with delicious.

'I think that's the best idea,' said Warren, doing the same thing.

The girls finished theirs and there was a collective silence.

'So what happens now?' said Les.

'Give it time,' said Clover. 'Be cool.'

'Yes. Be cool Les,' said Grace.

Les settled back, took a sip of his delicious, then turned to Warren. 'Okay Woz, old mate,' he said. 'Now that everybody's here. Do you know you're walking in your sleep?'

Warren screwed his face up at Les. 'I'm what? Ohh piss off.'

'I'm fair dinkum, Woz. Remember when I set that rat-trap last night? And I left it under the kitchen table?'

'Yeah,' nodded Warren.

'I got up this morning and it was in the fridge.'

'There was a rat-trap in the fridge?' said Clover. 'What? Still set?'

'Yeah,' nodded Les. 'I went to get some milk and it nearly took my bloody finger off.'

'Well, I didn't put the bloody thing in there,' declared Warren.

'But that's not all,' continued Les. 'When I got up on Saturday morning, our shaving gear was scattered all over the bathroom floor. And someone had pissed all over the seat. No prizes for guessing who.'

'Your shaving gear was all over the bathroom?' said Clover.

'Everywhere,' said Les. 'I cleaned it up and didn't say anything. But before that, I had to force my way out of my room.' Les turned to Warren. 'Because someone had jammed a bloody old horseshoe under my door.'

'You had a horseshoe jammed under your door?' said Grace.

'Yeah. I nearly had to break the door down to get out.'

'And you reckon I did it?' Warren looked at Les, quite put off.

'Well, of course you did. That's why you've been calling me Lucky Les all the time. I know your warped sense of humour, Woz.'

Warren looked directly at Norton. 'Les. Apart from the rat and the bear waking me, I've been sleeping like a log. I haven't moved. And where would I find a bloody horseshoe? And if did, I can think of a better place to stick it than under your door.'

'Woz. Get fair dinkum. You got it from under the house. Mate. I know it was only a joke,' smiled Les. 'And that's cool. But sleepwalking can be a worry.'

Warren stared at Les. 'I got a horseshoe from under the house? You moron. Remember last night in the kitchen? When it turned freezing cold?'

'The kitchen got cold?' said Clover.

'Yeah. Like a bloody morgue. So Einstein here said, "There must be a draught coming from under the house".' Warren turned to Les. 'And when I was walking to my room, I asked you, you goose — "What is under the house?" Because I haven't bothered to look.'

Les thought for a moment. 'Shit! You did too.'

'Hello,' said Warren. 'We've made contact with the lost tribe.'

'Well if that's the case' said Les, 'who ...?' Suddenly a strange, tingle ran up Norton's spine. He sat back in his seat, a surprised look on his face. 'Shit! What was that?'

Grace caught Clover's eye, then smiled serenely at Les. 'Why don't we leave it till tomorrow?'

'Yes,' agreed Clover. 'Why don't we talk about it in the morning, boys?'

Les blinked at the girls as if he was now looking at them through a shop window. 'Yeah,' he nodded. 'Why don't we.'

Warren was staring at something on the table. 'Yeah, good idea. Why don't we.'

Les looked around and the room had changed shape. There were no straight lines or sharp edges. Everything had been rounded off. The table, the fridge, the kitchen cabinets. It all looked as if it was moulded out of plasticine.

'Are you all right, Les?' asked Grace.

'Yeah,' nodded Les, staring at his drink. The ice cubes had lights in them and it was glowing in his hand. 'Yeah. I'm good,' he said, slowly.

'How are you Warren?' asked Clover.

'How am I?' replied Warren, looking around. 'I'm not sure. Did Tinkerbell just fly through here sprinkling stardust everywhere?' He looked at his hand. 'Hey. It's all over my fingers.' Warren blew on his fingers and started to laugh. 'Shit! Look at that,' he said.

'Why don't we take our drinks out onto the verandah, and have a look at the night,' suggested Grace.

'Sounds good to me,' said Les. 'Do you know the way from here?'

Grace smiled across at Clover, then back to Les. 'Follow us Les. It's not far.'

'Hey. Don't leave without me,' said Warren.

Les got up and followed the others down the hallway to find it had turned into a green, glowing tunnel. The ceiling had heightened and the floor was narrower, while the doors on either side looked like the entrances into an igloo. Around him the air seemed denser, almost like water, and Les felt as if he was wading as much he was walking. They stepped into the plasticine loungeroom and there were colours going everywhere. His ghetto blaster had grown legs and was singing to him, the piano looked like a whale and the bear standing on the whale's head seemed the same size as Les, with a big, friendly smile spread across its face. They walked out onto the verandah and Les leant against the railing with his drink and gazed up at the sky.

It was still cloudy. But in the clear patches the stars were buzzing round like fireflies. The rolling clouds looked like herds of cattle charging across the sky, then they turned into endless hectares of gigantic, pink, grey mushrooms. The water in the harbour had changed to blue, molten lava and the ocean looked like a huge indigo blanket covered with tiny, silver feathers and someone was shaking it. He turned to the surrounding buildings and they'd turned into funny, colourful drawings, swept by convections of more colour. It was beautiful. And it was all beautifully drawn. Les turned to the others.

'Hey. You know what it's like?' he said. 'It's like I've landed in Toon Town.'

The others had disappeared. Instead, Warren had turned into Mickey Mouse, complete with a huge pair of white gloves. Clover was Minnie Mouse in a pair of Doc Martens with her hair punked up. And Grace's Wrangler jacket was now a black leather Brando jacket and she looked like a cross between Barbarella and the Terminator.

Les started laughing. 'Holy Shit!' he said.

'What's the matter, Les?' asked Grace.

'You're not going to believe this.' Les told them what he was seeing.

'That's okay, Les,' said Grace. 'You know what you look like to me? Foghorn Leghorn. Wearing a Blues Brothers outfit.'

'I reckon Yogi Bear,' said Clover. 'In a tuxedo.'

'No, no. You're both wrong,' said Warren. 'It's Yosemite Sam in a white Elvis jump-suit.'

Les gave Warren a crazy look. 'Whooh! You make me so mad, you long-eared little varmint. I ought's to blast the hide clean offen' your fur bearin' carcass.'

Suddenly they all fell about laughing like they were going to piddle themselves. After a while they settled down and Les turned to the sky again. Now it was all pink and blue with chunky little yellow and white clouds edged with Mayan writing. He looked at the top of the railing running along the verandah and it had turned into a bright green railway line, with tubes of toothpaste for sleepers. Someone had left a white cup sitting on the railing. While everything round it was turning into all sorts of things and all kinds of colours, Les concentrated on the white cup, telling himself it was a white cup. Nothing else. And it stayed a white cup. Okay, Les told himself, as well as expanding your mind, the mushrooms work on your subconscious. But it's only a trip. You go along with it and have some fun. But just be cool and remember you can come back to reality. It's only your imagination. He left the cup and turned to the others, and for a moment they looked normal. Then they went back into cartoon form. Les looked across the street at a telephone pole and it turned into a gigantic, blue cactus. Then the cactus got up and walked away, crouched forward like Groucho Marx. Les could hear its footsteps sounding like someone beating on a bass drum as they faded into the distance. Les shook his head. At least I think it's my imagination.

'How are you handling things, Les?' asked Grace.

Les turned around and Grace was still Barbarella. 'Not too bad,' he replied. 'I just watched a telegraph pole turn into a cactus and walk away.'

'The boats on the jetty changed into storks a little while ago,' said Clover. 'And flew out to sea holding baby orang-utans in their beaks.'

'How are you going, Woz?' asked Les.

Warren had his eye on a moth circling the light on the verandah. 'I'm just watching this fighter jet. It's firing golden arrows all over the place. And they're exploding into showers of hundreds and thousands. It's unreal.'

'What about you, Grace?' asked Les.

'I'm into the Mandelbrot Set,' said Grace.

'The what?' said Les.

Grace pointed to the sky. 'Can you see an odd-looking black hole up there?'

Les stared up at the sky. 'Yeah. I think I can,' he said.

'Keep watching it,' said Grace.

Les stared intently at the black hole. At first it looked a silhouette of the bear. Then it turned into a fat little Buddha shape with a pointy cap. From out of the black hole flowed countless paisley patterns of every colour and design imaginable: they were continuously forming and re-forming as they spread across the sky into space. Million and billions of them. It was like watching an epiphany of never-ending, ethereal, coloured patterns pouring from a huge kaleidoscope. It was spiritual, metaphysical and the strangest, most surrealistically beautiful thing Les had ever seen.

'Holy smoke!' he said. 'Look at that.' Les turned to Grace. 'Is that the eye of God?'

'Sort of,' answered Grace. 'It's the Mandelbrot Set. Have a few Tiger Stripes and you don't need a computer to click into fractal geometry.'

'Whatever,' said Les, totally incredulous.

After staring at the amazing colours, Les turned to the house. The windows had changed into eyes and the door was now a mouth. One of the eyes winked at him and a huge, Rolling Stones tongue flicked out of the mouth. Four rats dressed in jockey colours came sliding off the tongue pulling a pumpkin coach with a boardrack full of surfboards. The coach flew off over the railing and disappeared towards the golf course which had turned into a Jurassic Park full of pink and green dinosaurs; they were strolling arm in arm across the links carrying paper umbrellas. Les watched them for a moment then looked at his watch. Although it had melted like in a Salvador Dali painting, Les could still tell the time and he was amazed how fast it had gone. Unlike smoking pot where time often slowed to a crawl — mushrooms sped things up.

'Shit! If we're going to the concert,' he said, holding up his watch, 'we'd better make a move. Look at the time.'

'Hey, you're right,' said Grace. She turned to the others. 'Will we get going?'

Warren was aghast. 'That concert and all those people. It's going to be a complete freak-out.'

Clover smiled and put her arm around him. 'It'll be fun. You wait and see.'

'What if you know who's in there,' said Les, ominously. 'He'll look like Godzilla.'

'Oh God!' wailed Warren. 'Don't say that.'

'It's all right,' said Grace, holding up a biro. 'I've got my disintegrator, death ray gun with me.'

They went inside and somehow Les was able to turn off the radio, find his guest pass, get the rest of his stuff together and turn the lights off except for the one above the front step. When the others got their things together they all rallied out the front before walking down the hill to the jetty.

Walking down the hill was like going down a ski slope. They all leaned to one side as they turned left at the bottom and slid past the boats at the jetty. It was a full-on Toon Town trip now. Everything was a drawing by Harry Crumb and everybody they saw was a cartoon character in strange, colourful clothes. Even the people's eyes poked half-a-metre out of their heads. They showed their passes and the security staff in black all looked like Darth Vader. Inside was pandemonium. There seemed to be cartoon characters running everywhere, honking horns and banging on drums. Music was coming from one of the tents and Les could see notes and cleft tones spinning high above the crowd. The weather was changing and amongst the patches of spinning stars the clouds were flying across the sky as in time-lapse photography.

'We have to remember this night,' said Les.

He handed his camera to a cartoon character in a blue zoot suit with a huge yellow fedora who was walking past and asked if they would take a photo. The character in the zoot suit was most obliging. Les gathered the others around and the character took two photos. Each time the flash went off it was like a phosphorous bomb exploding. Les thanked the character, retrieved his camera and turned to the others.

'What about drinks?' he asked.

'Yes. Good idea,' said Warren. 'I mean no. I mean yes. I mean ...'

'Ohh shut up, Warren,' said Les. 'Come and give me a hand.'

'I can't,' said Warren. 'I can't.'

'Yes you can. You stupid hippy. Come on.'

Les dragged Warren over to the drinks tent and got four delicious. Paying for the drinks was a trip in itself. The fifty dollar bill had turned into an Indian blanket and his change looked like playing cards and gambling chips. All the drinks were full of glow worms wearing snorkelling gear. With not much help from Warren, Les handed the drinks around then they followed Grace across to the blue tent. Somehow they got four seats together and managed to arrive just as Pete Cornelius and the DeVilles came out on stage.

'This guy's really good,' said Grace. 'He's only eighteen.'

'I don't know if I've heard of him,' replied Les.

'He's from Tasmania.'

Les looked up at the stage and it was a mess of lights going everywhere. Comets and shooting stars whirled above the band, then an Egyptian Pharaoh in a chariot drawn by four black horses galloped above the stage, before heading out through the top of the tent. Les tried to concentrate on the band. The lead singer was wearing a plain, dark blue shirt and black trousers. The bearded drummer had on a black T-shirt and jeans and the other guitarist was wearing a cap and a Levi's jacket. Next thing the lead singer turned into Zeke Wolf with this huge, bushy tail and the two others in the band turned into Heckle and Jeckle. Bloody hell, thought Les, and settled back in his seat as the band went straight into 'If You Be My Baby'.

The music didn't sound quite as deep and smooth as being stoned. But it was still great and the light show was fantastic. Zeke Wolf and Heckle and Jeckle were boogeying away on stage while a small crowd of cartoon characters bounced up and down in front of the band as the rest of the cartoon characters in the audience got into the music. Norton's delicious tasted like he was drinking liquid fire and he sipped away as the band did 'All My Heroes Are Dead', 'After School Blues', the old Johnny O'Keefe classic, 'She's My Baby'. Heaps of others and a sensational version of 'Riders On The Storm'. Then it was over. Les looked at his watch and again couldn't believe how fast the time was going. He turned to Barbarella, Micky and Minnie.

'What did you think?' he asked.

'Unreal,' answered Clover.

'I still don't know where I am,' said Warren.

'Yeah. Come to think of it. How did we finish up in here?' Les asked Grace.

Grace shrugged. 'We just did. Next up is Jo Jo Zep and The Falcons. They're the last act of the night. But I don't like our chances of getting a seat.'

'It doesn't matter,' said Clover.

'Yeah. I don't mind standing up,' said Les. 'In fact I don't care what happens one way or the other tonight. I'm having a ball.'

'That's good,' smiled Grace. 'But we'd better make a move. They're on in fifteen minutes.'

They left their seats and shuffled through the Toonies over to the booze tent. Les and Warren got another round of drinks and they joined the crowd standing outside the big tent. Les got Grace to hold his drink while he took his camera out and started taking photos of the crowd. They were still all Toonies in Toon Town clothing. But every now and again, one would slip back into almost human form and Les was convinced he was getting photos of their auras. One woman with long black hair had a blue, green and silver aura around her, radiating a metre from her body.

There was a great roar then the musicians came out on stage. Over the heads of the crowd Jo Jo Zep and The Falcons looked like the cast of Cirque du Soleil and Munchkins on steroids. Then they blasted off with 'Honey Dripper' and the Toonies all went mad.

Les was rocking and laughing along with the others when he looked away and noticed a skyscraper had broken off from Toon Town and was walking towards them. The skyscraper stopped in front of Norton, a big gap opened near the top floors and a voice boomed out.

'Hey Les! Can you do me a favour?'

Les squinted up at the skyscraper and it partly took on human form. 'Ohh yeah,' he answered. 'What is it, Norm?'

Norm handed Les a video recorder. 'You know how to work one of these?'

'Sure,' replied Les. Billy had one and he'd lent it to Les for a week. Les was thinking of buying one.

'I'm flat out. The Handbrake's hurt her ankle. Can you come backstage and video Jo Jo and Wilbur Wilde for me?'

'Righto,' said Les.

Norm turned to the others staring blankly up at him. 'I'll send someone over with some seats for you. Okay Les. This way mate.'

Les followed the skyscraper through the backstage entry, past several tents and offices and a guests' tent full of chairs and tables. There were staff standing around doing whatever it was they were doing, looking like shiny, black robots with mirrors for eyes and old FJ Holden radiator grills for mouths. Pounding music was thumping from above Norton's head. He followed Norm up a set of steps onto the back of the stage and stopped dead in his tracks.

On the left, surrounded by more robots in black, were all the mixing panels, glowing and blinking like the control room on a space ship. On the right Cirque du Soleil was blasting away loud enough to raise the dead, and in the middle was the crowd, swarms of frantic Toonies, twisting and turning and bouncing into and tumbling over each other. Then half the Toonies dissolved into snapping, carnivorous plants, wrapping themselves around the poles and spiralling up the sides of the tent. The plants in front of the stage changed back to Toonies with gorilla heads, wearing straw boaters and blazers. They all looked up at Les and started yammering, and hopping from one foot to the other beating their chests. Next thing, Les picked up the energy emanating from the crowd. It came at him in convections of shimmering light, almost knocking him off his feet. The skyscraper smiled over at Les.

'Okay Les,' it boomed over the crowd. 'Away you go. Start filming.'

Les looked at the video camera and it had changed into a Stinger surface to air missile launcher. 'Righto.' Les raised the camera to his eye, and pressed the button. A rocket fired out and exploded in a burst of flowers above the band as they slipped into 'The Shape I'm In'. After that, Les just winged it.

The band thumped out one song after another and the crowd kept changing into one shape after another; meanwhile, anti-aircraft fire exploded above their heads showering them with fruit salad shrapnel, as lights and rockets flew over the band and whirled round the tent. Through the viewfinder, Wilbur Wilde looked five metres tall and Joe Camilleri looked five metres wide. The rest of the band had turned into penguins wearing top hats, waddling around with their instruments on a skating rink made of rainbow-coloured ice edged with luminous coconut trees and gingerbread guard towers. A technician hit the smoke machine, the stage fogged up and the band all turned into a bunch of Jack the Rippers, wearing long capes, tartan top hats, mini-dresses and fishnet stockings. Les wandered around filming and doing his best to keep out of the band's way. He looked over and the skyscraper gave him the thumbs up. Les panned the camera over the crowd and seated near the side of the tent he could see Barbarella, Mickey and Minnie. They saw Les and waved and Les waved back.

What songs the band played Les wasn't sure. It was just loud, hot and smoky on stage and Les roamed around thinking he'd beamed down onto an alien planet. The band played 'Chained To The Wheel' and walked off past him. The skyscraper ambled over to the microphone, strangled it to death and told the Toonies to put their hands together for Jo Jo Zep and The Falcons. The Toonies did what they were told and Circus Soleil came back and did 'Rock Me Baby All Night Long' for an encore, and that was it. Everything seemed to be all over before it even started. Les filmed the band leaving the stage then walked across and handed the skyscraper back his video camera.

'Thanks for that, Les,' said Norm. 'How did you like it backstage?'

'It was great,' replied Les. 'Unreal.'

The skyscraper edged in a little closer. 'How's your back now?'

'My back?'

'Yeah.'

'Oh my back. It's good. It's still there behind me I think.'

Norm stared at Norton. 'Are you all right, Les?'

'Yeah,' nodded Les. 'As a bean. We had a smoke earlier. That's all.'

Norm winked. 'Don't turn up stoned tomorrow.'

'No. I'll be cool. Anyway, I'd better get back to Barbarella, Mickey and Minnie.'

'Who?'

'The Toonies I came with. I'll see you tomorrow, Norm,' smiled Les.

'Yeah . . . right.'

Les left Norm and worked his way back through the crowd to the others. They were still sitting at the side of the tent staring into space.

'Hey. How's things?' Les asked them.

They looked up at Les and Grace spoke. 'How did you finish up on stage?' she asked.

'Norm asked me to video the band,' replied Les. 'It was a madhouse. Were they any good?'

'They were great,' said Warren. 'And it was mad down here too.'

'How are you feeling now, Les?' asked Clover.

'All right,' replied Les. 'I'm starting to straighten out a bit.' He looked at his watch and shook his head. 'Shit! I can't believe how fast the night's gone.'

'Yes,' agreed Grace. 'Time certainly flies when it's all over the place. And you're in another dimension having fun.'

'Does it what,' agreed Les. 'And you're right about time. It seems to bend.'

'What are we doing now?' asked Warren.

'We'd best head for home,' said Clover. 'Mum will be along soon.'

'Righto,' agreed Les. 'Let's make tracks.' He helped Grace to her feet and they all started to make their way to the entrance.

No one said much on the way home. They were all starting to come down and everyone was in their own little world. Arm in arm they made it to the front of the house and stood around looking at each other.

'So what's doing tomorrow?' asked Les.

'I don't know,' said Warren. 'What's tomorrow?'

'Monday,' said Clover. 'We're going home. Remember?'

'Ohh yeah, that's right,' nodded Warren.

'Why don't we all have breakfast together before you leave?' suggested Grace.

'Yes. I'd like that,' said Clover.

'Good idea,' agreed Les. 'There's something I want to talk to you about too.'

'We'll talk over breakfast.' Grace snuggled up to Les and put her arms around him.

'Hey. Here's mum now,' said Clover.

The station wagon arrived out the front in a blaze of light with Clover's mother behind the wheel in her dressing gown. Clover said goodbye to Les, then kissed Warren goodnight and walked over to the car. Les smiled down at Grace.

'Well. I don't think I'll forget tonight in a hurry, Grace,' he said.

'No. Me either,' replied Grace.

'What time do you want to have breakfast?'

'About nine or so?'

'Sounds good to me,' said Les. 'I'll see you then.'

'Goodnight Les.'

Les gave Grace a tender kiss goodnight, then she walked across to join Clover. As she got to the car she called out, 'Don't forget to drink your water.'

'I won't,' Les assured her.

The boys waved them off, Les opened the door, then they walked inside to the kitchen and Warren turned on the light.

'Fuck! What a night,' blinked Les. 'I'm still seeing things.'

Warren looked a little drawn and pale. 'I don't think I'm in any hurry to do that again. It was all right. But at times there, I was just seeing too much weird shit.'

'You should have seen it up on that stage,' said Les. 'It was insane.'

Warren yawned and rubbed a hand across his neck. 'Mate. I'm going to have a snakes and hit the sack. I'm rooted.'

'I won't be far behind you, Woz.'

Norton went to his room and sat on the bed, still seeing coloured lights and stars similar to when you get a knock on the head or let out a violent sneeze. He changed into his tracksuit and heard Warren shuffling down the hallway.

'What time are we having breakfast?' Warren called out.

'Grace said around nine,' Les called back.

'See you then, Les.'

'Righto.'

Les went to the bathroom, then got the last bottle of mineral water, took it out to the kitchen and opened it. He didn't feel all that thirsty and it wasn't easy drinking a large bottle of mineral water in the middle of the night. But Les kept glugging and yawning away till it was all gone. Suddenly the temperature in the kitchen dropped down to below freezing. Shit, cursed Les, rubbing his arms as his breath immediately turned to steam. Here we go again. Back to bloody Siberia. This joint's fucked. Les was about to get up and go to bed when he glanced across the kitchen. A peculiar green glow was coming from under the front door and reflecting along the hallway. Les watched the strange light and shook his head. Fuckin hell, when do these bloody mushrooms wear off? he asked himself. Next thing, he heard a noise coming from around the cars. Feeling suspicious, he got up and opened the front door.

Les stared into the yard and all he could see at first was the same green glow. Then he noticed a slightly built, not very tall man standing near Warren's Celica. He was wearing a straw hat with a black ribbon around it, a crumpled, grey frock coat, matching trousers and lace-up boots. An untidy beard covered his face and perched on his nose were a pair of John Lennon glasses. Les wasn't sure in the light, but he looked to have blood on the sleeve of his coat and his left hand appeared to be missing. Whoever it was, he didn't say anything. He just stared silently at Les with an expression of sad anger in his eyes.

'Yeah, what do you want mate?' said Les.

The man with the beard continued to stare at Les without answering.

'What's up?' said Les. 'Do you want something? What are you hanging around the cars for? What do you want?'

Without saying anything, the man with the beard slowly raised his right arm and pointed away from the house towards the ocean.

Les screwed his face up. 'What . . . ?'

The man still kept his silence and simply stood in the green glow pointing south. Les figured he must be drunk and had been in a fight or something.

'Listen mate,' said Les bluntly. 'If you don't want anything, piss off. And get away from the cars. Go on. Fuck off.'

The man kept staring at Les then lowered his arm and started to walk away, still staring at Les over his shoulder. Finally, he disappeared into the darkness taking the green glow with him. Les waited for a moment, then shut the door, turned the light off in the kitchen and went to his bedroom.

Bloody hell! That's all I need, thought Les, after he switched off the bedlamp and climbed under the blankets — some drunken yobbo trying to steal one of the cars. Anyway, he'd better not come back. Unless he wants that empty bottle right between the eyes. Les gathered the blankets round his neck and shivered. Shit, it's fuckin cold in here. Les stayed still and started to warm up. Norton watched the last coloured lights exploding in his mind's eye and before long he had put the intruder behind him and was snoring peacefully.

Les blinked his eyes open before seven the next morning absolutely bursting for a piss. He rolled out of bed, hurried to the bathroom and hosed away like a draught horse. God! I didn't think that was ever going to finish, he thought, as he flushed the toilet. There must have been a gallon. Les splashed some water over his face and stared at himself in the mirror. Anyway, I'm up now. He cleaned his teeth then changed into his training gear and walked into the kitchen. While the kettle was boiling and the toast was browning, he stared at the floor and mulled over the previous night. His mind was still a bit gluggy. But slowly the cogs and wheels started turning and Les smiled round the kitchen. It had certainly been a night with a difference. He made a mug of tea, buttered his toast and walked down the hallway into the loungeroom. Everything looked normal and steady snoring was coming from Warren's bedroom. Les stepped out onto the verandah and took up his usual position, leaning against the railing.

The weather had cleared up. It was fairly warm, the southerly had turned light nor'-east and apart from a few clouds the sky was bright blue. A lovely day to be fishing off the jetty, walking around or having a surf. Not much of a day to be fighting some gorilla in a park, mused Les. He placed his mug of tea on the railing and touched his toes. He touched them again, swung his arms from side to side, and his brow furrowed. Something was wrong. Les did some squats then stretched his legs on the railing. He laced his hands behind his head, twisted his torso and did some side bends. Something was wrong all right. The pain and stiffness had completely vanished from his back.

'The bloody mineral water,' Les said, out loud. 'Grace. You doll.'

Les got down on his behind and did some crunches then rolled over and snapped off thirty press-ups, before jumping to his feet and running up and down on the spot. Not only had the pain in his back gone, all the other kinks in his body had disappeared too. From football, fighting, getting shot: even the sinus in his broken nose had cleared up.

'Shit! I can't remember ever feeling this good,' said Les. Ecstatically, he grinned up at the sky. 'Boss. What can I say? Thanks mate. And give that girl a medal.' Les quickly finished his tea and toast, put his cap and sunglasses on and tore off out the front door towards the golf links.

Les walked down Browning Street, stopped at the bottom and looked at the hill going up to the golf course. He took a breath then sprinted to the top like Sylvester Stallone taking the steps in *Rocky*. When he got there, he was barely puffing. Les felt he could run all day. He was about to take off again, then stopped. No. I'll put the run on hold for the time being. I've got a big day in front of me. And you never know who's around. Norton straightened his cap and set off across the golf links at a fast walk.

Les was moving that freely he felt his feet were hardly touching the ground and, before he knew it, he was overlooking Narooma Beach. He stopped to watch the people fishing near the rocks for a second, then started crisscrossing the golf links, stopping to do sets of push-ups and crunches or shadow box around the low-hanging branches under the trees. After a while Les checked his watch and decided to head back home. On the way, he found a metre of fence paling laying near a tree. He jammed one end in the ground, pushed the other against the tree then, taking a quick look around to make sure no one was watching, smashed a short right into the length of paling, snapping it in half. Les propped one of the shorter pieces of paling against the tree and whacked it with a short left. It only cracked. But there was plenty of power in his fist. Norton looked at the two pieces of wood for a moment then continued thoughtfully on his way.

The way Les felt, he knew he could kick Morgan Scully's arse to the Queensland border. And he couldn't wait to do it. But there was betting involved now, and most of the money would be on Morgan. If Les did too quick a demolition job on him, the punters might think he'd pulled a scam. Daddy was holding the prize money and running the show. But Les was still one out in a country town. If the locals got the shits at the result, anything could happen. This meant he'd have to carry Morgan for a while and make it look convincing without getting hurt. Which wouldn't be easy with an angry, big mug like Morgan. By the time Les got back to Browning Street, however, he had an idea.

Les still couldn't believe how good he felt as he walked in the driveway, when he stopped abruptly and took off his sunglasses. The rear window of Warren's car was smashed. Pieces of broken glass were scattered over the bonnet and sitting amongst the pieces on the back seat was a horseshoe. When he bolted out of the house earlier Les hadn't noticed. Les checked to make sure his car was all right, then walked over to the trees. He had a look around before taking another look at a Warren's car, then went inside and had a shower.

Les washed his training gear, hung it out on the verandah, changed into his blue cargos and a grey Hahn T-shirt then walked up to the newsagency. The idea he had earlier was just inside the door; a metal stand stacked with packets of cheap toys for kids. Amongst the Floating Eyeball, the Fly in an Ice Cube and Fart Powder, were packets labelled Vampire Blood Capsules: Scare Your Friends. Each packet contained four capsules of fake blood. Les bought two packets and the paper then walked back to the house. Warren was still in bed. Les poured himself a glass of water then went and banged on Warren's door.

'Hey Warren! Get out of bed.' Les banged on the door again. 'Warren. Are you awake?'

'Mmmrrgghhburrnngh,' came a horrible, strangled reply. 'Fuck! I am now.'

'Good. Get your arse out here. I want you to see something.'

There was more grumbling before Warren opened the door wearing his tracksuit and blinking at the light. 'What the fuck's up? What time is it?'

'Go and have a look at your car, Woz,' said Les.

'What?'

Warren shuffled off down the hallway and Les went out onto the verandah with his glass of water. He'd barely had two mouthfuls when a string of expletives echoed round the side of the house. Next thing, Warren came cursing up the hall way and out onto the verandah.

'Have you seen my fuckin car?' he howled.

'What do you think I got you out of bed for?' said Les.

'Who the fuckin hell did that?'

'I don't know,' answered Les. 'But there was a bloke hanging round out the front last night.' Les told Warren about chasing off the man with the beard before going to bed. 'It might have been him.'

'What a cunt,' said Warren.

'At least it's not your windscreen,' offered Les.

'Ohh yeah, great. You know how much a rear window is for a fuckin Celica.'

'No. The same as one for a piecost, I suppose.'

'A piecost?' said Warren. 'What's a fuckin piecost?'

'About two dollars fifty with sauce.'

'Ohh what's the fuckin use?' groaned Warren.

'Woz,' said Les. 'Why don't you go and have a shower and get ready. Grace and Clover will be here soon.'

'Yeah righto.'

Warren shuffled back to his bedroom then had a shower while Les read the paper in the kitchen. Les had just finished when a car pulled up in the driveway. He heard voices and a few moments later Grace and Clover walked in the front door. Clover had her bags with her. She left them in the hallway, then they both stepped into the kitchen, each wearing T-shirts and jeans.

'What happened to Warren's car?' asked Clover.

'I'm not sure,' said Les. 'Warren's inside. Maybe you should ask him?'

Clover walked off to the front bedroom leaving Grace in the kitchen. Les folded the paper and smiled up at her. 'Good morning Grace,' he said.

'Hi,' replied Grace. She gave Les a quick once up and down. 'So how are you this morning?'

'Come here,' Les indicated with his head.

'What?'

'Come here.' Grace came over and Les pulled her down onto his knee then kissed her all over her neck.

'Goodness,' flustered Grace. 'What was that for?'

Grace took a chair and Les told her about the pain in his back disappearing and how good he felt all round.

'You're a genius, Grace,' said Les. 'I don't know what to say.'

Grace was all smiles. 'That's great,' she said. 'I knew it would work.'

'Work? It's nothing short of a miracle.'

'And you sprinted up the hill?'

'I flew. My shadow was flat out keeping up with me.' Les rubbed his hands together. 'Poor bloody Morgan. He won't know what's hit him.'

Grace looked sagely at Les. 'Don't be too sure, Les. He's a big man. And I've seen what he can do to people.'

Les was about to say something when Clover and Warren walked into the kitchen. Warren was still wearing his tracksuit. But he looked much better after a shower.

'Warren tells me you had an intruder last night,' said Clover.

Grace turned to Les. 'An intruder?'

'Yeah. In the front yard.' Les pushed out a chair. 'Okay Clover. Grab a seat. I'd like to have a word with you. You too Grace.' Les waited for Clover and Warren to get comfortable then he zeroed in on Warren's girlfriend. 'Righto Clover, what's going on?'

'Going on?' replied Clover. 'How do you mean, Les?'

'How do I mean? All right,' said Les evenly. 'This house, both your little ears prick up when me and Warren mention things that keep happening. Like the bear, and the rat in the piano. And the cold. And you're always asking us how we slept.'

'So?' shrugged Clover.

'So,' repeated Les. 'Our stuff lying around the bathroom and the rat-trap in the fridge. And the horsehoe under my door. I thought that was Warren. But it wasn't.' Warren smiled, vindicated as Les pointed his finger at Clover. 'Anyway, forget all the other shit for the moment. But that horseshoe sitting on the back seat of Warren's car. It's the same one that was under my door. I threw it under the trees out the front. Now, if Warren didn't stick it under my door, who did?' Les narrowed his eyes at Clover. 'You? Grace? Elves?'

Clover glanced at Grace then looked directly at Norton. 'Okay Les,' she said. 'I'll give it to you straight. The place is haunted.'

Warren sat up in his chair. 'Haunted?'

'Yes. There's a presence in the house,' said Clover.

'That's right,' added Grace. 'The Merrigan house has a poltergeist. It's the town's best kept secret.'

'Well, I'll be buggered,' said Les. 'How bloody slow am I?'

The girls looked at Norton without saying anything.

'So what happened?' asked Les. 'Did someone get murdered in here?'

'No,' answered Grace. 'We think it's Edward Ruddle.'

'The surveyor?' Les stared at Grace for a moment. 'Hey wait a minute,' he said. Les hurried out to the table on the verandah and came back with Jasmine Cunneen's book. He sat down and flicked through the pages till he came to the photo of Edward Ruddle and Gwendolyn Monteith. 'That's him,' said Les, stabbing his finger on the page. 'That's the bloke I saw out the front last night. Only he was wearing a straw hat.'

'Edward actually appeared last night?' said Grace.

'Yeah,' answered Les. 'In this green cloud. I thought I was still tripping.'

'Oh my God!' said Clover. 'That was the ectoplasmic aura. You saw the real deal, Les.'

'Christ! A bloody ghost,' said Warren.

'What exactly was he doing out the front, Les?' asked Grace.

'Nothing really. He was just standing near the cars staring at me.' Les thought for a second. 'Then he held his hand up and pointed. Like he was trying to tell me something.'

'So what did you do?' asked Grace.

'I told him to piss off.'

'And did he?'

'Yeah. He just vanished into the night.'

'Then came back later,' said Clover.

'But why would he want to break my window?' asked Warren. 'I've never done anything to him.'

'This is the fifth day people have been in the house,' said Clover. 'That's when the presence starts to get violent. After the fourth day.'

'Terrific,' said Les.

'Now you know why we never rent the place,' said Clover. 'We can't rent it. We can't sell it. We can't do anything with it. We're stuck with it.'

'That's what happened to Eachan,' said Grace. 'Edward drove him insane.'

'Well, why didn't you tell us what was going on?' asked Warren.

'Yeah. You could have warned us,' agreed Les.

'Oh, you both would have laughed at me,' said Clover. 'Besides that,' she smiled, 'I wanted to know what went on in here.'

'Thanks Clover.' Les turned to Grace. 'Naturally you were in on this too?'

'Well, I'd heard so much about the place, Les,' answered Grace.

'So when it turned freezing cold in here at night,' said Warren, 'that was Edward cruising around.'

'Yes. That was the ectoplasm, sweetheart,' smiled Clover. 'Edward's cool vibe from the spirit world.'

'Shit!'

There was silence for a moment, then Les looked around the table. 'So what do we do now? Call Ghostbusters?'

'No,' said Clover, rising to her feet. 'We go and have breakfast. Grace has got something she wants to show you.'

'Yes. Let's have breakfast,' said Grace, also rising from her chair.

'Yeah, suits me,' said Les. 'Ghost or no ghost. I'm that hungry, I'd eat the arse out of a dead werewolf.'

They got their things and walked up to the restaurant. The girls were chatting away, quite pleased that thanks to Les they could now verify who the spirit was. Warren was glad he was getting out.

Carey's wasn't crowded and they were able to get a table near the window. They ordered breakfast, Les paid and they got their little wooden objects again. Les couldn't help but laugh when Warren got a pineapple. They sat down, the first coffees arrived, then they started talking about the night before and the mushrooms. Grace reminded them that they'd have a flashback sometime tomorrow.

The waitress brought the food over and the conversation swung back to the house. Clover told them how the presence never made itself felt before midnight. Why? She didn't know. The house had never been broken into or vandalised. The locals gave it a wide berth. Some kids from Sydney got in there once. One fell over the balcony and broke his leg. Another had his fingers crushed when a door slammed on them. A medium from Sydney stayed there two nights. Although she never identified the spirit, she said it was seeking something. But it was trapped around the house. And until it got what it sought, it would remain in the house and the violence would continue. Clover's parents avoided any publicity and apart from one small story in the local paper, they'd managed to keep everything away from the mainstream media. All up, it was a lovely old house. But it was also a giant pain in the arse — thanks to Edward. Their second coffees arrived and Les turned to Grace.

'Clover said you had something you wanted to show me?' he asked her.

'Yes.' Grace opened her bag and took out a small folder of photos. 'I only got these this morning. But remember when I came round the house and took some photos?'

'Last Friday?' said Les.

'That's right. And I took a couple of you standing in the doorway out on the verandah. Take a look.' Grace slid the photos over.

Les looked at the photos. They were good, happy snaps. He was facing the sun with a smile on his face and he looked fit and relaxed without posing.

'That's definitely me,' said Les. 'Handsome devil that I am.'

'Arguably,' said Grace. 'But have a look at the doorway off the lounge. Up on the right.'

Les peered at the photos. It was a little dark inside the house. Then he saw it, sticking out of the door jamb. A shadowy hand and wrist.

'Bloody hell!' exclaimed Les. 'Look at that. It's a hand.'

'Give me a look.' Warren picked the photos up from the table. 'Shit! It is too.'

'You can bet that's Edward's hand,' said Clover.

'Just letting us know he was around,' said Grace.

'Is it in any of the other photos?' asked Les.

Grace shook her head. 'No. Only those ones.'

Les continued to stare at the photos. 'That's one of the weirdest things I've ever seen.'

'Yes. Kind of spooky, isn't it,' said Grace.

Warren handed the photos back to Grace and turned to Les. 'Brrrhh,' he shuddered. 'I'm glad you're staying there Ugly, and not me.'

'Yeah. Not for much longer,' replied Les. 'I'm booking into a motel. Before Edward starts leaving funnel web spiders round the house or something.'

'I don't blame you.' Warren looked at his watch and turned to Clover. 'Well, Clover dearest,' he said. 'We'd better make a move. We've got a long drive home.'

'Yes,' she agreed. 'And it's going to be a breeze too.'

'Yeah,' nodded Warren. 'Thanks to Casper, the not so friendly, bloody ghost.'

'Hey Warren, how much money have you got on you?' asked Les.

'Money? About three hundred bucks.'

'Can you get any more on your Visa card?'

'Yeah. Another four hundred. Why?'

'You got any money on you, Clover?' asked Les.

'A couple of hundred,' she replied.

'Can you get some more from the ATM?'

'About the same as Warren. Four hundred.'

'Okay,' said Les. 'Can you give it to me? I'll give it straight back to you as soon as I get home.'

'What's with all the money?' asked Warren.

Les winked at Grace. 'I'm feeling pretty good. And I want to back myself this afternoon.'

'That's right,' said Warren. 'You've got to fight that relation of yours from Queensland. I forgot all about it.'

'And you want to ... back yourself?' said Clover.

'Yeah,' answered Les. 'I reckon I'm a chance to beat him.'

Clover shook her head. 'I've heard you're pretty good, Les. But Morgan Scully? Christ! He eats crowbars and shits barbwire.'

'You haven't been into those mushrooms again, have you Les?' asked Warren.

'No. But thanks for all your support,' said Les. 'A hanged man would get the same from a length of rope.'

'Sorry mate,' smiled Warren. 'It's just that I've seen the opposition.'

'So can I get the money?'

'Yeah, come on,' said Clover. 'There's a bank opposite the paper shop.'

They all rose from the table, then walked down to the lights and crossed the road to the ATM. With what Les came up with, they were able to raise two thousand five hundred dollars between them. Clover would call into Dalmeny on the way home and get some travelling money from her mother. Les counted the money in front of everybody, then they walked back to the house.

While Clover helped Warren pack his gear, Les got a whisk broom from the boot of his car, took the horseshoe from Warren's, placed it near the steps and brushed away the broken glass. Grace got a dustpan and broom from the kitchen and helped. Before long Warren's car was tidied up, his bags were in the boot with Clover's and everyone was standing in the driveway.

'Well Les,' said Warren. 'What can I say? Good luck with that big goose this afternoon.'

'Thanks Woz,' replied Les. 'I'll tell you all about it when I get home.'

'See you then, Ugly.'

Les gave Warren a pat on the shoulder, Clover gave Les a goodbye kiss on the cheek and kissed Grace goodbye, promising to keep in touch. Clover got in the car and Warren started backing down the driveway. He tooted the horn and they disappeared towards the highway.

Les turned to Grace. 'So what did you think of the boarder?'

'He's lovely,' she replied. 'They both are.'

'Yeah. They're all right, aren't they.'

Grace smiled at Les. 'So you're moving out of the house?'

'Yeah,' nodded Les. 'I'll book into a motel this afternoon. I'm not scared or anything, I'm absolutely terrified ... What if Edward turns out to be a raving poof?'

'If you're a good boy,' said Grace, pulling gently at Norton's belt buckle. 'I might let you stay in the spare room at Graceland tonight.'

Norton's eyes lit up. 'Fair dinkum?'

'Yes. But only tonight. I'll have to kick you out first thing tomorrow. Ellie gets here in the morning. And I want to spend the day with her.'

'Unreal,' said Les. 'I'll bring something with me.'

'Okay. That would be good.' Grace looked up at Norton for a moment. 'Les. If anything should go wrong this afternoon, ring me, and I'll be straight over.'

Les smiled back at her. 'Nothing should go wrong, Grace. But I'll ring you anyway.'

Grace let go of Les and opened her bag. She found her purse and handed Les a fifty dollar bill.

'What's this?' asked Les.

'That's my last fifty dollars till Ellie's grandmother gets here tomorrow,' replied Grace. 'I want to place a bet on you.'

'You want to back me with your last fifty dollars?'

'Why not? It's my money.'

Les looked at Grace for a moment then pocketed the fifty. 'I'll make sure you get extra good odds.'

'Thanks.' Grace fumbled for her keys. 'I have to go.' She ran her hand across Norton's cheek and kissed him goodbye then got in the Jackaroo. As she backed down the driveway, Grace poked her head out the window. 'Les. Be careful this afternoon.'

Les smiled and gave Grace a wave as he watched her drive off, then picked up the horseshoe and went inside.

Les placed Grace's fifty on his dressing table, shook his head, then put the horseshoe in the pantry and walked out onto the verandah. He watched the ocean for a while then looked at his watch and went back to the bedroom to change. Amongst his T-shirts was a plain white one with a small pocket on the front. Les wore that out over his training shorts, slipped on his thongs, packed his camera and a towel in his bag, then removed the capsules of fake blood from their packets. He placed four in the pocket of his T-shirt and the rest in his shorts, along with the twenty five hundred dollars. After a glass of water in the kitchen and a quick trip to the bathroom, Les put his Bugs Bunny cap and sunglasses on, picked up his bag and walked out the door, closing it softly behind him.

Les took the way to the park along the jetty. As he passed the baths, he noticed the hessian was still up but the tents had all been pulled down. Two men were standing at the side entry and there appeared to be quite a commotion inside. Les walked round the front to find a small queue at the entrance. Above the entrance a plastic sign said: GALA SPORTING EVENT. FIVE DOLLARS DONATION FOR THE LIONS CLUB. LUCKY DOOR PRIZE. Two women in jeans and jackets were standing behind a table taking donations and handing out tickets. Les joined the queue and waited his turn.

'What's the story, ladies?' he asked.

'The Lions Club is having a boxing match,' said one lady with dark hair. 'It's five dollars in and there's a lucky door prize.'

'Yeah. What's the lucky door prize?' asked Les.

'A special meat tray from the Lions Club.'

'Unreal. So who's fighting?'

'A man from Sydney and a local boy. They're both heavyweights. And it's a grudge match.'

'Sounds good,' said Les.

He fished a fifty from his pocket and handed it to the woman with dark hair. She gave him a ticket and counted his change into his hand.

'Thank you,' said the woman. 'And have a nice day.'

'I'm sure I will. Thanks.' Les pocketed his change and walked inside.

Along with the big tents, the food stalls had gone from the end of the park and in their place a large crowd had formed out from the fence. To the right was a small caravan with a table in front of it and standing next to a whiteboard, you couldn't miss Norm's bulk in a Blues Festival T-shirt. As Les approached he noticed Norm's wife and another woman, both wearing Blues Festival T-shirts, seated at the table taking bets and putting the money in a metal strongbox. Les strolled over and caught Norm's eye.

'Les, how are you mate?' he called out. 'Come over here.'

Les said hello to Marina and stepped behind the table. 'How are you, Norm?'

'Good mate. So who are you here with?'

'No one. I just paid my five dollars. Got my lucky door prize ticket, and joined the happy crowd.'

'You paid to get in?'

'Yeah. You're not bad, Norm. I'll want to get my money's worth.'

'Shit! Sorry about that, Les. Anyway, come over here.' Norm took Les behind the whiteboard. 'There's been a change in the rules.'

'Oh?'

'Yeah. It's going to be three five minute rounds with a minute in between. We had to open up the betting.'

'Open up the betting?' said Les.

'Yeah. Morgan's been backed into the red. This way they can bet which round it'll finish. Or if it'll go the distance. If it does go the distance, you get two minute's break. Then you fight to the finish.'

'Does Boofhead know what's going on?'

'Yeah.'

'And what are the odds?'

'Morgan's two to one on. You're fives.'

'Beautiful.' Les took out his money and handed it to Norm. 'There's twenty-five hundred there, Norm. Less the five dollars I had to pay to get in. Put the lot on me at five to one.'

'Righto. And I'll fix up the five bucks.'

'And Norm. No matter what happens. Don't stop the fight, unless I quit or I get knocked out. Okay?'

'Okay,' said Norm. 'And you needn't worry about getting a fair go. None of Morgan's mates'll try to step in. If they do, I got plenty of willing boys here that'll sort 'em out.'

'That's good,' said Les.

'So how are you feeling anyway?' asked Norm. 'Is your back any better? You must be pretty confident putting two and half grand on yourself.'

'Just call it incentive, Norm,' he replied. 'And yes. My back is a little better. But we'll just have to see what happens.'

'Morgan's keen. I know that,' said Norm.

'Where is the prick anyway?' said Les. 'It's past starting time.'

Norm stared over the crowd. 'Here he comes now.'

Les turned around to see Morgan storming through the crowd wearing a black tracksuit and Blundstones. He was with four mates and beneath his old, black, cowboy hat his face looked meaner and uglier than ever. As soon as he saw Les his eyes brimmed over with hatred.

'You're late, you big goose,' said Les, pointing to his watch. 'Where have you been? Pulling yourself in the shithouse?'

Morgan started to hyperventilate. 'I'm fuckin here now,' he rasped.

'I see you're still wearing that silly fuckin hat too,' said Les. 'Or have you been stealing tonneau covers off old utes?'

A cruel smile formed on Morgan's face. 'Oh, I made sure I wore my hat.'

Morgan's mates were looking at Les as if he was a dead man walking. Les noticed a hub-bub going through the crowd with the arrival of Morgan and there was a last minute surge at the betting table.

'Now, you know the rules, Morgan,' said Norm.

'Fuckin rules,' spat Morgan. 'I'd like to get into it right here and now.'

'No. You go over to other side of the ring where that chair is.' Norm pointed across the grass. 'That's your corner. You wait there. Okay?'

Morgan turned around and saw an outdoor chair sitting in front of the crowd. He gave Les one last filthy look then turned to his mates. 'Come on,' he grunted.

'And you take that one there, Les.' Norm pointed to another plastic chair on the opposite side of the ring. 'And seeing as you're on your own, Spike'll be your second.'

Les turned to a solid fair-haired bloke in a pair of shorts and a Blues Festival T-shirt standing behind him. It was the bloke that came up to see Norm about the blocked toilet on Friday night.

'Hello Spike,' said Les.

'G'day Les,' replied Spike. 'How are you?'

'Not bad,' smiled Les.

'Well. I suppose we may as well get into it,' said Norm.

'Yes,' agreed Les. 'Too late to get out of it.'

Les walked over to the his chair, placed his bag under it and sat down. He kicked off his thongs and took his cap and sunglasses off, then gave his arms a stretch and casually slipped a couple of blood capsules out of his shorts into his mouth. The crowd had surged forward and while he was getting his camera out of his bag, Les looked across the ring at Morgan's corner. Morgan had taken his jacket off and over his pants he was wearing a black, Jack Daniels T-shirt with the sleeves hacked off. He still had his Blundstones on and he'd handed his hat to the solid bloke with the moustache.

Les handed his camera to Spike. 'You know how to work one of these, Spike?'

'Yeah easy,' replied Spike. 'Me missus has got one.'

'Okay. Just take a few in the first round. Then take plenty in the second.'

'What about the third?'

'Spike. Something tells me there ain't gonna be a third.'

Marina had closed off the betting and the crowd had now formed an orderly ring. However, it was starting to get restless. Norm, the consummate showman, sensed this and strode into the middle of the ring carrying a bell. Seated in his outdoor chair, Les scanned the punters and was surprised to see a lot of elderly women. Standing behind Morgan were the four fishermen Les had belted in the hotel; all heavily bandaged and either wearing splints or carrying walking sticks. Les smiled across the ring and gave them a little wave. They declined to wave back. Norm rang the bell above his head and the crowd settled down.

'Okay,' boomed Norm. 'Youse all know why youse are here. And what it's all about. To help the local Lions Club. We're havin' a no holds barred, grudge match. Between local boy — Morgan Scully ...' Norm waited as a ripple of applause and several cheers from Morgan's sycophants ran through the crowd '... and a tourist down from Sydney. Les Norton.'

Another ripple of applause ran through the crowd, accompanied by booing and several shouts of 'Poofter. Fairy. G'arn, get back to Sydney — you red-headed poofter.'

'All right, settle down,' boomed Norm. 'Anyway. We wish both contestants well. And don't forget, after the fight we've got the lucky door prize. Thirty T-bone steaks and two scotch fillets. Donated by the Lions Club. Righto. Would the two contestants please come to centre ring.'

Les got up and walked across to Norm. So did Morgan. Standing in his bare feet Les was a good six inches shorter than Morgan and nowhere near as heavy. But he was just as wide across the shoulders. Morgan glared down at Les as Norm spoke.

'Righto boys. You both know the rules.'

'Apart from this goin' three rounds, there ain't no fuckin rules,' said Morgan.

'Them's the rules,' said Norm.

'Do we shake hands first?' asked Les.

'Get fucked,' said Morgan.

'What about a kiss?'

'Ring the fuckin bell, Daddy,' snarled Morgan, 'before I kill this cunt.'

'Righto boys,' said Norm. 'Back to your corners. And come out at the bell.'

Morgan stormed over and stood next to his mates. Les went back to his corner and sat down. Spike gave his shoulders a rub.

'How do you feel, Les?' he asked.

'Good as gold, Spike,' answered Les. 'Who'd you put your money on?'

'No one. Even though I don't like your chances. If I won any money backing that big arsehole, I'd be dirty on myself.'

'Spike,' smiled Les, 'I couldn't ask for a better man in my corner.'

Norm stood in the middle of the ring and pointed to Les and Morgan. 'Are you both ready?' Morgan and Les nodded. 'Okay. Let's get into it.' Norm rang the bell and stood back.

Les got up and moved to centre ring with his fists up. Morgan came charging out of his corner hissing and snarling and throwing monstrous haymakers. Each punch had immense power behind it and would have taken your head off. But they were that telegraphed, Les easily got under most of them and caught the rest on his arms. As Morgan threw another flurry of bombs, Les shuffled to the side and poked out a couple of soft left jabs that caught Morgan in the face and then a short right to his ribs that wouldn't have crushed a SAO biscuit.

Morgan brought his hands down and grinned fiendishly at Les. 'You got fuckin nothing.'

'I know,' said Les. 'But I'm doing my best. Give me a break.'

Morgan threw another flurry of bombs and let go a kick to Norton's stomach that would have crushed his sternum. Les slipped the kick and poked another two feeble lefts into Morgan's face.

'Go on. Smash him, Morgan,' came a voice from the crowd.

'Give it to the cunt, Morgan.'

'Stick it up him, Morgan. The poofter.'

Hello, thought Les, as he shuffled around Morgan. The crowd's getting restless. I think it's time I gave them what they came for. He moved towards Morgan as the big man fired a up a John Wayne special and a huge straight right came barrelling towards Les. Les rode the punch with his forehead, bit on the capsule then spun around and fell to the grass, spitting the crushed capsule out of his mouth in a huge spray of blood.

'Yeah. That's the way, Morgan,' screamed a voice from the crowd. 'Smash him.'

Down on his hands and knees, Les smeared vampire blood across his face as Morgan aimed a huge kick at his head. Les rolled with it and bit down on another capsule, spurting up blood like a fountain.

'Yeah. Kill him Morgan.'

'Atta boy Morgan. Kick his fuckin head in.'

Les spread some blood over his T-shirt, while slipping another two capsules from his pocket at the same time. He palmed them into his mouth then rose shakily to his feet and faced Morgan. Morgan charged in throwing punches like a mad man. Les blocked or ducked most of them, rode a big right with his forehead, then bit on another capsule and fell to the grass coughing up blood. Amazed at how much the capsules contained, Les smeared blood over his face, in his eyes and into his hair. He rubbed some more on his T-shirt, then lurched to his feet and defiantly shaped up to Morgan.

Morgan turned and smiled at the crowd then charged into Les again. Les poked out another two ineffective left jabs as Morgan let go with another huge right, a haymaker. Les rode it, bit the other capsule and teetered back, spraying blood from one end of the ring to the other.

By now Les was covered in blood from head to foot; it was an awful sight. Morgan loved it and his piggy eyes were glowing. He ran in and threw another flurry of punches just as Norm rang the bell to end the first round. Morgan threw another punch after the bell. Les ducked it and staggered across to his corner.

'Shit Les. Are you all right?' said Spike, as Les flopped down in his chair.

'Yeah. He hasn't laid a glove on me,' replied Norton.

'Hasn't laid a glove on you? Have you seen your face?'

'Couple of grass burns, that's all,' said Les, palming another two blood capsules into his mouth.

Norm came over with a worried look on his face. 'Les, I know you told me not to stop the fight. But mate, you're a mess. You could end up getting badly hurt.'

Les spat out a gob of false blood. 'Turn it up. He's as weak as piss. I can take him anytime I want.'

Spike looked up at Norm. 'What do you want to do, Daddy.'

'We'll go another round. But if he takes much more punishment I'll stop it. I'm not going to stand around and watch someone get killed.'

'Hey Spike,' said Les. 'How many photos did you take?'

'About six.'

'Okay. Go for your life during the next round.'

Norm took another worried look at Les, then went back to centre ring and rang the bell for the start of round two. Keen for action, the crowd surged forward.

Les rose wearily from his seat and shuffled towards centre ring. Morgan strode confidently out of his corner and Les shaped up just in time to walk into another one of Morgan's John Wayne specials. Riding it easily, Les bit on another capsule then fell to the ground spurting out more fake blood. He clambered to his feet before Morgan could boot him in the ribs and poked out another couple of ineffective jabs, as Morgan charged in throwing more, huge bombs. Les rode them or caught them on his arms and went down again. Soaked in blood, Norton dragged himself to his feet and stood groggily in front of Morgan like an exhausted bull waiting for the Matador's coup de grace. By now a change had come over the crowd. They all expected Morgan to win, but the fight was turning into a slaughter.

'Stop the fight,' came a voice from the crowd.

'Come on. He's had enough.'

'Yeah, somebody stop it.'

One woman shielded her eyes. 'Oh God! This is making me sick.'

Morgan looked at Les all battered and bloodied, then smiled and turned to his mates. 'Hey Rossy,' he called out. 'Give me my hat.'

The man with the moustache stepped across, and handed Morgan his black Akubra. Morgan put it on then stared into Les's blood filled eyes and tapped the brim.

'You know where this is going smartarse, don't you?' said Morgan.

Morgan stepped up to Les and brought a massive fist back to finish him off, when unexpectedly Les moved into Morgan and slammed his right knee into the big man's groin. Morgan went white and howled with pain. Les kneed him again then stepped back and, like a cobra striking, hammered two murderous left hooks into Morgan's face. Just as quickly, Les went underneath and thumped a left and right rip into Morgan's midsection. Suddenly an audible gasp of disbelief rippled through the crowd. With his fists still at the ready, Les stopped for a brief moment to study Morgan. He looked beaten already. His mouth was shredded and all his front teeth were smashed in; he was out on his feet, trying feebly to hold his throbbing balls and his fractured ribs at the same time. Smiling to himself, Les dropped his right knee, and with all his weight behind it, banged a right uppercut onto the point of Morgan's chin. The punch sent his hat flying and shattered his jaw like a tea cup. Morgan's eyes rolled back, he made a grab at thin air, then his legs went from under him and he pitched forward onto the grass slightly bumping into Les on the way. Les went down with him, then rolled aside at the last second as Norm rang the bell and the crowd started cheering. Ignoring the cheers, Les staggered to his feet wiping fake blood from his eyes and squinted blindly at the faces around him.

'What's going on?' he said. 'I can't see. Who won?'

With real blood pouring from him, Morgan lay crumpled on the grass at Norton's feet, unconscious. Even though a lot of the crowd had lost their money, they kept clapping and cheering at Norton's heroic effort. Morgan's dumbfounded mates came in to pick him up and Les caught the eye of the bloke with the moustache.

'Hey Rossy,' said Les. 'You got a minute?'

Morgan's mate stopped, and walked up to Les. 'What do you want?'

'Nothing really,' answered Les.

Without saying another word, Les hit Rossy in the mouth with a quick, straight right and followed it up with a bone crunching left hook. His mouth a mess and his cheekbone fractured, Rossy started to totter, when Les buried his left foot into his sternum. As he fell forward, Les brought his right knee up and spread Rossy's nose across his face like a handful of mince.

'Actually, that was for Warren,' smiled Les. He left Morgan's mate bleeding on the grass then walked across to his corner.

'Fair dinkum, Les. That's the gutsiest thing I've ever seen in my life,' said Spike. 'And you flattened Rossy too.'

'The last one was personal,' said Les, putting his watch and thongs back on. 'Did you get plenty of photos?'

'Yeah. I almost finished the roll.'

'Good on you.' Les took his camera from Spike and put it in his bag as Norm came over.

'Les,' he said, incredulously. 'You are un-fuckin-believable. I was ready to stop the fight and call an ambulance.'

'I told you I could take that big goose whenever I wanted to,' replied Les.

'Fuck me. Listen. Do you want us to get you a doctor?'

'A doctor?' said Les.

'Yeah. For your face. You're going to need a heap of stitches. You've probably lost some teeth too. I know Morgan has. So's poor fuckin Rossy.'

Les spat out a gob of vampire blood. 'Don't worry about it. I got some band aids back at the house.' He picked up his bag and put his sunglasses on. 'Where's the back way out of here, Norm? I want to piss off.'

'Over this way. I'll show you.' Norm turned to Spike. 'Spike. Keep an eye on the Handbrake and Louise will you. They got all the money.'

'Righto Daddy. Hey, I'll see you later, Les.'

'Yeah, see you Spike. And thanks for everything.'

Les skirted the crowd behind Norm and followed him out past several tents and caravans to the side entrance. The two blokes standing on either side saw Les covered in blood and stepped back horrified.

'Are you sure you don't want to see a doctor, Les?' asked a puzzled Norm.

'I'm positive,' said Les. 'But I will want to see you about my money.'

'Sure,' said Norm. 'I got to sort things out first. Can you come back later?'

Les thought for a second. 'How about I meet you up at the pub on Tuesday night about nine? McBride's. I'll get it then.'

'Okay Les. That'd be good. We'll have a beer.'

'In the meantime, can you give me a hundred bucks, Norm? That was all the money I had earlier.'

'Yeah. No worries.' Norm pulled out two fifties and handed them to Les.

'Thanks mate.' Les pocketed the hundred then whipped off his blood spattered T-shirt and put it in his bag. 'I'll see you tomorrow night.' Norton turned and double-timed it back to the house.

Les let himself in the door and dropped his bag in the hallway then stripped off and got under the shower. Bloody hell, he chuckled, as he watched all the fake blood swirling down the plughole. This is like the shower scene from *Psycho*. He washed all the fake blood out of his hair and everywhere else, then towelled off and checked himself out in the bathroom mirror. There were bruises on his arms and a couple on his forehead, plus a small mouse near his left eye. He'd skinned his knuckles on Morgan's teeth and there were minor grass burns on his elbows and knees. Too easy, smiled Les. Much better than Morgan. Getting belted'd be bad enough. But losing five grand as well. Shit! that would hurt. Les wrapped the towel around him and poured some bourbon over his knuckles in the kitchen sink, then changed into a clean pair of cargos and a dark blue, Cooktown Resort T-shirt. A beer would have gone down well. But Les thought he'd wait and ring Grace first with the news. He put his cap and sunglasses back on and walked down to the hotel.

McBride's was fairly crowded with people having a drink and a post-mortem after the fight. There was no one in the bottle shop and Les didn't expect anyone would recognise him. They'd all be expecting someone who looked like he'd just crawled out of a car wreck. There was a phone just inside the door. Les dropped some coins in and dialled

Grace's number. It was engaged. He tried twice more and gave up. Then he stepped over to a blonde girl in a black uniform behind the counter and bought a bottle of Turkey Flat Butcher's Block Mataro Shiraz and a bottle of Rosevear's Tasmania Riesling. He paid cash, then took the wine back to the house and put both bottles in the fridge. He had a glass of water then walked up to the butcher shop and bought a dozen, beautiful lamb cutlets, bacon and a few brisket bones. There was a phone box just up from the butcher's; Les dropped some coins in and this time Grace answered.

'Hello?'

'Grace. It's Les. How are you?'

There was a pause for moment. 'How am I? How are you?'

'Good as gold,' replied Les.

'What? You're all right?'

'Yeah. Never felt better in my life.'

'But ... I. Julie was at the fight. She said you won. But you took a terrible beating. There was blood everywhere. An ambulance came and everything. God, I was just on my way over.'

Les laughed. 'Are you sure she was at the same fight?'

'Les, don't fool around. Are you all right or not?'

'Yes Grace. I'm all right. Truly.'

'Okay,' answered Grace. 'If you say so.'

'So what time do you want me to call over?'

'Well. You may as well come over at six. And I'll finish what I was doing.'

'Righto.'

'Les, you're such a bastard. I don't know what to believe.'

'Ohh, that's nice isn't it,' said Les. 'You've just won a heap of money. I busted my poor arse to make sure you did. And you call me a bastard. Fair dinkum Grace, are all the women down here your age as horrible as you?'

'Les ...'

'Don't bother saying it Grace. I'll see you at six.' Les blew Grace a quick kiss over the phone and hung up. I wonder what I am going to tell Grace when I see her, he chuckled, as he headed home. The truth I suppose. It would make a nice change.

Back at the house, Les put the meat in the fridge and opened a bottle of beer. He took it out on the verandah, sat down and after a couple of mouthfuls, belched, looked around and shook his head. For a bloke that gets around a bit, he told himself, Christ, you're dumb at times.

That first night in the house: the piano playing in the middle of the night and things all over the kitchen the next morning, and I convince myself it's a rat. And the wiring's rooted in the bear. Everybody I meet, as soon as I mention the Merrigan house, they look at me like I got a face full of boils. Even the two old girls in the op-shop. I thought they were just a couple of old biddies the way they were going on. Then Grace and Clover. No wonder they wouldn't come inside after midnight. Everybody was in on the act bar me. And when I finally see Edward's ghost, I think it's a burglar and tell him to piss off. Les shook his head. I wonder what he's got the shits about though? Probably the bloody cold. Les raised his bottle to the house. Anyway Edward, you can shove the place up your freezing cold arse after tonight. I won't be here.

Les switched his thinking to more pleasant things. Like the fight. I wonder if Norm videoed it? I hope he did, he chuckled. I'll definitely get a copy to show Billy and the rest of them. They'll crack up. Les started thinking about Grace and her magic mineral water and the astonishing effect it had on him. It was liquid gold. He might ask her for a little more to take home with him. Les finished his beer and watched a couple of kids paddling a kayak across the clear, blue water in the lagoon. He had plenty of time before driving out to Grace's. Time for a little snorkelling.

Les was tossing up whether to have another beer first, when there was a brisk knock on the door. Hello, thought Les. I wonder who this is? He'd left the front door open and when he walked down the hallway an uneasy feeling settled in the pit of Norton's stomach. Standing on the steps were two tall men with grainy faces and brown hair, wearing white shirts, ties and dark trousers. One had his hair parted and wore a moustache. The other had a buzz cut. They weren't wearing guns. But Les knew they hadn't knocked on the door to sell him an insurance policy. As he approached, the two men looked at him suspiciously.

'G'day fellahs,' said Les, as pleasantly as he could. 'What can I do for you?'

'Les Norton?' said the one with the moustache.

'Yes. That's me,' replied Les.

'I'm Detective Bischof. And this is Detective Stenlake.'

Les shook his head and resigned himself once more to the inevitable. 'Okay. What have I done?'

'You haven't done anything,' said Detective Bischof.

'I haven't?' said Les.

'Well, you have done something,' said Detective Stenlake.

'Yeah. You did us a favour,' said his partner.

Les was a little puzzled. 'A favour?'

'Giving it to that prick Morgan Scully.'

'Oh.' Les brightened up. 'Well in that case ... Do you want to come inside? There's a cold one in the fridge.'

'No. That's okay,' said Detective Bischof. 'Actually, Daddy sent us round to see if you were okay. He was worried.'

'No, I'm okay,' said Les. 'Couldn't be creamier.' He looked at both detectives. 'So I gather you're not all that rapt in Morgan either.'

'Mate. We've been trying to nail that big lump of shit for years,' said Detective Bischof. 'And to see him get stitched up like that. It was music to our eyes.'

'And his mate Mick Ross,' added Detective Stenlake.

'So we just called in to see you're okay, and to shake your hand,' said Detective Bischof.

'My pleasure,' said Les, shaking both detectives' hands.

'We backed you too,' said Detective Stenlake.

'You did?'

'Yeah. We thought we'd done our dough too,' said Detective Bischof. 'Christ! You were taking an awful battering there at one stage.'

'Then I came good,' said Les.

'You sure bloody did,' agreed Detective Stenlake. He looked at Norton for a moment. 'Les. I have to be honest. A while ago, you looked like you'd been dragged under a train. Now you haven't got a mark on you? What ...?'

Les smiled at the two detectives. 'Let's just say I'm a quick healer.'

The two detectives shook their heads. 'All right. We'll leave it at that,' said Detective Bischof.

'Hey before you go,' said Les. 'What's Scully's caper? If you don't mind me asking?'

'Anything he can get his big, hairy hands into,' said Detective Bischof. 'But mainly cars.'

'Cars?' said Les. 'As in, driving them without the owner's permission?'

'Well put, Les,' smiled Detective Stenlake. 'Scully and his mates drive up to Sydney, or down to Melbourne, nick a couple of cars on the way and flog them at the other end.'

'They know exactly what they're doing,' said Detective Bischof. 'And they know we can't follow them around all the time.'

'Can't you put a bit of pressure on some of his team?' asked Les. 'There must be witnesses or someone dirty on him.'

Detective Stenlake shook his head. 'No one's game to say a word. Everyone's shit scared of him.'

'In the meantime,' smiled Detective Stenlake, 'at least we got something to laugh about when we see him.'

'He'll love that,' said Les.

'So when are you going back to Sydney, Les?' asked Detective Bischof.

'Wednesday,' answered Les. 'Probably early.'

'Well if you get a chance before you leave, call in and have a coffee or something.' Detective Bischof pointed. 'The cop shop's just over there.'

'Okay,' said Les. 'But I'll be down here again. I like Narooma. Next time I'm in town you can shout me a beer.'

'You're on,' said Detective Stenlake.

Les said goodbye to the two detectives and watched them get inside a white Holden Commodore. He gave them a wave as they drove off then went back to his seat on the verandah

Shit! What about that, thought Les. A visit from the wallopers. At least it was a friendly one for a change. Les gazed out over the water and tried to relax. But being a fringe dweller when it came to the law and dealing with the police, an uneasy feeling still lingered in the pit of Norton's stomach. He was about to have another beer and changed his mind. No, he told himself. I'm going snorkel sucking. That's the best way for a dude to chill out. He changed into his old shorts and rubber vest, got his gear together and walked down to the jetty.

The water was just as clear as Saturday and there were even more fish around. Les chased four, fat leather jackets around the piers with his camera and out in the channel he saw another two big stingrays. The blackfish were back munching on the weed and Les joined them for lunch. One came right up to his face mask and he actually pushed it aside with his hand. Les snorkelled around, having fun using up what film was left in the disposable camera, then got out and walked back to the house.

Les had a shave and a shower, rinsed his gear and, figuring it could be a bit brisk sleeping out at Grace's, changed into his dark blue tracksuit which could double as pyjamas. The sun was just starting to go down, but there was still plenty of time, so he got another beer and took it out on the verandah.

It was a beautiful, late afternoon and Les was in a good mood as he sat and enjoyed the view. Getting out of the house for the night and having dinner at Grace's was perfect. She'd probably turn the TV on after, or they might even watch a video. Les hadn't watched TV since he left Sydney and he wasn't missing it all that much. But sitting back after a meal and watching a video, with maybe a little hanky panky thrown in, would be absolutely delightful. He'd even offer to give Grace a back rub if she wanted.

Les was contentedly sipping his beer when he noticed that a yacht had come through The Bar with its sails furled and was motoring slowly up the channel towing a rubber ducky. The water in the channel was like glass and the sun setting behind the surrounding hills gave the surface a golden sheen, making it all a lovely picture as the yacht moved effortlessly through the water. The yacht had turned side-on to the house where the channel curved round in front of the jetty and Les was thinking of taking a photo, when he thought the yacht looked familiar. Instead of getting his camera from inside, Les got his binoculars and checked it out. It was the *Kerouac*. One of the yachts he'd seen going past Montague Island the day before.

'Hello. It's the *Kerouac*,' he smiled. 'Anyone seen Jack? He's probably on the road.'

Les continued to watch the yacht moving up the channel. There were two dark-haired men on deck wearing black tracksuits and trainers. Les could pick out their watches and moustaches, even the expressions on their faces. They weren't talking and appeared serious. But they were fit and looked as if they spent a lot of time in the sun. Les was gazing away when the same woman he'd seen before came up from the galley wearing a dark blue tracksuit; the hood was down and this time she wasn't wearing sunglasses. Les watched her step out onto the deck, stared into the binoculars, and gave a double blink. He fine-tuned the viewers and pressed the stabiliser button. There was no mistaking the haughty features and the swirl of bright, orange hair. It was Serina: the late Edwin's grieving ex-girlfriend. Well I'll be buggered, Les said to himself. You know it's funny, but just for a moment, I thought that was her yesterday. I wonder what she's doing down here? The bloody yacht race of course. She's obviously getting her thrill-seeking rocks off again. Pity she didn't fall overboard on top of that big shark I saw.

Les watched Serina walk over to one of the men near the stern, wrap her arms round his neck and kiss him on the lips. Nice to see her broken heart's starting to mend too, he mused. Les zeroed in on Serina just as she turned towards the house and for a few moments it was like looking right into her cool, green eyes. The yacht motored towards the bridge and Les put the binoculars down. Well, that's enough to turn you off your day, seeing her down here, he frowned. I just hope I don't bump into the moll. Because if she has another go at me now that Edwin's not around, I'll tell her to get well and truly fucked. Les looked at his watch. Anyway. I got better things to do than worry about that hump. He finished his beer and went inside.

Les put the meat, the wine and a few other things in his overnight bag, along with the white T-shirt covered in false blood bundled inside a plastic bag. He picked up the key and had a last look around the house.

'Okay Edward,' said Les. 'The place is all yours. Try not to wreck too much if you can help it.'

Les locked the front door then got in his car and drove off. He was smiling about something as he drove past the turn-off to Mystery Bay, and still thinking as he drove through the deserted streets of Central Tilba. In no time at all he was parked outside Grace's and walking up the front steps. Right on cue, Morticia came skidding around the corner barking and howling like an Andrewsarchus out of the ABC show *Walking with Beasts*.

'All right. Don't shit yourself, Morticia,' said Les. 'It's only me.' The dog settled down a little as it picked up Norton's familiar voice. But it still watched Les carefully as he took something out of his bag. 'There you go, you little shit.'

Les handed Morticia a juicy piece of brisket bone. The dog took it neatly and, with its tail stuck straight up in the air, trotted back round to its kennel. Les was about to knock on the door when Grace opened it wearing a pair of cut down Wranglers that clung to her backside like a coat of paint and a grey T-shirt with two cute little sugar gliders on the front. Her hair was shining and parted to one side and she wasn't wearing makeup. She stared at Les.

'Good evening, young lady,' said Les. 'Is your mother in?'

Grace continued to stare at Les. 'Come in,' she said.

Grace closed the door and Les followed her down to the kitchen. He placed his overnight bag on the kitchen table and smiled at Grace as she turned around.

'All right. What's going on?' said Grace.

'What do you mean?' asked Les.

'You know what I mean.'

'I'm not sure if I do,' said Les. 'But while I'm here Grace, have you got a washing machine?'

'Of course. Out in the laundry.'

'Good.' Les took the white T-shirt out of the plastic bag and threw it to Grace. 'Wash that for me will you.'

'Oh my God!' Grace recoiled, and let the blood spattered T-shirt fall to the floor. 'Take it away. Please.'

Les picked up the T-shirt and held it up in front of Grace. 'It's only vampire blood,' he laughed.

'It's what?'

'I'll tell you in a minute.' Les put the T-shirt back in the plastic bag and took out the two bottles of wine. 'Does that look any better?'

Grace seemed to recuperate. 'Oh yes. Very nice.'

'Good,' said Les. 'But first. Do I get a kiss? I mean. No slipping the tongue in or anything. Just one of those kisses ... women sort of give blokes when they're happy to see them.'

'Who says I'm happy to see you?'

'Yeah, fair enough. But could you pretend? Cause I'm happy to see you.'

Grace put her hands on Norton's hips and gave him the sweetest little kiss on the lips imaginable. Les opened his eyes and smiled.

'See that wasn't hard, was it.'

'Don't bet on it.' Grace let go of Les. 'I'll open the wine.'

'I brought some other goodies too.' Les took the meat from his bag and put it on the kitchen table.

'Goodness,' said Grace. 'You even brought bones for Morticia.'

'Grace. When Les Norton eats, everybody eats.'

Grace opened the Riesling, poured two glasses and handed one to Les. 'Cheers Big Ears,' she said.

'Yeah. Here's looking up your old address.'

The wine was very good: dry, delicate, with a tiny taste of citrus.

'Not too bad,' said Les.

'It's lovely.' Grace took another sip of wine and gave Les a once up and down. 'Okay George. I give up. Julie said you were an absolute mess. But apart from a little bruise near your eye, you haven't got a mark on you. And did you punch up a guy called Mick Ross too?'

Les nodded. 'Yeah. That'd be Rossy. The bloke that hit Warren.'

'God. He's almost as bad as Morgan Scully.'

'He sure wasn't looking too good, last time I saw him.'

'So what did happen? Unless that mineral water of mine's got some other, unknown, healing properties.'

Les had a mouthful of wine and grinned. 'It was fake blood.'

Les told Grace about buying the vampire capsules and putting them in his pocket then gave her a blow by blow description of the fight. He even told her about the police calling around. He didn't tell her about seeing Serina on the yacht. But when he'd finished, the bottle of wine was almost gone and Grace was holding her sides.

'Les Norton. You are an absolute bastard,' she said.

'Yes. I do have my moments of absolute bastardry,' agreed Les.

'And you went easy with him. Bloody Morgan Scully.' Grace shook her head. 'I can't believe that.'

'I was just feeling that good,' said Les. 'But for all his size and everything, he's slower than the Russian national anthem.'

'Then you knocked out Mick Ross too. God! You're not bad.'

'Yeah. Well I king hit him,' admitted Les.

Grace wrapped her arms around Les and kissed him again: a little longer this time. 'Come on tiger. Get your bag and I'll show you your room.'

The spare room was on the right past the bathroom. There was a single bed with a blue duvet and matching sheets and a window faced out onto the valley. Near the bed was a small dressing table, a few photos of old Central Tilba hung on the walls, and stacked against the walls on the yellow carpet were boxes of plain T-shirts.

'You'll be as snug as a little bug in a rug in here,' said Grace.

'Unreal,' said Les, dropping his bag on the bed. 'And I don't have to worry about bloody Edward. Thanks Grace.'

'You're welcome handsome. Now let's work out what to do with those lamb cutlets. They look good enough to eat.'

Grace basted the cutlets with chilli and coconut sauce and put them under the griller, then made some mashed kumera and a rocket salad with balsamic, honey dressing and shaved almonds. While everything was cooking, they talked about this and that and had a few cool ones. Les let Grace drink most of the red wine while he had a couple of cans of VB she had in the fridge. The meal was sensational and while they were eating Les told Grace he'd pick up her winnings at the hotel on Tuesday night.

'When are you going back to Sydney?' she asked.

'Wednesday,' replied Les. 'I'd like to stay a bit longer. But after all the drama, it might be best if I got going. I'll drop your money in first though.'

'That's all right,' said Grace. 'What time do you think you'll be leaving?'

'Around lunch time.'

'I'd like you to meet Ellie before you go.'

Les glanced across at the photo on the fridge. 'I'd like to meet her too. She looks like a real little sweetheart.'

'She is. Especially when she gets her own way.'

It didn't take long to wash and dry the dishes and put the leftovers in the fridge with glad-wrap. Grace was impressed at how domesticated Les was. Les said it came from living with Warren and they didn't make a bad casserole either when it came to a pinch.

'What do you feel like doing now?' asked Grace.

'I don't care Grace,' replied Les. 'You're the boss.'

'Would you like to watch a video?'

'Yeah righto,' said Les. 'What is it?'

'*Blow* with Johnny Depp. Julie loaned it to me.'

'Unreal. I missed it when it was on at the movies.'

'I want to see it again,' said Grace. 'Everybody should see it. If this movie wouldn't turn you off getting into cocaine, nothing would.'

'Yes,' agreed Les. 'You're guaranteed to finish up one of three ways getting into coke. Dead, broke or in gaol.'

'Right on.' Grace raised the last of her wine. 'Shall we have a joint first?'

'The "erb",' smiled Les. 'Why not "oman"?'

Grace already had a hot one rolled which they smoked in the kitchen before they went inside. It wasn't bad pot either; almost as good as Warren's. Les mellowed out on the lounge while Grace got the video together, then she sat down next to him.

'I've fast forwarded all the other stuff,' said Grace. 'So the movie will come straight on.'

'All right.'

Grace had a nice TV and it was tuned in through a good stereo. Les was laid back on the lounge feeling no pain when the movie came on. There was absolute silence for a few moments. Next thing, the Keith Richard riff from 'Can't You Hear Me Knocking', whacked out of the speakers and Les nearly fell off the lounge.

'Holy shit!' he yelled.

'Isn't that unreal?' laughed Grace.

'Christ!' said Les. 'I thought my bloody head was going to come off.' The movie began and Les started to laugh. 'I know why you wanted me to watch this,' he said. 'The bloke's called George.'

'Shh! Watch the movie,' said Grace.

By the time George and Tuna moved to California and started selling pot, Grace and Les were snuggling up to each other. When George's horrible mother shelved him to the wallopers, Les was massaging Grace's scalp and neck. Just after George met Pablo Escobar, Grace was sitting on a cushion in front of Les, and Les was rubbing her shoulders, sinking his thumbs into her rotator-cuffs while she was crooning. When George got shelved by his mates and copped thirty years for trafficking cocaine, Grace had her T-shirt off and Les was rubbing her back with hemp oil. By the time the video ended, they were both looking forward to bed.

'Would you like to tuck me in now, Aunty Grace?' asked Les. 'George has had a big day and he's tired.'

'All right snookums,' said Grace. 'Would you like your teddy bear too?'

'No. That's all right,' smiled Les. 'Just ted will do.'

Les followed Grace to the spare room where they got down to the naughty, naked nude, and climbed under the duvet. Les figured they'd had ample foreplay on the lounge. But he still wanted to give Grace's lovely ted a bit of a detail. He kissed her for a while, then ran his tongue down her neck, around her nipples, over her stomach and in between her legs; and then went for it. Grace kicked and squealed and got her rocks off before Les finally surfaced. Grace took hold of Mr Wobbly to give him a quick polish. But reluctantly, Les had to drag Grace away. If Grace's sweet lips had gone within cooee of Mr Wobbly it would have been a disaster. Instead, Les spread Grace's legs and slipped the angry little fellow into his favourite hiding place. On the rubber ball it was good. But in a nice firm bed with his back healed, Les was able to put the big ones in. Grace sighed and moaned. Les kissed her neck and lips while he worked steadily away. It was the sweetest lovemaking and Les wished he could go all night. But eventually it just got too good. Les arched his back, lifted Grace's legs and with Grace yelling encouragement, poured himself into her.

After a while Norton's chest stopped heaving and the stars spinning in front of his eyes faded away. He had his arm around Grace: Grace was snuggled up to his chest with her eyes closed.

Les half-opened one eye and looked at Grace. 'Shit! How good was that.'

Grace nodded. 'There's definitely nothing wrong with your back now. That's for sure.'

'I'm just going to close my eyes for a minute,' said Les.

'Okay,' said Grace.

Norton's snoring woke him up and it was pitch black. He groped around the bed to find Grace had gone and he was on his own. Isn't that lovely, he thought. I bring her two bottles of wine, lamb cutlets and back a winner for her. And she leaves me to sleep in the wet spot. Thank Christ I didn't waste my money on flowers. Les quietly used the bathroom, put his tracksuit on and climbed back into bed. It was lovely and warm under the duvet. Les pulled it up under his chin, smiled into the darkness and in no time the big Queenslander was snoring like a baby.

Les woke up the next morning to the smell of bacon cooking and Fleetwood Mac singing 'You Make Lovin' Fun', coming from the kitchen. He went to the bathroom, freshened up and walked into the kitchen. Grace was at the stove with her back to him. She'd just had a shower and put on a light blue tracksuit. Les sneaked up behind her and tickled her under the ribs. Grace tensed for a second and turned around.

'Hello George,' she smiled. 'How are you this morning?'

'Terrific.' Les slipped his arms around Grace and gave her a peck on the forehead. 'How's yourself. You look very sparkle-arkley.'

'I'm good. I was just about to call you. Did you sleep all right?'

'Yeah. Like a baby. That little bed was unreal.'

'Would you like a glass of ruby red grapefruit juice? I just squeezed some.'

'Reckon,' said Les. 'I love the stuff.'

From the fridge Grace got a pitcher of juice she'd sweetened with a little honey and poured two glasses. Les commented on how nice it was then sat down at the kitchen table and stretched.

'Ahh yes. Nothing like a nice leisurely breakfast,' he winked.

'Be as leisurely as you like, Les,' said Grace, turning off the griller. 'Just as long as you've got all this food shoved down your throat and your arse out the door in half an hour.'

'That's what I like about you, Grace,' smiled Les, taking another sip of juice. 'You're so romantic.'

Grace served Les a huge plate of scrambled eggs and bacon, along with fresh brewed coffee and toast, then joined him. The food was delicious and Les got into it, knowing Grace wanted to have everything out of the way by the time her daughter arrived. They had time to joke about last night and discuss the movie, before Les finally wiped his plate with a piece of toast, washed it down with a second cup of coffee and burped quietly into his hand.

'Grace, that was sensational,' he said. 'Thanks a lot.'

'That's quite all right,' replied Grace. 'I'm glad you enjoyed it.'

'I'm full. I know that.' Les rose from the table. 'Do you want a hand or anything?'

'No. That's all right.'

'Okay. I'll grab my bag and get going.'

By the time Les got his bag from the bedroom, Grace already had the dishes stacked in the sink and was running the hot water. She stopped what she was doing, smiled at Les and walked him to the door. Morticia was sprawled stomach down on the verandah. She looked up at Les, rolled her eyes back and gave her tail the slightest suggestion of a wag.

'I hate kicking you out like this, Les,' said Grace. 'But ...'

'Hey. No problems,' said Les. 'I understand. I'm just rapt you let me stay here for the night.' He put his arms around Grace and they had a quick kiss. 'I'll ring you. And I'll call in tomorrow with your winnings.'

Grace let go of Norton's hand. 'Okay. We might have lunch before you go back. The three of us.'

'Righto. See you then.' Les started off down the steps. 'See you, Morticia. You little shit.' The dog wagged its tail a fraction more and Les walked across to his car. He started the engine and bipped the horn as Grace waved him off. A few minutes later Les was driving through the quiet streets of Central Tilba towards the highway.

It was a beautiful spring day: warm and sunny, with a light breeze stirring the leaves in the surrounding trees and a scattering of fluffy, grey clouds moving across the sky. Les was patting his stomach and feeling good as he turned left onto the highway back towards Narooma. What a top day, he smiled. And how good was that breakfast? Christ! She gave me enough. Les put his foot down and overtook an old, blue Kombi wagon blowing smoke. So what have I got to do today, he thought, easing back on the accelerator. Oh yeah. Move into a motel. That's going to be a nice drag just for one night. And what about all that food we got left? Bugger Edward and his tantrums. Les cruised along thinking he might book into the motel he told Grace he was staying at when he first met her. He was smiling at the irony of this when he came to the Mystery Bay turn-off. Ohh yeah, thought Les. I'm not in any hurry. Why don't I check it out? Les hung a right and followed the road down past several small farms. The paddocks soon became trees and Les was driving into Mystery Bay before he knew it.

On the left, a narrow dirt road led into a small, deserted camping area, with a wooden pole placed across the entrance, near a council sign that read: CAMPING AREA CLOSED TILL FURTHER NOTICE. KEEP OUT. Les followed the bitumen up past a cluster of houses on the right to a low headland and a sign saying CAPE DROMEDARY NATIONAL PARK, did a U-turn then drove back into an empty parking area where another sign said MYSTERY BAY. He pulled up facing the ocean and had a look around.

Two beaches, split by a spit of sand and rock, formed a wide, sheltered bay edged with trees. Stony outcrops pushed away from the sand and all through the bay clumps of rock stuck out of the water to form small islands. The bay finished on the right, at the flat headland next to the national park, and on the left, finished down at a long ridge of jagged rock running out from the sand near an old, concrete boat ramp with a crack in the centre. The ridge of jagged rock formed a safe inlet between it and the low cliffs further around from the camping area, where a large cave at the water's edge opened up towards the bay. The tide was out and the water in the bay was crystal clear over the sand and the reefs running into deeper water; in the distance was Montague Island.

So this is Mystery Bay, mused Les. The place where Edward and his mates ate the pie. Les shook his head. Stuffed if I know how, he thought. It looks as safe as a bank out there. Les stared at the sun sparkling on the clear, blue water. One thing I do know — I feel terrific and this is a snorkel sucker's paradise. I'm going straight home to get my gear. Les reversed the car around and headed for Narooma.

Now that the long weekend was over and the Blues Festival had ended, Narooma was back to its sleepy, peaceful self. Les stopped to get the paper and some milk, before pulling up in the driveway at Browning Street. He got his bag, opened the front door and walked into the kitchen.

'Oh shit!'

Edward had been during the night and things were lying everywhere. Cutlery, plates, pots, pans, even the tea towels and pot scourers were scattered around the floor. However, there was no food. Trepidatiously, Les opened the fridge and the cupboards, but couldn't see any loaded rat-traps or knives poking out. Les put the milk away and looked in the pantry. The rat-traps were there. But the horseshoe was missing. Les walked down to the lounge room. His cassettes were scattered across the carpet and the bear was facing the wall. The horseshoe was jammed under the bedroom door.

'Ha-ha-hah! Fooled you, Edward. You fuckin goose,' said Les. 'Warren's gone home.'

Les pulled the horseshoe out from under the door, dropped it on the lounge and walked into his bedroom. All his clothes were tossed around the floor, along with the pillows and blankets and his new CDs. Les looked at the mess and shook his fist.

'Not happy — Edward.'

It was the same in the bathroom. His shaving kit was spread across the floor along with his towel and the roll of toilet paper. Les left it and went back back to the kitchen. Shit! Where do I start? Bugger it. I'll sort my tapes out first. Les walked down to the loungeroom and started replacing his cassettes into their numbered containers.

'Edward,' he muttered. 'You're a pain in the fuckin arse. You know that? And your girlfriend wears army boots.'

Les put the last cassette away and looked out the door at the sun shining on the lagoon. Ohh stuff this, he thought. It's too good a day. I'll clean the rest up later. Wasting no time, Les put his Speedos on under his shorts, got his gear and shoved it in his bag then locked the house and climbed into his car. Seconds later he reversed out into Browning Street and headed for the highway to Mystery Bay.

There was nobody around and this time Les chose the car park closer to the camping area. He got his bag, locked the car and started walking along the beach towards the old boat ramp. Half way up the beach was a big, grey log. Les thought he might leave his gear there. He walked up, dropped his bag on the sand then sat down on the log and figured out his game plan. It wasn't hard. Just snorkel around all those little islands, and maybe swim round the ridge sticking out from the beach, into the inlet where the cave was. I can't see any sharks hanging around here, he hoped. And if I do spot one, I can jump straight out onto one of those little islands. Les was about to gear up when he felt several drops of cold sweat form on his brow. Next thing, a tingle like an ice cube getting dropped down his back ran along his spine, the sunlight got brighter and the clouds started whizzing across the sky like they were being driven along by a cyclone.

'Hello,' said Les. 'I think this is that flashback Grace was talking about. Shit!'

Oh well. Nothing much I can do about it, he thought. Les sat down with his back against the log and made himself comfortable. Just kick back and take the merry-go-round, through Toon Town again. I wonder how long it'll go for?

This time, however, it wasn't like before. Instead of plasticine shapes and Toonies, everything started to spiral crazily, as if Mystery Bay was getting sucked into a vortex of raging colours, somewhere above the horizon. Next thing, there was flash of blinding white light, like a nuclear explosion, forcing Les to close his eyes and turn away from the speeding vortex. But even with his eyes shut the light was still blinding. After a while the light faded. Les blinked his eyes open and looked around.

The houses on the hill were gone, the roads were gone, the car parks had disappeared; so had the camping area and the old, concrete boat ramp, along with the log he'd been resting against. Now it was all trees. Huge trees towering up to the sky with trunks as wide as houses. Cedar, ash, red gum, blue gum, ghost gum, ironbark. Around the bottom of the trees, crystal clear streams trickled around moss-covered logs, shaded by huge, spreading ferns. Les was sitting on a beach at the edge of an ancient rainforest. From out of the rainforest, flocks of parrots and other birds screeched and dived through the air. Sulphur-crested cockatoos, rosellas, rainbow lorikeets, king parrots, turquoise parrots, corellas, bulbuls, kingfishers, kookaburras, magpies, orioles … All in countless numbers. Bush turkeys and lyrebirds moved around the streams, the sky above the ocean was alive with sea birds. A mob of red and grey kangaroos came bounding along the beach, straight through a mob of wallabies being chased into the rainforest by a pack of dingoes. All the little islands in the bay were coated in white and crammed with barking seals: big, fat brown ones, some with pups. Others were swimming between the islands or lying on the sand. A school of playful dolphins swam into the bay, had a quick look around then swam straight out again. The tide was high and the water in the bay was teeming with schools of fish, while the bottom was covered in black stingrays foraging through the sand. Montague Island was green in the distance and the ocean between the island and the mainland swarmed with whales, breeching and blowing water as they swam past.

Shit! What the fuck's going on, wondered Les? A movement behind him made Les turn around. Two wiry aboriginal men dressed in loincloths and carrying spears and small wooden shields appeared at the edge of the rainforest. Both had beards and tribal markings across their chests, and their hair was pushed back and bound tightly on top of their heads. Each man's teeth were sparkling white and their skin was as black and shiny as onyx. One pushed his spear in the ground and rested his right foot against his left knee, while the other pointed to something on the beach. He said something to the other man in their tribal dialect, then they turned around and disappeared back into the rainforest.

Les watched the two men leave and noticed movement in the branches of some nearby gum trees. They were crawling with koala bears. He turned back to the beautiful, blue ocean and the pristine landscape. Behind the ridge at the end of the beach was the cave. Now I know what's going on, Les told himself. Somehow those mushrooms have sent me back in time.

Everything was crystal clear and razor sharp, and Les gazed around in wonder, taking in the unique setting of beauty and tranquillity. It was nature at is gentlest and loveliest and Les hoped he was going to be there for hours. Suddenly, a sinister movement in the water over to his right made him sit up. From out of nowhere, six massive killer whales came charging into the bay. They were as big as locomotives and with their fearsome teeth and sleek, black bodies reflecting the sun, they made an awesome display of beauty and power as they slashed ominously through the water. And the pod knew exactly what it was doing. To cut off any escape, two whales swam towards the ridge jutting out from the sand, two moved behind the islands while the last two charged straight into the terrified seals. The herd immediately went into a barking, yelping panic. Some seals managed to clamber up onto the islands, others made it to the beach with their pups. Those that didn't, got ripped to pieces or were simply gulped straight down as the killer whales went into a feeding frenzy, turning the water into a churning, red boil of blood, guts and lumps of seal meat.

The killer whales gorged themselves on any seals they could find, except for one. It was too big and fat to clamber up onto the rocks and its escape to the beach was blocked by the killer whales. All it could do was bark and flounder around in the gore. The pod watched the terrified seal, before the biggest one swam up alongside it, and with one mighty flick of its tail, sent the seal spinning up in the air like a football. It tumbled around, end over end then splashed down in front of the other killer whales. The seal bobbed to the surface and another killer whale swam over, flicked its tail and belted the seal back across to the first killer whale. The seal splashed down again and the first killer whale flicked it back to the others. Singing to each other, the killer whales spread out, formed a circle, and started belting the hapless seal back and forth between them in a macabre game of shuttlecock. This was a side of nature Les had seen on TV, but forgotten about. Nature at its most savage. Les watched the callous display in fascinated horror when another movement made him spin around to the left.

Coming from the cliffs behind the inlet, a boat suddenly appeared on the scene. It was a wide-beamed, wooden clinker, with two men rowing in the middle, another seated in the bow with his back turned taking notes, and another man standing at the tiller. The three men in the front were all wearing plain calico shirts and pants, and straw hats with turned up brims and black bows dangling at the back. The man at the tiller had a beard and funny little glasses, and was wearing the same kind of straw hat over a grey frock coat with matching trousers. The two men in the middle kept rowing unawares towards the killer whales, while the man in the bow concentrated on his notes. The man at the stern noticed all the blood in the water, then saw the killer whales and started yelling and pointing. The man in front stood up and turned around and the two men in the middle stopped rowing. The boat's momentum, however, took it into the pod just as the biggest killer whale gave a powerful kick of its tail and sent the seal sailing high into the air. The huge, fat seal spun lazily above the water, then came down right in the middle of the boat like a bomb landing.

The wooden boat rocked crazily as the seal smashed straight through the bottom staves, sending the man in front head first over the bow and the two men rowing straight into the blood-stained water, along with their oars. The man with the beard gripped the tiller, but was somersaulted backwards over the stern. Wondering where their plaything had gone, the killer whales looked up and saw the men struggling in the water around their crippled boat. Les had read about killer whales in Eden helping whalers herd whales, even saving the men from drowning at times. However, this pod must have been the bad boys on the block. They simply looked at the four men in the water as fresh food items and charged straight in.

The first to get eaten were the men in calico. They hardly had time to scream before they were either torn to bits or swallowed whole. For his size, the man on the tiller could swim a little and was stroking furiously across the inlet towards the cave. He was going all right when the biggest killer whale loomed up behind him and took him all in one bite. All except for his left hand which was left floating on the surface. The killer whale turned around, still swallowing the man with the beard, and with a lazy flick of its tail inadvertently sent the hand sailing across the inlet towards the cave. There was a ring on one of the fingers and Les watched it glinting in the sun as the hand turned lazily through the air before landing in the right side of the cave. A few seconds later, the battered and bloodied seal floated to the surface behind the boat. Another killer whale saw it and charged in giving the seal a flick with its tail to get the game going again. The killer whale's aim was a bit out and this time the seal crashed into the cliff face above the cave, dislodging several rocks and some of the ceiling, before it tumbled lifeless onto the rocks at the entrance. The biggest killer whale, the leader of the pod, was tired of playing; it swam over and threw itself onto the dead seal, dragging it back into the water in its huge jaws, where it gobbled it down like a cat swallowing a goldfish. The leader then swam back to the others, clicked and sang something while leisurely blowing clouds of vapour into the air;

the rest then all followed the biggest killer whale towards Montague Island to see who they could terrorise out there. Behind them, the mother seals that had survived the slaughter were barking across the bay trying to find their pups, while the sea birds and school fish swarmed at any scraps in the blood-stained water. The clinker, its staves smashed outwards and the men's belongings still inside, was left drifting near the islands with its gunwales poking out above the water.

Les watched the empty boat moving slowly with the current, when the rushing vortex appeared out of nowhere and started spiralling above the horizon again, and everything around him began to evaporate. The rainforest and all the wildlife disappeared, to be replaced by materialising roads, car parks and houses. The whales out to sea vanished as the camping area reappeared behind him, along with the boat ramp and the old log on the beach. Before Les knew it, everything was back the way it was. He blinked at the sunlight as a family in a station wagon pulled into the parking area, then he wriggled across the sand and sat with his back against the log again.

Although it had all been no more than a shocking, psychedelic illusion in his mind, Norton's sense of shock was tinged with sadness. It was awful to see the seals and the men getting torn apart so brutally. But it was sad to think what had happened to the rainforest and all the wonderful wildlife. For just a short time, Les felt he'd caught a glimpse of paradise. Well I'll be buggered, thought Les. I didn't think the flashback would be like that. Shit that was real — too real, if you ask me. Several thoughts flashed through Norton's mind and his face turned quite serious. Something strange is going on here, he told himself. I'm picking up this weird vibe. Fuck it. There's something I have to do.

Les got up and walked down near the old boat ramp. It was a fair swim around the ledge to the inlet. But the tide was out, and an exposed shelf of rock on the other side of the ridge jutting out from the beach ran beneath the cliffs and finished above the water not far from the cave. Les went back to the log and changed into a pair of old shorts and a T-shirt. He slipped on his rubber booties, and with a small clasp knife in his pocket set off along the beach.

The shelf running round to the cave turned out to be jagged folds of slippery rock, poking up between pools of tangled seaweed and it was difficult to get a foothold. Somehow Les managed to clamber unsteadily over the rocks without twisting his ankle, to where the ledge ended. There he found another smaller cave, filled with smooth boulders and pebbles washed around by the waves, and on this side of the big one.

Between the two, they formed a lovely, blue grotto and a boat would have fitted in there easily, especially at high tide. Pity the boat crew couldn't have rowed in here and got in the cave, he mused. They would have been as safe as a bank. Les jumped off the rock shelf into waist deep water and waded across to the big cave, then scrambled up onto a ledge at the mouth and stepped inside.

The cave was big and gloomy with a small entrance at the other end and Les could make out the coloured, volcanic strata around the walls and ceiling; it looked like marble cake. The floor was rough under his feet and strewn with jagged rocks, and on the left side of the cave a wide rock ledge covered in pebbles and stones stuck out from the wall. Les stepped over to the right side of the cave and smiled. Apparently there'd been a big sea recently and most of the pebbles and stones had been washed away, leaving a trench running along the bottom of the wall. How lucky's that, thought Les. Even if it does turn out I'm wasting my time, I don't have to dig that far to waste it. Les got down on his knees and started scooping away the pebbles from the bottom of the trench.

It wasn't easy going with his bare hands and the pebbles kept rolling back into the trench. What Les really needed was a garden spade. But at least the stones were smooth and he didn't get any nicks or cuts. Les got down into the trench and kept digging away to the gentle sound of pebbles clicking against each other and waves lapping against the rocks outside. He scooped and dug until his legs got cramps, finding nothing but more and more pebbles. Les stopped to wipe a little sweat from his brow. So much for my psychedelic archeological dig, he smiled to himself. I should have known it'd be a waste of time. Oh well. Doesn't matter.

The tide was turning, and a wave hit the rocks out front with a noisy slap that echoed round the cave. Les was thinking of throwing in the towel when his fingers touched something under the pebbles. It felt like small pieces of driftwood. Carefully Les scooped away the pebbles and his eyes lit up. It was the skeleton of a hand, the bones discoloured with age. Not a big hand. But definitely a hand and still very much intact. Les picked it up and got out of the trench.

'Holy shit! I don't believe it.'

Les looked at the bony hand, feeling like he'd just won Lotto. I got to put it down somewhere and have a good look. He looked around the cave, thought maybe over on that ledge near the wall . . . Bubbling inside, Les started pulling his T-shirt off and walked over to the ledge. He laid his T-shirt across the rocks on top and placed the hand on it, then stared at the hand in amazement. Still sitting on the third finger was a ring. Well raise my rent, thought Les. I knew I picked up some weird vibe after that flashback. Wait till I tell Grace.

Les went to rest his foot on the ledge and it slipped off. He put his foot back and it slipped off again. Norton's brow creased. The sole of his booty was wet. But for solid rock, the ledge was awfully soft. Les left the hand and brushed away some rocks and pebbles. It wasn't a ledge. Underneath all the stones was a black tarpaulin that had been been daubed with brown, white, ochre and yellow to match the walls of the cave.

The tarpaulin was covering a mound roughly six metres by three and waist high. Les stepped over to the right side of the mound, kicked away the rocks and pebbles at the bottom then squatted down and lifted up the edge of the tarpaulin. Underneath were rows of neatly piled green sacks. Les took out his clasp knife and cut one open. Inside the sack were ten, clear, thick, plastic bags full of white powder. Les didn't know that much about powder drugs. But it was too white to be heroin and too fine to be speed. He let the tarpaulin down, stood up and shook his head in astonishment.

'Fuckin cocaine. I don't believe it.'

Les looked along the tarpaulin. How many sacks there were was hard to estimate. But each plastic bag would have been a kilogram, and at ten bags to a sack there would have to be at least a thousand bags under the tarpaulin. Probably two. Another chill ran up Norton's spine; and it wasn't from the mushies. For that amount of coke and the money involved, if the people behind the shipment found out you knew about it, they'd murder you as quick as look at you. Les replaced the rocks he'd kicked away, carefully wrapped the hand in his T-shirt, then walked across to the front of the cave and stepped back into the water. Holding the hand above his head, he waded over to the shelf, and with the help of an incoming swell hoisted himself up and made his way back along the rocks to the beach.

As calmly as he could, Les ambled back to the log, collected his gear and walked across to his car. He took his wet shorts off and with a few butterflies kicking around in his stomach, placed his things inside and started the engine. As he reversed slowly around and started to drive off, Les had a good look over the camping area and up the dirt road into the trees, then proceeded steadily along the road leading to the highway.

Minutes later he was speeding back to Narooma. Les didn't notice any cars following him so he slowed down. Before long he'd reached town safely and was pulling up in the driveway of the house. He picked up the

T-shirt, got his bag from the back seat and went inside, closing the door behind him. He placed the hand on his dressing table, then got a beer from the fridge: half went down in one huge gulp. Les took the rest out onto the verandah and sat down.

Well that was certainly a day with a difference, he told himself. Thanks to Clover's mushrooms, it looks like I've solved the mystery of Mystery Bay. But what about all that fuckin cocaine. Shit! Where did that come from? Thank Christ no one saw me, or I doubt if I'd be sitting here now. Les took a grateful sip of beer and winked up at the sky. Anyway, forget about the okey. They can shove it up their arse for all I care. Finding that hand's all I'm interested in. That was absolutely unbelievable. Extremely pleased with himself, Les finished his beer and had a quick shower.

After changing into a clean T-shirt and his blue cargos, Les placed the T-shirt with the hand on the bed and carefully unwrapped it. He looked at the hand from all angles before slipping the ring from the third finger. The ring was covered in grime after lying in the cave for all those years. But Les could see it was gold with jewels inlaid around the band and an inscription inside. Les took the ring into the bathroom, ran some hot water and washed it with soap. He dried it off then brushed it several times with toothpaste. After a while the ring came up almost like new. Les dried it off, got another bottle of beer and took the ring out to where he'd been sitting on the verandah.

It was stamped twenty four carat gold and inlaid with six tiny hearts made from black opal. The inscription inside read: *To Gwendolyn. All my love. Now and Forever. Edward.* As well as hardly being able to believe what he'd found, Les was also moved. Shit! That's really lovely, he smiled. And it's such a beautiful ring. Thoughtfully sipping his beer, Les turned the ring over in his fingers letting it catch the sun. You know, I've been bagging poor Edward, because, according to that photo, his fiance was a dog. But they say love is blind. And Edward must have really loved her. Les raised his beer to the house and took a sip. Good on him. Bad luck they never got to walk down the aisle together. Les slipped the ring onto the top of his little finger and shook his head in admiration as he watched the fire in the opals. An antique like this, he mused — solid gold and inlaid with black opal — it'd be worth a motza too. Smiling happily, Les finished his beer, then took the ring inside and placed it back on the finger he'd got it off. He wrapped the hand up in a white T-shirt that had been lying on the floor and put it back on the dressing table. Les left the mess in his room and walked out to the mess in the kitchen. Now all I have to do is clean up Edward's shit after him. Les couldn't help himself and called out to his bedroom.

'Hey Edward! Any chance of a hand?'

Les started with the cutlery. While he was putting it away, he decided against moving into a motel. It was too much trouble just for one night and he'd stay in the house. As for Edward? He'd just have to sort it out when he arrived. Les mulled over a couple of other things. But before long he started thinking about the huge pile of cocaine.

It had more than likely been brought in on a yacht, then transferred to the cave in a rubber ducky, he surmised. And whoever the team were they were pretty bloody smart and knew the area. That cave was ideal. Easy to get into by boat. But quite difficult otherwise. And if anybody did put their head in the cave, it was that dark, and the dope that well concealed, you wouldn't know it was there. It probably wouldn't be there long anyway. Les dropped some more spoons into a drawer. It's funny, he laughed to himself. But the team did me a favour. If they hadn't dug up all those rocks and pebbles to cover the tarpaulin, I probably wouldn't have found the hand. So I got that to thank them for. Les dropped the last fork into the drawer. And I thought the trench was caused by a big sea. Hey. Why wouldn't I? Les stared at the floor for a moment and started on the cups and saucers. Their timing was spot on too. The Blues Festival in town. The yacht race. You can bet they used those for cover. The camping area closed. He'd had a good look around as he was leaving. You could get a truck in there and lower a rope with a pulley over the cave easy. You'd have all the toot out and loaded up in no time. Not a soul around and the nearest house up the hill on the other side of the beach. Yes, conceded Les. Whoever they are, they're smart bastards all right. They covered their arse from just about every angle imaginable. If coke dealers weren't my particular cup of tea, and they would have shot me if they saw me, I'd almost say good luck to them. Almost. Les put the last plate in the top of the cabinet and caught his reflection in the small glass door. Suddenly the Wile E. Coyote light bulb above his head blinked on.

'Ooohh! What's that you say, Shintaro?' exclaimed Les.

Smart bastards on a yacht? With a rubber ducky? That know the area? Les's eyes narrowed. Did I see someone answering that description only just the other day? I sure did. Fuckin Serina. Orange hair and all. Les shut the cabinet door and sat down at the kitchen table.

Bloody Serina, thought Les. She'd got nicked over a shipment of coke in WA. She comes from Narooma. She'd know about that cave and everything else. She walked last time. Why not have another go? What's to stop her from driving down here, picking up that yacht in Bermagui, then helping to unload the coke after the race on Sunday night or something? There's yachts going everywhere. They just cruise into Narooma the next day, then move the coke out when it suits them. Les felt the hairs on his neck tingle. One shouldn't cast aspersions. But I reckon you could lay odds Serina's in that pile of coke up to her tits. Les folded his arms and frowned towards the hallway. Okay. I know it's personal between me and her. But I've always had my doubts about that low moll. Especially after what happened to Edwin. So has Eddie. Les shook his head glumly. Weird isn't it? One day I'm walking along Bondi and there's poor bloody Edwin dead on the sand. Next thing I'm watching teary-eyed Serina, down the beach with all Edwin's friends seeing him off. A few days after that, there she is. Coming up the channel in Narooma all over some other bloke. And sailing past Montague Island in a yacht race the day before. Les reflected on seeing the wisp of orange hair under her hood before the yacht tacked. Funny how I thought it was her too. Next thing, the light bulb started blinking above Norton's head again and he rose up from the table.

'The day Edwin ate the pie,' said Les, staring around the kitchen. 'What was my smart arse remark? Two drownings for the price of one?'

Les strode out of the house without closing the door, and hurried straight up to the Wagonga Dive Shop. Ian was behind the counter reading *Underwater* magazine. He looked up when Norton walked in and smiled.

'G'day Les,' he said cheerfully. 'How are you?'

'I'm good Ian,' replied Les. 'How's yourself?'

'All right. Bad luck about the other day, mate. The weather turned sour.'

'Yeah. It wasn't the best,' agreed Les.

Ian half-smiled. 'Neville said you weren't in the water long.'

'No. I never quite got to see the seals. Ian. Have you got a magnifying glass?'

'Yeah. There's one under the counter. I use it to go over maps.' Ian reached around under the counter and came up with an oblong-shaped magnifying glass with a little circle in the corner for closer scrutiny. 'Here you are.' Just a little curious, Ian handed the magnifying glass to Les.

'Thanks,' said Les. 'I won't be long.'

'Go for your life,' shrugged Ian.

Les walked across to Ray Bissett's photo and ran the magnifying glass over it. Big and all as the photo was, the extra magnification really brought it up; and if Les thought he saw anguish and despair on the divers' faces before, now he could almost read their minds. He moved the magnifying glass to the woman diver being sick. She had twin tanks on her back and was holding her mask and flippers in one hand. But the woman diver wasn't bent over being sick. She had her head down, walking away from the other divers towards the stairs leading up to the parking area on the point. And through the little circle in the magnifying glass, the lock of hair poking out from under the hood of her wetsuit wasn't light brown. It was orange. Les had another look to make sure, then walked over to the counter and handed Ian back his magnifying glass.

'Find what you were looking for?' asked Ian.

'Yeah,' nodded Les. 'Yeah. I did. Thanks Ian.' Les turned and left Ian to his magazine.

Les started thoughtfully back towards the house. The two beers had made him a little hungry. There was a cake shop just back from the hotel. Les walked down to buy a couple of depth charges.

The front window of the Seaview Bakery was stacked with wedding cakes, ham and cheese buns and other goodies. A bell rang over the flyscreen door as Les walked inside. Under the counter were racks of delightful-looking cakes, and the Seaview special — their famous banana muffins. A tall brunette in a white dress smiled at Les from behind the counter.

'Yes. What would you like?' she asked, politely.

Les pointed to the blackboard menu above the pie warmer behind the counter. 'Two steak and onion pies, please.'

'Rightoh.'

The woman put the two pies in two white paper bags, Les paid her and walked back to the house. He made a cup of tea, squirted some tomato sauce into the two pies and took everything out onto the verandah. The pies were very good. Les washed one bite down with a mouthful of tea, had another, and started thinking poignantly about Serina.

The low, rotten moll. That was her in Ray's photo. I reckon she's necked Edwin. And you don't need to be Sherlock Holmes with a magnifying glass to work out how.

She's swum across from Ben Buckler while Edwin was out surfing, timed it right, then just swum up and grabbed him. She'd know Edwin's distinctive surfboard. She'd know his movements on the day. She probably kissed him goodbye before she went and put her Scuba gear on.

And a superfit woman like Serina wearing twin tanks would get across Bondi Bay and back easy. Impossible? Me and Eddie did the same thing in Port Stephens. It took us a minute. Yes, concluded Les. I reckon that's how she did it. She might have even known that dive school would be there in the morning and used them for cover. But if that's how, why? Les started on his second pie, and chewed thoughtfully.

Knowing Edwin, I'd say he was the weakest link. Apart from smoking pot and maybe having a toot now and again, Edwin wasn't a dealer. But somehow he's got involved in the shipment. Being so close to Serina, he'd have to know what was going on. Maybe the team put pressure on him because he had an import business? Help wash the money or something? But the thought of risking twenty years in the puzzle hasn't appealed to a party boy like Edwin. So he's politely said include me out. Except coke dealers, as well as being mad raving paranoid, are completely ruthless. So rather than have a loose cannon running around, they've decided to off him. I don't care what anyone says, there's no way Edwin committed suicide. He was too popular and had too much going for him. No. Bottom line, Edwin's shit himself so the team's said he had to go. And Serina was the girl who knew the best way to do it. So she did. *Exeunt* Edwin.

Les finished his second pie and washed it down with the last of his tea, pleased with the way he'd worked things out. And he was pretty sure he was right. However, there was a downside to this. The thought of Serina killing Edwin and getting away with a multi-million dollar drug shipment began to burn Norton's arse something awful. So what should I do now, he asked himself? Les absently tapped his empty mug on the table. Well, I figure I've got three options.

One. I can be a concerned citizen and ring the police. Les shook his head vehemently. No. No fuckin way. There's a chance they'll tape my voice or something. And friendly or not, I've just had a visit from the wallopers. They know I've been down here. If the team get nicked, and I've been seen in the vicinity, I'm going to get involved somehow. And I've been seen in Serina's company a heap of times. Christ! We all had our photos in the local rag once sitting outside the Toriyoshi. Guilt by association? Conspiracy? What if the team finds out it was me that tipped off the cops? They might. What if the cops say no, I wasn't involved, but I'm called in to give evidence. No. No matter what, if I ring the cops, it's going to come back on me. I just know it. So that's out.

Two. I could burn it? Yeah. Swim out with a big pile of wood, some newspaper and box of matches. Or take some petrol. I'd need gallons.

Plus all the flames and fumes in the cave. If I didn't get burnt to death, I'd suffocate. No. Too dangerous. Plus all the flames and smoke coming out of the cave. By the time I got back to my car, some concerned citizen would see me driving away and take my number plate. So that's out. Three. I could swim out with my trusty little clasp knife and cut open all the bags? That'd only take me a week, while I'm covered in coke from head to foot. I'd end up with a huge noseful or a lung full. And that definitely ain't no good for one's health. Not to mention the team coming back and finding me in there. Les shook his head dejectedly. Apart from dynamiting the cave, there was nothing he could do. No. If it is you Serina, you've won. You've pulled off a big one. I only hope you choke on it. You orange-headed dropkick.

Les stood up and walked across to the railing. He leant against it, put everything out of his mind and stared out at the ocean and up the coast. This bloody Narooma certainly is a good spot, he thought. You could buy a weekender or a house down here for the right price too. A bit cold in the winter. But summer'd be fantastic. Only a few hours from Sydney and Aunty Grace just up the road. It's a thought. Les watched another fishing boat coming up the channel then peered down into the backyards of the houses below. One had a small fountain in it; in the form of a cherub, with little wings and bow and arrow, continuously piddling. That reminds me, thought Les. I've still got to clean the fountain out in my backyard. My back was too crook before. I'll do it as soon as soon as I get home. Fuck! The last time I did it, I nearly burnt the bloody house down. And everything else. Shit! Wasn't that a lot of fun?

Just like now, the solar pump had stopped working. And through Norton's negligence, the little pool round the fountain had got full of slime and turned into a breeding ground for mozzies. So Les had gone to a pool shop and bought a five litre container of Ozone Accelerator; enough to clean out an Olympic pool. He tipped a bit in the little pool round the fountain and put the container on the grass just as the phone rang. Les didn't bother to put the cap back on, and as he went to pick up the phone, knocked the container over without noticing. It was his mother on the phone ringing up from Dirranbandi to see how he was getting on in the big smoke. Les settled down for a cosy chat and before long he and the old girl got a bit of a roll on. Les was wandering around with the remote when he noticed clouds of steam and smoke coming from the backyard. He hung up on his dear, sweet mother and raced out to see what was going on. Half the container had poured into the soil and a crater had formed, billowing out smoke and steam like a small volcano.

The acrid fumes and the heat being generated were unbelievable. To make matters worse, the whole, burning, seething mess was heading towards the shed and the pile of wood under which Les had buried all his ill gotten gains.

Les had grabbed a hose and started pouring water into the crater. But that only seemed to make it worse. So he grabbed a shovel and started digging like a madman. Les almost dug up half the backyard before he finally got it under control. Even then, the crater kept steaming and giving off heat for hours. But it was a close thing. If the heat had got to the shed, full of paint, thinners and other inflammable items, it could have been a disaster. After that, Les just used a little chlorine in the fountain. The Ozone Accelerator that was left, along with the container, got tossed into a dump bin on a building site.

Les reflected as he gazed down at the cherub piddling away in the backyard below, and glanced at his watch. He took his mug to the kitchen then got his money and credit cards and walked up the road again. On the other side of the traffic lights, past the Wagonga Dive Shop, was a large hardware store and pool shop. It wasn't quite closing time. But the fair-haired bloke wearing a white shirt and standing behind the counter, looked as if he wished it was. He gave Les a tired smile as Les walked in.

'Yeah mate? How can I help you?' asked the bloke.

'Have you got ten litres of Ozone Accelerator?' asked Les.

'Should have. Wait'll I have a look out the back.'

Les waited patiently and looked at a couple of drills while the bloke in the white shirt went to a room at the rear of the store. He came back carrying two large, white containers with blue labels and placed them on the counter. It was the same brand Les had used when he almost burnt down Chez Norton.

'There you go mate,' said the bloke. 'Last two left. Otherwise you'd've had to've gone to Ulladulla.'

'Unreal, me old,' smiled Les. 'What's the damage?'

The bloke looked the price up in the book. Les paid with his credit card then took the two containers back to the house and left them in the bathtub.

Norton spent the rest of the afternoon cleaning up the house and packing his things while he mulled over his game plan. He'd be leaving early in the morning, so unfortunately he wouldn't be having lunch with Grace and her daughter. He'd call in with her winnings and maybe have a quick cup of coffee. But that would be all. However, there would be another time, Les assured himself. You could back it in. Les also decided against having dinner at the hotel. Olney had promised to cook him a good meal. But after the fight there on Thursday night and one thing and another, Les felt the less time spent in the hotel the better. Pick up his winnings, have a beer and come home. Then await the arrival of Edward, with his spiritual, irritable bowel syndrome. If things got out of hand, he'd drive down the road and sleep in his car. By the time Les had everything packed and cleaned up, it was dark and he was hungry again. There was enough eggs, ham, tomato, cheese and other things to make an omelette. Les cooked a monster over two beers and washed it all down with tea and toast. After cleaning up and packing the rest of the food into cartons, he dumped anything over in the bin then locked the front door and walked up to the phone box to ring Grace. He dropped the coins in the slot and got straight through.

'Hello?'

'Grace. It's Les. How are you.'

'Les. What's happening dude? How's things?'

'Terrific. You sound like you're in a good mood. Did Ellie arrive okay?'

'She sure did. Not long after you left.'

'That's good,' smiled Les. 'So what are you doing now?'

'Nothing,' replied Grace. 'Sitting in the kitchen reading a magazine. Why?'

'All right,' said Les. 'I'll get straight to the point. Grace. Did you have a flashback today?'

'Ohh shit yeah,' answered Grace. 'Lucky Ellie was down the road on her bike, with Morticia.'

'What happened?'

'What happened? Let's just say Les, the hills were alive ... with the sound of UFOs landing.'

Les laughed out loud. 'Grace. You're not going to believe this,' he said. 'But I got taken back in time.'

'You what?'

Les told Grace what he saw and about digging the hand up in the cave. He didn't mention the cocaine. But told Grace a big sea must have washed the rocks away under the wall of the cave and he didn't have to dig far. There was an audible silence at the other end of the line when he finished.

'So, what do you think of that Grace?' asked Les.

'Les ... that is the most fantastic thing I've ever heard,' answered Grace. 'You're psychic.'

'I don't know what I am. But the hand's sitting in my bedroom wrapped in a T-shirt with the ring on the third finger. And that's what was inscribed on the ring. I'll admit, I was touched when I read it.'

'Why wouldn't you be?' said Grace. 'That's beautiful.'

'Yeah, it is,' agreed Les.

'So what are you going to do with the hand? And the ring?'

Les thought for a moment. 'I'll let you know tomorrow.'

'Okay,' said Grace.

'And Grace,' said Les, 'I got a bit of bad news.'

'Bad news?'

'Yeah. I'll be heading back early tomorrow. I just rang home and something's come up at the club. So I won't be able to have lunch with you and Ellie.'

'Oh. That's a shame,' said Grace. 'I was looking forward to it.'

'Yeah. So was I,' said Les. 'But you know how it is when you're a gangster. These things happen.'

'Well, I don't know how it is Les, to be honest,' said Grace. 'I'm not a gangster. Am I a gangster's moll?'

'How about a gangster's friend,' said Les. 'I didn't move into a motel either.'

'Are you still in the house?'

'Yeah,' laughed Les. 'It could be a fun night.'

'Shit! Be careful,' advised Grace.

'I'll be okay,' said Les. 'So what time will you be up tomorrow?'

'Around seven. A bit earlier maybe.'

'Okay. I'll be out then. And Grace, do me a favour will you.'

'Sure. What is it?'

'Keep what I just told you between the two of us for the time being.'

'All right. No problems. I think that might be best anyway.'

'Good on you, Grace,' said Les. 'Okay. I got to go up the pub and get our money. Wish me luck with Edward tonight.'

'I will. And Les. If Edward does turn out to be a raving poof ...'

'Yeah?'

'Try and sleep with your back to the wall.'

'Thanks Grace. I'll see you tomorrow morning.'

'Bye.'

Les hung up and headed for home. Sleep with my back to the wall, he said to himself, shaking his head. Jesus, they're good aren't they.

Back at the house, Les checked everything again. The place was clean, he was sure he hadn't forgotten anything. His tapes were in order. Les snapped his fingers. Shit! That's what I forgot to bloody do. Get a photo of the hand. I don't think I got any film left. And everything's bloody closed now. He got his camera out of his bag, checked the window at the back and smiled. There were five shots left. Les took the hand out to the loungeroom, unwrapped it and sat it on the dressing table right under the light. He took three photos from different angles, a close up of the ring, and left one shot in the camera for luck. Les put the ring back on the bony finger, wrapped the hand in the T-shirt and left it sitting on the coffee table. He put the camera back in his bag and sorted out a few more things then, locking the door behind him, walked down to the hotel.

Les was running a bit late when he walked in the side door. The hotel was fairly crowded and you couldn't miss Norm standing at the corner of the bar with Spike and a couple of other blokes, all wearing jeans and T-shirts. A little further down was Morgan's uncle and a beefy bloke with a mullet, both in yellow, Big Rock Fishing Club, polo shirts. The bloke with the mullet was drinking a schooner. Morgan's uncle was drinking spirits through a straw. They saw Les walk in the door and blanched. Norm and Spike looked as if they'd had a few and gave Les a double, triple blink as he stepped up to them.

'G'day Norm. Hello Spike,' said Les, breezily. 'How's things?'

'Les?' said Norm. 'How are you?'

'Les?' Spike shook his head. 'It is you, isn't it?'

'Of course it's me,' said Les. 'Who were you expecting? Russell Crowe?'

Spike shook his head again. 'No. It's just that . . .'

Norm butted in. 'Les. The last time I saw you, you looked like they just pulled you out of a tank full of piranhas. Now you haven't got a mark on you. What the fuck's going on?'

'I'm a quick healer,' shrugged Les. 'I take lots of kelp tablets.'

'Yeah, all right,' said Norm, exchanging glances with Spike.

'Well,' said Les, rubbing his hands together 'Are you going to stand there like a stale bottle of piss Norm? Or are you going to buy me a beer?'

'Yeah, right,' replied Norm, downing the last of his schooner. 'What'll you have?'

'A schooner of New would be just fine thanks Norm.'

'Coming right up.'

Norm turned to the bar and got a round of drinks. Spike kept staring at Les. Les noticed he was getting some mystified looks from the other punters as well. Morgan's uncle and his mate were eyeballing him like he was the devil incarnate.

'So how are you, Spike?' said Les. 'Thanks for the other day.'

'No worries,' said Spike. 'Les. Like Norm said, something weird's going on here.'

Les patted Spike on the shoulder. 'Spike. Don't tell anyone. But I'm in league with the devil. Whooohhh.'

'I wouldn't bloody be surprised,' replied Spike.

Norm turned around with the drinks and handed Les his schooner. Les thanked him and raised his glass.

'Well. Here's to Narooma,' said Les. 'You blokes don't know how lucky you are living down here. It's the grouse.'

'Cheers Les.'

The beer was cold, fresh and delicious. Les took a good pull and licked his lips.

'So have you got my money, Norm?' asked Les.

Norm patted his jeans. 'I sure have.'

'Okay,' nodded Les. 'We'll get to that in a minute. The important thing is, who won the lucky door prize? I kept my ticket.'

Norm shielded his eyes and exchanged glances with Spike. 'Les,' said Norm, shaking his head. 'Please don't ask.'

'Why? What's up?'

Norm nodded to his left. 'You see who's down the other end of the bar?'

'Yeah,' replied Les. 'Morgan's uncle. The reason all that shit happened in the first place.'

'You see the bloke with him. That's Ambrose Migner. One of Morgan's mates.'

'Ohh yeah,' said Les, turning to the two men. 'I thought I recognised him. He was with Morgan the day they grabbed Warren.'

'He won it,' said Norm.

'Oh shit,' said Les, smiling into his beer. 'Which means … ?'

'That's right,' said Norm. 'Morgan's jaw's wired up. His uncle's jaw's wired up. Mick Ross, the other bloke you flattened, he's got no front teeth and his jaw's wired up too. They're all eating and drinking through a straw. And Ambrose has got a fridge full of choice steak waiting to go on the barbecue.'

'And he's not game to light the fuckin thing up,' grinned Spike.

Les shook his head, looked sage and raised his glass. 'You know, when I hear things like that, I truly believe there is something out there.'

'I'll drink to that,' said Norm, downing half his schooner.

Les smiled at Norm and Spike. 'Would you excuse me for a sec?'

With his beer in his hand, Les walked down to Mick and Ambrose.

'G'day,' smiled Les.

They both looked at Les and barely nodded their heads.

'Fair enough,' acknowledged Les. 'You can't cop me any more than I can cop you. But I just want to tell you something.' Les moved in a little closer and looked right into Mick Scully's eyes. 'Okay. I went a bit overboard with you and your mates in here on Thursday night. I should have just given you a backhander and left it at that. But you've got a fuckin big mouth bloke. And from what I can gather, you got what you deserved.'

Mick didn't say anything. But he got the picture. Les turned to Ambrose.

'So you're Ambrose. And you won the lucky door prize. Good luck to you Ambrose. Get into those steaks. Because after what you did to my mate, you're lucky you still got your fuckin teeth too.' Ambrose gulped into his beer. 'But I've had my fun,' said Les. 'I'll let it go at that. I just want you to give your big, boofheaded mate Morgan a message for me. Okay?'

'Yeah,' nodded Ambrose.

'Good,' said Les. 'Now listen. I'm not a fuckin waiter. I'm a horrible cunt. And if you. Or Morgan. Or any of your mates are thinking about a square up with me. Be very careful. Because if I even think you are, I'll be back here, with some cunts even more horrible than me. We won't fuck around. You won't even know we're here, until you're looking up, and we're shovelling dirt on you. You got that?'

'Yeah all right,' nodded Ambrose.

'Lovely,' said Les. 'And if you don't believe me, ask Daddy.' Les smiled at the two men. 'Have a nice evening. And enjoy all that grouse steak.'

'What was that all about?' asked Norm, when Les returned.

'I just gave Ambrose and Mick a message for Morgan,' said Les.

'I think I get the picture,' said Norm.

'I think they did too,' said Les. 'And if they don't believe me, I told them to ask you. Now what's happening? I think it's my shout.'

They laughed and joked about this and that. Norm said he hoped Les didn't mind him sending the cops round to the house. But he was worried. He thought Les was concussed and the ambulance was full. Les said that was okay; the two detectives were both good blokes. Norm and Spike still couldn't get over Norton's miraculous recovery. Les steered the subject around to Norm doing all right on the day because all the money was on Morgan. Finally, Les steered the subject around to his money.

'Well I may as well pick up my whack, Norm,' said Les.

'Okay. Here it is, right here.' Norm pulled a large, thick envelope from inside his jeans and handed it to Les.

'How much did you make it, Norm?' asked Les, weighing the money in his hand.

'Twenty five grand,' replied Norm.

'That's ... a bit more than I made it, Norm,' said Les.

'Let's just say, your arithmetic's a bit better than mine, Les.'

'Thanks Norm.' Les shook the big man's hand then finished his beer. 'Well, those two beers were delicious. And I'd love to stay. But I'm expecting someone.'

'No worries,' said Norm. 'When do you reckon you'll be in Narooma again?'

'Before the next blues festival. That's for sure,' smiled Les. Les shook hands with Spike and shook hands with Norm again. 'Thanks for all your help, Norm. I owe you one. And I'll say hello to George Brennan for you. See you mate. See you Spike.' Les turned to go when Norm called out.

'Hey Les! What did you say you took again? Kelp tablets?'

Les nodded. 'Them. And apricot oil. It works for me.' Les exited the hotel and walked back to the house.

Well that was good of Norm, thought Les, placing the money in his overnight bag. An extra five grand. He sure must have cleaned up. Les went to the bathroom then changed into his tracksuit and put on an extra pair of socks. He checked the front door was locked then left the light on in the loungeroom, kitchen and hallway. There was some soda water left in the fridge. Les made a delicious, had a sip then took it into his room. He switched on the bed lamp then lay back on the bed with *The Perfect Storm* and opened it to the page he'd marked.

'Into the Abyss. *The Lord bowed the heavens and came down, thick darkness under his feet. The channels of the sea were seen, and the foundations of the world were laid bare. Samuel. 22.'*

Shit! I think I could have done without that. Les sipped some more bourbon, started reading and waited.

It was zero visibility. The pilot had issued a mayday on the Air National Guard frequency that he was going to ditch the helicopter when Norton's bed lamp started flickering on and off. Les looked up as the other lights started doing the same thing. He closed his book and sat up.

A rapid vibration rattled the house and Norton's bed began to shake. In an instant, the temperature in the bedroom dropped to freezing; this was a damper, much clammier cold than before, and it sunk right into Norton's bones.

'Hello,' said Les, flippantly. 'Heee's baaacckk.'

Leaving great clouds of steam in his wake, Les stepped out into the hallway where it was even colder again. He rubbed his arms briskly, spreading more clouds of steam along the hallway through his chattering teeth, and watched the flickering lights. Next thing, an awful, anguished moan lowered through the house, accompanied by ghoulish laughter that seemed to come from everywhere. Les turned around and the doorway was suddenly framed by streams of fluorescent green light pouring through the sides and underneath. Les stared as the light coming from round the door intensified into a foggy, green glow in the hallway. In the centre of the glow, an eerie figure began to take shape. It was the coal-black outline of a man.

'G'day Edward,' said Les. 'Nice of you to drop in.'

Les was immediately answered by a powerful force hitting him in the chest like a crash tackle, knocking the wind out of him. Arms and legs flailing, Norton skidded backwards towards the loungeroom where he crashed heavily into the door frame, before falling face down in the hallway.

'Ohh shit!' grunted Les. 'That bloody hurt.'

Les rose to his knees and was straightaway grabbed by the scruff of the neck, dragged along the hallway and flung head first into the front door. He just had time to throw his arms out in front of him or his skull would have been split open against the heavy wooden frame. Les spun around, seeing stars, and landed on his rump with his back against the door.

'Shit!' spluttered Les, trying to shake the cobwebs from his brain. 'What are you fuckin trying to do, Edward. Kill me?'

Les felt himself being dragged to his feet by the front of his tracksuit before getting flung forward along the hallway. He hit the floor in a clumsy somersault, rolling over on his back wondering what day it was. He brought his head up as a massive weight fell across his body, pinning him to the floor. It was like all those bags of cocaine had been stacked on top of him, slowly crushing him, and he was powerless to move. Les tried to breathe, his chest heaving in short, choking gasps as if he was having a violent asthma attack. The weight got heavier, pressing Les against the floor, crushing the very life out of him. Les choked off a cry of pain and felt himself blacking out.

'Jesus Christ!' screamed Les, with what little air he had. 'Get off me Edward. You're killing me you cunt. I can't fuckin breathe.' The weight crushed Les further into the floor and his eyes started to swim. 'Edward,' gasped Les. 'Edward listen to me. I've got something for you. The ring. Edward ... the ring. With the little black opals. "To Gwendolyn ... All my love. Now ... and Forever ... Edward. Now ... and Forever ..." Edward. Ohh shit!' begged Les. 'Edward. Get off me. Please.'

The lights flickered crazily. The howling and moaning got louder along with the fiendish laughter. Then it stopped and the weight eased. His chest heaving up from the floor, Les groaned with relief and sucked in all the life-giving air he could.

'Ohh Jesus!' garbled Les, as the freezing cold air filled his lungs. 'Thank God!' Les was starting to get his breath back, when he was dragged bodily to his feet again and shoved against the wall. 'Okay, okay Edward,' panted Les. 'I've got it. It's all right. Just follow me.'

Clutching his midriff, Les staggered into the loungeroom. He picked up the T-shirt with the hand inside, turned around and lurched down the hallway to the front door, leaving clouds of steam hanging in the frigid, green glow behind him. He opened the door to find the green glow all round his car. Les put the T-shirt on the roof and unwrapped the bony hand. The hand immediately took on a glow of its own, the gold ring beginning to shine while the fire danced in the tiny opals. Les stood back from the car and pointed.

'Edward look!' he cried. 'There's your ring. Still on your finger where you kept it for Gwendolyn. The ring Edward. There it is. Look.'

Les drew back from the green glow swirling around his car as the same black shape that was inside appeared by the passenger side door. The eerie, green light swirled in the darkness and the shape became a little man with a beard, wearing a frock coat and trousers. Norton left him and backed inside the front door, slamming it shut behind him. With the green glow still radiating into the hallway from outside, he leant his back against the door and slowly got his breath back.

Les could never remember being so terrified. The invisible weight that had lain all over his body had almost crushed the life out of him. Another minute and Les knew he would have stopped breathing. And the supernatural strength he'd been up against was incredible. Les was a big, strong man. But the poltergeist had tossed him around the hallway like he was a rag doll. After a while Les settled down and noticed the green glow had stopped. He pushed himself away from the front door, got the bourbon from his room and gulped it down in the kitchen, then stared into the sink, grateful that what had happened appeared to be over. Les had played Edward and the supernatural a little lightly and almost paid the price. He turned off the lights in the house then went back to his room and flopped down on the bed exhausted. His chest hurt, so did his neck, and Les knew he'd have bruises all over him tomorrow. But at least he was alive. With the bed lamp still on, Les lay on his bed in the cold before finally dragging the blankets over him.

Suddenly, the cold went away and the room returned to normal. Not only that. A beautiful feeling of peace and tranquillity washed over Les leaving him warm and relaxed. Any pain or anxiety had vanished and his mind filled with beautiful thoughts and colours. It was sensational. Even the house around him seemed like a big, cosy old friend taking care of him. It was just a beautiful, beautiful feeling, like nothing Les had ever experienced. Instead of lying on the bed, Les felt as if he was floating above it. It was absolutely marvellous. Les reached over and switched off the light then closed his eyes and let his head sink into the wonderfully soft pillows. In no time, Norton fell into the deepest, most refreshing sleep imaginable.

Les blinked his eyes open the next morning to the delightful sound of magpies whistling in the trees alongside the verandah. He felt great after an exceptionally good night's sleep and was pleasantly surprised to find he had no bruises or aches and pains of any description. Les stared up at the ceiling and reflected on the previous night, but soon put the unnerving events out of his mind. He rolled out of bed and went to the bathroom. After flushing the toilet, he stepped across to clean his teeth and abruptly stopped in front of the sink. Someone had taken the soap and written something across the mirror in beautiful, old script. It was just one word.

Thankyou.

'That's all right, Edward,' said Les. 'Thanks for not killing me.'

There was one photo left in his camera. Les got it from the bedroom, angled it across the mirror so the flash wouldn't mask the writing and took the last shot. The camera started to wind back and Les reached for his toothbrush. After freshening up, he went back to the bedroom and changed into his blue cargos and the same T-shirt he had on the night before, then walked into the kitchen where another surprise was waiting for him. Sitting on the kitchen table was the horseshoe with the bear standing in the middle. Les smiled again and pushed the little bear in its fat stomach. Straight away it started singing 'Livin' La Vida Loca' and waving its arms around. Les waited till the bear finished then switched it off and sorted out some tea and toast. While he was waiting, he opened the front door and walked out to his car. His T-shirt was folded up on the roof of his car and the hand was gone. Les picked up his T-shirt and took it inside.

'Well Edward. I think you finally got what you were after,' smiled Les, closing the door behind him. 'Say hello to Gwendolyn for me.' He put the T-shirt into his room and went back to the kitchen.

Les got his tea and toast together and walked out onto the verandah. Unfortunately, the day didn't match his good mood. The sky had clouded over, it was cooler, and the southerly was blowing again. Not much of a day for the beach, figured Les, as he sipped his tea and watched two boats pass each other in the channel. He strolled along the verandah nibbling on a piece of toast, checking things out for the last time. I'm going to miss this old house, he thought. I hope Clover's parents don't sell it now that Edward's gone. I'd like to stay here again. Actually, they don't even know he's gone. I should keep quiet about it and make them an offer. Les laughed to himself. Knowing my luck though, another ghost would move in and take over from Edward. Les finished his tea and toast and rinsed his mug in the kitchen.

After checking everything was packed and ready to go, Les got his diving gear together and put it it the car with his overnight bag. He then took the two containers of Ozone Accelerator out of the bathtub and stowed them carefully in the boot. After locking the house, he put his cap and sunglasses on, climbed in the car and headed south, past the turn-off to Mystery Bay and on to Tilba. Apart from one or two people outside the garage, there was no one around and not much happening in Tilba. A few minutes later, Les pulled up in front of Grace's house and got out of the car with his overnight bag.

A pretty young girl was seated across the top of the front steps wearing a white, Stussy sweat shirt over a pair of yellow tracksuit pants and trainers. Her hair was long and lighter than Grace's and her face a little pointier. But she had her mother's eyes. Morticia was standing next to her rolling out a low, menacing growl, as if to say 'Yes. I know who you are and all that. Just don't try anything with the kid.' Les walked almost to the top of the stairs and stopped.

'Hello Morticia, you little dag,' he said, then turned to the girl. 'Hello. You must be Ellie.'

'That's right,' replied the girl. 'Are you George?'

'Yeah. That's me,' answered Les. 'Gorgeous George.'

Les offered Ellie his hand. She gave it the softest shake and giggled.

'You're even bigger than mummy said you were.'

'Big and ugly,' smiled Les. 'But I like dogs and I'm environmentally friendly.'

The girl looked evenly at Les. 'Mummy said you're from Sydney.'

'That's right. I live in Bondi,' said Les. 'Have you ever been there?'

'Once. When I was really little. Where do you know Mummy from?'

'Where? Oh, your mummy knows some friends of mine in Sydney. They like your mummy's T-shirts. We were down for the long weekend and we all had lunch together. I'm on my way back to Sydney now, and I just called in to say goodbye.'

'Are you going to stay for breakfast?'

Les shook his head. 'No. I'd like to. But I won't have time.'

Ellie put her arms around the dog's neck. 'Do you like Morticia?'

'I sure do,' said Les. He reached across and patted Morticia on the head. 'She's beautiful. Aren't you Morticia?' The dog half-closed its eyes and lolled its tongue around.

'I think she is,' said Ellie. The young girl stood up and smiled at Les. 'We're going round the back to play.'

'Okay,' said Les. 'Nice talking to you Smelly. I mean Ellie.'

The girl giggled again. 'You're funny. Come on Morticia.'

Les watched them run off around the verandah then looked across as the door opened and Grace stepped out wearing a tracksuit and her hair in a ponytail.

'All right, George,' she said. 'What lies have you been filling my poor, innocent, young daughter's head with?'

'None really,' replied Les. 'Just covering my arse as usual. And mum's. Actually she's a bit of a sweetheart.'

'I know.' Grace gave Les a quick kiss on the lips. 'Come inside.'

Les followed Grace down to the kitchen and placed his bag on the table.

'Would you like a cup of coffee?' she asked.

'I just had a mug of tea,' answered Les.

'Okay. How about a smoothie?'

'All right. Thanks.'

Grace took a jug from the fridge and poured Les what looked like a pink milkshake. 'Try that.'

Les took a mouthful and raised his eyebrows. 'Holy smoke! How good's this? What is it?'

'Custard apple and strawberry. I have to make them for the blonde or she starts whingeing. Good, aren't they?'

'Reckon!' Les swallowed some more and smacked his lips.

'So sit down,' said Grace. 'Tell me about yesterday. Surely you're not in that big a hurry.'

'Forget about yesterday,' said Les. 'Wait till I tell you about last night. I'm lucky to bloody be here.'

Les sat down at the table. Grace got her coffee and sat opposite while Les gave her the lowdown on everything, except finding all the cocaine in the cave. Grace had one sip of coffee and sat gobsmacked. When Les was finished, Grace's coffee was cold and she was shaking her head with a blank look on her face.

'Yeah,' said Les. 'I left the hand on the car. And there was the thank you on the bathroom mirror. I took a photo with the last shot left in the camera. As soon as I get them all developed, I'll send you some copies.'

'My God!' exclaimed Grace. 'What you told me yesterday was fantastic enough. But this on top of it.' Grace shook her head again. 'I don't know what to say.'

'Yeah. It's totally bizarre all right,' said Les. 'But I think I did the right thing. I'm sure that's all Edward wanted.' Les pointed above. 'Now he and Gwendolyn are out there somewhere on their honeymoon.'

'Yes. They probably are,' agreed Grace. 'Unbelievable.'

'Exactly,' nodded Les. 'That's why I think we should keep it between us for the time being. I'll tell Clover when I get home. And Warren. And that's it. Maybe one day, we'll sell the story to a magazine.' Les laughed into his glass. 'But I doubt if even a magazine'd believe me.'

'You know, Les,' said Grace. 'Even though it's a weird, crazy thing, it's also quite beautiful. The love between Edward and Gwendolyn. Don't you think?'

'I agree,' nodded Les. 'But there was no need for him to bring her around last night and let her sit on me.'

Grace threw back her head and laughed. 'God you're a bastard.' Grace settled and looked evenly at Les. 'So what's happening now, George? You're off back to Sydney, leaving me and Ellie behind like a couple of chattels?'

'Chattels? Jesus you're good,' protested Les.

'Doesn't matter,' said Grace. 'But I got you something to take back with you.'

'You have? Oh.'

Grace stood up and went to the loungeroom. She returned holding a white paper carry bag with Tilba Fashions printed on the side and handed it to Les.

'There you go, George,' she said.

Les opened the bag and took out a dark blue T-shirt. There were two parrots cuddling up on the front and a smaller one on the back with its wings spread. They had beautiful, soft blue faces, a hint of red on their green and blue wings and striking, gold breasts. Grace had captured their colours perfectly.

'Ohh Grace,' said Les. 'That's unreal. They're the same parrots I saw when I was tripping out yesterday too.'

'Turquoise parrots,' said Grace. 'Neophema pulchella. You don't see many around these days. Check out the one on the back.'

Les turned the T-shirt back over and peered at the open wings. Very, very subtly, Grace had printed his name along the feathers in blue and gold.

'Fair dinkum,' blushed Les. 'I don't know what to say. That's the nicest present anyone's ever given me. Thanks Grace.' Les reached over the table and planted a kiss on Grace's lips.

'That's all right,' she smiled.

Les looked at the T-shirt and shook his head. 'Honestly Grace. What did I do to deserve this?'

'I don't know,' said Grace. 'Because you're an absolute bastard.'

'I am too,' agreed Les. He carefully folded the T-shirt up and put it back in the bag. 'Anyway. I got something for you too. It ain't much. Just your winnings.' Les opened his overnight bag, took out an envelope and handed it to Grace. 'There you go, mate,' he smiled. 'Don't spend it all at once.'

'Thank you. This will come in very handy too. Believe you me.' Grace took the envelope, felt it and frowned. 'What ...?' She opened the envelope and her jaw dropped. 'My God! How much is here?'

'Twenty grand,' answered Les.

'Twenty thousand dollars!' Grace stared at Les. 'What? Are trying to tell me, you were ... four hundred to one?'

Les nodded. 'I told you I'd get you the best odds.'

'Bullshit! No.' Grace shook her head and pushed the envelope back across the table. 'I can't take this.'

'All right. Don't,' shrugged Les. 'And you can take your T-shirt and stick it in your arse too.'

They both looked up as Ellie came running into the kitchen.

'Mummy. Mrs Hillier's outside on Apples.'

'Okay,' flustered Grace. 'Tell her ... tell her I'll be out in minute.'

'All right.' Ellie ran out the same way she ran in.

'Mrs Hillier?' asked Les. 'Is that ... ?'

'Yes. The old girl from next door,' said Grace. 'She's ridden up to see Ellie.'

'Well, that could be my cue to get going.' Les stood up and placed the T-shirt in his overnight bag. 'Now if you'll walk me to the door. I'll take my beautiful T-shirt and be on my way.'

Grace looked at the envelope full of money sitting on the table then turned to Les. 'You are a bastard, Les. I hope you know that.'

'Grace. I told you before,' smiled Les. 'I'm not really. I just keep meeting people who bring the bastard out in me. You just happened to bring out a bit extra.'

Les followed Grace down the hallway and she stopped just inside the flyscreen door. Les imagined she wanted to give him a goodbye kiss. But not in front of Ellie or the neighbours. Les definitely wanted to give her one. And a good one at that. He dropped his bag on the floor as Grace put her arms around his waist and looked up into his eyes.

'So when are you fixin' on riding into town again, stranger?' she said.

Les put his arms around Grace and looked at her wistfully. 'Don't rightly know little lady,' he answered. 'But I reckon, between your eggplant parmigiana, your mineral water, your custard apple smoothies. All the this, that, and the other, not to mention you saving my neck ... I reckon I'll be a hankerin' to ride through here again real soon maam.'

'Do that stranger.'

Grace gave Les a long, lingering sweet kiss. Les held Grace tight and if her kiss had lingered a second longer, Les would have had trouble getting away. Finally, he reluctantly let Grace go and picked up his bag.

'I'll ring you tonight,' he said. 'After I get home.'

Les followed Grace out onto the verandah. His car was parked on the left, and over to the right Ellie and a woman in sunglasses were standing next to an old pinto mare with a sway back. The woman was as straight as a gun barrel and suited the denim shirt, old jeans and brown RM Williams she was wearing. A thick head of long, grey hair tumbled down from beneath a big straw hat. The horse had its head down nuzzling at Morticia who was playing with it.

'So that's your next door neighbour,' said Les. 'I wish I had some film in my camera. They'd make a great photo they way they're all standing there.'

'She's not bad for eighty-two, eh,' said Grace.

'No,' agreed Les. 'I love her old horse.' He held out his hand. 'Well, goodbye Amazing Grace,' he said formally. 'Thank you for everything.'

'Yes. You too, George,' replied Grace, shaking Norton's hand. 'Thank you for everything.'

Les pointed his finger at her. 'I'll ring you tonight.' He turned and walked across to his car.

Les caught the woman's eye and smiled at her as he waved to Ellie. The woman smiled back. Ellie smiled and waved back, Morticia barked and the horse whinnied. Les got in his car, tooted the horn and drove off. In the rear-vision mirror Grace was waving from the verandah. Minutes later, Les was driving under a leaden sky through empty Tilba, past the Hemp shop.

That's what I meant to get too, he regretted. Some hemp shirts. Grace looked great in hers. Impassively, Les turned left towards the highway. Grace looked good in anything, he thought. And I should be having lunch with her and Ellie. But no. Not me. I have to be a complete fuckin idiot. And then I have to get out of town because I can't mind my own fuckin business. Fair dinkum. When God was giving out heads, I think I was at the end of the queue and he gave me a pumpkin. Les turned left at the highway and in what felt like too short a time, pulled up in the car park near the camping area at Mystery Bay and cut the engine.

Compared to when it had been calm and clear before, today the water looked murky and the southerly had stirred up the ocean. The tide was higher also and choppy swells were breaking against the rocks and around the little islands. The only sign of life was an old bloke fishing at the other end of the bay and a woman walking a small, grey dog. Les shook his head at his own foolhardiness and got out of the car.

As soon as he opened the back door and started taking his clothes off, the butterflies started kicking around in his stomach again. He looked up into the camping area and couldn't see anybody. Les climbed into his rubber vest and his old shorts, put a hanky and his clasp knife in his pocket then opened the boot. He tied the necks of two containers together with a short piece of rope, then closed the boot and buried the car keys behind the front right tyre. Carrying his diving gear in one hand and the two containers of Ozone Accelerator in the other, Les set off along the beach with the southerly whipping at his ears, towards the ridge of jagged rock sticking out from the sand.

The shelf on the other side was covered over by the tide and waves were pushing into the inlet and up against the mouth of the cave. Les clambered over a narrow pinch in the ridge and rinsed the facemask in a small rock pool. He had another look around while he got into his diving gear, but apart from the two people at the opposite end of the bay he couldn't see anybody. Les picked up the two containers and shuffled to the water's edge, took a breath, then bit on his snorkel and plunged in.

The water was gloomy and the swells had stirred up the bottom. Huge beds of seaweed growing amongst the rocks swirled in the white water and visibility was down to barely a couple of metres. Clutching the two containers to his chest, Les kicked furiously towards the cave, waiting for a killer whale or something to appear from behind the seaweed rolling around in the white water and grab him. But apart from the odd kale swimming amongst the seaweed and a few rock cod moving around their caves, there were no other fish, let alone any sharks or killer whales. He bumped against some rocks just below the surface and got a snorkel full of water as a swell washed over him. Les swooshed it out, then the rocky, sandy bottom turned to pebbles washing against each other in the undercurrent and he was at the front of the cave. He saw a swell coming, went with it, swam straight up the rocks into the mouth and got to his feet.

Les hurried inside the cave, whipped off his mask and flippers, then carried the two containers over to the mound. He untied them and started brushing rocks from the tarpaulin. Once he'd removed enough, Les dragged the tarpaulin back to one end and the amount of cocaine sitting in the cave momentarily took his breath away. He took his hanky from his pocket, wrung it out and tied it around his face, then climbed up in the middle of the mound and made a hole amongst the sacks of cocaine. When it was big enough, he opened his clasp knife and started quickly slashing open the surrounding sacks and plastic bags. Soon cocaine was going everywhere, coating him in a thin, white crust. Les slashed open some sacks along the side of the mound and watched the fine, white powder tumble to the floor of the cave like flour. Satisfied he'd slashed open enough sacks, Les picked up the two containers, unscrewed the tops and started pouring Ozone Accelerator into the hole in the mound. The pool cleaner reacted to the cocaine in a flash, immediately turning the hole into a boiling, bubbling crater just like the one in his backyard. In seconds, clouds of smoking cocaine were rising up from the intense heat into the cave. Les climbed down and slashed open the sides of both containers then dumped them in the middle of the mound, letting the liquid pour out into the cocaine. He watched in astonishment as the two containers buckled and melted before his eyes. He folded up his clasp knife then grabbed the tarpaulin, running it back over the pile of sacks to keep the heat in, and tossing some heavy stones back on top for good measure.

It wasn't long before smoke started spewing up from under the edges of the tarpaulin and Les could see the mound moving and boiling underneath. Suddenly the ghastly, acidic fumes started seeping through Norton's wet hanky. Shit! Time I was out of here, he told himself. Les whipped off the hanky, held his breath while he hurried into his snorkelling gear, then flip-flopped over to the mouth of the cave and plunged straight into the water; he broke all records swimming back across the inlet to where he'd jumped in. Puffing a little, Les pulled himself up onto the rocks then took off his face mask and looked back to see clouds of steam rising from the mouth of the cave before they disappeared into the wind. Well, I reckon that'd have to be the world's biggest crack pipe, he smiled.

Les took off his flippers, walked back to the car and retrieved his keys. He was too excited to worry about the butterflies in his stomach as he took off his wet shorts and vest and wrapped a towel around his waist. But there was no one around and this time Les smiled at his good fortune. He put his T-shirt on, got behind the wheel and before long he was on his way back to Narooma.

Lee Kernaghan was twanging 'Texas QLD 4385' when Les pulled up in the driveway. Well that's that, he chuckled. Bad luck I won't be around when Serina and her gang put their heads in the cave. Try chopping that up on a mirror and shoving it up your hooter. That's if it is Serina, of course. But, too fuckin bad if it's not. Les turned off the engine and grabbed his gear. Now. Let's get the fuck out of Dodge.

Without wasting any time, Les had a quick shower, changed into the same clothes he'd had on and started packing everything into the car. What do I need for a souvenir, he thought? The horseshoe. That'll do. I've already got the bear and about half a million photos ready to get developed. Les put the horseshoe in the bag with his diving gear and put it in the boot along with everything else. He placed his overnight bag on the seat next to him and his tapes, then went inside and had a last look around the house. Yeah, I'm going to miss this old house, he told himself again as he walked along the verandah. Even allowing for Edward nearly killing me. It was fun. And what about that view? Les closed the door to the verandah and walked into the bathroom. He looked at the message on the mirror and decided to leave it. I'll tell Clover what happened when I get home and her parents can come round and take a photo in case my one doesn't turn out. Les had a last look in the kitchen, made sure all the lights and everything were turned off, then stepped outside and locked the front door. Now, all I have to do is take the key back to the op-shop. What were those two old girls' names again? Edith and Joyce. That's right. Jiggling the solid brass key in his hand, Les walked down to the op-shop.

The only other car in the side street was a white, dual cabin truck with ropes in the back, parked outside the cake shop. The op-shop was open for business. Les stepped inside. Edith was standing with her back to the door, wearing a pair of grey, woollen slacks and a black cardigan, and dusting some bricabrac when Les walked in. She didn't hear him, so Les called out cheerfully.

'Good morning! Is that you, Edith?'

Edith turned around and peered at Les through her red-framed glasses. 'Oh good morning, Mr Norton,' she smiled. 'How are you?'

'Good thanks,' replied Les. 'Where's Joyce?'

'She'll be in later.'

'Fair enough,' said Les. 'Anyway, I just called in to return the key. I'm on my way back to Sydney.' Les handed Edith the key. 'There you are.'

'Oh, thank you, Mr Norton.' Edith put the duster down, pocketed the key and straightened an imaginary knot in her grey hair. 'So did you enjoy your stay in the Merrigan house?' she asked, smiling congenially.

'Yeah, it was a blast,' replied Les, happily. 'I've never had such a good time in my life. Especially listening to that radio station that plays all the old songs.'

'Season FM,' said Edith.

'That's the one,' nodded Les. 'I can never get enough of Fred Upstairs and Ginger Rogers.'

'Yes. I like them too,' beamed Edith. 'And tell me, Mr Norton. Did you sleep all right at night in the house? Were the beds comfortable?'

'Comfortable? Edith, my bed was that comfortable, I was asleep the minute my head hit the pillow. I slept like a baby.'

'Oh isn't that nice,' said Edith.

'It was funny though,' said Les. 'One of the old tenants called in and stayed with me a couple of nights.'

'One of the old tenants, Mr Norton?' enquired Edith.

'Yeah. He used to live there. Nice bloke too. Edward Ruddle.'

'Edward Ruddle?' gasped Edith.

'Yeah. Not a very big bloke,' said Les. 'Wore a beard and funny little glasses. Said he was a surveyor.'

'Edward Ruddle the surveyor?' Edith put a hand over her mouth.

'That's him,' nodded Les. 'He said he'd been working down at Mystery Bay. He's getting married next week out at Bodalla to a girl named Gwendolyn Monteith. He showed me a photo of her. Big woman. A little plain. But nice.'

'Oh dear.'

'He invited me to the wedding too,' said Les. 'If didn't have to go home, I'd be out there with bells on. I love a bush wedding.'

'Mr Norton, I might have to sit down for a moment.' Edith plonked herself down in a cane chair near a rack of clothes.

'Anyway. I'd better get going,' said Les. 'Goodbye Edith. I'll see you next time I'm in Narooma.'

'Goodbye, Mr Norton.'

Les smiled and left the shop. As he did he noticed a white porcelain teapot near the door, with Narooma written on the side and a sketch of the jetty. He didn't really need it. But it was only three dollars and it'd make another good souvenir. The bell had just rung above the door to the cake shop and Les was standing on the footpath going through his pockets to see if he had the right change. He didn't notice a group of people standing outside the cake shop until he heard a familiar voice.

'Well, well, well ... If it isn't Bondi playboy and big shot underworld figure, Les Norton.'

Les looked up in the direction of the cake shop and didn't blink an eye. 'Oh, hello Serina,' he smiled.

'Hello, Les,' she said, deliberately.

Serina had stepped out of the cake shop followed by three swarthy, unsmiling men with unkempt black hair and thick moustaches. Like Serina, they were all wearing dark tracksuits and gym boots and carrying white paper bags and boxes from the cake shop. With her mane of orange hair, Serina stood out like a beacon.

'So what brings you to Narooma, Serina?' asked Les. 'Family?'

Serina exchanged glances with the three men. 'We're down here for a yacht race,' she replied.

'Oh, of course. The one from Bermagui to Ulladulla,' nodded Les. 'You're right into that sort of thing, aren't you.'

Two of the men said something to Serina and got into the white truck, leaving one man standing next to Serina.

'So what are you doing down here, Les?' asked Serina.

'I came down for the Blues Festival,' he answered.

'The Blues Festival?' Serina twisted her face up. 'That was over days ago.'

'Yeah, I know,' answered Les.

'So what's a big, swinging, city boy like you doing still hanging round a dump like Narooma?'

'I dunno, Serina,' answered Les. 'It's got me beat. But I was just on my way home when you saw me.'

Serina nodded to the op-shop. 'And did I just see you coming out of an op-shop counting your money?'

'Yes Serina,' Les nodded slowly. 'You did.'

Serina turned to the man next to her then gave Les a caustic once up and down. 'Well, we all know you're tight with a dollar, Les. But what's a guy who owns a home in Bondi, and works at the Kelly Club helping old Price Galese wash piles of money, doing in fucking op-shops?'

Les thought for a moment. 'I'm fucked if I know Serina, to be honest,' he replied. 'It's a dead set fuckin mystery to me.' Les gave her an oily smile. 'Anyway. If you'll excuse me. It's a long drive back to Sydney. And I have to get on the road. See you, Serina. Nice talking to you as always.' Les nodded to her friend. 'See you, mate.' Without waiting for a reply, Les turned and walked back to his car.

Les started the car, drove up the side street, then did a U-turn at the lights and stopped at the garage opposite the hotel. He got out and proceeded to fill the tank. Fuck it, Les cursed to himself as he stared at the numbers going round on the bowser. They've sprung me. Well, that's fucked that, hasn't it. And that's them behind the coke all right. The truck and the rope proves that. But fuck it. How's my bloody luck. Les kept looking at the bowser and out the side of one eye watched the white truck go past. Serina and her friends never gave him a second look. He followed the truck as it disappeared down the hill towards the park and unexpectedly the sun appeared from behind the clouds. On the other hand, thought Les, why has it fucked things? They don't know that I know about their coke. And I doubt if they picked up on my little innuendos outside the op-shop. I'm just a goose as far as Serina's concerned. And when they do find all their coke looking like a giant pile of steaming seal shit, what are they going to do? They're not going to race into the hardware store asking if somebody just bought ten litres of pool cleaner. They won't have a clue what happened. They'll just cut their losses and get to the shithouse out of Narooma. They could even think it's another drug syndicate trying to put them out of business.

The meter stopped running when Norton's tank filled and he replaced the nozzle on the bowser. In fact, smiled Les, I'm glad I bumped into Serina and her friends. I reckon they've just done me another favour. Les screwed his petrol cap back on and walked across to the office.

While the young bloke in the blue denim shirt was swiping his Visa card, Les searched his pockets again for change. He signed the receipt and pointed to a yellow pay phone near the door.

'Is that phone working all right, mate?' asked Les.

'Yeah. No problems,' replied the young bloke, handing Les his receipt.

'Thanks.'

Les walked over to the phone, dropped some coins in the slot and dialled. It didn't take long to get through.

'Hello?'

'Grace. It's Les. How are you?'

'Les? What ...?'

'Grace. You're not going to believe this. But I just rang home. And everything's sorted itself out at the club. Do you and the other chattel still want to have lunch?'

THE END

A MESSAGE FROM THE AUTHOR

Wat can I say? I gave Les Norton a year off, now he's back, bigger and better than ever. And nicer. Les might have been a bit of a dropkick in *Leaving Bondi* and a few Christians wrote in castigating me because he porked the girl from Victor Harbor while she was asleep. But if Les hasn't turned out to be a good bloke again in this one, I'll go back on the dole. He just rides off into the sunset at the end: then turns around and rides back again. I think you'll enjoy *Mystery Bay Blues*. I know I enjoyed writing it and had a great time in Narooma doing the research. What a top place. In fact I'm going back for the blues festival again this year and catch up with Neil Mummie and Rhonda. It's the best three days and nights of rock 'n' roll in Australia. They don't call it the friendly festival for nothing. Hey! It was worth writing a book about.

I have to thank all the people that came up to say hello on *The Ultimate Aphrodisiac* book tour. It was fantastic. Look up my website. You might see yourself there. Like the woman that came up to me in Lismore with the top of her dress full of baby possums. And what about Edith? Who drove all the way from Grenfell to Grafton to say hello and get some books signed. She was so nice I was in tears. We've been trying to contact her through the Grafton paper, but we can't. Anyway Edith, if you read this, write to me. There's some presents waiting for you.

The feedback from *The Ultimate Aphrodisiac* was all positive. Some people said it was my best book. Some even said it was the best book they'd ever read. For a grumpy old fart of an awther I was flattered, I can tell you. I've also been doing my best to answer all your letters and I'm catching up. But the other day I found a full box I'd put aside to take down to Narooma with me and forgot all about them. So some replies might be a bit slow coming. But I'm doing my best and I love hearing from you. It makes my day.

Robert G. Barrett, 2002

Rosa-Marie's
Baby

DEDICATION

To the Bali victims. Ours and theirs.
I'll leave it at that.

The quote on page 378 is from *Occult Visions of Rosaleen Norton*
by Keith Richmond. Reprinted with thanks.

Summer was officially over and it was a typical autumn afternoon in Sydney towards the end of March. A light north-westerly was blowing, taking the edge from any heat and humidity still lingering around, while it pushed the air pollution out to sea along with whatever clouds were drifting across the clear, blue sky above the city. After training earlier in the day with Billy Dunne, and lunch at the Diggers, Les was seated comfortably on a banana-chair in the backyard of Chez Norton wearing a pair of blue shorts and a white T-shirt, casually tossing grapes to a pair of water dragons that had decided to make his backyard, with its small fountain, their home. On his lap was a copy of *Nexus* magazine and an article he'd been reading about water-fuelled cars, while on the stereo inside, the Alabama 3 were growling out country, acid-house rock off their CD *Exile on Coldharbour Lane*. Les finished the article, smiled and shut his eyes as the CD cut out in the lounge room. It was Tuesday afternoon and he didn't have to be at work till Thursday.

On Monday there'd been a fire and explosion in the German restaurant next-door to the club. Water from the fire-hoses had poured into the club, mixed with decades of putrid Kings Cross grunge from when the pipes burst in the old building that housed the restaurant. Price cursed the fire brigade and the owners of the restaurant to the heavens, threatening all sorts of diabolical retribution. But there wasn't much he could do, except recarpet the club, get the smell out, then open up again on Thursday night before claiming five times the cost of repairs on insurance.

Not that work worried Les. If anything, the job seemed to get easier all the time and Les often enjoyed sitting in the new front foyer talking to Billy and the punters. Price still had to grease the odd palm here and there, but by paying taxes on his substantial rake-off from the card games and easing up on the hits and limb dislocations, Price had the Kelly Club humming along that close to legal, Les and the others were starting to think they were solid citizens. Besides an amiable work environment, Les also had other reasons to smile.

He was cashed up and fit as a fiddle. He still heard from Roxy, the friendly, good-looking blonde from Victor Harbor, who was now somewhere in Arnhem Land still working on her book. He'd been back to Narooma to see Grace and had a great time again down the south coast. He got on good with Grace's daughter Ellie, and shouted them a week in Sydney at the Swiss Grand. With Grace wearing one of her T-shirts tucked into a pair of tight hipsters, Les took her up to the club one night where she wowed everybody with her figure when he introduced her around, then wowed everybody again when she won several thousand dollars playing manilla. Now Grace was in California, taking Ellie to see Disneyland. She rang Les on Sunday night to say they were both having a good time except the queues were a bit punishing and driving around LA on the wrong side of the road was like a fun ride on its own.

So life was good. Les was happy, Grace was happy, Roxy was happy and, despite the frozen looks on their faces, Les was convinced the two water dragons munching grapes in his backyard were happy. The only person not happy at the moment was Price. However, two of his horses had got up on the weekend, so he'd probably be happy when the club reopened on Thursday night. Yes, smiled Norton as he soaked up the last of the afternoon sun on his banana-chair, life's good and everybody in the garden is rosy. Nevertheless, there was one person whose well-being gave rise to Norton's concern. The boarder. Norton didn't know if he was using the correct medical terminology, but he was firmly convinced Warren was an extrovoid schizophrenic.

They'd both been watching *Nero Wolfe* on the ABC. Warren taped it for Les while he was at work and Les liked the TV show about the fat, pompous private detective, set in New York during the forties. Warren, however, had become besotted. Especially with Nero Wolfe's dapper assistant, Archie Goodwin. Now the boarder was Warren Edwards, advertising executive by day, but when he went out at night he was Archie Goodwin, private eye. Right down to Archie's double-breasted suits, art-deco ties and two-tone shoes. Warren had even effected Archie Goodwin's mannerisms. His jaunty, shoulder rolling, chin up, elbows by his side walk — with added jaunt — and the way he spoke in clipped tones out of one side of his mouth. Les wasn't sure what had sent Warren into the darkened nightmare world of schizophrenia. Work? Flashbacks from the magic mushrooms down at Narooma? The super-strong pot he was cunningly growing in the backyard concealed amongst a bed of mint? Les glanced across at the tiny heads ripening in the sun alongside the back shed. Certainly Warren wasn't doing any harm, and he did resemble Timothy Hutton, the actor who played Archie Goodwin. And Clover didn't appear to mind Warren's dressing up like a 1940s private eye. Les also had to reluctantly admit Warren did look sharp when he and Clover stepped out at night, they'd even managed to get their photos in the social columns and 'Sydney Confidential'. But Warren's condition could become a worry. It wasn't that long ago he was getting around in a *Star Trek* uniform with a tri-corder, convinced he was Croden, a humanoid fugitive from Rhakar in the Gamma Quadrant. What if

Warren developed multiple personalities? What if he went drag? What if he decided to become Dolly Parton or Kylie Minogue? Les felt he'd better keep a close eye on Warren, AKA Archie Goodwin.

And talking about Warren. Archie would be home soon to get changed. He was taking Clover to the opening of some new night spot at North Sydney. Les glanced at his watch as the sun disappeared behind a bank of clouds. It wasn't getting any earlier and his stomach was starting to rumble like a pre-dawn artillery barrage. He folded his magazine and went inside.

Les had a shave then walked out to the kitchen and opened a large bottle of Grolsch from the two cases Warren had brought home from the advertising agency. He took a mouthful and peered into the fridge. Dinner for one shouldn't be too difficult. Frozen vegetables in the microwave and a juicy big T-bone in the George Foreman griller. Les soon got that together, ate it and was glancing through *Nexus* again and dunking arrowroot biscuits into a cup of Russian Caravan tea when he heard the front door open and Warren walked into the kitchen with Clover. Warren's dark-haired girlfriend was carrying a small overnight bag and looked neat in a green top cut low in the front and a pair of green slacks. Warren was wearing designer jeans with a horizontal-striped blue shirt hanging out over the top. He was holding a letter in one hand and had an odd smile on his face as he caught Norton's eye.

'Hello Woz,' nodded Les. 'Hello Clover.'

'How are you, sexy?' replied Clover.

Les dunked another biscuit in his tea. 'I'm good. Especially when I see you, gorgeous.'

Warren continued to stare at Les. 'So,' he said. 'The truth's finally out. You are an old drag queen.'

'I'm a what?' retorted Les.

'You've finally come out the closet, Les,' smiled Clover.

'Yeah, all right,' said Les indifferently. 'I used to be a cross-dresser. But I stopped, because every time I wore women's clothes I couldn't parallel park. What are you pair on about? I'm trying to enjoy a cup of tea and a biscuit in peace. Do you mind?'

'So what made you pick Rosa-Marie for a drag name?' said Warren.

Les screwed up his face. 'What?'

'Here Rosa.' He handed Les the envelope. 'I've just been down the post office, and this came for you.'

Les took a long manilla envelope from Warren. It was a little brown around the edges and addressed in neat, sloping handwriting to *Rosa-*

Marie Norton, Post Restante, Kings Cross, Sydney, NSW. Under that someone had stamped a finger pointing and roughly printed on it, TRY POST OFFICE BONDI. Les turned the letter over. In the same neat handwriting on the back it said, *From Emile Decorice, C/o PO, Te Aroha, New Zealand.* Les examined the front of the envelope again then knitted his eyebrows at something.

'Oh, I get the picture,' he nodded to Warren. 'It's some sort of gee-up. You've gone into Archie Goodwin mode again and we're playing back to the forties. You definitely need help, Warren.'

'What?' said Warren.

Les handed the letter back to Warren. 'Where'd you get the old threepenny stamp?'

Warren looked in the corner of the envelope. Beneath the circular blur where it had been stamped by the post office, was a green stamp with a crown on it that said *Australia, 3d.* 'Shit! It is too. I never even noticed. Hey, have a look, Clover.'

Clover stared at the envelope. 'Well, I'll be,' she said, genuinely surprised. 'It is too.'

'So just what are you trying to pull, kiddies?' said Les, returning to his *Nexus.* 'Though I will give you ten points for authenticity. The old stamp's a ripper.'

'We're not trying to pull anything,' said Warren. 'This letter was in the box with two others for me.'

Les took the letter and looked at it again. He used to get the odd letter addressed to him care of the post office at Kings Cross. So he told the post office to redirect any letters for Norton to the mail box at Bondi. However, he'd never received anything like this.

'Rosa-Marie Norton?' Les shook his head. 'Never bloody heard of her.'

'It might be one of your inbred relatives in Queensland,' said Warren.

'Why don't you open it?' said Clover.

'You can't go opening other people's mail, Clover,' answered Les.

'Why not?' said Clover. 'It's probably been lost in the dead-letter office or something.'

'Dead-letter office?' said Les.

'Yeah,' said Warren. 'These things happen. People often get letters and postcards sent as far back as the First World War. They get lost in the system.'

'Going by the stamp and the envelope, that has to be years old,' said Clover. 'Go on Les. Open it up.' She turned to Warren. 'Ooh! This could be exciting.'

Les stared at the envelope for a moment. 'Okay,' he shrugged. 'Why not?'

Les reached over to the kitchen drawer and got a knife. He carefully slit the envelope open and removed the contents as the others took a chair each on either side of him. It was a neatly written four-page letter.

Dear Rosa

Well, dreadful witch of Kings Cross, I hope this letter finds you as well as circumstances can prevail. I sent it care of the post office rather than your flat because I don't know how long you'll be in Melbourne. And you never know with the police always snooping about. I'll make this as brief as I can, but you know me. I am a poet who likes to express himself, so if I start to ramble I'm sure you won't mind.

They let me out of Callan Park just after you left for Melbourne. Those nervous disorders and headaches turned out to be a brain tumour. So I decided to make a quick exit out of Sydney. I sold everything and I'll be on the Wanganella back to New Zealand tomorrow. If anything should happen, I'd like to be with my family in Te Aroha. But what a time I had with you. We certainly showed them a thing or two in Australia. God, I wonder if this country, with its figleaf mentality, will ever change? Bugger them anyway.

In the meantime, you've certainly got your share of problems with the stupid bloody police and customs department, now opening an exhibition in Melbourne and having to have another abortion at the same time. I think it is a better idea you having it down there. Apart from the money, getting one in Sydney is disgusting and I would dread to see you finish with blood poisoning again. God, you were half dead in the awful flat behind St Luke's and the police still wanted to arrest you. It's hard to believe what the police have done to you at times. And me. Especially that fat, loathsome pig of a thing McBride. And for what? But, Rosa my treasure. I have some great news for you. I managed to put one over on the bastards. I saved three of your paintings before they could burn them. When they released me, I managed to find out where they were. So I simply put on a pair of white overalls, walked in like I owned the place, then wrapped them up in a blanket and just walked out again. They'd taken them out of the frames so it was easy. I even caught the tram back to the Cross with them. I hid them at Talbot's for a short while, then decided they would be better off out of Sydney altogether. The police are searching high and low for them.

Everyone in the kitchen finished reading the letter at the same time. Les placed it carefully on the kitchen table alongside the envelope and turned to the others.

'Well, what do you make of that?' he said.

Warren shook his head. 'I'm not sure what to make of it. It's ... it's weird.'

Clover pointed to the name on the front of the envelope. 'He called her the Witch of Kings Cross. Who was she? I've never heard of her.'

'Me either,' said Les. 'And I've been working up there for a while. But she must have been an artist and this Emile bloke's gone in and got her paintings.'

'Yeah, why would they want to burn them?' said Clover. 'That's a bit heavy, isn't it?'

'Because she was a witch, I suppose,' said Warren.

'Very funny, Warren,' said Clover.

'Shit! What a letter,' said Les. 'It's all in there, isn't it. Witches, a black mass. A priest, a bishop.'

'Opium, abortions, Callan Park,' said Warren.

'I wonder how old the letter is?' said Clover. 'I wonder if they're all still alive?'

'I'd say it's pretty old,' said Les. 'The trams stopped running years ago, for a start.'

'Yeah,' agreed Warren. 'And no one catches boats to New Zealand anymore.'

'What about Emile?' said Clover. 'I wonder who he was. Her boyfriend?'

'Sounds like it,' answered Warren. 'He's got her up the stick and pissed off to New Zealand when they let him out of the rathouse. The swine.'

'Except it turned out he had a brain tumour. Poor bugger,' said Clover.

'Where's Lorne?' asked Les.

'The other side of Melbourne,' said Warren. 'On the Great Ocean Road. We shot a Holden commercial down there once. It's nice.'

Clover shook her head slowly. 'You know, I'm getting a weird sense of deja vu about this letter.'

Les shook his head firmly. 'No. There's definitely no deja vu about it,' he said. 'But something like this did happen to me once before.'

'Yeah,' nodded Warren. 'Like when you sent me a postcard from Cooktown and you got here before it did.'

'I'll tell you what,' said Clover. 'Warren dearest, why don't you go and have a shower first, and I'll see if I can trawl something up on the internet.'

'Good thinking, Ninety-Nine.' Warren took a last look at the letter then headed for the bathroom.

'You reckon you'll find anything, Clover?' asked Les.

'You never know. Something might turn up.'

'Okay Clover. Have a nice time in cyberspace,' said Les.

Clover turned for Warren's room to fire up his computer. Les flicked through the old letter again before folding it up and replacing it carefully back in its envelope on the kitchen table. He got another beer from the fridge then took it into the lounge room and switched on the TV.

Well, if that old letter don't beat all, Les mused as he sat down to watch the ABC news. It could only happen to bloody me. Les had almost finished his beer when Clover walked into the lounge room.

'How did you go?' he asked her.

Clover shrugged and handed Les a single sheet of paper. 'That's all I could find.'

Just then Warren called out from the hallway. 'Righto. I'm finished.'

'I leave you with it.'

'Okay. Thanks, Clover.' Les began to read what was on the page.

Rosa-Marie Norton. The notorious Witch of Kings Cross. Born an only child in Wanganui New Zealand in 1920, she came to Australia with her parents in 1929 and went to school in Apollo Bay, Victoria, where her father worked as an engineer. When her parents moved to Sydney in 1934, she went to school at Asquith and studied art at East Sydney Technical College before moving to Kings Cross when her parents returned to New Zealand in 1940. Rosa-Marie then went on to become a bohemian artist and gained notoriety as the Witch of Kings Cross, where she painted macabre, satanic paintings and held black masses in her Roslyn Gardens apartment, much to the consternation of the church and the ultra-conservative Australian establishment of that time. She was arrested on numerous occasions and is the only Australian artist to have their paintings confiscated and burnt. Despite her dubious reputation, Rosa-Marie Norton was popular within the Australian art community and corresponded with famed overseas artists like Yves Tanguy and Salvador Dali, as well as occultists like Aleister Crowley. And studied the works of Eliphas Levi. Rosa-Marie Norton died in Sydney in 1951 leaving very little money. Yet one of her paintings, *Sleeping Beast*, was sold in Sydney recently for $50,000. Further information can be found in *The Mystical Mind of Rosa-Marie Norton* by Kenneth Raymond. At the bottom of the page was a fuzzy printout of a slender woman with dark hair.

Les read the page again then went back to watching TV. A few minutes later, Warren walked into the lounge room with Clover. Clover had the same clothes on except for a black satin jacket and a pair of tan

Doc Martens. Warren was wearing a dark blue, chalk-stripe, double-breasted suit, a dark blue shirt with a maroon, yellow and white tie, blue and white two-tone shoes. Sitting squarely on his head was an oyster grey snap-brim fedora with a blue hat band.

'My God!' said Les. 'It's *Natural Born Killers* meets *Bonnie and Clyde*.'

'Don't sweat it, pal,' said Warren out the side of his mouth. 'Punks like you are a dime a dozen where I come from.'

'Did you read the printout, Les?' asked Clover.

'Yeah. There wasn't a great deal,' replied Les. 'But thanks anyway, Clover.' Les offered the printout to Warren. 'You want to have a look, Woz? Sorry, I mean Archie.'

Warren's head shook slightly beneath his snap-brim fedora. 'Ain't got time, pal. I gotta go and close the Sorrelli case.'

Les drew back the sheet of paper. 'I should have known.'

Clover made an open-handed gesture. 'We have to go.'

'Okay. Have a good night,' smiled Les.

Les heard the door close and went back to the TV. After a while he tossed his empty beer bottle in the kitchen tidy and made a delicious. Warren had brought a video home from the agency, *O Brother, Where Art Thou?* Les slipped it in the VCR and settled back on the lounge.

Les enjoyed the movie. George Clooney and his two dumb mates were a hoot as the escaped convicts bumbling around the deep South during the Depression. The music was good, the singing was great and when the Soggy Bottom Boys finally got up on stage, Norton cracked up. He made a point to buy the CD with the soundtrack from the movie. But as much as Les enjoyed watching the video, every so often his eyes would drift back to the printout Clover had given him. When the video finished, Les made a mug of Ovaltine, washed up, then read both the letter and the printout again before switching off the lights and taking the letter and printout into his bedroom with him.

After he climbed into bed, Les scrunched his head back into the pillows and stared up at the darkened ceiling. What happened today had to be more than coincidence, he told himself. A letter like that doesn't just get lost in the system for years then turn up out of the blue. Was it an omen? A voice from beyond the grave? Divine intervention? Les needed to know more about Rosa-Marie Norton, the Witch of Kings Cross. And the best way to find out was to get that book by Kenneth Raymond. After a while Norton's eyes started to flicker and he drifted off into the cosmos.

Wednesday was a little warmer and the northerly had swung round more to the west. Norton was up around seven; Warren was still in bed snoring. Les changed into his old blue tracksuit, had some tea and toast then tossed his training gear and a towel into an overnight bag and drove down to North Bondi to meet Billy and Eddie for a workout. Billy was leaning against the railing opposite the Surf Club wearing a tracksuit much like Norton's and a pair of sunglasses.

'Where's Eddie?' asked Les.

'Something's come up and he had to go round to Price's,' answered Billy.

'Did he say what it was?'

Billy shook his head. 'No. He probably just wants Eddie to shoot the local fire chief.'

'Yeah. And old Karl that owns the restaurant.'

'If there's any real drama, we'll find out tomorrow night, I imagine.' Billy nodded to the Surf Club. 'What do you want to do first? Have a run?'

'Righto,' said Les. 'Then we'll get on the skis. You fancy a bit of breakfast at Speedos after?'

'Okay.' Billy feinted a left rip into Norton's ribcage and they walked across to North Bondi Surf Club.

They jogged six laps of Bondi then paddled four laps on their skis. After that they smashed into each other with a medicine ball inside the Surf Club. During the run Les decided not to say anything about the letter for the time being. In fact Les didn't talk about anything much when they were running, because Billy kept the pressure on. After the workout they strolled across to Speedos, found a table inside and had a late breakfast of mineral water, OJ and a pile of scrambled eggs and bacon washed down with creamy flat whites. On the way back to their cars Billy said he wouldn't be able to train the next morning as he was going to the dentist. Les said okay. He'd see him at work tomorrow night. They got in their cars and drove off.

Les stopped for the *Telegraph* on the way home, then changed into his blue shorts and a white Roosters T-shirt and had a read while his laundry was going around. The two water dragons were sitting under the Hills Hoist; he fed them a few grapes before going back inside to read the old letter and the printout again. Les had a think for a moment then wrote something down on a piece of paper, put it in his overnight bag and drove up to Bondi Junction via Birrell Street. He fluked a parking spot in Denison Street, right opposite Waverley Library. Norton had held a library card for as long as he could remember. On a rotten, cold, boring day in winter, Les liked nothing better than to kill a few hours in the library, going over big old books about ancient ruins and other countries and their people. And the new, fully modernised cream and brown building now housing Waverley Library was bigger and better than ever, plus the staff were always helpful and patient. Les locked the car and walked across to the tiled courtyard of the Ron Lander Centre.

The double doors swished open, Les turned left at the wide, flat marble-and-stainless-steel statue in the foyer and through the two security gates inside. There was a man standing behind a counter on the left and two women seated at their desks in the corner to the right: a blonde in a grey cardigan and a brunette in a maroon shirt with matching earrings. Les approached the lady in the maroon shirt.

'Yes. Can I help you?' she asked.

'Yes please,' answered Les, placing a piece of paper on the counter. 'I'm after this book. Do you have it?'

The woman looked at the name on the piece of paper then punched it into her computer. 'Yes we do,' she smiled. She pointed to the rows and rows of books behind Les and the section Ra–Sh. 'Just over there.'

'Thanks very much.'

Les started running his eyes up and down the spines of all the books. Raymond's book was a large coffee-table type sitting between *Belle On A Broomstick* by Pat Richardson and *Just Another Angel* by Mike Riley. Les took the book over to the self-checker, placed his library card in the slot, pressed the book's spine against the red tape, there was a thump as it registered and Les picked up his printout receipt. Before he dropped the book in his bag, Les had a closer look at the cover.

The book itself was wide and long. The cover was a fiendish yet beautiful woman's face, in all the swirling, devilish colours of the rainbow, looking at you from above a darkened skyline of burning buildings. She had gorgeous lips and sinister emerald eyes that leapt from the cover and transfixed the viewer with an hypnotic gaze. In striking red and white print, it said, *The Mystical Mind of Rosa-Marie Norton by Kenneth Raymond*. Les zipped his bag closed and walked back to his car.

Despite getting caught in a gridlock of cars near Waverley College and nearly getting T-boned at Ocean Street by a woman in a 4WD talking on a mobile phone, Les was whistling happily when he pulled up outside Chez Norton and stepped inside. Finding Raymond's book was easier than he expected. He looked at his watch and thought: why not? It was getting cloudy outside. He got a bottle of Warren's beer from the fridge and settled back in the lounge room with his book.

On the inside cover was a photo of Rosa-Marie Norton wearing a military-style shirt and a hand-painted tie. She was very attractive with thick, shiny black hair, sensuous lips and plucked eyebrows that arched up giving her a sinister haughtiness. But it was her eyes, dark and lidded, that exuded a tigerish sexuality that bored deep inside you.

Amongst the printed matter were pages of her paintings. Some were black and white, but most were done in wild swirls of fantastic burning colours and flames, like the face on the cover. The subject matter was mainly esoteric satanism. Devils with four eyes, faces that turned into tarantulas, snakes with cat's heads. Genies coming out of buildings, buildings walking away on chicken's legs. Camels with heads for humps, superbly muscled men with horse's or goat's heads and penises with snake's heads. Except for one painting of a baby on a bed of pink flowers surrounded by buck-toothed rabbits titled *Tanybryn*, it was paintings of horned men and panthers making love to beautiful, cloven-hoofed women, more devils and demons, piranhas with forked tongues and werewolves holding magic wands; with titles like *Snake Blood, Demon at Rest, Love in Hell, Tarantula Power, Hair Hair the Storm Demon*. The painting on the cover was titled *The Temptress*. Les had a last look at the cover, then turned to page one and read the first paragraph.

Rosa-Marie Norton occupies a position unique in the annals of Australian art history: that of Australia's most persecuted — and prosecuted — female artist. Amongst the incidents which contributed to this dubious honour were her position as the only woman artist to be charged with 'having exhibited obscene articles', the only artist in Australia to have had a book of her works prosecuted for 'obscenity', and also — and most outrageously — the only Australian artist (male or female) to have had her works destroyed by judicial sanction.

Les spent the rest of the day poring over Raymond's book. A stiff neck later and as the sun was starting to set, Les finished. He stretched, made a cup of tea and placed Raymond's book on the kitchen table next to the letter. Between the two, Les felt he'd been given a small window into Rosa-Marie's amazing life. Many people in the past had voiced their opinions on Rosa-Marie Norton, the Witch of Kings Cross. Les sipped his tea, sat back and tried to draw his own conclusions from what he'd read in Raymond's book.

She was years ahead of her time. And although totally outrageous, also an extremely talented artist. If she had been alive today she'd be rich and her works appreciated. Behind the devil and demon subjects of her art, the colours she created were brilliant and dazzling. One fellow artist had described her as a 'female van Gogh'. She disliked children and preferred cats to people, yet lived life to the full and, sexually, would be in anything. From sado-masochistic orgies to bondage and devil worship. Drink, drugs. You name it. Rosa always brought plenty to the party and would be the first there and the last to leave, in her colourful clothes, twirling a jewelled cigarette holder. She entertained local artists of both sexes and her fame and notoriety were well known overseas. If you could handle a brush and palette, liked kinky sex, drink and drugs and staying up for days on end, call in to Kings Cross and see Rosa. American, English and European artists would visit her and literally kneel at her feet. Men fell in love with her one after the other. She modelled for Norman Lindsay, and Jacques San was an American artist who fell passionately in love with her on a brief visit to Australia. When Rosa-Marie cast him aside, he almost drank himself to death before he packed up his paintings and returned to New York. She always had trouble selling her paintings. Yet a Bishop Thomas Elsworthy from Victoria bought two, supposedly to show his parish exactly what evil and depravity was all about. And from the sale of the two paintings Rosa was able to buy a car and spend an entire summer travelling around country New South Wales and Victoria.

Emile Decorice was a homosexual poet who shared a house with Rosa and was one of her closest and most devoted friends. The police persecuted him as well as her and had him committed to a mental institution. He went back to New Zealand only to catch pneumonia during the voyage and died a week after the boat docked in Auckland. Talbot was Talbot Houlcroft, the editor of an avant-garde magazine, *Guichet*. He, too, was a good friend of Rosa's and published her art and articles she wrote. He even published an expensive book of her art, but went broke when the authorities declared it 'offensive to public chastity and human decency' and had it banned. McBride was Sergeant Arthur 'Buster' McBride, a Kings Cross detective who constantly harassed Rosa-Marie and Emile. The newspapers and any muck-raking journalists of that time rarely left her in peace. They made headlines out of her smallest misdemeanour and wrote anything they could think of about her, mostly lies and sensationalism. According to Raymond, however, she gave an interview to a university paper in which she said she studied occultism and eastern philosophy and claimed she went along with the Witch of Kings Cross infamy because she enjoyed being a nonconformist in a conservative, Christian country like Australia. Plus it drew attention to her art, and any publicity was better than none.

She opened an exhibition in Melbourne that turned out a complete disaster and saw her once again charged with obscenity. One critic described her art as 'Stark sensuality running riot'. Another said, 'Rosa-Marie Norton paints with a lurid brush dipped in nightmares.' When the exhibition virtually closed overnight, Rosa-Marie was said to have broken down, then she disappeared from public view till she was arrested at Apollo Bay for urinating in a public place. She later showed up in Sydney and died not long after when she fell out of a tram in Taylor Square one night and broke her neck. Naturally this made headlines and a huge crowd of people and various identities from the art world and around Kings Cross attended her funeral. Her ashes were sent back to her family in New Zealand and most of her paintings simply disappeared. The biggest irony Les found was that, although she died broke, as well as that one painting selling for $50,000, the owner of a restaurant in Kings Cross that used to be a bohemian coffee lounge in the fifties found one of her paintings in an attic and knocked back an offer of $85,000 for it.

Les tapped his fingers on the book and looked at his watch. Warren would be home soon and the beer had put an edge on Norton's appetite. He got a pile of vegetables and rice together, then marinated some lamb chump chops in Taka Tala sauce. While the rice was cooking, Les perused Emile Decorice's letter again and did a little deducing.

Rosa-Marie and Emile had probably caught Father Bernard Shipley with his pants down somewhere, taken photos and decided to blackmail him. Bishop Elsworthy had bailed his priest out by buying two of Rosa-Marie's paintings. Rosa or Emile probably still kept a couple of photos, which was why Emile sent the paintings to Father Shipley for safekeeping. Rosa-Marie never got the letter Emile sent telling her. Emile died not long after he sent it. Rosa-Marie died not long after that. And Father Shipley still had the paintings. When he found out Rosa-Marie and Emile were both dead it would have been a blessed relief. No more connection with the Witch of Kings Cross and her deviate friend. There was no next of kin that Father Shipley would have been aware of and he was the only one who knew about the paintings. He could have destroyed them. But then again, he might not have. Les picked up the old letter and tapped it softly against the table. Well, if that's the case, he surmised, hidden somewhere in Lorne, Victoria, still bundled up in heavy green canvas quietly gathering dust and cobwebs, are two hundred grand's

worth of paintings. Possibly under an old church. Les slipped the chops onto
the griller as the front door opened and Warren walked into the kitchen
wearing a white-on-white shirt and a pair of black jeans.

'Woz,' said Les. 'How are you mate?'

'Rooted,' yawned Warren. 'I must have drunk enough margaritas last
night to fill a bathtub.'

'Good turn eh?'

'Too fuckin good,' Warren yawned again.

'Hey have a look at this,' said Les. 'I got a book on Rosa-Marie
Norton.'

'You did?'

Les showed Warren the book he got from the library and the printout
Clover had given him. Warren read the printout and started flicking
through the book.

'Christ!' he exclaimed. 'What about some of these paintings.'

'Yeah. She was a wild woman all right,' said Les. 'Wait till you read
her story.'

'I'm going for an Edgar. I'll flick through it before I have a shower.'

'Okay. You hungry?'

'Reckon. I had fuck-all for lunch.'

Warren went to the bathroom. Les set the table and got the dinner
together. Warren eventually walked back into the kitchen freshly shaven,
wearing his grey tracksuit. He put the book and printout on the table, got
a beer and smiled at Les.

'What a gal,' he said. 'I didn't read all of it. But didn't she like a root?'

'Yeah,' laughed Les. 'Rosa would have been in a shit sandwich if you
cut the crusts off.' He moved the book and started serving up the rice.
'You know, Warren, I've got a bit of a theory.'

'What? About Rosa-Marie Norton?'

'Yeah. I'll tell you about it while we're eating.'

While they were having dinner, Les referred to the book and the letter
and told Warren his theory about what happened to Rosa-Marie's paintings.
Warren hadn't read all the book and couldn't remember everything that was
in the letter. But he agreed Norton's theory did hold water.

'What about those artists that gave her a painting?' said Warren.
'Normo and the other bloke. Who were they?'

'Don't know,' answered Les. 'There's nothing in the book about them.
And that Yank, Jacques San, was just a pisshead she ate up and spat out.'

Warren picked up the book again. 'Look at that cover. Shit! She sure
had an eye for colour.'

'Yep,' agreed Les. 'She was a female van Gogh.'

When they'd finished eating, Warren made a pot of coffee and they had a cup each while the food went down.

'So what's doing tomorrow, Woz?' Les asked.

Warren shook his head. 'Don't ask. I have to be up at six. We're doing a shoot at Whale Beach in the morning.'

'Who for?'

'A rock band called Knife Edge.'

'Never heard of them,' shrugged Les.

'You're lucky,' said Warren. 'A greater bunch of no-talent, shit-for-brains adolescents with attitude I've yet to come across. I know what I'd like to shoot the pimply-faced cunts with. An AK-47.'

'Of course they won't look like that after you've finished with them,' said Les, sipping his coffee.

Warren looked Norton straight in the eye. 'Les. When you see this ad on TV, you'll think they're silverchair, the Rolling Stones and Oasis all rolled into one.'

'TV commercials,' said Les. 'The science of arresting human intelligence long enough to get money from it.'

'Right on, baby,' said Warren. 'And talking about TV. There's not a bad movie tonight on the ABC. The original *Thing From Outer Space*.'

'Shit! That old black and white clunker,' said Les. 'I remember my old man saying he saw that in Brisbane when he was a kid. And it scared the shit out of him.'

'That's understandable,' said Warren. 'If you get too frightened, you can sleep in my room.'

'Be a bit crowded in there with the three of us, wouldn't it, Woz?'

They washed up, then made a delicious each and took it into the lounge room. Warren produced his bong and packed a couple of cones, pulling them in with relish. He offered some to Les. Les shook his head and sipped his delicious. While they were waiting for the movie to start, Les turned and looked at the boarder.

'Hey Warren,' said Les.

'Hey yeah,' replied Warren.

'What do you think of this for an idea?'

Warren picked up his drink. 'Go on.'

'What if I was to go down to Lorne in Victoria. Take that old letter with me. Find Father Shipley. And tell him Rosa-Marie Norton was my mother. I'm the only son. I've come to collect my mother's paintings.'

Warren looked at Les and gave him a long, slow double blink. 'What did you just fuckin say?' he asked deliberately.

Les repeated what he'd just said. 'My name's Norton,' he added. 'I could show him a heap of ID. Plus I got my mother's letter ... Who's to say I'm not telling the truth? He'd probably be glad to get rid of the horrible bloody ... creations of the devil.'

After the two cones, Warren started laughing that hard he had a coughing fit. 'I don't fuckin believe you. That has to be the stupidest idea I've ever fuckin heard,' he spluttered. 'You're completely fucked.'

'Okay, sorry,' shrugged Les. 'It was just a thought.'

'Just a thought?' said Warren. 'And you've got the hide to bag me about making TV commercials. You fuckin moron. Get fucked!' Warren swallowed some of his drink. 'Jesus! What next?'

'All right,' said Les. 'Don't shit your pants. It was just an idea. I'm sorry I bloody asked.'

Suddenly Warren changed tack. 'No wait,' he said. 'I'm wrong. It's a good idea. Do it. Fly down to Melbourne. Hire a car and drive down to Lorne. I'll even see if I can work you a deal through the agency on a car. That's a terrific idea, Les. You're a genius.'

Les looked at Warren suspiciously. 'Yeah that'd be right. You only want to get me out of the house so you and Clover can play chasings up and down the hallway. You two-faced little cunt.'

'Shit Les. Whatever gave you that idea?'

'Yeah. I'm awake up to you. No, fuck you. I'm not going now. You can get fucked.'

'Gee! That's nice, isn't it,' said Warren.

'And just for that, I'll have some of your pot, too. Fuck you.'

Les pulled a couple of cones while Warren watched him out of the corner of his eye and laughed. Then they settled back to watch the movie.

Half stoned and half pissed, the old black-and-white clunker wasn't bad. Even for another 'America saves the world' saga. The dialogue was snappy, it had plenty of pace and the music did add a sense of menace. It wasn't scary. In fact when the thing showed up at the end, it reminded Les of the camp android in *Red Dwarf*. It finished and Warren stood up.

'Okay Les,' he said. 'I'm hitting the sack. I'll see you in the morning.'

'Not if you're getting up at six o'clock you won't,' yawned Les, switching off the TV. 'I'll probably see you before I go to work tomorrow night.'

'Whatever,' said Warren. 'Hey. I still reckon that's a good idea, going to Lorne to get those paintings. You should do it.'

'Yeah. Thanks Warren,' answered Les. 'I'll give it some more thought.'

Warren went to the bathroom, followed by Les, then they both went to bed. The booze and the cones had made Les tired and he always enjoyed an early night when he wasn't working. His head had hardly hit the pillow when he was snoring soundly.

Les slept in the next morning and got up around eight. Warren was long gone when Les walked into the kitchen and made some tea and toast. Outside it looked a little cloudy and the wind had come up. Les decided to brush the beach and have a run in Centennial Park. He got into his shorts, trainers and T-shirt, and drove up, parking outside the gates in York Road.

Not having to keep up with Billy, Les took his time jogging around the trees, nodding to the rangers and anybody else who cared to pass the time of day. While he was trotting along, Les figured Warren was right. It would be stupid going to Victoria looking for a batch of paintings that could be anywhere after all these years, and he deserved to be laughed, chaffed and poked shit at. It was a thought, though. Albeit a devious one. But Les was still curious about Rosa-Marie Norton. And if there was one person who'd know about Rosa-Marie Norton it would have to be Price. Les decided he'd bring the subject up when they had a drink after work, then casually produce the old letter from inside his jacket and see what sort of reaction he got. Les finished his run with a few sprints, did some crunches and drove home.

He didn't get cleaned up straightaway. Instead, he guzzled down a bottle of mineral water, put some old clothes and a pair of protective sunglasses on, and whipper-snipped the patch of lawn at the front of Chez Norton. When he'd finished there, he did Mrs Curtin's across the road and finished up doing Mrs Beaty's next door to her. They thanked Les and made him a 'nice cup of tea' then gave him GBH of the earhole about the cost of living and the local council. Before they could get too much of a roll on, Les said he had things to do, said goodbye then went inside and got cleaned up.

Les drank some more mineral water and changed back into his shorts and T-shirt. While he was having another glass of water Les had another quick look through the book. The author's Melbourne address was in the back. The Obelisk Bookshop, Brunswick Street, Fitzroy. Les decided he had to have a book for himself. He rang assistance, got the number and rang Melbourne.

'Good morning. Obelisk Bookshop,' came a man's voice on the other end.

'Yeah. Is Kenneth Raymond there please?' asked Les.

'Speaking.'

'I'd like to order a copy of your book, *The Mystic Mind of Rosa-Marie Norton.*'

'No worries. I have some in stock.'

'Okay. I'm ringing from Sydney. Can you send me one?'

'No worries. It'll be forty-five dollars with postage.'

'No worries,' smiled Les. He gave the author his name, address and credit card details.

'You say your name's Norton?' asked Raymond.

'Yeah. That's right,' said Les.

'No relation — surely?'

'No,' laughed Les. 'But I'm interested in her art. And her.'

'Yes. She was a fascinating woman all right,' said Raymond.

'She sure was,' agreed Les. 'How long before it will get here?'

'Oh. It should be there within a week.'

'Okey doke. Thanks a lot.'

'No worries.'

Yeah. No wuckin furries, Les smiled to himself. Good old Melbourne. Les got some money and left the house, locking the door behind him.

He went to the photo shop in Hall Street and xeroxed a copy of the letter, plus the envelope. Then Les went to the Hakoah Club and had a meal of matso ball soup, and veal schnitzel with creamed spinach and veg. Washed down with a coffee and a quick flutter on the keno in the Maccabi Bar. After losing a few dollars, Les walked home, full, contented and on top of the day. After putzing around the house sorting out his washing and a few things, it was time to iron a shirt, put on his black trousers and bomber jacket, have a cup of tea and get ready to be at work by seven-thirty. Warren wasn't home when he left. Les tucked the old letter inside his jacket, locked up and went out to his car. The traffic wasn't too bad and Les was parked in an office driveway down from the club and jogging up the club's stairs a little before seven-thirty. Billy was inside, dressed pretty much like Les, talking to Price and George. Price was wearing a single-breasted, cream suit with a yellow silk tie, George was in a blue yachting jacket, grey trousers and a regimental striped tie. Around them the staff were preparing for another night of gambling. Everybody said hello to Les. Les said hello back then stopped to take in the new two-tone blue carpet and the distinct smell of freshness in the air.

'Very nice, Price,' said Les. He pointed to the ceiling. 'You've even shouted the club a new chandelier.'

Price made a magnanimous gesture. 'You know me, big fellah. Money's no object when it comes to providing the best for my customers.'

Les nodded. 'Yes. It's doubtful Saddam Hussein would have spent as much on one of his palaces in Baghdad. Do you and Saddam have the same insurance company, Price?'

'No. Just the same accountant,' replied Price.

Les smiled. 'Hey. There's something I want to see you about after work, too.'

'Good. Because I want to see you about something myself. Has Eddie rung you at all?'

'No.'

'Doesn't matter. He'll be here later.'

Norton's antenna went up and started turning. 'You want to see me? Eddie was going to ring me? What's going on?'

'Nothing. You'll find out after work,' said Price.

'Okay.' Les turned to George. 'I like the yachting jacket, commodore. All you need is a monogrammed pocket and you'd look like a poker machine supervisor at the Double Bay Yacht Club.'

'All you need with that nose of yours is a white glove and you'd look like Michael Jackson,' replied George.

Les gave them all an indignant once up and down. 'Well I didn't come in here to be insulted by riff raff. I'm going down to the foyer where it's more suited to a man of my congeniality and bearing.'

'Yeah. Ball bearings,' said George.

Les turned and walked down to the foyer, pleased he'd managed to get a rise out of George so early in the night. Although Les had to admit, George didn't tap dance too bad and often gave as good as he got. Straightaway, a team of Hungarian Jews, very astute German whist players, came up that Les recognised. There were smiles and high-pitched Hungarian greetings all round as Les welcomed them inside, then they walked up the stairs just as Billy came down.

'So how was the trip to the dentist?' asked Les.

The boys had been going to a Vietnamese dentist at Double Bay named Jim Ho, who they called Uncle Ho. He was a fantastic dentist. An artist. And with a great sense of humour.

'How was it?' said Billy. 'An hour of misery and pain. And then you have to pay for the privilege. But check this crown.' Billy showed Les his new tooth in the front. It looked better than the original.

'Jees, he does a bloody good job,' agreed Les.

'Yeah. His wife just had a baby so he shouted me another shot of novocaine. I didn't feel a thing to be honest. Until I got the fuckin bill.'

Les had a stretch. 'So what's going on with Eddie and Price? You heard anything?'

Billy shook his head. 'No. Nothing.'

'Oh well,' said Les. 'I'll find out soon enough, I suppose.'

As usual the night went smooth as silk. The punters soon arrived to get in as much card-playing as possible before the club closed at twelve-thirty. Price only had a midnight licence, which suited everybody. But in that short space of time, hundreds of thousands, even millions of dollars changed hands on credit. The only drama was the usual hassle with young techno-heads coming up full of Ebeneezer thinking the Kelly Club was an exclusive disco. They'd all be dressed beautifully in expensive clothes, wearing the best cologne, their hair gelled up in the latest style, and Billy would tell them they couldn't come in because they didn't look cool enough and their clothes were so five minutes ago. Another of his put-downs was to tell them Kylie and Russell were inside with Nicole and Jodie. And if they saw people like them in the club they'd never come back. The ravers would leave absolutely shattered, wondering just how exclusive can one nightclub be? An hour before closing Eddie arrived wearing a black leather jacket, a char-grey polo shirt and black jeans.

'Hello ladies,' he said breezily as he stepped into the foyer. 'Sorry I couldn't make it on Wednesday. What's doing, anyway?'

'Not much, Eddie,' replied Billy. 'What's doing with you?'

'The same,' shrugged Eddie. He caught Norton's eye and smiled. 'Sort of.'

'I believe Price wants to see me after work,' said Les. 'Your name was mentioned too, Edward.'

'Yeah?' replied Eddie. He feinted a left hook to the big Queenslander's chin. 'We'll talk about it when we knock off.'

Eddie disappeared up the stairs and Les left it at that. A few more members arrived for a late flutter and before Les knew it they had the club emptied, the staff had gone home, the front door was locked and they were sitting in Price's office talking easily about this and that. Les was drinking Fourex, the others were drinking beer, scotch and vodka while Eddie was sipping a bottle of Pellegrino. They were talking about one of the Hungarians winning almost a hundred thousand and a likeable, retired Italian baker winning fifty thousand, when the conversation dwindled off. Les had a mouthful of Fourex, eased back in his seat and looked at Price.

'Okay, Price me old mate,' said Les. 'Let's get down to business. What did you want to see me about?'

Price took a sip of Glenfiddich and soda, then placed the glass on a coaster on his office table. 'Do you know a bloke called Latte Lindsey?'

'Latte Lindsey?' Les had to think for a moment. 'Yeah. I think I do,' he nodded. 'Tall, sort of sallow-faced dork, around thirty, with an egg-shaped head. Got a real slimy smile. Poses as an art dealer or something.'

'That's him,' said Price. 'Oily as a kerosene lamp.'

'Isn't he the bloke used to go training with Killer and the boys down at City Tatts? And they caught him nicking their dough out of the locker room.' Les turned to George. 'Your nephew Kevin marked all the money and he got sprung when they were having a shout.'

'You got him,' nodded George. 'He bolted out of the joint, otherwise they would have kicked the shit out of him.'

'Bad luck they didn't,' said Billy.

'How did he get the nickname Latte Lindsey?' asked Les.

'His parents are Poms, and he grew up in Pyrmont,' said Eddie. 'But he likes to swan around the coffee shops in Double Bay sucking down lattes. Always with his little finger sticking out.'

'Yeah, I know him,' said Les. 'I said hello to him one day up Bondi Junction, and he looked straight through me. Guess I was beneath his standing.'

'That's Latte,' nodded Eddie. 'The fuckin poser.'

'So what's Latte done to incur your wrath, Price?' asked Les.

'What's he done?' scowled Price. 'He sold my sister-in-law Kitty a painting for twenty-five grand that turned out to be a dud. It's worth about two fuckin mintie wrappers.'

'Nice,' said Les.

'I won't go into it,' said Price. 'But I want him shortened up.'

'And you want me and Eddie to do the shortening?' said Les.

'That's right,' said Price. 'There'll be a drink in it for you.'

'Shit! You're not gonna kill him, are you?' said Les. 'Honestly. I'm not into murder right now. And killing him won't get Kitty her twenty-five grand back.'

'No,' said Eddie. 'Not murder. Just a severe shortening up.'

'I don't expect to get Kitty's money back,' said Price. 'But Latte wears a twenty-five thousand dollar Bvlgari watch, and a twenty thousand dollar diamond pinky ring he snookered off a dope dealer who's in the can. I'll settle for that.'

Les thought for a moment. 'So what did you have in mind?'

'Latte's train's run out of track up here,' said Eddie, 'and he's living in Melbourne. I'm not sure where. But I know where he's putting his slimy head into an art sale down there this Saturday night.'

Les sipped his beer. 'Go on.'

'So I thought you and I might fly down to Melbourne on the weekend,' said Eddie. 'Discuss the finer details of Rembrandt and Picasso with Latte. Then fly straight home again.'

This was entirely unexpected and Norton's mind went into overdrive. But he had to be cool. Very cool.

'Shit I don't know,' he said, shaking his head reluctantly. 'I'm not all that keen. Things are going good up here at the moment. And I can't say I'm over-rapt in Melbourne.'

'Christ! It's only for a couple of nights,' said Price. 'You go down tomorrow. Eddie'll meet you on Saturday. You sort Shithead out and fly back Saturday night. And a nice drink for your trouble.'

'I can get someone else,' said Eddie. 'But I'd rather have you.'

'You fly down business class,' said Price. 'I'll put you up in a top hotel.'

'And you can go shopping in Melbourne,' said George. 'Think of all the grouse clothes you can buy. You won't have to get around looking like a grave robber anymore.'

'Shit! I'll go if you don't want to,' said Billy. 'There's a good night scene in Melbourne. It shits on Sydney.'

Les shook his head and looked at the floor. 'All right,' he finally nodded. 'I'll go. But on one condition.'

'What's that?' said Price.

'Arrange a rental car and book me into a pub at Lorne till Friday.'

'Lorne? What's the big attraction in Lorne?' asked Price.

'Nothing really,' shrugged Les. 'But I've always wanted to see the Great Ocean Road. And I've heard Lorne's a nice spot.'

Price shrugged and looked around the office. 'Done,' he said. 'George. Sort that out with Gary.'

'I'll ring Travelabout first thing tomorrow,' said George.

'I imagine,' drawled Les, 'you've already taken my answer for granted.'

Eddie grinned and handed Les an airline ticket from inside his leather jacket. 'I knew you wouldn't let me down. You're on the twelve-thirty flight with Qantas tomorrow. You're booked into the Southville in Collins Street. A limo'll pick you up at the airport. I'll be there Saturday afternoon around five. Call in to Gary's and pick up the other bookings on your way to the airport tomorrow.'

Price smiled and pushed two thousand dollars across his desk to Les.

'And that should keep you in sandwiches and flavoured milk till you get back.'

Les picked up the money and the airline ticket and pocketed them inside his jacket, next to the old letter. 'Okay,' he shrugged. 'Like they say in Melbourne, no worries.'

'The limo driver's name's Perry,' said Eddie. 'He's a mate of mine. He'll be coming with us on Saturday night. I'll explain everything when I see you down there.' Eddie smiled and wiggled his eyebrows. 'You'll like it.'

'It couldn't be any worse than nearly getting eaten by fuckin sharks,' replied Les.

'Okay,' beamed Price, rubbing his hands together. 'That's settled.' He picked up his drink and turned to Les. 'Now, Les. What was it you wanted to see me about?'

Les looked at Price. 'See you about? Oh, yes. I was thinking about getting my place re-carpeted. And I was wondering who you used here? They did a terrific job.'

Price turned to George. 'George. You know who they are.'

'Achmet's Flying Carpet Service,' said George. 'I've got their card here somewhere.'

'Unreal,' said Norton. 'Thanks, George.'

They had one or two more drinks, then locked up the club and went their separate ways. Eddie told Les he'd see him in Melbourne. Les told the others he'd see them when he got back from Victoria, and drove home.

Shortly after, Les was sitting in the kitchen at Chez Norton sipping on a mug of Ovaltine. The old letter was on the table in front of him next to the airline ticket and the two thousand dollars. Well, if that's not divine intervention, he asked himself, what is? That nutty idea I had earlier has just fallen into my lap, thanks to you-know-who. And even if it is nutty, what have I got to lose? Six days living it up in Victoria, courtesy of Price. Les smiled and raised his mug. To divine intervention — and Price Galese of course.

Les finished his Ovaltine, got changed and went to bed. As he buried his head into the pillows, he briefly pondered what clothes he should take.

Knowing Victoria, plenty of warm ones. Les gave a final yawn and before long he was snoring peacefully.

Friday was mild and clear when Les got out of bed around eight. He changed into a pair of shorts and a T-shirt, cleaned up and walked into the kitchen. Warren was seated in a pair of jeans and a red and brown striped shirt, finishing a cup of coffee before he left for work.

'G'day Woz,' said Les. 'How's things?'

'Great,' replied Warren. 'I'm even starting to believe there is a God after all.'

'Oh?' replied Les. 'How's that?'

'Knife Edge's bass player got electrocuted in Melbourne last night.'

'Electrocuted? Shit! Is he dead?'

'Unfortunately no. But they say he's got a wonderful glow about him.'

'You're a bloody sadist.' Les checked the plunger. The coffee was still warm so he poured himself a cup. 'Anyway, talking about Melbourne, Woz. Can I borrow that suitcase of yours with the wheels on it?'

'Sure. It's under my bed. I'll get it for you.' Warren looked at Les. 'What's that got to do with Melbourne?'

'Woz, I'm taking your advice. I'm flying to Melbourne. Renting a car. And I'm driving down to Lorne to find those paintings.'

'You're what?'

Les took a sip of coffee and a faraway look appeared in his eyes. 'Warren. I firmly believe that letter was more than just a letter. It was a message. A message from beyond. You say you're starting to believe in God, Warren. Well, glory be. So am I. And God has spoken. Telling me to seek the path to Lorne, and find those paintings.' Les stared fervently at Warren. 'Woz. There's a spiritual connection between me, Rosa-Marie Norton and those paintings. They were meant for me. And through the power of the Lord, and divine guidance, I'm going to take back what's mine. Warren, I'm on a mission from God. Oh glory hallelujah!'

Warren stared at Les in disbelief. 'You've gone mad, you fuckin ratbag.'

Les shook his head sincerely. 'Nay Warren. Not mad. Just guided by unseen forces. Mysterious forces, Warren, that you and I know nothing about. Praise the Lord.'

'Jesus Christ!' exclaimed Warren.

'Him too.' Les took another sip of coffee. 'Anyway, what are you blowing up about, you little prick? I won't be back till Friday. That gives you and Clover a week to run around the house dressed up as Adolf Hitler and Eva Braun. And whatever else you get up to when I'm not here.'

'I'll get the suitcase.' Warren went to his room and came back carrying a black suitcase with rollers and a folding handle and put it in the kitchen. 'There you are, Frodo. That should help you on your quest. Do you want something to bring the paintings back in too, young hobbit?'

'No, great wizard Gandalf. I'll manage, thank you,' replied Les.

Warren glanced at his watch. 'Well, I have to get to the pickle factory.' He looked suspiciously at Norton. 'You are going to Melbourne, aren't you? This isn't just a gee-up?'

'Fuckin oath I am, sinner. Rosa-Marie's calling out from heaven.'

'Heaven? She was a fuckin devil-worshipper.'

'Makes no difference to me. I'm on a mission from God.'

Warren shook his head. 'I'll see you when you get back.'

'See you then, Woz.'

The door closed, Les opened the fridge and organised two toasted ham and tomato sandwiches. He ate them with another cup of coffee, then took Warren's suitcase into his room, put it on the bed and started filling it with whatever he thought he'd need for the trip, including his mini-ghetto blaster. Halfway through packing, Les thought of something and looked at his watch. He walked out to the lounge room, found the number still sitting next to the phone and dialled Melbourne.

'Hello, Obelisk Bookshop. Kenneth Raymond speaking.'

'Yeah. It's Les Norton in Sydney. I ordered that book off you about Rosa-Marie Norton.'

'Oh yes, Mr Norton. I remember.'

'Don't bother sending it. I'm coming down to Melbourne on business. I'll pick it up.'

'Oh all right, Mr Norton.'

'I might even call in this afternoon.'

'No worries.'

'Exactly.' Les hung up and went back to his bedroom.

Norton finished packing, had a quick shower then changed into a pair of jeans, a denim shirt and his blue cotton bomber jacket. He checked to make sure he had his travel documents and everything else, put them in his overnight bag and rang a taxi. It didn't take long to arrive. Les had a last look around the house then locked up, took his luggage out to the taxi and gave the driver directions how to get to Travelabout in Clovelly and to wait outside. Gary was seated at his desk opposite the two girls in their red uniforms, looking his dapper self in a maroon shirt and a blue silk tie. He smiled his usual warm smile when Les walked in and sat down.

'So what have you got for me, Gary?' asked Les.

'Mate. For about an hour's notice I've got you the grouse. I've booked you into the Otway Plaza Resort in Lorne. Your own modern apartment just across from the beach. The Erskine Hotel's on the opposite corner.'

'Sounds all right,' said Les.

'And you pick up a Mitsubishi Magna from Thrifty at twelve o'clock on Sunday. You know where you're staying and all that?'

'Yeah. Eddie gave me my ticket last night. You wouldn't have a map showing how to get to Lorne, would you?'

'Sure have.' Gary handed Les two brochures and a folder. 'There you go. Everything you need's in there.'

Les took the folder and stood up. 'Thanks Gary.'

'Have a lovely time in Victoria, Les,' smiled Gary. 'The garden state.'

'No worries.' Les walked back to the taxi and they drove on to Kingsford Smith Airport.

There were no dramas checking in. Les bought the *Telegraph* and next thing he was in the Qantas Club, seated on a comfortable lounge chair, reading the paper, checking out the punters and stuffing himself with tea, sandwiches and little pieces of cake. Eventually, it was time to board QF 283 for Melbourne. Les grabbed a lolly on the way out and next thing he was sitting in business class sipping a mineral water.

By the time Les finished his mineral water the plane was airborne and a flight attendant handed him a menu. Les was that full of sandwiches and cake he didn't bother to look at it. Instead he went through the two maps Gary had given him. Lorne wasn't far from Melbourne. Through Geelong and follow the road past Torquay. Apollo Bay was a little further on. Fitzroy wasn't far from his hotel in Melbourne. He had plenty of time to pick up his book after he checked in. Les put his maps away, asked the attendant for another mineral water and took out the book he was reading. *Hell's Angel: The Life and Times of Sonny Barger and the Hell's Angels Motorcycle Club*. By the time the plane was getting ready to land, Les was convinced Sonny and his Hell's Angels were just a fun-loving bunch of lads who liked to take dope, sell dope, bash, stab and kill people and root sheilas and have barbecues. The only time Sonny ever got mildly upset was when somebody from another club stole his motorbike. So Sonny and his friends went over to the other club, bull-whipped each member one at a time, bashed them with spiked dog collars and broke their fingers with ballpeen hammers. Then stole their bikes, sold them and disbanded their club. The Angels even had a member called Norton Bob. How good was that? Les put his book away, got off the plane and walked to the baggage collection. Well, here I am in Melbourne, he thought, as he passed an advertisement for Four'N Twenty Pies.

At the bottom of the stairs were several limo drivers in black suits and caps holding signs, with one saying NORTON. The driver was in his forties and not as tall as Les, but very stocky, with a hard face and eyes like onyx ball bearings. His suit was immaculately cut and he was wearing three hundred dollar Mellers shoes.

'Are you Perry?' said Les.

'Yeah. You must be Les.' The limo driver offered a quick smile and shook Norton's hand. 'Let's get your luggage.'

They followed the other passengers around to the carousel. When they got there, Norton's bag was already on the conveyor behind several others.

Les went to pick it up when Perry took it easily and nodded for Les to follow him. They stepped through the sliding glass doors then turned left towards a car park. It was cloudy outside, but Les was surprised at the heat; much warmer than Sydney and punishingly humid. When they came to the shiny black BMW limousine, Les had a sweat up, however Perry still looked cool when he placed Norton's suitcase in the boot. He opened the back door and Les climbed into the beemer's air-conditioned comfort.

Les peered out the window as they drove along a flat stretch of open road and under a circled green and yellow sign saying CITY 43. Further on a sign to the left said BULLA RD and a blue sign said CITY SOUTH-EASTERN SUBURBS. Perry hardly spoke, but every now and again his mobile would ring. He'd listen, then whisper a few taciturn words. Watching in the rear-vision mirror, Les noticed the onyx ball bearings rarely moved more than a centimetre. They passed a long yellow girder jutting out over the road on the left, and on the right what looked like the bones of a gutted whale painted red. Les wasn't sure if it was modern art or something that had fallen off a Jumbo jet.

'Eddie tells me you'll be coming with us on Saturday night,' said Les.

Perry nodded. 'Yeah. I'll be doing the driving.' Then his phone rang again.

Further on it was houses and trams and Les noticed a long park on the left. 'Is that Albert Park?' he asked.

Perry shook his head. 'No, Royal Park. That's where the nuthouse is.'

'Right,' nodded Les.

Further on Les saw what looked like a bunch of hippies hanging around the front of a black and silver coffee shop. Perry said the university was just up the road. He pointed out an old cream and brown building as Melbourne Baths, then they were right in the centre of the CBD with its traffic and pedestrians. Perry swung into Collins Street and pulled up on the left outside a small lobby with a blue sign above saying SOUTHVILLE HOTEL.

'Here you are,' he said.

'Thanks.'

Les got out of the car. Perry opened the boot and took out his suitcase.

'I'll see you on Saturday night, Les,' he said.

'Yeah. See you then, Perry.'

The limo drove off and a porter in a blue vest took Norton's bag and details. Les perused Melbourne's hustle and bustle for a moment, then followed the attendant into a small lobby with two lifts. Les took the lift to reception and stepped out facing the windows to a bar and restaurant; reception was down to the left. Les walked up and put his folder on the desk. A polite young lady in blue got him to sign in, gave Les his swipe card and told him his bag would be up shortly. Les walked to another two lifts a little further on the left and noticed the hotel was built around several storeys of shopping arcade. The light pinged, Les took the lift to the twelfth floor and stepped out, almost running into a blonde woman in a yellow skirt and jacket, who seemed to be lost. She looked left then turned right; Les checked the room numbers arrowed on the wall and started following her.

The way to his room seemed to go on forever, and a metre or so in front of him, Les could sense the woman in yellow getting nervous. They went left, then right, left again, took another right then followed a long, quiet, deserted corridor. Norton's room was at the very end, the woman's was next door. Les passed her and swiped his lock while the woman fumbled with hers.

'I didn't mean to frighten you,' smiled Les. 'But this is my room.'

'Oh ... that's all right,' said the woman, still trying to swipe her lock. 'I wasn't all that worried.'

Les caught her eye. She was around thirty, with a soft face, a thin nose, pouty red lips and green mascaraed eyes. 'Well, you're a better woman than I am, Gunga Din,' said Les. 'Because if I had a big ugly gorilla like me stalking me down a corridor, and no one around, I'd be absolutely shitting myself.'

The woman returned Norton's smile then gave him a quick once up and down before he stepped into his room.

Norton's softly lit room was quite nice. Blue carpet pushed against white walls and on the left a white bathroom faced a wardrobe with full-length mirrors. There was a bench table and TV opposite a queen-size bed with a blue douvet, and at the far end, a set of blue curtains were drawn across a window looking down on the arcade. Les tossed his overnight bag on the bed, got a mineral water from the bar fridge and checked out the in-house dining menu. He was thinking the beef tenderloin with Bernaise sauce didn't sound too bad, when there was a knock on the door and his suitcase arrived. The porter placed it on a rack next to the wardrobe, Les thanked him, gave him two bucks and he left.

Les decided to have a beer while he unpacked. He took off his bomber jacket, got a can of VB from the bar fridge and was sipping it as he started hanging a few things up when there was another knock on the door. It was the woman he'd followed down the corridor. She still had her yellow skirt on, but she'd taken her jacket off and was wearing a thin, lacy white top, unbuttoned enough to show a nice pair of boobs tucked into a thin, lacy white bra.

'Hello,' said Les. 'Is there something I can do for you?'

'Yes,' replied the woman. 'I can't seem to get my suitcase open. Could you please help me?'

'Sure.'

Les took his swipe card and followed the woman into her room. It was identical to Norton's except for a red carpet and a red douvet. Sitting on her bed was a brown suitcase the same size as his.

'What's your name?' asked the woman.

'Sonny,' replied Les.

'I'm Sonia.'

'Nice to meet you, Sonia.' Les ran his hand over the suitcase. 'Where's the key?' he asked.

'Here you are.'

Sonia handed Les a small key. Les clicked open the locks then ran the zipper around the sides and opened the suitcase. All Sonia's clothes were packed neatly inside, and sitting on top was a huge pink vibrator shaped like a cock, with two stubby balls at one end under a black plug for the batteries.

'Hello,' said Les. 'What's this for? Protection? Shit, I'd hate to get hit over the head with it.'

'No,' smiled Sonia, turning to Les. 'It's for enjoyment. And I know where I like to get hit with it.'

'Oh? And just where's that?' asked Les.

'Right about here.'

Sonia lifted up her skirt to reveal she was wearing no knickers. Just a neatly trimmed ted like a tiny brown pine cone. Les gave it a double, triple blink and shook his head.

'I don't quite know what to say, Sonia,' he smiled. 'But from where I'm standing, that looks good enough to eat.'

'Well what's stopping you, Sonny?' Sonia smiled back. 'You're not on a Jenny Craig diet, are you?'

'Are you kidding?' answered Les. 'I'd give Henry the Eighth a run for his money.'

Les pushed Sonia's suitcase off the bed, eased her back down on the douvet then buried his face in her business and went for it like a Rottweiler eating topside mince.

Sonia howled and shook and grabbed Les by the hair, pushing his face in harder. Les licked and sucked and it wasn't long before Sonia's gargling had turned Les on and Mr Wobbly wanted in on the action. Sonia spread her legs as wide as she could without dislocating her pelvis while Les undid his belt. Suddenly Sonia gave a squeal of rapture and emptied out into Norton's face. Les came up for air, and before Sonia knew it Les had his fly undone and Mr Wobbly in her mouth. Sonia didn't mind one bit and sucked Mr Wobbly hard enough to drain the marrow out of Norton's bones. Sweat running down his face, Les slipped a pillow under Sonia's behind then slipped Mr Wobbly in and started going for it. He figured Sonia had got her rocks off quick enough and now it was his turn. He gave a succession of solid thrusts, then stiffened his legs and emptied out in a panting, snorting blaze of glory. Sonia yelled some more, shook a few times then lay back on the douvet in a mess of damp hair and crumpled clothes. Well that was okay, thought Les, getting his breath back. Now, let's see how this thing works.

Les reached down and got Sonia's vibrator from her suitcase. A twist of the black plug at the end and it started pulsating smoothly in Norton's hand. Les slipped it in between Sonia's legs and started running it over her clit. Sonia closed her eyes and settled back against the pillows. Les zapped away for a while then slid the monster vibrator inside her. Sonia gave a little squeal of joy and Les started pumping away.

Sonia's eyes began to flutter, her tongue lolled over her lips and her face twisted into a look of excruciating ecstasy. Les pumped the vibrator with great gusto before Sonia finally let go a scream loud enough to wake the dead and got her rocks off again. Les dropped the vibrator back in her suitcase, wiped Mr Wobbly on her skirt before tucking him back into his jeans then stood up, leaving Sonia lying on the bed looking like she'd been washed up on a beach.

'Well, Sonia,' he said, zipping up. 'I might go back to my room and finish unpacking. If that's all right with you.'

'Unnhhh, ghhh. Okay.'

'If you have any more problems with your suitcase, or anything else, you know where to find me. Just knock.'

'All right Sonny,' muttered Sonia, without opening her eyes.

'Goodbye Sonia.' Les bent down and gave her a kiss goodbye.

'Bye Sonny.'

Les left her and let himself out.

Back in his air-conditioned room, the unfinished can of VB was still reasonably cold. Les downed it in one go and opened another. He had a mouthful, belched, then walked into the bathroom and splashed some water on his face before staring at himself in the mirror. What did Clover say after we read that old letter? She felt a sense of deja vu. The last time I was in Melbourne I wasn't in my room five minutes and that motel owner — Mrs Bloody Perry — threw me up in the air. And if I remember right, she wasn't wearing any fuckin knickers either. Les shook his head. Buggered if I know. He finished his beer, stripped off and got under the shower.

After he towelled off, Les put on a pair of blue cargoes, a Blues Festival T-shirt and his trainers. He stuck his Bugs Bunny cap on, dangled his sunglasses from off the neck of his T-shirt, then tossed his camera into his overnight bag and took the lift to reception and the other lift to the lobby. Outside it was still oppressively hot. Les was going to catch a taxi but decided on a tram. He turned to a porter standing just outside the lobby.

'Hey mate! How do I get a tram to Brunswick Street, Fitzroy?'

The porter pointed to a tram stop in the middle of the road. 'Over there. Take the 112. I think there's one coming now.'

'Thanks mate.'

Les jogged across the road as the tram pulled up and climbed aboard a side door. The tram lurched off as he grabbed for a strap only to land against a ticket machine dotted with coloured numbers and directions. After he regained his balance, Les looked blankly at the machine before pushing two dollars in a slot and pressing a button marked Section Two.

He took his ticket and while he was strap hanging, watched the people fanning themselves with newspapers. That's another bloody thing, thought Les, the last time I was in Melbourne, it was bloody hot like this too. The tram swayed up Collins Street, angled around further on, then swung left into a wide thoroughfare flanked with side streets.

The busy road was full of brightly coloured clothing shops, record stores, coffee lounges, restaurants, bars and whatever. On one corner stood a drab-looking hotel and Les noticed a bar with flames on the window called The Bar With No Name. The street had an old-world charm about it and reminded Les of King Street, Newtown and Oxford Street, Paddington. He watched the numbers on the shop fronts, then alighted near a record store. The Obelisk Bookshop was back a little from a side street on the left, between a clothes store and a bottle shop. It had a blue-tiled front, purple doors and a white awning, and on either side of the front door were two large windows piled with books. A sign in one window said THE OBELISK BOOKSHOP. In the other, SECOND-HAND, OLD & RARE BOOKS. Les had a quick look at some of the titles and stepped inside.

The bookshop was deceptively big, with blue carpet, wood-panelled walls and high ceilings. Around the walls were rows and rows of ancient hardbacks and in the middle were tables full of books, surrounded by glass cabinets crammed with more old hardbacks. A doorway down to the left opened into another room and there was another room behind that. Just inside the door on the left was the counter and on the wall behind hung a framed print by Rosa-Marie Norton. Seated at a computer in a corner was a portly man with a young face and untidy dark hair. He was wearing a maroon shirt over a red T-shirt and as Les approached the counter, he looked up and smiled.

'Yes. Can I help you?'

'Are you Kenneth Raymond?' asked Les.

'That's me,' replied the owner.

'My name's Les Norton. I rang you from Sydney.'

'Oh yes. About the book on Rosa-Marie Norton. I have it right here.'

'Good on you,' said Les.

As the owner rummaged under the counter for the book, Les noticed a rack of Rosa-Marie Norton postcards. He picked out four and placed them on the counter.

'There you are,' said the owner, placing Norton's book on the counter.

'Unreal,' said Les, having a quick look. 'I'll take these postcards too.'

'No worries.'

'I'm Les anyway,' said Les, offering his hand.

The owner shook Norton's hand. 'Ken.'

'Nice to meet you, Ken.' Les watched as the owner put the postcards and book in a plastic bag. 'So you're an expert on Rosa-Marie, Ken.'

'Not really an expert,' replied the owner. 'But I've always admired her art. And I've almost finished a longer, more detailed biography on her.'

'Fair dinkum?' said Les. 'I enjoyed the book you've already done. Actually I borrowed it from a library. And I had to get one for myself.'

'Thanks. Though it really doesn't do her justice,' said Ken.

'Oh, I don't know,' said Les lightly. 'But she certainly was something else.'

'Yes,' agreed Ken. 'She certainly was. So how did you find yourself interested in Rosa-Marie?'

'Through the name at first,' smiled Les. 'Plus I work in Kings Cross and I've read a few articles about her. I've never seen any of her paintings though.'

'No. Most of them are in private collections,' said Ken.

Les handed the owner his Visa card. 'Ken. Do you mind if I ask you a few questions?'

'No. Not at all.'

'Rosa-Marie sold some paintings to a bishop. Is that right?'

'Yes. Bishop Thomas Elsworthy of Prahran. He bought them to show his parishioners exactly what the devil's work was all about. Then he threw them in the Yarra.'

'Was there ever any mention of a priest? Father Bernard Shipley? From Lorne?'

Ken shook his head. 'Not that I know of.'

'Okay,' said Les. 'Ken. You know when they were going to burn her paintings that time?'

'Yes. I certainly do.'

'I read where three of them went missing.'

Ken looked surprised. 'If they did, it's news to me. Where did you read that, Les?'

'Oh, just an article in a little paper up the Cross,' replied Les.

Ken shook his head. 'I doubt it. But if it is true, you'd never know. The police and the authorities at the time would never admit it.'

'Yeah, right,' nodded Les. 'Shit! She had some dramas with the police, didn't she? Especially a Detective McBride. Why was that?'

'Mainly because Rosa was considered a threat to the conservative establishment at the time,' said Ken. 'But McBride was high up in the vice squad and just hated Rosa and all her friends. He came to her house one morning with a warrant and Rosa was upstairs in the bathroom. She looked out to see who it was, and emptied a chamber pot over him.'

'She what?' said Les. 'Emptied a piss pot over him?'

'That's right. And when they charged her with assault police, she beat it. She said she was about to flush the contents. And when she looked out the window to see who it was downstairs, the po accidentally slipped on the sill.'

'She sounds like my kind of woman,' chuckled Les.

'She was something else all right,' said Ken. 'There was an American artist called Jacques San,' he continued.

'Yeah. Who was he?' asked Les.

'No one knew for sure,' said Ken. 'He wasn't in Australia long and claimed he was from New York. But he was an awful drunk and totally in love with Rosa-Marie. He grabbed a carving knife at one of her wild parties one night and threatened Rosa with it, yelling he was Jacques the Ripper.'

'Jacques the Ripper?' said Les.

'Rosa hit him over the head with a bottle,' laughed Ken. 'Took the knife off him and said, "No you're not. You're Jacques the Dribbler. Now fuck off." And he did. Back to America with all his paintings. Broken-hearted.'

'Fair dinkum? You said in your book, though, she had a way with men,' said Les.

'They absolutely fell at her feet, Les,' replied Ken.

'Would you know who two artists were, Ken, called Normo and Dobbo?' asked Les.

Ken thought for a moment. 'Can't say I do,' he replied. 'There was a coffee shop in Kings Cross called The Dobruja, that hung some of Rosa's paintings. Rosa and her friends used to call it "Dob's" for short. But I don't know of any artists by that name. Though Rosa would have known scores of artists that just came and went.'

'And she never mentioned a Father Shipley?'

'No. Not to my knowledge.'

'She had an exhibition in Melbourne, too,' said Les.

'Yes,' said Ken. 'It was an absolute disaster. Christ! She thought she had troubles in Sydney. They almost burnt her at the stake down here. She had the absolute audacity to show a woman's pubic hair in her paintings.'

'How disgraceful,' chided Les. 'And what happened when it folded?'

'Rosa just disappeared. Till she was arrested in Apollo Bay.'

'Yeah. For pissing in the street.'

'Actually, she collapsed and wet herself,' said Ken. 'But being who she was, they charged her with drunk and disorderly. There was a lot of rubbish written about her.'

'What was she doing in Apollo Bay?' asked Les.

'Probably staying with some old school friends and getting away from everything after what happened in Melbourne. She went to school in Apollo Bay where her father worked for a company laying telegraph cables. He was an engineer.'

'Right,' Les nodded slowly. 'And not long after that she fell out of a tram in Sydney and broke her neck.'

'Yes. Quite sad really,' replied Ken quietly.

'Yes it is,' agreed Les.

Les enjoyed talking to Kenneth Raymond. He was good-humoured and patently enthused in his world of old books and Rosa-Marie Norton. Plus he liked to share his knowledge with people. Especially any who were like-minded.

Ken turned to the painting hanging on the wall behind the counter. 'Poor Rosa. Apart from being a trifle eccentric, Les, she was just a brilliant artist. Years before her time.'

'A female van Gogh,' said Les.

'Yes. That's as good a description as any,' agreed Ken.

'And like van Gogh, she had trouble selling her paintings.'

'Yes. Ironic isn't it,' said Ken. 'And would you believe, Les, one of her paintings sold in Brisbane recently for one hundred and fifty thousand dollars.'

Les gave Ken a double blink. 'How … much did you say, Ken?'

'One hundred and fifty thousand dollars.'

There was a movement at the doorway and an elderly lady dressed in all white walked in. She looked at Les then turned to Ken standing behind the counter.

'Can I help you?' Ken asked her.

'I'm after a book of Beardsley prints,' the woman said.

Ken pointed to one corner in the shop. 'Have a look over there, under B. I'll be with you in a moment.'

'Thank you.'

Les watched the woman shuffle off then turned to the owner. 'Well, Ken,' he said. 'I'd better let you get back to work. Thanks for your help and everything.'

'No worries, Les. It was a pleasure,' smiled Ken. 'How long before you go back to Sydney?'

'Tomorrow,' replied Les.

'Call in again if you've got time. I'll be closing early tomorrow. We're having a soiree here tomorrow night.'

'A soiree?' said Les.

'Yes. Rare books and documents,' replied Ken. 'I've got one of Governor Phillip's diaries. Sketches by Banks the botanist. Some original Henry Lawson manuscripts. All that sort of thing. Very wine and cheese and a little social. But,' Ken shrugged and rubbed his hands together, 'it should turn a nice dollar.'

'Oh. Well good luck with it.' Les shook the owner's hand again. 'Nice to have met you, Ken. I'll see you again.'

'You, too, Les. Enjoy yourself in Melbourne.'

'I have so far.' Les put the plastic bag in his overnight bag and left Ken to attend to the woman in white.

There was a sudden screeching of brakes and the irritated beeping of a car horn as Les almost walked under a taxi crossing the street. He gave the cab driver a sheepish look and, still doing mental arithmetic, joined the other pedestrians walking along Brunswick Street. According to Norton's reckoning, 150,000 × 3 equalled 450,000. His nutty idea didn't sound so nutty after all. And that old bishop tossed two of her paintings in the river. One thing for sure, thought Les, when I get to Lorne, I'll find out what happened to those bloody paintings. Even if I've got to knock on every door in the joint.

Still plotting and scheming, Les walked on in the heat. Neatly dressed people were coming and going or seated in swish restaurants and coffee shops eating excellent cuisine while they sipped bottles of fine wine. Jewellery shops, music shops and clothes stores appeared to be doing good business and Les got another angle on Brunswick Street and its old-world charm. Double Bay with grunge. He stopped outside a trendoid clothing shop playing house music loud enough to give you internal bleeding and wiped the sweat from his eyes while he debated whether to take a couple of photos of Brunswick Street, when a tram suddenly clanged to a halt in front of him. There was a pool back at the hotel and more cold beers in the bar fridge. Les climbed aboard and when he was flung against the ticket machine after the tram took off, found another two dollars for his fare.

Back at the hotel Les changed into his Speedos and shorts and took the lift down to the swimming pool. The open-air pool area was at the end of another long stretch of corridors overlooking the arcade and Les had it all to himself. The pool was only small, but there was a sauna, and a weight station with mirrors stood on a floor of astro-turf. He left his towel on a banana-lounge and started pushing and lifting various pulleys, then did a set of crunches and sit-ups. When he finished, Les gulped down several plastic cups of water then flopped his sweaty body into the pool and just drifted.

Norton rolled on his back and spurted a mouthful of water into the air. Well, he thought, it's kind of hard to believe I'm in Melbourne. And it's harder to believe I've been tossed up in the air already. I wonder what Sonia's story is? But what a nice bloke that Ken Raymond was. Bad luck he couldn't lay any more informaish on me about those paintings. But at least now I've got my own book on Rosa-Marie Norton. Les closed his eyes, duck-dived to the bottom of the shallow pool and came up again. So what will I do now? I could go and check out the punters and the office girls. But I don't really feel like sitting in the heat and car fumes drinking coffee. And I don't feel like plonking my arse down in a smoky bar and getting half pissed either. It's not getting any earlier. Why don't I stay in my air-conditioned room, have a few cool ones, then order up some food and watch TV? Later on take a taxi or the 'bread and jam' back up to Brunswick Street and see what goes on there at night? I won't have a late one, though. I'd better be on the ball when Eddie arrives tomorrow. Les flopped around in the pool till a shy young Japanese couple joined him, followed by a pale, flabby businessman with a comb-over like several tufts of flattened roadkill sitting on his head. Norton smiled, let them have the pool and returned to his room.

After a shave and a shower, Les got back into his shorts and T-shirt, got a Crown Lager from the bar fridge and looked at the in-room dining menu. He went for a caesar salad, braised lamb shanks with veg and mash, sticky date pudding with butterscotch sauce and ice-cream plus coffee and rolls. Room service said that shouldn't be long. Les finished his first beer then had a bottle of Heineken and switched the TV on. By the time he'd finished his Heineken the food arrived. Les tipped the girl two bucks and ripped in.

There wasn't much on TV. Les checked the in-house movies and settled on *Monsters Inc*. For an animated movie, it was an absolute hoot and the take-outs at the end were an even bigger hoot. But the look on the little girl's face when the big monster frightened her, almost brought a tear to Norton's eye. Les got involved in the movie and by the time it finished, he'd knocked over another Heineken plus three mini-bottles of vodka and bourbon. He switched off the TV, pushed his dinner tray into the corridor then changed into a pair of Levis and the light blue T-shirt Grace had given him with a dark blue, short-sleeved hemp shirt over the top. He gave himself a last detail, got his camera and took the lifts down to the foyer. There was a taxi waiting out the front. Les piled in and before he knew the driver let him out in Brunswick Street, opposite the old hotel he'd noticed earlier.

The street had really come to life now. There were people everywhere and when Les walked into the large bar area of the hotel it was packed. He squeezed through the crowd, ordered a delicious and checked out the punters. They were all around thirty, casually dressed and what you'd expect to see in any popular hotel, anywhere in Australia. Two dumpy girls, one wearing a Union Jack T-shirt, the other a black vest and matching headband, commented on Norton's T-shirt. They were English tourists and pleasant to talk to. But it was just too hot and noisy in the hotel. Les bought them a drink and took their photo, then said he might catch up with them later and drifted off into the night.

After that Les roamed from bar to bar. They were all good, the people were friendly, plenty of attractive girls and the drinks were okay. There was no hassles about having to eat. You just walked in, had a delicious or three and walked out again. Billy was right when he said Melbourne had a good night scene.

Les lost count of how many bourbons he had roaming from bar to bar. But he was getting quite a glow up when he wandered into one that reminded him of Florida, and the old bordello they'd turned into a bar in Siestasota. Crystal chandeliers sparkled from under a red ceiling and gilt-edged mirrors and old paintings decorated the maroon walls. Antique furniture and plush velvet curtains added to the bar's elegance, and near the entrance was a beautiful fish tank surrounded by statues of Grecian women supporting urns filled with healthy indoor plants. Les got another delicious and noticed three people, two men and an older woman, sitting on a red velvet lounge under a frilly white lamp. One man, wearing a gold lamé suit and a pink shirt, had his face painted like a geisha and a pair of red horns on his head. The other man was wearing a multi-coloured kaftan and a snug, brightly feathered hat. His face was painted white also, except for a wide area across his eyes squared off in light blue and edged with red. The woman was wearing an emerald green crushed velvet dress adorned with layers of coloured beads. Les couldn't help himself. He walked straight up, said he was from Sydney and would they mind if he took their photo? They were only too delighted. Les snapped off two photos, thanked them, took a couple of the fish tank then finished his delicious and left.

Les ended up in The Bar With No Name. It was smaller and quieter than the others with comfortable old lounges and soft lights. Les got one more delicious and as it was going down, decided it was time to sling his hook. He told himself earlier he'd go easy. But Brunswick Street was such a good scene, what could he do? He finished his delicious and walked outside to get a taxi just as a tram pulled up. This'll do, thought Les, and climbed aboard, grabbing hold of a strap before he got speared into the ticket machine. While he fumbled around for a two-dollar coin, Les checked things out. There was only a handful of people seated up front. But sprawled at the rear were ten members of a pseudo-American street gang, dressed in baggy jeans, sloppy T-shirts, Snoopy Dog jackets, caps on back to front and gym boots. They were all around eighteen and full of attitude, and the only difference Les could tell from street gangs he'd seen in Sydney was this lot had pimplier faces and paler skin. A tall dark-haired one seated in front with his legs stuck out wearing baggy black jeans and a St Kilda FC cap, appeared to be the leader. A couple of the gang gave Les an indifferent once up and down, then ignored him. Les gave the gang a desultory once over and decided to ignore them as well. He fumbled around some more for a two-dollar coin, then didn't bother. If he got pinched for fare evasion, stiff shit.

The tram rattled and clanged on into the night, some people got off, then two stops later another street gang got on. They were dressed much the same as the gang already on the tram and they also appeared to have a tall dark-haired one as leader; only he was wearing baggy denim shorts and a Hawthorn FC cap. The two gang leaders made eye contact and from the 'giddy-up' it was obvious there was no love lost between the two gangs.

The leader of the first gang leapt to his feet. 'What the fuck are you doin' here?' he scowled.

'Fuck you cunt,' the leader of the second gang scowled back.

Les remembered Eddie once saying that when it came to hostilities and violence in Melbourne, they didn't muck around with Mexican stand-offs. The leader of the second gang aimed up a right-cross and punched the leader of the first gang straight in the mouth, splitting his lip. St Kilda cap cursed and immediately came back with a straight left, giving Hawthorn cap a bloody nose. Once the reception formalities were over, it was choose your partner and dance.

The two gangs ripped into each other at the back of the tram in a fury of punches, kicks, knees and elbows, with Norton hanging from a strap in the middle. They were all evenly matched and although they weren't inflicting any serious injuries, they were giving each other plenty of split lips, bloody noses, black eyes and ripped clothes. Hey, this is all right, thought Les, and whipped out his camera. He got off two photos when instinct made him turn around just as a member of the second gang threw a quick right and punched him in the jaw. It stung and Les didn't like it. In return, Les threw a wicked short right that was nothing like any of the other punches being thrown in the tram. It slammed into the kid's face, knocking out all his front teeth, before dumping him on his backside out cold. Half full of bourbon and livened up from the whack on the jaw, Les thought he might as well join in the festivities, too. He slung his camera round his neck, hung off the strap with one hand and started belting gang members from both sides with the other; they were all too busy fighting to see who was doing all the damage.

Les sunk a right into another kid, pulverising his bony jaw. The unfortunate gang member slid down the one he was fighting, who looked up, straight into another short right from Les that smashed the kid's nose across his face and dumped him out cold on the floor of the tram, along with the others. Two gang members were wrestling around in front of Les. Les sunk a short right into one's ribs and smiled as he felt them crack under his fist and heard a howl of pain from the hapless gang member. The kid slumped to the floor gasping for breath as Les changed hands on the strap and smashed a left hook into the other kid's face ripping apart his lips. Blood dribbling down his chin, the kid bounced off the gang members fighting behind him into another left from Norton that opened his right eyebrow to the bone. Les watched him fall to the floor then punched another gang member in the kidneys. The kid snapped to his feet, Les swapped hands on the strap again and decked him from behind with a right backfist, dislocating the kid's neck.

Les didn't feel like a hero thumping into the gang members. Quite the opposite if anything. They were all too busy fighting each other to know what was going on and he was bigger than any of them. But he and Billy had seen smartarse street gangs strutting around Bondi and Kings Cross causing trouble, and they always felt like sorting a few of them out. So although it mightn't have felt brave flattening one gang member after another, shit, it felt good.

Les swung around on the strap and sunk his right boot into one kid's balls then brought his knee up into his face, smashing his nose and knocking out several teeth. A spray of blood hit Norton and as the gang member hit the deck, his opponent looked up and saw who did it. Les poked his fingers in the kid's eyes, then kneed him in the balls. From side on Les left-hooked another gang member in the ear. Seeing stars, the kid wobbled and reached out with his left hand to hold onto a seat. Les grabbed the gang member's arm, brought his right knee up and broke it at the elbow. The kid yelped then fell down amongst the other gang members moaning and bleeding all over the floor.

The people up front had been yelling for the driver to stop the tram. But he kept going and the tram lurched down Collins Street. Les decked another three gang members and the fighting began to slow down, except for the two gang leaders still going for it in the aisle hammer and tongs. Les grabbed the pair of them by the scruff of the neck, pulled them apart and banged their faces together, smashing both their noses. Then he whacked their heads together, splitting Hawthorn cap's scalp open before dropping them on the floor with the others. The remaining gang members stopped fighting and stared at Les like he was The Thing when it smashed through the door of the ice station in the old movie he saw with Warren. Les looked down at the blood and broken bodies lying around him on the floor and figured it might be a good time to split. He turned to the gang members still staring at him in horror and took out his camera.

'Righto fellahs. How about a smile.'

Les took several photos of the gang members left on their feet and the ones lying on the floor, when the tram came to a stop near Melbourne Town Hall. The door opened, Les climbed over the bodies and stepped out. Coming up the road he could see police uniforms. Les went round the back of the tram and quickly crossed Collins Street, ducked over Swanston then hurried down Collins Street to the hotel, past the porter standing outside the lobby and into a waiting lift. The bar upstairs was empty, the woman at reception had her back turned and Les stepped into the lift. A few minutes later he was safely in his room.

Les didn't need any more booze. He got a bottle of mineral water and had a look at himself in the bathroom mirror. Apart from a few sore knuckles and a bruise on his jaw, he didn't have a scratch on him. But blood had spattered down his jeans and onto his T-shirt. Les stripped off, threw them in the shower and got in. He rinsed out all the blood then gave himself a good scrub and hung his clothes up on the pull-out line above the bath. After changing into a clean pair of jox and a T-shirt, he sat down on the bed, yawned and stared at the floor. Now that he'd settled down, Les realised how much booze he'd drunk. He yawned again then turned out the lights and got under the bed covers. That's another bloody thing, he pondered as he shoved his head into the pillows. The last time I was down here and caught a tram at night, I ended up in a fight. Les gave his head a shake. I don't know. It's got me stuffed. Next thing, he was snoring.

Les woke up late the next morning and a bit seedy. He climbed out of bed, got a bottle of mineral water from the bar fridge and switched on the electric jug. He saw his camera sitting next to the TV, rubbed his jaw and half smiled when he recollected the previous night's events. After getting cleaned up, he climbed into his Speedos and old shorts and made a cup of instant coffee, which went down well with a hotel biscuit. A run to sweat out last night's drink would have gone well. Instead, Les went down to the pool area, did a few sit-ups and stretches by himself and had a sauna. When he got out, he could smell the stale booze trickling down his body before he splashed into the pool. Starting to feel half human again, Les went back to his room and changed into his blue cargoes and a white Rip Curl T-shirt, ready for breakfast. He got his cap and sunglasses, tossed his overnight bag across his shoulder and caught the lift down to the lobby.

It was hot outside and Melbourne's CBD had come to life. Cars and trams were honking and clanging along the streets and crowds of people were cruising the footpaths. Over from the hotel was a small arcade. Les wandered across the road and walked inside. It was mainly clothing or jewellery stores before it angled right into a narrow lane with several cafes on either side. Les chose one with small round marble tables and wicker chairs outside and ordered scrambled eggs, bacon and a flat white from a waiter in a red T-shirt. The food arrived and there was plenty of it. But the chef had scrambled the eggs in an oily pan and they didn't go down too well in the heat. While he was eating, Les decided not to tell Eddie about what had happened last night or about the girl in the hotel. Knowing Eddie, he'd probably start banging on her door wanting a piece of the action, and it wouldn't have been any laughing matter if Les had got picked up after what happened on the tram. He had another coffee to cut the greasy eggs, paid the bill and walked back round to Collins Street. He had a quick look around, adjusted his cap and sunglasses and decided to spend a leisurely day shopping and wandering around the CBD before Eddie arrived.

It didn't take long for Les to understand why Melbourne was said to be the best place to shop in Australia. As well as the enormous variety and the quality, the streets and footpaths were wide and level, making it a breeze to get around. He walked down Elizabeth Street and found where he had to pick up his car the next day, and on the way back stopped at a small art gallery where some black T-shirts with a colourful little devil on the front caught his eye. Les bought one for himself and one each for Warren, Grace and Clover. A little further on was a coffee shop specialising in fruit juices. Les took a seat and ordered a Brazilian Special. It was pink and delicious with a hint of ginger and mint. He had two. He roamed through a huge department store into the shirt section. The best ones were around two hundred dollars, yet they were all made in China. Someone must be cleaning up, mused Les and bought six at a clothes store on a corner where you paid for two and got one for free.

In the heat, Les drank more fruit juice then found a newsagency selling Sydney papers. So he had a bowl of won ton in a noodle shop and a read. He watched a busker in a turban going for it on some strange instrument in a wide boulevard with a statue of a purse on the footpath. He handed his camera to some Japanese tourists and got his photo taken in the middle of three skinny bronze statues of three weird men with briefcases. A few slices of ham and some potato salad from David Jones food hall, a perv and a takeaway coffee later, and Les couldn't believe the day was shot. He had another fruit juice from a shop across the road from the bronze statues and went back to the hotel to put away his purchases and get out of the heat. His bed had been made and they'd restocked the bar fridge. Les opened a mineral water and started unpacking when the phone rang. It was Eddie.

'Eddie. What's happening mate?' said Les.

'Not much,' replied Eddie. 'I'm here. But I've got a couple of things to sort out. I'll be about an hour late.'

'No worries. This is the earliest you've been late for ages anyway.'

'Yeah, right,' said Eddie. 'So what have you been up to?'

'Not much,' lied Les. 'Had a couple of drinks last night. Did a bit of shopping today. I'm hanging in ready for tonight.'

'Good. We might have dinner at the hotel and I'll tell you what's going on then.'

'Okay. So I'll see you in about an hour. In my room?'

'Yep. See you then.'

Les hung up and had a mouthful of mineral water. An hour, he mused. When I put all this away, I've got time for another swim. Les finished unpacking then put his Speedos and old shorts on and caught the lift down to the pool. Again he had it on his own.

Les flopped around just cooling off. When he'd had enough he went back to his room, showered and shaved then changed into his spare jeans, trainers and a yellow polo shirt. He put his ghetto blaster on and got some station playing golden oldies, and with Norman Greenbaum pumping out 'Spirit in the Sky', lay back on the bed and started reading *Hell's Angel*. He was into a part about a fun-loving member of the club called Doug 'The Thug' Orr, who could snap a pair of handcuffs and shot his girlfriend through the head before they put him in the Napa Valley Madhouse, when there was a knock on the door. It was Eddie, wearing black jeans and a grey shirt with a button-down collar.

'Hello mate,' said Les. 'Come in.'

'Fuck! How hot is it?' said Eddie stepping into Norton's room.

'Yeah. I've been hitting the hotel pool. You want a beer or something?'

Eddie shook his head and pulled up a chair. 'I wouldn't mind one down the bar before we have dinner.'

'Suits me,' said Les, sitting down on the bed.

'So you met Perry,' said Eddie.

'Yeah. He doesn't say much,' replied Les. 'What time's he picking us up?'

'Nine. Out the front.'

Les glanced at his watch. 'We got plenty of time.' He gave Eddie a thin smile. 'So what's the story?'

'We're going to sort Latte out in Fitzroy. It's not far from here.'

'Fitzroy? I was up there yesterday,' said Les. 'Whereabouts in Fitzroy?'

'At a bookshop in Brunswick Street.'

'A … bookshop?' said Les.

'Yeah,' answered Eddie. 'Called the Obelisk. It's right up one end.'

'I thought we were going to an art exhibition?'

'So did I. But they're selling a whole lot of rare books and stuff. Shithead's going to be in there with a dodgy plan of Burley Griffin. I got the listings.'

'Shit! Won't somebody recognise us?' said Les.

'I got disguises,' said Eddie. He peered quizzically at Les. 'You look a bit worried, big fellah. What's up?'

'Oh nothing, Eddie. I was expecting an art gallery. That's all. You know, more room to get around. A bookshop sounds a bit … poky.'

'All the better,' said Eddie. 'I've checked this place out. Most of the action's going to be in the front room. We just run in. Do the biz. And run out again. Easy.'

'Yeah okay. If you say so, Eddie.'

Eddie looked at his watch. 'Anyway. Let's go and have a beer and a bite to eat. By then it'll be time to go.'

'Okay.' Les stood up. 'What I got on do?'

'Sensational.' Eddie followed Les and they got the lift down to the lobby.

The bar was roomy and bright and predominantly red and cream with red furnishings and a black and white mosaic floor. Windows on the left overlooked the arcade, the restaurant was on the right and the wooden bar faced the lobby area. Seated around the bar and tables was a small crowd of neatly dressed men and women. Eddie got two pots of VB and they chose a table with red velvet lounge chairs in a corner looking down on the arcade. They clinked glasses then took a sip each. Les tried not to appear trepidatious. But having to belt Latte in the bookshop had thrown him out. Ken the owner would have to be blind not to recognise him.

'Okay Eddie,' said Les. 'Fill me in a bit more about tonight. And what are these disguises?'

Eddie rubbed his hands together. 'Who's got everybody shitting themselves these days?' he asked Les.

'I don't know,' shrugged Les. 'The taxation department? Marilyn Manson? Osama bin liner or whatever his name is.'

'Right on, baby,' said Eddie. 'So we're going in dressed as Muslim terrorists.'

'We're what?' said Les.

'We're getting done up as Muslims. Perry's got the Arab gear waiting for us in his garage. And two Groucho masks.'

Les stared at Eddie in disbelief. 'Eddie. You are joking, aren't you?'

Eddie took a sip of beer and looked directly at Norton. 'Les. You can't tell me, when Saddam Hussein sucks on a cigar in those horn-rim glasses and his moustache, he doesn't look like Groucho.'

Les thought for a moment. 'A bit,' he conceded from over his beer.

Eddie raised his glass. 'There you go. What did I tell you?'

'So we're going to run into the bookshop and bash Latte. Wearing tea towels on our heads and Groucho masks.' Les closed his eyes. 'I don't believe it.'

'Hey. We're not going to bash him,' said Eddie. 'I'm going to cut his fingers off.'

'You're what?' said Les.

'Well, I got to get that pinky ring off his finger,' gestured Eddie. 'This is the quickest way. And while I'm at it, I'll cut his other one off too. You just hold him.'

'Shit!'

'Besides,' said Eddie, 'if we give him a hiding, it's only going to heal up. This is a little more permanent.' Eddie smiled and wiggled his eyebrows. 'See how Latte likes sucking on his lattes with a couple of Manly Warringahs missing.'

Les shook his head. 'Eddie,' he said, 'you are a deadset evil little cunt.'

'No I'm not,' replied Eddie. 'I'm a force technician.' He finished his beer and nodded to the bar. 'Your shout, dude.'

Les got another two pots, Eddie went to the gents and saw the head waiter about a table on the way back. They drank their beers and talked about this and that. Eddie said there were a couple more things he wanted Les to do when they hit the bookshop; he'd explain when they were getting changed in Perry's garage. They finished their beers and went round to the restaurant.

The head waiter, wearing a high-collared white shirt and black vest, was Tim. Tim was very friendly and sat them down at a polished wooden table near the centre of the restaurant, across from a section of curved windows overlooking Collins Street. The restaurant was almost full and softly lit, with tasteful furnishings and the same mosaic floor pattern as the bar. Next to where they were seated, a huge vase of flowers sat on a solid wooden table that doubled underneath as a wine rack. Les went for a dozen oysters and the veal cutlet on citrus risotto. Eddie had a dozen oysters and Moroccan spiced chicken on mashed potato with coriander salsa. They drank mineral water with their meal; no sweets, just coffee. The food was delicious and very filling with crispy bread rolls, and they were too busy enjoying it to say a great deal. But they did agree that although twenty-five thousand dollars was just a bet to Price, Latte Lindsey must be living in another world if he thought he could get away with dudding a member of Price's family for even a postage stamp. Latte should have stuck to robbing people he knew. They finished their coffees, charged the meal to Les's room then gave the waiter a twenty and caught the lift down to the foyer. They were there a minute when the BMW limo pulled up out the front. A porter opened the rear doors for them and they climbed in the back and drove off.

'How are you, Perry?' said Les.

'I'm all right, Les,' replied the driver, glancing at him in the rear-vision mirror. 'How's yourself?'

'Good.'

'Perry's is only a few minutes over the bridge from here,' said Eddie.

'Righto,' nodded Les.

Not a great deal was said in the limo. Perry and Eddie exchanged a few words. Les stared out the window at the passing cars and darkened buildings not having a clue where he was, except the water below when they crossed Queens Bridge must be part of the Yarra. They went under a freeway then down a long wide street flanked with neat houses, flats, small hotels and busy restaurants. They turned into a smaller street and pulled up in front of a wide cream-painted double garage under a red-brick two-storey house with an enclosed verandah. The garage door on the left swung up, the limo glided inside and a light came on when the door closed. They got out and Les had a look around.

Perry's garage was neat and tidy with white-washed concrete walls. A double fridge sat in one corner, there were drawers and cupboards and a long white workbench ran along one wall beneath a tool rack. A meat hook hung from the ceiling and in one corner was a battered green punchbag. In the other parking bay on the right sat a blue Holden sedan with tinted windows.

'Do a bit of bag work, Perry?' said Les, nodding to the punchbag in the corner.

'Perry used to be amateur welterweight champ of Victoria. Didn't you mate,' said Eddie.

Eddie threw a couple of left jabs at Perry. The limo driver weaved expertly and countered Eddie with a left and right to the mid-section.

'A while ago,' smiled Perry.

'Not that long ago, if you ask me,' said Les.

Perry took off his coat and cap and Les followed Eddie over to the workbench. Sitting near a lathe were two neat piles of clothes and two Groucho masks. Eddie picked up one pile of clothing and handed it to Les.

'Righto Fred Astaire,' said Eddie. 'Here's your top hat and tails.'

Eddie handed Les a red and white cotton headscarf edged with small white tassles, plus a ring of thick black cord that doubled over and secured it to your head. Along with a long-sleeved collarless brown cotton shirt that reached the floor and buttoned up to your chin.

Les turned to Eddie. 'What the …?'

'The head gear's called a kofia. The shirt's a dajdaja,' said Eddie. 'Put it on over what you're wearing.'

Les was sceptical. 'Yeah righto,' he said.

Les slipped the dajdaja on and was surprised how easily it fitted over what he was wearing. He buttoned it up then put on the kofia, doubling the ring of black cord above his forehead.

'And now,' said Eddie. 'The piece de resistance.'

Eddie handed Les one of the Groucho masks. He'd tinted the rubber nose darker, glued hair to the plastic moustache and changed the horn rims into sunglasses. Les put it on and turned to Perry, who was now wearing a hooded black tracksuit top and a blue baseball cap.

'How do I look, Perry?' asked Les. 'I feel like a nice Beechams Pill.'

'Have a look.'

Perry opened a wardrobe near the fridge. Les had a look in the full-length mirror behind the door and was pleasantly surprised. The Groucho mask didn't look that ridiculous and with the sunglasses hiding his eyes and the kofia masking both sides of his face, his own mother wouldn't have recognised him. Les stepped back from the mirror.

'Not too bad, I suppose. All I need is a pair of white shoes and I'd pass for a second-hand camel dealer.'

Eddie put his outfit on and walked over for a look in the mirror. He had the same red and white patterned kofia, but his dajdaja was white.

'Pretty good if you ask me,' said Eddie. 'What do you reckon, Perry?'

'Terrific,' said Perry. 'Laurel and Hardy of the Sahara.'

Perry closed the wardrobe door and Eddie turned to Les. 'Righto Les,' he said. 'Here's our game plan. As soon as we spot Latte, I'll give him a whack in the guts to settle him down. You grab him by his right arm and pin it down palm up on the nearest table full of books.'

'Okay,' nodded Les.

'I'll lop his right little finger off first and get the ring. Then you grab his left arm and pin it down. And I'll lop the other finger off and grab his watch.'

'Sweet as a nut.'

'Now all the while,' said Eddie, 'I'm going to be yelling and screaming and carrying on like a madman.'

'That's nothing new,' said Les.

'And I want you to just keep yelling out Aieee! Aieee!'

'Aiee? Aiee?' said Les.

'Yeah. You've seen those ratbags on TV when they're all running around screaming. Death to Israel. Death to America.'

'Yeah,' nodded Les.

'Same as that,' said Eddie. 'Only louder.'

'AIEEEE! AIEEE!' howled Les.

'That's it Les,' said Eddie. 'Beautiful.'

'AIEEE! AIEE!'

Perry opened a drawer and handed Eddie a cleaver. It was small but quite heavy with a black plastic handle. 'Here you are, Eddie,' he said.

Eddie slipped it under his dajdaja. 'Thanks mate.'

Perry gave them both a quick once up and down. 'You right?' he said.

'Yeah. Let's get going,' answered Eddie.

'Why not,' said Les. 'Aiee! Aiee!'

Perry opened the doors of the Holden and got behind the wheel. Les and Eddie piled in the back. The other garage door swung open and they drove off into the night. They went back over the river, through the CBD, and next thing they were following the traffic down busy Brunswick Street. The Obelisk Bookshop was all lit up when they went past, there was a reasonable crowd inside, and standing at the door was a dark-haired woman in a black dress meeting and greeting. Perry swung the Holden into the side street ahead on the left and stopped in a no parking zone on the corner with the engine running.

'Righto,' he said. 'Good luck, boys. I'll wait right here.'

'We won't be long,' said Eddie.

'Two snips of a lamb's tail,' smiled Les. 'Aiee! Aiee!'

They got out of the car and walked towards the bookshop. There were people around and Les expected Saudi Arabia's answer to Laurel and Hardy would get some strange looks. But compared to the two Grand Viziers whose photo Les had taken the night before, they were small potatoes and barely rated a second glance. Sitting on the footpath just before the old bookshop was a skinny old white dog with a happy slobbery face. It saw them and started to wag its tail.

'Hello, old fellah,' said Eddie as they strode past.

'G'day mate,' said Les and gave the old dog a pat on its bony head.

They reached the bookshop and the woman on the door must have thought they were wealthy Middle Eastern buyers; she ushered them inside with a slight bow of her head.

'Good evening, gentlemen,' she said.

'Yashmak,' grunted Eddie.

'Shalom,' smiled Les.

The front room of the Obelisk looked very wine and cheese, exactly as Ken the owner had said. The men were all wearing well-cut suits, the women were dressed in style, and everybody was sipping on a glass of white wine while a string quartet creaked out Mozart in the next room. Ken the owner was standing on the left in a dark blue suit with a red tie talking to a woman in yellow. Les gave a double blink from behind the sunglasses. It was Sonia, the girl next door. The owner saw Eddie and Les, gave them a second look then turned away, knowing it was impolite to stare. Over to the right, wearing a three-piece grey suit and a regimental striped tie windsor-knotted into a blue shirt with a white collar, was Latte Lindsey. There was no mistaking his egg head, jowly face and oily smile as he escorted a woman in a red floral dress across the room. He was walking measuredly, his left hand flat across his stomach and his right arm bent by his side with his index finger drooped towards the floor. He looked like the Duke of Bedford strolling through his drawing room about to take tea with the Duchess of Crawley. Eddie spotted him the same time as Les, gave Les a nudge in the ribs and went into action.

'There he is!' shrieked Eddie, in a whiney, high-pitched voice, pointing at Latte. 'The one who fornicates with dogs and desecrated the tomb of Kareem.'

'AIEE! AIEE!' howled Les.

'Seize the infidel,' yelled Eddie.

'AIEE! AIEE!'

The band played on out the back, but everything in the front room stopped as all eyes fell on Les and Eddie. Latte had a look of outraged indignation on his face when Eddie strode across the room and sunk a left rip into his solar plexus. Lindsey went white, his knees buckled and he started gasping for breath as Les grabbed him by his right arm and pinned it down on a stack of books piled on a table behind him.

'This man is a thief, a liar and a desecrator,' shrieked Eddie, pointing Latte out to everyone in the room.

'AIEE! AIEE!' howled Les.

'Death to thieves and liars,' shrieked Eddie. 'And all those who would desecrate the tomb of Kareem.'

'AIEE! AIEE!' yelled Les.

'Hold out the hand of the infidel desecrator,' yelled Eddie, whipping the cleaver out from under his dajdaja.

'Aiee! Aiee! Death to the infidel,' said Les.

Latte went even whiter when he saw the cleaver in Eddie's hand. 'Help me, somebody. Please,' he whined.

'Silence, dog,' shouted Eddie.

Les pushed Latte's right hand down on the books palm up, Eddie brought the razor-sharp cleaver down with a solid crunch and Latte's right little finger came off, spurting blood and shreds of nerve endings all over *Key to the System of Victorian Plants*, Von Mueller, black bound.

'Oh my God,' screamed Latte.

Everybody in the shop either gasped or screamed as Eddie quickly removed the ring, left the finger where it was and raised the cleaver again.

'Now hold out the other hand of the infidel,' shrieked Eddie.

'AIEE! AIEE!'

Les changed sides and forced poor Latte's left hand down amongst the books on the table. Eddie whipped off Latte's watch and brought the cleaver down again. Latte's other little finger came off and a gush of blood spurted across *In the Wake of the Windships*, Frederick William Wallace.

'Ohhhh, God help me,' Latte's anguished cry was pitiful to hear.

Eddie slipped the watch and ring under his dajdaja then picked up the two fingers as Les let go of Lindsey. Moaning with pain, Latte slumped on his backside against the book table, spurting blood all over the carpet.

'Let this be a lesson to all thieves and liars,' shrieked Eddie, holding the two fingers up in front of the horrified people in the shop. 'And all those who would desecrate the tomb of Kareem.'

'AIEE! AIEE!' howled Les.

Eddie gave Latte a parting smack in the teeth with the blunt edge of the cleaver, then slipped it under his dajdaja before turning to Les.

'Come, my brother. Now we must leave.'

'AIEE! AIEE!'

Les followed Eddie past the ashen-faced woman at the door and into the street. The old white dog was still sitting on the footpath. It saw them coming and started wagging its tail again.

'There you go, mate,' said Eddie, and tossed the fingers to the dog.

The old dog snapped them up, and started chewing hungrily.

'Good boy,' said Les. He gave the old dog a pat on the head, then followed Eddie back to the car and jumped inside.

'How did it go?' asked Perry, as they drove off.

'Easy as shit,' replied Eddie. He turned to Les. 'Mate. You were fuckin unreal back there,' he said, slapping Les on the back. 'Good on you.'

'I did my best,' shrugged Les. 'And I think I learned something tonight, too.'

'Yeah. What was that, Les?'

'If you know what's good for you, don't fuck with the tomb of Kareem.'

'Or the club of Galese,' winked Eddie.

Les and Eddie took their Groucho masks off as Perry swung the Holden into another side street then headed towards the CBD. Before long they crossed the Yarra again and were back inside Perry's garage. Les and Eddie got out of the car and removed their blood-spattered Arabian clothing while Perry unscrewed the number plates on the Holden and changed back into his driver's suit and cap. They left the two outfits on the floor then washed any blood off themselves in a sink near the fridge. Eddie washed the cleaver, then rinsed Latte's watch and ring and looked at them sitting in the palm of his hand.

'Hard to believe that ring's worth twenty grand, isn't it,' said Eddie.

'Yeah,' agreed Les. 'Not a bad-looking watch, though.'

'I have to drop Eddie off at the airport,' said Perry. 'What do you want to do, Les?'

Les thought for a moment. 'I don't feel like going straight back to the hotel. And Fitzroy's definitely brushed. There's a hotel on the water at St Kilda. I did a TV commercial there the last time I was down here.'

'The Boulevard?' said Perry.

'That's it. Can you drop me off there?'

'No worries.'

Perry got behind the wheel of the BMW, Eddie got in next to him, Les piled in the back and Perry reversed out of the garage.

Eddie and Perry were talking business in the front so Les just sat back and watched the cars and buildings go past, pleased how smoothly the night had gone and glad it was all over. Before long they were cruising down a wide, flat boulevard with houses on the right, trams in the middle and crowded bars, restaurants and hotels on the left. A tram rattled by at the end and Perry swung the limo left past several blocks of flats. Les got a glimpse of the darkened ocean before Perry pulled up in front of the old hotel.

'All right, Les,' he said. 'Here you are.'

'Thanks, Perry.' Les shook the driver's hand before he got out. 'Nice to have met you, mate.'

'You too, Les.'

'I'll see you back in Sydney, Les,' said Eddie. 'Have a good time in Lorne. Hey. And thanks for everything, big fellah. You're the best.'

'Any time, Eddie,' winked Les. 'I'll see you and the others when I get home.' Les watched as the limo drove off into the night then turned to the Boulevard Hotel.

It was the same as the last time Les was there. Big and white, windows overlooking the bay and stairs out the front. Only this time there were a lot more people around. Les walked up the stairs past two security men in jeans and T-shirts and stepped through the door.

Inside was crowded with casually dressed punters. The lounge area on the right was packed and a band on stage had just finished a bracket. People were swarming everywhere or seated under the stairs at the end or at what tables there were. On the paint-chipped walls were posters for different bands. Bugdust, The Chucky Monroes, They Might Be Vaginas. A girl with spiked dark hair walked past wearing a black T-shirt under a white singlet with I LIKE HARLOCKS SACKS across the front in red. There was a small bar on Norton's left with a sign above saying TONIGHT, BOB MARLEY BIRTHDAY BASH, CONRAD ROOM. Les went to the bar, got a delicious and stepped back into the crush. The Conrad Room was down to the left, and Les thought he'd check out the Bob Marley Bash.

The gig was down the end of a corridor and seven dollars in. It was hot, smoky and absolutely jam packed; you couldn't swing a mouse, let alone a cat. On stage at the far end a DJ in a Jamaican beanie was playing Bob Marley's 'Lion In Zion'. Les got pushed and shoved and the ice in his delicious melted before he had a chance to drink it. Les drank some then put the glass on a table and left the Bob Marley fans to it.

Back at the bar Les ordered another delicious. By the time he'd drunk half he'd had enough. It was a good night in the pub if you wanted to get half full on ink and rage. But being on his own and after what happened earlier, Les wasn't quite in the mood. He finished his drink and walked outside.

Still looking for a quiet sort of drink, Les noticed the other bar to the right of the stairs and decided to have a look in there. It was just as crowded as upstairs and in a corner on the right as you walked in, a three-piece punk band and a singer were all screaming their heads off under a sign saying 102.7 FM TRIPLE R. The band were all stripped to the waist and covered in tattoos, the bearded singer was wearing a buffalo-skin hat and a black and white dress that looked like it was made from an old string shopping bag. It was all 'Oi, oi, oi' head-banging, loud and fast. Les walked straight back outside, gulped in some fresh air and cleared his head. He was thinking of having a look in the bars he'd seen round the corner driving there, when a taxi cruised up out the front. It wasn't getting any earlier, and the bar might still be open at the hotel. Les got in and told the driver to take him to the Southville in Collins Street.

The taxi ride home was uneventful and after getting hosed the night before, Les felt he was doing the right thing having an early one. This time tomorrow I'll be in beautiful down-town Lorne, he yawned as they approached the lights of the CBD. The taxi pulled up in front of the hotel, Les paid the driver then returned the porter's greeting as he stepped through the lobby and into the lift. The bar was still open and about a dozen people were seated around the various tables. Alone at the bar a woman was staring balefully into her drink. There was no mistaking the yellow outfit and neat blonde hair. It was Sonia. Les walked over and stood next to her.

'Hello, Sonia,' he said. 'How are you?'

Sonia gave a start and looked up. 'Oh, Sonny. Hello.'

Les gave her a smile. 'So what's a nice girl like you doing in a place like this?'

Sonia stared into her drink and shook her head. 'Sonny. You wouldn't want to know,' she replied.

Les immediately took this as an invitation for him to stick around while she poured her heart out. He ordered a delicious then turned to Sonia. 'Okay if I join you?'

Sonia indicated to the bar stool alongside her. 'No worries.'

'Thanks.' Les sat down and had a pull on a particularly excellent delicious.

'Where have you been tonight, Sonny?' Sonia asked.

'I had dinner in the restaurant earlier,' answered Les. 'Then I went to St Kilda for a Bob Marley night. But it was too crowded, so I came back to the hotel. What about yourself?'

Sonia drew in a deep breath. 'I just saw one of the most awful things I've ever seen in my life.'

'What? A car accident?'

'If only.' Sonia stared directly at Les. 'Sonny. I just saw two Muslim terrorists chop a man's fingers off.'

'What?' Les looked horrified. 'You're joking,' he said.

Sonia shook her head. 'I wish I was,' she replied, and gulped down a mouthful of her drink.

Les took a sip of his delicious. 'Tell me what happened?' he asked.

'I was at a rare book sale in a bookshop at Fitzroy,' said Sonia.

'A rare book sale?'

'Yes. I work for a firm of solicitors in Geelong. They sent me down here to bid for a rare book.' Sonia indicated with her glass. 'That's why I'm staying at the hotel.'

'Go on,' said Les.

'I was standing in the bookshop talking to the owner, when these two Muslims came in and started screaming and carrying on like madmen.'

'What did they look like?'

'Like ... Muslims. Arab headgear, long shirts. Thick moustaches. A tall one and a short one. And they were both wearing sunglasses.'

'Sunglasses.'

Sonia nodded. 'The short one did all the talking. The big one just ranted like a lunatic and waved his arms around, yelling Aiee! Aiee!'

'Aiee! Aiee?' said Les.

'Yes,' nodded Sonia. 'Then they grabbed this poor man. Screamed out he was an infidel and a thief. Then held his arms down and chopped his fingers off.' Sonia shuddered. 'It was horrible. I've never seen so much blood in my life.'

'How many of his fingers did they cut off?' asked Les.

'I don't know. They took the fingers with them. But it was a lot. They were brothers, too. Because I heard the small one say to the big one, "Come on, brother. Let's get out of here."'

'Good heavens,' said Les, taking a pensive sip of his delicious. 'What's the country coming to?'

Sonia shook her head. 'They got some tablecloths and tried to patch the poor man up till the ambulance came. But you should have seen the blood. It was everywhere.'

'I can imagine, Sonia,' said Les. 'Shit! That must have been terrible for you.'

Sonia gulped down some more of her drink. 'It was. But you know the funny thing, Sonny?'

'No. What?'

'The man they attacked went into shock. And while we were waiting for the ambulance, the owner loosened his tie and took his coat off. And a Cayman Islands bank cheque fell out.'

Les stopped himself from sputtering into his drink. 'A Cayman Islands bank cheque?'

'Yes. And not only that,' said Sonia. 'They checked the item he had up for sale. And it turned out to be a bit foreign, too.'

'You're having me on.'

Sonia shook her head. 'No. The police came and took down all the details. I only just got here a little while ago. I had to give a statement.'

'Great day in the morning,' said Les.

'Yes. But not a very nice night.' Sonia drained her glass.

Les finished his delicious and pointed to Sonia's empty glass. 'Would you like another one, Sonia?'

'Yes. Thank you, Sonny. Brandy and lemonade.'

Les ordered two more drinks, clinked Sonia's glass and tried not to burst out laughing. Listening to Sonia relay the events at the bookshop had made his night. But the final wash-up with Latte was the icing on the cake. Price and Eddie would crack up when they found out.

'Well if you ask me,' said Les, 'maybe the bloke was a thief and an infidel and he got what he deserved.'

'Yes, but these people can't just come out here to Australia and make their own rules,' said Sonia.

'You're right, Sonia,' nodded Les. 'And I don't want to get into it, because you'll only think I'm prejudiced.'

'Oh. Why's that, Sonny?'

'Why? Because I'm Jewish. That's why.'

'Jewish?'

'Yes. Sonny's just my nickname. My real name's Solomon. Solomon Klinghoffer.'

'Oh,' replied Sonia, taking a thoughtful sip of her drink. 'So are you from ... Melbourne, Solomon?'

Les shook his head. 'Sydney. My family owns a supermarket at Rose Bay. And call me Sonny.'

'Okay. So what brings you to Melbourne, Sonny. Business?'

'No. Holidays. I just stopped in Melbourne to do a little shopping. And tomorrow I'm off to Lorne for a few days.'

'Oh? Geelong's not far from there. I'll have to give you my phone number. Maybe we could catch up?'

Les gave Sonia an oily smile. 'I'd very much like that,' he told her.

'Yes. There's some nice hotels there. Good restaurants. Where are you staying?'

'Otway Plaza Resort.'

Sonia looked impressed. 'Oh, lovely.'

With a couple of brandies under her belt, Sonia started to relax. After a couple of nice bourbons on top of what Sonia just told him, Les was beginning to feel the same way.

'Sonia', said Les. 'There's something I'd like to ask you.'

'Sure,' smiled Sonia. 'What is it, Sonny?'

'Well. Yesterday. I wasn't in my room five minutes and you knocked on my door with that ... Well, let's face it. That line about your suitcase. I mean. What was that all about? You certainly took me by surprise.'

Sonia looked a little embarrassed. 'Do you ever experience deja vu, Sonny?'

'Sometimes,' answered Les. 'But there's never any future in it.'

'Yes, okay. Well a year ago, the same thing happened to me in another hotel. This man followed me to my room and started to attack me. Luckily an army officer came out of his room and the man ran off. But I've been really scared when I'm alone in hotels ever since.'

'That's understandable,' said Les.

'When you were following me down the corridor. I was absolutely terrified. I thought I was going to faint at one stage. Then when you opened the door to your room, and you said what you did about ... me being a better woman than you are Gunga Din and all that. When I got inside I started laughing and couldn't stop. I was so relieved. It was like a huge weight off my shoulders. Then I just felt. I don't know. I just felt like confronting my fears. So I thought, bugger it.' Sonia smiled. 'And I knocked on your door. If that sounds stupid, I'm sorry.'

Les shook his head. 'No. It doesn't sound stupid, Sonia. I think it's great the way you buried your demons.' He clinked Sonia's glass. 'Good on you.'

'Thank you, Sonny.'

'The other thing I wanted to ask you, Sonia,' said Les.

'Yes.'

'What's with ... Señor Buzz? Where did he come from?'

Sonia blushed coyly. 'That's my woman's home companion, Sonny. I call him Max.'

'Max?'

'Yes. Short for Maximus.'

'Fair enough,' said Les.

'Geelong's not all that big, Sonny. And if you like a bit of nooky, like I do, it doesn't take long to get a reputation. So ...'

'Hey. Nothing wrong with masturbating, Sonia,' smiled Les. 'You're always in good company.'

'Right on, Sonny,' said Sonia. 'And might I say, Solomon, you handled Max wonderfully.'

Les made an open-handed gesture. 'What can I say, Sonia? Max did all the heavy lifting. I just gave directions.'

The barman told them they were closing now and would they like any last drinks. Les looked around and he and Sonia were the only ones left. He asked Sonia if she wanted another brandy. Sonia declined. She'd had enough, it had been a traumatic night and she was getting up early in the morning. But she was glad she had run into Sonny again. Les put the drinks on his tab and smiled at Sonia.

'Well, Sonia. Would you like me to walk you home? Or will I ring you a taxi?'

Sonia put her hand on Norton's knee. 'Why don't you walk me home. I might even get you to check my suitcase again.'

'Still giving you trouble, is it Sonia?' asked Les.

'It's a bugger, Sonny. I should never have bought the cheap darn thing in the first place.'

They caught the lift to their floor. Sonia put her arms around Les when the door closed and they slipped into an extremely passionate embrace, with lots of tongues going everywhere and plenty of heavy breathing. They were still going for it when the door opened on the twelfth floor and they continued to grope each other all the way to Sonia's room. As soon as they got inside, Sonia started getting her clothes off and Les got out of his jeans. They finished in the nude and Sonia didn't have a bad little body. Her bum was tight, her boobs sat neatly and there was even a hint of six pack. Mr Wobbly had one look and he was up and at 'em and rearing to go.

'You know, Sonny,' said Sonia, putting her arms around Les. 'We really shouldn't be doing this. I'm not on the pill ...'

'Yeah and I'm not wearing a raincoat,' said Les. 'But I've got a simply splendid idea.'

'What's that, Sonny?'

'I'll get Max. And we'll have a sixty-niner.'

'Ooh yes,' squealed Sonia. 'I'd like that.'

Sonia got the vibrator from her suitcase, put a little hand lotion on it and handed it to Les, then they got on the bed. Les swung himself around and next thing he was looking into Sonia's neatly trimmed lamington. He switched Max on and started buzzing it around Sonia's clit when he heard her laugh.

'What is it, Sonia?' asked Les.

'I was just thinking, Sonny,' chuckled Sonia. 'You definitely are Jewish.'

'Shalom.' Les started buzzing away then shuddered as he felt the sweet sting of Sonia's mouth around Mr Wobbly.

Les quite enjoyed his anomalous sixty-niner. Sonia's warm tongue and lips felt sensational and it was fun watching the vibrator sliding in and out of her ted. Sonia sounded like she was having a great time too and over the soft buzz of the vibrator Les could hear her snorting and moaning away. Les held off for as long as he could, but eventually he began to approach critical mass. Beneath him Sonia started getting her rocks off too. She gripped Norton's thighs, kicked her legs and the moaning turned into muffled growling noises. Les kept giving it to her with the vibrator when suddenly the kicking stopped and Sonia raised her pelvis, let go a muffled scream and fired off a rattling great broadside. Les screwed his face up in sweet pain and with a roar like a bull emptied out into Sonia's mouth a moment or two later. After they'd both orgasmed, Les climbed alongside Sonia and shakily placed Max near the clock radio next to her bed.

'Shit,' panted Les. 'That was an Exodus I won't forget in a hurry. I feel like the Red Sea just parted right up my blurter.'

Sonia's eyes were still rolling around in her head like marbles. 'God! What a way to go,' she spluttered. 'Mamma Mia!'

'And my mother wanted me to be a dentist,' said Les. 'Oi vey! If she was alive now, she'd roll over in her grave.'

Les lay on the bed for a while then gave Sonia a kiss on the lips, got up and climbed unsteadily back into his jeans. Sonia reached out to the hotel biro and writing pad next to the bed, wrote something down then got beneath the douvet. With his trainers and shirt in one hand Les sat down on the bed.

'Well I'd better get going, Sonia,' he said. 'I got a long walk home. And you have to get up early in the morning.'

'Okay, Sonny,' said Sonia. 'There's my phone number in Geelong.'

'Thanks.' Les pocketed the piece of paper and kissed Sonia again. 'I'll ring you when I'm settled in at Lorne.'

'Okay Sonny.' She returned Norton's kiss. 'I'll see you through the week. Don't forget to ring me.'

'No. I'll remember. See you then Sonia.' Les blew her a kiss and let himself out.

Back in his room, Les got out of his jeans, used the bathroom then cleaned his teeth. When he'd finished he gave the mirror a tired smile.

Hello Sol. How are they hanging, baby? Long and loose and out of juice?

Les turned off the lights, yawned and climbed under the sheets. What about Sonia, he mused as he closed his eyes. Even she's into this deja vu. Come to think of it, I lied my head off to those two women poets in the Blue Mountains and got a blow job. Les scrunched his head into the pillows. Include me out of deja vu. It's too spooky. Who wants to recollect on what might be waiting for you round the corner. The big Queenslander yawned again then he was snoring.

Les woke up the next morning, had a look at his watch and pushed his head back into the pillows. He generally slept in on Sundays, so he stayed in bed and dozed back off into dreamland before finally getting up and drinking a bottle of mineral water. He decided to have breakfast in his room then pack his gear and check out. He rang room service and ordered Bircher muesli, fruit, eggs Benedict and coffee, then climbed into his old shorts and went down to the pool. He splashed around and got the cobwebs out then by the time he caught the lift back to his room, changed into his blue shorts and a white Bob Dylan T-shirt Clover had given him, breakfast arrived. Les tipped the girl then started eating while the same radio station ran 'Love is in the Air' by John Paul Young into 'You Can Call Me Al' by Paul Simon.

The breakfast was very good. Les drank the last of the coffee then got his clothes from the bathroom and finished packing. He tossed a hotel biro and some stationery into his overnight bag, had a last look around then picked up his suitcase and got the lift to reception.

Yes, he told the smiling girl behind the counter, he enjoyed his stay at Southville, the food was great, the bed was comfortable and he'd recommend the hotel to his friends. After charging everything to Price, Les took his suitcase down to the lobby and told the porter he had to pick up a car; he'd be back later. No worries, Mr Norton. The name's Klinghoffer. Solomon Klinghoffer, squinted Les, as he flicked his sunglasses open and walked out into another hot sunny day.

If Melbourne's CBD was crowded the day before, Sunday was even busier. Every little cafe or restaurant was crowded, bookshops were doing a roaring trade and all the trendy clothing stores were full of customers with the techno music pumping at warp nine. At minute intervals a tram would clang to a stop and more people would get off armed to the teeth with credit cards, cash and cheque books. Maybe it's the heat's bringing them out, thought Les, flicking some sweat from his eyes. He cruised around killing time before walking up to the paper shop he had found yesterday and buying the *Sunday Telegraph*. A support lead on the front page of the Melbourne *Sunday Age* and two identikit drawings caught his eye. BRUTAL ASSAULT IN FITZROY. MUSLIM TERRORISTS ATTACK MAN AT RARE BOOK SALE. Les lowered his eyes and bought the *Age* then walked up to the fruit juice shop, got a Brazilian Special and sat down.

'Two terrorists, apparently Muslims, were involved in a violent confrontation at The Obelisk Bookshop in Brunswick Street, Fitzroy last night in which a man's fingers were hacked off.'

The story must have broken late because there were only a few paragraphs and the paper hadn't had a chance to beat it up yet. It just said how shocked onlookers saw the men run in shouting slogans denouncing Zionists and infidels before chopping the man's fingers off. There were a couple of eyewitness accounts fairly similar to what happened and at the end it said, '*The injured man, a resident of Brighton, is in a stable condition at Royal Melbourne Hospital where he is currently helping detectives with their inquiries.*' I'll bet he is, thought Les. There were a few more paragraphs and two identikit photos like Groucho Marx minus the cigar. Les kept the front page and tossed the rest of the paper into a bin. As he placed it in his overnight bag something ominous struck him. Oh no, he said to himself. I'm not saying nothing about anything. But the last time I was down here I made headlines when I blew up that church in Whittlesea, and I was described as 'solidly built of Middle Eastern appearance'. And what else did it say? '*The evil octopus of international terrorism has spread its tentacles from the Middle East to sleepy Whittlesea in Victoria.*' Les looked up at the sky. Sorry boss. But I ain't saying nothing to nobody. Les got another Brazilian and started on the *Telegraph*.

By the time Les finished the paper and two cappuccinos, it was time to pick up the car. Thrifty was a short walk along Elizabeth Street.

The car rental was busy, but before long it was Norton's turn. No worries, Mr Norton, smiled a polite lady in blue. Your car is waiting. May we see your licence and how much insurance do you want. Les showed his licence and wanted maximum insurance. More smiles and paperwork later and Les found himself behind the wheel of a silver Mitsubishi Advance with a map from Thrifty marked in highlighter showing how to get onto the M1 and out of town. Les followed the traffic up Elizabeth then turned into Collins and pulled up in front of the hotel. The porter had his suitcase waiting and Les was on his way.

The Advance handled smoothly and was very comfortable with plenty of zip. That was the good news. The bad news was, there was no cassette player, only a radio and CD player. Which meant Les couldn't listen to his tapes. Les left the radio off till he figured out where was what. But there were no dramas and before long he was down Collins, found Flinders, yada-yada-yada and he was on the M1 with the other Sunday drivers, going through Altona Meadows towards Geelong.

At a sign saying POINT COOK RD, Les put the radio on and got some station playing classical dirges: moaning cellos and creepy violins. It sounded like backing music to the shows on SBS about the Holocaust. Les brushed it and flicked round the dial. He saw a sign saying LITTLE RIVER and thought of the old LP *Diamantina Cocktail* when he hit on PBS Station 106.7 FM and got some good blues music. The DJ announced some tune Les had never heard before, Geoff Costanza and Jerry Lou, 'Jive Samba'. More good music and very few ads later and Les was driving past brown and grey countryside with few trees. 106.7 changed disc jockeys and went on a jazz trip. Near Geelong Les brushed Miles Davis and found 96.3 Reema FM. It was all soul music and seemed to be a happy-clapping, praise-the-Lord station. Les blew Sonia a kiss as he crossed a bridge bypassing Geelong and further on the road veered left at sign saying THE GREAT OCEAN ROAD, LORNE 62 KMS. Les drove past Geelong airport and the scenery changed to wide, flat plains running off to hills in the distance and lines of trees on either side of the road.

The traffic increased going through Torquay and besides the houses and shops, Les noticed all the huge surf outlets. Norton was right in the heart of waxhead territory. Some radio station was playing 'Baby Love' by Diana Ross and Les started singing along as he went past the turn-off to famous Bells Beach. He got a glimpse of the ocean then it all opened up into red and brown cliffs and scrubby green hills on one side of the road. And on the other, shallow reefs and long golden beaches dotted with surfers taking advantage of the offshore wind. Driving past on a beautiful sunny day, Les was impressed. The Great Ocean Road truly lived up to everything he'd heard about it. Les was crooning along behind the wheel to some other pop song when suddenly the radio station sprung Celine Dion on him wailing 'I Drove All Night'.

'Ohh shit!' howled Les. 'Where's the cyanide pill? Give me a razor.'

Les turned the radio off and drove on in silence. He went through Anglesea before arriving at a sign saying WELCOME TO LORNE, SURF COAST. In the distance Les glimpsed a town and a long pier running out to sea from a rolling green headland.

'Hello. Looks like I'm here,' smiled Les.

Les eased the Mitsubishi around several hairpin bends then drove on past houses nestled into the green hills on his right, with wide bay windows facing the ocean before a long curve of golden sand opened up on the left. Further along a small white suspension bridge crossed over a wide brown creek running into the sea, then the traffic slowed down as Les passed a supermarket set back amongst trees on the right. Next to a tiny alcove of shops and a caravan park to the right, the road crossed the Erskine River and turned left. On a corner next to some colourful studio apartments with weather vanes on the roof sat two Rubenesque statues of a bug-eyed blue woman and a bug-eyed green one. Les drove past them and a row of buildings being demolished then, opposite a resort on the beach, the road swung right into Mountjoy Parade: Lorne's main street.

The traffic was heavy and crowds of people were either lying on the beach, taking a swim or walking around in the sun. Through the trees

Les could see the ocean on his left and roughly a kilometre of shops and buildings on the right. An old two-storey picture theatre faced an open-air swimming pool and steep side streets ran up to the forested hills overlooking the town. A car park and a modern surf club sat inside the headland where the beach ended and on the other side of a roundabout in Mountjoy Parade, the Otway Resort faced the Erskine Hotel on the opposite corner. The mustard-coloured resort was three rambling storeys of sundecks facing the ocean and looked very swish. The olive-coloured hotel had a beer garden on top full of sheltered tables surrounded by glass railings and a lounge underneath encased in smoked-glass windows, all built to take advantage of the view. White marble steps ran up to the entrance and there was a drive-in bottle shop underneath.

Les drove past a white church set amongst trees on the right then followed the road alongside the ocean for another kilometre to the wooden pier he'd seen in the distance. It started at a seafood restaurant and a fish co-op then ran out towards a low headland where a handful of surfers were catching waves off a point break. At the end of the pier a number of people were fishing near a crane and boats chocked up on the wooden pylons. Across the road from the pier was another hotel that had been beautifully restored back to its old-world charm. Huge windows surrounded the entrance, beneath sweeping verandahs with yellow wrought-iron railings that faced the ocean. On top was a steep, tiled roof with a large windowed loft and two smaller ones. Lorne ended at a block of holiday units, a small restaurant and more homes built into the hills. Les pulled over opposite the hotel and did a U-turn then crawled along with the Sunday traffic back to the roundabout between the first hotel and the resort. He took a left at the start of a steep hill then swung right into the resort's driveway.

There was a circled flowerbed in the middle and plenty of room. Les got out of the car, stretched his legs and walked into reception, where a dark-haired man in a blue suit was standing behind a brightly lit desk talking to a beefy woman in white shorts. Les waited his turn and had a look around. Outside were more gardens and landscaped walkways running by an enclosed pool and a gymnasium. Everything was mustard-coloured stucco, quite modern and very well maintained. The beefy woman departed and it was Les's turn.

Not a problem, Mr Norton, smiled the man in the blue suit. Your room is on the second floor on the Anchorage level. Parking is underneath. One key opens the roller door, the other your room. The lift is down the end of the hallway. Thank you, Mr Norton. Enjoy your stay at Otway Resort. Sitting on a wooden table next to the reception desk was a bowl of Roma apples. Les took one and started chomping on it on the way back to his car. It was that crisp and full of juice he went back for another before driving down to the parking area and finding a spot near the lift. He got his bag from the boot then caught the lift to the second floor, found his room easily and let himself in.

Les was surprised to find his room was a modern one-bedroom unit. The bedroom was off the corridor on the right, then the bathroom and after that you stepped down past a modern kitchen into a large air-conditioned lounge room with two comfortable lounges and a TV. A sliding glass door opened up onto a sundeck with a great view of the beach. The unit was done out in beige and pastel colours with thick blue carpet, white curtains and prints on the walls. Les got his suitcase from where he left it near the front door and tossed it on the bed along with his overnight bag. There was another TV in his room and a desk with a lamp. He checked out the cream-tiled bathroom. There were plenty of soaps, shampoos and bath gels and at one end you stepped down to a spa bath and shower. Les felt one of the fluffy towels then walked out to the kitchen. There was plenty of room and everything else, plus a nice big fridge, and every appliance imaginable for preparing meals. And if you didn't feel like cooking, there was an extensive room service menu. Les got a drink of cold water from the fridge and looked around. Shit! How good's this, he thought. Gary's done it again. Les went back to the bedroom, opened his suitcase and took out his ghetto blaster. He set it up in the lounge room, chose a tape and with the Jive Bombers thumping 'JB Boogie' through the unit, started to unpack.

When he'd finished, Les was looking forward to a swim. He put his Speedos on under his shorts, tossed a towel and his camera into his overnight bag then took the lift to the lobby. From the resort it was just a short, sloping walk to the corner then across the road to the beach.

The beach was crowded and it was high tide with a nice wave running between the flags. Les asked a family stuffing themselves with sandwiches under a beach umbrella if they'd watch his bag then jogged down to the water's edge and dived in. The water was chilly compared to the last swim Les had had at Bondi. But it was all right once you got in. Les caught a few body waves, flopped around, got out and picked up his things. He thanked the family under the beach umbrella and managed to sneak a photo of them hogging into the sandwiches. He had a shower next to the car park then strolled off to take a look around and have a cup of coffee.

Lorne was a pleasant holiday resort full of boutique clothes shops and nice restaurants. It reminded him of Port Douglas, only the shops were all on one side of the road and there was a surf beach. He went into a real estate agency and helped himself to a small map of Lorne, then found a milk bar-cafe with outside seating and ordered a flat white from a pretty brown-haired girl in a black T-shirt. The coffee was that good, Les immediately ordered another and went over his map.

Lorne appeared to be split in two by the Erskine River. On one side was a golf course and a road leading out to Deans Marsh. This side was the shops and the resort. The beach sat in Loutitt Bay, and Corio Crescent where the church was, wasn't far from where he was staying. Les glanced at his watch and daylight saving in Victoria having slipped his mind, he was surprised how late it was. He paid for his coffees and left.

On the way back to the resort, some striped shirts in a window caught Norton's eye and a second-hand bookshop in a little old house up from the street looked interesting. Les bought some fruit, milk and a few things in a takeaway food store, checked out the menu in the restaurant under the resort, then crossed over to the hotel bottle shop and got a bottle of Jack Daniels, a dozen VB, ice and mineral water.

Back in his unit Les had a VB, listened to some music and put everything away. He didn't have a clue what was on TV, so he checked out the in-house movies then perused the room service menu. He rang down and ordered a prime rib steak with potato lasagne, a side salad, a caesar salad and oven-roasted asparagus with shaved parmesan. While he was waiting, Les had a hot shower and a shave, put his blue shorts back on and changed into a grey Winnipeg Blue Bombers T-shirt. The food arrived and the waiter placed it on the table near the balcony. Les tipped him, put the caesar salad in the fridge for later then sat down and ate the rest watching the movie he chose: *Billy Elliot*.

The movie was a ripper. By the time the kid got into ballet Les finished eating and had his first delicious. When the kid did a routine with the woman dance teacher to Marc Bolan's 'I Like to Boogie', Les got up and started dancing round the lounge room and Les almost burst into tears when the kid, now all grown up and starring in the Royal Ballet, leapt out onto the stage at the end. It was the feel-good movie of all time and after several Jack Daniels, Norton was feeling very good indeed.

Les put his tray out on the landing, finished another delicious and contemplated his navel. He could have an early night and maybe watch another movie. Or he could go and have a drink. The hotel was just across the road. Les decided to go for a stroll down the other end of town and walk the meal off then come back to the hotel. He locked the unit and, taking his camera with him, caught the lift to the lobby.

Outside, the evening felt pleasant and the sky was full of stars, however most of the daytrippers had gone home and there weren't many people around. Les strolled past the shops and several restaurants still ticking over then shuddered when he went by the old picture theatre and saw the feature movie was *The Two Towers*, the second part of *The Lord of the Rings*. Further on he found some unexpected action. A restaurant with a white front, a white door and wide windows facing the street, was going off. There were chairs and tables along the footpath with people seated having a drink and music was coming from inside. A blue sign above the door said: ROSA'S. The name alone told Les he had to have a drink there, so he stepped inside to get a cool one.

Rosa's had soft lighting and pastel tiles with pink and black murals on the walls and people were seated drinking coffee or finishing bottles of wine after their meals. A square of bar sat opposite the kitchen and in a corner on the right a young DJ was playing ambient house music. Les got a delicious then went back outside and sat down at an empty table to have a look around.

There were a few people on his left. But to Norton's right, a crowd of casually attired drinkers faced each other over a long wooden table. Les overheard their conversations and gathered most of them worked in the local catering industry. Everybody was drinking and nattering away, except for a girl seated at the end of the table next to Les, staring pensively into an empty glass. She had spiky black hair and soft grey eyes set in a pretty, if slightly hard-boiled, face and was wearing a black cotton jacket over a long-sleeved yellow T-shirt tucked into a short tartan dress, and black gym boots. On the table in front of her was a well-worn leather handbag and near her feet sat a blue travel bag. Les would have put her age at around twenty. Seated next to her was a tall girl with a long face and long brown hair, wearing a white jacket and Levis. The girl with the spiky hair seemed oblivious to the people around her as she stared into her glass and Les didn't have to be a mind reader to tell something was wrong. He had another mouthful of bourbon and took out his camera.

'Excuse me,' he said to the girl at the opposite table. 'Do you mind if I take your photo?'

The girl moved her eyes from her glass to Les. 'Did you say something?'

'Thanks,' said Les, and fired off a photo.

The girl blinked at the flash. 'What was that all about?' she said.

'Nothing really,' answered Les. 'It's just that I'm having such a good time sitting here. And you looked like you were having such a good time too. I had to take your photo.'

The girl stared wryly at Les. 'Having a good time? Are you fuckin kidding?'

'Okay,' shrugged Les. 'Maybe I'm a bad judge. But that's how it looked to me.' He finished his bourbon and stood up. 'Anyway. I'm going for another cool one. Can I get you something?'

The girl looked at Les for a moment. 'All right,' she said. 'Jack Daniels and soda, with a slice of orange.'

'That sounds all right,' said Les. 'I might have one of those myself. Watch my camera for me, will you.'

Les walked into Rosa's and got two bourbons. When he returned the girl was still staring into her glass so he put her drink in front of her.

'There you go,' said Les, taking his seat.

'Thanks,' replied the girl.

'No worries.' Les reached over and clinked her glass. 'Cheers,' he smiled.

The girl couldn't quite manage a smile. 'Yeah, cheers,' she said.

'So what's your name?' asked Les, after they'd each taken a sip of their drinks.

'Stepha.'

'Nice to meet you, Stepha. I'm Les.'

The girl gave a little nod and turned to Norton. 'Where are you from, Les?'

'Sydney.'

'Yeah? What brings you down here? I suppose you're a waxhead.'

Les shook his head. 'No. Just a holiday. Till Friday. What about you, Stepha? Where are you from?'

'Melbourne.'

Les nodded to Stepha's travel bag. 'You on holidays too? Or have you just been kicked out of home?'

'Yeah,' nodded Stepha derisively. 'You could bloody say that.'

Suddenly the long-haired girl next to Stepha put her head in. She was waving a glass of wine around and looked drunk. 'Oh, Stepha,' she said. 'I see you got a drink.'

'Yes,' answered Stepha. 'Les got me one. Les, this is Trish.'

Les raised his drink. 'Hello Trish.'

Trish gave Les a half once up and down. 'I suppose Stepha's been telling you all the trouble she's in,' gabbled Trish.

Les shook his head. 'No. We were just talking, that's all.'

'Well she's in some, aren't you, Stepha?'

'Yes, Trish. I suppose I am,' Stepha replied wearily.

Les smiled at Stepha. 'And I suppose it's none of my business, either.'

Trish turned to one of the windows and noticed something inside Rosa's. 'Nicole wants me,' she said. 'I'll be back.'

Les watched her leave then turned to Stepha who looked a little embarrassed. 'All right, Stepha,' said Les. 'I know it's none of my business. But what sort of trouble are you in? Are you involved with all the North Korean heroin they found in Lorne? Have you murdered someone? Done a kidnapping?'

'I'd settle for any of the above three,' replied Stepha.

'Fair dinkum? Shit! You must be in strife.' Les gave Stepha a congenial look over his glass. 'Do you want to tell me your troubles, Stepha? I'm a good listener.'

Stepha stared at her drink for a moment, then took a deep breath and turned to Les. 'All right, Les,' she said. 'If you want to know, I came down here to work the holiday season for three months.'

'Doing what?'

'Waitressing. The money's always good and so are the tips. Anyway, I met this guy and moved in with him. He seemed all right at first. Then he thought he owned me.'

'A control freak,' opined Les.

Stepha pointed to her eye and Les noticed a slight mouse. 'You better fuckin believe it.'

Les nodded slowly. 'I see. So what does this … chap do?'

'Burne. He's a bar manager. And he sells dope. Which I didn't know about at the time.'

'What? Smack? Coke?'

'Eccy mainly,' said Stepha. 'Plus speed. And a bit of hash.'

'The Lorne cartel,' said Les. 'So what's all the drama with the bar manager?'

'I got out of the house,' replied Stepha. 'I decided to leave Lorne early and I'm getting the bus back to Melbourne tomorrow morning. But when Burne finds out he'll come looking for me. As well as owning me, he reckons I stole some money off him too.'

'Right.' Les nodded to the bar. 'What about your girlfriend? Can't you stay with her?'

'Trish?' Stepha shook her head. 'She's not my girlfriend. And nobody else wants to get involved. Not with Burne.'

'Sounds like one tough hombre,' said Les. 'So what's the bottom line, Stepha?'

'The bottom line, Les?' Stepha had a mouthful of bourbon. 'The bottom line is I've got nowhere to stay tonight and Burne will finish work soon and come looking for me. All the cheap motels are booked out. So I'll most likely finish up sleeping on the beach. Then he'll probably be waiting for me at the bus stop in the morning.' Stepha raised her glass. 'Life's fuckin great, isn't it, Les.'

'Can't you go to the cops?' suggested Les.

'What are they going to do?' shrugged Stepha.

'Fair enough, I suppose.' Les shook his head then smiled at Stepha. 'Well. All I can say is, Stepha, I feel your pain, matey. I've got a bit of a problem myself.'

'You? What's your problem?'

Les nodded to his left. 'I'm staying in a fully furnished unit at the Otway Resort. Besides my bedroom, there's two big lounges. Two TVs, music. I've got a fridge full of beer, a bottle of Jack Daniels and a bag of ice. Tea and coffee. Oh, and there's bloody room service if I want it, too.' Les sipped his drink and stared into the glass.

Stepha peered derisively at Les. 'You got a fuckin unit in the Otway, with all the trimmings. And you call that a problem. Are you all right in the head?'

'I don't know,' answered Les. 'It's just that I got it all to myself. And it's too bloody big.'

Stepha moved a little closer to Les. 'You've got the place all to yourself?'

'That's right,' nodded Les. 'All on my lonesome.'

Stepha fished into her battered leather purse, came up with a twenty-dollar bill and looked pleadingly at Norton. 'Les. I haven't got a real lot of money on me. But I'll give you twenty dollars if you'll let me sleep on your lounge for the night.'

Norton took a sip of bourbon and looked evenly at Stepha. 'Make it twenty-five.'

Stepha fished out a five-dollar bill and handed the money to Les. 'Okay. Twenty-five it is.'

Les pocketed the money. 'Righto. When did you want to move in?'

'Now,' replied Stepha.

'Now?'

'Yeah right fuckin now. Before Burne shows up.' Stepha drained her drink and stood up. 'Come on let's go. There's nothing happening here anyway.'

'What about in the morning?' asked Les.

'I'll worry about that when the time comes,' replied Stepha, picking up her bag. 'At least I'll be safe tonight.'

'Okay,' shrugged Les. He finished his drink and stood up also. 'Do you want a hand with your bag?'

Stepha shook her head. 'No, I'm fine, thanks.'

Without saying goodbye to anyone, Stepha started off towards the resort with Les at her side. Les didn't quite know what to say. He felt like a heel taking the poor girl's money. However, there were no complications that way and if she got smart he could give it back and kick her arse out the door. But Stepha seemed all right and it was an awful predicament she was in. Nonetheless, Norton would be sleeping with his car keys, money and credit cards under his pillow. They walked on and by the time they passed the garage and got to the picture theatre on the opposite corner, Les found out Stepha was twenty-five and had a brother in the Navy. Les gave her the same spiel about his family owning a supermarket in Rose Bay. But added he'd just spent five years in the clergy.

'You were a priest?' said Stepha.

'That's right,' nodded Les. 'Father Les.'

'What denomination? Catholic? Anglican ...?'

Les shook his head. 'I don't really want to discuss it, Stepha,' he said. 'As far as I'm concerned, it was five wasted years of my life.' He smiled at her. 'I'd have been better off joining the Navy.'

'Yeah. Vince loves it,' said Stepha. 'He's just come back from the Gulf.'

'They do a bloody good job our armed services,' said Les. 'I've got no time for people that bag the military.'

'Good on you, Les.'

'Thanks, Stepha.'

They passed some phone boxes opposite a wire fence running past a church when Stepha slowed down and the expression drained from her face.

'Oh-oh,' she said.

'What's the matter?' said Les.

'Here comes Burne. Shit! And he's with Allan and fuckin Bucky too.'

Les stared ahead at three shadowy figures diagonally crossing the road towards them. The tallest one in the middle was wearing a cap, the others at his side appeared bare-headed and not much shorter. Les turned to Stepha and smiled.

'You know, Stepha,' he said. 'I had a feeling this was going to happen.'

'Look Les. Don't say anything. I think I can handle it. Christ!'

'If you say so,' replied Les. 'But I can be very diplomatic in these sorts of situations. Which is who?'

'Burne's the tall one in the cap. Allan's on the left. And Bucky's the solid one on the right.'

'Okey doke,' said Les.

'But leave it to me, Les,' said Stepha. 'There's no need for you to get involved.'

'Don't worry, Stepha,' Les assured her. 'They'll hardly know I'm here. Would you mind holding my camera for me?'

The three men approached. Burne was wearing a red Quicksilver cap, black jeans, and a white shirt hanging out over a black T-shirt. Bucky was squashed into a pair of faded Levis and a black Rolling Stones sweatshirt with the sleeves hacked off. Allan was wearing a grey tracksuit and a thick grey woollen beanie. They were all around thirty, they weren't small and no one was smiling when they stood in front of Les and Stepha. Burne looked positively filthy.

'Where the fuck are you going?' he barked at Stepha. 'I've been looking for you. You fuckin little moll.'

'Burne. Look, will you just listen,' pleaded Stepha.

Burne's two friends puffed up and gave Les a menacing once up and down, then figured he looked harmless enough and there were three of them if he was stupid enough to put his head in. Les smiled at the three men and decided to put his head in.

'Excuse me,' he said politely to Burne. 'Are you talking to Stepha?'

Burne glared at Les. 'Well, I sure ain't talking to you, dopey. So why don't you fuck off while you're in front?'

'Fair enough,' nodded Les. 'But you asked Stepha a question. Perhaps I can answer it for you.'

'You?' sneered Burne.

'Yeah.' Les pointed in the direction he and Stepha were walking. 'My parents own a holiday house just up the road. Stepha and I are on our way back there. To smoke some pot, snort a few lines of coke, drop a tab of acid and do a bit of crystal meth. Then we're going to boil up some Viagra. Shoot it. And fuck each other all night. After that I'm going to order a pizza with the money Stepha stole off you. And when we've finished eating it, I'm going to invite you over. And shove the cardboard box up your fat arse.' Les smiled at the three men before turning back to Burne. 'Now you know, Burney boy. You happy?'

Stepha gave Les a double blink. The three men exchanged glances then Burne sucked in his breath and snarled a reply.

'What?'

Les knew he was in Victoria and there wouldn't be any huffing and puffing, so he whacked Burne in the face with a crisp straight left. Not hard enough to knock him out. But hard enough to stun him and make his nose bleed, giving Les a few moments with just his two mates. Les decided to get rid of Bucky first.

Bucky and Allan started for Les. Norton weaved to the side and Bucky walked straight into a diabolical left hook from the big Queenslander that had all Norton's shoulder behind it. Bucky's eyes rolled back as his front teeth fell out in a gush of blood, then his knees went and Bucky landed on his rump and one elbow somewhere between Mars and Disneyland. Allan let go a flurry of good, hard punches landing a couple on top of Norton's bobbing head. He set himself to throw some more when Les moved in and banged a short right under Allan's heart, stopping him in his tracks. Les followed up with two filthy left hooks that tore Allan's face open and almost jolted his head off, then belted another short, bone-crushing right into his ribs. Out on his feet and in an awful lot of pain, Allan closed his eyes and turned away. Using his right arm, Les grabbed him in a standing reverse headlock, bent down and sent Allan cartwheeling over his shoulder. Allan's beanie flew off and he crashed heavily on his face near the phone boxes, out cold and oozing blood across the footpath.

By now Burne had shaken away the cobwebs and noticed his two mates lying on the footpath. He snarled angrily, wiped some blood from his face and threw a solid left and right at Norton. Les caught them both on his arms, crouched slightly then moved into Burne and brought his knee up hard into Burne's groin. Burne let out a howl of pain and started to double up. Les whacked him with a couple of left uppercuts, knocking Burne's cap off, then pushed Burne's head down and smashed another two knees into his face. As Burne started to buckle, Les grabbed him by the scruff of the neck and the back of his jeans and banged his head noisily into the corner of the nearest phone booth. Burne collapsed unconscious on the footpath next to Allan, then rolled over and the metal corner of the phone booth had split his forehead open from his hairline to the bridge of his nose. Bucky was still lying on the footpath on one elbow with blood pouring out of his mouth, wondering through glazed eyes what year it was and who was prime minister. Les walked over and booted him hard in the face, leaving him sprawled on his back out cold. Les had a quick look up and down the street and noticed that luckily there were no other people around. He turned to Stepha, who was still standing near the wire fence holding his camera.

'Well, Stepha,' gestured Les innocently. 'I did my best to be diplomatic.'

Stepha looked at the bleeding, unconscious men lying on the footpath and nodded her head. 'Yeah. Yeah you did.' She turned to Norton. 'Les. Do you mind if I do something?' asked Stepha.

'No. Go for your life,' shrugged Les.

'Thanks.' Stepha handed Les back his camera then walked over and kicked Burne in the groin, then kicked him in the head. 'That's for Friday night. You fuckin bastard!' Burne didn't feel a thing. Stepha kicked him in the balls again then spat in his face. 'Arse-fuckin-hole!' She turned to Les. 'Okay. Let's go.'

Les thought for a moment. 'Yeah, righto,' he said. 'But your friends look a bit untidy lying here in the street. Hold on a sec.' The wire fence in front of the church was only waist high. Les dragged Burne, Allan and Bucky across, then flipped them over onto the other side, leaving them lying on the church grass. 'That's better.' He gave Stepha a smile. 'Now let's head for home.'

'Yes, let's.'

'You sure you don't want me to carry your bag?'

'No. It's quite all right, thank you.'

'Okey doke.'

They walked on in silence. Les wiped any blood from him with his hanky. Stepha slung her bag over her shoulder. They got as far as the resort restaurant on the corner, when Stepha suddenly dropped her bag on the footpath and stared questioningly at Les.

'All right Father Les,' she demanded. 'Just what the fuck are you? Some kind of Shaolin fuckin monk or something? And don't give me any shit about being diplomatic. You're about as diplomatic as a fuckin wrecking ball.'

'What are you talking about?' asked Les.

'What am I talking about?' Stepha pointed back to where they'd just come from. 'I've seen Bucky knock guys out with one punch. Allan does tae-kwon-do. And Burne's fitter and tougher than both of them. Which is more or less what attracted me to the prick in the first place.'

'Go on,' said Les.

'But you just bashed the shit out of them. Like they were three girl guides selling jam lamingtons. What's your story — boy?'

'I dunno,' shrugged Les. 'I watch a lot of Jackie Chan videos.'

'Ohh fuckin bullshit!'

'All right. Don't shit your pants,' smiled Les. 'I'll tell you when we get upstairs. Anyway, you needn't talk. I saw what you did back there. You vicious little monster.'

'Vicious little? ... Yeah, all right.' Stepha humphed and picked up her bag then followed Les to the resort.

A man behind the desk wearing a neat grey suit and red tie smiled up when he saw them walk into the foyer.

'Good evening, sir,' he said.

Les returned the man's smile. 'How are you, mate?'

'Evening, madam.'

'Hi,' said Stepha.

They caught the lift to the Anchorage level in silence. Les found his key, then they walked across the landing; Les opened the door and switched on the light.

'Ohh wow!' said Stepha. 'This place is really cool.'

'Yeah, it's not bad,' agreed Les, closing the door. He tossed his camera on the bed then pointed out the bathroom and kitchen to Stepha as they followed the corridor down to the lounge room. Les nodded to the lounge nearest the TV. 'I reckon that's the most comfortable of the two. I'll get you a blanket and pillows from my room.'

Stepha placed her bag near the TV and flopped on the lounge. 'Ohh yeah. This'll do me. Thanks Les.'

'No wuckin furries.' Les rubbed his hands together. 'Well, I'm going to have a drink. You want one?'

'Thanks. I might go to the loo first.'

Les made two Jack Daniels with soda and sliced up an orange. He gave them a stir and added the orange as Stepha came back from the bathroom.

'You got a spa bath in there,' she said.

'Yeah,' nodded Les. 'I haven't tried it yet.' He pushed Stepha's drink across the bar top in the kitchen. 'There you are.'

Stepha sat down on a bar stool round the other side, picked up her drink and clinked Norton's glass. 'Thanks Les,' she said.

'That's okay, Stepha,' replied Les. 'Cheers.'

'Yeah, cheers.' Stepha had a mouthful, blinked at the kick then looked directly at Les. 'Righto Mike Tyson,' she said. 'A little bit of explaining please. And forget the Jackie Chan videos.'

'All right.' Les came round and sat down on a bar stool next to Stepha. 'The monastery where I was studying was right out the back of New South Wales. A couple of the other priests were Korean and into all that martial arts stuff. So a couple of us started training with them. There wasn't much to do after prayer. And I finished up training about five hours a day for five years. Plus I'm fairly fit.' Les shrugged his shoulders. 'That's about it. No big deal.'

'No big deal?' said Stepha. 'Shit! I'm glad I'm not Burne and his mates. And how about showing me that one where you threw Allan over your shoulder. That was so cool.'

'Yeah, I might later,' said Les, sipping on his bourbon. 'But just don't ask me any more about the church. It's a bit of a sore point with me.'

'Okay. No worries.'

Les looked evenly at Stepha. 'Do you think there'll be any dramas with the police over what happened tonight?'

'I doubt it,' answered Stepha. 'The cops have got their eye on Burne. And Bucky's on bail for assault. And there's no way they'll admit just one guy beat them up.'

'Good,' nodded Les. 'And you won't have to worry about catching the bus in the morning either. In fact you don't even have to leave.'

Stepha shook her head. 'I've already lined up a job in Melbourne. But yeah, you're right. I can catch the bus in peace now.' She clinked Norton's glass. 'Thanks to Father Les. The fighting priest. Ooh, sorry. Don't mention the church.'

'That's okay.' Les walked across to the ghetto blaster. 'You fancy a bit of music?'

'All right. What have you got?'

'This.' Les pressed play on his ghetto blaster and Bernard Ellison started cranking 'Fistful of Dirt'.

'Hey. This is all right,' said Stepha. 'Rock 'n roll.'

'It's good for your soul,' smiled Les.

They chatted away about this and that as the tape played. Les bullshitted about the family store in Rose Bay and how he'd been out of circulation up until a couple of months ago. Stepha told him about life in Box Hill, where she lived in Melbourne, working in Lorne and how she wasn't much of a judge when it came to men. After a couple more drinks and knowing she was rid of the bar manager, Stepha loosened up. She also started taking a bit of a shine to Les, her knight in shining armour and new landlord.

'For an ex-priest, you sure know a lot about drugs, Les,' smiled Stepha. 'That pay you gave Burne cracked me up. If I hadn't been so worried at the time I would have burst out laughing. Boil up some Viagra. Where did you get that from?'

'I dunno,' Les smiled back. 'I was amped up, and it was just the first thing that came into my head. I'm not into drugs. Though I've smoked pot.'

'You have?'

'Yeah. It was growing all over the place out west. We used to make scones with it. I think that was what made me give up the priesthood.'

Stepha gave Les a quick once up and down. 'Would you like a smoke now? I got some hash joints in my bag. Courtesy of Burne.'

'Sure why not,' shrugged Les. 'We'll smoke 'em out on the sundeck.'

'Unreal.'

Stepha went to her travel bag, found a plastic container and came up with two small joints and a lighter. Les walked across to the sundeck, opened the sliding glass door and they stepped outside with their drinks. Stepha stuck a joint in her mouth, lit it, took a hit and handed it to Les.

'There you go,' she said from behind a curl of smoke.

'Thanks.' Les took the glowing joint and had a hit.

They finished the joint fairly quickly. Stepha stubbed it out and lit the other one.

'Drug City Mamma,' said Les.

'Just call me Amphetamine Annie,' said Stepha.

They finished the second joint and took their drinks inside. Stepha sat on the lounge near her bag and kicked off her shoes. Les sprawled back on the one opposite. It wasn't long before the hash kicked in and Les began to relax on what felt like a very comfortable lounge. The music sounded better and Stepha started to look like Miss Universe.

'So how was that, Les?' said Stepha, grinning like a Cheshire cat from the other side of the room.

'Very good,' Les nodded slowly. 'Very good indeed. Hey, if you get the munchies later, there's some biscuits in a cupboard, and a caesar salad in the fridge.'

'Thanks Les,' said Stepha.

Les started to slip deeper into the cosmos. He stretched and smiled around the unit too. 'You know, it's funny,' he said slowly. 'Just a few hours ago I was in Melbourne having a Brazilian. Now I'm in Lorne having a Jackies and smoking Johnny.'

Stepha spluttered into her bourbon. 'What did you just say you were having in Melbourne, Les?' she asked incredulously.

'A Brazilian,' replied Les.

'A Brazilian? Oh my God!' Stepha fell back on the lounge and started giggling like she was going to wet herself.

Les stared at her completely confused. 'What's the matter? Did I say something funny?'

'A Brazilian?' giggled Stepha.

'Yeah. It's a bloody fruit drink,' said Les.

'A fruit drink. Oh shit! I don't believe it.'

Les shook his head. 'Bloody hell!' he said. 'The hash wasn't that good.'

Stepha straightened up and wiped her eyes. 'Les. Do you know what a Brazilian is?'

'Yeah. I just told you. A sweet, pink, fruit drink. With mint in it. Christ!'

Stepha shook her head. 'No it's not. Well maybe. But this is a Brazilian.'

Stepha pulled up her tartan dress, took off a pair of lacy blue knickers, then lay back on the lounge with her legs apart.

'That's a Brazilian, Les,' she said. 'A waxed fanny.'

Les gave Stepha's bald ted a double blink. 'Holy mother of God,' he said. 'Where did you get that?'

'In Melbourne. Haven't you ever seen one before?' asked Stepha, holding her legs apart.

'No. I told you. I've been out of circulation for five years,' replied Les.

'It ain't just a fruit drink, baby,' said Stepha.

'Evidently not,' said Norton. 'All right if I have a closer look?'

'Be my guest,' invited Stepha.

With his drink in one hand, Les crawled across the room on his hands and knees and stared into Stepha's freshly plucked business. In his confused state Les couldn't think what it resembled. He gave it a little poke with his finger.

'What a ripper,' said Les. 'It looks like … like a plate of veal schnitzel without the crumbs.'

'Oh Lord!' squealed Stepha.

Les shook his head. 'I'll tell you what though, Stepha,' he grinned. 'It might not be the same Brazilian I was talking about. But it sure looks just as pink and sweet.'

Les took a sip of his drink then pushed his face into Stepha's lamington and found it slightly spiky. But very chewy and very delectable; and you didn't have to pick pubic hairs out of your teeth. He gave it a reasonable going over while Stepha moaned and groaned on the lounge. After a while Les came up for air.

'Hey, this is all right,' he said to Stepha. 'Forget macadamias and peanuts. From now on, I'm a certified Brazil nut.'

'Yeah, well don't stop,' panted Stepha.

Les stood up. 'Hang on a minute,' he said. 'I got an idea. Don't go away.'

Les hurried to the bathroom, had a quick leak and ran the bath. He came back into the lounge room where Stepha hadn't moved.

'Hey. You feel like a spa bath?' asked Les.

'Yes. That would be good,' replied Stepha. 'Now how about ...'

'Coming right up,' said Les. 'Sorry. Make that going right down.'

Les finished his drink and got stuck into Stepha's business again, like he was the guest of honour at a cannibal feast. Stepha sighed and howled then started to kick her legs before emptying out into Norton's face. Les gave a howl of approval and came up with his eyes sparkling and his face looking like an iced Danish.

'Oh baby that's a what I like. Shake it, but donnn't break it.'

'Shit! What hit me?' heaved Stepha. 'Father Les. You're a beast.'

'Hey. What did I say,' frowned Les.

'Yeah, right. Don't mention the church.'

'Exactemondo. Now come on, Miss Brazil. Let's go for a surf.'

'Whatever you like.' Stepha smiled sweetly up at Les. 'But how about a kiss first, huh?'

'Why certainly, my child,' smiled Norton.

Les put his arms tenderly around Stepha and met her lips coming towards him. They were lovely and soft and Stepha had a hot, spicy tongue. After a while he opened his eyes and smiled into Stepha's.

'Come on,' he said. 'Let's get in the spa. It should be about ready.'

'I'll see you in there,' smiled Stepha.

Les went to his room and got out of his clothes, then padded down to the bathroom. The spa had filled perfectly and the temperature was ideal. He got a bottle of spa crystals, dumped them in the water then ran the jets and watched the crystals foam up like clouds of white fairy floss, bubbling and crackling as they burst into the steam. He put his foot in the water, then slowly climbed into the spa bath and lay back against one side, closed his eyes and sighed as the jets of water softly massaged his body.

'Ohh yeah. How good's this.'

'Did you say something?'

Les looked up and Stepha was standing by the side of the spa, naked. She had a whippy little body and pert boobs. Her skin was pale and across her ribs were several purple bruises. Norton looked at them for a moment and wished he'd smashed the bar manager's head into the phone box a couple more times. Nevertheless, the boot in the balls Stepha gave him would give Burne something to think about when he woke up.

'I was just saying,' said Les, 'how sweet it is. Give me your hand. The floor's a bit slippery.'

Stepha took Norton's hand and lowered herself into the spa. 'Ohh yeah,' she smiled. 'This is unreal.'

'All part of the service, ma'am,' said Les.

Les poked his legs out and felt Stepha's legs resting on top of his. He closed his eyes, leant his head against the side of the spa and let the sweat run down his face while the jets of water gently massaged his body. Stepha did the same. Les dunked his head under the warm water for a while and so did Stepha, then they sat in the spa smiling happily at each other. Les switched off the jets and it went quiet in the bathroom. The music drifted in from the lounge room and Les recognised the song as Johnny Lang bopping 'If This Is Love'.

'Hey Stepha,' said Les.

'Hey yes,' answered Stepha.

Les tilted his head to one side. 'How about a kiss, huh?'

Stepha batted her eyelids. 'Why Les,' she answered. 'I never thought you'd ask.'

Stepha drifted across the spa and Les put his arms around her then they got into a steamy kissing session that matched the atmosphere in the bathroom. Stepha sucked Norton's tongue and kissed him all over the face, Les kissed her neck and bit into it leaving a love bite under her ear as big as a fifty-cent coin. As Les kissed Stepha and felt her in his arms, he got the impression that beneath the bad language and the rough exterior, Stepha was just a little battler who only wanted to love and be loved in return. Plus she had a good, honest heart. She didn't have much money and she could have taken advantage of Les and put it straight on him to stay the night. But she offered Les what she could spare. Then found the extra five dollars when he niggardly asked her for it. And when Burne showed up, she told Les it was her problem. He didn't have to get involved. Les could have easily walked away and left her. And when Les didn't, she got between them and faced up to Burne, knowing she'd only cop it again. That showed plenty of heart. And a lot of honesty. Yes, thought Les, as he kissed Stepha's eyes and gave her a big, big hug. The cheeky little waitress from Melbourne was all right.

Somebody else in the spa, however, had different feelings about the cheeky little waitress from Melbourne. Mr Wobbly. He'd been sitting up under the bubbles just biding his time. Now the evil little monster wanted in on the action. And why waste another minute. Les eased Stepha against the side of the spa bath, spread her legs then got between them and entered her, finding the little waitress firm and warm. Les then did his best to return Stepha's honesty as sweet as he could, for as long as he could.

The steaming water churned in the spa, the bubbles rose and fell and water spilled over the side. Stepha held Les round the neck, sighed and went with him, kissing the big red-headed Queenslander tenderly. It was all too good; and after the hash joints, it was even better. Les got his arms under Stepha's legs, held her against the side of the spa then thrust as hard and as deep as he could, and with a moan of pure ecstasy that echoed Stepha's squealing, poured everything he had into her. The water in the spa bath swirled from side to side, bubbles went everywhere, then it all settled down just as the tape cut out in the lounge room.

They lay together in the spa and shared a few kisses till eventually the water temperature began to drop.

'Well what do you reckon, Stepha?' said Les. 'We go to bed? I'm not used to all this and I'm about knackered.'

'Yes,' agreed Stepha. 'I'm tired too.'

They got out of the spa bath, wrapped towels around themselves, Les pulled the plug and they walked out to the lounge room. Les smiled at Stepha and put his arms around her.

'Look,' he said. 'You can sleep in bed with me if you want. But I had a huge meal earlier and a few drinks. So I'll be farting and snoring all night. You'd be better off sleeping on your own. But please yourself.'

'That's all right,' replied Stepha. 'I understand. You've had a root. Now I can piss off. Would you like me to sleep out on the landing?'

'Okay. Bring the paper in with you in the morning.' Les scrabbled Stepha's hair. 'Hang on. I'll get you a pillow and blankets.'

Les went to his room and changed into a clean T-shirt and jox then came back with two blankets and two pillows from the wardrobe. Stepha put on a black Freddie Mercury T-shirt, a pair of grey tracksuit pants and woolly socks.

'Here you are Baby Bunting.' Les lay Stepha on the lounge, put the pillows under her head and tucked the blankets up under her chin. 'Now. Are we all warm and snug?'

'Yes thank you,' said Stepha.

'Good. What time does the bus leave in the morning?'

'Ten-thirty.'

'Unreal,' smiled Les. 'We can have a nice breakfast before you go.'

'Okay. Hey Les.'

'Yes.'

'Do I get a goodnight kiss?'

'Oh, I don't see why not,' replied Les.

Les lifted Stepha's chin up gently and left her with a long, lingering kiss. 'How was that?'

'That was just fine.' Stepha rolled over on her side as Les turned out the lights. 'Hey Les,' she said, from under the blankets.

'Yes Stepha.'

'I like you, Father Les. You're really nice.'

Les smiled at Stepha's silhouette in the darkness. 'Thank you Stepha. You're rather nice yourself. I'll see you in the morning.'

Les went to his bedroom, closed the door and switched off the light, not bothering to put his money and credit cards under the pillow when he got into bed. Well, apart from having to take those three mugs to task, he yawned, I'd call that a pretty good night. And I think somebody else enjoyed themselves too. Les smiled and thought about Stepha when the wind picked up across the landing and began flicking at the window curtains on the opposite side of the room. Outside Les could hear the ocean breaking along the beach. Norton yawned again and scrunched his head into the pillows. In seconds he was snoring happily.

Norton's sleep was disturbed the next morning by the sound of his door opening. He was awakened a few seconds later by something getting under the douvet and curling up against his back.

'Stepha,' blinked Les. 'What's ...?'

'I just came in for a cuddle. That's all,' said Stepha.

'No worries.' Les took Stepha's arm and wrapped it round him. 'How are you this morning?'

Stepha nuzzled his neck. 'Good.'

'Did you sleep all right?'

'Yes thanks. I got up to go to the loo and found that caesar salad. Gee it was nice.'

'Yeah? Did you leave me any?'

'I meant to.'

'No wonder Burne kicked you out of the house.'

Stepha pinched Les through his T-shirt and it hurt. Les chuckled into the pillow and closed his eyes. A few moments went by then Stepha started rubbing Miss Brazil against his back. A couple of minutes of this and Mr Wobbly began to think Stepha had got into bed for a bit more than a cuddle. He was soon up and about and somehow managed to roll Les over on his back and find his way into Stepha's mouth. Stepha gave

Les a diabolical polish then got on top. Les gave a shudder of delight as Stepha came down on him. It felt that good he could have kissed her. So he did. Stepha kissed him back then started grinding away. Les smiled up and watched Stepha's hair swaying rhythmically from side to side then closed his eyes and went along for the ride.

It was a fantastic way to commence the morning and Les would have liked to have gone on till lunchtime. However, Stepha revved up then came down too hard and too often in one long burst and Les let go with a howl that rattled the windows. Stepha eventually got off and lay down alongside Les. Norton's heart had settled down and Mr Wobbly was flopping around, a mere husk of his former, finely chiselled self.

'How was that?' purred Stepha.

'For just a cuddle. Not real bad,' answered Les. 'What would have happened if you'd've come in wanting a root?'

Stepha gave Les another pinch. 'You big shit. No wonder they kicked you out of the church.' She got up and dropped the douvet over Norton's face. 'I'm going to have a shower.'

Les smiled and lay under the douvet for a while then got up and sat on the edge of the bed. Shit! Am I imagining things, he shivered. Or is it cold in here? He glanced up at the windows above the TV and it looked very gloomy on the landing. Les got up, wrapped a towel around himself then walked down to the lounge room, drew back the curtains and opened the sliding glass door onto the balcony. Outside it was drizzling rain, the wind was blowing onshore and it was grey and gloomy all the way to the horizon. He closed the door and turned around just as Stepha walked into the lounge room wrapped in towels.

'What a miserable bloody day,' said Les.

'You're only saying that because I'm leaving,' smiled Stepha. 'Aren't you, darling pet.'

'You're right.' Les gave Stepha a kiss on the forehead then headed for the shower.

Stepha was standing in the lounge room wearing a pair of jeans, the same black jacket zipped up over a black T-shirt and a huge grey beanie, when Les came down wearing his blue tracksuit. His hair was combed and he'd squirted himself with deodorant, but he hadn't bothered to shave. He walked up to Stepha and put his arm around her.

'Well Stepha,' he said. 'Parting is such sweet sorrow. But we got plenty of time for breakfast. You hungry?'

'After one lousy caesar salad. What do you reckon?' said Stepha.

'Why are you such a romantic, Stepha?' asked Les.

'It's you, Father Les,' she smiled. 'You've taken away all my pain. And filled my cold, cold heart with love.'

'I'll carry your bag for you.'

Arm in arm, Les and Stepha caught the lift to the lobby, sharing a kiss or two on the way down. Rather than enter the restaurant through the resort, Les walked Stepha outside to see if the weather was as bad as it looked from the balcony. It was. And as they rounded the corner past the pine trees, the rain got heavier. They jogged up a short flight of stairs, then stepped through the chairs and tables in front of the restaurant. Les slid the glass door open and they stepped inside.

The restaurant was called Michael's. It had soft lights set in a white ceiling and was painted in shades of tan to match the resort. The counter was on the right and in the middle was a buffet breakfast. Coffee and tea was against the wall behind. Les gave the girl at the counter his room number then he and Stepha walked past the other diners and found a table in a corner facing the ocean. Les placed Stepha's bag against the wall and nodded at the buffet.

'Why don't we just attack?' he suggested.

'Good idea,' nodded Stepha. 'I'm going to get a cup of tea first.'

After tea and fruit juice they got into the Bircher muesli and fruit, then proceeded on to bacon and eggs with all the trimmings plus hot buttered toast washed down by cups of tea and coffee. From the look on Stepha's face as she ate a third piece of toast with apricot jam, she hadn't done too bad for twenty-five dollars. They talked about different things, Les got Stepha's mobile phone number and it was a very leisurely, very enjoyable breakfast. However, time always flies when you're having fun.

'Stepha,' said Les. 'You've worked down here a few times and you know your way around.'

'Yeah. That's right,' replied Stepha.

'If I wanted to find out ... say something about old Lorne. Where would I go? The council? They got a historical society round here or something?'

Stepha pointed down the street. 'You know the second-hand bookshop in the laneway?'

'Yeah. The little wooden house back off the street.'

'That's it,' nodded Stepha. 'See the lady that runs it. Mrs Totten. She's lived here all her life and knows everything there is about the place. I get my books off her and she's a real old sweetheart. She'll look after you.'

'Thanks Stepha,' said Les.

Stepha looked at her watch. 'Shit! I'd better get going. The bus'll be here any minute.' She smiled at Les. 'I wish I wasn't going now.'

Les returned Stepha's smile and put his hand on hers. 'I wish you weren't either.'

They finished the last of their tea and coffee, Les picked up Stepha's bag and paid the bill while she went to fix her non-existent make-up. They walked outside and by the time they joined the other people huddled at the bus stop, the bus was coming down the hill, its windscreen wipers beating away at the swirling rain. It squealed to a halt and the door swished open, several passengers got off and the people at the bus stop filed on, happy to be getting out of the cold. Les handed Stepha her bag, put his arms around her and gave her a warm kiss goodbye.

'Listen, Stepha. Before you go,' said Les. 'I've got something for you.' He fished into his tracksuit and came up with a twenty-dollar bill. 'There's your twenty dollars back. I'm keeping the other five for the caesar salad.'

'What? You miserable bastard,' said Stepha. 'If I'd have known that I wouldn't have eaten it.'

Les fished into the other pocket of his tracksuit and handed Stepha an envelope. 'My phone number's in there. Give me a ring sometime.'

Stepha took the envelope, felt it then took a peek inside. 'There's money in here,' she said. 'Shit! Are some of those fifties?'

'They're all fifties,' said Les.

Stepha shook her head and pocketed the envelope. 'Why did you have to go and do that, Les? You big prick.'

'I dunno,' shrugged Norton. 'It's a prick of a day. And I guess you've left me in a prick of a mood. What can I say?'

The rain pattered down on Stepha's beanie, dripped onto her face and blended in with two smears of warm salty water trickling from the corners of her eyes. 'For a priest, you're certainly something else. Aren't you — Father Les.'

The other people had got on the bus and Les could see the driver trying his best to look patient. 'Next time I see you, I'll tell you a bit more about myself.' He gave Stepha a quick kiss on the lips and pulled down her beanie. 'Now go on. Get on the bus, you little shit. Before you catch pneumonia.'

Stepha picked up her bag and got on the bus and the door swished shut behind her. She sat down at a window seat and stared out at Les. Les smiled up through the rain, blew her a kiss and waved. Stepha waved back, then the bus began to move off. She was still staring out the window at Les when it went past the old picture theatre. Les watched the bus disappear round the bend then shoved his hands in the jacket pockets of his tracksuit and walked back to the unit.

Once inside, Les switched the kettle on and walked into the lounge room, noticing Stepha had folded the blankets neatly and left them on the lounge. He stared out across the balcony at a rotten cold day and suddenly the unit felt awfully empty. The kettle boiled, Les made a cup of tea and took the blankets and pillows back to his bedroom.

Les sipped his tea, took his tracksuit top off and put on a grey sweatshirt with his GAP anorak on over the top. He tossed a few things in his overnight bag, took it out to the kitchen, then finished his cup of tea looking over the map of Lorne he got at the real estate agency. Corio Crescent was up a hill behind the main street. Okay, thought Les. Let's see how we go. He rinsed his cup, put his cap on, and caught the lift down to the car park.

The Mitsubishi purred into life, Les checked his map and tuned the radio to 106.7 FM. The reception was a little scratchy and the woman DJ was on a bluegrass trip, playing Yank Ratchell a'plunking 'Cigarette Blues'. It was a bit hokey for Norton's taste. But anything had to be better than listening to Who Da Funk, or hearing 'Hotel California' for the two hundred thousandth time between ads for junk food and electrical appliances. The roller door was up, Les drove out into the rain, went down the hill then turned left into Mountjoy.

There was hardly any traffic. Les took a left at a motel then drove up the hill and turned right at the local police station, before passing an ambulance station and a school. All the houses were spread out on hilly open blocks surrounded by trees, and Corio Crescent was a deadend running into bush. Number two was on the corner. It was a big old weatherboard building painted white and set back in a yard full of tall blue gums. A white picket fence, divided by a wooden gate framed with pine logs, ran around part of the yard, and a concrete path led to a set of steps going up to a vestry out the front. Either side of the vestry was an enclosed verandah beneath an A-frame roof with a satellite TV dish on the side. A blue and gold sign hanging above the gate said MADONNA BACKPACKERS LORNE. Seated on a milk crate beneath the apex at the top of the stairs, a woman in a red flannelette shirt and jeans was washing a small white dog in a yellow plastic bathtub. Les switched off the engine and got out of the car. He stood in the rain for a moment looking at the old wooden building before opening the gate and hurrying along the path and up the stairs out of the rain. The woman looked up as Les stepped under the apex.

'Not much of a day,' commented Les.

'No,' agreed the woman, pouring water over the dog's head. 'Chewy's enjoying it even less.'

The woman was an overweight blonde, with a plump, happy face; the dog was a Maltese terrier with a flat, miserable face. Standing reluctantly in the soapy water, it was that miserable it didn't even acknowledge Norton's presence, let alone bother to bark at a stranger.

'Chewy? That wouldn't be short for Chewbacca, would it?' said Les.

'Yes. The little shit. He rolled in something earlier. God, the stink was enough to make you sick.' She gave the dog another splash of water then lifted it out of the tub. Chewy shook himself, gave his owner a filthy look then ran off around the verandah. The woman wiped her hands on a tea towel and looked at Les. 'So what can I do for you?'

'Have you got something to do with this place?' asked Les.

'Yes. I'm the owner,' replied the woman. 'With my husband. Are you looking for a room?'

'Actually,' said Les. 'I'm looking for a church.'

The woman gave a little laugh. 'Well you're a bit late,' she said.

'Late?' said Les.

'Years bloody late.'

'Years?'

'Yeah,' said the woman. 'This used to be a church, till the priest died. Then some sculptors turned it into a studio. Before me and my husband bought it and started up a backpackers. We kept the old name.'

'That's right,' said Les. 'It used to be the Church of the Blessed Madonna. And the priest's name was Father Shipley.'

The woman shook her head. 'No. It wasn't Shipley. It was Marriott.'

'Marriott?'

'That's right,' said the woman. She got up off the milk crate, rubbed her legs and looked curiously at Les. 'What did you want the old church for, anyway?'

'Well,' said Les. 'My name's Norton. Les Norton. And my late mother, Rosa-Marie Norton, had some paintings sent here from Sydney to a Father Shipley for safekeeping. It was a long time ago. But I was sort of ... hoping they might still be here.'

The woman looked at Les somewhat amused. 'Have you come all the way from Sydney to find these paintings?'

'That's right,' answered Les.

'Well, all I can say is, mate, you've come a long way for nothing.'

The woman picked up the bathtub and emptied it out into the garden at the side of the stairs. Les felt like he'd been kicked in the stomach.

'If you don't mind, ma'am,' said Les. 'What's your name?'

'Sirotic,' replied the woman. 'Maureen Sirotic.'

'Mrs Sirotic. There wouldn't be an old storage shed or something round the back would there?'

'There would,' replied Mrs Sirotic. 'But I can tell you now, there's no paintings in there. When the sculptors moved out they practically stripped the place bare. Anything they did leave, we either threw out or burnt.'

'Fair dinkum?' said Les bleakly.

'Fair dinkum,' repeated Mrs Sirotic. 'But seeing you've come such a long way, you're welcome to have a look around when my husband comes back from Geelong. But you'd only be wasting your time.'

Les looked at the owner and knew when he'd tossed tails. 'No, that's all right, Mrs Sirotic. I'll take your word for it. But thanks for your help anyway.'

'No worries,' said the owner.

The dog appeared from around the verandah and decided to bark at Les. Les felt like giving it a kick in the arse. The owner told it to keep quiet then turned to Les.

'Are you staying in Lorne?' she asked.

'Yes. Till Friday,' replied Les. 'At the Otway Resort.'

'Well, why don't you ask the priest at the church just up from there. He was friends with Father Marriott. He might be able to help you, and he lives on the premises.'

'Okay. I will. Thanks.' Les gave the woman a brief smile then turned and trotted down the stairs.

A gust of wind hit the trees and a shower of wet leaves fell around Les as he opened the car door. He got inside and stared back at what was once the Church of the Blessed Madonna. Well wouldn't that root you, he cursed to himself. I've been kneecapped right from the word go. I should have bloody known. Les started the engine, the radio came on and Harry Manx began moaning 'Lay Down My Worries'. Ohh get fucked, you whingeing hillbilly prick, Les cursed again. He reversed round and headed back into town.

Les found the church easily enough, did a U-turn and pulled up in front under a pair of towering eucalypts. It was set in neat surroundings edged with trees, and made from white weatherboard like the first building, except the vestry stood at the end and it was built side-on to the road. Stained-glass windows ran along the side, under a grey roof with a cross on top, and a sign out front said CHURCH OF THE HOLY BLOOD, SURF COAST PARISH, VICAR:

ENOCH RATHBONE. There was a driveway on the left and near the driveway a man in yellow plastic coveralls, glasses and a dirty white cap was working a whipper snipper. Les got out of the car and walked over to him.

'Excuse me,' said Les.

The man turned down the whipper snipper and looked at Les. He had a three-day growth and horrible brown teeth that said he rolled his own and smoked plenty of them. 'Yeah mate,' he wheezed. 'What's up?'

'I'm looking for the vicar,' said Les. 'Is he around?'

The man indicated to the driveway. 'He's down the back.'

'Thanks mate.'

The man continued whipper snipping and Les walked up the driveway, coming to a garage at the end. To the right, a white-panelled house was built onto the back of the church, and behind the garage a permalum storage shed stood on one side of a grassy yard opposite an open greenhouse full of roses. Inside the greenhouse, a big man was standing at a table pruning a magnificent yellow rose. Les walked over and approached him quietly.

'Excuse me. Are you Vicar Rathbone?' asked Les.

The man slowly turned around and stared at Les. He had an impassive, jowly face, dark fire-and-brimstone eyes topped by thick black eyebrows and a head of unruly black hair. He was wearing a yellow shirt and black trousers under a green apron that came up to his chest and in a gloved hand was a pair of secateurs. Les gave him a double blink. Shit! Where's Warren? I've found Nero Wolfe.

'Yes. I am he,' boomed the vicar, in a voice that matched his eyes.

'My name's Les Norton,' said Les. 'Mrs Sirotic sent me around.'

'Mrs Sirotic? Oh yes. From the backpackers.'

'That's her.' Les offered his hand and the vicar gave it a quick shake.

'So what is the purpose of your visit, Mr Norton?' asked Vicar Rathbone.

'Mrs Sirotic said you were a friend of Father Marriott.'

'That's right. Father Marriott had the Church of the Blessed Madonna. Until sadly he was taken from us.'

'Taken?' said Les. 'What happened?'

'A motor accident,' answered Vicar Rathbone. 'William was knocked off his pushbike.'

'Oh. That's no good,' said Les.

'Indeed not sir. He was a good man, Father Marriott.'

Les gave an understanding nod. 'Vicar Rathbone. Would you know a priest called Shipley? Father Bernard Shipley.'

'I would,' replied the vicar. 'He had the church before William.'

'Is Father Shipley still …?'

Vicar Rathbone shook his head. 'Hardly. We laid Bernard to rest many years ago, over in Lorne cemetery. I read the eulogy.'

'Oh. What happened to Father Shipley?'

'The Lord called him,' orated Vicar Rathbone. 'And he went to his arms.'

'As good a place to be, vicar,' said Les solemnly.

'Indeed.' The vicar went back to pruning the beautiful yellow rose sitting in its pot on the table. 'So Mr Norton,' he said. 'What exactly is it you want from me, sir, on this rather inclement day?'

'All right, vicar.' Les gave Vicar Rathbone the same spiel he gave Mrs Sirotic. The vicar listened politely, although he seemed more interested in his roses than listening to Les. 'The thing is, vicar, my mother may not have been a well-known artist, but she was very gifted. And those paintings mean a lot to my family, in sentimental value.'

The vicar digested all Les said and waited before answering. 'I understand the purpose of your visit, Mr Norton,' he replied sagely. 'I also respect your family values, and you have certainly come a long way. But how can I possibly be able to help you?'

'Well,' said Les. 'I just thought the paintings might have finished up in your care. Seeing you knew both Father Shipley and Father Marriott. Mrs Sirotic suggested it actually.'

'She did?' said the vicar.

Les turned to the white permalum shed behind the garage. 'There's a storage shed over there, vicar. If I was to make a donation to the church, do you think I could have a look inside?' Les produced a one-hundred-dollar bill from his pocket and Vicar Rathbone's fire and brimstone eyes lit up like halogen lamps.

'I don't see why not,' replied the vicar. He dropped the secateurs on the table and deftly snatched the hundred from Norton's hand. It disappeared under the vicar's apron and was replaced by a set of keys. 'Follow me, my boy.'

'Thanks, vicar.'

Les followed Vicar Rathbone over to the storage shed. The vicar opened the door, found a switch on the wall and the storage shed lit up under several fluorescent lights hanging from the ceiling. There was any amount of junk and objects the church had saved, and like the vicar's roses, most of it was laid out neatly on tables. The remainder was stacked around the walls or propped up in corners.

'Start wherever you wish,' offered the vicar.

'Thanks,' said Les.

With the vicar watching him like a hawk, Les started rummaging through all the junk. There were old heaters, furniture, wicker chairs, boxes of crockery. Piles of magazines, car parts, an organ, battered violin and guitar cases and two milk crates full of old albums. Les absently flicked through a few. Patti Page, The Ink Spots, Perry Como, Bing Crosby, the soundtrack from *West Side Story*.

Next to the mandatory piles of *National Geographics* and *Reader's Digests*, were two paintings. Norton's eyes lit up as he moved them out from the wall. One was Christ on the cross. The other was the Virgin Mary, complete with a shiny white halo. Les put them back against the wall.

The more he looked around, the more Les realised nearly everything in the shed was left over from church sales. He dropped a Snoopy doll back into a box of toys and turned to the vicar still watching him from the door.

'Well, they're definitely not in here, vicar,' said Les.

'I could have told you that, Mr Norton,' replied the vicar. 'But I had no desire to curb your enthusiasm.'

Yeah. Or miss out on the lazy hundred. 'That's okay,' said Les. 'I appreciate your help anyway. Hey, vicar. There's a church down the road. Who's in charge of that one?'

'Saint Fabian's?' replied the vicar. 'Reverend Kimball Pillinger.'

'I may as well call in there, too,' said Les.

The vicar nodded sagely. 'Yes, why not. Kim knew Father Marriott.'

'And are there any other churches around here?' asked Les.

'There's one on the other side of town, in Falls Terrace. I don't know who runs it now.'

'Doesn't matter,' said Les. 'I'll call in there too.'

The vicar switched off the lights and opened the door. Les stepped outside into the rain and the vicar locked the door behind them.

'Good luck, Mr Norton,' said the vicar. 'God willing, you will find your mother's paintings.'

'Yes,' smiled Norton. 'I can see her looking down from heaven now, telling me to keep searching. Goodbye, Vicar Rathbone.'

Les walked down to the car and the vicar went back to his roses. Brown teeth had taken a breather and was standing under a tree puffing on a roll-your-own. Les gave him a nod and got in the car. Well, another out, thought Les, as he started the engine. And I got a feeling there's going to be plenty more. With the Wildwood Valley Boys howling 'Are You On The Right Road?' Les drove down to the next church, finding a parking spot between the phone boxes and the old picture theatre. He switched off the engine and got out of the car.

Walking past the phone boxes, Les noticed the rain had washed away any blood from last night's activities and in the daytime St Fabian's was a lovely old church. Built in white weatherboard like the others, it was bigger, with higher stained-glass windows and topped by a green roof with green turrets. The sloping grounds were lovingly maintained and full of beautiful flower beds and rockeries. A set of stone steps with a white railing ran up to the church and behind on the right was a white weatherboard house. A sign near a gate in the wire fence said ST FABIAN'S, LORNE, CONSOLIDATING CHURCH OF AUSTRALIA, MINISTER: REVEREND KIMBALL PILLINGER. Where Les had dumped Burne and his mates the previous night, a man wearing a plastic raincoat was standing under an umbrella staring down at the grass. Through the plastic raincoat Les could make out a pair of black trousers, a black cardigan and a white priest's collar. I think that could be my man, surmised Les. He let himself in the gate and walked over.

'Excuse me,' said Les. 'Are you Reverend Pillinger?'

The man turned around under his umbrella. He was stockily built with thinning brown hair going grey, and came up to Norton's chin. He had a plump, ruddy face and slightly bloodshot eyes, and a thick red nose and veiny cheeks suggested the good reverend didn't mind a tipple at the altar wine now and again.

'Mmhh? What was that?' he said vaguely.

'Are you Reverend Pillinger?' repeated Les.

'Yes, yes. That's me. Are you from the police?'

'No. Vicar Rathbone sent me down,' said Les.

'Oh.'

'Why? What's the matter?' inquired Les. 'Is something wrong?'

'There was a nasty accident outside the church last night,' answered Reverend Pillinger. 'A car jumped the gutter and knocked three young men over the fence.'

'Fair dinkum?' said Norton. 'Was anybody seriously hurt?'

'Seriously enough,' replied Reverend Pillinger. 'One young man has a broken jaw and several teeth missing. The others are quite knocked about too, I believe.'

'Gee. That's no good,' sympathised Les. 'And a car accident, you say, reverend?'

'Yes. It's rather strange, though,' ruminated the reverend. 'The police thought they might have been in a fight. But one of the lads said a 4WD hit them, and sped off.'

'Did they get the number?'

'Unfortunately no,' said Reverend Pillinger. 'Actually I was just saying a prayer for the victims when you walked up.'

'Very thoughtful of you, reverend.' Les decided not to go in with the hard sell too early. 'I believe the same thing happened to Father Marriott too,' he said.

'Yes. That was quite tragic,' said Reverend Pillinger. 'Poor William was riding his pushbike at night without a light, and a tow truck hit him.'

'You can never be too careful,' said Les. 'Did you know Father Marriott well, reverend?'

'Yes. We used to study the Bible together and go fishing. He only had a small diocese. But he was a lovely man. Sorely missed.'

'What about Father Bernard Shipley, reverend. Did you know him?'

'Not very well. I hadn't been here long before he passed away. And he was often in Apollo Bay.'

'Right,' Les nodded slowly.

'So why did Enoch send you down here?' enquired Reverend Pillinger. 'And might I say, you're a fine stamp of a lad. Footballer are you?'

'Yes,' smiled Les. 'But not Aussie Rules, I'm sorry to say.'

Reverend Pillinger drew closer. 'Between you and me, I don't like rules. Kick basketball, I call it. But say that around here and they'll hang you.' Reverend Pillinger drew Les into his confidence. 'I'm a Rugby Union man myself.'

'The game they play in heaven, reverend,' said Les. 'But I have to confess. I used to play Rugby League.'

'Close enough.' Sharing his umbrella with Les, Reverend Pillinger turned and started walking up to the church residence. 'Now, where were we?' he said. 'Oh yes. Enoch sent you down. Exactly what for, Mr ...?'

'Norton. Les Norton. From Sydney.'

Les gave Reverend Pillinger much the same spiel he gave the other two. Reiterating that because of the mutual connection between the different ministers in Lorne, Shipley or Marriott might have left his mother's paintings at another church when the one in Corio Road folded. Again Les offered a donation if he could look through the church's storage area. The good reverend said that wasn't necessary, but Les insisted he take fifty dollars.

When they reached the house, it was white weatherboard like the church. There was a storage room built underneath and a set of steps ran up to the front door and an enclosed verandah. Reverend Pillinger appeared deep in thought as he stepped across to a door beneath the house.

'Paintings you say, Mr Norton?' he said.

'Yes. Six of them,' replied Les. 'Bound up in green canvas.'

The reverend nodded thoughtfully. 'You know, something like that rings a bell.'

'It does?' said Les.

'Yes, yes.'

At that moment a white-haired lady wearing a grey twin set and a kitchen apron over a checked woollen skirt came down the stairs.

'Reverend Pillinger. You're wanted on the phone,' she said. 'It's Reverend Whittle in Bendigo.'

'Thank you, Mrs Hardaker.' The reverend found a set of keys in his trousers and opened the door. 'The light switch is just inside the door, Mr Norton,' he said. 'Have a good look around. I'll be back directly.'

'Okay, Reverend Pillinger. Thanks a lot.' Les stepped into the storage room and groped around for the light switch. Shit! I wonder what he means by 'rings a bell' thought Les. Don't tell me the bloody things are in here. Les found the switch and turned on the light.

The storage room was as big as the previous one, but just a single, weak light bulb hung from the ceiling, and instead of things being laid out neatly or placed on tables, they were scattered everywhere or piled on top of each other. Old fuel stoves, wheelbarrows full of rusty tools, wooden boxes that could have contained anything. Boxes of toys, a couple of old computers, coils of chicken wire, a rusty ab-rocker, even a clothes dummy with an arm missing. Shoes, clothes, men's hats and ladies' bonnets, handbags, blankets, rolls of carpet. Junk of every description and more leftovers from church bazaars, all gathering dust and cobwebs. Next to a shelf full of Mills and Boon novels and a carton of knitting patterns were several milk crates full of albums. Les checked some out. Lawrence Welk and his Champagne Music, *Listening and Dancing*. Lester Lanin, *House Party. Cocktails and Conversation*, Jan August at the Piano. What? mused Les. No Radiohead or Groove Armada?

Les scoured through the junk finding everything from Monopoly sets to a framed photo of Mao Tse-tung. But no sign of any paintings. The cobwebs stuck to Norton's clothes, the dust made him sneeze and the dim light had him squinting. An enjoyable time it was not. Les looked at his watch, wondering where Reverend Pillinger had got to when a movement in the doorway caught his eye.

'How are you going, Mr Norton?' asked the reverend, stepping into the storage room.

'Yeah. Real good,' answered Les sarcastically.

'Sorry I'm late returning,' said Reverend Pillinger. 'But believe me, when Joe Whittle gets going, there's no stopping him. Then Mrs Hardaker insisted I have a cup of tea.'

'That's okay,' said Les.

'So, have you come across anything?'

'Not so far,' said Les. 'Hey reverend. What did you say before? About something ringing a bell?'

'Yes. Over here in the corner,' he replied. 'You did say there were six paintings bound in green canvas. Didn't you?'

'That's right,' said Les.

'Well there's something like that, been sitting here for years,' said the reverend. 'I've never bothered to see what it is.'

Norton's eyes lit up. 'Yeah?'

Reverend Pillinger led Norton over to a corner of the storage room and started pulling away a pile of rugs next to a hat stand. Beneath the rugs was a dirty green canvas bundle tied with rotting black rope. There was no name on the canvas bundle, but it was old and thick with dust and when Les gave the reverend a hand to lift it up, he could definitely feel wooden frames.

'There's a table by the door,' said the reverend. 'Help me over there with them.'

'It's okay, reverend,' said Les. 'I can manage.' Les picked up the old bundle and followed the reverend over to a table near the light switch. The reverend cleared a few things away and Les placed the bundle gently on top.

'There should be a knife somewhere,' said the reverend.

'It doesn't matter.'

Les grabbed the rope and gave it a sharp tug; it was that old it disintegrated in his hands. Brimming with expectation, Les carefully unwrapped the canvas under the watchful eye of Reverend Pillinger. When he'd finished, they both stared at the contents. Sitting on the table were eight old ouija boards.

'Damn ouija boards!' exclaimed Reverend Pillinger. 'I never knew these infernal contraptions were down here.'

'They definitely ain't paintings, are they,' gritted Les.

'My word, they are not,' declared the reverend. 'And they'll go on the fire this afternoon. The devil's work, if you ask me.'

Les felt deflated and would have much preferred not to have found anything at all. All he wanted now was to get out of the gloomy storage room with its dust and junk and away from Reverend Pillinger. Les turned to the reverend and gave him a thin smile.

'Reverend. I have to get going,' he said. 'Thanks for your help.'

'Not at all, Mr Norton,' replied Reverend Pillinger. 'Would you care for a cup of tea before you leave?'

Les shook his head. 'No, thank you. See you later, reverend.'

Norton left Reverend Pillinger with his ouija boards and stepped out of the storage room into the fresh air. He turned his collar up against the wind then strode quickly across the church grounds back to the car, pressed the remote and got inside, shutting the door firmly behind him.

The rain came down and Les stared up at the leaden sky. Bloody ouija boards. Fair dinkum, boss. Why do that to me? Les took out his hanky and wiped away the dust and rain from his face. Well, what now? The church of the great unknown, over the other side of town, and waste more of my time. Les checked his map then started the car and headed for Falls Road, while some hillbilly band called the Bluegrass Cardinals started honking a song over the radio he didn't catch the name of.

Once he'd crossed the bridge over the Erskine River and veered left onto Deans Marsh Road, Les began to see the ironic side of things and a thin smile creaked across his face. What about the boys saying they were hit by a car. Bloody Stepha. She wasn't wrong. I'll give her a ring later. Les hung a left up a hilly road and thought he might 'cruise the hood' before he found Falls Road.

It was steeper than the other side of town, with the same nice homes on big blocks of land, only with more trees. Les drove past a flock of sulphur-crested cockatoos picking at the grass on the side of the road, then the road climbed through a sloping golf course and he came to a sign on the edge of a large parking area saying LORNE COUNTRY CLUB, VISITORS WELCOME. The golf club was on the right and on the far side of the parking area was a tennis court. The rain eased off, Les parked next to a set of steps at the tennis court and got out of the car with his camera.

There was no one on either tennis court and a handful of cars in the parking area. Les walked along the back of the tennis court then stopped at the edge of the fairway. From high on the golf course the view was magnificent. Even on a dismal day Les could see right across Lorne to the jetty and the old hotel and back to the surrounding green mountains. He took a couple of photos then walked over to the car and drove back down the hill.

Les followed his little map and Lorne Cemetery appeared on the left behind a fenced-off dirt parking area surrounded by trees. All the graves sloped down to the treeline and faced the ocean and around the corner, two gates sat opposite the houses across the road. Falls Road was further down on the right. Les drove past a row of houses to a corner to where the road levelled off, and several houses along on the left was the church.

Compared to the others, it was very humble. Just a brown wooden building in a yard surrounded by trees, and a low cyclone-wire fence separating it from the houses next door. A square of yellow window panes with a white cross on them faced the street, the entrance ran up on the left and a driveway led through the trees to what looked like a rickety wooden shed at the back. Les pulled up and switched off the motor. Apart from the rain and a few magpies whistling in the trees, there were no other sounds and no one about. Les took his overnight bag from the back seat and got out of the car.

Behind the fence, the front yard was full of leaves and needed mowing and along the side were small piles of rubbish. Next to the front gate a faded yellow sign on a chipped brown background said CHURCH OF FUNDAMENTAL ADORATION, LORNE, DEACONESS: BRITNEY SKENRIDGE. Les let himself in the front gate and got a feeling Deaconess Skenridge definitely wasn't a profit preacher. He closed the gate behind him and followed the dirt driveway to the shed at the rear.

The shed was built from old brown palings, had a sagging roof and wasn't much bigger than a garage. On the side was a rickety door bolted with a rusting padlock. Les gave it a tug then glanced at another pile of rubbish stacked alongside the back fence. Beneath the bricks and rubbish was half a metre of steel rod from a building site. Les picked it up and put it in the lock, gave it a twist and the lock snapped easily. He kept the piece of metal and pushed the door open.

There was no light inside. But enough coming in to make out a dirty, concrete floor and a cobweb-strewn ceiling. Les took a torch from his overnight bag and ran it around the shed. Stacked alongside one wall were a couple of push-blade mowers, and a birdcage sitting on an old suitcase. In the middle was a canoe with a hole in it, a pushbike with two flat tyres and a coffee table stacked with magazines. Along the other walls were more piles of wood, tins of paint and a whipper snipper resting against an old table strewn with tins of screws and nails. Pinned to the wall above the table was a poster of the Geelong Cats. Les had another quick look around then turned off the torch and exited, locking the door behind him as best he could.

Before he left, Les stopped under the entrance at the side of the church and took an empty envelope from his overnight bag. He put a fifty-dollar bill inside, printed DONATION on the front and slipped it under the door. After walking back to the car, Les had one last look at the little church sitting quietly in the rain, then drove back into town. He didn't bother about the radio.

When Les turned into Mountjoy Parade, he was wet, cold and ready to kill for a cup of hot coffee. He parallel-parked facing the beach, got his overnight bag and walked across to the same coffee shop. After ordering a flat white from inside he picked a table out the front and sat down. An attractive dark-haired girl in black brought his coffee out; Les added sugar and took a very enjoyable sip. He had another sip then got a notepad and biro from his bag and jotted down a few things; all negatives surrounded by doodling.

The day had been a waste of time and money. However, Les couldn't think of anywhere else to look for the paintings except in the old churches. Les still doubted if Father Shipley destroyed the paintings, and he would never have hung them; if the customs department was going to burn them, they'd be too raunchy. There was another possibility: he left them to someone when he died. If that was the case, then the paintings could be anywhere. Talk about looking for a needle in a haystack. But Reverend Pillinger said Father Shipley was often in Apollo Bay. So tomorrow would be much like today. Visit the churches down there, give whoever the same spiel, along with a donation, and with a bit of luck the paintings might turn up. A lot of luck. Norton finished his coffee and went inside to order another.

Les resumed his seat and was wondering where the day had gone when a different girl, wearing black jeans and a black leather jacket, came out of the doorway with his coffee. She had shiny black hair cut in a fringe and appeared just as attractive as the other girl, when she came across the footpath. Unexpectedly, an elderly man wearing a hat and raincoat, darted past and knocked her from behind. The girl with the fringe slipped in the wet and Les copped most of his flat white down the front of his anorak; the rest went over the table.

'Oh shit!' exclaimed the girl. 'I'm so sorry.'

Les flicked at the coffee on his plastic jacket. 'That's all right,' he said good-naturedly. 'I'm wearing plenty of wet weather gear.'

'Look. Let me get a cloth,' said the girl.

She straightened the cup and saucer, went inside and returned with a wettex and a tea towel. Les took the tea towel while the girl wiped the table.

'I really am sorry,' she said.

'Don't worry about it,' said Les, wiping coffee off his jacket. 'I won't get you the sack.'

'There's no chance of me getting the sack,' said the girl, wringing coffee out of the wettex. 'I don't work here.'

'That figures,' said Les.

'Now don't be like that,' smiled the girl.

'So what are you doing if you don't work here?' asked Les. 'Rehearsing for a part in The Three Stooges run a coffee shop?'

'No. I just called in to see my girlfriend. She was on the phone. So rather than see a nice gentleman like you waiting out here in the rain, I brought your coffee out for you.'

'Well raise my rent,' said Les. 'Don't you know how to butter people up. You can tip as many cups of coffee over me as you like.'

'I'll get you another one,' smiled the girl.

'Thanks.'

The girl took the tea towel off Les and went inside. A few minutes later she was back with another coffee and the same thing happened again. This time it was a woman in a yellow mackintosh pushing a pram. The girl managed to straighten up and save the coffee. But it was close.

Les recoiled slightly. 'Hey listen. I was only joking before,' he said.

The girl carefully placed the coffee in front of Les. 'Golly! I don't think it's my day.'

'You're not Robinson Crusoe there,' said Les.

The girl looked at Les and smiled. 'Enjoy your coffee,' she said.

Les returned her smile. 'I will. Thanks very much.'

The girl went inside, Les drank his coffee and stared absently at the rain on the ocean. For some reason holiday resorts always seemed worse than anywhere else when the weather turned sour. His mind completely in neutral, Les finished his coffee, left some money on the table then picked up his overnight bag and walked back to the resort.

When Les got inside the unit and tossed his bag on the bed, it suddenly dawned on him that he'd left the car opposite the coffee shop.

'Shit!' he cursed. 'Now I'll have to go back and get the bloody thing.'

No, bugger it, he thought. I'm having a shower first. Les climbed out of his damp clothes, wrapped a towel around himself and walked down to the lounge room. He switched on the ghetto blaster, and with Jools Holland and Marianne Faithfull getting into 'You Got To Serve Somebody', stepped into the bathroom.

After a miserable, cold day, Les took his time under the shower. He had a few bruises on his arms and the odd lump on his head from the fight on Sunday night and he was enjoying the hot, steamy water running over his body. It would have been nicer if Stepha was in there with him, helping him save water while he showered with a friend. But it was still pretty good. Les got out and had a shave then changed into a pair of jeans and a dark blue Easts T-shirt and made a cup of tea. It wasn't cold in the unit and after he switched on the TV, Les sat on the lounge watching the news and pondered what to do. Why not ring Stepha and see how she's going? He got her mobile number from his bedroom and picked up the phone. After dialling he got the usual message saying the mobile phone he'd called was switched off. Ring back later. Les replaced the receiver and sipped his tea. Hang on. What about Sonia in Geelong? I promised I'd give her a call. He found Sonia's number and dialled.

'Hello. You've rung Sonia. I'm not home. Please leave a message and I'll call you back. Thank you.'

'Sonia. It's Solomon. How are you? I'm in room 202 at the Otway Resort, Lorne. Call me when you get a chance.'

Les rinsed his cup and thought about having a couple of nice draught beers then dinner. There was a hotel just across the road. But he had to go and get the car. Why not drive up to the old hotel near the jetty, check it out and have a couple in there? Les put his black leather bomber jacket on, locked the door and caught the lift down to the lobby.

Outside, the rain had eased off but it was still a cold, bleak night and there was no one around as Les walked briskly down to the car. He got behind the wheel and minutes later pulled up in front of the Great Ocean Hotel, which was lit up like an ocean liner in the night and looked beautiful from the road. Les locked the car and stepped up to the entrance under the archway.

Inside, the hotel had been revamped with an ultra-modern interior that contrasted tastefully with the outside. A restaurant on the right faced a roomy lounge with polished wooden tables sitting on a polished wooden floor. The walls and ceiling were ivory white and around the walls were asymmetrical mirrors, panels of black riverstone and sepia photos of old Lorne. Rear of the lounge was the bar and behind the bar, a mirror reflected back to the doorway. The bar top was perspex with coloured lights underneath. Soft lights sat in the corners next to healthy indoor plants and music was playing softly from speakers hidden in the ceiling. Despite the delightful atmosphere there wasn't a soul in the place. Les pulled up a black padded stool, sat at the bar and waited. Before long a dark-haired man in a blue shirt and black trousers appeared from a doorway behind the bar.

'Sorry mate,' he said. 'I was doing something out the back.'

'That's okay,' replied Les.

'What can I get you?'

Les looked behind the bar then pointed to a pilsener glass and a Carlton Draught tap. 'One of those full of that, thanks.'

'No worries.'

The beer arrived and it was chilled and delicious. Les left his change on the bar and the man walked out the back again. Les decided to have a wander around with his beer and look at some of the old photos.

There were shots of the old hotel, beached whales and stranded sailing ships, all blown up and clear as the day they were taken. Down a step left of the bar and along a short corridor, another room with a bar full of coloured lights looked out over the ocean. In the middle of the room several small lounges faced a fireplace. Three girls in black were seated on two of the lounges having a quiet drink and a cigarette. Les guessed by their outfits they'd just finished work somewhere. One of them turned around and caught Norton's eye. It was Trish, the girl who'd been seated next to Stepha outside Rosa's. Les blanked her. But she got up and walked over, holding a glass of white wine.

'Hello,' she said evenly.

Les looked at her like she was trying to sell him insurance. 'Hello,' he replied. 'Do I know you?'

'Trish. I was with Stepha last night. You left with her.'

Les gave her a false double blink. 'Oh yes. I remember now. I'm sorry.'

Trish gave Les a surreptitious once up and down. 'Where did you go with Stepha?'

'Go?' replied Les. 'Nowhere. I walked up the road with her and put her in a taxi. She went to a friend's house.'

'Oh? Did you hear what happened last night?'

Les looked mystified. 'No. I was only talking to Stepha for a few minutes before a taxi came along. Do you know if she got the bus all right this morning? She seemed quite worried about it.'

'Yes. Evidently she did,' said Trisha. 'So what did you do after Stepha left in the taxi?'

'Me? I went home to bed. It was getting late and I was tired.'

'Where are you staying?'

'Staying? Falls Road. Up near the cemetery. I'm down here visiting my sister.'

'And you don't know anything about last night?' said Trish.

Les shook his head. 'I wouldn't have a clue. Why, what's up? Is Stepha all right?'

'It's not about Stepha.'

'Well, you've lost me, Trish.' Les looked at his watch. 'Anyway. If you'll excuse me. I have to meet someone in the restaurant. Nice talking to you.'

'Yes,' replied Trish.

Les turned and walked back to the other bar. Fancy bumping into her, he mused. And what about the third degree. You can bet she's friends with those three dills I belted last night. They can have her. When he got to the other bar a girl wearing a black uniform was seated having a cup of coffee. It was the same girl who tipped the coffee on him earlier. Well, well, well, Les smiled to himself. Isn't it just my night for bumping into old acquaintances. He resumed his seat one stool down from the girl, where his change was still sitting on the bar.

'Hello,' said Les. 'If it isn't Larry out of The Three Stooges. I'm not going to wear that cup of coffee too, am I?'

The girl turned to Les. She had lovely hazel eyes and a whippy body under her uniform and was even more attractive than Les had noticed earlier.

'Oh hello,' she said cheerfully. 'How are you?'

'Good thanks.' Les took a sip of beer. 'Are you working here?'

'Yes. In the restaurant.'

'Looks like you've got it easy tonight.'

'Yes. It's dead,' agreed the girl. She looked at Les over her coffee. 'So what brings you up here? It's not much of a night.'

'I wanted to check the place out. So I came up for a couple of quiet beers,' replied Les. 'I'm glad I did. It's a terrific old hotel.'

'Yes. The new owners did a great job restoring it.'

'There's nothing wrong with the beer either,' said Les.

'Hey, you were really nice this afternoon when I spilled your coffee on you,' said the girl. 'Generally if that happens, people start jumping up and down like it's the end of the world.'

'What was I going to do?' shrugged Les. 'It was an accident. And I could see you were proficiency challenged.'

'Proficiency challenged,' laughed the girl. 'You're a cheeky bugger. What's your name?'

'Les. What's yours?'

'Claire.'

'Nice to meet you, Claire.'

'You too, Les.'

'So what sort of work do you do in here, Claire?' asked Les.

'Tonight I'm in the restaurant,' replied Claire. 'Thursday night I'm singing up here.'

'You're a singer? Unreal. What? You play a guitar and all that?'

'Yep. Sure do.'

Les raised his glass. 'Good on you. It must be terrific to have talent. Any particular sort of music?'

'Oh. I do a bit of Sheryl Crow. k.d. lang. Kasey Chambers.'

'Yeah? I don't mind all three,' said Les. 'I might come up and see you.'

'Why don't you,' said Claire. 'We get a few in here on Thursday night.'

'All right. You got me,' said Les.

Claire gave Les a short once up and down as he had a mouthful of beer. 'Where are you from, Les?'

'Sydney. I'm here till Friday. I got a unit at the Otway.'

'Really? I've heard it's very swish in there,' said Claire.

'It is.' Les took another sip of beer and smiled at Claire. 'You might like to call round and hear some music. You like blues? Rock 'n roll?'

'Of course I do.'

'Well. I got a ghetto blaster and some good tapes. If you want to come back for a cool one before I leave, you're more than welcome.'

'I might just do that when I finish on Thursday night,' smiled Claire. She looked at Les for a moment. 'Do you like a little puff, Les?'

'Does a honey bee like a little buzz, Claire?'

'I'll see you up here Thursday night.' Claire glanced at her watch. 'Well, I'd better get back to work. We're doing a stock-take.'

Les pointed to his empty glass. 'Can you get me another beer before you go?'

'Sure.'

Claire got Les another beer then disappeared out the back. Les had a mouthful and looked into his glass, a tiny smile flickering around his eyes. Thursday night with Claire, eh. There's not enough O's in smooth to describe you, is there Norton. Les caught his reflection in the mirror and grinned. Queenslander.

Les relaxed with his beer and listened to the music coming out of the hidden speakers, finding it laid back and very easy to listen to. He had another sip of beer and his stomach started to rumble. He thought of checking out the restaurant menu then decided he may as well order room service back at the resort and watch a movie. The food at the resort was very good and he could have a meal at the hotel on Thursday night.

Les was halfway through his beer and he still had the place to himself when a movement in the bar mirror caught his eye. Maybe it was coincidence. Or maybe Trish had got on a mobile or something. But Bucky, the bloke he'd belted the night before, had just walked in with two other blokes. Les kept his back to the door and checked them out in the mirror as they approached the bar. Bucky looked solid in a Levi jacket and jeans, except his jaw was wired up and he had two glorious black eyes. His two mates weren't quite as solid. But they were tall and fit. One bloke with fair hair was wearing a black leather jacket and jeans. The other had a black mullet and a black leather jacket over a pair of grey trousers. They both had lean, sallow faces and hard eyes and something in their walk that got Norton's radar going. They saw Les sitting at the bar and appeared to take no notice. Les casually sipped his beer and stared ahead as the three men sat down two stools away on his right; the fair-haired bloke nearest to him, Bucky in the middle and the Mullet on Bucky's right. The man in the blue shirt came out and one of the men ordered three Bacardi and cokes. They got their drinks and the man in the blue shirt went out the back again. The fair-haired bloke gave Les an impassive once up and down then the three men settled into a quiet conversation. Well, thought Les. They haven't particularly come in here looking for me. And Bucky hasn't noticed who I am. I reckon if I keep my head down, I'll be able to finish my beer and get out of here without any dramas. And return on Thursday night looking the goods. Les finished his beer then stood up and pocketed his change, leaving something on the bar for Claire. Bucky absently noticed Les in the mirror and suddenly squeezed a painful double blink from behind his blackened eyes. He motioned to his mates, mumbled something through his wired-up jaw, and pointed at Les. Oh well, thought Norton regretfully. So much for no dramas. Because I'm not letting them follow me out to the car. Especially those two pricks in the leather jackets.

Les took a quick step across then reached down and grabbed the legs of Bucky's stool with both hands and yanked it out from under him. Bucky's legs shot up in the air and he flew back, hitting his head against the bar rail before landing under the bar seeing a lot of stars through a lot of pain. Les brought the stool up over his shoulder then swung it against the side of the fair-haired bloke's face. It knocked him violently off his stool and he slammed into the bar then fell on the floor next to Bucky, out cold. The bloke with the mullet jumped up and reached under his leather jacket just as Les hurled the bar stool into his chest knocking all the wind out of him. The Mullet clutched at his solar plexus gasping for breath and from somewhere under his leather jacket a knife fell out and clattered on the floor. Les left it there then quickly picked up the stool he'd been sitting on, raised it above him and banged it down over the Mullet's head like a mallet. The Mullet's eyes glazed over and he landed on his backside against the bar then slumped over on top of the others, out like a light. Les looked at the three men stacked neatly on the floor and brought the stool up again to give them another serve, the Mullet in particular. But there was no visible blood and no one had seen anything. Les decided to leave it at that. He replaced the bar stools, then picked up the knife and put it in his pocket just as Claire appeared from out the back. She couldn't see what was on the floor in front of the bar. But she saw Les standing there and smiled.

'You're leaving?' she said.

'Yeah,' nodded Les, zipping up his leather jacket. 'I'm driving. And it's best not to take the risk.'

'Smart thinking,' agreed Claire. She looked curiously at Les. 'I thought I heard noises out here?'

Les pointed to Bucky and his mates lying on the floor. 'Yeah. I don't know what happened,' he replied frankly. 'These blokes were sitting having a quiet drink. Then they fell off their stools. Maybe they're epileptics or something?'

Claire looked down over the bar. 'Good Lord!' she said. 'I'd better get the manager.'

'Yeah,' agreed Les. 'A glass of water might be an idea too. Okay Claire. I'll see you on Thursday night.'

'Yes,' Claire replied absently. 'I'll see you then Les.'

Norton walked back to the car, got straight in and quickly drove home. Minutes later he was standing in the kitchen having a delicious. Alabama 3 were quietly bopping 'Reachin' on the ghetto blaster and Les was softly crooning along with the lyrics, the knife sitting on the kitchen bar top. It was ten centimetres long, with a black handle and a tiny, serrated knob on the blade so you could flick it open with one hand. Well fuckin beat that, mused Les. I can't go anywhere without getting into strife. Australia just isn't big enough for me. And even though I swore I wouldn't mention bloody deja vu again, the same thing happened to me in Adelaide. Some bloke I belted turned up at a pub in Victor Harbor with his mates, and I had to fight them too. But at least they didn't have knives. Les sipped his bourbon and stared at the deadly little weapon sitting on the bar. Yeah. I knew there was something about those two blokes. If they'd have followed me outside, that could have finished up in my back. And you can bet his mate had one too. Pair of pricks. Les drained his bourbon and patted his stomach. Anyway. I got more important things on my mind than Bucky and his mates. Dinner. It's getting late, and I ain't been fed.

Les made another delicious then rang room service and ordered two dozen oysters kilpatrick, braised lamb shanks with parmesan mash and port wine jus, a side salad and oven roasted potatoes with rosemary and garlic. Plus a frozen chocolate mousse with creme anglaise. He changed into his blue tracksuit then kicked back in front of the TV while he waited for room service.

His food arrived before long. The waiter placed it on the table, Les tipped him then ripped in. It was delicious, the two beers had put an edge on his appetite and Les ate every morsel; when he'd finished he could hardly move. But he managed to make another delicious before turning on the in-house movie, *Austin Powers — The Spy Who Shagged Me*.

It wasn't the worst movie Les had ever seen. But it was up there with them. Inane dialogue and non-stop corny sexual innuendos mixed with ghastly colours and atrocious music. It was that bad it got Les in. Or maybe it was Elizabeth Hurley's boobs. Send up or not, it was a dog. And when it finished Les couldn't work out for the life of him why a good actor like Tim Robbins would take a part in such a stinkerrollah. Les shook his head in disgust then turned everything off and went to his room.

Les thought about reading for a while. But the huge meal and dud movie had flattened him. He yawned, switched off the bedlamps and got under the douvet. Oh well. Tomorrow, my quest takes me to Apollo Bay. I wonder what sort of shit I'll get into down there? Knowing my luck, deep and thick. Les yawned again, shoved his head into the pillows and before long he was sawing wood.

The rain had temporarily eased to windswept drizzle and it was another cold, bleak day when Les got up the next morning and stared out over the balcony. Although he'd slept in his tracksuit, he didn't bother changing. He just cleaned himself up, put his gym boots on then got the lift down to the lobby and took the stairway from the resort down to the restaurant.

After a fruit juice and coffee, Les had a chuckle over his breakfast as he reflected on last night's events in the old hotel. I wonder if Trish came across Bucky and his mates lying on the floor after I left? I'd like to have seen the look on her face if she did. Norton finished his breakfast with one more cup of good coffee and went back to his unit.

His sweatshirt had dried out, so he put that back on with his anorak over the top. After checking his overnight bag and taking a look at the road map, Les put his cap on and took the lift to the parking area. When he opened the car door and went to throw his overnight bag inside, he noticed the damp, rusty piece of iron inside it was rubbing against everything. Near another car were several sheets of newspaper. Les put them on the back seat and lay the length of iron on top. He started the motor and turned on the radio to find the station was playing blues music. Les drove out of the garage then took a right at the roundabout, and with Eric Clapton crooning 'Got You On My Mind', headed for Apollo Bay.

The road was even windier than driving down from Melbourne, with steeper cliffs and hills overlooking the ocean. Coming off the sea, a strong breeze was pushing the rain up against the cliffs like huge billowing clouds of steam. Les didn't see many beaches. Mainly glimpses of pretty little bays with small green rivers running into them between rocky headlands. And only glimpses. The road was full of hairpin bends and he wasn't game to take his eyes off it for a second. The surrounding hills and cliffs also made the radio reception a bit iffy. However, the rain suddenly stopped, although there was absolutely no sign of any sun.

Les drove through Wye River and glimpsed several odd-looking long-necked animals amongst some cattle high up on a hill. They were alpacas. The last time Les had seen an alpaca was in Wagga Wagga, when he was minding the Murrumbidgee Mud Crabs for Neville Nizeguy. He slowed down as he approached the small hamlet of Kennett River then slowed right down when he noticed a white police car parked near a shower block in a dirt parking area on his left. Next thing a uniform cop stepped out from in front of the patrol car holding a STOP sign. Les turned in and pulled up alongside him. The cop had a ruddy face lined from the weather with tufts of scrubby red hair poking out from under his cap, and from the way he towered over the car, Les tipped he was an Aussie Rules player.

'Good morning, sir,' he smiled. 'I'm Constable Hitchon. Apollo Bay police. Have you been drinking at all?'

Les looked up at the cop and shook his head. 'Sober as a judge, officer.'

The cop continued to smile. 'Would you mind blowing into this, sir?'

'Sure,' said Les.

The cop pushed a breathalyser unit through the car window. Les blew into it and it came up negative.

'May I see your driver's licence, sir?' asked the cop.

'Sure,' repeated Les.

Les took his wallet out from beneath his anorak and handed the cop his New South Wales driver's licence. The cop noticed all the money in the wallet and looked at Les as he carefully examined the licence.

'Are you the owner of the vehicle, sir?' the cop asked.

Les shook his head again. 'No. It's a rental. I got it in Melbourne.'

The cop handed Les his licence back, glanced at Norton's overnight bag then noticed the length of iron on the back seat. 'What's the iron bar for, sir?'

Les half turned around. 'That? I found it in the car park where I'm staying. And I've been using it to knock the mud off my shoes.'

'Where are you staying, sir?'

'The Otway Resort in Lorne. I'm down here on a holiday.'

'May I examine the contents of your bag, sir?'

'Sure.'

Les sat the bag on his lap and opened it up. The cop gave it a perusal noticing the torch and Norton's camera.

'A torch, sir?'

'I always carry a torch with me,' shrugged Les.

The cop nodded. 'Would you mind stepping out of the vehicle, sir?'

'If you want.' Les switched off the engine and apprehensively got out of the car.

The cop gave Les a heavy once up and down. 'Would you please open the boot, sir?' he said.

'Sure.'

Les reached into the car and pulled the button. The lid swung open and Les stepped round to the back of the car while the cop examined the boot. It was spotlessly clean and empty.

'You can close the boot, sir,' said the cop.

Les shut the boot and turned to the cop. 'Is there a problem, officer?'

'No. No problem.' The cop gave the car another once over then smiled at Les. 'Enjoy your stay in Victoria, sir.'

Les returned the cop's smile. 'Thank you, officer. I'm sure I will.'

Les got back in the car, the cop waved him on and Les drove off. In the rear-vision mirror he noticed the cop writing something down in a notebook. Well what the fuck was that all about, wondered Les as he went round another bend. Suddenly he clicked his fingers. That big heroin bust they just had down here, when they boarded that North Korean freighter. There was a body and a shitload of heroin on a beach near Lorne. And only last week they found another forty-five kilograms buried on some other beach. No wonder they're pulling cars up. And me, driving a rental and coming from New South Wales, especially with my big boofhead. I'd stick out like ... like an alpaca's knackers. But, smiled Les, apart from smoking two grouse hash joints with a good little sort, I have got nothing to do with wretched drugs and the misery they bring. Les drove on with the radio playing something inaudible in the background.

The road climbed up and Les got snatches of a sensational view as he drove past Cape Patton Lookout. He drove through more tiny hamlets with names like Wongarra and Skenes Creek, then the road levelled off, curved once or twice, and just as the rain started up again a long white beach flanked by trees opened up on the left and he came into Apollo Bay.

Unlike Lorne, the surrounding hills facing the ocean were much further away from the road and the bay ended at a breakwater and harbour. A large red-brick house, built up off the road on the right with a sign out the front saying OLD CABLE STATION MUSEUM, was the first thing Les noticed as he drove by, then came blocks of land, houses, and holiday units before the shops started: a garage, restaurants, clothes stores, etc. Les passed a large, modern hotel and a park alongside the beach opposite dotted with wooden statues, before coming to an older hotel near the end of the shops. Although Apollo Bay's shopping centre was longer than Lorne's, it wasn't as developed, and still had an easygoing, country town look about it. The shops ended at a war memorial in the middle of the road near the local police station, then the road continued south. Les pulled over on a rise where a sign said MARENGO. Cattle were grazing in open marshes on the right and in the grey distance Les could see a cemetery overlooking the ocean. He did a U-turn and came back into Apollo Bay.

On the right, a golf course ran alongside the harbour, and across the road was a large red-brick church. Not far up the road from the war memorial was another church built from white weatherboard. Hello, smiled Les. We're in business already. He drove slowly along the strip then pulled up outside a coffee shop next to a real estate agency. Les got out of the car and walked into the real estate. It wasn't very big and behind a desk sat a dark-haired woman in a beige dress. Les stepped up to the counter and caught her eye.

'Excuse me,' he said. 'I was looking at some houses in your window. Would you have a map of Apollo Bay?'

The woman pointed to some flyers on a rack near the door. 'Help yourself.'

'Thanks.' Les took one out and came back and placed the map on the counter. 'Actually,' he said, 'I'm trying to buy a house for my mother who's very religious. Could you mark where the local churches are for me?'

'Certainly.' The woman got up with a biro and made three crosses on the map. 'There's two just down there. And another further round in Sandstock Road.'

'Thanks very much,' smiled Les.

'No worries.'

Les got back in the car and drove down to the big brick church he'd noticed opposite the golf course. He stopped in a driveway out front, took the piece of iron from the back seat, put it back in his overnight bag and got out of the car.

The church was high and wide and set in well-kept grounds surrounded by flowerbeds. A set of concrete steps ran up to an open door behind a white archway at the front, and next to the archway a sign said CHURCH OF OUR BLESSED LADY, MINISTER: FATHER RUPERT STRECKETSEN. Les figured there was no need to go inside the church, so he walked around the back.

Built onto the rear of the church was a red-brick house surrounded by thriving flowerbeds. One was full of huge white roses shimmering with rain drops. Opposite the house was a garage and two small toilet blocks, and near these was a brick storage shed with a green wooden door. There was no one around and no sounds coming from the house. Les walked up the steps and knocked on the door. There was no answer, so he knocked again. Les gave it a third knock then walked over to the storage shed. He had a good look around then took the length of iron from his overnight bag to prise it open. Suddenly a thought occurred to Les. When the cop pulled him over earlier, he questioned him about the iron bar on the back seat and the torch in his bag. If a local church reported a break-in, that cop would remember him for sure. And after leaving footprints, tyre prints and fingerprints all over the place, it wouldn't be five minutes before the local wallopers were banging on his door at the resort. And besides getting nicked, if he did happen to find the paintings, the police would confiscate them. All of a sudden Les was up shit creek. He was about to let go a string of expletives then remembered he was on sacred ground. He turned and walked back to the car. Les sat behind the wheel staring out the windscreen at the rain for a while, then started the car and drove down to the white-panelled church he noticed driving in. He pulled up out the front, turned off the motor and checked it out.

Two small wooden buildings, almost side by side on a neatly kept lawn, faced the street from behind a low brick wall. They both had stained-glass windows set in panels and the larger building on the right had a vestry out front. A concrete driveway ran between the two buildings to a residence at the rear, and a sign in the left-hand corner of the front yard said SAINT QUILLAN'S CHURCH, MINISTER: REVEREND BRANDER CROMWELL. Les got out of the car and walked along the driveway.

The residence was separate from the church, with windows along the side and a set of steps running up from a garden to a front door on the right. Between the residence and the smaller building on the left, was a wooden storage shed as big as a double garage with a flat tin roof and a wooden door at the end. Les checked the lock then walked up to the residence and knocked on the door. Again no answer and no sounds from inside. He knocked twice more then went back and had another look at the lock on the storage shed. It was just a lock and Les was sorely tempted. Instead, he shook his head ruefully and walked back to the car.

Oh well, thought Les, as he stared morosely out the windscreen. One church to go. And you can bet there'll be no one there either. Bloody hell! Where would anyone be, on a prick of a day like this? He checked the map and drove off towards Sandstock Road.

The last church was on an open block of land where the houses thinned out into trees running up towards the surrounding hills. It was a yellow weatherboard A-frame featuring a row of stained-glass windows along the side and a white vestry in front with a wooden cross on top. Built onto the back of the church was a residence, and a garage on the right faced a wooden storage shed on the left. A slab walkway led from a gate in a fence out front up to the vestry and the residence, and a driveway cut through the trees to the garage. The grounds were well maintained with beds of flowers running along either side of the walkway, and the church had just been given a fresh coat of paint. Les pulled up near the front gate, switched off the engine and got out of the car. On a white wooden sign board behind the gate it read CHURCH OF THE HOLY ORDER, MINISTER: DEACON LORIMER BROCKENSHIRE. Les followed the wooden walkway up to the residence and was about to take the steps to a door at the rear, when a man in a pair of khaki overalls stepped out of a side door in the garage carrying a stepladder. He had a lean, acned face with thick fair hair swept straight back from his forehead along with a fervent, God-fearing look in his eyes and reminded Les of a young Jerry Lee Lewis. When he saw Les, he stopped and placed the stepladder on the ground as if it was a shield between them and stared at Les suspiciously.

'Is there something I can do for you?' he said in a raspy voice that sounded like a loud whisper.

'Yes. I was hoping to see Deacon Brockenshire,' said Les.

'Deacon Brockenshire isn't here at the moment.'

'He's not?'

The man shook his head. 'All the ministers from Apollo Bay are arranging the funeral of a colleague in Portland. They won't be back until Friday at the earliest.'

'Oh,' replied Les, figuring out why nobody had answered when he knocked on the other doors. 'So are you the caretaker, mate?' Les asked.

'Yes. I'm Deacon Brockenshire's nephew. Uriah.'

'Nice to meet you, Uriah. My name's Les. Les Norton.' Uriah nodded, but he didn't reply or accept Norton's attempted handshake. In his God-fearing eyes, Norton looked like a philistine at the gate. 'All right, Uriah,' said Les. 'I'll tell you why I'm here.'

Les gave Uriah the usual spiel, adding a bit more about the sentimental value the paintings meant to his family and how the family had sent him a long way at great trouble and expense. He ended by offering a one-hundred-dollar donation to the church if he could take a peek in the storage shed. Uriah listened intently and Les thought for a moment he detected a brief sign of sympathy in Uriah's God-fearing eyes.

'I understand your position, Mr Norton,' Uriah said. 'But under no circumstances could I let you look through the storage shed without the deacon being here.'

'The deacon has to be here,' said Les.

'Absolutely.'

'And you couldn't just open the door and let me have a quick look around?'

Uriah shook his head slowly and adamantly. 'Not without my uncle's permission, and my uncle being here.'

From the look in Uriah's eye and the way he stood behind the stepladder, Les figured Uriah would lay down his life before he'd let him in the storage shed. And with God on his side, Uriah would probably fight like ten men if he had to protect the church's property.

'Right,' nodded Les.

'If you come back when my uncle returns from Portland, possibly he could arrange something. But definitely not until then. I'm sorry, Mr Norton.'

Les turned to the shed for a second. For some reason he had a feeling about this one. But he'd identified himself. So even if he did fight Uriah to get in, he'd be up for assault, as well as break and enter. And he couldn't sneak back and break in, either. Les found himself snookered behind the black. Unless he wanted to take the odds to spending time in a cold hard Victorian prison for the dud rap of assaulting a church worker and breaking into church property.

'All right, Uriah,' said Les. 'Thanks for your help. I'll come back later.'

'Do that, Mr Norton.'

Uriah picked up the stepladder and walked over to the house. Les returned to the car and got inside as the rain temporarily eased into drizzle.

Well, wouldn't that root you, scowled Les, looking back at the church. A quiet wet day. No one around. I could have knocked over those storage sheds like piggy banks. But between that copper pulling me over, and Uriah on the scene, I've been well and truly fucked. And maybe it's just the old forbidden fruit thing. But I got a feeling about this one. Les glanced at his watch and felt the cold seeping into his damp clothes. Fuck it, he cursed silently. And fuck heading straight back to Lorne. I'll have a cup of hot coffee and a sandwich in Apollo Bay first. Les started the car and headed into town.

He found a parking spot right outside a neat little coffee shop next to a camping store, and got out of the car with his overnight bag. A sign above the footpath with a girl's face wearing a sailor's hat said SAILOR GIRLS, CONSCIOUS CUISINE. There were sheltered fold-up chairs out the front and several Tibetan prayer flags hung above a wide doorway; on one wall inside were several racks of books, on the others murals and Eastern bric-a-brac. Les scanned the blackboard menu and ordered a pina colada muffin and a mug of flat white from a dark-haired man in black, then sat at a table next to three girl backpackers talking in Scandinavian. He took his notebook out of his overnight bag and started sourly doodling.

Les didn't have to doodle much to tell himself he'd struck out again; badly. Yesterday was just a waste of time. But today he'd been completely rooted. Mainly by bad timing. If he'd have left five minutes later or five minutes earlier, the cop might not have pulled him over. And if Uriah had of been somewhere else, the paintings could possibly be sitting in the boot of the car. Les looked up and gave the proprietor a thin smile as his order arrived, then drank his coffee and ate his muffin while his mood increasingly matched the weather.

So what now, Norton asked himself. The answer: nothing. It was all over Red Rover. Unless he wanted to stick around till the priests came back from Portland. And with the weather well and truly set in, that would be a real fun time. Even Thursday night with Claire had lost its allure. And she'd probably change her mind by then. No. The best idea would be to cut his losses, go home and come back another time. Catch an early flight to Melbourne, hire a car, check the churches out in Apollo Bay and fly home. You'd do it in a day. Les finished his coffee and ordered another one. By the time it arrived another thought occurred to him. The ministers in Apollo Bay obviously stuck together. Now that he'd been down there asking about the paintings, what was to stop the ministers from looking for them? And if they found them, keep them? A few phone calls and they'd soon find out Les wasn't Rosa-Marie's son. He could get stuffed and the paintings would be considered a gift from the Lord. Along with a nice little earner for the local ministers.

Les now wished Father Shipley had either burnt the paintings, sold them, or shoved them in his arse, and also wished he'd never got the letter in the first place. He was also looking for someone to blame for what had turned out to be a complete waste of time and effort. Warren? No. Father Shipley? It was all his fault for getting involved with Rosa-Marie in the first place. The dope. Les finished his coffee, paid the bill and sourly headed for Lorne.

The drive back was no joy either. The rain came down heavier than ever at Wongarra and Les finished up stuck behind a council truck just past Cape Patton. The radio reception was bad the entire trip and all he got was scratchy parts of songs he'd never heard, like Leonard Cohen's 'There Is A War On' and The Infernos' 'Cry Cry Cry'. And Les was in too lousy a mood to even change the station. Just outside of Lorne, the council truck finally decided to pull over and let everyone past.

After a slow, punishing drive squashed behind a seat belt, the two mugs of coffee had gone right through Les and when he made it to the old hotel opposite the jetty, he was absolutely bursting for a leak. But Norton's mood had overtaken him. He drove straight past the resort and down the main street, crossed the bridge, then veered left and started climbing towards the golf links. A left turn here and a right turn there and soon Les found what he was looking for. Lorne cemetery. He stopped the car in front of the gates, got out and strode through the small one.

Left of the gate was a sheltered table with a list of all the graves and the names of the people buried in the cemetery engraved on it in alphabetical order. Les quickly scanned the names and found Father Bernard Shipley. Row 11, Plot 28. With the cemetery to himself, Les started off in the rain down through the graves.

There were elaborate ones and plain ones, recent ones and some going back to 1850. There was even a Ruby Blanche Norton buried there. Father Shipley's was almost at the end of the row going towards the tree line. It was just a simple plot edged in moss-stained stone with a faded stone cross. There were no dates. But inscribed beneath the cross was FATHER BERNARD SHIPLEY. LOVED BY ALL. ESPECIALLY THE PEOPLE AT THE CABLE STATION. Underneath that it said, SO HE BRINGETH THEM UNTO THE HAVEN WHERE THEY WOULD BE.

'Well, good on you, Bernie boy,' said Les, undoing his fly. 'Now I'm going to bringeth you something for causing me all this trouble. And for getting caught with your hand up Rosa-Marie's dress. You Bible-bashing hypocrite.'

Les closed his eyes with joyous relief and pissed all over Father Shipley's grave, giving it a good going over before squirting and shaking the last drops on the epitaph. When he'd finished, Les tucked Mr Wobbly back into his jox and tied up his tracksuit pants. Although he felt wonderfully relieved after emptying his bladder, suddenly Les didn't feel all that thrilled. He watched some of the steaming froth get washed off the grave by a gust of wind-blown rain and actually felt quite disgusted with himself.

'Now why did I have to go and do that?' Les turned to the leaden sky and nodded sagely as the rain hit him in the face. 'You're right, boss. That was a bit out of order. Sorry.'

There was a bottle-brush tree at the edge of the cemetery. Les walked over and picked four yellow sprigs off the tree then walked back to the grave and placed them below the epitaph.

'My apologies, Father Shipley,' Les said quietly. 'I dunno what brought the nark out in me. Maybe it's the weather? Have a good sleep.' Les made a quick sign of the cross and walked back to the car.

So what now, Les asked himself as he stared out the windscreen once again. Have a hot shower, grab a bite to eat and get ready for another exciting night watching TV. And pack my gear ready to piss off early. To be honest, I'll be glad to get home. Shit! And won't Archie Goodwin give me a nice bagging when I get back. Warren'll feed off this for ages. Clover, too. The worst part is, I can't tell them I was going down to Melbourne anyway. Bloody hell! I've certainly put my head in a moose with Woz and his girl this time. Hang on a minute, talking about girls. What about Stepha? Didn't Stepha say something about a woman in a bookshop? Mrs Totten? She knows everything about down here? I can't see how she can help me. But what have I got to lose by calling in for five minutes and just saying 'g'day'? Les started the car and drove back into Lorne. He angle-parked across from the shops then locked the car and jogged across the road.

Les had noticed the bookshop before. It was a tiny wooden house, painted olive, set back off the main road in a laneway near the paper shop. A large window faced the street on the right and a set of steps ran up to a small landing in front of a doorway on the left. In the middle was a chimney stack with a sign on it saying OCEAN ROAD BOOK EXCHANGE. Thick vines grew alongside the wall in the laneway and amongst the groundcover out front stood a couple of small trees. Les jogged up the stairs and opened the door and a small bell tinkled overhead as he stepped through.

Inside, tables and Balinese wicker shelves stacked with books were spread over a polished wooden floor or standing against the walls. A couple of bird mobiles hung from the ceiling and sitting along a cornice were several abstract paintings without frames. The books were all listed in order: humour, history, action, romance, etc, and the little shop had a lovely, dusty ambience about it that made you want to spend hours just browsing. In a corner on the left a counter stood in front of a doorway leading out the back and seated in front of an old-style till, a little old lady was writing something down in a notebook. Les approached her slowly and smiled.

'Hello,' he said.

The little old lady looked up. She was in her eighties at least, short and stooped with signs of arthritis in her hands. Her face was lined with just a tiny bit of blue mascara round her eyes and her hair was grey and short and brushed down either side of her face. A pink cardigan hung across her shoulders over a blue top and a pair of blue woollen slacks, and asleep in her lap was an old tortoiseshell cat. The little old lady might have been getting on in years, but when she looked up, Les noticed her hazel eyes were as bright as buttons.

'Hello,' she said, returning Norton's smile.

'Are you Mrs Totten?'

'Yes. That's me.'

'My name's Les, Mrs Totten. Les Norton. Stepha sent me to see you. Dark-haired girl, works as a waitress. She said she gets her books here.'

'Yes. I know Stepha,' said Mrs Totten. 'She's a lovely girl. Likes lots of thrillers. John Grisham and Robert Ludlum.'

'They're a bit heavy for me,' said Les.

'Oh? And what sort of books do you like, Les?'

'Well,' shrugged Les. 'At the moment I'm reading *Hell's Angel*, the story of Sonny Barger.'

'I only just finished reading it,' said Mrs Totten. 'What a good book. He was a bit of a villain, that Sonny.'

Les gave Mrs Totten a double blink. 'You read that?'

'I read all sorts of things,' smiled Mrs Totten.

'I suppose you would,' replied Les, taking a quick look around the bookshop. 'Anyway, Mrs Totten,' he said. 'I didn't really come here to talk to you about books. I came to see you about something else.'

'Oh? And what was that?' asked Mrs Totten.

'I'm from Sydney, Mrs Totten,' answered Les. 'But Stepha said you know quite a bit about the area around here.'

'Yes. My late husband was the postmaster here for many years. And I've always maintained an interest in Lorne and parts of the coast. I got a little book together a few years ago.'

'All right. Well, I'll tell you what's going on, Mrs Totten.'

Without going into too many details, Les told the bookshop owner where he was staying and how he met Stepha, then gave her the usual spiel about the paintings. He told her about calling into the local churches and how he couldn't get into the storage sheds belonging to the churches in Apollo Bay because the ministers were all down at Portland. Mrs Totten listened intently, but something in the way she looked at him with those bright hazel eyes gave Les the impression she only half believed him.

'So that's what's going on, Mrs Totten,' concluded Les. 'I don't know if you can help me. But Stepha suggested I call in and see you anyway.'

Mrs Totten didn't say anything at first. The cat woke up, yawned and stretched then jumped off Mrs Totten's lap and went out the back. Mrs Totten watched it disappear through the doorway then looked up at Les.

'Well, you've been to all the churches there are, Les,' she said. 'So I can't help you there. But I did know Father Shipley.'

'You did?' said Les.

'Yes,' nodded Mrs Totten. 'A very nice man. Always doing things for people. Though he could be a bit of a devil at times if he wanted to,' she added with a knowing smile. 'He's been dead for years now.'

'Yes. I actually visited his grave,' said Les.

'That was nice of you.' Mrs Totten flicked a piece of cat fur from her lap. 'But apart from knowing Father Shipley when I was younger, I don't see how I can help you.'

'That's all right, Mrs Totten,' said Les. 'I didn't really expect you to.'

'However, I think I know someone who can.'

'You do?'

'Yes. Tania Settree,' said Mrs Totten. 'She runs an orphanage not far from where you're staying.'

'Oh?'

'She might not be able to help you actually find the paintings, but I'm sure she can get you into the church storage sheds in Apollo Bay.'

'She can?' said Les. 'Hey, that'd be unreal.'

Mrs Totten smiled up at Les. 'But it's going to cost you.'

'Sure,' said Les, reaching for his pocket. 'How much?'

Mrs Totten shook her head. 'You'll have to give Tania a small donation towards the orphanage.'

'Sweet as a nut,' said Les. 'It'd be a pleasure.'

'And you have to take me to the pictures.'

'The pictures?' said Les.

'Yes,' said Mrs Totten. 'We've got a lovely old theatre here in town. But I have trouble getting up the stairs.'

'Hey, no problems, Mrs Totten. I can do that. When did you want to go, and what do you want to see?'

'Tonight. And I want to see *The Two Towers*. The sequel to *The Fellowship of the Ring*.'

Les felt like he'd just been hit in the face with a huge, frozen tuna. '*The … Two Towers?*' he said quietly.

'Yes. I absolutely loved the first one,' beamed Mrs Totten. 'And I can't wait to see the sequel. And going with a lovely young man like you makes it even better.'

'All right, Mrs Totten,' said Les. 'What time does it start?'

'The film starts at seven-thirty. If you can call back here at seven-fifteen, that would be lovely. In the meantime, I'll make some phone calls.'

'Okay, Mrs Totten. Sounds good.' Les gave the bookshop owner a thin smile. 'I'll see you here at quarter past seven.'

'Wonderful,' said Mrs Totten. 'I'll see you then.'

Les turned and left the bookshop, then drifted across the road in the rain back to the car. He opened the door and slumped over the steering wheel.

Les had seen *The Fellowship of the Ring* with Warren and Clover. Clover had free tickets. It was after seeing the movie, Les realised there was something wrong with him and he possibly needed some sort of counselling. It was one of the biggest-grossing movies of all time. The books sold in millions and the producers spent millions making a spectacular film with fantastic special effects. Yet Les hated it. He actually put it down as the worst movie he'd ever seen. Three tedious hours of stupifyingly boring waffle and an annoying, cock-eyed dwarf who needed a good bath.

Go here, go there. The river of blood. The castle of doom. The pub with no beer. Your life shall be forfeit. Oh great wizard of Middle Shitville. Where does our quest lead? Your journey will be long and fraught with many dangers. Blah, blah, blah.

The clunker seemed to go on forever. When it finished, Clover said it was okay. But she wouldn't like to sit through it again. Les told the others exactly what he thought of it. Warren didn't like it. But said he did just to nark Les. Now Les had to sit through another three punishing hours of the sequel. He stared out the window up to the sky.

'Why, boss? Why?' he pleaded. 'What did I do? Did I not return and put flowers on the priest's grave? Has not my quest down here been fraught with disappointment and misery enough?' With a heavy heart, Les started the engine and drove back to the resort.

The first thing Les did was have a shave and a shower. He watched the news then changed into his Levis, one of the shirts he bought in Melbourne with blue and brown diagonal stripes, and his black leather jacket. Even if he was in for a night of misery, he figured he may as well look half all right for Mrs Totten's sake. She *was* a bit of an old sweetheart. By then it was time to eat. Les thought he might have a change from room service and sample the cuisine at the local over a couple of cool ones. He locked up and caught the lift down to the lobby.

The hotel was directly across the road. A set of steps led from the footpath up to the beer garden and a bar facing the stools and tables. There was a dining room inside on the left and the kitchen and servery were along a corridor to the right. It had stopped raining, but it still looked a little wet to eat outside. Les walked into the servery to see what was on offer.

Behind the counter was a blackboard menu as well as the normal one. Les gave them both a quick peruse and ordered a dozen oysters kilpatrick and chicken schnitzel with chips and salad from a blonde girl in white, got his number and walked round to the bar. The hotel had Stella Artois on tap, Les got a pot and stepped round to the dining room, straight into a couple with a baby in a pram that was putting on a horrendous screaming and crying fit. Although the noise was louder than a brick saw and drowned out any other sound in the dining room, the baby's parents seemed completely oblivious to it. Les turned around and found a table outside that was sheltered and dry enough and sat down with his beer.

The beer was beautiful and a pot lasted barely a minute. Les got another one and downed the last of that just as the girl brought the oysters out. They were delicious, so was the schnitzel and by the time he'd finished eating, Les had sunk four beers. He ordered a double Jack Daniels with a beer chaser and drank it standing on the balcony staring out over the beach, then placed the empty glasses on a table and looked at his watch. Okay, he told himself, a boozy glow coursing through his body. I think I'm ready now to handle another three hours of *Conan the Barbarian* meets *Camelot*. Les zipped up his jacket and strolled down to the bookshop.

The light was on inside but the door was locked. Les gave a knock and Mrs Totten appeared from out the back. She'd brushed her grey hair to one side, added a tiny touch of mascara and looked very lady-like in a pair of grey woollen slacks, a black polo neck sweater and a green silk scarf with a horse design on it round her shoulders. In one hand was a small handbag, in the other an umbrella.

'I don't think you'll need the umbrella, Mrs Totten,' said Les when she opened the door. 'It looks like the rain's stopped.'

'Oh, you never know,' replied Mrs Totten, stepping out onto the landing and locking the door behind her. 'It might start again.'

'Do you live here?' asked Les.

'Yes. I have a flat out the back. Luke and myself,' she replied.

'Luke?'

'My cat.'

'Right.' Les smiled and gave Mrs Totten a quick once up and down. 'I'll tell you what,' he said. 'You've brushed up pretty good for a young country girl. I hope I don't have to fight too many blokes off tonight.'

'And might I say, Les, you look very handsome yourself,' smiled Mrs Totten. 'That's a lovely jacket.'

'Thank you, Mrs Totten,' said Les. 'So how did you go?' he asked. 'Did you make those phone calls?'

'I certainly did,' replied Mrs Totten. 'I'll tell you about it later.'

'Okey doke,' said Les. He offered Mrs Totten his arm. 'Well, just latch onto this, good-looking. And let's show the locals what style's all about.'

'Yes. Why don't we.'

Mrs Totten took Norton's arm and they proceeded to the picture theatre. Although it was like a trip to the gallows for Les, he still felt good helping the old lady down the road, and while she hobbled a bit from age, Mrs Totten was stepping out as she hung off Norton's huge arm, enjoying the occasion. They got to the theatre and Les helped Mrs Totten up the steps, through the wide glass doors, then up an equally wide flight of stairs to the ticket office where they joined the queue. Mrs Totten opened her bag to get her purse.

'Mrs Totten, please,' said Les. 'What will people think? I don't mind being your toy boy. But I refuse to be your gigolo.'

Mrs Totten gave Les a friendly slap on the arm. 'Oh you're a cheeky devil,' she said, closing her bag. 'I knew that the minute I saw you.'

Les pointed a finger at her. 'And no kissing on the first date, either.'

Les got the tickets and, knowing the marathon in front of him, stocked up on popcorn, mineral water and choc-tops for both of them, then helped Mrs Totten upstairs to their seats.

The picture theatre was big and grand and done out in lots of light brown with soft lighting. The carpet in the aisles was thick, the seats were comfortable and the old theatre would have been something else in its day. Even now it still maintained an air of old-time class. For a Tuesday night, there was a reasonable crowd, and Les and Mrs Totten sat down two seats back from the balcony. Mrs Totten took a pair of glasses from her bag then put them on and watched the screen advertising intently while she got into her choc-top. The ads finished, the lights dimmed then the curtain drew back to the crashing sound of flutes and harps. Les sunk back in his seat with his popcorn, and prepared for the worst.

Difficult as it was for Les to believe, the sequel was even worse. Go here, go there, cross that, climb those, ford this. There was absolutely no plot. Just three separate bunches of dorks with long hair and funny feet dressed like park winos, looking for who knew what? Only this time, one bunch of dorks had a thing tagging along with them that looked like a cross between a gecko on steroids and Marilyn Manson. And right in the middle of all the sword-rattling, shield-banging crap was the cock-eyed dwarf; and he still hadn't had a bath.

Mrs Totten, however, loved the movie. She oohed and aahhed and punched Les on the arm or slapped him on the leg with excitement. And when the trees got up and started walking around, Mrs Totten sighed and clutched her breast in rapture. Despite his misery, Les did get some satisfaction from the movie watching Mrs Totten having a good time. It was a buzz seeing the old lady enjoying herself to the hilt. Finally, after what seemed like a year, the film mercifully ended with one of the dork bunch and the gecko pitching up to the camera for another sequel. Then the curtain closed, the lights came on and Les straightened up in his seat bursting to go to the toilet.

'Well, what did you think of that, Les?' asked Mrs Totten.

'Yeah, just great,' replied Les, flicking popcorn from the front of his jacket. 'Almost as good as the first.'

'I thought it was better.'

'Maybe.'

Les helped Mrs Totten to her feet and they walked up the aisle then down the stairs to the landing. Les excused himself and made a dash for the gents. After hosing out the steaming remains of the Stella Artois and two bottles of mineral water, he rejoined Mrs Totten.

'Okay good-looking,' he said, happy now that his ordeal was over. 'Let's get you home before your parents start to worry about you.'

'And I'll make you a nice cup of tea,' said Mrs Totten.

'That I would like,' said Les.

With Mrs Totten's umbrella in one hand and her on his other arm, Les walked the old lady back to the bookshop and followed her through the front door. They went round the tables of books then through another door into a small kitchen with slate floor tiles, a shiny stainless-steel sink and a dishwasher set into a black granite top. A window opened onto the laneway, several small paintings hung round the walls, and beneath the kitchen table in front of the fridge Mrs Totten's cat was curled up on a rubber mat. It blinked a couple of times when she turned on the light then stretched and went back to sleep. Mrs Totten put the kettle on and turned to Les. 'I'll just change into a pair of slippers,' she said. 'Make yourself comfortable.'

'Okay,' said Les.

Les sat down at the kitchen table, careful not to kick the sleeping cat, then Mrs Totten came back and started fussing around getting the tea together.

'What about those talking trees,' she said, placing a cup in front of Les.

'Yes,' replied Les. 'I nearly fell out of my seat when they walked out of the forest.'

'They saved the day too, when the river burst,' said Mrs Totten.

'They sure did,' agreed Les. 'Now Middle Earth is once again safe from the forces of evil.'

Before too long Mrs Totten had a pot of tea with a crocheted doily on it sitting on the table along with a plate piled with slices of lemon and coconut sponge cake. She poured Les a cup of tea and told him to help himself to the cake. The tea hit the spot and the cake was sensational. It made Norton a little homesick for his mother's house in Dirranbandi. Les complimented Mrs Totten on her cake, they chit-chatted some more about the movie, then Mrs Totten slid a piece of paper across the table to Les.

'That's the woman's name and mobile phone number and the address,' said Mrs Totten. 'The orphanage is not far from where you're staying. She's expecting you round ten-thirty tomorrow. All you have to do is drive her to Apollo Bay and back.'

'Good as gold,' said Les. 'Thanks very much, Mrs Totten.'

Mrs Totten smiled at Les over her cup of tea. 'No worries,' she said, taking a delicate sip. 'She's a lovely person, Tania. Even though she's had a terrible lot of misfortune in her life.'

'She has?' inquired Les.

'Yes. I'll tell you a little about her.'

'Okay. If you'd care to.'

'Tania was an orphan herself,' said Mrs Totten. 'There used to be an orphanage in Apollo Bay. Before it burnt down.'

'None of the kids were burned, were they?' said Les.

'No. Everybody was saved, except the head nun, Sister Manuella. She never got burned though. A beam fell on her and broke her neck.'

Les shook his head. 'That's no good.'

'There were only a dozen or so children in the orphanage,' continued Mrs Totten. 'And when it burnt down they all managed to get adopted. Tania went with a local family. The Walmsleys. He was the town butcher.'

'I used to work in meatworks,' smiled Les.

Mrs Totten nodded over her tea. 'Tania eventually married a man named Grant Currie. He was a surveyor. And they had two children. A son, Grant Junior. And a daughter, Angie.'

Les looked at the piece of paper. 'I thought her name was Settree?'

'That was her second husband, Frank. He was an electrician,' said Mrs Totten. 'Her first husband died in Melbourne. He took Angie to visit his mother, and he fell under a train at Flinders Street Station.'

'Crikey!' said Les.

'Then not long after that, her son Grant Junior and Angie were out fishing, and young Grant fell out of the boat and drowned.'

'Poor bloody woman,' sympathised Les. 'So what happened to husband number two? The electrician.'

'He was electrocuted,' said Mrs Totten.

'Yeah. Well, that's an occupational hazard in that game,' said Les.

'Yes. But Frank was taking a bath. And a hair dryer accidentally fell in the water.'

'Cripes! I'd certainly call that misfortune,' said Les.

'Tania never remarried,' said Mrs Totten. 'She lives alone with her daughter and runs the orphanage.'

'What a sad sort of life,' said Les.

'Yes. But she's happy now. Even if running the orphanage is a constant battle. Although Angie's a little strange.'

'Her daughter?' said Les.

'Yes. She's nineteen. But keeps very much to herself. I don't think she's … you know. But she doesn't seem to like boys or men very much. Actually it's funny you're after your mother's paintings. Because Angie likes to paint.'

Les looked directly at Mrs Totten. 'Not devils or witches? Or anything like that?'

'No. Nothing like that,' laughed Mrs Totten. 'I've seen her paintings. It's all abstract dribble. She's never sold any and I wouldn't hang them in the shop. But don't tell Tania or her daughter I said that.'

'My lips are glued,' replied Les.

They both finished a second cup of tea at the same time just as Les polished off a third piece of cake. Mrs Totten smiled at him.

'Les, I hate to be an ungrateful host after all you've done for me tonight, but I'm awfully tired now.'

'Hey. No worries, Mrs Totten,' said Les. 'I understand. In fact I'm quite tired myself, after all that sword-fighting and dodging blazing arrows and axes and things.'

She placed a hand on his. 'I'll walk you to the door.'

Les stood up, sneakily leaving a fifty-dollar bill under his saucer. 'When I get back from Apollo Bay tomorrow,' he said. 'I'll call in and tell you how I went. We might have another cup of tea. And,' Les wiggled his eyebrows, 'maybe just another slice or two of your lemon sponge cake.'

'That would be lovely,' beamed Mrs Totten.

Mrs Totten walked Les to the front door and opened it. She looked up at Les then put her arms around him and hugged him. Resting on his chest, her head didn't even come up to the big Queenslander's chin.

'Les, I had a wonderful time tonight,' she said. 'You're a true gentleman. Thank you ever so much.'

Les went all funny inside. 'Hey,' he said, gently rubbing the old lady's bony back. 'Don't you think I had a good time. How often do I get to take a good sort out and see a grouse movie?'

Mrs Totten looked up again and waved a finger at Les. 'You're only saying that because it's true.'

'You're on to me, sweetheart,' smiled Les. He placed his hands on Mrs Totten's shoulders and gave the bookshop owner a kiss on the forehead. 'I'll see you tomorrow, Mrs Totten, and thanks very much for your help.'

'It was a pleasure.'

Mrs Totten closed the door, Les put his hands in the pockets of his jacket and walked towards the resort. When he rounded the corner he looked up and behind a bank of clouds a sprinkling of stars twinkled against the deep indigo of the night sky. Look at that, smiled Les. The rain's cleared up. Truly it is an omen from the great wizard of ... wherever that old fart with the silly hat comes from.

Once inside, Les changed into his tracksuit and cleaned his teeth, then had a cold glass of water in the kitchen. Bloody hell, he yawned, as he rinsed the glass. I don't know about Mrs Totten being tired. But I'm absolutely rooted. Christ! Why not? That movie'd be enough to root anybody. Still. The night wasn't a complete disaster. As well as being a real old sweetheart, Mrs Totten was a big help. And what about that lemon sponge cake. I should have snookered a couple of pieces when I was leaving.

Les switched off the lights in the hallway, then the ones in his room and climbed under the douvet. Well, I wonder how I'll go tomorrow, he thought as he shoved his head into the pillows. I'll more than likely strike out again, I suppose. And I wonder what Widow Settree'll be like? You couldn't bet enough money she'll whinge and whine about her miserable life all the way to Apollo Bay and back. Fair dinkum. If my quest hasn't been long and fraught with shit, I'm a cocky-eyed dwarf with a hygiene problem. Les yawned again then pulled the douvet up round his ears and in minutes he was snoring his head off.

Les slept in the next morning. When he finally got up and looked out over the balcony, the rain had stopped and patches of blue were appearing between the clouds, however the wind was gusting onshore and it was still cold. He raised an arm and sniffed his tracksuit. After sleeping in it since he'd arrived in Lorne, it was starting to get rather minty. Nothing anyone would notice in the restaurant, however. Les cleaned himself up, put his gym boots on, then caught the lift to the lobby and strolled down to have breakfast. The girl on the counter knew him by now and smiled a nice hello when Les gave her his room number. He found a table facing the beach then ripped into the usual, washed down with ample amounts of fruit juice and coffee.

Norton was in a fairly good mood as he ate, even though today was just a case of hope for the best and expect the worst. He had a good feeling about the last church in Apollo Bay. And if it turned out another no-result, at least he was going home and it was all over. He got a chuckle when he remembered how Mrs Totten punched and prodded him when she got excited during the movie, and got even more of a chuckle when he felt the slightest, tiniest bruise on his thigh. Les finished breakfast and went back to his unit, whistling.

Although his faithful, blue tracksuit needed a drink, Les felt it was no good wearing anything clean if he was going to be crawling around dusty storage sheds. And it wasn't as if he was taking the lady from the orphanage to Doyle's for a seafood dinner. He left it on, gave himself a few good squirts of deodorant then, making sure he had everything he needed in his overnight bag, caught the lift down to the parking area.

The Mitsubishi purred into life. Les gave it a few moments to warm up while he checked his map of Lorne, then switched the radio on and drove out of the car park. As he took a right at the roundabout, a barbershop quartet began harmonising beautifully through the speakers.

'Her vaginnnna. Her vaginnnna.

Just a quick reminder, take a peek in her vagina, if she's hur-a-ur-ting.

Brother you can betcha, gonorrhoea is gonna get you, without war-a-ar-ning.'

'What the fuck?' exclaimed Les. 'Has this radio station gone mad? Bloody hell! That's all I need playing when I pull up at the orphanage.' Les shook his head, switched the radio off and drove on up the hill.

The way to the orphanage was behind the white church where he met Vicar Rathbone. Les drove along a tree-lined street, then turned left and pulled up amongst some trees, just back from a driveway in a steep, deadend near some nice homes. The orphanage was on a long, wide sloping block of land facing the ocean. It was a rambling old two-storey building with a tiled roof supported by columns set along wide verandahs that commanded a million-dollar view of the ocean. Huge bay windows were spaced along the verandahs, the grounds were enclosed by stone walls, and there was a yard at the rear full of trees surrounded by a low green wooden fence. In the middle of the yard was a white wooden building with a flat roof, windows along the side and a door at the front. The driveway led up to a wide green gate that opened into a circular courtyard with a flowerbed in the middle. Les guessed the building to be heritage listed and possibly a hundred years old. It had seen better days and needed maintenance here and there. But it was still nothing short of magnificent.

Les got out of the car and walked over to the gate. As he did, he noticed a curtain draw back in the wooden building behind the orphanage and someone watching him all the way. Les opened a door in the gate and stepped into the courtyard. There was a laundry and a shed behind the orphanage and parked to one side of the courtyard was a plain, battered, black kombi-wagon. Les couldn't see a back door and he wanted to check out the view. So he walked quietly around the top verandah, past windows hung with thick blue curtains. Behind one of the curtains Les glimpsed a lounge room filled with furniture and a TV; the rest were bedrooms. When he got to the front of the orphanage Les stopped and reminded himself to bring his camera with him when he brought the woman who ran the orphanage back from Apollo Bay. The view had to be seen to be believed.

He followed the verandah past more blue-curtained windows around to the other side of the old home, stopping at a wide screendoor in front of a kitchen. All the while Les was expecting to hear children playing or making a noise of some description. But apart from a few magpies and kookaburras making their presence known, and the sound of the breeze stirring the surrounding blue gums, there was silence. Les rapped on the kitchen door and took a peek through the flyscreen.

The kitchen was quite big and although there was no light on, Les could make out an open range gas stove, a stainless steel fridge, and a wooden floor with a long wooden table sitting in the middle. Pots and pans and other cooking utensils hung over the stove, and around the walls long shelves of crockery sat above wooden cabinets with glass fronts. The sort of kitchen you would expect to find in a restaurant or place that catered for a number of people. From a corridor behind the kitchen a slender woman appeared on the left, wearing a white shirt and a grey cardigan over a long, grey, tartan skirt. She was holding a mobile phone in one hand and a pair of round-rimmed glasses in the other and opened the door as soon as she saw Les.

'Come in,' the woman said quietly. 'I won't be a moment.'

'Okay, thanks,' replied Les.

Les stepped inside and while the woman leant against one end of the table talking into the mobile, discreetly checked her out. She was about average height, wore no make-up and had a thin, plain face with worry lines radiating from a pair of soft hazel eyes. Her short black hair was clean and shiny and tucked behind her ears with two small combs and although Les couldn't see much grey amongst the black, guessed her age as approaching a hard-working fifty. Two thin hands poked out from under her cardigan and a glimpse of skinny white ankle poked out from below her long woollen skirt. The woman blinked constantly as she spoke on the phone and after she put her glasses on once she'd finished talking, looked very Miss Prissy. She walked nervously over to Les and kept her head slightly bowed when she spoke, giving Norton the impression of a woman who felt ill at ease around men; even a little frightened.

'You must be Mr Norton?' she blinked.

'That's right,' Les smiled softly. 'Les Norton. Are you Mrs Settree? The lady that runs the orphanage?'

'Yes. That's right.'

Les offered her his hand. 'Pleased to meet you, Mrs Settree.'

The woman gave Norton's hand a gentle shake. 'Thank you, Mr Norton.'

Les shook his head. 'I should be thanking you.'

Mrs Settree blinked and looked at Les for a moment. 'I'm sorry if it's a little dark in here,' she apologised. 'But we keep the lights off to try and save on electricity.'

'Good idea, Mrs Settree,' commended Les. He ran his eyes from the kitchen to the corridor running behind. 'It's very quiet,' said Les. 'I was expecting to see kids running everywhere.'

'All the girls have gone camping at Lake Colac while there's a break in the weather,' said Mrs Settree. 'They'll be back tomorrow afternoon.'

'How many girls are there?' asked Les.

'At the moment, twenty.'

'Are they very old?'

'Ten to fifteen,' replied Mrs Settree.

'Right,' said Les. He ran his eyes around the kitchen. 'Gee, it's a beautiful old house, Mrs Settree.'

'Yes. Would you like to have a look around?' she asked.

'I would,' said Les. 'But how about when we get back from Apollo Bay?'

'Very well,' said Mrs Settree. 'Can I get you something? A cup of tea? A glass of water ...?'

'No. That's all right, thanks,' said Les. He smiled at Mrs Settree. 'So Mrs Totten told you what's going on?'

'Yes. You're looking for some paintings.'

'That's right. My mother did them a long time ago. The family thinks they still might be down here.'

'Well, I certainly hope you find them,' said Mrs Settree.

'Yes. I've come a long way,' said Les.

Mrs Settree blinked at Les a couple of times from behind her glasses. 'I'll get my handbag and scarf and we'll get going.'

'When you're ready, Mrs Settree,' said Les. 'There's no mad hurry.'

Mrs Settree turned and walked off to the right down the corridor at the back of the kitchen. She returned a minute or two later with a grey tartan scarf round her neck and holding a small black leather handbag.

'I'm ready,' she said.

'Okay,' replied Les. 'Let's go.' He held the kitchen door open, Mrs Setttree stepped through and they followed the verandah round to the back of the orphanage.

'Aren't you going to lock the door?' asked Les.

'My daughter Angie's here,' replied Mrs Settree. 'She'll look after things.'

'Okey doke.'

Les followed Mrs Settree across the courtyard then through the door in the gate and up to Norton's car. Les opened the door for her, she thanked him then got inside and did up her seatbelt and Les did the same. Les started the motor and absently switched the radio back on as he did a U-turn to go back up the hill. Through the four-speaker system the barbershop quartet started harmonising melodically again.

'It's beginning to look — a — lot — like — syphillis.'

'What the ...?'

Les stabbed at the dash and switched the radio off, then turned to Mrs Settree apologetically. However, everything appeared to have gone over her head and she just sat there like Miss Prissy, buckled up, clutching her handbag and staring out the windscreen. Les came back down behind the church to get onto the main road and drove for a while before speaking.

'So how long have you known Mrs Totten?' he asked.

'Oh, many years now,' replied Mrs Settree.

'She's a bit of a sweetheart,' said Les.

'Yes she certainly is. God bless her,' agreed Mrs Settree.

'She's not bad on her feet either,' chuckled Les. 'Do you know what she did to me?'

'No.'

Les told Mrs Settree how Mrs Totten cajoled him into taking her to the movies. But it had been fun watching her have a good time and she made him a nice cup of tea later. Her sponge cake was good too.

'*The Two Towers?*' said Mrs Settree.

'Yeah,' replied Les. 'Have you seen it?' Mrs Settree shook her head. 'Did you see the first one?' Mrs Settree shook her head again and Les was going to tell her she'd hadn't missed much.

'To take even ten girls to the pictures would cost a fortune,' said Mrs Settree. 'And I couldn't just go on my own.'

'Yes. I hadn't thought of that,' said Les. 'Anyway, Mrs Totten also threatened me if I didn't give a donation to the orphanage.'

'You're not obliged to, Mr Norton,' said Mrs Settree. 'But it would be greatly appreciated if you did.'

'That's okay,' said Les. He put his foot down a little as they began to leave Lorne behind them. 'So how long have you been running the orphanage, Mrs Settree?'

'Quite a few years now,' replied Mrs Settree. 'And you can call me Tania if you like, Mr Norton.'

'Okay. So how do you get on, Tania?'

'Get on? We simply get on as best we can,' replied Tania.

'Fair enough,' said Les. 'So who owns the building? It's in a beautiful spot.'

'The Church of the Holy Blood.'

'Is that the white one near the hotel?'

'Yes. Vicar Rathbone.'

'I met him,' said Les. 'He seemed like a nice man. Do they charge you much rent?'

'Not really,' replied Mrs Settree. 'I took over the home at the end of a one-hundred-year lease.'

'How long have you got to go on the lease?' asked Les.

'Five years,' said Mrs Settree.

'Five years,' said Les. 'What happens then?'

'Vicar Rathbone intends to sell the building.'

Les half smiled. 'They always do. So what'll happen to you and the kids?'

'I'm not sure,' replied Mrs Settree. 'But we're hoping something will turn up.'

'How much will they sell the building for?'

'The vicar's been offered over a million dollars.'

'I can see why,' said Les.

'Yes,' nodded Mrs Settree. 'It's in a prime position, as they say.'

The lady from the orphanage still kept looking straight ahead at the road, never making eye contact with Les when she spoke, and Les couldn't remember meeting a woman so mousy. But there was something about Mrs Settree he liked, so he thought he'd try and get her out of her shell.

'Mrs Totten said you were in an orphanage yourself,' said Les.

'Yes,' replied Mrs Settree. 'And I can't say they were the best years of my life either.'

'They weren't?'

Tania shook her head grimly. 'No. Not at all.'

Les thought for a moment. 'And might I hazard a guess, Tania,' he said, 'and suggest you took over the orphanage to see the girls there got a better go than you did.'

Tania slowly turned to Les. 'That's exactly right, Mr Norton,' she said.

'Well good for you, Tania. Well done. You're a deadset gem.'

Tania blinked at Les. 'It's funny,' she said. 'But I don't mind talking to you, Mr Norton. You have a polite honesty about you.'

'Well thank you, Mrs Settree,' smiled Les. 'That's quite a compliment. And I like talking to you also.'

'Oh? Why's that Mr Norton?'

'You're a person who gives of themselves, Tania. You don't see much of that where I come from. And I can tell you're honest, too.'

Tania went back to staring out the windscreen. 'There was another reason I took over the orphanage,' she said.

'Oh? Why was that?' asked Les.

'To get away from my husband.'

'Your husband?'

'Yes. He … he used to beat me.'

Les screwed his face up. 'Beat you? Christ! There's not much to beat.'

'Grant didn't seem to think so,' said Tania.

Les thought he might get Mrs Settree's version of what Mrs Totten had told him about her. 'So what happened to your husband?' he asked.

'He fell under a train,' answered Tania.

'Serves him bloody right,' said Les.

'In front of our daughter, too,' said Tania.

'Shit! That would have been traumatic for her,' said Les.

'Actually, Angie handled it quite well.'

'Right.' Les put his foot down to head off another council truck before it could pull out from the side of the road and slow him down. 'Did you ever remarry, Mrs Settree?'

'Yes. And Frank was almost as bad as my first husband. He even hit Angie.'

'He did? And what happened to him?' asked Les.

'Frank got electrocuted.'

'Well. I suppose it serves him right, too,' said Les.

'Possibly,' said Tania. 'But it's not a very nice thing to say.'

'It's not very nice to hit women, either,' said Les. 'Except in self-defence of course,' he added with a smile. 'In fact I thought I was going to have to give Mrs Totten a rabbit-killer last night. She got a bit excited during the movie and kept belting into me. I even had a bruise on my arm this morning,' Les sniffed.

'Bless her,' smiled Tania.

'Yes, the old darling.' Les slowed the car right down for a hairpin bend. 'She said you had a son who died. Is that right?'

'Yes. Grant Junior. He was out fishing with Angie and drowned.'

'Gee. That's bad luck,' said Les.

'He was a strange boy, though, young Grant,' said Tania. 'A lot like his father in many ways.'

'How do you mean?' asked Les.

'He was violent. My son Grant actually hit me on several occasions. And he used to hit Angie too.'

'Crikey! You've sure had it tough, Tania,' said Les.

'It was bad at times,' nodded Tania.

Les slowed down for a small white bus full of backpackers. 'So I imagine you and your daughter would be very close now?' said Les.

'Very close,' answered Tania. 'In fact I often think of Angie as my little guardian angel.'

'That's nice.'

Les now understood why Tania was nervous around men, and being stuck in a car next to a gorilla like him wouldn't have been a day at the beach for her. Conversely, it was a pleasant surprise to know she liked him. Les felt at this point it might be an idea to change the subject.

'So how come you can get into these church storage sheds in Apollo Bay, Tania?' he asked.

'The ministers let me have a key in case I need something for the orphans. Blankets, toys. Different little things.'

'That's decent of them,' said Les.

'Except for The Church of the Holy Order. But the caretaker's there. And he'll let me in.'

'Is that Uriah?' said Les.

Tania turned to Les. 'Yes. You met Uriah?'

'Yeah, yesterday,' said Les. 'Only for a few minutes.'

'How did you find him?'

'Find him? Polite,' said Les. 'A little wild-eyed. But polite.'

'Yes. That's one way to describe Uriah,' agreed Tania. She stared out the windscreen as Les manoeuvred the Mitsubishi around two hairpin bends then turned to Les. 'So tell me a little about yourself, Mr Norton.'

'Me? Okay,' smiled Norton. 'And you can call me Les if you want to.'

Les told Tania mostly the truth. He came from Queensland, worked at the Cross in Sydney and had a house in Bondi. By the time he got to Warren and Clover and different things, Les was driving into Apollo Bay.

'You lead quite an interesting life, Les,' said Tania.

'It has its moments,' agreed Les.

Traffic was light. But because the weather had improved there were more people around than the day before and the council was working on the road.

'We may as well go to the big brick church first,' suggested Les, driving past a lollipop-man in an orange vest.

'The Church of Our Blessed Lady,' said Tania. 'I know it well.'

'Daht's de one, 'oman,' said Les.

'I beg your pardon, Mr Norton?' said Tania.

'Nothing, Tania,' smiled Les. 'I was just trying out my Jamaican. I'll tell you about that on the way home.'

Les took a left at the war memorial, then pulled up on the grass at the rear of the church opposite the golf course. He took the torch from his overnight bag and followed Tania around to the storage shed. She took a key from her bag, turned it in the lock and the door creaked open. Having been there before, Mrs Settree quickly found the light switch near the door.

The shed lit up and apart from the usual junk, it was mostly gardening essentials stacked neatly on tables or resting against walls. In the middle of the shed was an old grey Morris Minor convertible up on blocks.

'Hey, look at that,' said Les. 'It's not in bad nick, either.'

'Rupert's been going to get that on the road for years,' said Tania. 'One of the parishioners gave it to him.'

'He should,' said Les, shining his torch along the dash. 'It's a classic.'

'Yes,' agreed Tania. 'Can I help you at all, Mr Norton ... Les?'

'No. I'll be okay thanks,' replied Les.

Les started rummaging through what there was. Boxes of books, LPs, old clothes, suitcases, etc. There was everything from the old car to old Victa lawn mowers. But nothing remotely resembling a bundle of old paintings.

'No sign of any paintings, Mr Norton?' asked Tania.

Les shook his head. 'No. Fried egg, I'm afraid.' Norton turned the torch off and wiped his hands on the sides of his tracksuit. 'We go and have a look at the one up the road, past the war memorial?'

'Saint Quillan's.'

'Yeah. That's it.'

Tania locked the door and they walked back to the car. Les opened the door for her first, then got in and they drove the short distance to the white-panelled church with the low brick wall out the front. They got out of the car and Les followed Tania across to the storage shed. She found another key, turned it in the lock and the rickety wooden door almost fell off its hinges when it swung open.

There was no light inside; Les switched his torch on to find the shed was crammed mostly with old building materials. Bits of wood, sheets of corrugated iron going rusty, saws, sledgehammers, post-hole diggers. All placed on a dirty concrete floor spread with tins of paint, oil, weed killer and boxes of nails and screws or whatever. Again Tania offered to help. Les said it was okay, and started walking and crawling around with his torch. All he got for his trouble was a couple of skinned knuckles and more dirt on his tracksuit.

'Nothing again, Mr Norton?' said Tania.

Les let go a couple of robust sneezes. 'No,' he said. 'But there's plenty of dust and cobwebs.'

Les took out his handkerchief to blow his nose and wipe where he'd skinned his knuckles, then flashed the torch up around the ceiling. There was nothing there except some old rope, several blackened hurricane lamps and a rusty double-handed rip-saw. Les switched off the torch and turned to Mrs Settree.

'Well. One to go.'

'The Church of the Holy Order,' said Tania.

'Yeah. Let's call in and see Uriah.'

'Uriah's a nice boy,' said Tania as they stepped out of the shed. 'But I think he needs to get out more often.'

'Yes,' agreed Les. 'All work and no play makes Jack a dull boy. Or whoever the case may be.'

Tania locked the door to the storage shed and they walked back to the car. Although he'd struck out again with the last two churches, Les didn't feel so disappointed having the woman from the orphanage for company, and he still had a good feeling about the last church. They got in the car and proceeded on to Sandstock Road.

The yellow church looked a lot brighter in the sunshine and so did the flowers along the pathway. Les stopped the car in front of the gate, then he and Tania got out and took the slab path past the vestry and round to the residence. The sound of someone tapping metal was coming from the garage. They walked across and Tania knocked on the side door. A few seconds later Uriah appeared at the door in his khaki overalls. As soon as his God-fearing eyes fell on Mrs Settree, a slick formed on Uriah's forehead and he started to hyperventilate. He stared at her, then came out of the garage with one eyebrow twitching and his top lip curling like Benny Hill when he used to play the fat perv in the round glasses and beret on TV, ogling the bikini girls.

'Good morning Uriah,' smiled Mrs Settree. 'How are you today?'

Uriah's eyes bored into Tania as if he had Superman's X-ray vision, and if Les wasn't mistaken, the deacon's nephew had a roaring boner poking against his overalls.

'I'm good, Mrs Settree,' Uriah replied, in a rasping growl. 'Real good. How are you this truly wonderful day?'

'Fine thank you, Uriah.' Tania indicated to Les. 'You met Mr Norton?'

Uriah hadn't noticed Les standing beside her. 'Oh yes,' he panted. 'Mr Norton. Good day, sir. How are you?' Uriah glanced at Les before quickly riveting his gaze back on Tania.

'I'm all right thanks,' said Les cheerfully. 'And is that a Bible in your overalls, Uriah? Or are you just happy to see Mrs Settree?'

Uriah turned back to Les. 'What was that?' he rasped.

'I said, you've got your overalls on again, Uriah,' smiled Les. 'And you're a man of the Bible, who's happy when he's working. Which is good to see.'

'Yes, yes. I do. I mean, I am, yes,' drooled Uriah, his God-fearing eyes immediately clicking back onto Tania.

'Good for you mate,' said Les. Yeah. And if I wasn't around, you'd be all over poor Mrs Settree like ants at a picnic. You happy-clapping ratbag.

'Mr Norton's here to look in your storage shed for some paintings, Uriah,' said Tania. 'Is that all right?'

'Yes. I got your message earlier, Mrs Settree,' wheezed Uriah. 'That's quite all right. And Mr Norton explained things to me yesterday.'

'That's right,' said Les. 'And I appreciate what you're doing for me too, Uriah. Don't you worry about that.'

'I'll get the key,' said Uriah.

Uriah ogled Tania again, like the crazy little weasel in the Bugs Bunny cartoons always trying to steal the chickens off Foghorn Leghorn, then hobbled off to the residence on three legs. Les turned to Tania and smiled.

'Nice young man,' said Les.

'Yes,' said Tania. 'But if ever I'm here with Uriah, I always feel a little uncomfortable. I don't know why. Maybe it's just my imagination.'

'Maybe,' said Les. 'But I think you're right when you said he should get out a bit more.'

'You think so?' blinked Tania.

'I'm sure so,' Les nodded. 'Right out. Like Mars or Pluto.'

Uriah returned holding a key. He'd managed to tuck his roaring boner up under his overalls and was walking straighter. However, the lust in his God-fearing eyes for Tania hadn't receded one bit. If anything, it burnt brighter as he ogled her again.

'Here's the key,' he panted.

'Thank you, Uriah,' said Tania.

'Good on you mate,' said Les.

Uriah opened the door to the storage shed then switched on the light and they followed him inside. Les had a quick look around and gave a double, triple blink. There was lots of junk stacked neatly around the shed. But sitting on a wide bench taking up one wall was a small army of garden gnomes. They weren't ordinary garden gnomes. They'd all been repainted in bright colours, and their little gnome faces had been changed. There was an Alice Cooper gnome, a Marilyn Manson gnome, a Keith Richards gnome. Adolf Hitler, Joseph Stalin, Saddam Hussein, Whoopi Goldberg. There was a Boy George gnome and four gnomes painted like KISS, right down to Gene Simmons with his monster tongue hanging out. There was even a gnome amongst the others that looked suspiciously like Mrs Settree.

Les turned to Uriah. 'All ... your own work, Uriah?' he asked.

'Yes,' nodded Uriah. 'Do you like them?'

'Yeah,' nodded Les. 'They're great.'

'They're my little friends,' said Uriah.

'Uriah's very talented,' blinked Tania.

'I can certainly see that,' said Les. 'Why don't you put them outside in the sun, Uriah?' he asked.

'Uncle Lorimer doesn't like me to,' replied Uriah. 'He thinks they're evil. But I sneak them out sometimes. I'm just waiting for the paint to dry on Dame Edna. And I'm going to put them all out this afternoon. And we'll have a little tea party.'

'Just like Alice in Wonderland,' smiled Les.

'Yes,' Uriah smiled back. 'Just like Alice in Wonderland.'

'I'll start looking for the paintings.'

Les began searching around the storage shed, watching Uriah out the corner of his eye edging up to Tania, while she nervously shuffled away from him before he could start humping her leg.

If the paintings had been there they would have been easy to find because Uriah had the storage shed as clean as a whistle and everything was packed and sorted away neatly. Amongst the boxes of books, videos, records, golf bags, maps, mirrors, irons, coffee machines, crockpots, lamps, beer steins, old bottles and whatever, there wasn't a speck of dust or a cobweb. There was also no sign of any paintings or anything resembling a bundle of paintings. Norton's heart sank. This was it. The last blast. There was nowhere else now. He looked under the table full of gnomes, stood up and shook his head. And I had a feeling about this place. Les stared at a Johnny O'Keefe gnome in a leopardskin coat, red shoes and a string bow-tie. Some bloody feeling.

'Nothing again, Mr Norton?' asked Tania. She was standing not far from Les, keeping a small stack of school desks between her and a heaving Uriah.

'No. Nothing unfortunately,' said Les.

'Oh. I'm so sorry,' said Tania.

'Yeah,' nodded Les. He gave Tania a weary smile. 'So we may as well get going. Unless you want to stay here and talk to Uriah for a while. I can get a coffee and come back.'

'Yes, yes,' nodded Uriah. 'Mrs Settree could stay here with me.'

Tania latched onto Les's arm like she was going to tear it out of its socket. 'Mr Norton. Don't you dare ...' She let go of Norton's arm and composed herself. 'I mean. Don't you dare think I would stay here alone with Deacon Brockenshire's nephew. My goodness! I'm old enough to be his mother. What would people say?'

'No, no,' whined Uriah. 'It's all right, Mrs Settree. You can stay.'

Les turned to Uriah. 'I'm afraid I have to agree with Mrs Settree, Uriah,' he said. 'A small town. People could get the wrong idea and construe that as some kind of subliminal incest.'

Uriah shook his head emphatically. 'No, no,' he said.

'Yes, yes,' nodded Tania just as emphatically.

Les stepped across and pushed the side door open. 'After you, Mrs Settree.'

'Thank you, Mr Norton,' breathed Tania.

Tania stepped outside and Uriah pushed in front of Les behind her. Les came out, closed the door and followed them down the slab path to the car.

Mrs Settree was walking fairly quickly with Uriah breathing down her neck. Les watched Uriah slip one hand inside his overalls then start stumbling along behind her, having a full-blown game of pocket billiards. They got to the gate and Uriah stopped as Tania opened it before she hurried across to the passenger side of the car. Les stepped past Uriah, closed the gate then turned around and smiled.

'Well, thanks for your help, Uriah,' said Les. 'Enjoy your tea party this afternoon.' Les squinted up as the sun appeared between the clouds. 'Looks like you've got a nice day for it.'

'Yes, thank you, Mr Norton,' wheezed Uriah as he kept furiously playing pocket billiards under his overalls. The veins started to bulge out round his temples, and he stared desperately over at Tania. 'Goodbye Mrs Settree,' he wailed.

Tania was holding onto the car door as if her life depended on it. 'Goodbye Uriah,' she called back. 'Be sure and say hello to your Uncle Lorimer for me.'

The second Les opened the car door for her, Tania got inside and quickly buckled up. With an eye still on Uriah, Les strolled round to the driver's side and opened the door just as Uriah's knees buckled and he gripped the gate with one hand for support. His blond hair flew back, then he let go a long, anguished groan of ecstasy and, seconds later, a huge wet patch started soaking through the front of Uriah's khaki overalls. Les climbed behind the wheel and turned to Tania, who was staring anxiously out the windscreen.

'Well, I guess that's that, Mrs Settree,' Les started to say.

Tania nodded to the keys in Norton's hands. 'Don't you think you should start the car, Mr Norton,' she suggested.

'Yeah, righto.' Les put the key in the starter and kicked the motor over. 'One thing, Tania,' said Les as he buckled up. 'At least the car doesn't suffer from premature ignition.'

Norton's mind was elsewhere as they drove back towards the main road. The Church of the Holy Order was the last roll of the dice and now Les realised it was all over. Still, he told himself. Nothing ventured, nothing gained. And at least he had a go. Les missed the turn-off he'd taken on the way out and was now driving along another road to the left, still deep in thought. Tania wasn't saying anything either.

Houses were thin and it was mostly sparse brown fields pushing up to the surrounding hills. Les pulled up at a crossroad and noticed on the left a large block of land with a weathered grey sliprail fence in front taking up the corner. A white metal sign in front of a tree next to a locked gate on a dirt driveway said BLUE DOLPHIN GALLERY. The driveway led to a glimpse of buildings obscured by tall green fir trees. Les turned to Tania and noticed she was staring at the dashboard and looked quite downcast.

'Are you all right, Tania?' he asked.

Tania turned to the driveway. 'That's where the orphanage used to be,' she answered.

'The one you were in?' said Les.

'Yes. Saint Benedicta's.'

'Looks like it's an art gallery now.'

'Yes.' Tania turned away and stared melancholically out the windscreen.

Les figured Mrs Settree had no desire to get out and reminisce about her childhood, and having figured out where he was, he turned right and eventually got back onto Sandstock Road.

'Mrs Settree,' asked Les as they drove along. 'What would you say to a nice cup of coffee right now?'

Tania brightened up. 'Yes. I'd like that very much,' she said.

'There's a nice little place in Apollo Bay sells good coffee and pina colada muffins. I was in there yesterday.'

'Sailor Girls,' said Tania.

'That's it,' answered Les. 'We'll hit there. And have a cuppa.'

'Lovely,' said Mrs Settree. They drove past some colourful wooden houses, then Tania turned and smiled at Les. 'Well, Mr Norton, I must say, you seem quite happy, despite your disappointment at not finding your mother's paintings.'

'Yeah, well, what can you do?' shrugged Les. 'You just got to cop it on the chin. It's not the end of the world.'

'No. But I imagine your family will be very disappointed as well. Having sent you all this way and everything.'

Les smiled at Tania. 'They'll just have to cop it on the chin too.'

It didn't take Les long to find his way back into town and there was a parking spot two down from Sailor Girls. He got out of the car, opened the door for Tania and they walked back to the coffee shop. There were a number of people seated out the front, but the same table Les had the day before was empty and Les pulled a chair out for Tania.

'Now. What can I get you, Mrs Settree?' he asked.

'A pina colada muffin and a mug of flat white, please,' she replied. 'Is that all right?'

Les gave Tania a wink. 'I'm going to have exactly the same thing myself.'

Les went to the counter and ordered then returned to the table. He sat down and smiled at Tania.

'Well, Tania. Despite not finding the paintings, you've been a great help, and I really appreciate you going to the trouble you have. I know how busy you must be, with the orphanage and all that.'

'That's all right, Mr Norton,' Tania replied. 'I enjoyed the drive down. And I enjoyed your company.'

'Thank you Mrs Settree,' said Les. 'And I'll make sure I leave a donation when we get back to the orphanage.'

'Whatever you can spare will do, Mr Norton,' said Tania, looking a little embarrassed.

'I can spare something, Tania,' Les assured her. 'And I'd like to take some photos when we get back too, if that's all right.'

'Of course, Mr Norton. It would be a pleasure.'

A tall curly-haired girl in black brought their order over. Les thanked her then he and Tania sugared their coffees and started in.

'So do you come down here much?' asked Les.

'Every now and again,' replied Tania, enjoying her muffin and coffee. 'Something gets donated I can use at the orphanage. And we bring the girls down to play netball or hockey.'

'Did you play sport when you were younger?' asked Les.

'I was quite a good runner,' replied Tania. 'I actually represented my school in the state titles. But I hurt my ankle bushwalking, and it was never the same.'

'Yeah. I got a crook knee from football,' said Les. 'It's okay now. But they're never a hundred per cent.'

'I used to like running too,' said Tania. 'Especially on a cold, crisp day.'

'Yeah,' nodded Les. He took a sip of coffee and looked at Mrs Settree. 'Did you ever know Father Shipley, from the Church of the Blessed Madonna, Tania?' he asked her.

'Yes,' replied Tania. 'But I never really got on with him. Right up until his death.'

'Oh?' said Les. 'How do you mean?'

'I don't know,' shrugged Tania. 'He'd say hello and that. But he always seemed to avoid me, for some reason.'

'Avoid you?'

'Mmhh. Even when I was young. He had a small sailboat, and he'd often take the other girls out sailing. But he'd never take me.' Tania made a tiny gesture with one hand. 'I mean. It's not as if I was ever rude to him. Or anything like that.'

'Yeah. People can be funny at times,' said Les. 'Actually I visited his grave yesterday. I left some flowers on it.'

'That was thoughtful of you, Mr Norton,' said Tania.

'Well, I was in Lorne,' said Les, magnanimously. He looked at Mrs Settree over his mug for a moment. 'It said on his grave, "Loved by all. Especially the people at the cable station." And something about? "So he … bringeth them unto the haven — where they would be." I'm kind of curious what all that's about.'

Tania looked back at Les. 'I'm not overly religious,' she said. 'But the piece about, "unto the haven" is a passage from the Bible. Father Shipley saved almost twenty men from drowning once.'

'Fair dinkum?'

'Yes. He was quite an avid sailor,' said Tania. 'And he often used to sail his small boat from Lorne to Apollo Bay. He sailed down here one morning, just as a big storm blew in from Bass Strait and a timber vessel overturned. Father Shipley saved all the crew, except for one, and brought them into Apollo Bay. The government gave him a medal.'

'Go on,' said Les.

'And he was also involved with the old telegraph cable station. Before it became a museum.'

'I noticed it on the way in,' said Les. 'What did you say it was? A telegraph cable station? What's that?'

'Before satellite technology came in. The original telegraph cable across to Tasmania was laid from here,' said Tania. 'It was completed in the thirties. But the building's over a hundred years old.'

'Is that right?' said Les.

'You may not think so, Mr Norton. But at one time almost everything came into Apollo Bay by ship. The roads in those days were little more than bullock tracks.'

'Really?' said Les.

'Oh yes. There was no Great Ocean Road then,' said Tania. 'And when the telegraph cable finally became obsolete, Father Shipley made sure the government would never sell the old building. So it would preserve the area's heritage. Then after he died it became a museum.'

Les stopped eating his muffin and looked directly at Mrs Settree. 'Did you say a museum, Tania?'

Tania smiled at Les. 'I feel I know what you're thinking, Mr Norton. But believe me, I've been in there on many an occasion with the children. And there's no paintings. Lots of old photos. But no paintings.'

Les watched Mrs Settree sip her coffee. 'Tania, did Father Shipley have any other connection with the old telegraph station? Apart from getting it preserved as a museum?'

'Oh yes,' replied Mrs Settree. 'He helped with the maintenance. Baptised the workers' babies. Took care of any widows whose husbands died on the job. Considering his parish was in Lorne, he spent a lot of time in Apollo Bay.' A coy smile formed on Mrs Settree's face. 'It was rumoured he was having an affair with one of the widows. And that she had a son to him, who became a well-known detective in Melbourne.'

Les kept his eyes on Mrs Settree. 'Does the museum have a storage shed?' he asked her.

'Yes. An old building out the back,' she replied. 'No one ever bothers much about it.'

'You wouldn't have a key to the storage shed, Tania?' asked Les.

Tania shook her head. 'No. But my friend Mrs Sheridan has. She's one of the museum's volunteer caretakers.'

'Any chance of getting the key off her?' asked Les.

'I don't see why not. She runs a gift shop with her daughter just a few doors up the road. I'll go and ask her.' Mrs Settree picked up her handbag and rose from the table.

'Do you want me to come with you?' asked Les.

'No. Stay here, Mr Norton, I'll only be a few minutes.'

'Okay.'

Les watched Mrs Settree walk off to the left and drummed his fingers on the table. Dear Father Shipley. Acting the good samaritan at the telegraph station while he was porking a lonely widow on the side. Mrs Totten said he was a bit of a devil. He could have sailed down here with the paintings and stashed them somewhere to get them out of Lorne. Maybe there was another roll left in the dice yet. Mrs Settree returned and sat down looking rather pleased with herself. She opened her handbag and took out a solid brass key tied by a strip of leather to a piece of wood with MUSEUM printed on it.

'Here it is, Mr Norton,' she smiled.

'Hey. Well done, Mrs Settree,' said Les. 'Thanks for that.'

'Do you wish to go there now?' asked Mrs Settree.

'Yeah. Why not?' said Les. He got up to pay the bill and they walked out to the car.

It was only a short drive back up the main road to the Cable Station Museum. Les swung left up a driveway then reversed round into a gravel parking area with a fir tree in the corner. He turned off the engine and had a look through the windscreen.

The old single-storey red-brick building was quite big and set in a large fenced-off block of land overlooking the ocean. A yellow double-door stood at the front between four whited-over windows, and there was a side entrance down to the left. A wide patch of grass ran down the right side and scattered around the grass or against the fence and the side of the building, were old wooden signs with WARNING: TELEGRAPH CABLE on them along with piles of greying timber and lumps of rusting metal. Les stopped the engine, took his overnight bag from the back seat and they got out of the car.

'Where to?' Les asked Mrs Settree.

'This way, Mr Norton.'

Les followed Mrs Settree down the left side of the building past the side entrance, then past a garage and, further along, a large concrete water tank. Where the block of land ended back from the water tank, an old sandstone building with a tarred roof pushed into the hill behind the cable station. There were no windows, but at the front was a sturdy greying wooden door with a rusty keyhole in it.

'Crikey,' said Les. 'It's a solid, big old thing.'

'Yes,' agreed Mrs Settree. 'They built them to last in those days.'

'Did they ever,' muttered Les.

Mrs Settree took the key, put it in the keyhole and gave it a turn. She gave it another hard turn. Got her strength back and gave it another.

'Oh dear!' she said. 'It won't open.'

'Give me a go.'

Les gripped the key and gave it a good twist. It might have moved, except the hole was full of corrosion from the salty air. Les removed the key, opened his bag and took out a small can of WD40.

'I'm a good boy scout, Tania,' said Les. 'I'm always prepared.'

'Yes. You certainly are, Mr Norton,' smiled Mrs Settree.

Les gave the keyhole a good squirt, then squirted some over the key. After waiting a moment or two, he put the key in and tried again. A couple more turns plus a bit of gentle persuasion and the lock clicked. Les pushed the door with his foot and it creaked partially open. He handed Mrs Settree back the key, then picked up his overnight bag and took out his torch.

'After you, Mrs Settree,' he said.

'Thank you.' Mrs Settree put the key back in her bag and blinked at Les. 'I've never been in here before.'

Les gave her a wink. 'There's always a first time for everything, Tania.'

Les pushed the door open and followed Mrs Settree inside. He shone the torch around the wall next to the door and found an old brass light fitting. Mrs Settree switched it on and a bulb sputtered a few times from behind a metal grille in the ceiling before filling the room with just as many shadows as light.

'Shit a brick!' said Les. 'Where do you start?'

Piled around the room, or lying on the cobblestone floor, were age-old objects covered in dust and cobwebs. Mostly to do with seafaring. Next to a wooden rudder in the middle, were halliards, capstans, brass portholes and enough parts stacked on top of each other to make a small sailing boat. In one corner was a sulky with its wheels removed and resting against it, along with a saddle. And in another corner was a ship's boiler with an anchor and a broken bowsprit sitting on top. There were huge springs, coils of rope, marlin spikes and block-and-tackles. And wooden and metal objects, with pieces of wood and metal screwed or bolted onto them that had Les completely mystified as to what they were ever used for. Lying on a padlocked metal trunk against one wall was a hard hat and diving suit, and stacked on a battered wooden set of drawers against another wall was a pile of lead ballast. On a wooden sea-chest against another wall was a ship's bell, a compass and a small anchor. Mrs Settree was examining something that resembled an extra-long handled machete.

'What's that?' asked Les.

'I think it's a flenser,' said Mrs Settree.

'A flenser?'

'Yes. For slicing up whales.'

'Ohh yuk!' said Les.

'Yes,' nodded Mrs Settree. 'The children and I are against whaling too.'

Les flashed his torch around the room and over the ceiling. 'Well, the sooner I start looking, the sooner we're out of here, I suppose.'

'Yes,' agreed Mrs Settree, wrapping her cardigan around her. 'It's not very warm in here.'

Les began going through all the old gear, flashing his torch in every nook and cranny. There was everything from big brass rings to little wooden plugs. Iron spikes to pieces of iron grate. He even uncovered an old wooden leg. But nothing even resembling a green canvas bundle of old paintings. Mrs Settree had been helping too and she couldn't find anything either.

'I'm afraid I can't see your paintings, Mr Norton,' she said, poking at a pile of old hemp rope.

'No,' said Les. 'It looks like I've struck out again.'

Norton walked over to the chest of drawers and pulled one out. It was full of copper nails. The rest were full of wooden dowels, small tools and other old junk. He pushed the last drawer in and turned to the wooden sea-chest. He looked at it, thought for a moment, then walked over and gave it a kick. The old wooden chest sounded a little empty inside.

'Hello?' said Les.

'You've found something, Mr Norton?' said Mrs Settree.

'I don't know. Maybe.'

The sea-chest wasn't locked. Les took the ship's bell and compass off and lay them on the floor. The lid had tightened up over the years. But Les was able to put his back into it and wrench the lid open. Inside was a stack of folded white canvas.

'Hello, hello, hello!' said Les.

Mrs Settree came over and watched Les pulling aside the canvas. He got halfway down and stencilled across one of the folds was MIZZEN LOWER SHROUDS. Les pulled a few more folds aside, then pushed them back in and dropped the lid.

'What was it?' asked Mrs Settree.

'Just an old sail,' replied Les.

'Oh dear,' sympathised Mrs Settree. 'What a shame.'

'Yeah.'

Les put the bell and compass back on the sea-chest and turned to the metal trunk. It was black and dented here and there with rust poking through the paint, around a metre and a half square and secured by a solid brass padlock on the front. Les walked over and gave it a kick. It didn't sound quite as empty inside as the wooden chest. Les looked at the lock then picked up a metre-long iron spike he had noticed lying on the cobblestones.

'Mrs Settree. What's that down there?' said Les, pointing behind the chest of drawers.

'Down here?' Mrs Settree walked over and peered behind the chest of drawers.

While Mrs Settree was looking the other way, Les jammed the iron spike in the lock, got a good grip and quickly wrenched it open. He placed the iron spike back on the cobblestones as Mrs Settree looked up from the old chest of drawers.

'I can't see anything, Mr Norton,' she said.

'Must've been my imagination,' said Les. 'Sorry.' He turned to the metal trunk. 'Hey, this old metal box isn't locked. I may as well have a look and see what's inside.'

'Yes. Why not?' agreed Mrs Settree.

Les lay the hard hat and diving suit on the floor then removed the broken lock and creaked open the old iron trunk. It, too, was filled with folded layers of white canvas. Across the top layer was stencilled MAIN ROYAL SAIL.

'It's another bloody sail,' said Les.

'Dear oh dear,' said Mrs Settree.

Les pulled a couple of layers out, then shoved his hand down one side of the metal trunk. He got down a fair way and felt tightened rope amongst the sails. Les got his hand under the rope and gave it a tug and found it was attachcd to something solid. He pulled several more layers of canvas sail out of the metal trunk and, sitting on the remaining layers of white canvas, was a bundle of green canvas a good metre square, bound with white rope. Les took hold of the rope with both hands and lifted the bundle out of the trunk. It was about a metre thick and, when Les lay it on the floor, he felt wooden frames along the sides.

'Holy bloody shit!' yelled Les. 'I think it's them.'

'The paintings?' said Mrs Settree.

'Yeah. Look. You can see where something's been painted over on the front. But maybe there might be something on the other side.' Les turned the canvas bundle over and, printed neatly on the back, was *From: Guichet Magazine, Bayswater Road, Kings Cross.*

'Yes,' howled Norton. 'It's bloody them all right. That's Talbot's place in the Cross, where Emile sent them from.'

Mrs Settree looked mystified. 'I don't quite follow you, Mr Norton.'

'Don't worry, Tania,' said Les. 'This is them all right. You bloody little beaut.' Les stared at the bundle of paintings lying on the cobblestones and felt like breaking into a dance. 'I'm a genius,' he shouted. 'A bloody genius.' He grabbed Mrs Settree and planted a kiss on her cheek. 'Genius. Hah-hah. Hah-hah-hah!'

Mrs Settree blushed and put her hands to her face. 'And they're definitely your mother's paintings?' she said.

'My oath they are,' said Les. 'After all these bloody years.'

Mrs Settree clutched at her breast and looked a little faint. 'Oh my Lord!' she gasped. 'This is so exciting.'

'Is it what,' said Les.

'Nothing like this has ever happened to me before in my life,' said Mrs Settree. 'I do believe I feel quite dizzy.'

'I think I'm getting half a horn,' said Les. 'Anyway,' he said. 'We won't unwrap them here. We'll do it back at the orphanage. What do you reckon?'

'If you wish, Mr Norton.' Mrs Settree put her hand on Les's arm. 'Oh, I'm so happy for you, Mr Norton,' she smiled. 'This is marvellous.'

'Yeah. And I got you to thank, Tania.' Les gave Mrs Settree another kiss on the cheek. 'God bless you, sweetheart.'

'Mr Norton. Please,' blushed Mrs Settree. 'You're making me all embarrassed.'

'Good,' grinned Les. 'All right, Tania,' he said. 'Let's get out of here, and I'll put the paintings in the boot of the car.'

'Very well,' said Mrs Settree.

Les repacked the sails then closed the trunk and piled the old diving gear back on top. He picked up the paintings and carried the bundle through the door. Mrs Settree locked it behind them, then joined Les as he placed the paintings in the boot of the car.

'I'll have to take the key back to Mrs Sheridan, Mr Norton,' she said.

'Yeah, no worries,' said Les, closing the boot.

He opened the door for Mrs Settree then got behind the wheel and they headed back into Apollo Bay. Les was absolutely beside himself. Mrs Settree looked flustered and kept waving her hand in front of her face. She stopped for a moment and turned to Les.

'Mr Norton,' said Mrs Settree.

'Yes Tania,' replied Les brightly.

'Would you mind terribly if I was to have a little drink in town? I feel quite heady. There's a hotel not far from Mrs Sheridan's.'

'No. Not at all,' replied Les. 'In fact I might have a light myself. This calls for some sort of a celebration.'

'We could have a celebration back at the orphanage tonight, if you like. There'll only be Angie and myself there. I'll cook you dinner. I'm quite a good cook, too, people tell me.'

'Okay,' said Les. 'That's sounds good. I'll bring a bottle. Does your daughter drink?'

'Yes. Red wine.'

'Okay. Red wine it is.'

The Apollo Breeze Hotel was cream and brown with stairs running up to two entrances, and took up a corner of the main street next to a blue and white supermarket. Les did a U-turn and found a parking spot outside the supermarket. He got out of the car and walked with Mrs Settree as far as the hotel, then waited outside the stairs on the left. As he absently watched the people walking past Les couldn't believe his luck. He was right. Shipley must have brought the paintings down in his boat. The cable station was right across the road from the water and if anybody asked what the canvas bundle was, he would have said sails. And what a great spot to keep them. Locked in a trunk, in a place no one would ever enter, hidden amongst old sails no one would ever use. He removed his name just as a precaution and that's where they stayed. Rosa-Marie and Emile died without contacting him, and Father Shipley died taking his secret to the grave. And that's where the paintings would have stayed. Except for the world's greatest non-professional detective, Sherlock Holmes Norton, finding them. Les smiled across to the Mitsubishi. Now there was around half a million dollars worth of paintings sitting in the boot of a rental car. Hold on to them for a few years and they could be worth anything. Les had finally cracked the big one. The world was his oyster: mornayed, kilpatrick or on the half shell with pepper and a wedge of lemon. Any way you want it. Thanks mainly to a skinny old Miss Prissy who ran an orphanage. And what would be an appropriate remuneration for an old bag of bones running an orphanage, mused Les as he watched Mrs Settree walking back down the street towards him. I could pull fifty thousand out of that hole in my backyard without even missing it.

'Everything okay, Tania?' asked Les as Mrs Settree stopped in front of him.

'Yes,' replied Mrs Settree. 'I didn't say anything about the paintings. I said you were looking for an old map.'

'Good idea,' said Les. 'Okay. Let's go and throw a few double OP rums down our throats. Arhh, arhh, me heartys,' he growled.

'Oh, I don't know about that,' said Mrs Settree. 'But I'd like a nice gin.'

Les escorted Mrs Settree up the stairs and through the doors. There was a bar and food servery on the right, with model boats and ship's lanterns and wheels round the walls, that looked a little crowded. To the left was a smaller, quieter bar with a covered-over pool table, a fireplace in the corner and tables and chairs next to several windows offering a nice view of the street. Les sat Mrs Settree down at a table two back from the fireplace.

'What would you like, Tania?' he asked.

'A gin and tonic please,' she answered. 'Is that all right?'

'It sure is.'

Les walked over to a bar panelled with red cedar and ordered a pot of Carlton light and a double gin and tonic. He smiled at the other people round the bar while he waited, then took the drinks back to the table and sat down.

'Well cheers, Tania,' he said, clinking her glass.

'Yes. Cheers … Les,' she replied.

Les took a sip of beer and put his glass down. Mrs Settree had a swallow of gin and gave several blinks.

'Ooh, this is lovely,' she said, putting her glass down. 'Just what the doctor ordered.'

'Yeah. Me too,' said Les, taking another sip.

Mrs Settree had another mouthful of gin. 'What I can't understand, Mr Norton,' she said, 'is why Father Shipley erased his name from the front of the canvas. And why he hid the paintings?'

'Oh, probably for safekeeping or something,' said Les. 'Who knows? Things were different in those days.'

'And what did you say the address was on the back? A magazine?'

'Yes. My mother used to be an illustrator on it. She must have left the paintings there and … somehow they finished up down here.'

'Who was Emile?' asked Mrs Settree.

'A friend of Mum's,' answered Les. 'Another artist.'

'Oh.'

Les finished his beer and was surprised to see Mrs Settree finish her gin and tonic at the same time. 'Would you like another one?' he asked.

'Yes.' Mrs Settree took her handbag and went to stand up. 'I'll get them.'

'No. Let me,' said Les. 'After what you've done, the least I can do is shout you a couple of drinks.'

'Very well, Mr Norton. If you insist. Thank you.'

Les got two of the same and when he returned, noticed Mrs Settree's face was starting to get a bit of a glow up. He put the drinks on the table then sat down and clinked Mrs Settree's glass again.

'Well, at least you've got your paintings, Mr Norton,' said Mrs Settree. 'Your family will certainly be so proud of you.'

'Yes,' smiled Les. 'I can just see the look on one particular person's face when I walk in now.'

'What will you do with them? Just hang them?'

'Oh yeah. One for me. The rest for the others.'

'How many paintings are there?' asked Mrs Settree.

'Six,' replied Les. 'Three are Mum's. And three are by other artists.'

'And are you still going to unwrap them back at the orphanage first, Mr Norton?'

'Reckon,' said Les. 'After all your help, you deserve to be there for the unveiling.'

Knowing the nature of Rosa-Marie's paintings, especially ones they were going to burn, Les regretted having said that. But it was a bit late now. And if Mrs Settree got blown away by the contents, there wasn't much he could do. He only hoped it didn't affect a home-cooked meal that night.

'Angie would like to see them too,' said Mrs Settree.

'Yes. Your daughter's a painter, too, I believe,' said Les. 'What's she like?'

Mrs Settree smiled. 'I don't know a great deal about art, Mr Norton,' she replied. 'But she's different. Very ... colourful. And she has her own style.'

'That's good,' said Les.

'That's Angie's studio out the back. She lives in it and guards it like Fort Knox. She hardly ever lets anyone in there.'

Les raised his glass. 'Secretive creativity.'

'Yes. That's my Angie. God love her.'

'Your little guardian angel.'

'My little guardian angel,' nodded Mrs Settree. 'I don't know what I'd do without her.'

Les asked Mrs Settree one or two things about the orphanage before they finished their drinks, then Mrs Settree made a trip to the Ladies and they walked out to the car. Les was going to put the radio on, but he changed his mind. Minutes later they were out of Apollo Bay and on their way back to Lorne.

Les was almost jumping out of his skin as he cruised along with the ocean on his right. But he drove slowly and kept himself alert, carefully steering the Mitsubishi around any hairpin bends. The last thing he wanted, after all the trouble he'd gone to, was an accident and the car bursting into flames with thousands of dollars' worth of paintings in the boot. Les didn't feel all that good inside, telling poor Mrs Settree a heap of lies. But when he sent her down a big fat cheque, Les felt that would make up for any minor indiscretions on his part. Les was whistling softly to himself as he pulled over to let a young bloke in an old hotted-up black Kingswood roar past, when he noticed Mrs Settree had suddenly gone very quiet. He glanced across and she was totally expressionless, just staring out the windscreen at the road ahead. Les manoeuvred his head around, had a good look and noticed tears were streaming down her cheeks. Ohh yeah, thought Les. Good old gin. The world's happiest drink.

'Are you all right, Mrs Settree?' he asked quietly.

Mrs Settree gave her head a tiny nod. 'Yes,' she whispered.

'You're crying, Tania.' Les found himself quite concerned. Mrs Settree didn't just have the sniffles. Tears were pouring out of her and in between sobs her thin shoulders would shudder under her cardigan.

'What's the matter, Tania. I didn't say anything to upset you, did I?'

'No. It's not your fault, Mr Norton,' cried Mrs Settree. 'It's just that driving past where the orphanage used to be. It brought back all the terrible memories.'

'Shit! I'm sorry, Tania,' said Les. 'I wasn't watching and I took a wrong turn.'

'Please don't blame yourself, Mr Norton. You're kind.' Next thing Mrs Settree turned to Les and completely broke up. Tears poured down her cheeks and sobs racked her poor skinny body. 'Oh, Mr Norton,' she wailed. 'They beat me there. They beat me so bad. They were so cruel to me. Oh, I'm sorry, Mr Norton,' howled Mrs Settree. 'But they were.'

'That's all right, Tania,' soothed Les. 'Let it all go.' He took his hanky out and handed it to Mrs Settree. 'Who beat you?'

Mrs Settree dabbed at her eyes with the hanky. 'The nuns. The nuns beat me.'

'The nuns?' said Les. 'The nuns beat you?' said Les. 'I ...?'

'They beat me. They whipped me. They made me sleep in the toilets with all the smell.' More violent sobs racked Mrs Settree's body. 'They poured buckets of urine over me. They locked me in closets. I had to sleep out in the rain and cold. I slept in filth with the animals. They starved me. When it was hot they locked me in the toolshed without any water. And I was just a little girl,' cried Mrs Settree. 'A poor little girl.'

'Shit!' said Les. Mrs Settree's description of life at the orphanage was quite graphic and he found himself getting stirred up. 'The low rotten bastards,' he growled. 'That's bloody awful.'

'All the beatings they gave me,' sobbed Mrs Settree. 'When I got married and my husbands beat me, I didn't know any better. I thought it was the way life was. Until Angie told me I didn't have to take it.'

'Good for bloody Angie,' said Les.

'But Sister Manuella was the worst,' sobbed Mrs Settree. 'She beat me with a strap once and I couldn't sit down for almost a week. She broke coathangers on me. Rulers. Punched me. Dragged me down the stairs by my hair. I had so many bruises.'

'Sister Manuella?' said Les. 'Mrs Totten said she was the one who got her neck broken when the orphanage burnt down. Is that right?'

Mrs Settree turned to Les and for a brief moment a fierce gleam shone through the tears in her eyes. 'Yes. That was an unfortunate accident. Wasn't it.'

Norton's eyebrows rose. 'Yes. I imagine it was.' He slowed down for a hairpin bend, then put his foot down as the road rose above the ocean. 'So why did the nuns beat you all the time, Tania?'

'They said I was evil,' replied Mrs Settree. 'And I had the devil in me. They said my mother was a witch. And I was going to burn in hell.'

Norton turned slowly to Mrs Settree. 'What did you just say? The nuns said your mother was a witch?'

'Yes. All the time,' sobbed Mrs Settree. The tone in her voice now sounded like a little girl talking. 'Sister Manuella even made me wear a witch's hat and sit on a broomstick in front of all the other children. She wouldn't even let me go to the toilet. And when I'd wet myself she'd rub my face in it. Even the other children cried. Oh, it was so horrible.'

Les was trying to keep his eyes on the road and look at Mrs Settree at the same time. 'Tania,' he asked. 'How old are you?'

'I'm not sure,' sobbed Mrs Settree. 'The nuns kept it a secret from me. But I think I'm around fifty.'

'Fifty,' said Les.

'I think so,' sniffed Mrs Settree. 'I'm not really sure. But I do know one thing. I know what my real name is,' she said, a hint of triumph in her voice.

'Your real name?' said Les.

'Yes,' nodded Mrs Settree. 'I've always been called Tania. But when the Walmsleys adopted me, one of the nuns told my foster parents that when my mother left me at the orphanage, she gave them an envelope with some money in it. And a note that said, *Please look after Tanybryn.*'

'Tanybryn?' said Les.

'Yes. And Sister Manuella said it was an evil name. And changed it to Tania.'

'Did you ever find out who your mother was, Tania?' asked Les.

Mrs Settree shook her head and dabbed at her eyes with Norton's hanky. 'No. But I think she must have come from around Apollo Bay. Because Tanybryn's a little hamlet not far away. It's very pretty. I sometimes go out there and just sit.' Mrs Settree turned to Les. 'And often, it feels like my mother's there. Watching over me.'

Les drove on in silence till he found a space at the side of the road and pulled the car over. Mrs Settree looked up through her tears.

'What's the matter?' she asked.

Les stared at Mrs Settree for a moment trying to find the right words. 'Tania,' he said. 'I know this is a pretty lousy time to be telling you this. But I haven't been completely honest with you.'

'Oh?' Mrs Settree looked genuinely surprised. 'You haven't?'

Les shook his head. 'No. I haven't. And fair dinkum. I'm really sorry.'

'What ...?'

'Tania. You told me Father Shipley kept away from you. Is that right?'

'Yes,' nodded Mrs Settree. 'He used to avoid me, for some reason.'

Les reached over to the back seat and got his overnight bag. He sat it on his lap and took out the book on Rosa-Marie Norton. Inside the pages was a copy of the letter Warren had brought home from Bondi post office. He opened it up and handed it to Mrs Settree.

'Tania,' said Les. 'I want you to read that. Then I want you to have a look at this book. But read the letter first. Okay?'

'All right, Mr Norton,' said Mrs Settree, looking a little mystified behind her bloodshot eyes. 'If you insist.'

Mrs Settree dried her eyes, then adjusted her glasses and began reading. Les pulled out from where he'd parked and drove on in silence, staring impassively at the road ahead. His mind was working overtime, and if he was right, everything had suddenly turned pear-shape. Les drove on, and the further he went, the more numbed he felt. Mrs Settree finished the letter and, still holding it open in her hands, turned to Les.

'This letter, Mr Norton,' she said in a puzzled tone. 'It's ... it's quite remarkable. But I don't quite understand what it's got to do with me.'

Les found himself searching for the right words again. 'Mrs Settree. Warren, the bloke I live with, brought it home from the post office. It had been lost in the dead letter office for years. But because my name's Norton, I finished up with it.'

Les told Mrs Settree the truth. How he got the letter, and borrowed the book from the local library and found out how much the paintings were worth. Then, without telling Mrs Settree about what happened in Melbourne, told her how he decided to come to Lorne to see if he could find the paintings. And after lying through his teeth to almost everybody he'd met, found them with her help.

'So Rosa-Marie Norton wasn't your mother?' said Mrs Settree.

'No, she wasn't,' confessed Les.

'Oh? I don't quite know what to say, Mr Norton.'

'But I do know whose mother she was,' said Les.

'Whose?' asked Mrs Settree.

Les looked directly at Mrs Settree. 'Yours.'

'Mine?' gasped Mrs Settree. 'Oh, don't be ridiculous.'

'Tania. Put the letter away,' said Les. 'And open up that book. To page six, I think.'

Mrs Settree neatly folded the letter then picked up the book on Rosa-Marie Norton. 'My goodness,' she said. 'Look at this cover.'

'Yes. She was one wild artist all right,' said Les.

Mrs Settree turned to page six and spread the book open. 'Dear me!' she said. 'If these are her paintings, she was more than wild.'

'Yeah. But have a look at the one with the baby and all the bunnies and things.'

Mrs Settree perused the pages from behind her glasses. 'Oh, this one is quite nice,' she said.

'Yes it is,' agreed Les. 'Now have a look what it's called.'

Mrs Settree squinted at the photo in the book then slowly turned to Les. '*Tanybryn?*'

'That's right,' said Les. 'That painting was Rosa-Marie Norton's secret tribute to you. The daughter she left behind.'

'Nooooo,' said Mrs Settree.

'Yes,' nodded Norton emphatically. 'She didn't come to Melbourne to have an abortion. She was too scared of getting blood poisoning again. She came down and put on an exhibition. Then she came to Apollo Bay to have you.'

'Me,' blinked Mrs Settree.

'Yes you,' said Les. 'Christ! It all adds up. The nuns knew who your mother was and took it out on you. Shipley must have known, too, and that's why he kept away from you. He might have even thought you were his daughter. Then there's the name. Tanybryn. Rosa-Marie grew up down here, and the place probably meant something to her. She would have known a local doctor who'd deliver her baby on the quiet. And she'd have known about the orphanage. So she left you there without knowing what a bunch of bastards the nuns were. Rosa-Marie and Emile had blackmailed Shipley at one time. And that's why Emile sent the paintings to him. Which is why Shipley hid them so well. He couldn't bring himself to destroy them. But he was terrified somebody would find them and connect them to him. Rosa-Marie died not long after that. So did Emile Decorice. And nobody would have known nothing. Only for that letter arriving at my place. And me, being the scheming low bastard that I am, always on the hunt for an easy dollar, I came down here looking for them. And ended up finding them.'

Mrs Settree stared at the photo of *Tanybryn*. 'Mr Norton. This is just unbelievable.'

'Unbelievable?' Les looked at Mrs Settree. 'It's more than that. It's horrible. Because even though it breaks my bloody heart to tell you this, Tania, those paintings in the boot belong to you.'

'Me?'

'Yeah.' Les laughed derisively. 'Wouldn't it give you the shits.'

Mrs Settree shook her head. 'This is all too much for me,' she said, and closed the book.

'Tell me about it,' said Les.

Mrs Settree stared at the book cover then turned to Les. 'Is there a photo of Rosa-Marie Norton in here?' she asked.

'Yeah. On the second page,' said Les.

Mrs Settree opened the book again and her bloodshot eyes almost bulged through her glasses. 'Oh my God!' she cried. 'Is that her?'

'That's her,' said Les. 'Rosa-Marie Norton. The Witch of Kings Cross.'

'Oh my God!' Mrs Settree closed the book and fell back against the seat. 'I think I'm going to faint.'

'There's a bottle of mineral water in my bag,' said Les. 'Have a drink.'

Mrs Settree's hands were shaking that bad as she got the bottle out, she could hardly get the cap off. She gulped some down and patted at her chest then cautiously opened the book again and took another look at the photo.

'And that's Rosa-Marie Norton?' said Mrs Settree softly.

'Yep. That's her, Tania,' said Les. 'Your dear sweet mother, Tania.'

'Oh my good God!' said Mrs Settree. 'Oh my God! This is all too much for me.'

'Yeah. Your mother was a bit out there,' agreed Les. They went round a bend and Les recognised a familiar part of the road. 'Anyway. We'll be back at the orphanage soon,' he said. 'And we'll unwrap the paintings and see what we've got.' Les gave Mrs Settree a sickly smile. 'What you've got.'

While Mrs Settree flicked gingerly through the book on Rosa-Marie Norton, Les drove on in silence, not knowing whether to laugh or cry. There was a fortune in paintings in the boot of the car, and it looked like he was going to have to give them to Mrs Settree. It was the only right thing to do. The money they'd bring would help her and the kids when they got booted out of the orphanage. But it would have looked a lot better in his bank account. What about poor, innocent Mrs Settree, though, thought Les. The last thing she would have been expecting was to find out who and what her mother was after all this time. It also looked like sneaky old Father Shipley might have been her father, too. Before Les knew it, he was approaching the pier and coming into Lorne. He hung a left near the church, drove up the hill and next thing he'd pulled up in the orphanage driveway.

'Well. Here we are,' said Les, switching off the motor.

Mrs Settree looked up from the book. 'Oh. We are too.' She closed the book and turned to Les. 'There's quite some interesting things in here,' she said. 'Do you mind if I show Angie?'

'No. Bring my bag with you,' said Les. 'I'll get the paintings.'

They got out of the car. Mrs Settree waited while Les got the paintings from the boot, then opened the door in the gate for him and they walked round to the kitchen. Mrs Settree opened the flyscreen.

'Round to the left, Mr Norton,' she said. 'Put them in the lounge room. I'm going to make a cup of tea. Would you like one?'

'How about a coffee?' said Les. 'Milk and two sugars.'

'If you want.'

Les followed a corridor with a tattered blue runner into a large cedar-panelled lounge room full of furniture that had seen better days. Three old grey Chesterfield lounges and a half-a-dozen lounge chairs of different shapes and patterns were sitting on several stained scatter-rugs. And about the same number of vinyl chairs sat round an old varnished table that had been cut down and turned into a long coffee table. A huge marble fireplace faced the blue-curtained windows looking out over the ocean from across the verandah, and to the side was a TV and a cheap stereo with a small CD stacker. Rock posters and a poster of the Sydney Swans were blue-tacked to the walls, church sale lamps sat in the corners and cheap light fittings hung from the ceiling, replacing what had probably once been chandeliers. Les placed the paintings on a lounge near one of the windows and turned on the lights at a switch near the door.

The green canvas bundle was tied securely. But the knots in the old white rope were thick and easy enough to get your fingers into, so there was no need for a knife. Les started pushing and pulling around and before long he'd loosened the knots. He was starting to undo them when Mrs Settree walked into the lounge room with his overnight bag over her shoulder, carrying a tray with two white mugs on it and a plate of mixed biscuits. She placed the tray on the coffee table and put the overnight bag next to it.

'Here you are, Mr Norton,' she said. 'Yours is the biggest mug.'

'That'd be me all right. Thanks.' Les turned and smiled at Mrs Settree. 'So how are you feeling now, Tania? You all right?'

'Yes. I'm a little better,' replied Mrs Settree. 'But my word, Mr Norton. This has certainly been a bolt out of the blue.'

'Yeah. I can understand that,' nodded Les. He picked up his coffee and took a sip. It was instant. But it was all right.

Mrs Settree sat down in one of the vinyl seats and sipped her coffee.

'Do you need a knife, Mr Norton?' she asked.

Les shook his head. 'No. I've just about got it undone already.'

'Oh good.' Mrs Settree looked up at Les. 'I must admit, Mr Norton, even though I'm absolutely flabbergasted, it's still very exciting.'

'Yeah,' muttered Les. He drank some more coffee, put the mug on the table and went back to the green canvas bundle. 'Anyway. Let's see what's in here. And see what all the fuss was about.'

Les dug at the knots and his strong fingers soon had them undone. He removed the rope and put it to one side, then carefully unfolded the canvas. Inside were six paintings, a metre square, three were in plain, wide, pinewood frames. Rosa-Marie's were in the middle with the others surrounding them, as Emile Decorice had described in the letter. Les placed the three other paintings on the floor, leaning against the lounge, then spread Rosa-Marie's across the lounge facing away from the window and stood back.

'Oh my God!' gasped Mrs Settree.

Les picked up his coffee and ran his eyes over the paintings. 'Yeah,' he nodded appreciatively. 'I think I know why they wanted to burn your mother's paintings years ago.'

On the right was a painting of a man, half eagle, half human, with an enormous erection, having sex with a woman, half tiger and half human, with massive breasts and nipples. The background was a whirlwind of amazing colours and strange, esoteric little figures with bulging eyes. On the left were two Medusa-type women with snakes for hair. Only the snakes were all soft penises. The women had huge bushes of pubic hair and growing out of the pubic hair were more snake-penises. Flying around in the background were sinister masturbating little cherubs with devil's horns poking out of their heads. The painting in the middle was a circle of stupid-looking fat pigs wearing policemen's hats and tunics, all sodomising each other. In the middle of the unbroken circle, one of the pigs was wearing a judge's wig and robes. Dancing around in the background on stumpy little legs with stumpy little genitals hanging down were moneybags with the old pounds and shillings signs on them and cunning, laughing faces. Although the subject matter in the paintings was open to discussion, the figures were wonderfully and skilfully composed and, as usual, the colours were fantastic.

'Are you absolutely positive this woman was my mother, Mr Norton?' said a shocked Mrs Settree.

'Absolutely positive, Tania,' answered Les. 'That's her all right.' Les pointed to the name. 'But, before you condemn anybody, Tania, just remember the old saying, never mind the quality, feel the width. Those paintings are worth a packet.'

'Dear me. I wouldn't like the children to see them.'

Les shrugged. 'I suppose so. But shit, the bloke I work for would love to hang that middle one in his office.'

'Yes. I noticed in one section of the book Rosa-Marie Norton didn't have a great deal of affection for the police.'

'Neither does this bloke.' Les put his mug of coffee down and turned to Mrs Settree. 'Well. They're your mother's paintings, Tania. What do you reckon?'

'I'm … I'm lost for words,' blinked Mrs Settree.

'Yeah. I see what you mean,' said Les. 'Anyway. Why don't we have a look at the others, and see what they're like?'

'Very well,' agreed Mrs Settree.

Les picked up the first one, had a look then placed it on a lounge chair. It was four people seated at a bar. Two men and two women. The colours were soft, yet eye-catching, and the people were all dressed in the style of the forties. The men wore hats and ill-fitting double-breasted suits; the women had print dresses and cheap hats. The four figures all had sad, almost comical faces. Poking out from under the frame was painted in fine, white lettering WILLIAM. The rest was obscured by the frame. Les stared at the painting and picked his chin.

'I've seen paintings by this bloke before,' he said. 'When I've been browsing through different books up at the library. Where's that letter?'

'It's a very nice painting,' said Mrs Settree.

'Yeah.' Les took the letter from his overnight bag, found what he was looking for and pointed excitedly. 'That's it. "Dobbo left a painting for you." That'd be a nickname. I'll bet that's a William Dobell. He was friends with Rosa-Marie from the Cross. She used to model for him. Shit!'

'I think I've heard of him,' said Mrs Settree.

'Yeah. He had a drama with the art establishment over the Archibald Prize.'

'Is it valuable?' asked Mrs Settree.

'Valuable?' said Les. 'Are you kidding? It's probably worth more than the others put together. Christ! What else is here?'

Les picked up the next painting. It was like a biblical scene of a half-a-dozen wide-hipped and buxom nude women seated out in the open on rugs, or standing holding parasols. Some were wearing hats or sandals. One of the women was holding a lion on a lead and in the background, two men in ancient Egyptian clothing were seated on horses. The colours were bright and the figures all had a casual haughtiness about them. At the bottom of the painting, just NORM was visible. The rest of the name was cut out by the wide frame.

'That one's a little risqué,' said Mrs Settree. 'It's quite nice, though.'

Les put the painting on another lounge chair and picked up the letter from where he'd placed it on the coffee table. 'There it is,' he said, stabbing his finger at the letter again. '"Normo". Another nickname. That's got to be a Norman Lindsay. Rosa-Marie used to model for him too. Holy shit!'

'I think I've heard of him,' said Mrs Settree. 'There was a movie?'

'Yeah. *Sirens*.'

'That's it,' said Mrs Settree. 'He was quite famous — I think.'

'Quite famous?' said Les. 'Just a bit. Bloody hell. This is worth a heap too.' Les put the letter back and picked up the last painting.

'Oh my God!' gasped Mrs Settree.

Les ignored her for the moment and placed the painting on another chair. It was just a mass of coloured lines and dots. As if the artist had squeezed the paint over the canvas like toothpaste. Nevertheless, in garish patterns of reds and blues and yellows and whites, the painting had a colourful intricateness about it that drew your attention. In the corner was written JACKSON. Like the others, the rest of the name was covered by the cheap frame. Les picked up the letter, looked at it, then dropped it back on the table.

'Oh no,' groaned Les. 'No. This isn't happening.' He turned to Mrs Settree who was staring at the painting. 'Mrs Settree,' said Les. 'In that letter Emile Decorice refers to a drunken bullshit artist called Jacques San. It was probably a false name he was getting around under. And in the book it says how he fell in love with Rosa-Marie, and she turfed him out. She called him Jacques the Dribbler. There was a movie about an artist with Ed Harris. Because of his style of painting, they used to call him Jack the Dripper. I was singing the lyrics the other night from the song by Alabama 3. "Reachin": "Talking like Soprano, Thinking like …" oh shit!' Les turned to Mrs Settree, who was still staring at the squiggly painting. 'You'd have to pull the frame off to be sure. But I'll bet my life that's a bloody Jackson Pollock. And if it is, it's worth millions.' Les threw back his head and tore at his hair. 'Bloody millions.'

Mrs Settree continued to stare at the painting. 'This Jackson Pollock,' she said. 'Was he having an affair with my mother?'

'Yeah. Pretty heavy too,' said Les. 'He was in love with her.'

Mrs Settree turned to Les. 'Mr Norton, I'd like to see my daughter. And I want you to meet her too.'

Les stared morosely at the last painting. 'Yeah, righto. Why not.'

Mrs Settree stood up and Les followed her along the hallway and out through the kitchen. What have I done, he asked himself as they walked down the verandah to the courtyard. I've just turned this skinny old bat into a multimillionaire. And it should be me. Me. Shit! She's got to give me one fuckin painting.

A set of steps ran from the courtyard up to a gravel path crossing the land behind the orphanage, to a door at the front of the white building in the middle of the block. The door was painted bright red, with a brass knocker shaped like a monkey. A sign in Gothic print above the knocker read WELCOME TO ANGELA'S WORLD OF THE WEIRD AND WONDERFUL. Mrs Settree rapped on the door then pushed it ajar.

'Angela,' she said. 'Can I come in?'

'Yes. Come in, Mum,' replied a deep female voice from inside.

Mrs Settree opened the door, Les followed her through and she closed it behind them.

Inside was one big room made into an art studio, with a partitioned-off kitchen and bedroom at the rear. There were dark curtained windows on either side and a single fluorescent bulb in the ceiling, next to several mobiles of bats and spiders, partially filled the room with milky white light. A lounge, a small stereo and a TV sat along the left-hand side of the room and on the other side were shelves of gothic bric-a-brac and a bookshelf stacked with magazines, novels and hardbacks. Several abstract paintings hung on the walls, along with some weird posters and painted masks, giving the place an atmosphere of sinister gloom. The floor was covered in cheap green carpet and spread across the carpet was a large paint-spattered canvas tarpaulin. A girl dressed in a black top and a maroon velvet miniskirt over black stockings and blue Doc Martens was standing to one side of the tarpaulin, holding a can of paint in one hand and a long, skinny paintbrush in the other. A black beret was shoved on her head and a white cigarette holder with a roll-your-own in it, poked out from one side of her mouth while she dripped yellow paint onto a piece of plywood sitting in the middle of the tarpaulin. The young girl was very attractive, with loose black hair, sensuous purple glossed lips and plucked eyebrows that arched up, giving her a sinister haughtiness. Two obsidian green eyes peered down at what she was doing and, despite the girl's youth, she was the spitting image of Rosa-Marie Norton. Les gave a double blink and realised why Mrs Settree had reacted the way she did when she saw the photo in the book. He then noticed the painting on the floor and the ones hanging on the walls were in the same drip style as the Jackson painting sitting in the lounge room.

'Angela,' said Mrs Settree. 'This is Mr Norton. Mr Norton, this is my daughter Angie.'

'Hello … Angela,' said Les.

The girl nodded impassively and the obsidian green eyes studied Norton intently. 'Hello Mr Norton,' she said. 'How are you?'

'I'm good thanks, Angela,' replied Norton, hiding his shock and an icy feeling the girl had sent up and down his spine. 'And you can call me Les, if you like.'

'Whatever,' answered the girl.

'Angie. Stop what you're doing,' said Mrs Settree. 'And come into the lounge room. I've something interesting to show you.'

'Interesting?' said Angela.

'Yes. Mr Norton and I uncovered some paintings in Apollo Bay. And they were done by my mother.'

'Your mother?' said Angela, screwing up her face.

'Yes. I've found out who my mother was,' said Mrs Settree. 'Your grandmother. I think I've also found out who my father was, too, Angie.' Mrs Settree turned to Les then pointed out the drip paintings around the walls and smiled. 'What do you think, Mr Norton?'

Les stared at the paintings and shook his head in amazement. 'Yeah. I think I know exactly what you mean, Tania.'

Angela looked curiously at her mother, then suspiciously at Les. 'Okay,' she said, putting down the paint and paintbrush and leaving her cigarette holder in an ashtray near the bookcase. 'Let's go inside.'

Mrs Settree opened the door and Les followed them outside then back down the path to the orphanage. As they walked through the courtyard and into the kitchen, Les felt a sinister sense of deja vu. A mother and daughter in a deserted bay near Cooktown that he'd never told anyone about. They stepped into the lounge room and Mrs Settree pointed to the paintings.

'Well, Angela,' she said. 'What do you think?'

Angela studied the paintings then pointed to the ones by Rosa-Marie Norton. 'Who did these?' she asked. 'They're so cool.'

'This woman.' Mrs Settree took the book from Norton's overnight bag and handed it to her daughter. 'Rosa-Marie Norton. My mother. And I want you to read this letter.' Mrs Settree handed Angela the copy of the letter, then turned to Les. 'Would you like another cup of coffee, Mr Norton?'

'Yeah, righto,' replied Les. 'That'd be nice.'

Mrs Settree took the two mugs out to the kitchen leaving Les alone with Angela. Angela looked at the book then began reading the letter. Les sat on a lounge chair feeling very uncomfortable and as he watched Angela out of the corner of his eye, his mind started racing again. Mrs Settree returned with another mug of coffee and placed it on the coffee table as Angela finished reading the letter.

'Well, Angela,' said Mrs Settree. 'What do you think? It appears she never came down to Melbourne to have an abortion at all. She came down for her exhibition. And to have me. Then she left me at Saint Benedicta's.'

Angela nodded slowly and folded up the letter. 'Quite amazing,' she said. 'Quite amazing.' She turned to her mother. 'So how did all this come about, Mum?'

'I'll explain it to you in detail later, Angie,' said Mrs Settree. 'But see the comparison between that painting and yours.'

'Yes, I do,' said Angela quietly. 'That's quite amazing.'

'Mr Norton said it's by an artist named Jackson Pollock. And it's worth millions. Not only that. It appears he was my father. Your grandfather.'

Angela studied the painting and looked at the name half-hidden on the bottom. 'What an amazing coincidence,' she said composedly.

'Yes. Isn't it,' said Mrs Settree.

Angela turned to Les. 'And you say these paintings are worth millions of dollars, Mr Norton?'

'I'm positive,' answered Les.

'Does anybody else know they're here?' asked Angela.

'No. Just the three of us, Angela,' said Les.

Mrs Settree smiled at her daughter. 'Anyway, Angie. Mr Norton's coming around for tea tonight and a few drinks. We can all talk about it then.'

Angela looked at her mother for a moment, then turned to Les with a half-smile on her face, and her snake-like green eyes glowed for a second in a shaft of light coming through the window. 'You're calling round tonight … Les,' she said easily.

'Yes. Your mother's going to cook something special for me,' said Les.

'And we're going to drink some wine,' said Mrs Settree. 'Have a little celebration.'

'You're going to have a few drinks, Les?' said Angela.

'Ohh yeah,' said Les. 'Why not?'

'Well, leave your car,' said Angela. 'I'll come round and get you. Where are you staying?'

'At the Otway Resort,' said Les. 'Room 202.'

'I know it,' said Angela. 'I won't call up to your room. I'll park in the driveway out the front. And you can come down.'

'Okay,' said Les.

Angela turned to her mother. 'What time, Mum?'

Mrs Settree turned to Les. 'What time suits you, Mr Norton?'

Les looked at his watch. 'Oh. About an hour. Is that okay?'

'That would be fine,' said Mrs Settree.

'Yes. Excellent,' said Angela.

Les got to his feet and rubbed his hands together. 'All right,' he said to Angela and Mrs Settree. 'Well look, I imagine this has been a big day for both of you, and you want to talk about things in private. I'll go home and get cleaned up.'

'Okay Les,' said Angela. 'I'll see you out the front of the resort in an hour.'

'No worries.' Les left them with the copy of the letter. But picked up the book on Rosa-Marie Norton and put it in his overnight bag. 'I'll bring this back with me,' he said. 'I just want to have a look at a couple of things.' He turned to Angela. 'Your mother said you like red wine, Angela?'

'Yes. Especially burgundy.'

'There's a bottleshop across the road from the resort,' said Les. 'I'll get something extra grouse.'

'Thank you Mr Norton,' smiled Angela.

'I'll walk you to the door,' offered Mrs Settree.

Les shook his head. 'No. That's all right,' he said, picking up his overnight bag. 'I know my way out.' Les pointed to the mug of coffee still sitting on the coffee table. 'Look at that. I didn't even drink my coffee.' Les gave the women a warm smile. 'See you in an hour.'

'See you then Les,' they chorused.

Les left them in the lounge room and walked up to the car. He got behind the wheel and stared down at the orphanage for a moment before starting the engine. Minutes later Les drove into the resort. He didn't bother going down to the car park. He left the car in the driveway out front then walked inside and straight up to the reception desk. The dark-haired man in the blue suit recognised him and smiled.

'Mr Norton,' he said. 'There's a message here for you.' The man got a piece of paper and placed it on the desk. 'It's from a Miss Sonia Rouvray in Geelong. She asked for a Mr Klinghoffer. But insisted it was your room.'

'That's okay,' said Les. 'I know what it's all about. Anyway. I just got a phone call from Sydney, and I have to go home. So I'll be checking out early.'

'Oh. All right Mr Norton. No problems,' said the man in the blue suit. 'When did you wish to check out?'

'In about thirty minutes. I'll get my bags. And I'll be right back.'

'Not a problem, Mr Norton.'

'Thanks.' Les turned and walked down to the lift. On the way he read the note. *Solomon. I can be there tonight. Call me. Sonia.* Les screwed the message into a ball and and dropped it in a bin next to the lift.

As soon as he was inside his unit, Les began hurriedly packing things into his suitcase and getting rid of what he didn't need. He kept what was left of the bourbon, but left the beer in the fridge. And he didn't bother to get changed. Yes, Les told himself as he gathered up his tapes and unhooked the ghetto blaster, a nice mother and daughter duo, that one. Mum's not so bad. But what about the daughter? Where do you start? How about daddy number one that used to hit Mummy and fell under a train. Angie handled the trauma okay. Why wouldn't she? She pushed him off the platform. And husband number two. The stepdaddy that also used to beat Mummy. An electrician, and he finished up with a hair dryer in his bath. Mummy's little 'guardian angel' to the rescue again. Then there was the brother. Grant Junior. He used to hit both Mummy and his sister. Till his sister took him fishing. Which brings us to Sister Manuella. Who used to beat poor young Tanybryn. 'That was an unfortunate accident. Wasn't it.' Okay. I don't blame Tania for setting fire to the orphanage and breaking Sister Manuella's neck. I would have done the same thing. But that daughter? I don't know about witches or things, but I saw the devil in those pretty green eyes. Les shoved the last of his socks and underwear into his suitcase and zipped it up. 'Does anybody else know about the paintings, Mr Norton? You going to have a few drinks, Mr Norton? Leave your car at the resort, Mr Norton. Les. I'll come and get you.' Yeah, thought Les. It's getting dark now. No one would notice that old black kombi pull up out the front, and me getting into it. Bloody hell! If I went round to that orphanage tonight, after Angie's got into her mother's ear about those millions of dollars' worth of paintings, I'd either get poisoned, cop a knife in the back or get hit over the head from behind. Or they'd probably just push me off the balcony. 'Stand here, Mr Norton. Where we can take a better photo.' I know one thing. No one would ever see me again. There'd be places in that orphanage you could hide an elephant.

I suppose I could just run in and grab a couple of paintings and piss off. But all they'd have to do is ring the police and have me nicked. Mrs Settree can prove they're her paintings more than I can. No. Even though it breaks my poor Queensland heart. They can have the fuckin things. It's all going to a good cause. And all in all, Mrs Settree's okay. I'll leave things as they are. Les checked around the unit, then glanced at his watch. Look at that. I've got a good twenty minutes up my sleeve before Rosa-Marie's baby gets here. Or granddaughter. Or whatever she is. I really don't give a shit. Les picked up his bags and caught the lift down to the lobby. Ten minutes later he had checked out and was turning left at the roundabout down from the resort.

Halfway along Mountjoy Parade Les slowed down for a bus and one last feeling of deja vu crept over him. Almost the same thing happened to him at Yurriki near Murwillumbah, when he found the painting hidden in the farmhouse and he gave it to Perigrine. And it turned out to be a van Gogh worth millions. Then before Perigrine could send him a thank you note written on a huge cheque, Perigrine got blown up, along with the painting. And Les missed out on another fortune. Now it had happened again. Only worse. Les watched the lights over the Erskine River disappear in the rear-vision mirror and a tiny tear rolled down his cheek.

'Bugger deja vu,' sniffed Les. 'You can stick it in your arse. It's nothing but the same bloody thing, over and over again. AIEEE!'

THE END

Firstly I have to thank everyone who came along to the *Mystery Bay Blues* book signing. Especially the people in Merimbula and Newcastle. They made me feel like visiting royalty. When I get down on my knees in front of the queue and say, 'I'm not worthy, I'm not worthy,' I mean it. And an apology to the woman in the bookshop at Narooma for causing her cash register to seize up. She sold more books in the short time I was there than she would in a month. Luckily my publicist was quick-witted enough to throw a bucket of cold water in the till and we got it going again.

To all those nice people writing to me, I'm doing my best to write back. You haven't been ignored. There's just a lot of letters, that's all. And to all the mad people who write to me — yes, you know who you are. It doesn't worry me if you're on medication and counselling. But could you please settle back, take another pill or whatever and try to write a little more clearly. I don't mind deciphering gibberish and the ravings of people who are a strawberry or two short of a punnet. But if I can't read it, it's impossible. Fair dinkum. At times I believe the government's Subsidised Prescription Drug Program has got a lot to answer for amongst some of my readers.

Also, to my many readers enjoying a vacation care of Her Majesty and wanting books for their libraries, plus the people from Words On Wheels: I'm doing my best. But crime appears to be a growth industry at present, and there's a lot of punters bunged up in various nicks all over Australia. I can only get so many books. Write to Bryce Courtney and ask him for some. He's always waffling on about how good reading is. On second thoughts, don't bother. The puzzle's hard enough as it is, without clubbing yourself in the head with one of Bryce's wheel-chocks. Ask your librarian to order in some books by Charles Bukowski. Charles tells it like it is.

About this book: some of those churches around Lorne and Apollo Bay are real and some aren't, I just changed the names around. But that radio station, 607.5 FM PBS, is for real. When I heard those dirty ditties I had to put them in the book somehow. But what a good radio station. Between the ditties and the Tibetan monks chanting mantras, they play some great music. If you live around Melbourne give it a listen and become a subscriber. If I lived down that way I would.

Rosa-Marie Norton is a fictitious character, but Rosaleen Norton was a real person and an absolutely fascinating character, as well as a great artist who bordered on genius and gave the establishment of the day a well-deserved finger. The cover of this book is actually one of her paintings, *The Goddess.* If you want to read a book about a totally outrageous woman who was years before her time, Keith Richmond, co-owner of the Basilisk Bookshop in Brunswick Street, Fitzroy in Melbourne, is the authority on Rosaleen Norton. He should have a comprehensive biography on Rosaleen Norton, the Witch of Kings Cross, finished by the end of the year. After spending some time with Keith, I'm certain it will be a fascinating and interesting book, and I can't wait for it to come out.

People have been writing in to the publishers telling me it's about time I got my finger out and updated my website. They're right, too. I'm getting a bit slack. So I'm going to attack it shortly and you'll see photos from my trip to the Norfolk Island Writers' Festival, where I wowed them and Dr Colleen McCullough baked me a chicken dinner at her house. She fair dinkum did. And when I got back I addressed the troops of the DFSU at Randwick Barracks. The Deployed Forces Support Unit. What a great team of men and women and what a great day I had. These people make me so proud to be an Australian. Even when they got me and my publicist and shoved us into gas masks, Kevlar vests and helmets. We looked like Darth Vader and Mickey Mouse standing next to each other.

What more can I say? I hope you like the latest Les Norton. I had a lot of fun hanging out in Melbourne and travelling along the Great Ocean Road doing my research. It's a beautiful part of Australia down there. Plus I think I rose to a new low in filth and sunk to new heights of violence to keep everybody happy. And Les managed to leave everybody happy in the end. Except him. I'll do my best again next year. See you then, and thank you for reading my books.

Robert G. Barrett, 2003